Cutting for Stone

Cutting for Stone

A NOVEL

Abraham Verghese

Alfred A. Knopf   New York

THIS IS A BORZOI BOOK
PUBLISHED BY ALFRED A. KNOPF

ISBN-13: 978-1-61523-386-1

Manufactured in the United States of America

For George and Mariam Verghese

Scribere jussit amor

And because I love this life
I know I shall love death as well.
The child cries out when
From the right breast the mother
Takes it away, in the very next moment
To find in the left one
Its consolation.

—Rabindranath Tagore,
  from *Gitanjali*

Cutting for Stone

The Coming

A FTER EIGHT MONTHS spent in the obscurity of our mother's womb, my brother, Shiva, and I came into the world in the late afternoon of the twentieth of September in the year of grace 1954. We took our first breaths at an elevation of eight thousand feet in the thin air of Addis Ababa, capital city of Ethiopia.

The miracle of our birth took place in Missing Hospital's Operating Theater 3, the very room where our mother, Sister Mary Joseph Praise, spent most of her working hours, and in which she had been most fulfilled.

When our mother, a nun of the Diocesan Carmelite Order of Madras, unexpectedly went into labor that September morning, the big rain in Ethiopia had ended, its rattle on the corrugated tin roofs of Missing ceasing abruptly like a chatterbox cut off in midsentence. Overnight, in that hushed silence, the *meskel* flowers bloomed, turning the hillsides of Addis Ababa into gold. In the meadows around Missing the sedge won its battle over mud, and a brilliant carpet now swept right up to the paved threshold of the hospital, holding forth the promise of something more substantial than cricket, croquet, or shuttlecock.

Missing sat on a verdant rise, the irregular cluster of whitewashed one- and two-story buildings looking as if they were pushed up from the ground in the same geologic rumble that created the Entoto Mountains. Troughlike flower beds, fed by the runoff from the roof gutters, surrounded the squat buildings like a moat. Matron Hirst's roses overtook the walls, the crimson blooms framing every window and reaching to the roof. So fertile was that loamy soil that Matron—Missing Hospital's wise and sensible leader—cautioned us against stepping into it barefoot lest we sprout new toes.

Five trails flanked by shoulder-high bushes ran away from the main hospital buildings like spokes of a wheel, leading to five thatched-roof bungalows that were all but hidden by copse, by hedgerows, by wild eucalyptus and pine. It was Matron's intent that Missing resemble an arboretum, or a corner of Kensington Gardens (where, before she came to Africa, she used to walk as a young nun), or Eden before the Fall.

Missing was really *Mission* Hospital, a word that on the Ethiopian tongue came out with a hiss so it sounded like "Miss*ing*." A clerk in the Ministry of Health who was a fresh high-school graduate had typed out THE MISSING HOSPITAL on the license, a phonetically correct spelling as far as he was concerned. A reporter for the *Ethiopian Herald* perpetuated this misspelling. When Matron Hirst had approached the clerk in the ministry to correct this, he pulled out his original typescript. "See for yourself, madam. *Quod erat demonstrandum* it is Missing," he said, as if he'd proved Pythagoras's theorem, the sun's central position in the solar system, the roundness of the earth, and Missing's precise location at its imagined corner. And so Missing it was.

NOT A CRY or a groan escaped from Sister Mary Joseph Praise while in the throes of her cataclysmic labor. But just beyond the swinging door in the room adjoining Operating Theater 3, the oversize autoclave (donated by the Lutheran church in Zurich) bellowed and wept for my mother while its scalding steam sterilized the surgical instruments and towels that would be used on her. After all, it was in the corner of the autoclave room, right next to that stainless-steel behemoth, that my mother kept a sanctuary for herself during the seven years she spent at Missing before our rude arrival. Her one-piece desk-and-chair, rescued from a defunct mission school, and bearing the gouged frustration of many a pupil, faced the wall. Her white cardigan, which I am told she often slipped over her shoulders when she was between operations, lay over the back of the chair.

On the plaster above the desk my mother had tacked up a calendar print of Bernini's famous sculpture of St. Teresa of Avila. The figure of St. Teresa lies limp, as if in a faint, her lips parted in ecstasy, her eyes unfocused, lids half closed. On either side of her, a voyeuristic chorus peers down from the prie-dieux. With a faint smile and a body more muscular than befits his youthful face, a boy angel stands over the saintly, voluptuous sister. The fingertips of his left hand lift the edge of the cloth covering her bosom. In his right hand he holds an arrow as delicately as a violinist holds a bow.

Why this picture? Why St. Teresa, Mother?

As a little boy of four, I took myself away to this windowless room to study the image. Courage alone could not get me past that heavy door, but my sense that she was there, my obsession to know the nun who was my mother, gave me strength. I sat next to the autoclave which rumbled and hissed like a waking dragon, as if the hammering of my heart had roused the beast. Gradually, as I sat at my mother's desk, a peace would come over me, a sense of communion with her.

I learned later that no one had dared remove her cardigan from where it sat draped on the chair. It was a sacred object. But for a four-year-old, everything is sacred and ordinary. I pulled that Cuticura-scented garment around my shoulders. I rimmed the dried-out inkpot with my nail, tracing a path her fingers had taken. Gazing up at the calendar print just as she must have while sitting there in that windowless room, I was transfixed by that image. Years later, I learned that St. Teresa's recurrent vision of the angel was called the transverberation, which the dictionary said was the soul "inflamed" by the love of God, and the heart "pierced" by divine love; the metaphors of her faith were also the metaphors of medicine. At four years of age, I didn't need words like "transverberation" to feel reverence for that image. Without photographs of her to go by, I couldn't help but imagine that the woman in the picture *was* my mother, threatened and about to be ravished by the spear-wielding boy-angel. "When are you coming, Mama?" I would ask, my small voice echoing off the cold tile. *When are you coming?*

I would whisper my answer: "By God!" That was all I had to go by: Dr. Ghosh's declaration the time I'd first wandered in there and he'd come looking for me and had stared at the picture of St. Teresa over my shoulders; he lifted me in his strong arms and said in that voice of his that was every bit a match for the autoclave: "She is CUM-MING, by God!"

FORTY-SIX AND FOUR YEARS have passed since my birth, and miraculously I have the opportunity to return to that room. I find I am too large for that chair now, and the cardigan sits atop my shoulders like the lace amice of a priest. But chair, cardigan, and calendar print of transverberation are still there. I, Marion Stone, have changed, but little else has. Being in that unaltered room propels a thumbing back through time and memory. The unfading print of Bernini's statue of St. Teresa (now framed and under glass to preserve what my mother tacked up) seems to demand this. I am forced to render some order to the events of my life, to say it began here, and then because of this, that happened, and this is how the end connects to the beginning, and so here I am.

WE COME UNBIDDEN into this life, and if we are lucky we find a purpose beyond starvation, misery, and early death which, lest we forget, is the common lot. I grew up and I found my purpose and it was to become a physician. My intent wasn't to save the world as much as to heal myself. Few doctors will admit this, certainly not young ones, but subconsciously, in entering the profession, we must believe that ministering to others will heal our woundedness. And it can. But it can also deepen the wound.

I chose the specialty of surgery because of Matron, that steady presence during my boyhood and adolescence. "What is the hardest thing you can possibly do?" she said when I went to her for advice on the darkest day of the first half of my life.

I squirmed. How easily Matron probed the gap between ambition and expediency. "Why must I do what is hardest?"

"Because, Marion, you are an instrument of God. Don't leave the instrument sitting in its case, my son. Play! Leave no part of your instrument unexplored. Why settle for 'Three Blind Mice' when you can play the 'Gloria'?"

How unfair of Matron to evoke that soaring chorale which always made me feel that I stood with every mortal creature looking up to the heavens in dumb wonder. She understood my unformed character.

"But, Matron, I can't dream of playing Bach, the 'Gloria' . . . ," I said under my breath. I'd never played a string or wind instrument. I couldn't read music.

"No, Marion," she said, her gaze soft, reaching for me, her gnarled hands rough on my cheeks. "No, not Bach's 'Gloria.' Yours! Your 'Gloria' lives within you. The greatest sin is not finding it, ignoring what God made possible in you."

I was temperamentally better suited to a cognitive discipline, to an introspective field—internal medicine, or perhaps psychiatry. The sight of the operating theater made me sweat. The idea of holding a scalpel caused coils to form in my belly. (It still does.) Surgery was the most difficult thing I could imagine.

And so I became a surgeon.

Thirty years later, I am not known for speed, or daring, or technical genius. Call me steady, call me plodding; say I adopt the style and technique that suits the patient and the particular situation and I'll consider that high praise. I take heart from my fellow physicians who come to me when they themselves must suffer the knife. They know that Marion Stone will be as involved after the surgery as before and during. They know I have no use for surgical aphorisms such as "When in doubt, cut it out" or "Why wait when you can operate" other than for how reliably they reveal the shallowest intellects in our field. My father, for whose skills as a surgeon I have the deepest respect, says, "The operation with the best outcome is the one you decide not to do." Knowing when not to operate, knowing when I am in over my head, knowing when to call for the assistance of a surgeon of my father's caliber—that kind of talent, that kind of "brilliance," goes unheralded.

On one occasion with a patient in grave peril, I begged my father to operate. He stood silent at the bedside, his fingers lingering on the patient's pulse long after he had registered the heart rate, as if he needed the touch of skin, the thready signal in the radial artery to catalyze his decision. In his taut expression I saw complete concentration. I imagined I could see the cogs turning in his head; I imagined I saw the shimmer of tears in his eyes. With utmost care he weighed one option against another. At last, he shook his head, and turned away.

I followed. "Dr. Stone," I said, using his title though I longed to cry out, *Father!* "An operation is his only chance," I said. In my heart I knew the chance was infinitesimally small, and the first whiff of anesthesia might end it all. My father put his hand on my shoulder. He spoke to me gently, as if to a junior colleague rather than his son. "Marion, remember the Eleventh Commandment," he said. "Thou shall not operate on the day of a patient's death."

I remember his words on full-moon nights in Addis Ababa when knives are flashing and rocks and bullets are flying, and when I feel as if I am standing in an abattoir and not in Operating Theater 3, my skin flecked with the grist and blood of strangers. I remember. But you don't always know the answers before you operate. One operates in the now. Later, the retrospectoscope, that handy tool of the wags and pundits, the conveners of the farce we call M&M—morbidity and mortality conference—will pronounce your decision right or wrong. Life, too, is like that. You live it forward, but understand it backward. It is only when you stop and look to the rear that you see the corpse caught under your wheel.

Now, in my fiftieth year, I venerate the sight of the abdomen or chest laid open. I'm ashamed of our human capacity to hurt and maim one another, to desecrate the body. Yet it allows me to see the cabalistic harmony of heart peeking out behind lung, of liver and spleen consulting each other under the dome of the diaphragm—these things leave me speechless. My fingers "run the bowel" looking for holes that a blade or bullet might have created, coil after glistening coil, twenty-three feet of it compacted into such a small space. The gut that has slithered past my fingers like this in the African night would by now reach the Cape of Good Hope, and I have yet to see the serpent's head. But I do see the ordinary miracles under skin and rib and muscle, visions concealed from their owner. Is there a greater privilege on earth?

At such moments I remember to thank my twin brother, Shiva— Dr. Shiva Praise Stone—to seek him out, to find his reflection in the glass panel that separates the two operating theaters, and to nod my thanks because he allows me to be what I am today. A surgeon.

According to Shiva, life is in the end about fixing holes. Shiva didn't speak in metaphors. Fixing holes is precisely what he did. Still, it's an apt metaphor for our profession. But there's another kind of hole, and that is the wound that divides family. Sometimes this wound occurs at the moment of birth, sometimes it happens later. We are all fixing what is broken. It is the task of a lifetime. We'll leave much unfinished for the next generation.

Born in Africa, living in exile in America, then returning at last to Africa, I am proof that geography is destiny. Destiny has brought me back to the precise coordinates of my birth, to the very same operating theater where I was born. My gloved hands share the space above the table in Operating Theater 3 that my mother and father's hands once occupied.

Some nights the crickets cry *zaa-zee, zaa-zee*, thousands of them drowning out the coughs and grunts of the hyenas in the hillsides. Suddenly, nature turns quiet. It is as if roll call is over and it is time now in the darkness to find your mate and retreat. In the ensuing vacuum of silence, I hear the high-pitched humming of the stars and I feel exultant, thankful for my insignificant place in the galaxy. It is at such times that I feel my indebtedness to Shiva.

Twin brothers, we slept in the same bed till our teens, our heads touching, our legs and torsos angled away. We outgrew that intimacy, but I still long for it, for the proximity of his skull. When I wake to the gift of yet another sunrise, my first thought is to rouse him and say, *I owe you the sight of morning.*

What I owe Shiva most is this: to tell the story. It is one my mother, Sister Mary Joseph Praise, did not reveal and my fearless father, Thomas Stone, ran from, and which I had to piece together. Only the telling can heal the rift that separates my brother and me. Yes, I have infinite faith in the craft of surgery, but no surgeon can heal the kind of wound that divides two brothers. Where silk and steel fail, story must succeed. To begin at the beginning . . .

PART ONE

*. . . for the secret of the care of the patient
is in caring for the patient.*

Francis W. Peabody, October 21, 1925

CHAPTER I

The Typhoid State Revisited

Sister Mary Joseph Praise had come to Missing Hospital from India, seven years before our birth. She and Sister Anjali were the first novitiates of the Carmelite Order of Madras to also go through the arduous nursing diploma course at the Government General Hospital, Madras. On graduation day my mother and Anjali received their nursing pins *and* that evening took their final vows of poverty, celibacy, and obedience. Instead of answering to "Probationer" (in the hospital) and "Novitiate" (in the convent), they could now be addressed in both places as "Sister." Their aged and saintly abbess, Shessy Geevarughese, affectionately called Saintly Amma, had wasted no time in giving the two young nurse-nuns her blessing, and her surprising assignment: Africa.

On the day they were to sail, all the novitiates rode from the convent in a caravan of cycle-rickshaws to the harbor to send off their two sisters. In my mind's eye I can see the novitiates lining the quay, chattering and trembling with excitement and emotion, their white habits flapping in the breeze, the seagulls hopping around their sandaled feet.

I have so often wondered what went through my mother's mind as she and Sister Anjali, both just nineteen years old, took their last steps on Indian soil and boarded the *Calangute*. She would have heard stifled sobs and "God be with you" follow her up the gangway. Was she fearful? Did she have second thoughts? Once before, when she entered the convent, she'd torn herself away from her biological family in Cochin forever and moved to Madras, which was a day and a night's train ride from her home. As far as her parents were concerned, it might just as well have been halfway across the world, for they would never see her again. And now, after three years in Madras, she was tearing herself away from the family of her faith, this time to cross an ocean. Once again, there was no going back.

A few years before sitting down to write this, I traveled to Madras in search of my mother's story. In the archived papers of the Carmelites, I found nothing of hers, but I did find Saintly Amma's diaries in which the abbess recorded the passing days. When the *Calangute* slipped its mooring, Saintly Amma raised her hand like a traffic policeman and, "using my sermon voice which I am told belies my age," intoned the words, "Leave your land for my sake," because Genesis was her favorite book. Saintly Amma had given this mission great thought: True, India had unfathomable needs. But that would never change and was no excuse; the two young nuns—her brightest and fairest—were to be the torchbearers: Indians carrying Christ's love to darkest Africa—that was her grand ambition. In her papers, she reveals her thinking: Just as the English missionaries discovered when they came to India, there was no better way to carry Christ's love than through stupes and poultices, liniments and dressings, cleansing and comfort. What better ministry than the ministry of healing? Her two young nuns would cross the ocean, and then the Madras Discalced Carmelite Mission to Africa would begin.

As the good abbess watched the two waving figures on the ship's rail recede to white dots, she felt a twinge of apprehension. What if by their blind obedience to her grand scheme they were being condemned to a horrible fate? "The English missionaries have the almighty Empire behind them . . . but what of my girls?" She wrote that the seagulls' shrill quarreling and the splatter of bird excreta had marred the grand send-off she had envisioned. She was distracted by the overpowering scent of rotten fish, and rotted wood, and by the bare-chested stevedores whose betel-nut-stained mouths drooled bloody lechery at the sight of her brood of virgins.

"Father, we consign our sisters to You for safekeeping," Saintly Amma said, putting it on His shoulders. She stopped waving, and her hands found shelter in her sleeves. "We beseech You for mercy and for Your protection in this outreach of the Discalced Carmelites . . ."

It was 1947, and the British were finally leaving India; the Quit India Movement had made the impossible come about. Saintly Amma slowly let the air out of her lungs. It was a new world, and bold action was called for, or so she believed.

. . .

THE BLACK-AND-RED FLOATING PACKET of misery that called itself a ship steamed across the Indian Ocean toward its destination, Aden. In its hold the *Calangute* carried crate upon crate of spun cotton, rice, silk, Godrej lockers, Tata filing cabinets, as well as thirty-one Royal Enfield Bullet motorcycles, the engines wrapped in oilcloth. The ship wasn't meant to carry passengers, but the Greek captain did just that by housing "paying guests." There were many who would travel on a cargo ship to save on passage, and he was there to oblige by skimping on crew. So on this trip he carried two Madras nuns, three Cochin Jews, a Gujarati family, three suspicious-looking Malays, and a few Europeans, including two French sailors rejoining their ship in Aden.

The *Calangute* had a vast expanse of deck—more land than one ever expected at sea. At one end, like a gnat on an elephant's backside, sat the three-story superstructure which housed the crew and passengers, the top floor of which was the bridge.

My mother, Sister Mary Joseph Praise, was a Malayali from Cochin, in the state of Kerala. Malayali Christians traced their faith back to St. Thomas's arrival in India from Damascus in A.D. 52. "Doubting" Thomas built his first churches in Kerala well before St. Peter got to Rome. My mother was God-fearing and churchgoing; in high school she came under the influence of a charismatic Carmelite nun who worked with the poor. My mother's hometown is a city of five islands set like jewels on a ring, facing the Arabian Sea. Spice traders have sailed to Cochin for centuries for cardamom and cloves, including a certain Vasco de Gama in 1498. The Portuguese clawed out a colonial seat in Goa, torturing the Hindu population into Catholic converts. Catholic priests and nuns eventually reached Kerala, as if they didn't know that St. Thomas had brought Christ's uncorrupted vision to Kerala a thousand years before them. To her parents' chagrin, my mother became a Carmelite nun, abandoning the ancient Syrian Christian tradition of St. Thomas to embrace (in her parents' view) this Johnny-come-lately, pope-worshipping sect. They couldn't have been more disappointed had she become a Muslim or a Hindu. It was a good thing her parents didn't know that she was also a nurse, which to them would mean that she soiled her hands like an untouchable.

My mother grew up at the ocean's edge, in sight of the ancient Chinese fishing nets cantilevered from long bamboo poles and dangling over the water like giant cobwebs. The sea was the proverbial "breadbasket" of her people, provider of prawns and fish. But now on the deck of the *Calangute,* without the Cochin shore to frame her view, she did not recognize the breadbasket. She wondered if at its center the ocean had always been this way: smoking, malevolent, and restless. It tormented the *Calangute*, making it pitch and yaw and creak, wanting nothing more than to swallow it whole.

She and Sister Anjali secluded themselves in their cabin, bolting the door against men and sea. Anjali's ejaculatory prayers startled my mother. The ritualized reading of the Gospel of Luke was Sister Anjali's idea; she said it would give wings to the soul and discipline to the body. The two nuns subjected each letter, each word, line, and phrase to *dilatatio, elevatio,* and *excessus*—contemplation, elevation, and ecstasy. Richard of St. Victor's ancient monastic practice proved useful for an interminable ocean crossing. By the second night, after ten hours of such close and meditative reading, Sister Mary Joseph Praise suddenly felt print and page dissolve; the boundaries between God and self disintegrated. Reading had brought this: a joyous surrender of her body to the sacred, the eternal, and the infinite.

At vespers on the sixth night (for they were determined to carry the routine of the convent with them no matter what) they finished a hymn, two psalms, and their antiphons, then the doxology, and were singing the Magnificat when a piercing, splintering sound brought them to earth. They grabbed life jackets and rushed out. They were met by the sight of a segment of the deck that had buckled and pushed up into a pyramid, almost, it seemed to Sister Mary Joseph Praise, as if the *Calangute* were made of corrugated cardboard. The captain kept his pipe lit and his smirk suggested his passengers had overreacted.

On the ninth night, four of the sixteen passengers and one of the crew came down with a fever whose flesh signs were rose spots that appeared on the second febrile day and that arranged themselves like a Chinese puzzle on the chest and abdomen. Sister Anjali suffered grievously, her skin burning to the touch. By the second day of illness she was raging in feverish delirium.

Among the *Calangute*'s passengers was a young surgeon—a hawk-eyed Englishman who was leaving the Indian Medical Service for better pastures. He was tall and strong, and his rugged features made him look hungry, yet he avoided the dining room. Sister Mary Joseph Praise had run into him, literally, on the second day of the voyage when she lost her footing on the wet metal stairs leading up from their quarters to the common room. The Englishman coming up behind her seized her where he could, in the region of her coccyx and her left rib cage. He righted her as if she were a little child. When she stuttered her thanks, he turned beet red; he was more flustered than she by this unexpected intimacy. She felt a bruising coming on where his hands had clutched her, but there was a quality to this discomfort that she did not mind. For days thereafter, she didn't see the Englishman.

Now, seeking medical help, Sister Mary Joseph Praise gathered her courage to knock on his cabin. A faint voice bid her to enter. A bilious, acetone odor greeted her. "It is me," she called out. "It is Sister Mary Joseph Praise." The doctor lay on his side in his bunk, his skin the same shade as his khaki shorts, his eyes screwed shut. "Doctor," she said, hesitating, "are you also with fever?"

When he tried to look at her, his eyeballs rolled like marbles on a tilting plate. He turned and retched over a fire-bucket, missed it, which didn't matter, as the bucket was full to the brim. Sister Mary Joseph Praise rushed forward and felt his brow. It was cold and clammy, not at all feverish. His cheeks were hollowed, and his body looked as if it had shrunk to fit the tiny cabin. None of the passengers had been spared seasickness, but the Englishman's affliction was severe.

"Doctor, I am wanting to report a fever that has affected five patients. It comes with rash, chills, and sweats, a slow pulse and loss of appetite. All are stable except for Sister Anjali. Doctor, I am most worried about Anjali . . ."

She felt better once it was off her chest, even though other than letting out a moan the Englishman made no response. Her eyes fell on a catgut ligature that was looped around a bed rail near his hands and that displayed knot thrown on top of knot, ten-score of them. The knots were so plentiful that the thread stood up like a gnarled flagpole. This was how he had logged the hours, or kept track of his bouts of emesis.

She rinsed out the bucket and put it back within his reach. She mopped the mess on the floor with a towel, then she rinsed the towel out and hung it up to dry. She brought water to his side. She withdrew, wondering how many days it had been since he'd eaten anything.

By evening he was worse. Sister Mary Joseph Praise brought sheets, towels, and broth. Kneeling, she tried to feed him, but the smell of food triggered dry heaves. His eyeballs had sunk into their orbits. His shriveled tongue looked like that of a parrot. She recognized the room's fruity odor as the scent of starvation. When she pinched up a skin fold at the back of his arm and let go, it stayed up like a tent, like the buckled deck. The bucket was half full of clear fluid. He babbled about green fields and was unaware of her presence. Could seasickness be fatal, she wondered. Or could he have a *forme fruste* of the fever that afflicted Sister Anjali? There was so much she did not know about medicine. In the middle of that ocean surrounded by the sick, she felt the weight of her ignorance.

But she knew how to nurse. And she knew how to pray. So, praying, she eased off his shirt which was stiff with bile and spit, and she slid down his shorts. As she gave him a bed bath, she was self-conscious, for she'd never ministered to a white man, or to a doctor for that matter. His skin displayed a wave of goose bumps at the touch of her cloth. But the skin was free of the rash she'd seen on the four passengers and the one cabin boy who had come down with fever. The sinewy muscles of his arms bunched together fiercely at his shoulder. Only now did she notice that his left chest was smaller than his right; the hollow above his collar-bone on the left could have held a half cup of water, while that on the right only a teaspoon. And just beyond and below his left nipple, extending into the armpit, she saw a deep depression. The skin over this crater was shiny and puckered. She touched there and gasped as her fingers fell in, not meeting bony resistance. Indeed, it appeared as if two or perhaps three adjacent ribs were missing. Within that depression his heart tapped firmly against her fingers with only a thin layer of hide intervening. When she pulled her fingers away, she could see the thrust of his ventricle against his skin.

The fine, translucent coat of hair on his chest and abdomen looked as if it had drifted up from the mother lode of hair at his pubis. She dispassionately cleaned his uncircumcised member, then flopped it to one side and attended to the wrinkled and helpless-looking sac beneath. She washed his feet and cried while she did, thinking inevitably of her Sweet Lord and His last earthly night with His disciples.

In his steamer trunks she found books dealing with surgery. He had penned names and dates in the margins, and only later did it occur to her that these were patients' names, both Indian and British, mementos to a disease he'd first seen in a Peabody, or a Krishnan. A cross next to the name she took as a sign the patient had succumbed. She found eleven notebooks filled with an economical handwriting with slashing down-strokes, the text dancing just above the lines and obeying no margin save for the edge of the page. For an outwardly silent man, his writing reflected an unexpected volubility.

Eventually she found a clean undershirt and shorts. What did it say when a man had fewer clothes than books? Turning him first this way and then that, she changed the sheets beneath him and then dressed him.

She knew his name was Thomas Stone because it was inscribed inside the surgical textbook he'd placed at his bedside. In the book she found little about fever with rash, and nothing about seasickness.

That night Sister Mary Joseph Praise negotiated the heaving passageways, hurrying from one sickbed to the next. The mound where the deck had buckled resembled a shrouded figure and she averted her eyes. Once she saw a black mountain of a wave, several stories high, and the *Calangute* looked poised to fall into a hole. Sheets of water smashed over the bow, the noise more terrifying than the sight.

In the middle of the tempestuous ocean, groggy from lack of sleep, facing a terrible medical crisis, her world had become simplified. It was divided into those with fever, those with seasickness, and those without. And it was possible that none of these distinctions mattered, for very soon they might all drown.

She awoke from where she must have drifted off next to Anjali. In what seemed like the next instant she awoke again, but this time in the Englishman's cabin where she'd fallen asleep kneeling by his bed, her head lolling on his chest, his arm resting on her shoulder. In the time it took her to recognize this, she was asleep again, waking at daybreak finding herself on the bunk, but on its very edge, pressed against Thomas Stone. She hurried back to Anjali to find her worse, her respirations now sighing and rapid. There were large confluent purple patches showing on Anjali's skin.

The anxious faces of the sleepless crew and the fact that one fellow had knelt before her and said "Sister, forgive my sins!" told her that the ship was still in danger. The crew ignored her pleas for help.

Frantic and frustrated, Sister Mary Joseph Praise retrieved a hammock from the common room because of a vision she had in that fugue state between wakefulness and sleep. She strung it in his cabin between porthole and bedpost.

Dr. Stone was a dead weight and only the intercession of St. Catherine allowed her to drag him from bunk to floor, then feed him, one body part at a time, onto the hammock. Answering more to gravity than to the roll of the ship, the hammock found the true horizontal. She knelt beside him and prayed, pouring her heart out to Jesus, completing the Magnificat which had been interrupted the night the deck had buckled.

Color returned first to Stone's neck, then his cheeks. She fed him teaspoons of water. In an hour he held down broth. His eyes were open now, the light coming back into them, and the eyeballs tracking her every movement. Then, when she brought the spoon up, sturdy fingers encircled her wrist to guide the food to his mouth. She remembered the line she'd sung moments before: "He hath filled the hungry with good things, and the rich He hath sent empty away."

God had heard her prayers.

A pale and unsteady Thomas Stone came with Sister Mary Joseph Praise to where Sister Anjali lay. He gasped at the sight of the wide-eyed and delirious nun, her face pinched and anxious, her nose sharp as a pen, the nostrils flaring with each breath, seemingly awake and yet completely oblivious to her visitors.

He knelt over her, but Anjali's glassy gaze passed right through him. Sister Mary Joseph Praise watched the practiced way he pulled down Anjali's lids to examine her conjunctivae, and the way he swung the flashlight in front of her pupils. His movements were smooth and flowing as he bent Anjali's head toward her chest to check for neck stiffness, as he felt for lymph nodes, moved her limbs, and as he tapped her patellar tendon using his cocked finger in lieu of a reflex hammer. The awkwardness Sister Mary Joseph Praise had sensed in him when she had seen him as a passenger and then as a patient was gone.

He stripped off Anjali's clothes, unaware of Sister Mary Joseph Praise's assistance as he dispassionately studied the patient's back, thighs, and buttocks. The long sculpted fingers that probed Anjali's belly for the spleen and liver seemed to have been created for this purpose—she couldn't imagine them doing anything else. Not having his stethoscope, he applied his ear to Sister Anjali's heart, then her belly. Then he turned her to one side and pressed his ear against her ribs to listen to the lungs. He took stock, then muttered, "Breath sounds are diminished on the right . . . parotids enlarged . . . she has neck glands—why? . . . Pulse is feeble and rapid—"

"It was a slow pulse when the fever started," Sister Mary Joseph Praise offered.

"So you mentioned," he said sharply. "How slow?" He didn't look up.

"Forty-five to fifty, Doctor."

She felt he had forgotten his illness, forgotten even that he was on a ship. He had become one with Sister Anjali's body, it was his text, and he sounded it for the enemy within. She felt such confidence in his being that her fear for Anjali vanished. Kneeling by his side, she was euphoric, as if she had only at that moment come of age as a nurse because this was the first time she had encountered a physician like him. She bit her tongue because she wanted so much to say all this and more to him.

"Coma vigil," he said, and Sister Mary Joseph Praise assumed he was instructing her. "See how her eyes keep roving as if she's waiting for something? A grave sign. And look at the way she picks at the bedclothes—that's called carphology, and those little muscle twitches are *subsultus tendinum*. This is the 'typhoid state.' You'll see it in the late stages of many kinds of blood poisoning, not just typhoid . . . But mind you"—and he looked up at her with a little smile that belied what he said next—"I am a surgeon, not a medical man. What do I know of medical matters? Except to know that this is *not* a surgical illness."

His presence had done more than reassure Sister Mary Joseph Praise; it calmed the seas. The sun, which had been hiding, was suddenly at their back. The crew's drunken celebration indicated how grave the situation had been just hours before.

But though Sister Mary Joseph Praise did not want to believe this, there was little Stone could do for Sister Anjali, and in any case, nothing to do it with. The first-aid box in the galley held a desiccated cockroach—its contents had been pawned by one of the crew at the last port. The medicine chest which the captain used as a seat in his cabin seemed to have been left over from the Dark Ages. A pair of scissors, a bone knife, and crude forceps were the only things of use within that ornate box. What was a surgeon like Stone to do with poultices, or tiny containers of wormwood, thyme, and sage? Stone laughed at the label of something called *oleum philosophorum* (and this was the first time Sister Mary Joseph Praise heard that happy sound even if in its dying echo there was something hard-edged). "Listen to this," he said, reading: " 'containing old tilestones and brickbats for chronic costiveness'!" That done, he heaved the box overboard. He'd removed only the dull instruments and an amber bottle of *laudanum opiatum paracelsi*. A spoonful of that ancient remedy seemed to ease Sister Anjali's terrible air hunger, to "disconnect her lungs from her brain," as Thomas Stone explained to Sister Mary Joseph Praise.

The captain came by, sleepless, apoplectic, spraying saliva and brandy as he spoke: "How dare you dispose of shipboard property?"

Stone leaped to his feet, and at that moment he reminded Sister Mary Joseph Praise of a schoolboy spoiling for a fight. Stone fixed the captain with a glare that made the man swallow and take a step back. "Tossing that box was better for mankind and worse for the fish. One more word out of you and I'll report you for taking on passengers without any medical supplies."

"You got a bargain."

"And you will make a killing," Stone said, pointing to Anjali.

The captain's face lost its armature, the eyebrows, eyelids, nose, and lips all running together like a waterfall.

Thomas Stone took charge now, setting up camp at Anjali's bedside, but venturing out to examine every person on board, whether they consented to such probing or not. He segregated those with fever from those without. He took copious notes; he drew a map of the *Calangute*'s quarters, putting an *X* where every fever case had occurred. He insisted on smoke fumigation of all the cabins. The way he ordered the healthy crew and passengers around infuriated the sulking captain, but if Thomas Stone was aware of this he paid no attention. For the next twenty-four hours he didn't sleep, reexamining Sister Anjali at intervals, checking on the others: keeping vigil. An older couple was also quite ill. Sister Mary Joseph Praise never left his side.

Two weeks after they left Cochin, the *Calangute* limped into the port of Aden. The Greek captain had the Madagascar seaman hoist the Portuguese flag under which the ship was registered, but because of the shipboard fever the *Calangute* was promptly quarantined, Portuguese flag or no Portuguese flag. She was anchored at a distance, where, like a banished leper, she could only gaze at the city. Stone bullied the Scottish harbormaster who had pulled up alongside, telling him that if he didn't bring a doctor's kit, bottles of lactated Ringer's solution for intravenous administration, as well as sulfa, then he, Thomas Stone, would hold him responsible for the death of all Commonwealth citizens on board. Sister Mary Joseph Praise marveled at his outspokenness, and yet he was speaking for her. It was as if Stone had replaced Anjali as her only ally and friend on this ill-fated voyage.

When the supplies came, Stone went first to Sister Anjali. Making do with the crudest of antisepsis, with one scalpel stroke he exposed the greater saphenous vein where it ran just inside Sister Anjali's ankle. He threaded a needle into the collapsed vessel that should have been the width of a pencil. He secured the needle in place with ligatures, his hands a blur as he pushed one knot down over another. Despite the intravenous drip of Ringer's lactate and the sulfa, Anjali didn't make a drop of urine or show any signs of reviving. Later that evening, she died in a final dreadful paroxysm, as did two others, an old man and old woman, all within a few hours of one another. For Sister Mary Joseph Praise the deaths were stunning, and unforeseen. The euphoria she felt when Thomas Stone had risen and come to see Anjali had blinded her. She shivered uncontrollably.

At twilight, Sister Mary Joseph Praise and Thomas Stone slipped the shrouded bodies over the rail, with no help from the superstitious crew who wouldn't even look their way.

Sister Mary Joseph Praise was inconsolable, the brave front she'd put up shattering as her friend's body splashed into the water. Stone stood beside her, unsure of himself. His face was dark with anger and shame because he had not been able to save Sister Anjali.

"How I envy her," Sister Mary Joseph Praise said at last through tears, her fatigue and sleeplessness combining to release custody of her tongue. "She's with our Lord. Surely that is a better place than this."

Stone bit off a laugh. To him such a sentiment was a symptom of impending delirium. He took her by the arm and led her back to his room, lay her down on his bunk, and told her she was to rest, doctor's orders. He sat on the hammock and watched as life's only sure blessing—sleep—came to her, and then he hurried off to reexamine the crew and all passengers. Dr. Thomas Stone, surgeon, did not need sleep.

TWO DAYS LATER, with no more new cases of fever, they were finally allowed off the *Calangute*. Thomas Stone sought out Sister Mary Joseph Praise before disembarking. He found her red-eyed in the cabin she'd shared with Sister Anjali. Her face and the rosary she clutched were wet. With a start he registered what he had failed to before: that she was extraordinarily beautiful, her eyes big and soulful and more expressive than eyes had a right to be. His face grew warm and his tongue wouldn't unstick itself from the floor of his mouth. He shifted his gaze to the floor, to her travel bag. When he finally spoke it was to say, "Typhus." He'd looked in his books and given the matter a great deal of thought. Seeing her puzzlement, he said, "Indubitably typhus." He had expected the word, the diagnosis, would make her feel better, but instead it seemed to fill her eyes with fresh tears. "*Most* likely typhus—of course a serum test could have confirmed it," he stammered.

He shuffled his feet, crossed and uncrossed his hands. "I don't know where you're going, Sister, but I'm heading to Addis Ababa . . . it's in Ethiopia," he said, mumbling into his chin. "To a hospital . . . that would value your services if you were to come." He looked at her and blushed again, because the fact was he knew nothing about the hospital he was going to or whether it could use her services, and because he felt those moist dark eyes could read his every thought.

But it was her own thoughts that kept Sister Mary Joseph Praise silent. She remembered how she'd prayed for him and for Anjali, and how God had answered just one of her prayers. Stone, risen like Lazarus, then brought his entire being into understanding the fever. He'd barged into the crew's quarters, run roughshod over the captain, and bullied and threatened. Doing the *wrong* thing, as Sister Mary Joseph Praise saw it, but in pursuit of the *right* thing. His fierce passion had been a revelation to her. At the medical college hospital in Madras where she trained as a nurse, the civil surgeons (who at the time were mostly Englishmen) had floated around serene and removed from the patients, with the assistant civil surgeons and junior and senior house surgeons (who were all Indian) trailing behind like ducklings. At times it seemed to her they were so focused on disease that patients and suffering were incidental to their work. Thomas Stone was different.

She felt his invitation to join him in Ethiopia hadn't been rehearsed. The words had slipped out before he'd been able to stop them. What was she to do? Saintly Amma had identified a Belgian nun who had broken away from her order, and who had made a most tenuous foothold in Yemen, in Aden, a foothold that was in jeopardy because of the nun's ill health. Saintly Amma's plan was for Sister Anjali and Sister Mary Joseph Praise to start there, perched above the African continent, and to learn everything they could from the Belgian nun about operating in hostile climates. From there, after correspondence with Amma, the sister-sisters would head south, not to the Congo (which the French and Belgians had covered), not to Kenya, Tanganyika, Uganda, or Nigeria (the Anglicans had their fingers all over those souls and disliked competition), but perhaps to Ghana or Cameroon. Sister Mary Joseph Praise wondered what Saintly Amma might say to Ethiopia.

Saintly Amma's vision now felt like a pipe dream, a vicarious evangelism so ill informed that Sister Mary Joseph Praise was embarrassed to mention it to Thomas Stone. Instead she said in a breaking, hopeless voice, "I have orders to Aden, Doctor. But I thank you. Thank you for all you did for Sister Anjali." He protested that he'd done nothing.

"You did more than any human being could do," she said and took his hand in both of hers and held it. She looked into his eyes. "God be with you and bless you."

He could feel the rosary still entwined in her fingers, and the softness of her skin and the wetness from her tears. He recalled her hands on him, washing his body, dressing him, even holding his head when he retched. He had a memory of her face turned to the heavens, singing, praying for his recovery. His neck grew warm and he knew his color was betraying him a third time. Her eyes showed pain, and a cry escaped her lips, and only then did he know that he was squeezing her hands, grinding the rosary against her knuckles. He let go at once. His lips parted, but he didn't say anything. He abruptly walked away.

Sister Mary Joseph Praise couldn't move. She saw that her hands were red and beginning to throb. The pain felt like a gift, a blessing so palpable that it rose up her forearms and into her chest. What she couldn't bear was the feeling that something vital had been plucked out and uprooted from her chest when he walked away. She'd wanted to cling to him, to cry out to him not to leave. She had thought her life in the service of the Lord was complete. There was, she saw now, a void in her life that she'd never known existed.

THE MOMENT she stepped off the *Calangute* onto the soil of Yemen, Sister Mary Joseph Praise wished she'd never disembarked. How absurd it had been for her to have pined to come ashore all those days they'd been quarantined. Aden, Aden, Aden—she'd known nothing about it before this voyage, and even now it was no more than an exotic name. But from the sailors on the *Calangute,* she gathered that one could hardly go anywhere in the world without stopping in Aden. The port's strategic location had served the British military. Now its duty-free status made it the place to both shop and find one's next ship. Aden was gateway to Africa; from Africa it was gateway to Europe. To Sister Mary Joseph Praise it looked like the gateway to hell.

The city was at once dead and yet in continuous motion, like a blanket of maggots animating a rotting corpse. She fled the main street and the stultifying heat for the shade of narrow alleyways. The buildings looked hewn from volcanic rock. Pushcarts loaded impossibly high with bananas, with bricks, with melons, and even one carrying two lepers weaved through the pedestrian traffic. A veiled, stooped old woman walked by with a smoldering charcoal stove on her head. No one glanced at this strange sight, saving their stares instead for the brown-skinned nun walking in their midst. Her uncovered face made her feel stark naked.

After an hour during which she felt her skin puffing up like dough in an oven, after being directed this way and that, Sister Mary Joseph Praise arrived before a tiny door at the end of a slitlike passage. On the rock wall was a pale outline of a signboard recently removed. She offered a silent prayer, took a deep breath, and knocked. A man yelled in a hoarse voice, and Sister Mary Joseph Praise interpreted the sound as invitation to enter.

Seated on the floor next to a shiny balancing scale, she saw a shirtless Arab. All around him, reaching to the ceiling, were great bales of bundled leaves.

The hothouse scent stifled her breathing. It was a new scent for her, this scent of khat: partly cut grass, yet with something spicier behind it.

The Arab's beard was so red with henna she thought he'd bled into it. His eyes were lined like a woman's, reminding her of depictions of Salahuddin, who'd kept the Crusaders from taking the Holy Land. His gaze took in the young face imprisoned in the white wimple, and then those hooded eyes fell to the Gladstone bag in her hand. A heave of his body produced a vulgar laugh through gold-trimmed teeth, a laugh which he cut off when he saw the nun was about to collapse. He sat her down, sent for water and tea. Later, in a mixture of sign language and bastardized English, he communicated to her that the Belgian nun who'd lived there had died suddenly. When he said that, Sister Mary Joseph Praise began shivering again, and she felt a deep foreboding, as if she could hear death's footsteps rustling the leaves in that hothouse. She carried a picture of Sister Beatrice in her Bible, and she could see that face in her mind's eye, now metamorphosing into a death mask, and then to Anjali's face. She forced herself to meet the man's gaze, to challenge what he said. *Of what? Who asks "of what" in Aden? One day you are well, your debts are paid, your wives are happy, praise Allah, and the next day the fever gets you, and if it opens your skin up to the heat which your skin has fought off all these years, you die. Of what? Of what doesn't matter. Of bad skin! Of pestilence! Of bad luck, if you like. Of good luck, even.*

The building was his. Green khat stalks flashed in his mouth as he spoke. The old nun's God had been unable to save her, he said, looking up to the ceiling and pointing, as if He were still crouching there. Sister Mary Joseph Praise's eyes involuntarily followed his gaze, before she caught herself. Meanwhile, his muddy eyes dropped from the ceiling to her face, to her lips, and to her bosom.

IF I KNOW THIS MUCH about my mother's voyage, it's because it came from her lips to the ears of others and then to mine. But her tale stopped in Aden. It came to an abrupt halt in that hothouse.

What is clear is that she embarked on her journey with faith that God approved of her mission and would provide for and protect her. But in Aden, something happened to her. No one knew what exactly. But it was there that she understood that her God was also a vengeful and harsh God and could be so even to His faithful. The Devil had shown himself in Sister Anjali's purple, contorted death mask, but God had allowed that. She considered Aden an evil city, where God used Satan to show her how fragile and fragmented the world was, how delicate the balance between evil and good, and how naïve she was in her faith. Her father used to say, "If you want to make God laugh, tell him your plans." She felt pity for Saintly Amma, whose dream of enlightenment for Africa was vanity that cost Anjali's life.

For the longest time all I knew was this: after an unknown period of time that could have been months or even a year, my mother, aged nineteen, somehow escaped Yemen, then crossed the Gulf of Aden, then went overland perhaps to the walled and ancient city of Harrar in Ethiopia, or perhaps to Djibouti, then from there by train she entered Ethiopia via Dire Dawa and then on to Addis Ababa.

I know the story once she arrived at Missing Hospital. There were three spaced knocks on the door to Matron's office. "Come in," Matron said, and with those two words Missing was on a course different than anyone could have imagined. It was at the start of the short rains, when Addis was stunned into wet submission, and when after hours and days of the sound and sight of water, one began hearing and seeing things. Matron wondered if that explained this vision of a beautiful, brown-skinned nun, standing, but just barely, in the doorway.

The young woman's recessed, unblinking brown eyes felt like warm hands on Matron's face. The pupils were dilated, as though, Matron would think later, the horror of the journey was still fresh. Her lower lip was ripe, as if it might burst at the touch. Her wimple, cinched at the chin, imprisoned her features in its oval, but no cloth could restrain the fervor in that face, or conceal the hurt and confusion. Her gray-brown habit must have once been white. But, as Matron's eyes traveled down the figure, she saw a fresh bloodstain where the legs came together.

The apparition was painfully thin, swaying, but resolute, and it seemed a miracle that it was capable of speech, when it said in a voice heavy with fatigue and sadness: "I desire to begin the time of discernment, the time of listening to God as He speaks in and through the Community. I ask for your prayers that I may spend the rest of my life in His Eucharistic Presence and prepare my soul for the great day of union between bride and Bridegroom."

Matron recognized the litany of a postulant entering the order, words she herself had uttered so many years ago. Matron replied automatically, just as her Mother Superior had done, "Enter into the joy of the Lord."

It was only when the stranger slumped against the doorpost that Matron came out of her trance, running around her desk to grab her. Hunger? Exhaustion? Menstrual blood loss? What was this? Sister Mary Joseph Praise weighed nothing in Matron's arms. They took the stranger to a bed. Under the veil, the wimple, and habit they found a delicate wicker-basket chest and a scooped out belly. A girl! Not a woman. Yes, a girl who'd only just bid good-bye to childhood. A girl with hair that was not cut short like that of most nuns but long and thick. A girl with (and how could they not notice?) a precocious bosom.

Every maternal instinct in Matron came alive, and she kept vigil. She was there when the young nun woke up in the night, terrified, delirious, clinging to Matron once she knew she was in a safe place. "Child, child, what happened to you? It is all right. You are safe now." With such soothing words, Matron comforted her, but it was a week before the young nun slept alone and another week before the color returned to her face.

When the short rains ended, and when the sun turned its face to the city, as if to kiss and make up and say it was after all its favorite city for which it had reserved its most blessed, cloud-free light, Matron led Sister Mary Joseph Praise outdoors. She was to introduce her to the Missing People. The two of them entered Operating Theater 3 for the first time, and an astonished Matron watched as the stern and serious expression of her new surgeon, Thomas Stone, crumbled into something akin to happiness at the sight of Sister Mary Joseph Praise. He was blushing, taking her hand in his and crushing it till tears came to the young nun's eyes.

My mother must have known then that she would stay in Addis Ababa forever, stay in Missing Hospital and in the presence of this surgeon. To work for him, for his patients, to be his skilled assistant, was sufficient ambition, and it was an ambition without hubris, and God willing, it was something she could reasonably do. A return journey to India through Aden was too difficult to contemplate.

In the ensuing seven years that she lived and worked at Missing Hospital, Sister Mary Joseph Praise rarely spoke about her voyage and never about her time in Aden. "Whenever I brought up Aden," Matron said, "your mother would glance over her shoulder, as if Aden or whatever it was she left behind had caught up with her. The dread and terror on her face made me loath to ask again. But it scared me, I'll tell you. All she said was, 'It was God's will that I come here, Matron. His reasons are unknowable to us.' There was nothing disrespectful about that answer, mind you. She believed that her job was to make her life something beautiful for God. He had led her to Missing."

Such a crucial gap in the history, especially that of a short life, calls attention to itself. A biographer, or a son, must dig deep. Perhaps she knew that the side effect of such a quest was that I'd learn medicine, or that I would find Thomas Stone.

SISTER MARY JOSEPH PRAISE began the task of the rest of her days when she entered Operating Theater 3. She scrubbed and gloved and gowned and stood across the table from Dr. Stone as his first assistant, pulling on the small retractor when he needed exposure, cutting the suture when he presented the ends to her, and anticipating his need for irrigation or suction. A few weeks later, when the scrub nurse couldn't be there, my mother filled in as scrub nurse *and* first assistant. Who knew better than a first assistant when Stone wanted a scalpel for sharp dissection, or when gauze wrapped around his finger would do. It was as if she had a bicameral mind, allowing one half to be scrub nurse, shuttling instruments from the tray to his fingers, while the other side served as Stone's third arm, lifting up the liver, or holding aside the omentum, the fatty apron that protected the bowels, or with a fingertip pushing down edematous tissue just enough for Stone to see where his needle was to take a bite.

Matron would peek in to watch. "Pure ballet, my dear Marion. A heavenly pair. Totally silent," Matron said. "No asking for instruments or saying 'Wipe,' 'Cut,' or 'Suction.' She and Stone . . . You never saw anything quicker. I suspect that we slowed them down because we couldn't get people off and on the table quickly enough."

For seven years Stone and Sister Mary Joseph Praise kept the same schedule. When he operated late into the night and into the morning, she was across from him, more constant than his own shadow, dutiful, competent, uncomplaining, and never absent. Until, that is, the day when my brother and I announced our presence in her womb and our unstoppable desire to trade the nourishment of the placenta for the succor of her breasts.

CHAPTER 2

The Missing Finger

THOMAS STONE HAD a reputation at Missing for being outwardly quiet but intense and even mysterious, though Dr. Ghosh, the hospital's internal medicine specialist and jack-of-all-trades, disputed that last label, saying, "When a man is a mystery to himself you can hardly call him mysterious." His associates had learned not to read too much into Stone's demeanor, which a stranger might think was surly when in fact he was painfully shy. Lost and clumsy outside it, inside Operating Theater 3 he was focused and fluid, as if it was only in the theater that body and soul came together, and where the activity within his head matched the terrain outside.

As a surgeon, Stone was famous for his speed, his courage, his daring, his boldness, his inventiveness, the economy of his movements, and his calmness under duress. These were skills that he'd honed on a trusting and uncomplaining population, briefly in India, and then in Ethiopia. But when Sister Mary Joseph Praise, his assistant for seven years, went into labor, all these qualities vanished.

On the day of our birth, Thomas Stone had been standing over a young boy whose belly he was about to open. He held his hand out, palm up, fingers extended to receive the scalpel in that timeless gesture that would forever be the measure of his days as a surgeon. But for the first time in seven years, steel had not slapped into his palm the instant his fingers opened; indeed, the diffident tap told him someone other than Sister Mary Joseph Praise stood across from him. "Impossible," he said when a contrite voice explained that Sister Mary Joseph Praise was indisposed. In the preceding seven years there hadn't been a time when he'd stood there without her. Her absence was as distracting and maddening as a bead of sweat about to fall into his eye when he was operating.

Stone didn't look up as he made his keyhole incision. Skin. Fat. Fascia. Split the muscle. Then, using blunt dissection, he exposed the glistening peritoneum, which he incised. His finger slithered into the abdominal cavity through this portal and rooted for the appendix. Still, with each step, he had to wait for a fraction of a second, or wave off the proffered instrument in favor of another. He worried about Sister Mary Joseph Praise even if he was unaware that he was worrying, or unwilling to admit it.

He summoned the probationer, a young, nervous Eritrean girl. He asked her to seek out Sister Mary Joseph Praise and remind her that doctors and nurses couldn't afford the luxury of being ill. "Ask her"— the terrified probationer's lips were moving as she tried to by-heart his message—"kindly ask her, if . . ." His eyes were free to look at the probationer, since his finger was now sounding the boy's insides better than any pair of eyes. ". . . if she recalls that I returned to the operating theater the very next day after performing a ray amputation on my own finger?"

That event took place five years before and was an important milestone in Stone's life. His own curved needle on a holder had nicked the pulp of his right index finger while he worked in a pus-filled belly. He'd immediately stripped off his glove, and with a hypodermic needle, he had injected acriflavine, precisely one milliliter of a solution diluted 1:500, down the tiny track the errant needle had traveled. Then he'd infiltrated the fluid into the surrounding tissue as well. The orange dye transformed the digit into an oversize lollipop. But despite these measures, in just hours a creeping red wave extended down from the fingertip and into the tendon sheath in the palm. Despite oral sulfatriad tablets and, later, at Ghosh's insistence, injection of precious penicillin into his buttocks, scarlet streaks (which were the hallmark of streptococcal infection) showed at his wrist, and the epitrochlear lymph node behind the elbow became as big as a golf ball. The rigors had made his teeth chatter and the bed shake. (This later became an aphorism in his famous textbook, a Stonism as readers called it: "If the teeth chatter it is a chill, but if the bed shakes it is a true rigor.") He had made a quick decision: to amputate his own finger before the infection spread farther, and to do the operation himself.

The probationer waited for the rest of his message, while Stone drew the wormlike appendix out of the incision and straightened up like a fisherman who'd reeled his quarry onto the deck. The few bleeders Stone snapped off with hemostats, like a marksman firing at pop-up ducks, while also clamping off the blood vessels to the appendix. He tied these off with catgut, his hands a blur, until all the dangling hemostats were removed.

Stone held up his right hand for the probationer's inspection. Five years after the amputation, the hand looked deceptively normal, though on closer study the index finger was missing. The key to this aesthetically pleasing result was that the metacarpal head—the knuckle of the missing finger—had been cut away, too, so that no stump was visible in the *V* between thumb and middle finger. It was as if the fingers had simply moved over one notch. Four-fingered custom gloves added to the illusion of normalcy. Far from being a disadvantage, his hand could negotiate crevices and tissue planes that others could not, and his middle finger had developed the dexterity of an index finger. That, together with the fact that his middle finger was longer than his former index finger, meant he could tease an appendix out from its hiding place behind a cecum (the beginning of the large bowel) better than any surgeon alive. He could secure a knot in the deepest recess of the liver bed with just his fingers, where other surgeons might resort to a needle holder. In later years, in Boston, he famously punctuated his admonishment to his interns of "*Semper per rectum, per anum salutem,* if you don't put your finger in it, you'll put your foot in it," by holding up the former middle finger, now elevated to the status of index finger.

Those who trained with Stone never overlooked the rectal exam on their patient, not just because Stone had drilled into their heads that most colon cancers are in the rectum or sigmoid, many within reach of the examining finger, but also because they knew they'd be fired for this omission. Years later in America, a story circulated about one of Stone's trainees, a man named Blessing, who, after examining a drunk in the emergency room and taking care of whatever the problem was, returned to his call room. As he was about to sleep, he remembered that he hadn't done a rectal exam. Guilt and fear that his chief would somehow discover his lapse moved him to get up and go out into the night. Blessing tracked the patient down to a bar, where for the price of a beer the man agreed to drop his pants and be digitally examined—be "blessed" as the event came to be described—and only then was the young doctor's conscience eased.

THE PROBATIONER IN Operating Theater 3 on the day of Sister Mary Joseph Praise's labor and our birth was a pretty—no, a *beautiful*—

young Eritrean girl. Sadly, her humorless intensity, the dedication she showed to her training, made people forget her youth and her looks.

The probationer hurried off to find my mother, not pausing to question the propriety of the message she carried to Sister Mary Joseph Praise. Stone, of course, would never have imagined the message might be hurtful. As is so often the case with shy yet talented people, Stone was generally forgiven what Dr. Ghosh called his social retardation. The glaring gaps that in a bowel repair could have been fatal were overlooked when they occurred in such a personality; they weren't an impediment to him, only an irritation to others.

At the time of our birth the probationer was not yet eighteen, with a tendency to confuse penmanship and keeping a neat medical record (and thereby pleasing Matron) with the actual care of patients.

Being seniormost of the five probationers in Missing's nursing school had been a matter of pride for her, and most days she managed to push to the back of her mind the fact that her seniority was only because she was repeating her year, or, as Dr. Ghosh put it, because she was "on the long-term plan."

Orphaned as a child by smallpox, which had also left a faint lunar landscape on her cheeks, the probationer had from a young age addressed her self-consciousness by becoming excessively studious, a trait encouraged by the Italian nuns, the Sisters of the Nigrizia (Africa), who raised her in the orphanage in Asmara. The young probationer displayed her studiousness as if it were not merely a virtue but a God-given gift, like a beauty spot or a supernumerary toe. What promise she'd shown in those early years, sailing through church school in Asmara, skipping grades, speaking fluent official Italian (as opposed to the bar-and-cinema version spoken by many Ethiopians, in which prepositions and pronouns were dispensed with altogether), and able to recite even her nineteen-times table.

You could say the probationer's presence at Missing was an accident of history. Her hometown of Asmara was the capital city of Eritrea, a country which had been an Italian colony from as far back as 1885. The Italians under Mussolini invaded Ethiopia from Eritrea in 1935, with the world powers unwilling to intercede. When Mussolini threw his lot in with Hitler, his fate was sealed, and by 1941, Colonel Wingate's Gideon Force had defeated the Italians and liberated Ethiopia. The Allies gave Emperor Haile Selassie of Ethiopia a most unusual gift: they tacked on the very old Italian colony of Eritrea as a protectorate of newly liberated

Ethiopia. The Emperor had lobbied hard for just this, so that his land-locked country could have the seaport of Massawa, not to mention the lovely city of Asmara. The British perhaps wanted to punish the Eritreans for their long collaboration with the Italians; Eritrean *askaris,* thousands of them, were part of the Italian army and had fought their black neighbors and died alongside their white masters.

For the Eritreans to have their lands handed to Ethiopia was an unimaginable wound, akin to giving liberated France to England merely because the people of both countries were white and ate cabbage. When, a few years later, the Emperor annexed the land, the Eritreans at once began a guerrilla war for their liberation.

But there were some advantages to Eritrea being part of Ethiopia: the probationer won a scholarship to the country's only nursing school in Addis Ababa, at Missing Hospital, the first young person from Eritrea to be so rewarded. The trajectory of her scholastic progress to that point was spectacular and unprecedented, a model for all youth; it was also an invitation to fate to stick a foot out and trip her.

Yet it wasn't fate that stymied the probationer when she came to her clinical years, and it wasn't her clumsiness with the Amharic language, or with English, since she soon overcame these obstacles and became fluent. She discovered that memorization ("by-hearting," as Matron called it) was of no help to her at the bedside, where she struggled to distinguish the trivial from the life threatening. Oh yes, she could and did recite the names of the cranial nerves as a mantra to calm her own nerves. She could rattle off the composition of *mistura carminativa* (*one* gm of soda bicarb, *two* ml each of spirit of ammonia and tincture cardamom, *point six* ml of tincture of ginger, *one* ml of spirit of chloroform, topped off with peppermint water to *thirty* ml) for dyspepsia. But what she couldn't do, and it annoyed her to see how effortlessly her fellow probationers could, was develop the one skill Matron said she lacked: *Sound Nursing Sense.* The only reference to this in her textbook was a statement so cryptic, more so after she memorized it, that she'd begun to think it was put there to antagonize her:

> Sound Nursing Sense is more important than knowledge, though knowledge only enhances it. Sound Nursing Sense is a quality that cannot be defined, yet is invaluable when present and noticeable when absent. To paraphrase Osler, a nurse with book knowledge but without Sound Nursing Sense is like a sailor at sea in a

seaworthy vessel but without map, sextant, or compass. (Of course, the nurse without book knowledge has not gone to sea at all!)

The probationer had at least gone to sea—she was sure of that. She was determined to prove that she did have map and compass, and so she would regard every assignment as a test of *her* skills, an opportunity to display Sound Nursing Sense (or to hide the lack of it).

SHE RAN AS IF *jinn* were chasing her, through the sheltered walkway between the theater and the rest of the hospital. Patients and relatives of those being operated on that day were squatting or sitting cross-legged on either side of her path. A barefoot man, his wife, and two small children shared a meal, dipping fingers into a bowl lined with *injera* on which a lentil curry had been poured, while an infant, all but hidden by the mother's *shama,* suckled at the breast. The family turned in alarm as she ran by, and it made her feel important. Across the yard she could see women in white *shamas* and bright red and orange head scarves crowding the outpatient benches, looking at that distance like hens in a chicken coop.

In the nurses' quarters she ran up the stairs to my mother's room. When she knocked there was no answer, but the door was unlocked. In the darkened room she saw Sister Mary Joseph Praise under the covers, her face turned toward the wall. "Sister?" she called softly, and when my mother moaned, the probationer took that to mean she was awake. "Dr. Stone sent me to tell you . . ." She felt relieved to have remembered all the parts of the message. She waited for a response, and when my mother didn't volunteer one, the probationer imagined that my mother might be annoyed with her. "I only came because Dr. Stone sent me. I'm sorry to disturb you. I hope you feel better. Do you need anything?" She waited dutifully, and after a while, she eased out of the room. Since there was no return message for Dr. Stone, and since her pediatric nursing class was about to start, she did not return to Theater 3.

IT WAS EARLY AFTERNOON by the time Stone went to the nurses' quarters. He had finished the appendectomy, then two gastro-jejunostomies for peptic ulcer, three hernia repairs, one hydrocele, a subtotal thyroid resection, and a skin graft, but by his standards it had been tortuously slow. An ordeal. With knitted brow he ascended the stairs. He understood that his swiftness as a surgeon depended to a large degree—more than he'd ever imagined—on the skills of Sister Mary Joseph Praise . . . Why did he have to think about these things? Where was she? That was the point. And when would she be back?

There was no answer when he knocked. It was the corner room on the second floor. The compounder's wife came charging up to protest this trespass by a male. Though Matron and Sister Mary Joseph Praise were the only nuns at Missing, the compounder's wife acted as if she had been denied her true calling. With a sash low over her brow and a crucifix as big as a revolver, she looked like a nun. She considered herself a quasi warden of the nurses' hostel, the keeper of the Missing virgins. She had a spider's sense for a male footstep, an incursion into her territory. But now, seeing who it was, she backed away.

Stone had never been inside Sister Mary Joseph Praise's room. When she typed or worked on the illustrations for his manuscripts, she came to his quarters or to his office adjoining the clinic.

He turned the handle, calling out, "Sister? Sister!" He was met by a miasma at once familiar and alarming, but he couldn't place it.

He groped for the switch and swore when it eluded him. He stumbled to the window, bumping into a chest of drawers. He swung the glass-paned portion of the window in, and then pushed back the wooden shutters. Daylight flooded the narrow room.

On top of the chest of drawers was a heavy mason jar that drew the sun's rays. The amber fluid within reached all the way to the chunky lid which was sealed with wax. At first he thought the jar might hold a relic, an icon. A carpet of gooseflesh swept down his arms, as if recognition came to his body before it came to his brain. There, suspended in the fluid, the nail delicately pivoting on the glass bottom like a ballerina on tiptoe, was his finger. The skin below the nail was the texture of old parchment, while the underbelly displayed the purple discoloration of infection. He felt a longing, an emptiness, and an itch in his right palm which only that missing finger could relieve.

"I didn't know—" he said turning to her bed, but what he saw made him forget what he was going to say.

Sister Mary Joseph Praise lay in agony on her narrow cot. Her lips were blue. Her lusterless eyes were focused beyond his face. She was deathly pale. He reached for her pulse, which was rapid and feeble. An uninvited memory from the *Calangute* voyage of seven years before came flooding over him: he recalled the feverish and comatose Sister Anjali. A cold sensation spread from his belly to his chest. He was overcome by an emotion that as a surgeon he had rarely experienced: fear.

His legs could no longer support him.

He fell to his knees by her bed. "Mary?" he said. He could do nothing but repeat her name. From his lips, Sister Mary Joseph Praise's name sounded like an interrogation, then an endearment, then a confession of love spun out of one word. *Mary? Mary, Mary!* . . She did not, could not, answer.

An old man's palsy overtook his hands as they reached for her face. He kissed her forehead. In that extraordinary and unstoppable act he realized, not without a twinge of pride, that he loved her, and that he, Thomas Stone, was not only capable of love, but that he had loved her for seven years. If he'd been blind to his love, perhaps it was because it had happened as soon as he met her on those slippery stairs, it had happened when she had nursed him, bathed him, tried to revive him on the *Calangute.* It had happened when she'd held him in her arms and wrestled and dragged his dead weight to a hammock and then spoon-fed life back into him. It had happened as they crouched over Sister Anjali's body. But love reached its apogee when Sister Mary Joseph Praise came to work alongside him in Ethiopia, and then it had never wavered. Love so strong, without ebb and flow or crests and troughs, indeed lacking any sort of motion so that it had become invisible to him these seven years, part of the order of things outside his head which he had taken for granted.

Did Mary love him? Yes. Of this he felt certain. She had loved him, but following his cue—always following his cue—she'd said nothing. And what had he done all these years? Only taken her for granted. *Mary, Mary, Mary.* Even the sound of her name was a revelation to him since he'd never called her anything but Sister. He was sobbing, terrified of losing her, but that, too, he saw was his selfishness, *his* need for her manifesting itself again. Would he have the chance to make amends? How stupid could a man be?

Sister Mary Joseph Praise barely registered his touch. Her cheek was hot against his. He lifted the sheet. A generous swelling of her belly met his eyes.

It was an axiom of his that any swelling in a woman's abdomen was a pregnancy until proven otherwise. But his mind overrode that thought, refusing to consider it—this was a nun, after all. Instead he came to

a snap diagnosis of bowel obstruction . . . or free fluid in the peritoneal cavity . . . or hemorrhagic pancreatitis . . . *some* sort of abdominal
catastrophe . . .

Maneuvering through the door frame, then trying not to bump her
feet on the banister, his sobs changing to grunts of effort, he carried her
out from her quarters, and then down the path to the operating theater.
She felt heavier to Stone than she had a right to be.

There was a question the chief examiner had posed to him when he
appeared for the Royal College of Surgeons viva voce after passing his
written examinations in Edinburgh: "What first-aid treatment in shock
is administered by ear?" His answer "Words of comfort!" had won the
day. But now, in place of reassuring and soothing words that would have
been humane and therapeutic, Stone yelled for help at the top of his
voice.

His shouts, taken up by the keeper of the virgins, brought everyone
including Gebrew the watchman, who came running from the front
gate, along with Koochooloo and two other unnamed dogs at her heels.

The sight of the blubbering, helpless Stone shocked Matron just as
much as the sight of Sister Mary Joseph Praise's terrible state.

Lord, he's done it again, was Matron's first thought.

It was a well-kept secret that Stone had on three or four occasions
since his arrival at Missing gone on a drunken binge. For a man who
rarely drank, who loved his work, who found sleep a distraction, who had
to be reminded to go to bed, these episodes were mystifying. They came
with the suddenness of influenza and the terror of possession. The first
patient on the morning list would be on the table, ready to be put under,
but there'd be no sign of Stone. When they went looking for him the
first time they found a babbling, disheveled white man, pacing in his
quarters. During these episodes he did not sleep or eat, slipping out in
the dead of night to replenish his supplies of rum. On the last occasion
this creature had climbed the tree outside its window and perched there
for hours, muttering like a cross hen. A fall from that height would have
cracked its skull. Matron, when she had seen those bloodshot, mongoose
eyes staring down at her, fled, leaving Sister Mary Joseph Praise and
Ghosh to keep vigil and to try to talk him down, get him to eat, to stop
drinking.

As abruptly as it started, in two days, no more than three, the spell
would be over, and after a very long sleep Stone would be back at work as
if nothing had happened, never making any reference to how he'd incon-
venienced the hospital, the memory of it erased. No one ever brought it

up to him because the other Stone, the one who rarely drank, would have been hurt and insulted by such inquiry or accusation. The other Stone was as productive as three full-time surgeons, and so these episodes were a small price to pay.

Matron came closer. Stone's eyes were not bloodshot and he didn't reek of spirits. No, he was unhinged by Sister Mary Joseph Praise's condition, and rightly so. As Matron turned her attention from Stone to Sister Mary Joseph Praise, she nevertheless felt a ghost of satisfaction: at last the man had bared his soul, displayed his feelings for his assistant.

Matron ignored Stone's ramblings about volvulus or ileus or pancreatitis or tuberculous peritonitis. "Let's go to the theater," she said, and when they were there, she said, "Lay her on the operating table."

He set her down and Matron saw a sight she had seen seven years before: blood soaked Sister Mary Joseph Praise's dress in the region of her pubis. Matron's mind raced back to Sister Mary Joseph Praise's first arrival from Aden, and how blood on her habit then had caused similar concern. Matron had never asked the nineteen-year-old, point-blank, what caused the bleeding. The irregularity of the stain on that occasion had invited the observer to read meaning in its shape. Matron's imagination had constructed so many scenarios to explain that mystery. In the ensuing years, memory had changed the event from mysterious to mystical.

Which was why Matron now glanced at Sister Mary Joseph Praise's palms and breast as Stone laid her down, as if she half expected to see bleeding stigmata, as if that first mystery had grown into this second mystery. But no, the only blood was at the vulva. Lots of blood. With dark clots. And bright red rivulets that ran down the thighs. Matron had no doubt, as blood dripped to the floor: this time it was secular bleeding.

Matron seated herself between Sister Mary Joseph Praise's legs, willfully ignoring the stomach swelling that loomed in front of her. The labia were engorged and blue, and when Matron slid her gloved finger in, she found the cervix fully dilated.

Of blood there was much too much. She swabbed and dabbed and pulled down on the posterior vaginal wall for a better view. When a piteous sigh emerged from her patient's lungs, Matron almost dropped the speculum. Matron's chest was pounding, her hands shaking. She leaned forward, tilted her head again to peer in. There, like a rock at the bottom of a mud pit, a stone of the heart, was a baby's head.

"Lord, she's," Matron said, when she could finally speak, gasping at the sacrilegious word that threatened to choke her and which her mouth could no longer contain, "pregnant."

Every observer I later talked to remembers this moment in Theater 3, when the air stood still, when the loud clock across from the table froze and a long, silent pause followed.

"Impossible!" said Stone, for the second time that day, and even though it was incorrect and hardly the thing to say, it allowed them all to breathe again.

But Matron knew she was right.

She would have to deliver this baby. Dr. K. Hemlatha—Hema to all of them—was out of station.

Matron had delivered hundreds of babies. She reminded herself of this now to try and keep herself from panic.

But how was she to push away not just her qualms but her confusion? One of her own, a bride of Christ—pregnant! It was unthinkable. Her mind refused to digest this. And yet the evidence—an infant's skull— was there, right before her eyes.

The same thought distracted the scrub nurse, the barefoot orderly, and Sister Asqual, who was the nurse anesthetist. It caused them to trip over one another and knock down an intravenous drip as they scurried around the table, readying the patient. Only the probationer, who was mortified that she had failed that morning to recognize this crisis when she visited Sister Mary Joseph Praise, didn't stop to wonder how Sister Mary Joseph Praise got pregnant.

Matron's heart felt as if it might gallop right out of her chest. "Lord, what worse circumstance can you construct for a delivery? A pregnancy that's a mortal sin. A mother-to-be who is like my own daughter. Massive bleeding, ghostly pallor . . ." And all this when Hema, Missing's only gynecologist, not only the best in the country, but the best Matron had ever seen, was away.

Bachelli up in the Piazza was marginally competent in obstetrics but unreliable after two in the afternoon, and his Eritrean mistress was deeply suspicious of him leaving on "house calls." Jean Tran, the half-French, half-Vietnamese fellow in Casa Popolare, did a bit of everything and smiled a lot. But assuming they could be reached, it would still be a while before either man would come.

No, Matron had to do this herself. She had to forget the implications of the pregnancy. She had to breathe, concentrate. She had to conduct a normal delivery.

But that afternoon and evening, normal would elude them.

. . .

STONE STOOD BY, his mouth open, looking to Matron for direction, while Matron sat facing the vulva, waiting for the baby to descend. Stone alternately crossed his hands in front of him and then dropped them by his sides. He could see Sister Mary Joseph Praise's pallor increasing. And when Nurse Asqual in a panicked voice called out the blood pressure—"systolic of eighty, palpable"—Stone wobbled as if he might faint.

Despite uterine contractions which Matron could feel through the belly and see in Sister Mary Joseph Praise's contorted face, and despite the fact that the cervix was wide open, nothing happened. A baby's head high up in the birth canal with the cervix flattened like a gasket around it always reminded Matron of the shaved scalp of a bishop. But this bishop was staying put. And meanwhile, such bleeding! A dark and messy pool had formed on the table and tidal eddies of blood came out of the vagina. Blood was to delivery rooms and operating theaters what feces were to tripe factories, but even so it seemed to Matron that this was a lot of blood coming out.

"Dr. Stone," Matron said, her lips quivering. A bewildered Stone wondered why she was calling on him.

"Dr. Stone," she said again. For Matron, Sound Nursing Sense meant a nurse knowing her limits. *For God's sake, she needs a Cesarean section.* But she didn't say those words because with Stone it could have the opposite effect. Instead, her voice low, her head drooping, Matron pushed down on her thighs to bring herself to her feet and to vacate her spot between Sister Mary Joseph Praise's legs.

"Dr. Stone. Your patient," she said to the man who everyone believed to be my father, putting in his hands not only the life of a woman that he chose to love, but our two lives—mine and my brother's—which he chose to hate.

CHAPTER 3

The Gate of Tears

WHEN SISTER MARY JOSEPH PRAISE felt the herald cramps of labor, Dr. Kalpana Hemlatha, the woman I would come to call my mother, was five hundred miles away and ten thousand feet in the air. Off the starboard wing of the plane Hema had a beautiful view of Bab al-Mandab—the Gate of Tears—so named because of the innumerable ships that had wrecked in that narrow strait that separated Yemen and the rest of Arabia from Africa. At this latitude, Africa was just the Horn: Ethiopia, Djibouti, and Somalia. Hema traced the Gate of Tears as it widened from a hairline crack to become the Red Sea, spooling north to the horizon.

As a schoolgirl studying geography in Madras, India, Hema had to mark where coal and wool were produced on a map of the British Isles. Africa figured in the curriculum as a playground for Portugal, Britain, and France, and a place for Livingstone to find the spectacular falls he named after Queen Victoria, and for Stanley to find Livingstone. In future years, as my brother, Shiva, and I made the journey with Hema, she would teach us the practical geography she had taught herself. She'd point down to the Red Sea and say, "Imagine that ribbon of water running up like a slit in a skirt, separating Saudi Arabia from Sudan, then farther up keeping Jordan away from Egypt. I think God meant to snap the Arabian Peninsula free of Africa. And why not? What do the people on this side have in common with the people on the other side?"

At the very top of the slit a narrow isthmus, the Sinai, thwarted God's intention and kept Egypt and Israel connected. The man-made Suez Canal finished the cut and allowed the Red Sea to connect with the Mediterranean, saving ships the long journey around the Cape. Hema would always tell us that it was over the Gate of Tears that she had the awakening that would change her life. "I heard a call when I was in that plane. When I think back, I know it was you." That rattling, airborne tin can always seemed an improbable place for her epiphany.

HEMA SAT ON THE WOODEN BENCH SEATS that ran lengthwise on both sides of the ribbed fuselage of the DC-3. She was unaware of how badly her services were needed just then at Missing, the hospital where she had worked for the last eight years. The drone of the twin engines was so loud and unrelenting that half an hour into the flight she felt as if the sound inhabited her body. The hard bench and choppy ride were raising blisters on her behind. Whenever she closed her eyes, she felt as if she were being hauled across a rutted landscape in the back of a bullock cart.

Her fellow travelers on this flight from Aden to Addis Ababa were Gujaratis, Malayalis, French, Armenians, Greeks, Yemenis, and a few others whose dress and speech did not as clearly reveal their origins. As for her, she wore a white cotton sari, a sleeveless off-white blouse, and a diamond in her left nostril. Her hair was parted in the middle and gathered with a clip at the back, and loosely braided below.

She sat sideways looking out. She saw a gray dart below—the shadow cast by the plane on the ocean. A giant fish she imagined was swimming just below the surface of the sea, keeping pace with her. The water looked cool and inviting, unlike the interior of the DC-3, which had grown less steamy but was still thick with the mingled scents of the human freight. The Arabs had the dry, musty smell of a grain cellar; the Asians contributed the ginger and garlic; and from the whites came the odor of a milk-soaked bib.

Through the half-open curtain to the cockpit she could see the pilot's profile. Whenever he turned to glance at his cargo, his bottle-green sunglasses seemed to swallow his face, only his nose poking through. The glasses had been perched up on his forehead when she boarded, and Hema had noted then that his eyes were red like a rodent's. The odor of juniper berry on his breath advertised his fondness for gin. She'd developed an aversion to him even before he opened his mouth to herd his passengers onto the plane, snapping at them—"Allez!"—as if they were subhuman. She bit her tongue then, because this was the man about to take them aloft.

His face and jug ears resembled a figure a child might draw with crayon on butcher paper. But the details were beyond a child: the fine arbor of blood vessels on his cheeks; muttonchop sideburns dyed boot-polish black; the white ring of *arcus senilis* around his pupils; gray eyebrows that betrayed his pretense at youthfulness. She wondered how a man could look in the mirror and not see the absurdity of his own appearance.

She studied her own reflection in the porthole. Hers was a round face, too, the eyes widely spaced with a doll's pert nose. The red *pottu* in the center of her forehead stood out. Her cheeks had a Martian tint cast on them by the cobalt-blue water below, and the hint of green in her eyes—unusual for an Indian—was accentuated. "Your gaze encompasses all men, makes your most ordinary glance seem intimate, carnal," Dr. Ghosh had told her, "as though you are ravishing me with your eyes!" Ghosh was a tease and forgot what he said as soon as the words rolled off his tongue. But this statement of his lingered with her. She thought of Ghosh's fur-covered limbs and shuddered. Body hair was one of her pet dislikes, or so she'd believed. She knew it was a fatal prejudice for an Indian woman. His was like a gorilla coat, the chest tendrils poking out through his vest and peeking up above his shirt collar. "Ravishing? You wish, you lecher," she said now, smiling as if Ghosh were sitting across from her.

She had to give him this much: if she stared fractionally too long at a man, she attracted more attention than she intended. It was partly why she used spectacles with large wire frames, because she thought they made her eyes seem closer together. She liked the exaggerated Cupid's bow of her upper lip, but not her cheeks, which she felt were too chubby. What to do? She was a big woman. Not fat, but big . . . Well, maybe a bit fat, and she'd certainly put on a kilo or two or three in India, but how could she help that in the face of a mother's astonishing cooking? Because of my height, I get away with it, she told herself. Wearing a sari helps, of course.

She grunted, remembering how Dr. Ghosh had invented a special term for her: *magnified*. Years later, when Hindi movies with their song and dance became all the rage in Africa, the ward boys in Addis Ababa would call her Mother India, not in mockery, but in reverence for the tearjerker of the same name starring Nargis. *Mother India* had run for three straight months at the Empire Theater and then moved to the Cinema Adowa; that, too, without the benefit of subtitles. The ward boys could be heard singing "Duniya Mein Hum Aaye Hain"—"We've Arrived in This World"—though they didn't understand a word of Hindustani.

"And if I'm *magnified*, what term shall we apply to you?" she said, carrying on the imaginary conversation, surveying her old friend from head to foot. He was not a conventionally good-looking man. "How about 'alien'? I mean it as a compliment. I say 'alien,' Ghosh, because you are so unaware of yourself, of your looks. There's a seduction in that for others. Alien becomes beauty. I'm saying this to you because you're not here. To be around someone whose self-confidence is more than what our first glance led us to expect is seductive."

Mysteriously, during her holidays, Ghosh's name kept popping up in her conversations with her mother. Despite Hema's lack of interest in marriage, her mother was terrified that her daughter would end up with a non-Brahmin, someone like Ghosh. And yet as Hema neared thirty, her mother had begun to feel that any husband was better than no husband at all.

"You say he's not handsome? Does he have good color?"

"Ma, he's fair . . . fairer than me, and he has brown eyes. Bengali, Parsi, and God knows what other influences in those eyes."

"What is he?"

"He calls himself high-caste Madras mongrel," she said, giggling. Her mother's frown threatened to swallow her nose, and so Hema had changed the subject.

Besides, it was impossible to construct a Ghosh for someone who'd never met him. She could say that his hair was combed flat and parted in the middle, looking sleek and smart for about ten minutes in the morning, but after that, the hairs broke loose like rioting children. She could say how at any time of the day, even after he had just shaved, black stubble showed under his jaw. She could say that his neck was nonexistent, squashed down by a head shaped like a jackfruit. She could say he just looked short because of a slight belly whose size was exaggerated in the way he leaned back and swayed from side to side as he walked, which drew the eye away from the vertical. Then there was his voice, unmodulated and startling, as if the volume knob had frozen on its highest setting. How could she convey to her mother that the sum total of all this made him not ugly, but strangely beautiful.

Despite the rash on the backs of his hands—a burn, really—his fingers were sensual. The ancient X-ray machine, a Kelley-Koett, had caused the rash. Just thinking of the "Koot" made Hema's blood boil. In 1909, Emperor Menelik had imported an electric chair, having heard the invention would efficiently get rid of his enemies. When he discovered it needed electricity, he simply used it as a throne. Similarly, the big Kelley-

Koett had come in the 1930s with an eager American mission group that soon realized that, even though electricity had arrived in Addis Ababa, it was intermittent and the voltage insufficient for such a temperamental beast. When the mission folded, the precious unpacked machine had been simply left behind. Missing lacked an X-ray machine, and so Ghosh reassembled the unit and matched it to a transformer.

No one but Ghosh dared touch the Koot. Cables ran from its giant rectifier to the Coolidge tube, which sat on a rail and could be moved this way and that. He worked the dials and voltage levers until a spark leaped across the two brass conductors, producing a thunderclap. The fiery display had caused one paralyzed patient to leap off the stretcher and run for his life; Ghosh called that the Sturm und Drang cure. He was the Koot's keeper, repairing it, babying it so that three decades after the company went under, the Koot was still operational. Using the fluoroscopy screen, he studied the dancing heart, or else he defined exactly where a cavity in the lung resided. By pushing on the belly he could establish whether a tumor was fixed to the bowel or abutted on the spleen. In the early years he hadn't bothered with the lead-lined gloves, or a lead apron for that matter. The skin of his probing, intelligent hands paid a visible price.

HEMA TRIED TO IMAGINE Ghosh telling *his* family about her. *She's twenty-nine. Yes, we were classmates at Madras Medical School, but she's a few years younger. I don't know why she never married. I didn't get to know her well till we were interns in the septic ward. She's an obstetrician. A Brahmin. Yes, from Madras. An expatriate, living and working in Ethiopia these eight years.* Those were the labels that defined Hema, and yet they revealed little, explained nothing. The past recedes from a traveler, she thought.

Sitting in the plane, Hema closed her eyes and pictured her schoolgirl self with the twin ponytails, the long white skirt, and white blouse under the purple half sari. All Mrs. Hood Secondary School girls in Mylapore had to wear that half sari, really nothing more than a rectangle of cloth to coil around the skirt once and pin on the shoulder. She'd hated it, because one was neither child nor adult but half woman. Her teachers wore full saris while the venerable headmistress, Mrs. Hood, wore a skirt. Hema's protests triggered a lecture by her father: *Do you not know how fortunate you are to be in a school with a British headmistress? Do you not know how many hundreds have tried to get in there, offered ten times the money, but were turned down by Miz-Iz-Ood. She goes by merit only. Would you prefer the Madras corporation school?* And so, each day she put on the hated uniform, feeling half dressed, and feeling as if she were selling a piece of her soul.

Velu, the neighbor's son who'd once been her best friend, but who had turned insufferable at ten, liked to perch on the dividing wall and tease her:

> The girls who come from Miz-Iz-Ood, parlez-vous?
> The girls who come from Miz-Iz-Ood, parlez-vous?
> The girls who come from Miz-Iz-Ood,
> Haven't grown their womanhood,
> Inky Pinky parlez-vous!

She ignored him. Velu, who was as dark-skinned as she was light, said, "So proud you are of being fair. Monkeys will nibble your sweet flesh thinking it is jackfruit on a jackfruit tree, mind you me!" There she was, eleven years old, setting off for school, dwarfed by her Raleigh bicycle, trading barbs with Velu. Her books were in a tasseled *sanji* slung over her shoulder, the strap running between her breasts. Already in her posture and in her steady pedal strokes there were signs of a certain immutability.

The bicycle, once so tall and perilous, soon shrunk beneath her. Her breasts thrust out on either side of that *sanji* strap, and hair sprouted between her legs. (If that was what Velu had meant about not growing her womanhood, she had proved him wrong.) She was a good student, a captain in net ball, a senior prefect, and showing promise in Bharatnatyam, finding in herself a talent for recapitulating a most intricate dance sequence after being shown it just once.

She felt neither an obligation to join the herd nor any urge to try to stand out from it. When a close friend told her she always looked cross, she was surprised and a little thrilled that she could pull off such misdirection. In medical school (in full sari and now riding the bus) this quality grew stronger—not crossness, but independence and misdirection. Some classmates considered her arrogant. She drew others to her like acolytes only for them to discover she wasn't recruiting. The men needed pliancy in their women friends, and she couldn't bring herself to act coy or silly for their sakes. The couples who huddled in the library behind oversize anatomy atlases and whispered themselves into the notions of love amused her.

I had no time for such silliness. But she did have time for trashy novels set in castles and country houses with heroines named Bernadette. She fantasized about the dashing men of Chillingforest and Lockingwood and Knottypine. That was her trouble then—she dreamed of a *greater* kind of love than the kind displayed in the library. But she was also filled with a nameless ambition that had nothing to do with love. What exactly did she want? It was an ambition that wouldn't let her compete for or seek the same things others sought.

When, as a student at Madras Medical College, Hema had found herself admiring her professor of therapeutics (the lone Indian in a school where, even as independence approached, most of the full professors were British), when she found herself moved by his humanity, his mastery of his subject (*Face it, Hema; it was a crush*), when she found herself wishing to be his understudy and found him encouraging, she deliberately chose another path. She was loath to give anyone that kind of power. She chose obstetrics and gynecology instead of his field, internal medicine. If the professor's field was limitless, requiring a breadth of knowledge that extended from heart failure to poliomyelitis and myriad conditions in between, she chose a field that had some boundaries and a mechanical component—operations. Of these there was a limited repertoire: C-sections, hysterectomies, prolapse repair.

She'd discovered in herself a talent for manipulative obstetrics, becoming expert at divining just how the baby was hung up in the pelvis. What other obstetricians perhaps dreaded, she relished. Blindfolded, she could distinguish the left from the right forceps and apply each in her sleep. She could see in her mind's eye the geometry of each patient's pelvic curve and match that to the curvature of the baby's skull as she slid the forceps in, articulating the two handles and confidently extracting the baby.

She went overseas on a whim. But it broke her heart to leave Madras. She still cried some evenings, picturing her parents taking their chairs outdoors to wait for the sea breeze which, even on the hottest and stillest of days, blew in at dusk. She left because gynecology, at least in Madras, remained a man's domain, and, even on the eve of independence, a British domain, and she had no chance at all for a civil service appointment to the government teaching hospital. It was strange and yet it pleased her to think that she, Ghosh, Stone, and Sister Mary Joseph

Praise had all at one time or another trained or worked at the Government General Hospital in Madras. A thousand five hundred beds and twice that number under the beds, between the beds—it was a city by itself. In it Sister Mary Joseph Praise had been a budding novitiate and probationer; perhaps they'd even walked past each other. And incredibly, Thomas Stone, too, had a brief tenure at Government General Hospital, though since the maternity section was quite separate, there'd been no reason for his path to cross with Hema's.

She'd left behind Madras, left behind labels of caste, gone so far away that the word "Brahmin" meant nothing. Working in Ethiopia, she tried to make a visit home every third or fourth year. She was returning after her second such visit. Seated in the noisy airplane, she found herself rethinking her choices. In the last few years she'd come close to defining the nameless ambition that had pushed her this far: *to avoid the sheep life at all costs.*

Missing had felt familiar when she first arrived there, not unlike the Government General Hospital in India, but on a much smaller scale: people waiting in line, the families camping out under trees, waiting with the infinite patience of those who have little choice but to wait. She'd been kept busy from her first day. If the truth be known, she secretly relished the emergencies, the situations where her heart was in her mouth, where the seconds ticked off, where a mother's life hung in the balance, or a baby in the womb, deprived of oxygen, needed a heroic rescue. In those moments she did not have existential doubts. Life became sharply focused, meaningful just when she wasn't thinking of meaning. A mother, a wife, a daughter, was suddenly none of these things, boiled down to a human being in great danger. Hema herself was reduced to the instrument required to treat them.

But of late she felt the huge remove between her practice in Africa and the frontiers of scientific medicine epitomized by England and America. C. Walton Lillehei in Minneapolis had just that year begun an era of heart surgery by finding a way to pump blood while the heart was stopped. A vaccine for polio had been developed, though it had yet to make its way to Africa. At Harvard in Massachusetts, a Dr. Joseph Murray had performed the first successful human kidney transplant from one sibling to another. The picture of him in *Time* showed an ordinary-looking chap, unpretentious. The portrait had surprised Hema, made her imagine that such discoveries were within every doctor's reach, within her reach.

She'd always loved the story of Pasteur's discovery of microbes, or Lister's experiments with antisepsis. Every Indian schoolchild dreamed of being like Sir C. V. Raman, whose simple experiments with light led to a Nobel Prize. But now she lived in a country that few people could find on the map. ("The Horn of Africa, on the upper half, on the eastern coast—the part that looks like a rhino's head and points at India," she'd explain.) And fewer still knew of Emperor Haile Selassie, or if they remembered him for being *Time* magazine's Man of the Year in 1935, they didn't remember the country whose cause he pleaded at the League of Nations.

If asked, Hema would have said, *Yes, I'm doing what I intended to do; I'm satisfied.* But what else could one say? When she read her *Surgery, Gynecology & Obstetrics* (each month's volume arriving by sea mail weeks after publication, bruised and stained in its brown wrapping), the innovations read like fiction. It was exciting yet deflating, because it was already old news. She told herself that her work, her yeoman contribution in Africa, was somehow connected to the advances described in *SG&O*. But in her heart she knew that it wasn't.

A NEW SOUND REGISTERED. It was the scrape and rattle of wood on metal. The tail of the plane was packed with two giant wooden crates and stacks of smaller square tea chests, banded with tin strips stamped LONGLEITH ESTATES, S. INDIA. Netting hooked to skeletal struts restrained the cargo from falling on the passengers, but not from sliding around. Her feet and those of her fellow passengers rested on bulging jute sacks. Fading military logos were stenciled on the floor and on the silver fuselage. American troops in North Africa once sat here and contemplated their fate. Patton himself perhaps sat on this plane. Or perhaps this was a relic from the French colonies in Somalia and Djibouti. The carrying of passengers felt like an afterthought for this new airline with its hand-me-down planes and ancient pilots. She could see the pilot arguing into the microphone, gesticulating, pausing to listen to the reply, then barking again. The passengers who were close to the cockpit frowned.

Once again Hema craned her neck to see if her crate with the Grundig was visible, but it wasn't. Every time she thought about her extravagant purchase she felt a pang of guilt. But buying the radio-cum–record player had made the night she spent in Aden almost tolerable. A city built on top of a dormant volcanic crater, hell on earth, that was Aden, but at least it was duty-free. Oh yes, and Rimbaud had once lived there—and never wrote another line of poetry.

She'd picked out the spot for the Grundig in her living room. Most definitely it would have to be under the framed black-and-white print of Gandhi spinning cotton. She'd have to hunt for a quieter location for the Mahatma.

She imagined Ghosh nursing his brandy, and Matron, Thomas Stone, and Sister Mary Joseph Praise drinking sherry or coffee. She pictured Ghosh leaping to his feet as the dazzling opening chords of "Take the 'A' Train" poured from the Grundig. Then came the cheeky melody—the last tune in the world that you'd have predicted to follow. Those opening chords, though . . . how they stayed with her. And how she resisted them! She resented the chauvinism of Indians who could only admire things foreign. And yet, she heard those chords in her sleep, found herself humming them during her ablutions. She heard them now in the plane. Strange dissonant notes thrown together, wanting resolution, and somehow they captured America and Science and all that was bold and brash and daring and exciting about America (or at least the way she imagined America to be). Notes pouring out of the skull of a black man whose name was Billy Strayhorn. Stray . . . horn!

Ghosh had introduced her to jazz and to "Take the 'A' Train." "Wait . . . watch! See?" he said, the first time she heard the melody after the chords. "You have to smile. You can't help it!" And he was right, the tune was so catchy and upbeat—how fortunate she was that her first introduction to serious Western music should be that tune. Still, she'd come to think of it as her song, her invention, and it annoyed her that he'd been the one to bring her to it. She laughed at the strangeness of liking Ghosh so much, when she wanted so much to dislike him.

BUT JUST AT THE MOMENT she was thinking these thoughts, anticipating her arrival in Addis Ababa . . . she found herself suddenly invoking Lord Shiva's name: the plane, the DC-3, the trustworthy camel of the frontier sky, was shuddering as if mortally wounded.

She looked out. The propeller on her side fluttered to a stop, and a puff of smoke came out of the beefy engine cowling.

The plane pitched to starboard and she found herself plastered against the window. All around her passengers screamed, and a thermos flask bounced on the cabin wall, spilling tea as it clattered away. She clutched around for a handhold, but then the plane righted itself and seemed to stop in midair, before beginning a steep descent. No, not a descent, her stomach corrected her—this was a fall. Gravity reached its tentacles out and grabbed the silver cylinder with its cantilevered wings. Gravity promised a water landing. Or, since the plane had wheels, not floats, a water smashing. The pilot was shouting, not in panic, but in anger, and she had no time to think how strange this was.

When, years later, she'd look back at this moment of change, look at it clinically ("Milk the history! Exactly when and exactly how did it start? Onset is everything! In the *anamnesis* is the diagnosis!" as her professor would say), she would see that her transformation actually took place over many months. However, it was only as she was falling out of the sky over the Bab al-Mandab that she understood that change had come.

A LITTLE INDIAN BOY fell on her bosom. He was the son of the only Malayali couple on board—teachers in Ethiopia, no doubt; she could tell that in a single glance. This knock-kneed fellow, five, maybe six, years old in oversize shorts, had clutched a wooden plane in his hand from the moment he came on board, protecting it as if it were made of gold. His foot had become wedged between two jute sacks, and when the plane righted itself, he fell onto Hema.

She held him. His puzzled look collapsed into one of fear and pain. Hema spotted the curve in his shin—like bending a green stick, the bone too young to snap clean. She took all this in even as her body registered that they were plunging, losing altitude.

A young Armenian, bless his practicality, scrambled to free the leg. Incredibly, the Armenian was smiling. He tried to tell her something— a reassurance of sorts. She was shocked to see someone calmer than herself when all around the cries of passengers made the situation worse.

She lifted the little boy to her lap. Her thoughts were both clear and disconnected. The leg is already straightening but there is no doubt that it is fractured and the plane is going down. She stopped his stunned parents with an outstretched palm and clamped a hand on the mouth of the wailing mother. She felt the familiar calmness of an emergency, but she understood the falseness of that feeling, now that it was her life at stake.

"Let him be with me," she said, removing her hand from the woman's face. "Trust me, I'm a doctor."

"Yes, we know," the father said.

They squeezed in next to her on the bench. The boy didn't cry; he only whimpered. His face was pale—he was in shock—and he clung to her, his cheek against her bosom.

Trust me, I'm a doctor. She thought it ironic that these would be her last words.

Through the porthole Hemlatha saw the white crests getting closer, looking less and less like lace on a blue cloth. She had always assumed that she would have years to sort out the meaning of life. Now, it seemed she would only have a few seconds, and in that realization came her epiphany.

As she bent over the child she realized that the tragedy of death had to do entirely with what was left unfulfilled. She was ashamed that such a simple insight should have eluded her all these years. *Make something beautiful of your life.* Wasn't that the adage Sister Mary Joseph Praise lived by? Hema's second thought was that she, deliverer of countless babies, she who'd rejected the kind of marriage her parents wanted for her, she who felt there were too many children in the world and felt no pressure to add to that number, understood for the first time that having a child was about cheating death. Children were the foot wedged in the closing door, the glimmer of hope that in reincarnation there would be some house to go to, even if one came back as a dog, or a mouse, or a flea that lived on the bodies of men. If, as Matron and Sister Mary Joseph Praise believed, there was a raising of the dead, then a child would be sure to see that its parents were awakened. Provided, of course, the child didn't die with you in a plane crash.

Make something beautiful of your life—this whimpering little fellow with his shiny eyes and long eyelashes, his oversize head and the puppy-dog scent of his unruly hair . . . he was about the most beautiful thing one could make.

Her fellow passengers looked as terrified as she felt. Only the Armenian shook his head at her, and smiled as if to say, *This isn't what you think it is.*

What an idiot, Hema thought.

An older Armenian—his father perhaps—was impassive, staring straight ahead. The older man had looked morose on boarding and his mood now was no better, and no worse. Hema found herself amazed that she should notice such trivial details at a time like this when, instead of deconstructing faces, she should be bracing for the moment of impact.

As the sea rushed up to meet the plane, she thought of Ghosh. She was shocked when a flood of tender feelings for him overcame her, as if *he* were about to die in a plane crash, as if *his* grand adventure in medicine and *his* carefree days were ending and with it any chance of his achieving the thing he wanted most: to marry Hema.

CHAPTER 4

The Five-F Rule

Y OUR PATIENT, DR. STONE," Matron said again, vacating the stool between Sister Mary Joseph Praise's legs. Seeing his face, she wondered if he was about to throw something.

Thomas Stone was an occasional flinger of instruments, though never in front of Matron. It was rare that Sister Mary Joseph Praise ever handed him the wrong implement, but from time to time, a hemostat failed to release with light counterpressure, or a Metzenbaum didn't cut at its tip. He had good aim; one spot on the wall of Operating Theater 3, just above the light switch and perilously close to the glass instrument cabinet, was his usual target.

No one but Sister Mary Joseph Praise took it personally—she would be crestfallen, even though she tested every instrument before she put it in the autoclave. Matron insisted the throwing was a good thing. "Feed him a ratchetless hemostat from time to time," she said to Sister Mary Joseph Praise. "Otherwise he'll keep it bottled up till it comes oozing out of his ears and we'll have a right mess then."

The plaster above the light switch had stellate pits and scratches as if a firecracker had gone off there. The strike on the wall occurred after the word "COMPLETELY" and before the word "USELESS!" left his mouth. Once in a great while he exploded at Nurse Asqual, the anesthetist, if the patient were too lightly under or had been given too little curare so that the belly muscles clamped down like a vice on his wrists as he fished inside the abdomen. More than one etherized patient had woken in holy terror hearing Stone bellow, "I'll need a pickax if you can't give me more relaxation down here!"

But at this moment, with Sister Mary Joseph Praise's lips ashen, her breathing shallow, her eyes seeing past him, her unrelenting bleeding, and then with Matron having passed the baton to him, Stone was speechless. He was experiencing the helplessness that patients' relatives must feel, and he didn't like it in the least bit. His lips trembled and he felt shame at how his wet face displayed his emotions. But more than that he felt fear, and an astonishing paralysis of thought which only shamed him further.

When he finally spoke it was to say in a quavering voice, "Where is Hemlatha? Why isn't she back? We need her," which was an act of uncharacteristic humility.

He swiped at his eyes using the back of his forearm, a childlike gesture. Matron watched in disbelief: instead of taking the stool she offered, he retreated. Stone walked to the wall that bore the marks of his anger. He struck his head on the plastered surface, a head butt worthy of a mountain goat. His legs wobbled. He clung to the glass cabinet. Matron felt obliged to murmur "Completely useless" on the off chance that if his violence had meaning, God forbid it should fail for lack of its accompanying mantra.

True, Stone could have done a Cesarean section, though, strangely for a tropical surgeon, it was one of the few operations he hadn't done. "See One, Do One, Teach One" was a chapter heading in his textbook, *The Expedient Operator: A Short Practice of Tropical Surgery*. But what his readers didn't know, and what I learned only many years later, was that he had an aversion to anything gynecological (not to mention anything obstetrical). It stemmed from his final year of medical school, when he did what was unheard of: he bought his very own cadaver so that he could master the anatomy he had already learned so well on a shared cadaver in his first year of medical school. The male poorhouse specimen of his first-year anatomy class had been ancient and shriveled with ghostly muscles and tendons, such being the common tender of Edinburgh anatomy theaters. He'd shared that body with five other students. But he lucked out with the cadaver he purchased in his final year: a well-fed, middle-aged female, a type he associated with the linoleum factories in Fife. Stone's dissection of the hand was so elegant (with just the tendon sheath exposed on the middle finger, while on the ring finger he carried it further to lay open the sheath and show the tendons of *flexor sublimis* like the wires of a suspension bridge, the *profundus* tendon coursing between them) that the anatomy professor preserved it to show the first-year students. For weeks Thomas Stone toiled over his cadaver, spending more time with her than he had with any other female save his mother. He felt an ease with her, a fluency that came from intimate knowledge. On one side, he had filleted her cheek to the ear, tying the flap back with sutures to expose the parotid gland and the facial nerve passing through, its branches splayed out like a goose's foot, hence the name *pes anserinus*. On the other side of the face he'd removed all subcutaneous tissue and fat to reveal the myriad muscles of expression whose concerted movements in life had conveyed her sorrow, joy, and every emotion in between. He didn't think of her as a person. She was simply knowledge embodied, embalmed, and personified. Every evening he folded back the muscles and then the skin flaps dangling on narrow hinges, and then he spread the formalin-soaked rags over her to ensheathe her. Sometimes when he fastened the rubber sheet around her and tucked the edges in, it reminded him of his mother's ritual of putting him to bed. Back in his room, his solitude and loneliness always felt more acute.

On the day he removed the bowel to expose the aorta and kidneys, he saw her womb. It wasn't the shriveled purse he expected to find, sunk into the bowl of the pelvis. Instead, it peeked above the pelvic brim. A few days later he turned to the pelvis, his *Cunningham's* dissection manual open to the new section. He proceeded step by step, marveling at the book's genius as it unpeeled and unroofed and taught as it went. *Cunningham's* dictated a vertical slice through the front of the uterus and then the operator was to gently pry the uterus open. He did, and out fell a fetus, its head a little bigger than a grape, eyes tightly shut, limbs folded in like an insect. It dangled on the umbilical cord like an obscene talisman on a headhunter's belt. He could see the mother's cervix destroyed and black, from infection or gangrene. The catastrophe that befell this woman was memorialized in formalin.

Stone barely made it to the sink before his dinner came up. He felt betrayed, as if someone had been spying on him. All this time he'd imagined he and she were alone. He couldn't go on. He couldn't even look at her, or fold her back up or cover her. The next day he asked the puzzled attendant to dispose of the cadaver even though the dissection of the pelvis was incomplete and the lower limbs were untouched. But Thomas Stone was done.

At Missing Hospital, because of Hema, Stone never had to venture into the territory of the female reproductive organs. That area he conceded (and it was atypical for him to concede anything) to her.

He and Hemlatha were civil, collegial, and even friendly outside the operating theater. After all, Missing only had three physicians—Hema,

Stone, and Ghosh—and it would've been awkward if they didn't get along. But in Operating Theater 3, Hema and Stone managed to provoke each other. Hema's style was precise and careful—a living example, Matron thought, of why more women should be surgeons. Matron sometimes believed she saw Hemlatha listening and *then* thinking when with a patient in the clinic, rather than trying to do both things at once. Hema was a surgeon who would throw four casts to her knots where others might be content with three. She never left the operating room until her patient awoke from anesthesia. Her surgical field was as neat and tidy as an anatomical demonstration with vulnerable structures carefully identified and moved out of harm's way and with bleeding meticulously controlled. To Matron the field looked static, yet alive, like a painting by Titian or da Vinci. "How can a surgeon know where she is," Hema was fond of saying, "unless she knows where she has been?"

For Stone, minimal handling of tissue was what counted the most, and he had no time for the aesthetic of the surgical field. "Hema, if you want pretty, dissect cadavers," he once told her. "Stone, if you want bloody, become a meat cutter," she said. So vast was his experience and the practice that he put into his craft that his nine fingers could find their way in a bloody field in which no landmarks were visible to others; his movements were economical and precise, and his results were excellent.

On those rare occasions when a woman with the mud of the field still fresh on her feet was brought in with a bull-gore wound that extended into the pelvis, or when a bar girl came with a knife or bullet wound near the uterus, Hemlatha and Stone would scrub together and enter the abdomen à deux, fussing at each other, bumping heads, and at times rapping each other's knuckles with the handle of the hemostat. Matron said she kept a register of which surgeon had stood on the right side at the last joint exploration, and she made sure they took turns. While Hemlatha meticulously resected uterus or repaired a bladder tear, Stone, who could not carry a tune, nevertheless whistled "God Save the Queen," which riled Hema. If Stone went first, Hemlatha would talk about the famous surgeons of years past—Cooper, Halsted, Cushing—and what a shame it was that tropical surgeons showed no sign of that great surgical legacy.

Stone didn't believe in glorifying surgeons or operations. "Surgery is surgery is surgery," he liked to say, and on principle he would no more look up to a neurosurgeon than down on a podiatrist. "A good surgeon needs courage for which a good pair of balls is a prerequisite," he had even written in the manuscript of his textbook, knowing fully well that his editor in England would take it out, but enjoying the experience of putting those words on paper. Stone had found a volubility, a combativeness and forcefulness, in his writing that he didn't show in his speech. "Courage? What's this you write about 'courage'?" Hema asked. "Is it *your* life you are risking?"

A Cesarean section was technically not beyond Stone's abilities. But on that fateful day, the *thought* of taking scalpel to Sister Mary Joseph Praise—his surgical assistant, his closest confidante, his typist, his muse, and the woman he realized he loved—terrified him. She was already in appalling shape, pale and clammy, her pulse so thready that he believed anything he did would send her over the precipice. On a stranger, he might not have hesitated to try a Cesarean section. "The doctor who treats himself has a fool for a patient" was an adage he knew well. But what about a doctor who performed an unfamiliar operation on a loved one? Was there an adage for that?

Increasingly, since the publication of his textbook, Stone had taken to quoting from it, as if his own written word had greater legitimacy than his unpublished (and heretofore unspoken) thoughts. He'd written, "The doctor who treats himself has a fool for a patient, *but there are circumstances when he has no recourse...*" He had gone on to chronicle the tale of his own ray amputation, how he'd performed a nerve block on his right elbow, and then, with Sister Mary Joseph Praise "helping," he had made the incision into his flesh, his left hand doing some of the work while Sister Mary Joseph Praise stood in for his right. He realized as he watched her make the bone cuts that she could do much more than assist if she chose to. It was the anecdote of the amputation, together with his picture in the frontispiece, his fingers—all nine of them—forming a steeple in front of his chin, which had made the book so successful. There were so many extant surgery texts that it was surprising how popular *The Expedient Operator* (or *A Short Practice*, as it was known in some countries) had become. For a tropical surgery book, most of its sales took place in nontropical countries. Perhaps it was its quirkiness, its biting tenor, and the often sharp and unintended humor. He drew only on his experience or his careful interpretation of the experience of others. Readers pictured him as a revolutionary, but one who operated on the poor instead of preaching land reform. Students wrote him adoring letters, and when his dutiful responses (penned by Sister Mary Joseph Praise) didn't match the gushy, confessional tone of their letters, they pouted.

The illustrations in the textbook (all drawn and lettered by Sister Mary Joseph Praise) had a simple quality, as if done on a napkin; no attempt was made at getting proportion or perspective right, but they were models of clarity. The book was translated into Portuguese, Spanish, and French.

Daring operations performed in darkest Africa—that was how the publisher had described the book on the back cover. The reader, knowing nothing about the "dark continent," filled in the blanks, pictured Stone in a tent, a kerosene lamp held up by a Hottentot providing the only light, elephants stampeding outside while the good doctor recited Cicero and excised a part of himself as blithely as if he were cutting for stone on the body of another. What neither the reader nor Stone would accept was that his self-amputation was as much an act of conceit as it was an act of heroism.

"YOUR PATIENT, Dr. Stone," Matron said for the third time.

Stone took the spot between Sister Mary Joseph Praise's legs that Matron vacated, though, after all that, Matron seemed reluctant to let him by, as if she didn't want him to sit there any more than he wanted to sit. It wasn't a vantage point that he was accustomed to, at least not often with a woman. With men, he sat there to repair a watering-can scrotum, and in both sexes he might be seated to drain rectal abscesses, or to ligate and excise hemorrhoids or *fistula-in-ano*. But otherwise, he was a surgeon who was rarely seated.

When Stone clumsily parted the labia, blood poured out. He adjusted the gooseneck lamp and then his own neck to sight up the birth canal.

He tried to remember the citrus rule from his student days. What was it? Lime, lemon, orange, and grapefruit corresponded to four, six, eight, and ten centimeters of dilation of the cervix. Or was it two, four, six, and eight? And was there a grape or plum involved?

What he saw made him turn pale: the cervix was past grapefruit, on its way to melon. And there, as if at the bottom of a bloody well, was a baby's head, the tissues around it flattened. The fine wet black hair on the skull reflected the theater lights.

At that moment it was as if someone who'd lain dormant within Stone took over.

If there was a connection between him and the poor infant within, it was something that Stone didn't see. Instead, the sight of that skull agitated him. Fear was driven out by anger, and anger had its own perverted reasoning: What cheek this invader had to put Mary's life in jeopardy! It was as if he'd spotted the corpse of a burrowing mole that had attacked Mary's body, and the only way he could bring her relief was to extract it. The sight of that bright scalp wrought no tenderness from Thomas Stone, only revulsion. And it gave him an idea.

"Find the enemy and win the firefight" was a saying of his.

He had found the enemy.

"*F*latus, *F*luid, *F*eces, *F*oreign Body, and *F*etus feel better out than in," he said aloud, as if he'd just invented the phrase. In his book he had called it the Five-F rule. He drove himself to his terrible decision. Far better, he decided, to drill a hole in the skull of the mole—he'd already stopped thinking of it as a baby—than to experiment on Sister Mary Joseph Praise by doing a Cesarean, an operation that was both unfamiliar and one that he feared would kill her in her fragile state. The enemy was more a foreign body, a cancer, than it was a fetus. No doubt the creature was dead. Yes, he would tap that skull, empty its contents, crush it just as if he were crushing a bladder stone, and then he'd pull out the deflated head which was the part that was hung up in the pelvis. If need be, he'd use scissors on its collarbones, scalpel on ribs; he would grab, slash, slit, and smash whatever fetal part obstructed delivery, because only by getting *it* out could Mary be out of her misery and the bleeding cease. Yes, yes—better out than in.

Within the boundaries of his irrational logic, this was a rational decision. *Doing the wrong thing to do the right thing,* as Sister Mary Joseph Praise might have said.

To a shocked and horrified Matron, the man who sat between Sister Mary Joseph Praise's legs didn't resemble *their* fierce, shy, and exceedingly competent Thomas Stone. This man had nothing in common with Thomas Stone, FRCS, author of *The Expedient Operator.* His place had been taken by this desperate, agitated fellow who did not look like a Fellow of the Royal College of Surgeons, but rather someone for whom the letters FRCS could mean (as Dr. Ghosh often claimed they did) "Farting Round the Country-Side."

Stone, animated now, consumed by a sense of mission, propped *Munro Kerr's Operative Obstetrics* open, cookery-book fashion, on the down slope of Sister Mary Joseph Praise's protuberant belly. "Damn it, Hemlatha, you picked a hell of a time to be away," he said aloud, feeling his courage return.

Two blasphemies, Matron noted. "Custody of the tongue," she murmured under her breath. She took her own pulse because despite her faith in the Lord she was anxious about the heart flutter that had turned up in the last year like a surprise guest. Her heart was skipping beats now and she felt faint.

The strange instruments that Stone had requested and that Matron dug up from an old supply closet refused to be tamed by his hands. "Where the devil is Ghosh?" he shouted, because Ghosh often pitched in to help Hema with abortions and tubal ligations, and, as a jack-of-all-trades, he had more experience with a women's reproductive anatomy than Stone. Matron once again sent a runner over to Ghosh's bungalow, more to placate Stone than with any faith that Ghosh was back. Perhaps she would have done better to send the maid to inquire at the Blue Nile Bar or its vicinity for the *banya* doctor. But even an inebriated Ghosh could counsel Stone that what he was about to do was not the act of an expedient surgeon but an idiotic one, and that his decision was wrong, his logic illogical. Matron felt this pregnancy, this birth, was somehow her fault—some inattention on her part had resulted in this. Still, she also assumed in the face of torrential bleeding that the child was long dead. Had she believed for a moment that the child was alive (she knew nothing about twins), she would have intervened.

Stone cocked his head from side to side, trying to match *Munro Kerr's* illustrations of instruments—Smellie scissors, Braun's cranioclast, Jardine's cephalotribe—with the objects he juggled in his hand. His tools were distant cousins of the ones depicted in the book, but clearly designed for the same sinister purpose.

With two Jacobs clamps, he grabbed the oval of my brother's scalp. "I see you in the depths, burrowing creature! Damn you for torturing Mary," he muttered. Then, using scissors, he cut the skin between the two clamps and gave the intruder its first introduction to pain.

His next move was to try to put the cephalotribe—the skull crusher—on the head. This awkward medieval instrument had three separate pieces. The middle was a spear meant to go deep into the brain, cutting a big opening in the skull as it did so. Flanking it were two forcepslike structures to clamp to the outside of the skull. Once all three pieces were in place, their stems interlocked to form a single handle with convenient finger indentations. Stone would be able to crush *and* grip the skull so it wouldn't slide away. Out would come the intruder.

It was cool in the operating theater, but sweat from his brow trickled into his eyes and wet his mask.

He tried to drive the spear in.

(The child, my brother, Shiva, sheltered for eight months and already hurting from the cut of scissors on his scalp, cried out in the womb. I pulled him to safety as the spear slid over the skull.)

Stone decided it would be easier if he first applied the outer two blades of the cephalotribe, *then* dragged the head within reach, and *then* inserted the spear. His hands were clumsy in this awkward space. Matron shuddered at the damage he might be doing to Sister Mary Joseph Praise's tissues and to the baby as he jammed each piece past an ear until, finally, he had the skull in his grasp, or thought he did.

Matron was close to dropping. "It is the duty of the nurse to assist and anticipate the doctor's every need." Wasn't this what she herself preached to her probationers? But it was all wrong, all wrong, and she didn't know how to begin to turn it around. She was sorry she ever dug out the instruments. A humane obstetrician invented these instruments for mothers with the most desperate needs, not for desperate physicians. A fool with a tool is still a fool. In Stone's hands the instruments had taken over, and they were doing the thinking for him. Matron knew that nothing good could ever come out of that.

CHAPTER 5

Last Moments

A<small>T THE VERY LAST SECOND</small>, just as she braced for the plane to smash into the water, Dr. Hemlatha saw the ocean give way to dry scrubland.

And before she could digest this, the plane flared to a touchdown over shimmering asphalt, squealing its tires, wiggling its tail, and, when it bled off its speed, scampering down the runway like a dog unleashed.

The passengers' relief turned to bewilderment and embarrassment, for the most godless among them had prayed for divine intervention.

The plane stopped, but the pilot continued arguing with the tower while dragging on a cigarette, even though he had made a big point of turning on the NO SMOKING light after they landed.

The little boy whimpered, and Hema rocked him with an adeptness she didn't know she possessed. "I'm going to put a *tiny, tiny* bandage on your leg, okay? Then the hurt will be all gone." The young Armenian somehow found a cane, and the two of them fashioned a splint.

When the throb of the engine ceased, Hema felt the silence within the cabin press on her eardrums. The pilot looked around, a smirk on his face, as if he were curious to see how his passengers had held up. Almost as an afterthought, he said, "We are stopping to pick up some bagg-aje and some Very Important People. This is Djibouti!" He smiled and showed his bad teeth. "They did not give me permission to land unless it is emergency. So I make an engine failure." He shrugged as if modesty prevented him from accepting their accolades.

Hemlatha was startled to hear her own voice shatter the silence.

"Baggage? You bloody mercenary. What do you think we are? Goats? You just shut down an engine and drop out of the sky like that and stop in Djibouti? No warning? Nothing?"

Perhaps she should have been grateful to him, happy to be alive, but in the hierarchy of her emotions, anger was always trumps.

"Bloody?" the pilot said, turning red. "Bloody?" he said, clambering out of the cockpit, white knees knocking under his safari shorts, as he struggled free.

He stood before her, huffing from the effort. He seemed to take far more exception to "bloody" than "mercenary." His contempt for this Indian woman was greater than his anger. But he had raised his hand. "I will offload you here, insolent woman, if you don't like it." Later he would claim that he had raised his hand merely as a gesture, with no intent to strike her—God forbid that he, a gentleman, a Frenchman, would strike a woman.

But it was too late, because Hemlatha felt her limbs move as if by their own volition, fueled by anger and indignation. She felt as if she were observing the actions of a stranger, of a Hemlatha who had not previously existed. The new Hemlatha, whose license on life had just been renewed and its purpose defined, came to her feet. She was as tall as the pilot. She could see the tiny feeder vessel in the starburst on his left cheek. She pushed her glasses up on her forehead and met him eyeball to eyeball.

The man squirmed. He saw she was beautiful. He fancied himself a lady's man, and he wondered if he'd blown the opportunity to have drinks with her at the Ghion Hotel that evening. Only now did he notice the people huddled over the whimpering boy. Only now did he notice the father's rage, and the clenched fists of some of the other passengers who had lined up behind her.

What a specimen, Hema thought as she studied him. Spider angiomas all over his exposed skin. Eyes tinged with jaundice. No doubt his breasts are enlarged, his armpits hairless, and his testes shriveled to the size of walnuts—all because his liver no longer detoxifies the estrogen a male normally produces. And the stale juniper-berry breath. Ah yes, she thought, coming to a diagnosis beyond cirrhosis: a gin-soaked colonial resisting the reality of postcolonial Africa. If in India they still are cowed by all of you, it is from long habit. But there are no such rules on an Ethiopian plane.

She felt her rage boil over, and it was directed not just at him but at *all* men, every man who in the Government General Hospital in India had pushed her around, taken her for granted, punished her for being a woman, played with her hours and her schedule, transferred her here and there without so much as a please or by-your-leave.

Her proximity to him, her encroachment of sacred *bawana* space, rattled him, distracted him. But his hand was still up there. And now, as if he just noticed it, he moved the hand, not to strike her, he would claim, but as if to determine whether it really was his hand and to see if it still answered to his commands.

The upraised hand was insult enough, but when Hema saw it start to move, she reacted in a manner that made her blush when she recalled it later.

Hemlatha's fingers shot up the pilot's shorts and locked around his testicles, only his underwear intervening. There was an ease to her movements which surprised her, and an ease to the way the gap between her thumbs and index fingers allowed passage for the spermatic cords that connected balls to body. Years later she would think that what she did was conditioned by her surroundings, by the propensity in East Africa for *shiftas* and other criminals to lop off their victims' testicles. *When in Rome* . . .

Her eyes burned like a martyr's. Sweat changed the *pottu* on her forehead from a dot to an exclamation mark. She had worn a cotton sari for the heat, and earlier, when she had been seated, she had hiked it to her knees—modesty be damned—and now that she was standing it stayed that way, outlining her thighs. Sweat glistened on her upper lip as she squeezed to extract the same measure of distress and fear the Frenchman had caused her.

"Listen, sweetie," she said (deciding that there was indeed testicular atrophy and also trying to recall *tunica albugineae,* and *tunica* something else, and vas deferens, of course, and that craggy thingy at the back, whatsitcalled . . . epididymis!). She saw his shoulders sag and the color drain out of his face as if she'd opened the spigot below. Dampness quite different from sweat appeared on his forehead. "At least your syphilis isn't far advanced because you can feel testicular pain, huh?" His upraised hand came floating down and then hesitantly, almost lovingly rested on her forearm, pleading with her not to increase the pressure. A cathedral of silence descended on the plane.

"Are you listening now?" she said (thinking that she didn't really want to know a man's anatomy this way). "Are we talking as equals? . . . My life in your hands and now your family jewels in mine? You think you can terrify people like that? That little boy broke his leg because of your stunt."

She turned her head toward the other passengers but, keeping her eye on Frenchie's face, said, "Anybody have a sharp knife? Or a Gillette?"

The rustle she heard might just have been the cremaster muscles of all the males on board involuntarily reeling their dangling sperm factories back up to shelter.

"We were unauthorized . . . I had to . . . ," the pilot wheezed.

"Take your wallet out right now and pay for this child," Hema said, because she didn't believe in IOUs.

When he fumbled with the notes, the young Armenian grabbed the wallet and handed it to the boy's father.

One of the Yemenis, finding his voice, let out a stream of profanities, wagging his finger in the pilot's face.

Hema said, "Now, you refund the plane tickets for the boy and his parents. And you get us back in the air very soon, . . . otherwise, you will not only be a eunuch, but I will personally petition the Emperor to make sure that even a job as a camel driver, let alone flying khat, will be much too good for you."

They heard the cargo door open and sharp exclamations from the coolies milling around outside.

The Frenchman, his eyeballs sinking in their sockets, nodded mutely. France had colonized Djibouti and parts of Somalia, and they had even jockeyed with the English in India before settling for a foothold in Pondicherry. But on this steamy afternoon, one brown soul who would never be the same again, and who had Malayalis, Armenians, Greeks, and Yemenis backing her, showed she was free.

"Well, how can one be sane in hot weather?" Hemlatha said to no one in particular, letting go and making for the outside to wash her hands, stifling her laughter.

CHAPTER 6

My Abyssinia

HEMA FIXED HER EYES on the ground below, watching for the transition of brown scrub and desert into steep escarpment announcing the lush, mountainous plateau of Ethiopia. Yes, she thought. This is my home now. My Abyssinia, which sounded to her so much more romantic than "Ethiopia."

The country was in essence a mountain massif that rose from the three deserts of Somaliland, Danakil, and Sudan. Even now Hema felt a bit like a David Livingstone or an Evelyn Waugh exploring this ancient civilization, this stronghold of Christianity which, until Mussolini's invasion in '35, was the only African nation never to be colonized. Waugh, in his dispatches to the London *Times* and in his book, referred to His Majesty Haile Selassie the First as "Highly Salacious," seeing cowardice in the Emperor's leaving the country in the face of Mussolini's advance. Hema's reading of Waugh was that he couldn't accept the notion of African royalty. He couldn't accept that the bloodlines of Emperor Haile Selassie, extending back as they did to the Queen of Sheba and King Solomon, made the Windsors or the Romanovs look like carpetbaggers. She didn't think much of Waugh or his book.

The new passengers who climbed aboard at Djibouti were Somalis or Djiboutians (and really, she thought, what difference was there between the two, other than a line drawn on a map by some Western cartographer). They chewed khat and smoked 555s and despite their doleful, muddy eyes they were happy. Crammed into the plane, which by now was altogether too familiar to Hema, was khat, great bales of it being hauled back to Addis Ababa. It was all very strange, since khat usually traveled in the opposite direction: grown in Ethiopia, around Harrar, and exported by rail to Djibouti and then by air to Aden. That lucrative khat trade route was responsible for the birth of Ethiopian Airlines. She overheard that some problem with the railway and road transport, as well as the urgent need for large quantities of khat for a wedding, prompted this reverse export and the unscheduled stop. Khat had to be chewed within a day or so of its harvest, or else it lost its potency. Hema pictured the Somali, Yemeni, and Sudanese merchants in the tiny souks that anchored every street and byway, and the owners of the bigger shops of the Merkato in Addis Ababa, eyeing their Tissot watches, snapping at their shop boys as they waited for this shipment. She pictured the wedding guests with mouths too parched to spit, but spitting and cursing all the same, telling one another that the bride was uglier than they remembered, and the big mole on her neck must mean she'd also inherited the miserliness of her father.

Hema imagined telling her mother about the pilot business. It made Hema laugh, which made the Somali sitting opposite her, one of the newcomers, smile.

Madras had been hot and humid for the three weeks that Hema was there, but it was heaven compared with Aden. Her parents' three-room house in the neighborhood of Mylapore, very near the temple, had seemed spacious to her as a girl, but on this visit if felt claustrophobic. Though she regularly sent her parents bank drafts, she'd been dismayed to find no improvements in the house since her last visit. The interior paint had peeled to form abstract patterns while the kitchen, blackened with smoke, resembled a darkroom. The narrow street outside which rarely saw a car was now a noisy thoroughfare, and the compound wall showed no trace of whitewash but instead was the color of the earth on which it stood. Only the garden had benefited from the passage of time with the bougainvillea hiding the house from the street. The two mango trees had become huge and heavy with fruit. One was an Alphonso and the other a hybrid with flesh that felt rubbery at first bite but then melted in the mouth like ice cream.

The sole decoration in the living room was, as it had always been, the Glaxo powdered-milk calendar hanging on a nail. The overfed blue-eyed Caucasian baby had never grown up. The caption read "Glaxo Builds Bonny Babies." It was enough to make any breast-feeding mother feel guilty that she was starving her infant. As a child Hema had barely registered the Glaxo baby. Now the calendar drew her eye and her ire. What an insidious presence that brat had been in her life. An interloper with a false message. Hema took down the calendar, but the pale rectangle on the wall called attention to itself in a way the baby never had. No doubt once Hema left, another Glaxo baby would find its way back there.

During her brief vacation, Hema had the house painted and ceiling fans installed. Sathyamurthy, the father of her old childhood nemesis, Velu, peered over the fence as workmen carried in a Western-style commode to be cemented over the footpads of the Indian toilet. He sniggered and shook his head. "It's not for me, you old coot," Hema said in English. "My mother's hips are bad." And Sathyamurthy answered in the only English phrase he knew, "Goddamn China, kiss me Eisenhower!" He smiled and waved, and she waved back.

THE SOMALI ACROSS FROM HER wore a shiny blue polyester shirt and a gold watch that swung on his stick wrist. His toes, protruding from sandals, glowed like polished ebony. He looked familiar to Hema. Now, he bowed, grinned, and displayed his fingers as if bidding at an auction as he said, "Three kids, two shots, one night!"

She remembered. His name was Adid. "I say, are you still doing double duty these days?"

His ivory teeth lit up the plane's dim interior. He said something to his friends. They smiled and nodded sagely. Such strong teeth they have, Hemlatha thought. She admired his blackness, a color so pure that there was a purple tinge to it. The headmistress at her school, Mrs. Hood, had been porcelain white, and the schoolgirls believed that if they touched her, their fingers would come away white; with Adid, she imagined they would come away black. Adid's regal manner, the slow play of expressions on his face, each thought matched by a lip-eyebrow combo, gave Hema the bizarre idea that she'd like to suck his index finger.

She'd last seen Adid in a headdress and flowing robes in the casualty room at Missing, unflappable, even though his pregnant wife was convulsing. When Hemlatha unwrapped the shrouds of cotton she found a young, pale, anemic girl. Her blood pressure was sky-high. This was eclampsia. While Hemlatha was in Theater 3 delivering this wife of her firstborn by Cesarean section, Adid disappeared and returned with an older wife, also in labor, who proceeded to deliver in the horse-drawn gharry beside the outpatient steps. Hemlatha ran out in time to cut the cord. She pushed on the wife's belly, but instead of the afterbirth, a twin popped out. Adid's smile when he saw the second child, the third total, reached from ear to ear. Hema suggested he wear a banner across his chest that said ONE NIGHT, TWO SHOTS, THREE KIDS. Adid had laughed like a man who'd never heard the word "worry."

"Yes, yes," he said now, raising his voice to be heard over the drone of the engines. He had the clipped, French-accented diction of a Djiboutian. "A man is only as rich as the number of children he fathers. After all, what else do we leave behind in this world, Doctor?"

Hema, who'd been thinking along similar lines just minutes before, decided she was a pauper by that yardstick. She said, "Amen. You must be a millionaire many times over then."

An impish expression stole across his face, and with waggling brows and using just his eyes he pointed down the bench to a woman veiled and swathed in red-and-orange cotton robes. A very pale, henna-painted foot showed. Hemlatha guessed her to be a Yemeni. Or else a Muslim from Pakistan or India.

"And she is . . . ?" Hema said, hoping it would not be impolite to ask about her nationality.

Adid nodded vigorously. "Three more months at least. And one more expecting at home!"

"I tell you what," Hema said, looking pointedly at Adid's groin, "I'll ask Dr. Ghosh to give you a special rate on a vasectomy, two for one. It will be cheaper than doing a tubal ligation on all the begums."

The Gujarati couple across from her looked up scowling at Adid's thigh-slapping laughter.

"Why don't you bring the wives to the antenatal clinic?" Hema asked. "A smart man like you shouldn't wait till they get into trouble. You don't want them to suffer."

"It's not my choice. You know how these women are. They won't come until they are unconscious," he said simply.

True enough, Hemlatha thought. Years before, an Arab woman in the Merkato was in labor for days, and the husband, a rich merchant, brought Dr. Bachelli to see her. But rather than allow a male doctor to see her, she wedged her body behind the bedroom door so that any attempt to open it would crush her. The woman died alone, behind that door, an act much admired by her peers.

Because Hema was hungry, and to annoy the Gujaratis further, she accepted some leaves of khat from Adid and tucked them into her cheek. It was something she'd never have dreamed of doing before, but events of the last few hours had changed things.

The khat was bitter at first, but then the pulpy mass became almost sweet and not unpleasant. "Wonder of wonders," she said aloud, as her face took on the chipmunk bulge and her jaw fell into the lazy, slewing rhythm of the thousands of khat chewers she had seen in her lifetime. Like a pro, she used her handbag as an elbow bolster and she brought her feet up to the bench, one knee flat, the other under her chin. She leaned toward Adid, who was surprisingly chatty.

". . . and we spend most of the rainy season away from Addis, in Aweyde, which is near Harrar."

"I know all about Aweyde," Hema said, which wasn't true. She'd driven there years before on a holiday to see the old walled city of Harrar. What she remembered about Aweyde was that the entire town seemed nothing more than a khat market. The houses were hopelessly plain, not a trace of whitewash. "I know all about Aweyde," she said again, and the khat made her feel that she actually did. "The people there are rich enough to each drive a Mercedes, but they won't spend a cent to paint their front door. Am I right?"

"Doctor, how could you know these things?" Adid said, astonished.

Hema smiled, as if to say, *Very little escapes me, my dear man.* And then she was thinking of the Frenchman's balls, of rugaeform folds, of the median raphe that separated one bollock from the other, of the dartos muscle, the cells of Sertoli. Her mind was racing, hyperaware.

The cabin was no longer hot, and it felt good to be heading home. She wanted to say to Adid: When I was a medical student, we had to do this test on patients to check for *visceral* pain. Visceral pain is different from when you bump your knee, for example. Visceral pain comes from the inside, from the body's organs. It's a pain that is tough to characterize, poorly localized, but painful all the same. Anyway, as students we had to squeeze the testes to check for intact visceral pain, because diseases like syphilis can cause the loss of visceral pain sensations. One day, at the bedside of a patient with syphilis, the professor picked on me to demonstrate visceral pain. The men in our group were snickering. I was bold then—I didn't hesitate. I exposed the balls— the testes, excuse me. The patient had advanced syphilis. When I squeezed, the man just smiled at me. Nothing. No pain. No reaction. So I squeezed harder—really hard. Still nothing. But one of my male classmates fainted!

Adid grinned, as if she *had* told him this story.

THE PLANE DESCENDED, slipping into and out of the scattered clouds over Addis Ababa. The dense forests of eucalyptus trees at first concealed the city. Emperor Menelik had imported eucalyptus years before from Madagascar, not for its oil, but as firewood, the lack of which had almost made him abandon his capital city. Eucalyptus had thrived in the Ethiopian soil, and it grew rapidly—twelve meters in five years, and twenty meters in twelve years. Menelik had planted it by the hectare. It was indestructible, always returning in strength wherever it was cut down, and proving ideal for framing houses.

The trees revealed clearings with circular, thatch-roofed *tukuls* and a thorn enclosure to keep the animals penned in. Then, at the edge of the city, she saw corrugated-tin-roofed houses, abundant and closer together. A church with a short spire came into view, and then the city proper. There was Churchill Road starting at the railway station and making a steep rise to the Piazza, with a handful of cars and buses plying its slope. This glimpse of the city center, which looked so modern, made her think of Emperor Haile Selassie. He'd brought about more change in his reign than the country had undergone in three centuries. Down at street level, his portrait—the hook nose, the thin lips, the high brow—would be in every house. Hema's father was the Emperor's biggest fan because just before World War II, as Mussolini stood ready to invade, Emperor Haile Selassie warned the world of the price of standing by and allowing Italy to invade a sovereign country like Ethiopia; such inaction, he said, would fuel the territorial ambitions of not just Italy but Germany. "God and history will remember your judgment," he said famously before the League of Nations, and they did. It made him the symbol of the little guy who'd stood up to the bully (and lost).

"You see Missing Hospital, madam?" This from Adid who peered over her shoulder.

"Missing is missing," she said.

Near the airport an entire hillside had turned to a flaming orange from the blooming of the *meskel* flower which told her that the rainy season must have ended. Another hillside was covered with lean-tos and shacks of corrugated tin, the colors rust brown or a darker corrosive hue. Each shack shared a wall with its neighbor, so that collectively they looked like long irregular railway carriages that snaked across the hill, sending buds and offshoots in all directions.

THE FRENCHMAN BUZZED low over the strip so that the customs agent could get on his bicycle and shoo stray cows from the runway. He circled and landed.

Cars and vans in the bile-green colors of the Ethiopian police raced up to the plane, along with every functionary of the Ethiopian Airlines staff. The cargo door was yanked open, and frantic hands rushed to unload the khat. They tossed the bundles into a VW Kombi, then into a three-wheeler van, and when those were full, they stuffed the police cars, and they all raced off, sirens sounding. Only then were the passengers allowed to disembark.

The engine of the blue-and-white Fiat Seicento whined as the six-hundred milliliter engine, which gave it its name, strained to carry Hemlatha and her Grundig. She'd personally supervised the loading of the big crate onto the roof rack.

It was a perfect sunny afternoon in Addis, and it made her forget that she was more than two days overdue at Missing. The light at this altitude was so different from Madras, suffusing what it graced rather than glaring off every surface. There was no hint in the breeze of rain, though that could change in an instant. She caught the woody, medicinal odor of eucalyptus, a scent that would never do in a perfume but was invigorating when it was in the air. She smelled frankincense, which every household threw onto the charcoal stove. She was glad to be alive, and glad to be back in Addis, but she didn't know what to make of the wave of nostalgia that overcame her, an unfulfilled longing that she could not define.

With the end of the rains, makeshift stalls had popped up selling red and green chilies, lemons, and roasted maize. A man with a bleating sheep draped around his neck like a cape struggled to see the road in front of him. A woman sold bundles of eucalyptus leaves used as cooking fuel for making *injera*—the pancakelike food made from a grain, *tef.* Farther on Hema saw a little girl pour batter on a huge flat griddle which sat on three bricks with a fire underneath. When the *injera* was ready, it would be peeled off like a tablecloth, then folded once, twice, and once more, and stored in a basket.

An old woman in the black clothes of mourning stopped to assist a mother sling her baby onto her back in a pouch made out of her *shama*—the white cotton cloth that men and women alike wrapped around their shoulders.

A man with withered legs that were folded into his chest swung stiff armed along the dirt sidewalk. He had blocks of wood with a handle in each hand, which he planted on the ground, and then he swung his bottom forward. He moved surprisingly well, like the letter *M* marching down the road. Her brief absence made these sights a novelty again.

A herd of mules overladen with firewood trotted along, their expressions docile and angelic in the face of the whipping they were getting from the barefoot owner who ran with them. The taxi driver leaned on his horn. Despite the high whine of the engine, the taxi managed only to crawl along like another overburdened beast.

A lorry carrying sheep, the poor animals so crowded together they could hardly blink, overtook them. These were the lucky animals being *carried* to slaughter. Before Meskel, the feast celebrating the finding of Christ's cross, huge herds of sheep would arrive in the capital, the animals wobbly from exhaustion, barely surviving this march to the feast table. Then, in the days after Meskel, one neither heard nor saw any sheep. Instead the skin traders walked the streets and alleys shouting, *"Ye beg koda alle!"*—"The sheep's hide whoever has!" A household would hail him, and after some haggling, he'd drape another skin over the ones that he was already shouldering and resume his cry.

Suddenly Hemlatha noticed children everywhere as if they'd been invisible all these years. Two boys were racing their crude metal hoops, using a stick to guide and push, weaving this way and that and making motorcar noises. A toddler with railroad tracks of snot connecting nose to lip watched with envy. Its head had been shaved to leave a traffic-island tuft in front; Hema was told when she first came to Ethiopia that this strange haircut was so that if God chose to take that child (and He took so many), the tuft gave Him a handle by which to lift it to heaven.

The child's mother stood outlined by the bead curtain of a *buna-bet*—coffeehouse—though it was really a bar, offering things more potent than coffee. At night the bar would glow within from the tube lights, painted green, yellow, and red, and the woman, transformed by that hour, would offer drinks and her company. An espresso machine on a zinc bar established the class of an establishment—this was a legacy of the Italian occupation. The woman's flat eyes fell on the cab, then on Hema, and her expression hardened as if she had seen a competitor. She lifted her gaze to the strange container on the taxi's roof, and then she looked nonchalantly away as if to say, *I'm not the least bit impressed*. She might be an Amhara, Hema thought, with that walnut skin, the high cheekbones. She is so pretty. Probably a friend of Ghosh. A comb was stuck in her hair as if she were taking a break from teasing it into shape. Her legs shone from Nivea. She might even swallow a dab or two of Nivea now and then, in the belief it lightened the complexion. "For all I know, it works," Hema said, though she shuddered at the thought.

Between the newer cinder-block buildings were huts, the wattle walls unpainted and revealing their sticks, straw, and mud. All it took was a pole stuck in the ground with an empty can inverted over the top to say, This, too, is a *buna-bet*, and though we don't have an espresso machine, and though we sell homebrewed *tej* and *talla* instead of bottled St. George beer, we offer the same services as the other.

The oldest profession in the world raised no eyebrows, even with Hema. She'd learned it was futile to object—it would have been like taking exception to oxygen. But the consequences of such tolerance were evident to her: tubal and ovarian abscesses, infertility from gonorrhea, stillbirths, and babies with congenital syphilis.

On the main road Hema saw a work crew of grinning, dark-skinned, big-boned Gurages supervised by a laughing Italian overseer. The Gurage were southerners with a well-deserved reputation for being hard-working and willing to take on what the locals wouldn't. Gebrew, when he needed extra hands at Missing, would simply step out of the front gate and yell "Gurage!" though of late, that could be seen as insulting, so it was safer to shout "Coolie!"

The crew was barefoot but for the overseer and one man who had squeezed into ill-fitting plastic shoes, having cut holes in them for his big toes. By all rights Hema should have been incensed by this sight of black laborers and a white overseer, and she wondered why she wasn't; maybe it was because the Italians who stayed behind in Ethiopia after it was liberated were so easygoing, so ready to mock themselves, that they were hard to resent. Life for the Italians was what it was, no more and no less, an interlude between meals. Or maybe that was just the way of being that they found worked best in their circumstance. Hema saw the laborers stand still as soon as the overseer turned away. A snail's pace, but nevertheless, schools, offices, a grand post office, a national bank, were coming up to match the grandeur of Trinity Cathedral, the Parliament Building, and the Jubilee Palace. The Emperor's vision of his European-style African capital was taking shape.

PERHAPS IT WAS BECAUSE the Emperor was still on her mind, and because her taxi was at the intersection where, in place of the string of shops, there once stood a gallows, but suddenly Hema was thinking about a scene that haunted her.

It was at this very spot in 1946 that she and Ghosh, in their first months in Addis, had come upon a crowd blocking the road. Standing on the running board of Ghosh's Volkswagen, Hema had seen a crudely constructed frame and the three dangling nooses. A modified Trenta Quattro with military markings had pulled up. Three handcuffed Ethiopian prisoners on the flatbed were hauled to their feet. The men were coatless, but otherwise, in their shirts, shoes, and pants, they looked as if they'd been interrupted while having dinner.

An Ethiopian officer in Imperial Bodyguard uniform read from a piece of paper and tossed it aside. Hema watched, fascinated, as he put the noose over each head and positioned the knot to one side, behind the ear. The condemned seemed resigned to their fate, which was in itself a form of extreme bravery. The bearing of a tall older man made Hema certain the prisoners were military. This graying but upright prisoner spoke to the Imperial Bodyguard officer who inclined his head to listen. He nodded, and removed the noose. The prisoner then leaned over the truck and held his handcuffed wrists out to a weeping woman. She removed a ring from his finger and kissed his hand. The prisoner stepped back, looked down like an actor searching for his mark onstage, then bowed to this executioner, who returned the gesture and replaced the noose with the delicacy of a husband garlanding his new bride.

Hema didn't understand what she was seeing, not then anyway. She half believed it to be a form of theater. The violence of what followed—the truck roaring away, the thrashing forms, the awkward and impossible angle of head on chest, the mad rush of onlookers to tear off the dead men's shoes—was less disturbing than the idea that she was living in a country where such things could take place. Sure, she'd seen brutality, cruelty, in Madras, but they took the form of neglect and indifference to suffering, or they took the form of corruption.

The event left Hema sick for days. She contemplated leaving Ethiopia. There'd been nothing about it in the *Ethiopian Herald,* no comment the government wished to make. The men had been planning revolution, so people said, and this was the Emperor's response. He was keeping a fragile country on course.

Hema had never forgotten the reluctant executioner, a handsome man, his temples forming a sharp angle with his brow so his head was shaped like a hatchet. His nose was flattened at its base as if from an old fracture. She remembered his stately bow to the condemned before he carried out his orders. She'd felt pity and even respect for him. The conflict between his duty and his compassion was revealed by that gesture. Had he refused to follow orders, his neck would have been stretched. Hema was sure he'd acted against his conscience.

Maybe this is what keeps me in Addis all these years, Hema thought, this juxtaposition of culture and brutality, this molding of the new out of the crucible of primeval mud. The city is evolving, and I feel part of that evolution, unlike in Madras, where the city seems to have been completed centuries before I was born. Did anyone but my parents notice that I left? "Why don't you stay in India? There are so many poor women who die needlessly here in Madras," her father had said halfheartedly on this visit. "You want me to give free service to the poor from this house?" she said. "If not, then get me a job. Let the City Corporation hire me, or the Government Medical Service. If my country needs me, why is it that they don't take me?" They both knew the answer: jobs went to those willing to grease palms. She sighed, causing the taxi driver to look over. She was reliving the pain of saying good-bye to her parents yet again.

The sight of barefoot peasants carrying impossible head loads and horse-drawn gharries plying the roads maintained the aura and mystique of this ancient kingdom that almost justified the fabulous tales of Prester John, who wrote in medieval times of a magical Christian kingdom surrounded by Muslim lands. Yes, it might be the era of the kidney transplant in America and a vaccine for polio due to arrive even in India, but here Hema felt she'd tricked time; with her twentieth-century knowledge she had traveled back to an earlier epoch. The power filtered down from His Majesty to the Rases, the Dejazmaches, and the lesser nobility, and then to the vassals and peons. Her skills were so rare, so needed for the poorest of the poor, and even at times in the royal palace, that she felt valued. Wasn't that the definition of home? Not where you are from, but where you are wanted?

AT ABOUT TWO in the afternoon, her taxi pulled up to the chukker-brown gates of Missing, a world unto itself.

The rock wall enclosed the hospital grounds and hid the buildings. Eucalyptus towered over the wall, and where there was no eucalyptus there were firs and jacaranda and acacia. Green bottle shards poked up from the mortar at the top of the wall to dissuade intruders—robbery and petty theft were rampant in Addis—though the sight of roses lapping over the wall softened this deterrent. The wrought-iron gate covered with sheet metal was normally kept closed, and pedestrians were admitted through the smaller, hinged door in the gate. But now the big gate was wide open, as was the pedestrian flap.

Inside, Hema saw that Gebrew's sentry hut door and shutter were also open, and when they crested the hill, she could see that every visible window and door in Missing's outpatient building was open, too; in fact, she could see Gebrew, the watchman (who happened to be a priest), in the process of propping open the woodshed door with a rock.

Spotting the taxi, he came running, his army surplus overcoat flapping, his white priest's turban dwarfing his small face, his fly wand, cross, and beads clutched in one hand. He seemed to be trying to shoo the taxi away. Gebrew was a nervous chap given to rapid speech and jerky movements, but he was far more agitated than was his norm. He looked stunned to see her, as if he'd never expected her to come back.

"Praise-God-for-bringing-you-safely, welcome-back-madam, how-are-you-are-you-well? God-answered-our-prayers," he said in Amharic. She matched him bow for bow as best she could, but he wouldn't stop until she said, "Gebrew!"

She held out a five-birr note. "Take bowl to Sheba Bar and fetch please *doro-wot*," she said, naming the delectable red chicken curry cooked in Ethiopian peppers—*berbere*. Her Amharic was crude, and she could only speak in the present tense, but *doro-wot* was a term she'd mastered early. And *doro-wot* had occupied her dreams her last few nights in Madras, after so many days of a pure vegetarian diet. The *wot* came poured onto the soft crepelike *injera* and there would be more rolls of *injera* which Hema would use to scoop up the meat. The curry would have soaked into the *injera* that lined the bowl by the time Gebrew brought it. Her mouth watered just thinking of the dish.

"Indeed-I-will-madam, Sheba-is-best, blessed-is-their-cook, Sheba-is—"

"Tell me, Gebrew, why be doors and windows open?" Now she noticed his nails and fingers were bloody, and his sleeves had feathers sticking to them, and feathers were caught up in his fly swish.

It was then that Gebrew said, "Oh, madam! This is what I have been trying to tell you. Baby is stuck! The baby. And Sister! And the baby!"

She did not understand. She'd never seen him so worked up. She smiled and waited.

"Madam! Sister is borning! She is not borning well!"

"What? Say again?" Perhaps being away and not hearing Amharic had made her misunderstand.

"Sister, madam," Gebrew said, alarmed that he didn't seem to be getting through, and thinking volume and pitch might help, though what came out was a squeak.

"Sister" in Missing always referred to Sister Mary Joseph Praise, for the only other nun there was Matron Hirst, who went by Matron, while all the other nurses were addressed as Nurse Almaz or Nurse Esther, and not Sister.

To Hema's astonishment, Gebrew was crying, and his voice turned shrill. "Passage is closed! I tried everything. I opened all the doors and windows. I split open a chicken!"

He clutched his belly and strained in a bizarre imitation of parturition. He tried English. "Baby! Baby? Madam, baby?"

What he tried to convey was clear enough; there was no mistaking it. But it would have been difficult for Hema to believe it in any language.

CHAPTER 7

Fetor Terribilis

THE DOORS TO THE OPERATING THEATER burst open. The probationer shrieked. Matron clutched her chest at the sight of the sari-clad woman standing there, hands on her hips, bosom heaving, nostrils flaring.

They froze. How were they to know if this was their very own Hema, or an apparition? It seemed taller and fuller than Hema, and it had the bloodshot eyes of a dragon. Only when it opened its mouth and said, "What bloody nonsense is Gebrew talking? In God's name, what is going on?" did their doubts vanish.

"It's a miracle," Matron said, referring to the fact of Hema's arrival, but this only further confused Hema. The probationer, her face flushed and her pockmarks shining like sunken nailheads, added, "Amen."

Stone stood and unfurrowed his brows at the sight of Hema. Though he didn't say a word, his expression was that of a man who, having fallen into a crevasse, spotted the bowline lowered from the heavens.

Hema, recalling this event many years later, said to me, "My saliva turned to cement, son. A sweat broke out over my face and neck, even though it was freezing in there. You see, even before I digested the medical facts, I'd already registered that smell."

"What smell?"

"You won't find it any textbooks, Marion, so don't bother looking. But it's etched here," she said, tapping her head. "If I chose to write a textbook, not that I have any interest in that kind of thing, I'd have a chapter on nothing but obstetric odors." The smell was both astringent and saccharine, these two contrary characteristics coming together in what she'd come to think of as *fetor terribilis*. "It always means a labor room catastrophe. Dead mothers, or dead babies, or homicidal husbands. Or all the above."

She couldn't believe the amount of blood on the floor. The sight of instruments lying helter-skelter—*on* the patient, next to the patient, on the operating table—assaulted her senses. But most of all—and she'd been resisting this—she couldn't accept the fact that Sister Mary Joseph Praise, sweet Sister, who should have been standing, gowned, masked, and scrubbed, a beacon of calm in this calamity, instead lay all but lifeless on the table, her skin porcelain white and her lips drained of all color.

Hema's thoughts became dissociated, as if they were no longer hers but instead were elegant copperplate scrolling before her in a dream. Sister Mary Joseph Praise's left hand lying supine on the table drew Hema's eye. The fingers were curled, the index finger less so, as if she'd been pointing, when sleep or coma overcame her. It was a posture of repose that one rarely associated with Sister Mary Joseph Praise. Hema's eyes would be drawn to that hand repeatedly as the hour unfolded.

The sight of Thomas Stone brought her back to her senses and galvanized her. Seeing Stone in the hallowed place between a woman's legs that was reserved for the obstetrician rankled Hema. That was *her* spot, her domain. She shouldered him aside, and in his haste he knocked the stool over. He tried to explain what had happened: finding Sister, their discovery of her pregnancy and then her obstructed labor, the shock, the bleeding that never stopped—

"*Ayoh*, what is this?" she said, cutting him off, her eyes round with alarm, brows shooting up and her mouth a perfect O. She pointed at the bloody trephine and the open textbook resting by Sister Mary Joseph Praise's belly. "*Books* and whatnots?" She swiped them aside, and they clattered to the floor, the sound reverberating off the walls.

The probationer's heart hammered against her breast like a moth in a lamp. Not knowing where to put her hands, she stuffed them in her pockets. She reassured herself that she had no part in the books and whatnots. Her failure (and she was beginning to see this) was a failure of Sound Nursing Sense; she'd missed the gravity of Sister Mary Joseph Praise's condition when she delivered Stone's message. She'd assumed that others would look in on Sister Mary Joseph Praise. No one had been aware that Sister Mary Joseph Praise was that ill, and no one had told Matron.

SISTER MARY JOSEPH PRAISE moved her head, and Matron believed that she was at least transiently aware that Matron held her hand. But so relentless was her pain that Sister couldn't acknowledge Matron's kindness.

In his hands I saw a large golden spear and at its iron tip there seemed to be a point of fire.

Matron's guess from the fragments she could understand was that Sister Mary Joseph Praise's mumbled words were perhaps the words of St. Teresa that they both knew so well.

I felt as if he plunged it into my heart several times, so that it penetrated all the way to my entrails. When he drew it out, he seemed to draw them out, and left me inflamed with a great love for God. The pain was so severe, it made me moan several times. The sweetness of this intense pain is so extreme, there is no wanting it to end, and the soul is not satisfied with anything less than God.

But unlike St. Teresa of Avila, Sister Mary Joseph Praise surely *did* want the pain to end, and just then, Matron said, the pain seemed to loosen its grip on her belly, and Sister sighed and clearly said, "I marvel, Lord, at your mercy. It is not something I deserve."

A brief period of lucidity with roving eye movements followed, along with more attempts at speech, but it was unintelligible. Light splashed into the room, and Matron said it was as if a shroud that had formed in front of her face melted away. In that moment, as Sister Mary Joseph Praise looked around OT3—her operating theater for all these years—Matron thought the young nun realized that *she* was now the patient to be operated on and that the odds were against her.

"Perhaps she felt she *deserved* to die," Matron said, guessing at my mother's thoughts. "If faith and grace were meant to balance the sinful nature of all humans, hers had been insufficient, and so what she felt was shame. Still she must have believed, even with all her imperfections, that God loved her and forgiveness awaited her in His abode, if not on earth."

Matron wondered if it scared my mother that she might die in Africa, a continent away from her birthplace. Perhaps deep in her—perhaps deep in every being—there lingers a desire to bring the circle of life back to its starting point, which in her case was Cochin.

Then Matron heard my mother clearly whisper *"Miserere mei, Deus"* before sound left her. Matron carried her through the rest of the psalm in Latin, serving as her voice box while Sister Mary Joseph Praise's lips moved: ". . . Behold, I was shapen in iniquity; and in sin did my mother conceive me . . . Purge me with hyssop, and I shall be clean: wash me, and I shall be whiter than snow . . ."

When she finished, Matron said the shroud was back. The light was slipping away from her world.

"PICK UP THE STOOL, Stone," Hema barked. "And you," Hema said, snapping her fingers at the probationer, "get your hands out of your pockets."

Stone set the stool upright just as Hemlatha eased down onto it. The key bunch Hema had fished out to open her house was now tucked into the waist of her sari, and it jingled as she settled herself. Under the theater lights the diamond in her nose sparkled. Strands of loose hair fell over her ears and in front of her eyes; through pursed lips she blew these wayward locks aside. She squared her shoulders, squared them to the horror and the unloveliness of what was before her. In that gesture she slipped off the mantle of the traveler and put on that of the obstetrician. The task ahead, however difficult, dangerous, or unpleasant, was hers and hers alone.

Hema felt herself gasping for air. Her lungs would need a week to acclimatize. She'd come from sea level in Madras to an operating room 8,202 feet above sea level, not counting the stool on which she sat. Her nostrils flared with each inhalation, like a thoroughbred after the quarter mile.

But her breathlessness came also from what was before her eyes. Gebrew hadn't lost his mind or imbibed too much *talla;* he'd been telling the truth. The everyday miracle of conception had taken place in the one place it should not have: in Sister Mary Joseph Praise's womb. Yes, Sister Mary Joseph Praise was pregnant, had been for months before Hema left for India! And not just pregnant, but now in extremis. And the father? Who else? She glanced at Stone's gray face.

But why not? she thought. Why should I be surprised? "The incidence of cancer of the cervix," she remembered her professor saying, "is highest in prostitutes, and *almost* zero in nuns. Why almost zero and not zero? Because nuns are not born nuns! Because not all nuns were chaste before they became nuns! Because not all nuns are celibate!" That's neither here nor there, Hema admonished herself, while she thrust her hands into gloves that Matron produced.

The probationer recorded in the chart the arrival of Dr. Hemlatha. She chastised herself for not thinking of the gloves.

Hemlatha spread her own legs. Her feet were swollen from the long flight. She flexed her toes against the straps of her sandals and pawed the ground to get good purchase on the bloody floor. With the fingers of her left hand she spread the labia. Then, with a motion made simple by countless repetitions, her right hand pulled down on the posterior rim, opening the birth canal to view.

"Rama, Rama, this is a bloody Stone Age utensil," Hemlatha shouted as she carefully disengaged first one half and then the other half of the skull crusher, slipping them over and then off the baby's ears. When the bloody instrument was free, she looked at it with distaste and flung it aside.

Matron felt relief. Whatever happened, at least now a real obstetrician was in charge. She couldn't help but note how Hemlatha and Stone had reversed roles: Hema was now the shouter and the flinger.

Matron offered the history that Sister Mary Joseph Praise had been in severe pain, great spasms of it, and then the pains had suddenly ceased and she'd seemed almost lucid, talking . . . but now she had deteriorated again.

"My God," Hema said, knowing that in nature pains don't cease till a baby is out, "it sounds like a uterine rupture." It would explain all the blood on the floor. Placenta previa—a placenta plastered over the exit to the womb—was another possibility. Neither possibility was good. "When did you stop hearing the fetal heart sounds?" No one replied.

"Pressure?"

"Sixty by palpation," the nurse anesthetist said, after a pause, as if she expected someone else to volunteer the number that she was responsible for.

Hema peered around Sister Mary Joseph Praise's swollen belly to fix Nurse Asqual with a withering look. "Are you waiting for it to get to zero before you breathe for her? Put in a tracheal tube. Connect it to the hand bellows. If she wakes, give her some intravenous pethidine. Tell me when you're done. Where's Ghosh? Have you sent for him?" Nurse Asqual busied herself, grateful for step-by-step instruction because her mind had seized.

"And who has gone for blood? What! Nobody? Am I dealing with idiots here? Go! Run! Run!" Two people charged for the door. "Round up anyone and everyone to give blood. We need lots of blood!"

Hema insinuated two fingers of her right hand around the fetal skull. With her other hand she pushed down on Sister Mary Joseph Praise's belly. She peeked over the rise of the abdomen at Sister's face; it had gone gray, grayer than Stone's.

Nurse Asqual, her hands shaking, managed to insert the tracheal tube. With every squeeze of the air bag, Sister's engorged breasts heaved up.

Hema's hands were like extensions of her eyes as she explored the space that she thought of as the portal to her work; fingers inside took their soundings, helped by the hand on the outside. She closed her eyes, the better to receive what her fingertips conveyed about the pelvic width, the baby's position. "What have we here . . . ?" she said aloud. Indeed, the baby was head down, but what was this? Another skull?

"Good God, Stone?" Hemlatha said, snatching her hand out as if she'd touched a hot coal.

Stone looked on, not understanding, but afraid to ask. She fixed her gaze on Stone, her face taut, waiting for a reply, *any* reply, and prepared to shout it down when it came.

"Better out than in?" Stone mumbled, thinking she meant his skull-crushing attempts.

"Damn it, Thomas Stone, don't quote me your idiot book. Do you think this is a joke?" Stone, who didn't at all see this as a joke, who in fact saw that everything Hema was doing was something he could have and should have done, turned crimson. Hema turned back to probe once more that calamitous space in Sister Mary Joseph Praise's body where *two* lives were in jeopardy. Her words were like body blows directed at Stone.

"*One* prenatal visit? Could you have let me see her for at least *one* prenatal visit? I'd have canceled my trip. Look at the soup we are in! Miracle, my foot. Completely avoidable . . . *completely avoidable*," the last two words delivered like lashes.

Stone stood as if in front of the headmistress. Hema seemed to expect him to speak and so he stammered, "I didn't know!"

Hemlatha's jaw dropped. She stared at him. There was a part of her that was incredulous at the idea of Stone impregnating Sister Mary Joseph Praise—who could imagine that? But the cynicism of the obstetrician who has seen everything crept back in. "You're thinking virgin birth, Dr. Stone? Immaculate conception?" She came around the table. "In that case, guess what, Mr. Expedient Operator? This is better than the manger in Bethlehem. This virgin is having twins!" She paused to let it sink in. "For goodness' sake, couldn't you have done a Cesarean section?" Her singsong intonation rose at the end, leaving the words "Cesarean section" hanging over Stone's head.

"Gloves and gown, quick!" Hemlatha shouted. "C-section tray here. Wake up, all of you! Do you not want to save her? Hurry! Hurry! Hurry!"

She repeated this in Amharic—"*Tolo, tolo, tolo!*"—in case English wasn't getting through.

The authority of her words kept them from retreating into the shock that had paralyzed them. "And you nurses standing around all starched and useless," Hemlatha said, as she pulled on a sterile gown and donned fresh gloves (there wasn't time to wash), "couldn't you have said something to him? Matron?" Matron looked to the floor.

"How long ago did the fetal heart sounds stop? What was the fetal heart rate?"

"It happened too quickly. We—"

"Oh, shut up, Stone. One of you give me a straight answer. Otherwise all of you shut up. Pressure now?"

"Barely sixty."

"Where's the blood? Am I dealing with deaf as well as dumb people? Answer me?"

The hospital had no blood bank, just a pint or two if one were lucky, kept in a refrigerator. Patients' families were reluctant to give blood. Hema once pressed a husband to give blood for his wife, and he'd refused outright. When she suggested that his wife would surely give blood for him if the tables were turned, he said, "You don't know my wife. She's waiting for me to die to take my cows and property." Time and again, she and Ghosh and Stone and Matron would donate their own blood and prevail on some of the nurses to do the same. At least once a year Ghosh would take his car and round up members of his cricket team to give blood.

"Has no one thought about blood?" Hema said again. "All of you who aren't needed here, go at once and give blood. This is one of our own, for God's sake. Go, now. No, not you Stone! Get gloved, man, for goodness' sake. Make yourself useful. What was the fetal heart rate?"

The probationer kept her eyes focused on the chart, terrified at the idea of giving blood and not daring to look up. And she knew that no one had *listened* for a fetal heart. They'd been too preoccupied with the mother. The probationer drew a line through her "C-section indicated" entry, sensing that it reflected badly on Matron. It was no consolation to see Dr. Stone standing frozen, eyes downcast, like a dog who'd disobeyed its master, every instinct telling it to slink away but knowing that the slightest movement would only bring more punishment.

Hema saw that Sister Mary Joseph Praise's face was losing all color, the eyelids lowered to quarter mast, the hooded gaze now unfocused, a look that was so often a precursor to death.

"Pressure?"

"Can't find it . . ."

"Doesn't matter, pour in blood, splash some iodine here, let's go!" With that she ripped open the sterile tray, grabbed the scalpel, and slashed through the skin—no time for sterility even—a vertical cut below the navel. Hema still couldn't believe what she was doing, or whom she was cutting.

She half expected Sister Mary Joseph Praise to sit up in protest.

Instead she heard the thud of a body falling and turned in time to see Matron crumpled on the floor.

CHAPTER 8

Missing People

"CUSTODY OF THE BODY" was the first thing out of Matron's mouth when she revived. She'd passed out for probably fewer than five seconds; everyone was in the same position, but now staring down at her. The probationer ran over to help. Despite Hema's protests, Matron clawed and kneed her way onto the anesthetist's stool, shouting, "I'm *not* leaving!" They were too busy to argue.

She sat near the board that tethered Sister Mary Joseph Praise's arm, blood finally running from a bottle into a vein. Matron reached for that hand, bending over it, studying Sister Mary Joseph Praise's fingers. She didn't want to look at what the doctors were doing, their red gloves reaching in Sister's belly. Matron still felt light-headed.

As she massaged Sister's fingers to still the shaking in her own, the words came to Matron unbidden: "Instruments of God." Sister Mary Joseph Praise had beautiful fingers, slender and soft, each a delicate sculpture. Even at rest they spoke of fine motor skills. Matron's by contrast were doughy white, the knuckles large and red as if someone had taken a ruler to them; the knobby excrescencies on the fingers spoke of nothing but age and toil and the caustic soaps and scrubbings which were the first tools of her profession; the fire burst of wrinkles on her palms spoke of her love for the Ethiopian soil and her willingness to plant and weed and dig alongside Gebrew. He was guard, gardener, odd-job man, and priest, and he believed Matron had no business dirtying her hands.

Matron felt her body shaking. Lord, you can take me, she thought. But wait till they're done because I don't want to distract them again. How she longed for a cup of coffee made from their own plant grown on Missing soil. She loved the gritty feel of the stone-ground bean against her teeth, and the way it rolled down the throat like lead shot. The Italians had left behind their passion for *macchiato* and espresso so that every café in Addis served these beverages. Matron had no use for any of that. *Missing* coffee, brewed traditionally, that's what sustained her through the day, and what she needed right now.

Tears tracked down into the crevices at the angles of her mouth. One of my Cherished Own, she thought; the daughter I can never have, now with child ... So many times at Missing, Matron had become privy to an unspeakable secret revealed by catastrophic illness. Impending death had a way of unexpectedly unearthing the past so that it came together with the present in an unholy coupling. *But Lord,* she cried out silently, *You could have spared us this. Spared her!*

As she stroked the younger woman's skin, Matron thought of the impulse that had made Sister Mary Joseph Praise choose to hide her body under a nun's habit or under scrub suit and mask. It hadn't worked; her covering exaggerated what little flesh was exposed. When a face was so lovely, lips so full, even a veil couldn't block its sensuality.

A few years after Sister Mary Joseph Praise's arrival, Matron thought that the two of them should give up the white habit. The Ethiopian government had closed down an American mission school in Debre Zeit for proselytizing. Matron was in the business of running a hospital, not converting souls; she decided it might be politically smart to forgo nun's habit. But when she'd seen Sister Mary Joseph Praise leaving Operating Theater 3 in a skirt and blouse, Matron wanted to run out and cover her with a sheet. W. W. Gonafer, Missing's laboratory technician, standing next to Matron, had also seen Sister Mary Joseph Praise walk by in mufti. He'd frozen like a setter pointing to quail, a flush creeping from his collar to the roots of his hair, as if lust were a companion fluid to blood. Matron had decided then that nuns at Missing should remain in habit.

A sudden exclamation that could have been from Hema or from Thomas Stone startled Matron, brought her back to the present. She jerked her head up, and before she could stop herself, she looked ... What she saw made her shudder and feel as if she'd keel over again. She dropped her head down between her shoulders, closed her eyes, and forced her mind to find another focus ...

Matron had no saint whom she modeled herself after, someone to call on at these times. To think of St. Catherine of Siena drinking the pus of invalids—oh! how that disgusted her. Matron thought of such displays as a particular Continental weakness, and she was impatient with *celestial billing and cooing,* bleeding palms and stigmata. And as for St. Teresa of Avila . . . why, she didn't have anything against Teresa. She didn't grudge Sister Mary Joseph Praise her adulation of Teresa. But secretly she agreed with Dr. Ghosh, the internal medicine physician at Missing, that St. Teresa's famous visions and ecstasies were probably nothing but forms of hysteria. Ghosh had shown Matron photographs that Charcot, the famous French neurologist, had taken of his patients with hysteria at the Salpêtrière hospital in Paris. Charcot believed that these delusions sprung from a woman's uterus—*hystera* in Greek. His patients, who were all women, stood in smiling poses—provocative poses, Matron thought—that Charcot had labeled "Crucifixion" and "Beatitude." How could anyone smile in the face of paralysis or blindness? *La belle indifférence* was what Charcot called this phenomenon.

If Sister Mary Joseph Praise had visions, she wasn't one to *speak* about them. Some mornings, Sister Mary Joseph Praise had looked sleepless, her bright cheeks, her floating carriage, suggesting her feet strained to remain earthbound. Perhaps that explained her equanimity while working shoulder to shoulder with Thomas Stone, a man who for all his talents gave little encouragement to those who labored with him.

Matron's faith was more pragmatic. She'd found in herself a calling to help. Who needed help more than the sick and the suffering, more so here than in Yorkshire? That was why she came to Ethiopia a lifetime ago. The few photographs, mementos, books, and certificates Matron brought with her had over the years been pilfered or mislaid. She never worried over this—one Bible, after all, would do just as well as the next. The essentials were also easily replaceable: her sewing kit, her watercolors, her clothes.

But she'd come to value the intangibles: the position she had grown to in the city where she was "Matron" to everyone, even to herself; the resourcefulness she'd discovered that allowed her to make a cozy hospital—an East African Eden, as she thought of it—grow out of a disorganized jumble of rudimentary buildings; and the core group of doctors whom she'd recruited and who by long association had evolved into her Cherished Own. The umbilical cord that had connected her to the Society of Holy Child Order, to the Sudan Interior Mission, had shriveled and fallen off. They were all now self-exiled prisoners at Missing—she and her Cherished Own.

Missing Hospital wasn't its name, of course, and now and then Matron tried to correct people, teach them to say "Mi-*shun*" instead of

"Missing." But in truth that year it wasn't even Missing; it was either Basel Memorial or Baden Memorial—she had to consult the paper taped to her desk to be sure—named after a generous church in either Switzerland or Germany. The Baptists of Houston were big donors, but they weren't at all concerned about naming the hospital. Dr. Ghosh liked to say that the hospital had as many forms as a Hindu god. "On any given day, only Matron knows which hospital we work in, and if we are walking into the Tennessee Baptist outpatient clinic, or the Texas Methodist outpatient clinic, so how can you blame me for being late— I have to get out of bed and go *find* my place of work. Oh, Matron, *there* you are!" Prisoners they all were, Matron thought, smiling despite herself; Missing People who could hardly choose their cell mates. But even for Ghosh, who was without doubt one of the strangest of God's creations, Matron felt a maternal affection. And the parallel anxiety that comes with such an impish child.

MATRON SIGHED and was surprised to hear words tumble out of her mouth, and she felt the others in the operating theater staring at her. Only then did she realize that her lips had been busy shaping prayers. Since turning fifty, Matron had noticed such dissonances and disconnections between her thought and action; they were becoming common. For example, at inopportune moments her mind busied itself pasting images into a mental scrapbook. Why? When would she ever have occasion to recall all these memories? At a testimonial dinner? On her deathbed? At the pearly gates? She'd long ago stopped thinking literally about such matters. Her father, a miner who had lost himself in alcohol and the darkness of the tunnels, had loved the words "pearly gates." On his tongue it sounded like the name of a blowsy woman, one of many that had come between him and his conjugal duties.

Still, Matron was sure of one thing: the image she witnessed when she'd inadvertently looked up a short while before, that was one she'd never ever forget. What happened was this: the sun had suddenly freed itself from behind a cloud, and by some accident of elevation and season presented itself directly on the ground-glass window of Operating Theater 3. Lambent and white, it had bounced off the walls, reflected off glass, metal, and tile, and there it was just when Hema or Stone or whoever it was made a loud exclamation, which was what had made Matron look up. That was when Matron saw them all bent over like hyenas over carrion, peering into Sister Mary Joseph Praise's open abdomen and its scandalous contents. She saw the light nosing its way between elbow and hip. Then the sunbeam fell directly on Sister Mary Joseph Praise's gravid uterus, which bulged out of the bloody wound like an obscenity on a saint's tongue. A blue-black collection of blood—a hematoma—stretched the broad ligament of the uterus, and it glowed in the light like the Host. Matron felt that this had been the sun's intent all along—to find the unborn. *We have seen each other anew. We are unmasked.* Yes, it was the kind of event that might be termed a "miracle"—except that nothing *happened;* the laws of nature weren't suspended (which Matron felt was the sine qua non for miracles). But it was as if the twins' place in the firmament as well as in the earthly order of things had been secured for them even before they were born; she knew that nothing—not even the familiar scent of eucalyptus, or the sight of its leaves thrust into a nostril, or the drumroll of rain on corrugated tin roof, or the visceral odor of a freshly opened abdomen—could ever be the same again.

CHAPTER 9

Where Duty Lies

HEMA WIELDED HER SCALPEL like a woman on fire. No time to tie off bleeders, and, in any case, very little bleeding along the way—not a good sign. She opened the glistening peritoneum and quickly positioned retractors to hold the wound edges back. The uterus bulged out of the wound. Then, before her eyes, it seemed to swell and turn luminous . . . She stood frozen, until she realized it was because the sun had suddenly struck the frosted window and lit up the table. In all her years operating at Missing, she couldn't remember that happening before.

Just as Hema feared, there was a lateral tear in the uterus. Blood had filled the broad ligament on one side. That meant that once she got the babies out, she'd have to do an emergency hysterectomy, no easy task in pregnancy, what with the uterine arteries being tortuous, thickened, and carrying half a liter of blood a minute. Not to mention the massive blood clot shimmering in the light, growing before her eyes and gloating at her like a smiling Buddha, as if to say, *Hema, I have completely distorted the anatomy, dissection is going to be bloody difficult, and your landmarks will all be gone. But come on in anyway, why don't you?*

Hema believed in numerology; next to one's name, nothing was as important as numbers. What is it about this day? she asked herself. It's the twentieth day of the ninth month. No fours or sevens in there . . . Airplane almost crashes, a child breaks his leg . . . I crack a Frenchman's nuts . . . What more, I say, what more?

She rapped Stone's knuckles with a scissors. "Stop!" He was fumbling with an oozing vessel when she needed him to retract.

She incised the uterus and tried to deliver the twin who sat higher in the uterus but was nevertheless head down, upside down. This twin would have been the second to come out had delivery proceeded through the birth canal, but now it would be the firstborn. But strangely, this twin, hand jammed against its cheek, wouldn't budge.

She extended the uterine wound.

She suctioned the infant's mouth.

She drew a sharp breath that inverted her mask against her lips because she could see the problem.

The babies were joined at the head. A short, fleshy tube passed from the crown of one to the other, a tube that was narrower and of a darker hue than the umbilical cords. They were tethered together, but there was a fatal tear in this stalk, a jagged opening caused no doubt by Stone's fishing with the basiotribe. And from this rent, what little blood the two infants possessed was pumping out.

Please God, she thought, let this be only a blood vessel, and a minor one at that. Let there be no brain or meninges or ventricle or cerebral artery or cerebrospinal fluid or whatnot in it. She spoke aloud to Stone now, to the room, to God, and to the twins whose lives, if they survived, might be irrevocably affected by this decision: "They could have seizures the minute I cut this. One twin could bleed out and the other overfill with blood. They could get meningitis . . ."

This was a technique surgeons used when difficult decisions had to be made: think aloud for your assistant because it might help clarify the issues for yourself. And theoretically it gave the assistant time to point out her faulty reasoning, though she wasn't about to take an opinion from the man responsible for this blunder. A careful decision was needed so as not to blunder again. It was often the *second* mistake that came in the haste to correct the first mistake that did the patient in.

"No choice," she said. "I have to cut." She put clamps across the stalk where it emerged from each infant's scalp. She invoked Lord Shiva's name, held her breath, and cut above each clamp, bracing herself for something terrible.

Nothing happened.

She tied off the stumps. She cut the umbilical cord and easily pulled out the first infant, a male. She handed it to the gowned and gloved probationer who stood nearby. This baby had been spared his father's probings. Then she pulled out the other infant—again a boy, an identical twin, whose scalp was bloodied from Stone's knife and whose skull would have been crushed had she not arrived.

Both infants were tiny, three pounds at best. Clearly less than full term. A month premature, perhaps more. Neither infant cried.

Distracted now by heavy oozing from Sister Mary Joseph Praise's soggy, friable uterus, Hema turned back from infants to the mother.

"What is her BP?" Hema asked, peering over the drapes, first at Nurse Asqual, and then at Sister Mary Joseph Praise's face. The anesthetist, the whites of her eyes showing like saucers, shook her head. Beautiful Sister Mary Joseph Praise's face now looked bloated and lifeless. "More blood! For God's sake. Pour it in!" Hema shouted.

As she toiled in the now deflated cavity of the belly, Hemlatha remembered that when she'd handed over the second baby to the probationer, she had been surprised to find the probationer still standing there, holding the first, a blank look on her face. But Hema had no time to worry about that. Once the babies were out, her duty as an obstetrician was to turn completely to Sister Mary Joseph Praise; her duty was to the mother.

CHAPTER 10

Dance of Shiva

WE TWO UNNAMED BABIES, newly arrived, were without breath. If most newborns meet life outside the womb with a shrill, piercing wail, ours was the saddest of all songs: the stillborn's song of silence. Our arms weren't clamped to our breasts; our hands did not make fists. Instead, we were limp and floppy like two wounded flounders.

The legend of our birth is this: identical twins born of a nun who died in childbirth, father unknown, possibly yet inconceivably Thomas Stone. The legend grew, ripened with age, and, in the retelling, new details came to light. But looking back after fifty years, I see that there are still particulars missing.

After labor stalled, I dragged my brother back into the womb and out of harm's way as lances and spears came at him through our only natural exit. The attack ceased. Then I remember—and I believe I do—the muffled voices, the tugging and sawing outside. As the rescuers neared us, I recall the blinding glare and strong fingers pulling at me. The shattering of the darkness and the silence, the deafening racket outside was so great that I almost missed the moment when we were physically separated, when the cord connecting my head to Shiva's fell away. The shock of that parting lingers. Even now, what I think about the most isn't that I lay there without breathing, immobile in the copper basin, born to the world, yet not alive—instead, I recall only the parting from Shiva. But, to return to the legend:

The probationer unloaded the two stillborns into a copper basin used to hold placentas. She carried the basin to the window. She made a notation in the delivery chart: *Japanese twins connected by the head but now disconnected.* In her eagerness to be useful, she completely forgot her ABC's: Airway, Breathing, and Circulation. Instead, she thought of what she had read the previous night about jaundice of the newborn and the helpful role of sunlight. She'd memorized that passage. She wished she had read about Japanese twins (the word "Siamese" eluded her) or asphyxiated babies, but the fact was she hadn't; she'd read about jaundice. But then, as she set the basin down, she realized that for sunlight to work, the babies had to be alive, which these weren't. Her sorrow and shame made her confusion worse. She turned away.

The twins lay face-to-face, feeling the basin's galvanic touch against their skin. In the chart the probationer used the words "white asphyxia" to describe their deathly pallor.

The sun, which had stage-lit the room moments before, now honed in on the basin.

The copper glowed orange. Its molecules became agitated. Its *prana* rose into the infants' translucent skin and passed into their doughy flesh.

HEMLATHA DISSECTED the broad ligaments, then clamped the uterine arteries, praying that she wouldn't accidentally clamp the ureters and shut down the kidneys in that bloody mess. "Quick, quick, quick!" She was tempted to smack Stone on the forehead instead of on the knuckles. "Retract properly, man!"

She followed his gaze to Sister Mary Joseph Praise's head, which bobbed like a rag doll's as the anesthetist tugged at her arm to find another vein. Matron, teary and lost in her grief, stroked Sister Mary Joseph Praise's other hand.

When Hema finally delivered the uterus, clamps and all, into a basin, she saw no pulsations in the abdominal aorta. Her hands, steady till now, shook as she loaded a syringe with Adrenalin and attached a three-and-a-half-inch needle to it. She lifted Sister Mary Joseph Praise's left breast, hesitated for a moment, invoked God's name again, then plunged the needle between the ribs and into the heart. She pulled the plunger back, and a mushroom of heart blood appeared in the syringe. Whenever I've had to resort to adrenaline to the heart it has never worked, Hema said to herself. Not once. Maybe I do it as a way to signal to myself that the patient is dead. But surely it must have worked, somewhere, with someone. Why else was it taught to us?

Hemlatha prided herself on being methodical in an emergency, keeping her cool. But she stifled a sob now as she waited, her right hand buried in Sister Mary Joseph Praise's abdomen, palm down, just over the spine, waiting for a throb in the aorta, a slap to register in her fingers. She couldn't forget that this was dear Sister's heart she was trying to jump-start, and whose life was slipping away. They'd shared the bond of two Indian women in a foreign land. The bond extended back to the Government General Hospital in Madras, India, even though they hadn't known each other there. To share a geography and a landscape of memory made them sisters, a family. And Hema could see her sister's hands turning blue, the nail beds dusky, and the skin turning dull. It was the hand of a corpse, and holding it was Matron, her head bowed as if she were asleep.

Hema waited longer than she might have under normal circumstances. It was some time before she could bring herself to say, her voice breaking, "No more. We have lost her."

IT WAS DURING this hiatus of activity in the room that the firstborn, the one who'd been spared a skull puncture, signaled its presence. It rapped its hands on the copper basin. It brought its left heel down to produce a muffled gong. Now that it had come wholly forth from a dying womb, it reached both arms skyward and then to its right, to its brother. *Here I be,* it announced. *Forget the shoulds and coulds and might haves and hows and whys. I am sympathetic to the situation, the circumstance, and in due course we can explore the details, and, in any case, Birth and Copulation, and Death—that's all the facts when you come down to brass tacks . . . I've been born, and once is enough. Help my brother. Look! Here! Come at once! Help him.*

Hemlatha ran over at this summons, saying "Shiva, Shiva," invoking the name of her personal deity, the God whom others thought of as the Destroyer, but who she believed was also the Transformer, the one who could make something good come out of something terrible. Later she would say that she'd assumed the worst about the twins. One of them had his head bloodied, and then there was the matter of her dividing the fleshy tube that connected them, and God knows how much distress they'd been in before she cut them free of the womb. But she'd also assumed that Matron or the probationer or both would be reviving the infants while she worked on the mother, though she recalled seeing Matron seated and immobile.

The probationer was mortified at the sound of a baby that had come alive right behind her back, confounding her most basic clinical assumptions. The child was no longer white, but pink, and *not* jaundiced. The other infant was a robin's egg blue, and it was still and unmoving as if it were the discarded chrysalis from which the crying baby had emerged. Matron, hearing that newborn cry, jumped off her stool. Her glance let the probationer know she was a hopeless case. Hemlatha went to work on the twin that was unmoving while Matron hastened to clean up the living one.

THE BREATHING TWIN gazed out from the copper vessel. Its puffy newborn eyes surveyed the room, trying to make sense of its surroundings.

There stood the man everyone took to be the father, a tall, sinewy white man, looking lost in his own theater. The father's hands were preternaturally pale from the talc that lingered on them after he'd stripped off his gloves. His fingers were clasped together in a posture shared by surgeons, priests, and penitents. His blue eyes were set deep in the orbits under a ledge of a brow which could make him look intense, but on this day made him look dull. From the shadows sprung the great ax blade of a nose, a nose that was sharp, in keeping with his profession. His lips were thin and straight as if drawn with a ruler. Indeed, the face was all straight lines and sharp angles, coming to a point in a lancet shaped chin, as if it had all been carved out of a single square of granite. His hair was parted on the right, a furrow that originated in boyhood with every follicle tamed by the comb to know exactly which direction it was to tilt. The top was cut unevenly, as if after saying, "A short back and sides," he'd risen from the chair when that was accomplished, despite the barber's protests. It was the kind of obstinate, determined face that with a spyglass held to the eye and a ponytail wouldn't have been out of place on the deck of an English man-of-war. Except, of course, for the tears rolling freely down the cheeks.

And from that tear-stained face, a voice emerged: "What about Mary?" startling everyone because it had been silent for so long. The measured syllables had the quality of a slow fuse.

"I'm sorry, Thomas. It is too late," said Hemlatha as she suctioned the infant's pharynx, then pushed air into the baby's lungs, her movements speedy and almost frantic. The irritation with Stone was gone from her voice, and pity had taken its place. She stole a glance at him over her shoulder.

A wrenching noise emerged from Stone's mouth, the cry of an unsound mind. He'd been a passive observer and a worthless assistant ever since Hema's arrival. Now he leaped forward and grabbed a scalpel from the tray. He placed a hand on Sister Mary Joseph Praise's chest. Hemlatha thought of restraining him and then decided it wasn't prudent to approach a man wielding a knife.

Stone lifted Sister Mary Joseph Praise's breast. The motto of those pioneers of resuscitation, the Royal Humane Society, resounded in his ears: *Lateat scintillula forsan*—a small spark may perhaps be hidden.

He pushed the breast up and out of the way, and under his knife a red gash appeared between the fourth and fifth ribs. He drew the knife over the wound again, and yet again till he was through muscle. If he was clumsy earlier, his movements now were those of a man incapable of tentative strokes. He cut the cartilages that connected the two ribs to the breastbone. He spread the ribs and watched in disbelief as his ungloved hand slid out of sight and into the still warm cavity of her chest. The spongy lung he pushed away. And there, under his fingers like a dead fish in a wicker basket, was Sister Mary Joseph Praise's heart. He squeezed, surprised at its size, barely able to encircle it. Meanwhile, he exhorted the nurse anesthetist to keep pushing air into her lungs, not to stop.

His right hand was buried within her thorax, but his eyes were on Sister Mary's engorged left breast, which he held out of the way with his left hand. The breast felt firm, unlike the slippery, soft heart. He saw blotchy blue shadows creep into her face, a hue that her brown skin shouldn't have been capable of. Her abdomen had collapsed, its surface crinkled like an airless balloon, its two halves splayed open like a book whose spine had given way.

"God? God? God?" Stone cried with every squeeze, calling on a God he had renounced once and didn't believe in. But Sister Mary believed, rising before dawn to pray, and lingering in prayer at night before she slept. Every beat of her life and each day of her calendar had been filled with God events, and no morsel of food entered her mouth without God's blessing. *Make your life something beautiful for God.* If Thomas Stone never understood it, he respected it, because it was the same quality she brought to the operating theater, and to the textbook she'd helped him with. That was why he called out God's name now, because if there was a God, God bloody well owed His devoted servant, Sister Mary Joseph Praise, a miracle. Otherwise, God was the shameless fraud Stone had always found Him to be. "If you want me to believe, God, I'll give you another chance."

The theater doors swung open.

All eyes turned to the figure that entered.

But it was only wide-eyed Gebrew, priest, servant of God, and watchman. The covered bowl he carried held the *injera* and *wot,* and their scent was added to that of placenta, blood, amniotic fluid, and meconium. Gebrew had hesitated to come into this sanctum sanctorum. He held the food container in front of him, unsure if it were the ingredient that might save the day. His eyes almost popped out of their sockets when he saw, on the altar of this hallowed place, Sister Mary Joseph Praise opened like a sacrificial lamb with Stone's hand in her chest. He started to shake. He put the food on the floor, squatted down against a wall, pulled out his beads, and swayed in prayer.

Stone redoubled his efforts. "I demand a miracle and I want it right now," he said, his body rocking back and forth. He kept it up even when the heart had turned mushy in his hand, and he was shouting now. "The bloody loaves and fishes . . . Lazarus . . . the lepers . . . Moses and the Red Sea . . ." Gebrew's chanting in ancient Geez matched Stone, call and response, as if Gebrew were translating because in this hemisphere God didn't know English.

Stone looked up to the ceiling, prepared for the tiles to part and for an angel to intercede where surgeons and priests had failed. All he saw was a black spider hanging down from its web, with its compound eyes taking in the scene of human misery below. Stone's shoulders slumped, and though his hand was still in Sister Mary's thorax, he was now merely caressing her heart, no longer squeezing. His chest heaved, tears falling onto the body of Sister Mary Joseph Praise. His head fell forward so it rested on his arms, which rested on Sister's chest. No one dared approach. They were transfixed by the sight of their surgeon so defeated, so destroyed.

AT LONG LAST he looked up, seeing as if for the first time the green tile going halfway up the wall, the swinging green door to the autoclave room, the glass instrument case, the bloody uterus with its necklace of hemostats lying in the green towel, the blue-black placenta right next to it on the specimen table, and the jade-colored ground-glass windows through which sunlight filtered. How did these things dare to exist if Mary did not?

That was when his eyes fell on the twins, no longer in their copper throne; that was when he saw the orange halo of light that surrounded the two boys. Somehow both children were alive, bright-eyed, one of them seeming to study him, the second one now as pink as the first.

"Oh no, no, no," he said in a pitiful voice. "No. *That* was not the miracle I asked for!" When he withdrew his hand from Mary's body it made a gurgling sound. He left the theater.

He came back with a long broom. He brushed the spider off the ceiling, and then, with his heel, he ground it into the tile.

Matron understood he was intent on blasphemy; in case the arachnid was God, he was killing God.

"Thomas," Hemlatha said, using his first name, which sounded strange on her tongue in Operating Theater 3, because they were always formal here. By this time both babies were in Hema's arms, wiped off and suctioned and swaddled in receiving blankets. The one in whose skull Stone had tried to drill a hole had aspirated some amniotic fluid but now seemed recovered; there was a big pressure dressing in place over the head wound. The other child showed only the stump of the flesh-bridge that had connected him to his brother, a stump now tied off with umbilical cord suture.

Hemlatha had established that the boys could move their limbs, neither of them was cockeyed, and they seemed to hear and to see. "Thomas," she said, approaching, but he cringed. He turned away. He would not look.

This man she thought she knew well, seven years a colleague, now stood bent as if he'd been gutted.

That, she said to herself, is visceral pain. As angry as she'd been with him, the depth of his grief and his shame moved her. All these years, she thought, it should have been clear to us that he and Sister were a perfect match; maybe if we'd encouraged them it could have been something more. How often did I see Sister assisting him in surgery, working on his manuscripts, taking notes for him in the outpatient department? Why did I assume that was all there was to it? I should have reached over and smacked him at my dinner table. I should have shouted at him, Don't be blind. See what you have in this woman! See how she loves you. Propose to her! Marry her. Get her to discard her habit, renege on her vows. It's clear her first vow is to you. But no, Thomas, I didn't do it because we all assumed that you were incapable of anything more. Who knew that this much feeling was hidden in your heart? I see it now. Yes, now we have these two as proof of what was in your hearts.

The two bundles in her arms propelled her forward, because they were, after all, his, and even as she thought that, she was still fighting her own disbelief. Surely he wouldn't try to deny that fact. She couldn't back away from this moment; she had to force the issue—who else could speak for these children? Stone was a fool who lost the one woman in the world fated for him. But now he had gained two sons. And Missing would rally round these infants. He'd have lots of help.

She moved closer.

"What shall we name these babies?" She could sense the uncertainty in her voice.

He appeared not to hear. After a pause, she repeated the question.

Stone thrust his chin at her, as if to say she could name them whatever she wanted. "Please get them out of my sight," he said very softly.

He kept his back turned on the infants to gaze once more at Sister Mary Joseph Praise. Which was why he missed the way his words fell on Hema like hot oil; he didn't see the flames of anger shooting out of her eyes. Hema would misread his intentions, and he hers.

Stone wanted to run away, but not from the children or from responsibility. It was the mystery, the *impossibility* of their existence that made him turn his back on the infants. He could only think of Sister Mary Joseph Praise. He could only think of how she'd concealed this pregnancy, waiting, who knows for what. In response to Hema's question, it would have been a simple thing for Stone to say, *Why ask me? I know no more than you do about this.* Except for the certainty that sat like a spike in his gut that it *was* somehow his doing, even though he had no recollection how or where or when.

Sister Mary Joseph Praise lay lifeless and unburdened of the two lives she had carried, as if that had been her sole earthly purpose. Matron had pulled down Sister Mary Joseph Praise's eyelids, but they would not stay closed. The half-mast eyelids, the unseeing gaze, hammered in the reality of her death.

Stone took one last look. He wanted to remember her not as Sister, not as his assistant, but as the woman he should have declared his love for, the woman he should have cared for, the woman he should have wed. He wanted the ghoulish image of her corpse burned into his brain. He had negotiated his way through life by work, and work, and more work. It was the only arena in which he felt complete and the only thing he had to give Sister Mary Joseph Praise. But at this moment work had failed him.

The sight of her wounds shamed him. There'd be no healing, no scars to form, harden, and fade on her body. *He* would bear the scar, he would carry it from the room. He'd known only one way of being, and it cost him. But he would have been willing to change for her had she only asked. He would have. If only she could have known. What did it matter now?

He turned to leave again, glancing around as if to seal in his memory this place in which he'd polished and elevated his art, this place that he'd furnished to suit his needs and that he thought was his real home. He took it all in because he knew he'd never ever return. He was surprised to find Hema still standing behind him, and again the sight of the bundles she carried made him recoil.

"Stone, think about this," Hema said. "Turn your back on me if you want, because I'll have no use for you. But don't turn your back on these children. I won't ask you again."

Hema held her living burden and waited on Stone. He was on the verge of speaking to her honestly, of telling her all. In his eyes she saw pain and puzzlement. What she didn't see was any recognition of the infants as being connected to him. He spoke like a man who'd just been hit on the head. "Hema, I don't understand who . . . why they are here . . . why Mary is dead."

She waited. He was circling around a truth that might emerge if she waited. She wanted to grab his ears and shake it out of him.

At last he met her gaze, refusing to look down at the infants, and what he said wasn't what she wanted to hear. "Hema, I don't want to set eyes on them, ever."

The last of Hema's restraint fell away. She was livid for the children, furious that he seemed to think this was just his loss.

"What did you say, Thomas?"

He must have known a battle line had just been drawn.

"They killed her," he said. "I don't want to set eyes on them."

So this is how it will be, Hema thought, this is how we shall pass from each other's lives. The twins mewled in her arms.

"Whose are they, then? Aren't they yours? So didn't you kill her, too?"

His mouth opened in pain. He had no answer, so he turned to leave.

"You heard me, Stone, *you* killed her," Hema said, raising her voice so that she drowned out every other sound. He flinched as the words lashed into him. It pleased her. She felt no pity. Not for a man who wouldn't claim his children. He pushed the swinging door so hard it shrieked in protest.

"Stone, you killed her," she shouted after him. "These are your children."

THE PROBATIONER BROKE the ensuing silence. She was trying to anticipate, so she opened a circumcision tray and pulled on gloves. The one thing Matron allowed her to do without supervision was to use the foreskin guillotine.

But instead of praising her, Hema pounced on her. "My goodness, girl, don't you think these children have had quite enough? They're preemies! They are not out of danger. Want them to be chip-cock-Charlies on top of all this? . . . And you? What have you been doing all the time, eh? You should've been worrying about their swallowing ends, not their watering cans."

HEMA ROCKED THE TWINS, thrilled by their breathing selves, by their peaceful smiles, the opposite of the usual anxious, panicked face of a newborn. Their mother lay dead in the same room, their father had run, but they knew nothing of that.

Matron, Gebrew, the nurse anesthetist, and others who had gathered were weeping around Sister's body. Word had spread to the maids and housekeepers. Now a funeral wail, a piercing *lululululululu* ripped through the heart of Missing. The ululations would continue for the next few hours.

Even the probationer began to show the first inkling of Sound Nursing Sense. Instead of struggling to appear to be something she was not, she wept for Sister, who was the only nurse who really understood her. For the first time the probationer saw the children not as "fetuses" or "neonates" but instead as motherless children, like herself, children to be pitied. Her tears poured out. Her body slumped as if the starch had vanished not just from her clothes but from her bones. To her amazement, Matron came and put an arm around her. She saw not just sadness but fear in Matron's face. How could Missing go on without Sister? Or without Stone? For surely he was never coming back, that she could see.

Hemlatha shut out the sobbing around her as she rocked the babies, and then she began to croon, her anklets jingling faintly like castanets as she shifted weight from one foot to the other. She felt the loss of Sister Mary Joseph Praise as acutely as anyone, and yet she felt guided—perhaps this was Sister's doing—to give her all at this moment to the two infants. The twins were breathing quietly; their fingers fanned over their cheeks. They belonged in her arms. How beautiful and horrible life is, Hema thought; too horrible to simply call tragic. Life is worse than tragic. Sister Mary, bride of Christ, now gone from the world into which she just brought two children.

Hema thought of Shiva, her personal deity, and how the only sensible response to the madness of life in this her thirtieth year was to cultivate a kind of madness within, to perform the mad dance of Shiva, to mimic the rigid masking smile of Shiva, to rock and sway and flap six arms and six legs to an inner tune, a tabla beat. *Thim-thaga-thaga, thim-thaga-thim, thim-thaga* . . . Hema moved gently, knees flexing, tapping her heels, then her forefoot in time to the music in her head.

The bit players in Theater 3 regarded her as if she were mad, but she danced on even as they tidied the corpse, she danced as if her minimalist gestures were shorthand for a much larger, fuller, reckless dance, one that held the whole world together, kept it from extinction.

Ridiculous, the thoughts that came to her as she danced: her new Grundig, Adid's lips and his long fingers, the thump of Matron falling over, the revolting feel of the Frenchman's balls but the satisfaction in seeing the color flee his face, Gebrew with chicken feathers stuck to him. What a journey . . . what a day . . . what madness, so much worse than tragic! What to do except dance, dance, only dance . . .

She was surprisingly graceful and light on her feet, the neck and head and shoulder gestures of Bharatnatyam automatic for her, eyebrows shooting up and down, eyeballs flitting to the edges of their sockets, feet moving, a rigid smile on her face, and all this while holding the babies in her arms.

Outside the hospital, as the light faded, the lions in the cages near the Sidist Kilo Monument, anticipating the slabs of meat the keeper would fling through the bars, roared with hunger and impatience; in the foothills of Entoto, the hyenas heard and paused as they neared the edge of the city, three steps forward and one back, cowardly and opportunistic; the Emperor in his palace made plans for a state visit to Bulgaria and perhaps to Jamaica, where he had followers—Rastas—who took their name from his precoronation name of Ras Teferi and who thought he was God (an idea he didn't mind his own people believing, but when it came from so far away and for reasons that he didn't understand, made him wary).

. . .

THE LAST FORTY-EIGHT hours had irrevocably altered Hema's life. She had two infants squinting up at her from time to time as if to confirm their arrival, their good fortune.

Hema felt light-headed, giddy. I won the lottery without buying a ticket, she thought. These two babies plugged a hole in my heart that I didn't know I had until now.

But there was danger in the analogy: she'd heard of a railway porter at Madras Central Station who won lakhs and lakhs of rupees, only to have his life fall apart so that he soon returned to the platform. When you win, you often lose, that's just a fact. There's no currency to straighten a warped spirit, or open a closed heart, a selfish heart—she was thinking of Stone.

Stone had prayed for a miracle. The silly man didn't see that these newborns *were* miracles. They were obstetric miracles for surviving his assault. Hema decided to name the first twin to breathe Marion. Marion Sims, she would tell me later, was a simple practitioner in Alabama, USA, who had revolutionized women's surgery. He was considered the father of obstetrics and gynecology, the patron saint; in naming me for him, she was both honoring him and giving thanks.

"And Shiva, for Shiva," she said, naming the child with the circular hole in his scalp, the last to breathe, the child she had labored over, a child all but dead until she had invoked Lord Shiva's name, at which point he took his first gasp.

"Yes, Marion and Shiva."

She tacked on "Praise" to both names, after their mother.

And finally, reluctantly, almost as an afterthought, but because you cannot escape your destiny, and so that he wouldn't walk away scot-free, she added our surname, the name of the man who had left the room: Stone.

PART TWO

When a pole goes into a hole
it creates another soul
which is either a pole
or a hole

Newton's Fourth Law of Motion (as taught by the Mighty Senior Sirs of Madras Christian College during the initiation/ragging of A. Ghosh, Junior Pisser Kataan, Batch of 1938, St. Thomas Hall, D Block, Tambaram, Madras)

below, which resembled a certain fallen dictator's potbelly, that gave it its name. Set into its side was a metal cavity so that whenever the stove was lit, water was heated. Almaz grumbled about having to split wood, then stoke the fire in Mussolini—all for what? To make one cup of that vile powder coffee for the *getta*? (In the mornings Ghosh preferred instant to the semisolid Ethiopian brew.) But it wasn't the coffee he valued as much as the hot water for his bath.

He drew the blanket over his head as Almaz stagger-stepped to the bathroom, hefting the steaming cauldron. "*Banya* skin!" she muttered in Amharic. Amharic was all she ever spoke, though Ghosh suspected she understood more English than she let on. After emptying the cauldron into the bathtub, she finished the thought: "It must be so sickly to require washing every day. What misfortune the *getta* doesn't have *habesha* skin. It would stay clean without the need for all this scrubbing."

No doubt Almaz had been to church this morning. When Ghosh first came to Ethiopia, as he walked down Menelik Street, a woman across the road stopped and bowed to him and he waved back. Only later did he realize that her gesture was aimed at the church across the way. Pedestrians bobbed before a church, kissing the church wall thrice and crossing themselves before going on. If they'd been chaste, they might enter. Otherwise they stayed on the other side of the street.

Almaz was tall with oak-colored skin and a shield-shaped face. Her oval eyes sloped down to the bridge of her nose, giving her a sultry, inviting gaze. Her square chin contradicted that message, and this hint of androgyny brought her admiring looks. She had large but shapely hands, wide hips, and buttocks that formed a broad ledge on which Ghosh believed he could balance a cup and saucer.

She was twenty-six when she came to Missing with labor pains, nine months pregnant, her cheeks flushed with pride because *this* baby she would carry to term, unlike all the others that had failed to take root in her womb. In the prenatal clinic visits, nursing students had twice recorded FHSH (Fetal Heart Sounds Heard) in the chart. But on the day of her putative labor, Hema heard only silence. Hema's exam revealed that the "baby" was a giant fibroid of the uterus and the FHSH nothing but a rattle in a probationer's brain.

Almaz refused to accept the diagnosis. "Look," she said, fishing out an engorged breast and squeezing forth a jet of milk. "Could a tit do that if there were no child to feed?" Yes, a tit could do that and more if its owner believed. It took three more months with no true signs of labor and an X-ray that showed no baby's skull, no spine, for Almaz to concede. At the surgery, which she at last agreed to, Hema had to remove both the fibroid and the uterus which it had swallowed. In the town of Sabatha they still waited for Almaz to return with the baby. But Almaz couldn't bear to go back. She stayed on and became one of the Missing People.

He heard Almaz return and the jangle of a cup and saucer. The scent of coffee made him peek from under his tent.

"Is there anything else?" she asked, studying him.

Yes, I need to tell you that I am leaving Missing. Really, I am! I can't let Hema play me like a harmonium. But he didn't say this; instead, he shook his head. He felt Almaz understood intuitively what Hema's absence did to him.

"Yesus Christos, please forgive this sinner, but he was out drinking last night," she said as she stooped to pick up a beer bottle from under the bed. Alas, Almaz was in a proselytizing mood. Ghosh felt as if he were eavesdropping on her private conversation with God. What a bad idea it had been to give the Bible to anyone but priests, Ghosh thought. It made a preacher out of everybody.

"Blessed St. Gabriel, St. Michael, and all the other saints," she continued in Amharic, confident he would understand, "for I prayed for master to be a new man, for him to one day give up his *dooriye* ways, but I was wrong, your venerable holinesses."

It was the word *dooriye* that tricked Ghosh into speaking. It meant "lout," "lecher," "reprobate"—and it stung him to hear that word.

"What gives you the right to address me this way?" he said, though he didn't really feel the anger his voice carried. He was about to add, *Are you my wife?*—but choked those words off. To his perpetual shame, he and Almaz had been intimate twice over the years, both times when he was drunk. She'd lain down, lifted, and spread, grumbling even as her hips fell into rhythm with his, but no more than she grumbled about the coffee or hot water. He'd decided that grumbling with Almaz was the language of both pleasure and pain. When they were spent she'd sighed, pulled her skirt down, and asked, "Will there be anything else?" before leaving him to his guilt.

He loved her for never holding those two episodes against him. But it had given her the license to nag him, to raise her grumbling to a steady pitch. That was her prerogative, but the saints help anyone else who addressed him in that tone; she defended him, his belongings, and his reputation with her tongue and with her fists and feet if necessary. Sometimes he felt that she owned him.

"Why do you harass me like this?" he said, the fire gone from his voice. He knew he'd never have the courage to break the news of his leaving to her.

"Who said I was talking to you?" Almaz replied.

But when she left he saw the two aspirins in the saucer with his coffee, and his heart melted. *My greatest consolation,* Ghosh thought, *for only the hundredth time since his arrival in Ethiopia, has been the women of this land.* The country had completely surprised him. Despite pictures he'd seen in *National Geographic,* he'd been unprepared for this mountain empire shrouded in mist. The cold, the altitude, the wild roses, the towering trees, reminded him of Coonoor, a hill station in India he'd visited as a boy. His Imperial Majesty, Emperor of Ethiopia, may have been exceptional in his bearing and dignity, but Ghosh discovered that His Majesty's people shared his physical features. Their sharp, sculpted noses and soulful eyes set them between Persians and Africans, with the kinky hair of the latter, and the lighter skin of the former. Reserved, excessively formal, and often morose, they were quick to anger, quick to imagine insults to their pride. As for theories of conspiracy and the most terrible pessimism, surely they'd cornered the world market on those. But get past all those superficial attributes, and you found people who were supremely intelligent, loving, hospitable, and generous.

"Thank you, Almaz," he called out. She pretended not to hear.

IN THE BATHROOM Ghosh felt a sharp pain as he peed and was forced to cut off his stream. "Like sliding down the edge of a razor blade using my balls as brakes," he muttered, his eyes tearing. What did the French call it? *Chaude pisse,* but that didn't come close to describing his symptoms.

Was this mysterious irritation from lack of use? Or from a kidney stone? Or was there, as he suspected, a mild, endemic inflammation along the passage that carried urine out? Penicillin did nothing for this condition, which waxed and waned. He'd devoted himself to this question of causation, spending hours at the microscope with his urine and with that of others with similar symptoms, studying it like the piss-pot prophets of old.

After his first liaison in Ethiopia (and the only time he'd not used a condom), he had relied on the Allied Army Field Method for "post-exposure prophylaxis," as it was called in the books: wash with soap and mercuric chloride, then squeeze silver proteinate ointment into the urethra and milk it down the length of his shaft. It felt like a penance invented by the Jesuits. He believed the "prophylaxis" was partly behind the burning sensations that came and went and peaked on some mornings. How many other such time-honored methods out there were just as useless? To think of the millions that the armies of the world had spent on "kits" like this, or to think that before Pasteur's discovery of microbes, doctors fought duels over the merits of balsam of Peru versus tar oil for wound infection. Ignorance was just as dynamic as knowledge, and it grew in the same proportion. Still, each generation of physicians imagined that ignorance was the special provenance of their elders.

There was nothing like a personal experience to tilt a man toward a specialty, and so Ghosh had become the de facto syphilologist, the venereologist, the last word when it came to VD. From the palace to the embassies, every VIP with VD came to consult Ghosh. Perhaps in the county of Cook in America, they'd be interested in this experience.

AFTER HE BATHED and dressed, he drove the two hundred yards to the outpatient building. He sought out Adam, the one-eyed compounder, who, under Ghosh's tutelage, had become a natural and gifted diagnostician. But Adam wasn't around, and so he went to W. W. Gonad, a man of many titles—Laboratory Technician, Blood Bank Technician, Junior Administrator—all of which were to be found on a name tag on his oversize white coat. His full name was Wonde Wossen Gonafer, which he'd Westernized to W. W. Gonad. Ghosh and Matron had been quick to point out the meaning of his new moniker, but it turned out that W.W. needed no edification. "The English have names like Mr. Strong? Mr. Wright? Mr. Head? Mr. Carpenter? Mr. Mason? Mrs. Moneypenny? Mr. Rich? I will be Mr. W. W. Gonad!"

He was one of the first Ethiopians Ghosh had come to know well. Outwardly melancholic, W.W. was nevertheless fun-loving and ambitious. Urbanization and education had introduced in W.W. a gravitas, an exaggerated courtliness, the neck and body flexed, primed for the deep bow, and conversation full of the sighs of someone whose heart had been broken. Alcohol could either exaggerate the condition or remove it entirely.

Ghosh asked W.W. to give him a B_{12} shot; it was worth a try—even placebos had *some* effect.

As he readied the syringe, W.W. made clucking noises. "You must be sure to always use prophylactics, Dr. Ghosh," he said and immediately turned sheepish, because W.W. was hardly one to proffer such advice.

"But I do. After that first time I've never had unrubberized intercourse. Don't you believe me? That is why I don't understand this burning some mornings. And you, sir? Why don't you use a condom, W.W.?"

Gonad wore heel lifts that made him walk with an ostrichlike pelvic tilt. He teased his hair into a lofty halo that would one day be called an Afro. Now, he pulled himself to his full five foot one and said haughtily, "If I wanted to make love to a rubber glove I would never have to leave the hospital."

IF GHOSH HAD BEEN AWARE that at this very moment Sister Mary Joseph Praise was in distress in her quarters, he'd have rushed to help; it might have saved her life. But at that point no one knew. The probationer had yet to deliver her message, and when she did, she failed to tell anyone how sick Sister was.

Ghosh made leisurely rounds with the ward nurse and the probationers. He pointed out a sulfa rash to the newest probationers, removed ascitic fluid from the belly of a man with cirrhosis. The outpatient clinics then took most of the day, except for a formal lecture to the nursing students on tuberculosis. Keeping busy helped him forget about Hema, who should have been back two days ago. He could think of only one explanation for her delay, and it depressed him.

In the late afternoon, Ghosh drove out of Missing. He missed by a few minutes the hue and cry when Thomas Stone carried Sister Mary Joseph Praise out of the nurses' hostel.

HE PARKED near the towering Lion of Judah, a landmark for the area near the railway station. Carved out of blocks of gray-black stone, with a square crown on its head, that cubist lion resembled a chess piece. The eye slits beneath the low brow stared across the plaza; the sculpture gave this part of town an avant-garde sensibility.

Ghosh stepped into the chromed and lacquered world of Ferraro's, where a haircut cost ten times as much as at Jai Hind, the Indian barbershop. But Ferraro's, with its frosted-glass window and red-and-white-striped barber's pole, was rejuvenating. The mirrored walls, the necklace of globe lights, the oxblood leather chair with more knobs and chrome levers than Missing's operating table—you could only get this at the Italian establishment.

Ferraro, dazzling in his collarless white smock, was everywhere: behind Ghosh to slip off his coat, alongside him as he led him to the chair, then in front of him to slip on the gown. Ferraro chatted in Italian and it didn't matter that Ghosh knew only a few words; the conversation was offered as background music, not requiring a response. He felt at ease with the older man. "Beware of a young doctor and an old barber" went the saying, but Ghosh thought both he and Ferraro were in good hands.

Ferraro had soldiered in Eritrea before becoming a barber in Addis. Had they shared a common language, there was much that Ghosh would have asked. He'd have loved to hear about the 1940s typhus epidemic during which some brilliant Italian official decided to douse the whole city with DDT, getting rid of lice and the typhus. How had the Italians handled VD in the troops who couldn't possibly have confined themselves to the six Italian ladies in Asmara who were the official garrison *puttanas*?

He felt an urge to confide in Ferraro, to tell him how his chest ached with jealousy; how he was leaving the country because of a woman who didn't take his love seriously. Ferraro made a soft clucking noise, as if he had intuited the problem and its gender; easing the chair into a reclining position was Ferraro's first step to finding a solution. Neither man could have guessed that at that moment Sister Mary Joseph Praise's heart had stopped beating.

Ferraro gently draped the first hot towel around Ghosh's neck. When the last towel was in place, blotting out all light, Ferraro fell tactfully quiet. Ghosh heard him tiptoe to where he'd parked his cigarette, and then the sound of his exhaling smoke.

If I could have a valet, this would be my man, Ghosh thought. One never doubted for a moment that it was Ferraro's destiny to be a barber; his instincts were perfect; his baldness was inconsequential.

GHOSH EMERGED in a cloud of aftershave. Driving away, he took in the sights as if for the last time: up the steep slope of Churchill Road and past Jai Hind to the traffic light where a balancing act between accelerator and clutch was required before the light turned green. He turned left and went past Vanilal's Spice Shop, Vartanian's Fabrics, and stopped at the post office.

The leper child who staked out this territory where foreigners abounded had blossomed into a teen seemingly overnight. Her perky breasts pushed through her *shama* while the cartilage of her nose had collapsed to form a saddle nose. He put a one-birr note into her clawed hand.

He turned at the sound of castanets. A *listiro*, bottle caps threaded onto a nail on his shoe box, looked up at him. Ghosh stood against the post office wall along with a half-dozen other men who were smoking or reading the paper while *listiros* worked like bees at their feet. The Italians are responsible for this, too, Ghosh thought: people getting their shoes shined more often than they bathe.

It was starting to drizzle, and the *listiro*'s elbows flew like pistons. On the nape of the boy's neck, Ghosh noticed a patch of albino-white skin. Surely not the collar of Venus? So young, and already with scars of healed syphilis? *Venereum insontium*—"innocently acquired" syphilis— was still in the textbooks, though Ghosh didn't believe in such a thing. Other than congenital syphilis where the mother infected the unborn child, he believed that *all* syphilis was sexually acquired. He'd seen five-year-olds at play mimicking the act of copulation with each other and doing a good job of it.

A sudden cloudburst sent Ghosh scrambling to his car. The rain washed off a coat of ennui that had enveloped the Piazza. The streetlights came on and reflected off the chrome of passing cars. The Ambassa buses turned a vivid red. On the rooftop of the three-story Olivetti Building (which also housed Pan Am, the Venezia Ristorante, and Motilal Import-Exports) the neon beer mug filled up with yellow lager, foamed over in white suds, then went dark before the cycle started again. That sign had been a source of such wonder when it was first put up. The barefoot men driving their sheep into town for Meskel festival had stopped to watch the show, knotting up traffic as the herd got away from them.

AT ST. GEORGE'S BAR, rain dripped off the Campari umbrellas onto the patio. It was packed inside with foreigners and locals who felt the ambience worth the prices. The glass doors held in a rich scent of cannoli, biscotti, chocolate *cassata*, ground coffee, and perfume. A gramophone blended into the chatter of voices, the tinkle of cups and saucers, and the sharp sounds of chairs scraping back and glass smacking on Formica-topped tables.

He had just sat down at the bar when he saw Helen's reflection in the mirror—she was seated at a far corner table. She was shortsighted and probably wouldn't see him. Her fair features were striking against her jet-black hair. She was paying no attention to her companion, who was none other than Dr. Bachelli. Ghosh's instinct was to leave at once, but the barman stood waiting, so he asked for a beer.

"My God, Helen, you are beautiful," Ghosh muttered to himself, studying her reflection. St. George's didn't employ bar girls, but it had no objections to the classier women coming in. Helen's legs were crossed under her skirt, the skin of her thighs white as cream. He remembered those generous glutei that obviated any need for a supporting pillow. A mole on her jawline added to her distinction. But why was it the prettiest half-caste girls—the *killis*, as they were often called, though the term was derogatory—put on this air of being above it all and bored?

Bachelli, his silk kerchief flowing out of his cream coat and matching his tie, appeared much older on this night than his fifty or so years. His carefully sculpted pencil mustache and his expression of equanimity, cigarette in hand, bothered Ghosh because he saw in it his own inertia, the thing that had kept him in Africa so long. Ghosh was fond of Bachelli; the man was not a great physician, but he knew his limits in medicine, though he didn't always know his limit in alcohol.

Just a week ago, Ghosh had been shocked to see Bachelli drunk and singing the "Giovinezza," goose-stepping down the middle of the road in the heart of the Piazza. It was near midnight, and Ghosh had stopped his car then and tried to get him off the street. Bachelli became loud and boisterous, screaming about Adowa, which was enough to get him beaten up if he persisted. Bachelli was lost in the memory of boarding his troop ship in Naples in 1934; he was a young officer again in the 230th Legion of the National Fascist Militia, off to fight for Il Duce, off to capture Abyssinia, off to expunge the shame of being defeated at the battle of Adowa by Emperor Menelik in 1896. At Adowa, ten thousand Italian soldiers, with as many of their Eritrean *askaris*, poured down from their colony to invade and take Ethiopia. They were defeated by Emperor Menelik's barefoot Ethiopian fighters armed with spears and

Remingtons (sold to them by none other than Rimbaud). No European army had ever been so thoroughly thrashed in Africa. It stuck in the Italian craw, so that even men who weren't born at the time of Adowa, like Bachelli, grew up wanting vengeance.

Ghosh didn't understand any of this till he came to Africa. He hadn't realized that Menelik's victory had inspired Marcus Garvey's Back to Africa Movement, and that it had awakened Pan-African consciousness in Kenya, the Sudan, and the Congo. For such insights, one had to live in Africa.

The Italians never forgot their humiliation, and so on the next try, some forty years later, Mussolini took no chances; his motto was *Qualsiasi mezzo!*—win by any means. The monkey-maned Ethiopian horsemen with leather shields and spears and single-shot rifles found the enemy was a cloud of phosgene gas that choked them to death, Geneva protocol be damned. Bachelli had been part of that. And looking at Bachelli's face, so flushed with liquor and pride, as he did his victory march in the Piazza, Ghosh had realized it must have been Bachelli's proudest moment.

Ghosh sat trying to be inconspicuous at the bar, but watching the couple in the mirror. When Ghosh first met Helen, he'd fallen madly in love with her—for a few days. Every time Helen saw him she'd say, "Give me money, please." When he asked for what, she'd blink and then pout as if the question were unreasonable. She'd say, "My mother died," or "I need abortion"—whatever came into her head. Most bar girls had hearts of gold and eventually married well, but Helen's heart was of baser metal.

Poor Bachelli was smitten by Helen and had been for years, even though he had a common-law Eritrean wife. He gave Helen money. He expected and accepted her selfishness. He called her his *donna delinquente,* offering the mole on her cheek as proof. Ghosh meant to ask Bachelli if he actually believed anything in Lombroso's abominable book, *La Donna Delinquente.* Lombroso's "studies" of prostitutes and criminal women uncovered "characteristics of degeneration"—such things as "primitive" pubic hair distribution, an "atavistic" facial appearance, and an excess of moles. It was pseudoscience, utter rubbish.

Ghosh slipped out abruptly without finishing his beer, because suddenly the idea of making small talk with either of them that evening was intolerable.

. . .

THE AVAKIANS WERE LOCKING UP their bottled-gas store, and beyond their shop the lights of the Piazza, the transitory illusion of Roma, came to an end. Now it was all darkness, and the road ran past the long, gloomy, fortresslike stone wall that held up the hillside. A gash in the moss-covered stones was Säba Dereja—Seventy Steps—a pedestrian shortcut to the roundabout at Sidist Kilo, though the steps were so worn down that it was more a ramp than stairs, treacherous when it rained. He drove past the Armenian church, then around the obelisk at Arat Kilo—another war monument at a roundabout—past the Gothic spires and domes of the Trinity Cathedral and then the Parliament Building, which took its inspiration from the one on the banks of the Thames. At the Old Palace, because he was not quite ready to head home, he turned down to Casa INCES, a neighborhood of pretty villas.

He wasn't in the mood for the Ibis or one of the big bars in the Piazza that employed thirty hostesses. He saw a simple cinder-block building up ahead. It appeared to be partitioned into four bars. There were hundreds of such places all over Addis. A soft neon glow showed from two doorways. A plank forded the open gutter. He chose the door on the right, pushing through the bead curtain. It was, as he had suspected given the size, a one-woman operation. The tube light had been painted orange, creating a womblike interior, exaggerated by the frankincense smoking on the charcoal brazier. Two padded bar stools fronted a short wooden counter. The bottles on the shelf on the back wall were impressive—Pinch, Johnny Walker, Bombay gin—even if they were filled with home-brewed *tej*. His Majesty Haile Selassie the First, in Imperial Bodyguard uniform, gazed down from a poster on one wall. A leggy woman in a swimsuit smiled back at His Majesty from a Michelin calendar.

What little floor space remained held a table and two chairs. Here the barmaid sat with a customer who held her hand; the man seemed intent on keeping her attention. Just when Ghosh decided there was no point in staying, she wrenched her hand free, scraped her chair back, stood, and bowed. High heels to show off her calves. Dark polish on her toenails. Very pretty, he thought. The smile seemed genuine and suggested a better disposition than Helen's. The other man pushed sullenly past Ghosh and left without a word.

The land of milk and honey, Ghosh thought. Milk and honey, and love for money.

Now she and Ghosh traded how-are-yous and I-am-wells, bowing, the deep excursions diminishing till the last few were mere inclinations of the head. Ghosh eased onto the bar stool as she circled behind the counter. She was perhaps twenty, but with big bones, and the fullness of her blouse suggested she had mothered at least one child.

"Min the tetaleh?" she asked, thrusting her finger at her mouth, in case he didn't understand Amharic.

"I deeply regret that I drove your admirer away. Had I known he was here, or how much he cared for you, I could never have intruded on such a tryst."

She gasped with surprise.

"Him! He wanted to keep that one beer going till daylight without buying me one. He is from Tigre. Your Amharic is better than his," she said, gushing, relieved that it would not be a night of sign language.

Her gauzy white cotton skirt ended just below her knees. The colorful border was repeated on the piping of the blouse, and again in the frill of the *shama* over her shoulders. Her hair was straightened and permed, a Western do. A collar of tattoos in the form of closely spaced wavy lines made her neck look longer. Pretty eyes, Ghosh thought.

Her name was Turunesh, but he decided to call her what he was in the habit of calling all women in Addis: Konjit, which meant "beautiful."

"I'll have blessed St. George's. And please serve one for yourself. We must celebrate."

She bowed her thanks. "Is it your birthday, then?"

"No, Konjit, even better." He was about to say, It is the day that I have freed myself from the chains of a woman who has deviled me for over a decade. The day I have decided my sojourn in Africa ends and America awaits.

"It is the day I have set eyes on the most beautiful woman in Addis Ababa."

Her teeth were strong and even. A rim of upper gum showed when she laughed. She was self-conscious about this because she brought her hand to her mouth.

Something inside him melted at the sound of her happy laughter, and for the first time since waking that morning, he felt almost normal.

When he first arrived in Addis Ababa he'd sunk into a deep depression. He considered leaving at once because he'd found that he'd completely misunderstood Hema's intentions in sending for him. What he thought was the triumphant conclusion of a courtship that began when they were interns in India turned out to be in his head alone. Hema thought she was just doing Ghosh (and Missing) a favor. Ghosh hid his embarrassment and humiliation. It was the time of the long rains and that alone was enough to make a man kill himself. The Ibis in the

Piazza saved him. He'd been looking for a drink and was attracted by an entrance with an arch of ivy that was festooned with Christmas lights. He could hear music from within and the sounds of womanly laughter. Inside, he thought he'd died and returned as Nebuchadnezzar. In those Ibis women—Lulu, Marta, Sara, Tsahai, Meskel, Sheba, Mebrat— and in the sprawling bar and restaurant that occupied two floors and three enclosed verandas, he found a family. The girls welcomed him like a long-lost friend, restoring his good humor, encouraging the joker in him, always happy to sit with him. Feminine good looks were as abundant as the rain outside; skin tones ranged from café au lait to coal. The few half-caste women at Ibis had white or olive-toned skin and blue-brown, or even green, eyes. The coming together of races generally produced the most exotic and beautiful fruit, however the core was unpredictable and often sour.

But of all the qualities of the women he met in Addis, the most important was their acquiescence, their availability. For months after his arrival in Addis, well after his discovery of the Ibis and so many other bars like it, Ghosh was celibate. The irony of that period was that the one woman he wanted rejected his advances, while all around him were women who never said no. He was twenty-four and not totally inexperienced when he arrived in Ethiopia. The only intimacy he'd ever had in India was with a young probationer by the name of Virgin Magdalene Kumar. Shortly after their three-month affair ended, she left her order and married a chap he knew (and presumably changed her name to Magdalene Kumar).

"Hema, I am only human," he murmured now as he did every time he thought he was being unfaithful to her.

He reached across and felt the flesh under Konjit's ribs, pinching up a skin fold.

"Ah my dear, should we send for dinner? We need to put flesh on you. And sustenance for what we are about to do tonight. It is, I will confess to you, my very, very first time."

Had she been an older woman (and many one-woman bars were run by older women who had saved money for their own place after working somewhere grand like the Ibis), he would have used a different tone, one that was less direct, more courtly—a gentler form of flattery. But with her, he had settled on the naughty schoolboy approach.

When she reached to feel his hair, rub his scalp, Ghosh purred with contentment. On the radio the muffled twang of a *krar* repeated a six-note riff from a pentatonic scale that seemed common to all Ethiopian music, fast or slow. Ghosh recognized the song, a very popular one. It was called "Tizita"; there was no single equivalent English word. *Tizita* meant "memory tinged with regret." Was there any other kind, Ghosh wondered.

"Your skin is beautiful. What are you? *Banya?*" she asked.

"Yes, my lovely, I am indeed Indian. And since nothing about me other than my skin is beautiful, you are gracious to say so."

"No, no, why do you say that? I swear on the saints I wish I had your hair. I can't get over your Amharic. Are you sure your mother is not *habesha?*"

"You flatter me," he said. He'd learned a little Amharic in the hospital, but it was only through tête-à-têtes like this that he became fluent. He had a theory that bedroom Amharic and bedside Amharic were really the same thing: *Please lie down. Take off your shirt. Open your mouth. Take a deep breath* . . . The language of love was the same as the language of medicine. "Really, I only know the Amharic of love. If you sent me outside to buy a pencil, I wouldn't be able to do it, for I lack those words."

She laughed and again tried to cover her lips. Ghosh held her hands, and so she drew her lower lip up as if to hide her teeth, a gesture he found nubile and touching.

"But why hide your smile? . . . There. How beautiful!"

Much, much later, they retired to the back room; he closed his eyes and pretended, as he always did, that she was Hema. A most willing Hema.

THE MIST WAS inches off the ground when he emerged, and it had brought with it a funereal silence and bone-chilling cold. He took a leak by the roadside. A hyena laughed, whether at his action or his equipment he couldn't be sure. He spun around and saw lupine retinas shining from the trees beyond the first set of houses. He ran while trying to zip up, unlocked his car, and jumped in. He quickly started the engine and moved off. A peeing man had to worry about more than hyenas. *Shiftas, lebas, madjiratmachi,* and all sorts of villains were a threat after midnight, even in the heart of the city and near paved roads. Just the previous month, two men had robbed, raped, and then cut off an Englishwoman's tongue, thinking its absence would prevent her from tattling. Another victim of a robbery had his balls cut off—a common enough practice— in the belief that he would have no courage left to extract revenge. They were the lucky ones. The rest were simply murdered.

THE GATES OF MISSING were wide open when he got back, which was strange. He pulled up to his cottage, slid the car into the open-sided shed. As his lights shone on the rock wall, he slammed the brakes, terrified by what he saw: a ghostly white figure rose from a squat to stand before his headlights, the eyes reflecting back a shimmering red, just like the hyena's eyes. But this was no hyena, but a weeping, bereft Almaz who had clearly been waiting for him.

"Hema, Hema, what have you done," he muttered to himself, convinced that the worst had happened and Hema had returned married. Why else would Almaz stay so late except to tell him this? She and the whole world knew how he felt about Hema. The only person who didn't know was Hema.

The ghostly figure ran over to the passenger side, opened the door, and climbed in. Bowing her head and in the most formal tone and without meeting his eyes, she said, "I am sorry to bring you bad news."

"It's Hema, isn't it?"

"Hema? No. It is Sister Mary Joseph Praise."

"Sister? What happened to Sister?"

"She is with the Lord, may He bless her soul."

"*What?*"

"Lord help us all, but she is dead." Almaz was sobbing now. "She died giving birth to twins. Dr. Hema arrived but could not save her. Dr. Hema saved the twins."

Ghosh stopped hearing after her first mention of Sister and death. He had to have her repeat what she said, and then repeat again everything that she knew, but each time it came down to Sister being dead. And something about twins.

"And now we can't find Dr. Stone," she said at last. "He is gone. We *must* find him. Matron says we must."

"Why?" Ghosh managed to ask when he found his tongue, but even as he said that he knew why. He shared with Stone the bond of being the only male physicians at Missing. Ghosh knew Stone as well as anyone could know Stone, except, perhaps, Sister Mary Joseph Praise.

"Why? Because he is suffering the most," Almaz said. "That is what Matron says. We must find him before he does something stupid."

It's a bit too late for that, Ghosh thought.

CHAPTER 12

Land's End

THE MORNING AFTER the births and the death, Matron Hirst came to her office very early as if it were any other day. She'd slept but a few hours. She and Ghosh had driven around, hunting for Thomas Stone late into the night. Stone's maid, Rosina, had kept a vigil in his quarters, but there had been no sign of him.

Matron pushed away the papers stacked on her desk. Through her window she could see patients lined up in the outpatient department, or rather she could see their colorful umbrellas. People believed the sun exacerbated all illnesses, so there were as many umbrellas as there were patients. She picked up the phone. "Adam?" she said, when the compounder came on the line. "Please send word to Gebrew to close the gate. Send patients to the Russian hospital." Her Amharic, though accented, was exceedingly good. "And Adam, please deal with the patients who are already in the outpatient department as best you can. I'll be asking the nurses to make rounds on their wards and to manage. Let the probationers know that all nursing classes are canceled."

Thank God for Adam, Matron thought. His education had stopped at the third grade, which was a shame, because Adam could have easily been a doctor. Not only was he adept at preparing the fifteen stock mixtures, ointments, and compounds which Missing provided to outpatients, he also had uncanny clinical sense. With his one good eye (the other milky white from a childhood infection) he could spot the seriously ill among the many who came clutching the teal-blue graduated Missing medicine bottles, ready to have them refilled. It was a sad fact that the commonest complaint in the outpatient department was *"Rasehn . . . libehn . . . hodehn,"* literally, "My head . . . my heart . . . and my stomach," with the patient's hand touching each part as she pronounced the words. Ghosh called it the RLH syndrome. The RLH sufferers were often young women or the elderly. If pressed to be more specific, the patients might offer that their heads were spinning (*rasehn yazoregnal*) or burning (*yakatelegnal*), or their hearts were tired (*lib dekam*), or they had abdominal discomfort or cramps (*hod kurteth*), but these symptoms were reported as an aside and grudgingly, because *rasehn-libehn-hodehn* should have been enough for any doctor worth his salt. It had taken Matron her first year in Addis to understand that this was how stress, anxiety, marital strife, and depression were expressed in Ethiopia— somatization was what Ghosh said the experts called this phenomenon. Psychic distress was projected onto a body part, because culturally it was the way to express that kind of suffering. Patients might see no connection between the abusive husband, or meddlesome mother-in-law, or the recent death of their infant, and their dizziness or palpitations. And they all knew just the cure for what ailed them: an injection. They might settle for *mistura carminativa* or else a magnesium trisilicate and belladonna mixture, or some other mixture that came to the doctor's mind, but nothing cured like the *marfey*—the needle. Ghosh was dead against injections of vitamin B for the RLH syndrome, but Matron had convinced him it was better for Missing to do it than have the dissatisfied patient get an unsterilized hypodermic from a quack in the Merkato. The orange B-complex injection was cheap, and its effect was instantaneous, with patients grinning and skipping down the hill.

THE PHONE RANG, and for once Matron was grateful. Normally she hated the sound because it always felt like a rude interruption. The small Missing switchboard was still a novelty. Matron had declined an extension in her quarters, but she thought it was important to have phones in the doctor's quarters and the casualty room. Even this phone in her office she considered a luxury, but now she grabbed the receiver, hoping for good news, news about Stone.

"Please hold for His Excellency, the Minister of the Pen," a female voice said. Matron heard faint clicks, and imagined a little dog walking on the wooden floors of the palace. She stared at the stacks of Bibles against the far wall. There were so many they looked like a barricade of shiny, cobbled rexine.

The minister came on, asked about Matron's health, and then said, "His Majesty is saddened by your loss. Please, accept his deepest condolences." Matron pictured the minister standing, bowing as he spoke into the phone. "His Majesty personally asked me to call."

"It is most kind, most kind, of His Majesty to think of us . . . at this time," Matron said. It was part of the Emperor's mystique and a key to his power that he knew everything that went on in his empire. She wondered how word had reached the palace so soon. Dr. Thomas Stone with Sister Mary Joseph Praise assisting had removed a pair of royal appendices, and Hema had performed an emergency Cesarean section on a granddaughter who didn't make it to Switzerland. Since then a few others in the royal family came to Hema for their confinement.

Matron only had to ask, the minister said, if there was something the palace could do. The minister didn't touch on the manner of Sister's death, or the fate of the two babies.

"By the way, Matron . . . ," he said, and she was alert because she sensed this was the real reason for the call. "If by any chance a military . . . a senior officer comes to Missing for treatment, for surgery in the next day or so, the Emperor would like to be informed. You can call me personally." He gave her a number.

"What sort of officer?"

She took the silence to mean the minister was giving thought to his answer.

"An Imperial Bodyguard officer. An officer who has—shall we say— no need to be at Missing."

"Surgery, you say? Oh, no. We've closed the hospital. We have no surgeon, Minister. You see Dr. Thomas Stone . . . is indisposed. They were a team, you see . . ."

"Thank you, Matron. Please let us know."

She mulled over the call after she hung up. Emperor Haile Selassie had built up a strong, modern military, consisting of army, navy, air force, and the Imperial Bodyguard. The Bodyguard was a force as large as the others, the equivalent of the Queen's Guard in England who stood outside Buckingham Palace. But just like the Queen's Guard, the Imperial Bodyguard wasn't merely a ceremonial unit; its professional soldiers and its units were no different than the rest of the armed forces, and trained for battle. Up-and-coming cadets from all the services went to Sandhurst or West Point or Poona. But those sojourns had a way of expanding one's social conscience. The Emperor feared a coup by these young officers. Having the second- or third-largest standing armed force on the continent was a matter of pride, but it was also potentially dangerous to his reign. The Emperor deliberately kept the four services in competition with one another, kept their headquarters far apart, and he transferred generals who were getting too powerful. Matron sensed some such intrigue—why else would the Minister of the Pen call personally?

The minister had no idea what it meant for Missing not to have a surgeon, Matron thought. Before Thomas Stone's arrival, Missing could handle most internal medicine and pediatric patients, thanks to Ghosh, and it tackled complicated obstetric and gynecologic conditions, thanks to Hema. Over the years a number of other doctors had come and gone, some of them capable of surgery. But Missing never had a fully trained and competent surgeon till Stone. A surgeon allowed Missing to fix complex fractures, remove goiters and other tumors, perform skin grafts for burns, repair strangulated hernias, take out enlarged prostates or cancerous breasts, or drill a hole in the skull to let out a blood clot pressing against the brain. Stone's presence (with an assistant like Sister Mary Joseph Praise) took Missing to a new level. His absence changed everything.

THE PHONE RANG again a few minutes later, and this time the sound was ominous. Matron brought the instrument gingerly to her ear. *Please God, let Stone be alive.*

"Hello? This is Eli Harris. Of the Baptist congregation of Houston . . . Hello?"

For a call from America, the connection was crystal clear. Matron was so surprised that she said nothing.

"Hello?" the voice said again.

"Yes?" Matron said gruffly.

"I'm speaking from the Ghion Hotel in Addis Ababa. Could I speak to Matron Hirst?"

She held the receiver away, covering the mouthpiece. She felt panicked. And confused. What on earth was Harris doing here? She was accustomed to dealing with donors and charitable organizations by mail. She needed to think quickly, but her mind refused to cooperate. At last, she took her hand away and brought the phone up. "I'll pass the message on, Mr. Harris. She will call you back—"

"May I know who is speaking—"

"You see, we have had a death of one of our staff. It might be a couple of days before she calls you." He started to say something, but Matron hung up abruptly. Then she took the receiver off the hook, glaring at it, daring it to ring.

The Baptists of Houston were of late Missing's best and most consistent funders. Matron sent out handwritten letters every week to congregations in America and Europe. She asked that her letter be forwarded to others if they were unable to help. If a reply came expressing any interest, she immediately mailed them Thomas Stone's textbook, *The Expedient Operator: A Short Practice of Tropical Medicine*. Though expensive to mail, it was better than any prospectus. Donors, she found, always had a prurient interest in what could go wrong with the human body, and the photographs and illustrations (by Sister Mary Joseph Praise) in the book satisfied that desire. A picture of a strange creature with the face of a pig, the furriness of a dog, and with small, myopic eyes accompanied the chapter on appendicitis, and Matron always put her letter there as a bookmark. The legend read "The wombat is a burrowing, nocturnal marsupial found only in Australia, and the only reason to mention it is the dubious distinction it has in joining man and apes in ownership of an appendix." The book, more than any exchange of letters, had won the Houston Baptists' support.

Ghosh arrived half an hour later, shaking his head. "I went to the British Embassy. I drove around the city. I went to his house again. Rosina's there and she hasn't seen him. I walked all over Missing's grounds—"

"Let's take a ride," Matron said.

As they drove down to Missing's gate, they saw a taxi coming up the hill carrying a white man. "That must be Eli Harris," Matron said, sliding down in the passenger seat with an alacrity that surprised Ghosh. She told him about Harris's call. "If I remember correctly, I got Harris to fund a project that was your idea: a citywide campaign against gonorrhea and syphilis. Harris has come to see how we are doing."

Ghosh almost steered them off the road. "But we have no such project, Matron!"

"Of course not." Matron sighed.

Ghosh never looked his best in the morning, even after a bath and shave. He hadn't had time for either of these. Dark stubble swept up from his throat, detoured around his lips, and reached almost to his bloodshot eyes.

"Where are we going?" he said.

"To Gulele. We need to make funeral arrangements."

They rode in silence.

THE GULELE CEMETERY was on the outskirts of town. The road cut through a forest where the dense overhanging canopy of trees made it feel like dusk. Suddenly the forbidding wrought-iron gates loomed before them, standing out against the limestone walls. Inside, a gravel road led up to a plateau thick with eucalyptus and pine. There were no taller trees in Addis than in Gulele.

They trudged between the graves, their feet crunching and crackling on the carpet of leaves and twigs. No urban sounds or voices were to be heard here; only the stillness of a forest and the quiet of death. A fine drizzle wet the leaves and branches, then gathered into big drops that plopped on their heads and arms. Matron felt like a trespasser. She stopped at a grave no larger than an altar Bible. "An infant, Ghosh," she said, wanting to hear a living voice, even if it was only hers. "Armenian, judging by the name. Lord, she died just last year." The flowers by the headstone were fresh. Matron began a Hail Mary under her breath.

Farther down were the graves of young Italian soldiers: NATO À ROMA, or NATO À NAPOLI, but no matter where they were born they were DECEDUTO AD ADDIS ABABA. Matron's vision turned misty as she thought of them having died so very far from home.

John Melly's face appeared to her, and she could hear "Bunyan's Hymn." It was the hymn they had played at his funeral. At times the tune found her; the words came to her lips unbidden.

She turned to Ghosh, "You know I was in love once?"

Ghosh who already looked troubled, froze where he stood.

"You mean . . . with a man?" he said at last, when he could speak.

"Of course with a man!" She sniffed.

Ghosh was silent for a long time, then he said, "We imagine we know everything there is to know about our colleagues, but really how little we know."

"I don't think *I* knew I loved Melly until he was dying. I was so young. Easiest thing in the world is to love a dying man."

"Did he love you?"

"He must have. You see he died trying to save me." Her eyes welled up. "It was in 1935. I'd just arrived in the country, and I couldn't have picked a worse time. The Emperor fled the city as the Italians were about to march in. The looters went to town, pillaging, raping. John Melly commandeered a truck from the British Legation to come and get me. You see, I was volunteering at what is now Missing. He stopped to help a wounded person on the street, and a looter shot him. For absolutely no reason." She shuddered. "I nursed him for ten days, and then he died. One day I'll tell you all about it." Then, uncontrollably, she had to sit down, her head in her hands, weeping. "I'm all right, Ghosh. Just give me a minute."

She was mourning not Melly as much as the passage of the years. She'd come to Addis Ababa from England after getting restless teaching in a convent school and running the student infirmary; she'd accepted a post with Sudan Interior Mission to work in Harrar, Ethiopia. In Addis, she found her orders were canceled because the Italians had attacked, and so she had simply attached herself to a small hospital all but abandoned by the American Protestants. During that first year she'd watched as soldiers—some of the young men buried here—as well as Italian civilians poured in to populate the new colony: carpenters, masons, technicians. The peasant Florino became Don Florino when he crossed the Suez. The ambulance driver reinvented himself as a physician. She had carried on, just as the Indian shopkeepers, the Armenian merchants, the Greek hoteliers, the Levantine traders had carried on during the occupation. Matron was still there in 1941, when the Axis's fortunes turned in North Africa and in Europe. From the Hotel Bella Napoli's balcony, Matron watched Wingate and his British troops parade into town, escorting Emperor Haile Selassie, who was returning after six years of exile. Matron had never set eyes on the diminutive Emperor. The little man seemed astonished by the transformation of his capital, his head swiveling this way and that to take in the cinemas, hotels, shops, neon lights, multistory apartment buildings, paved avenues lined with trees . . . Matron said to the Reuters correspondent standing beside her that perhaps the Emperor wished he'd stayed in exile a little longer. To her chagrin, she was quoted verbatim (but fortunately as an "anonymous observer") in every foreign paper. She smiled at that memory.

She rose, brushed away her tears. The two of them trudged on.

They walked down the path between one row of graves, then back up another.

"No," Matron said abruptly. "This'll never do. I can't imagine leaving our cherished daughter in this place."

Only when they broke out into the sunlight did Matron feel she could breathe.

"Ghosh, if you bury me in Gulele, I'll never forgive you," she said. Ghosh decided silence was the best strategy. "We Christians believe that in the Lord's Second Coming the dead will be raised from the grave."

Ghosh was raised a Christian, a fact that Matron never seemed to remember.

"Matron, do you sometimes doubt?"

She noticed that his voice was hoarse. His eyelids sagged. She was reminded again that this was not her grief alone.

"Doubt is a first cousin to faith, Ghosh. To have faith, you have to suspend your disbelief. Our beloved Sister believed . . . I worry that in a place as damp and disconsolate as Gulele, even Sister will find it hard to rise when the time comes."

"What then? Cremation?"

One of the Indian barbers doubled as a *pujari* and arranged cremations for Hindus who died in Addis Ababa.

"Of course not!" She wondered if Ghosh was being willfully dense. "*Burial.* I think I might know just the place," Matron said.

THEY PARKED AT Ghosh's bungalow and walked to the rear of Missing, where the bottlebrush was so laden with flowers that it looked as if it had caught fire. The property edge was marked by the acacias, their flat tops forming a jagged line against the sky. Missing's far west corner was a promontory looking over a vast valley. That acreage as far as the eye could see belonged to a *ras*—a duke—who was a relative of His Majesty, Haile Selassie.

A brook, hidden by boulders, burbled; sheep grazed under the eye of a boy who sat polishing his teeth with a twig, his staff near by. He squinted at Matron and Ghosh and then waved. Just as in the days of David, he carried a slingshot. It was a goatherd like him, centuries before, who had noticed how frisky his animals became after chewing a particular red berry. From that serendipitous discovery, the coffee habit and trade spread to Yemen, Amsterdam, the Caribbean, South America, and the world, but it had all begun in Ethiopia, in a field like this.

An unused bore well occupied this corner of Missing. Five years before, one of the Missing dogs had fallen into the well. Koochooloo's desperate yelps brought Gebrew. He fished her out by dangling a noose around her, almost lynching her in the process. The well needed to be sealed over. In supervising that task, Matron found used prophylactics and cigarette butts around the rock wall; she'd decided the area was in need of redemption. Coolies cleared the brush and planted native grass seedlings. In two months a beautiful green carpet surrounded the well.

Gebrew tended to this lawn, squatting, crab walking, grabbing a fistful of grass with his left hand and sweeping under it with the sickle in his right hand.

It was Sister Mary Joseph Praise who identified the wild coffee bush by the well. But for Gebrew's regularly nipping the top buds, it would have grown out of reach. With a few old outpatient benches brought to this lawn it became a place where even Thomas Stone temporarily abandoned his cares. Cigarette in hand, mind adrift, he'd smoke and watch while Sister Mary Joseph Praise and Matron fussed with their plants. But before too long he would grind his cigarette into the grass (a practice which Matron thought vulgar) and march off as if to some urgent summons.

Matron prayed silently. *Dear God, only You know what will become of Missing now. Two of ours are gone. A child is a miracle, and we have two of those. But for Mr. Harris and his people, it won't be that.* For them it would be shameful, scandalous, a reason to pull out. Missing had no income to speak of from patients. It relied on donations. Its modest expansion of the last few years came because of Harris and a few other donors. Matron had no rainy-day fund. It was against her conscience to hold back money when money allowed her to cure trachoma and to prevent blindness, or give penicillin and cure syphilis—the list was endless. What was she to do?

Matron studied the view in every direction. She wasn't registering what she saw because her thoughts were turned inward. But gradually, the valley, the scent of laurel, the vivid green colors, the gentle breeze, the way light fell on the far slope, the gash left by the stream, and above all this the sweep of sky with clouds pushed to one side—it had its effect on her. For the first time since Sister Mary Joseph Praise's death, Matron felt a sense of peace, a sense of certainty where there had been none. She was certain that this was the spot—this was where the long voyage of Sister Mary Joseph Praise would end. She remembered, too, how in her first days in Addis, when things had looked so bleak, so terrifying, so tragic with Melly's death—it was at those moments that God's grace came, and that God's plan was revealed, though it was revealed in His time. "I can't see it Lord, but I know You can," she said.

CHAPTER 13

Praise in the Arms of Jesus

T HE BAREFOOT COOLIES were jovial men. Told by Ghosh what their task would be, they made clucking sounds of condolence. The big fellow with the prognathic jaw shed his fraying coat; his shorter companion pulled off his tattered sweater. They spat on their palms, hefted the pickaxes, and set to it; *happened-had-happened* and *be-will-be* as far as they were concerned, and though it was a grave they were digging, it guaranteed the night's bottle of *tej* or *talla* and perhaps a bed and a willing woman. Sweat oiled their shoulders and foreheads and dampened their patchwork shirts.

The sky had started off bluffing, convoys of gray clouds scurrying across like sheep to market. But by afternoon a perfect blue canopy stretched from horizon to horizon.

GHOSH, SUMMONED to the casualty room by Matron, spotted a lean and very pale white man waiting by a pillar. Ghosh kept his head down, certain this was Eli Harris, and thankful that the man's back was to him.

Inside, Adam pointed to a curtain. Ghosh heard regular grunting, coming with each breath and in the rhythm of a locomotive. He found four Ethiopian men standing there, three in sports coats and one in a burly jacket. They were gathered around the stretcher, as if in prayer. All four had spit-shined brown shoes. As they squeezed out to make room for Ghosh, he glimpsed a burgundy holster under a coat.

"Doctor," the man lying on the table said, offering his hand and trying to rise, but wincing with the effort. "Mebratu is my name. Thank you for seeing me." He was in his thirties, his English excellent. A thin mustache arched over a strong mouth. Pain had given him a peaked expression, but it was nevertheless an extraordinary, handsome face, the broken nose adding to its character. He looked familiar, but Ghosh couldn't place him. Unlike his companions, he seemed stoic, not fearful, even though he was the one in pain.

"I tell you, I have never hurt like this." He grinned from ear to ear as if to say, A man is going along when out of the blue comes a banana peel, a cosmic joke that leaves you upended and clutching your belly. A wave of pain made him wince.

I can't possibly see you today. Beloved Sister has died and any minute I expect someone to tell me they have found Dr. Thomas Stone's body. For God's sake go to the military hospital. That was what Ghosh wanted to say, but in the face of such suffering he waited.

Ghosh took the proffered hand and while supporting it he felt for the radial artery. The pulse was bounding at one hundred and twelve per minute. Ghosh's equivalent of perfect pitch was to be able to tell the heart rate without a watch.

"When did this start?" he heard himself say, taking in the swollen abdomen that was so incongruent on this lean, muscled man. "Begin at the beginning . . ."

"Yesterday morning. I was trying to . . . move my bowels." The patient looked embarrassed. "And suddenly I had pain here." He pointed to his lower abdomen.

"While you were still sitting on the toilet?"

"Squatting, yes. Within seconds I could feel swelling . . . and tightening. It came on like a bolt of lightning."

The assonance caught Ghosh's ear. In his mind's eye he could see Sir Zachary Cope's little book, *The Diagnosis of the Acute Abdomen in Rhyme.* He'd found that treasure on the dusty shelf of a secondhand bookstore in Madras. The book was a revelation. Who knew that a medical text could be full of cartoon illustrations, be so playful, and yet provide serious instruction? Cope's lines regarding sudden blockage of the normal passage through the intestine came to him:

> . . . *rapid onset of distention*
> *Will certainly attract your keen attention.*

He asked the next question, even though he knew the answer. There were times like this when the diagnosis was written on the patient's forehead. Or else they gave it away in their first sentence. Or it was announced by an odor before one even saw the patient.

"Yesterday morning," Mebratu replied. "Just before the pain began. Since then no stool, no gas, no nothing."

Sometimes a bowel-coil gets out of place
By twisting round upon a narrow base . . .

"And how many enemas did you try?"

Mebratu let out a short sharp laugh. "You knew, huh? Two. But they did nothing."

He wasn't just constipated but obstipated—not even gas could pass. The bowel was completely obstructed.

Outside the cubicle the men seemed to be arguing.

Mebratu's tongue was dry, brown, and furred. He was dehydrated, but not anemic. Ghosh exposed the grotesquely distended abdomen. The belly didn't push out when Mebratu took a breath. In fact it moved hardly at all. This is my work, Ghosh thought to himself as he pulled out his stethoscope. This is my grave-digging equivalent. Day in and day out. Bellies, chests, flesh.

In place of the normal gurgling bowel sounds, what he heard with his stethoscope was a cascade of high-pitched notes, like water dripping onto a zinc plate. In the background he heard the steady drum of the heartbeat. Astonishing how well fluid-filled loops of bowel transmitted heart sounds. It was an observation he'd never seen in a textbook.

"You have a volvulus," Ghosh said, pulling his stethoscope off his ears. His voice came from a distance, and it didn't sound like it belonged to him. "A loop of the large bowel, the colon, twists on itself like this—" He used the tubing of his stethoscope to demonstrate first the formation of a loop, then the twist forming at the base. "It's common here. Ethiopians have long and mobile colons. That and something about the diet predisposes to volvulus, we think."

Mebratu tried to reconcile his symptoms with Ghosh's explanation. His mouth turned up; he was laughing.

"You knew what I had as soon as I told you, right, Doctor? Before you did all these . . . other things."

"I suppose I did."

"So . . . will this twist untwist by itself?"

"No. It has to be untwisted. Surgically."

"It's common, you say. My countrymen who get this . . . what happens to them?"

At that moment, Ghosh connected the face with a scene he wished he could forget.

"Without surgery? They die. You see, the blood supply at the base of the loop of bowel is also twisted off. It's doubly dangerous. There's no blood going in or out. The bowel will turn gangrenous."

"Look, Doctor. This is a terrible time for this to happen."

"Yes, it *is* a terrible time," Ghosh burst out, startling Mebratu. "Why here, if I may ask? Why Missing? Why not the military hospital?"

"What else have you understood about me?"

"I know you're an officer."

"Those clowns," he said, nodding his chin in the direction of his friends outside. "We don't do a good job of dressing as civilians," Mebratu said, wryly. "If their shoes aren't spit polished they feel naked."

"It's more than that, actually. Years ago, shortly after I arrived here, I saw you conduct an execution. I'll never forget that."

"Eight years and two months ago. July the fifth. I remember it, too. You were there?"

"Not intentionally." A simple drive into the city had turned into something else when a large crowd on the road had forced him and Hema into being spectators.

"Please understand, it was the most painful order I ever carried out," Mebratu said. "Those were my friends."

"I sensed that," Ghosh said, recalling the strange dignity of both the executioner and the condemned.

Another wave of pain traveled over Mebratu's face and they both waited till it passed. "*This* is a different kind of pain," he said, trying to smile.

"You should know," Ghosh said, "that earlier today the palace called. They asked Matron to inform them if a military person came here for treatment."

"*What?*" Mebratu swore and tried to sit up, but the movement made him yell in pain. His companions rushed in. "Did Matron tell the palace?" he managed to ask.

"No. Matron told me she wouldn't turn you away knowing that you had nowhere else to go."

The patient relaxed now. His friends had a quick discussion, and then they remained in the room.

"Thank you. Thank Matron for me. I am Colonel Mebratu, of the Imperial Bodyguard. You see we had plans, a few of us, to meet on this date in Addis. I came from Gondar. When I got here I found the meeting had to be called off. We feared we were . . . compromised. But I didn't get the message till I was already here. Before I left Gondar, yesterday, my pain began. I saw a physician there. Like you, he must have known what I had, but he told me nothing. He told me to come back and see him in the morning and that he wanted to check me again. He must have told the palace, or else why would they call the hospitals in Addis? Hanging will also be my fate if I am discovered in Addis. You must treat me. I can't be seen at the military hospital today."

"There is another problem," Ghosh said. "Our surgeon has . . . he has left."

"We heard about your . . . loss. I am sorry. If Dr. Stone can't do it, then you have to."

"But I can't—"

"Doctor, I have no other options. If you don't do it, I die."

One of the men stepped forward. With his light beard, he looked more like an academic than a military man. "What if your life depended on it? Could you do it?"

Colonel Mebratu put his hand on Ghosh's sleeve. "Forgive my brother," he said, then smiled at Ghosh as if to say, *You see what I have to do to keep peace?* Out loud he said: "If something should happen, you can say in good faith that you knew nothing about me, Dr. Ghosh. It's true. All you know about me are all the things you guessed."

GHOSH DIALED Hema's quarters. It occurred to him that Colonel Mebratu and his men must have been plotting some kind of a coup. What else could the secret meeting in Addis have been about? Ghosh was faced with a conundrum: How did one treat a soldier, an executioner, who now was engaged in treason against the Emperor? But of course, as a physician, his obligation was to the patient. He felt no dislike for the Colonel, though he could do without the brother. It was difficult to dislike a man who bravely suffered physical pain and managed to retain his manners.

Over the hum of the receiver, Ghosh could hear the blood rushing into his ear with every heartbeat.

Hema's brusque "Hello" told him she was scowling. "It's me," he said. "Do you know who I have here tonight?" He told her the story. She interrupted before he could finish: "Why are you telling me this?"

"Hema, did you hear what I just said? We have to operate. It's our duty."

She wasn't impressed.

He added, "They're desperate. They have nowhere else to go. They have guns."

"If they are so desperate, they can open the belly themselves. I am an obstetrician-gynecologist. Tell them I just had twins and I'm in no condition to operate."

"Hema!" He was so mad that words would not come out. At least in the business of patient care, she was supposed to be on his side.

"Are you minimizing what I have on my hands?" she said. "What I've gone through just yesterday? You weren't there, Ghosh. So now these children's every breath is my responsibility."

"Hema, I'm not saying . . ."

"*You* operate, man. You've assisted him with volvulus, haven't you? I've never operated on volvulus." By "him" she meant Stone.

The silence was punctuated only by the sound of her breathing. Does she not care if I get shot? Why take this attitude with me? As if I'm the enemy. As if I caused the disaster she walked into when she returned. Did I invite the Colonel here?

"What if I have to resect and anastomose large bowel, Hema? Or do a colostomy? . . ."

"I'm postpartum. Indisposed. Out of station. Not here today!"

"Hema, we have an obligation, to the patient . . . the Hippocratic oath—"

She laughed, a bitter, cutting sound. "The Hippocratic oath is if you are sitting in London and drinking tea. No such oaths here in the jungle. I know my obligations. The patient is lucky to have you, that's all I can say. It's better than nothing." She hung up.

GHOSH WAS an internal medicine specialist through and through. Heart failure, pneumonia, bizarre neurological illness, strange fevers, rashes, unexplained symptoms—those were his métier. He could diagnose common surgical conditions, but he wasn't trained to fix them in the operating theater.

In Missing's better days, whenever Ghosh popped his head into the theater, Stone would have him scrub and assist. It allowed Sister Mary Joseph Praise to relax, and for Ghosh, being the first assistant to Stone was a fun change from his routine. Ghosh's presence transformed the cathedral hush of Theater 3 to a carnival racket, and somehow Stone didn't seem to mind. Ghosh asked questions left and right, cajoling Stone into talking, instructing, even reminiscing. At night, Ghosh sometimes assisted Hema when she did an emergency C-section. Rarely, Hema sent for him when she performed an extensive resection for an ovarian or uterine cancer.

But now he found himself alone, standing in Stone's place, on the patient's right, scalpel in hand. It was a spot he hadn't occupied for many years. The last time he stood on the right was during his internship when, as a reward for good service, they let him operate on a hydrocele while the staff surgeon stood across and took him through each step.

On his instruction the circulating nurse passed a rectal tube into the anus, guiding it up as high as it would go.

"We better start," he said to the probationer who was scrubbed, gowned, and gloved on the other side of the table, ready to assist him. Her faint pockmarks were hidden by cap and gown. Even though her lids were puffy, she had beautiful eyes. "We can't finish if we don't start so we better start if we're to finish, yes?"

> *A very large incision should be made*
> *—of small ones in such cases be afraid—*
> *The coil brought out, untwisted by a turn*
> *—a clockwise turn as you will quite soon learn—*
> *And then a rectal tube is upward passed—*
> *Thereon there issues forth a gaseous blast . . .*

With the colon swollen to *Hindenburg* proportions it would be all too easy to nick the bowel and spill feces into the abdominal cavity. He made a midline incision, then deepened it carefully, like a sapper defusing a bomb. Just when panic was setting in because he felt he was going nowhere, the glistening surface of the peritoneum—that delicate membrane that lined the abdominal cavity—came into view. When he opened the peritoneum, straw-colored fluid came out. Inserting his finger into the hole and using it as a backstop, he cut the peritoneum along the length of the incision.

At once, the colon bullied its way out like a zeppelin escaping its hangar. He covered the sides of the wound with wet packs, inserted a large Balfour retractor to hold the edges open, and delivered the twisted loop completely out of the wound onto the packs. It was as wide across as the inner tube of a car tire, boggy, dark, and tense with fluid, quite unlike the flaccid pink coils of the rest of the bowel. He could see the spot where the twist had occurred, deep in the belly. Gently manipulating the two limbs of the loop, he untwisted, clockwise, just as Cope said. He heard a gurgle and at once the blue color began to wash out of the ballooned segment. It pinked up at the edges.

He felt through the bowel wall for the rectal tube that Nurse Asqual had inserted. He fed it up like a curtain rod in a loop. When the tube reached the distended bowel, they were rewarded with a loud sigh and the rattle of fluid and gas hitting the bucket below. "And down the coil contracts and you will see, the parts arranged more as they ought to be," Ghosh said, and the probationer, who had no idea what he was talking about, said, "Yes, Dr. Ghosh."

Ghosh flexed his gloved fingers. They looked competent and powerful—a surgeon's hands. You can't feel this way, he thought, unless you have the ultimate responsibility.

After he closed, as he was stripping off his gloves, he saw Hema's face in the glass of the swinging doors. It disappeared. He charged after her. She ran, but he soon caught up with her in the walkway. She stood panting against the pillar. "So?" she said when she could speak. "It went well?"

They were both grinning. "Yes . . . I just untwisted the loop." He couldn't hide the pride and excitement in his voice.

"It could twist again."

"Well, his choice was either me or nothing, since the other doctor here would not help."

"True. Good for you. I've got to go. Almaz and Rosina are watching the babies."

"Hema?"

"What?"

"You would have helped if I got into trouble?"

"No, I was just stretching my legs . . ." Despite herself, a twinkle showed in her eyes. "Silly. What did you think?"

With Hema, even sarcasm felt like a gift. He fought the instinct to jump forward, the eager puppy, too ready to forget the cuffing it had received minutes before.

"Just yesterday," Hema said, "I drove past the spot where we saw that first hanging, and I thought about it . . ." She seemed to study him meditatively. "Have you eaten anything today?"

That was when he noticed: His beloved, his Madras-returned, unmarried beauty, was more *magnified* than ever. There were succulent rolls visible between sari and blouse. The skin under her chin was gently swollen like a second mons.

"I've not eaten since you left for India," he said, which was almost true.

"You've lost weight. It doesn't look good. Come by and eat. There's food, tons of it. Everybody keeps bringing food."

She walked off. He studied the way the flesh on her buttocks swung this way, and that, about to sail off her hips. She'd brought back from India more of herself to love. It was the worst time for this, but he was aroused.

He dressed and found himself thinking about the operation again. Should I have tacked the sigmoid colon to the abdominal wall to prevent it twisting again? Didn't I see Stone do this? Colopexy, I think he called it. Had Stone spoken to me about the danger of a colopexy and warned against it, or had he recommended it? I hope we took out all the sponges. Should have counted once more. I should've taken one more look. Checked for bleeders while I was at it. He recalled Stone saying, *When the abdomen is open you control it. But once you close it, it controls you.* "I understand just what you mean, Thomas," Ghosh said, as he walked out of the theater.

IT WAS LATE EVENING before the hospital staff gathered by the gaping cavity in the earth, now shored up with timber. There was no time to waste, because by Ethiopian tradition, no one eats till the body is interred. That meant the nurses and probationers were starving. The casket arrived on the shoulders of orderlies treading the same path down which Sister Mary Joseph Praise would come to sit in this grove. Hema trailed behind the pallbearers, walking with Stone's maid, Rosina, and with Ghosh's maid, Almaz, the three of them taking turns carrying the two infants who where bundled up in blankets.

They laid the casket down by the edge of the grave, and removed the lid. There were sobs and strangled cries as those who had yet to see the body pressed closer.

The nurses had dressed Sister Mary Joseph Praise in the clothes the young nun first donned when she pledged body and soul to Christ—her "bridal" dress. The arching, hooded veil was to show that her mind was not on earthly things but on the kingdom of heaven; it was the symbol of her being dead to the world, but in the gathering mist it was no longer a symbol. The starched guimpe around her neck hung down like a bib. Her habit was white, interrupted by a plaited white cord. Sister Mary Joseph Praise's hands emerged from the sleeves and met in the middle, the fingers resting on her Bible and a rosary. Discalced Carmelites originally shunned footwear—hence the term "discalced." Sister Mary Joseph Praise's order had been practical enough to wear sandals. Matron had left her feet bare.

Matron chose not to call Father de la Rosa of St. Joseph's Catholic Church, because he was a man who had a disapproving manner even when there was nothing to disapprove, and there was plenty here. She almost called Andy McGuire from the Anglican church; he would have been a comfort and most willing. But in the end Matron felt that Sister Mary Joseph Praise would have wanted no one but her Missing family to see her off. The same instinct led Matron to ask Gebrew earlier that day to prepare to say a short prayer. Sister was always respectful of Gebrew, even though his being a priest was incidental to his duties as watchman and gardener; she would have appreciated how much it honored and consoled Gebrew to be called on in this fashion.

In the cool and very still air, Matron held up her hand. "Sister Mary Joseph Praise would have said, 'Don't grieve for me. Christ is my salvation.' That must be our consolation as well." Matron lost her train of thought. What else was there? She nodded at Gebrew who was immaculately dressed in a white tunic extending to his knees, trousers underneath, and tightly coiled turban on his head. These were the ceremonial clothes he wore only on Timkat, the day of the Epiphany. Gebrew's liturgy was in ancient Biblical Geez, the official language of the Ethiopian Orthodox Church. With great effort, he kept his singsong recitation short. Then the nurses and probationers sang Sister Mary Joseph Praise's favorite hymn, one she had taught them and which they favored in morning chapel in the nurses' hostel.

> Jesus lives! Thy terrors now
> Can no longer, death, appall us;
> Jesus lives! By this we know
> Thou, O grave, canst not enthrall us.
> Alleluia!

They all pushed forward, straining for a last look before the lid was nailed in place. Gebrew would say later that Sister Mary Joseph Praise's face glowed, her expression was peaceful, knowing her ordeal on earth was over. Almaz insisted that a lilac scent emerged as the lid went down.

Ghosh felt a message being conveyed to him. Sister seemed to be saying, *Make good use of your time. Don't waste more years pursuing love that might never be reciprocated. Leave this land for my sake.*

Hema, standing close, vowed silently to Sister Mary Joseph Praise that she'd look after us as if we were her own.

With ropes under the casket, the coolies lowered Sister into her grave. The heavy stones required by Ethiopian tradition were handed down to the taller coolie whose feet were perched on either side of the coffin. The stones were to keep hyenas out.

At last the two men pushed the earth back to fill in the grave, the service all but over. All but the ululations.

Shiva and I, so new to life, were startled by that unearthly sound. We opened our eyes to contemplate a world in which so much was already amiss.

CHAPTER 14

Knowledge of
the Redeemer

THE DAY AFTER THE FUNERAL, Ghosh rose early. For a change his waking thoughts were not about Hema but about Stone. As soon as he was dressed, he went straight to Stone's quarters, but he found no sign that the occupant had returned. Deflated, he went to Matron's office. She looked up expectantly. He shook his head.

He was eager to see his postoperative patient and check his handiwork. He'd been a reluctant surgeon, but now the anticipation he felt was a revelation to him. It must have been a feeling Stone had regularly enjoyed. "This could be addictive," he said to no one in particular.

He found Colonel Mebratu sitting on the edge of the bed, his brother helping him dress. "Dr. Ghosh!" Mebratu said, smiling like a man without a care in the world, though he was clearly in pain. "My status report: I passed gas last night, stool today. Tomorrow I will pass gold!" He was a man used to charming others, and even in his weakened state, his charisma was undiminished. For someone fewer than twenty-four hours out of surgery, he looked great. Ghosh examined the wound, and it was clean and intact.

"Doctor," the Colonel said, "I must return to my regiment in Gondar today. I can't be gone for much longer. I know it's too soon, but I don't have a choice. If I don't show my face I will be under even deeper suspicion. You don't want to save my life only for me to be hanged. I can arrange for intravenous fluids at home, whatever you say."

Ghosh had opened his mouth to protest, but he realized he could not insist.

"All right. But listen, there is a real hazard of the wound bursting if you strain. I'll give you morphine. You must travel lying flat. We'll arrange intravenous fluids, and tomorrow you can sip water and then clear liquids the next. I will write it all down. You will need the stitches removed in about ten days." The Colonel nodded.

The bearded brother clasped Ghosh's hand and bowed low, muttering his thanks.

"Will you travel with him?" Ghosh said.

"Yes, of course. We have a van coming. Once he is settled, I'll go to my new posting in Siberia." Ghosh looked puzzled. "I am being banished."

"Are you also in the military?" Ghosh said.

"No, as of this moment, I am nothing, Doctor. I am nobody."

Colonel Mebratu put his hand on his brother's shoulder. "My brother is modest. Do you know he has a master's degree in sociology from Columbia? Yes, he was sent to America by His Imperial Majesty. The Old Man wasn't happy when my brother was attracted by the Marcus Garvey Movement. He didn't let him pursue a Ph.D. He summoned him back to be a provincial administrator. He should have let him finish."

"No, no, I came willingly," the brother said. "I wanted to help my people. But for that I am off to Siberia." Ghosh waited, expecting more.

"Tell him why," the Colonel said. "It's a health matter, after all."

The brother sighed. "The Health Ministry built a public health clinic in our former province. His Imperial Majesty came to cut the ribbon. Half my budget for the district was consumed to make everything look good along His Majesty's route. Paint, fences, even a bulldozer to tear down huts. As soon as he left, the clinic closed."

"Why?"

"The budget for the clinic was spent!"

"Did you not protest?"

"Of course! But no replies to my messages. The Health Minister intercepted them. So, I reopened the health center myself. It took about ten thousand birr. I got a missionary doctor in a town fifty miles away to come once a week. I had a retired army nurse doing dressings, and I found a midwife to move there. I got supplies. The local bootlegger gave me a generator. The people loved me. The Health Minister wanted to kill me. The Emperor summoned me to Addis."

"How did you get the money?" Ghosh asked.

"Bribes! People would bring over a big *injera* basket, with more money in it than *injera*. When I used the bribes for a good purpose, they gave me more bribes because they were worried that I would expose them."

"You told this to His Majesty?"

"Ah! But that is complicated. Everyone is whispering in his ear. 'Your Majesty,' I said, when I got my audience. 'The health center needs a budget to keep going.' He acted surprised."

"He knew," the Colonel interjected.

"He heard me out. Those eyes give away nothing. When I was done, His Majesty whispers to Abba Hanna, the Minister of the Purse. Abba Hanna scribbles in the record. And the other ministers, have you seen them? They are in a state of constant terror. They never know if they are in their master's favor or not.

"His Majesty thanks me for my service to that province, et cetera, et cetera, and then I bow and bow and walk backward. I meet the Minister of the Purse at the rear of the room, and he gives me three hundred birr! I need thirty thousand, or even three hundred thousand, I could use. For all I know the Emperor said one hundred thousand and Abba Hanna decided it was worth only three hundred. Or was three hundred the Emperor's idea? And who do you ask? By then, the next petitioner is telling his story, and the Minister of the Purse is running back to take his position near the Emperor.

"I tried to shout from the back of the room, 'Your Majesty, did the minister make a mistake?' My friends dragged me away—"

"Otherwise you wouldn't be around to tell us this story," the Colonel said. "My foolhardy brother."

The Colonel turned serious, his eyes on Ghosh as he took Ghosh's hand in both of his. "Dr. Ghosh. You're a better surgeon than Stone. A surgeon in hand is worth two who are gone."

"No, I was lucky. Stone is the best."

"I thank you for something else. You see, I was in terrible pain all the way from Gondar to here. The journey going back is going to be easy by comparison. The pain was . . . I knew whatever this was would get worse, would kill me. But I had options. I came to you. When you told me that for my fellow countrymen, if they have to suffer this, they simply die . . ." The Colonel's face turned hard, and Ghosh could not be sure if it was anger or if he was holding back tears. He cleared his throat. "It was a crime to close my brother's health center. When I came to Addis Ababa for this meeting with my . . . colleagues, I was prepared to listen. But I wasn't sure. You could say my motives were suspect. If I wanted to be part of a change, was it for the best of reasons, or just to grab power? I'm telling you things you can never repeat, Doctor, do you understand?"

Ghosh nodded.

"My journey, my pain, my operation . . . ," the Colonel went on, "God was showing me the suffering of my people. It was a message. How we treat the least of our brethren, how we treat the peasant suffering with volvulus, *that's* the measure of this country. Not our fighter planes or tanks, or how big the Emperor's palace happens to be. I think God put you in my path."

Later, when they had left, Ghosh realized how he'd been so predisposed to dislike Colonel Mebratu, but the opposite had happened. Conversely, as an expatriate, it was easy to project benevolent qualities on to His Majesty. Now he was less sure.

MR. ELIHU HARRIS was dressed all wrong. That was the first thing Matron noticed when he closed the door behind him and stepped up to her desk and introduced himself. He had every right to be annoyed, having visited Missing on the two previous days without meeting Matron. Instead, he seemed grateful to see her, worried about intruding on her time.

"I had no idea you were coming, Mr. Harris," Matron said presently. "Under any other circumstance, it would have been a pleasure. But you see, yesterday, we buried Sister Mary Joseph Praise."

"You mean . . ." Harris swallowed hard. His mouth opened and closed. He saw such sorrow in Matron's eyes, and he was embarrassed to have overlooked it. "You mean . . . the young nun from India? . . . Thomas Stone's assistant?"

"The very same. As for Thomas Stone, he has left. Vanished. I am very worried about him. He is a distraught man."

Harris had a pleasant face, but his overdeveloped upper lip and uneven front teeth left him just short of handsome. He fidgeted in his chair. He was doubtless yearning to ask how all this had happened, but he didn't. Matron understood he was the sort of man who, even when he had the upper hand, didn't know how to press for his rights. As he stood before her, his soft brown eyes reluctant to engage, her heart softened to him.

So Matron told Harris everything, a rush of simple sentences that were weighed down by what they conveyed. When she was finished, she said, "Your visit comes when we are at our worst." She blew her nose. "So much of what we did at Missing revolved around Thomas Stone. He was the best surgeon in the city. He never knew that it was because of the people he operated on in the royal family, in the government, that we were allowed to go on. The government makes us pay a hefty annual fee for the privilege of serving here, can you imagine? They could if they want simply close us down. Mr. Harris, even your giving us money was because of his book . . . This might be the end of Missing."

As Matron talked, Harris sank farther back in the chair, as if someone had a foot on his chest. He had a nervous habit of patting his cowlick, even though it was not in danger of falling.

There are people in the world who were cursed by bad timing, Matron thought. People whose cars break down on the way to their wedding, or whose Brighton holiday is invariably ruined by rain, or whose crowning day of private glory is overshadowed by and forever remembered as the day King George VI died. Such people vexed the spirit, and yet one was moved to pity because they were helpless. It wasn't Harris's fault that Sister had died or Stone had disappeared. Yet there he was.

If Harris wanted an accounting of money, she had nothing to show him. Matron submitted progress reports under duress, and since what donors wanted to spend on had no link to the reality of Missing's needs, her reports were a form of fiction. She'd always known a day like this would come.

Harris choked, then coughed. When he recovered, with much throat clearing and fumbling with his handkerchief, he came indirectly to his business with Matron. But it wasn't what Matron imagined it would be.

"You were right about our plan to fund a mission for the Oromo, Matron," Harris said. Matron faintly recalled a mention of this in a letter. "The doctor in Wollo sent me a telegram. The police have occupied the building. The district governor will do nothing to evict them. The supplies are being sold. The local church has been preaching against us, saying we are the devils! I had to come to straighten things out."

"Pardon me for being blunt, Mr. Harris, but how could you have funded it sight unseen?" She felt a pang of guilt as she said this, since Harris hadn't seen Missing till now. "If I recall, I wrote to say that it was unwise."

"It's my fault," Harris said, wringing his hands. "*I* prevailed on my church steering committee . . . I haven't told them yet," Harris said, almost in a whisper. Clearing his throat and finding his voice he added, "My intentions . . . , I hope the committee will understand, were good. We . . . I hoped to bring knowledge of the Redeemer to those who do not have it."

Matron let out an exasperated sigh. "Did you think they were all fire worshippers? Tree worshippers? Mr. Harris, they *are* Christians. They are no more in need of redemption than you are in need of a hair straightening cream."

"But I feel it's not true Christianity. It's a pagan sort of . . . ," he said, and patted his forehead.

"Pagan! Mr. Harris, when *our* pagan ancestors back in Yorkshire and Saxony were using their enemies' skulls as a plate to serve food, these Christians here were singing the psalms. They believe they have the Ark of the Covenant locked up in a church in Axum. Not a saint's finger or a pope's toe, but the Ark! Ethiopian believers put on the shirts of men who had just died of the plague. *They saw in the plague a sure and God-sent means of winning eternal life, of finding salvation.* That," she said, tapping the table, "is how much they thirsted for the next life." She couldn't help what she said next. "Tell me, in Dallas, do your parishioners hunger like that for salvation?"

Harris had turned red. He looked around as if for a place to hide. But he wasn't completely done. Men like him became stubborn with opposition, because their convictions were all they had.

"It's actually Houston, not Dallas," he said softly. "But, Matron, the priesthood here is almost illiterate—Gebrew, your watchman, doesn't understand the litany that he recites because it is in Geez, which no one speaks. If he holds to the Monophysite doctrine that Christ had only a divine nature, not a human one, then—"

"Stop! Mr. Harris, do stop," Matron said, covering her ears. "Oh, how you vex me." She came around the table, and Harris drew back as if he worried that she might box his ears. But Matron walked to the window.

"When you look around Addis and see children barefoot and shivering in the rain, when you see the lepers begging for their next morsel, does any of that Monophysitic nonsense matter the least bit?"

Matron leaned her head on the windowpane.

"God will judge us, Mr. Harris, by"—her voice broke as she thought of Sister Mary Joseph Praise—"by what we did to relieve the suffering of our fellow human beings. I don't think God cares what doctrine we embrace."

The sight of that plain, weathered face pressed against the glass, the wet cheeks, the interlocking fingers . . . it was for Harris more powerful than anything she had said. Here was a woman who could give up the restrictions of her order when it stood in the way. From her lips had come the kind of fundamental truth which, because of its simplicity, was unspoken in a church like Harris's where internecine squabbling seemed to be the purpose for the committee's existence, as well as a manifestation of faith. It was a small blessing that an ocean separated the doers like Matron from their patrons, because if they rubbed shoulders they'd make each other very uncomfortable.

Harris stared at the stack of Bibles by the wall. He hadn't seen them when he first walked in.

"We have more English Bibles than there are English speaking people in the entire country." Matron had turned from the window and followed his gaze. "Polish Bibles, Czech Bibles, Italian Bibles, French Bibles, Swedish Bibles. I think some are from your Sunday-school children. We need medicine and food. But we get Bibles." Matron smiled. "I always wondered if the good people who send us Bibles really think that hookworm and hunger are healed by scripture? Our patients are illiterate."

"I am embarrassed," Harris said.

"No, no, no. Please! People here love these Bibles. They're the most valuable thing a family can possess. Do you know what Emperor Menelik, who ruled before Haile Selassie, did when he fell ill? He *ate* pages of the Bible. I don't think it helped. This is a land where paper—*worketu*—is much valued. Did you know that among the poor, marriage consists simply of writing two names on a piece of paper? And to divorce, why you just tear up the paper. Priests will give out pieces of paper with verses on them. The paper is folded over again and again until it is a tiny square and then these are wrapped in leather and worn around the neck.

"I was happy to give away Bibles. But the Interior Minister saw it as proselytizing. 'How can it be proselytizing when no one can read? Besides it is the same faith as yours,' I said. But the minister disagreed. So now the Bibles pile up, Mr. Harris. They breed in the toolshed like rabbits. They spill over into our storerooms and into my office. We use them as support for bookshelves. Or to paper the walls of the *chikka* huts. Anything at all, really!"

She walked over to the door and beckoned him to join her outside. "Let's take a walk," she said. "Look," Matron said when they were in the hallway, pointing to a sign above a door: OPERATING THEATER 1. The room was a closet, jammed full of Bibles. Wordlessly she pointed to another room across the way which Harris could see was a storeroom for mops and buckets. The sign above it read OPERATING THEATER 2. "We have only one theater. We call it Operating Theater 3. Judge me harshly, if you will, Mr. Harris, but I take what I am given in God's name to serve these people. And if my donors insist on giving me another operating theater for the famous Thomas Stone, when what I need are catheters, syringes, penicillin, and money for oxygen tanks so I can keep the single theater going, then I give them their operating theater in name."

At the steps of the Missing outpatient department the bougainvillea was in full bloom, concealing the pillars of the carport so that the roof appeared to be cantilevered.

A man hurried by, bundled in a heavy white wrap over a ragged military overcoat. His white turban and the monkey-mane fly-swish in his hand made him stand out.

"That's the very Gebrew we were talking about," Matron said as Gebrew spotted them and stopped and bowed. "Servant of God. And watchman. And . . . one of our bereaved."

Harris was surprised at Gebrew's relative youth. In one of her letters, Matron wrote of a Harrari girl of twelve or thirteen who had been brought in, moribund, a cut umbilical cord trailing out from between her legs. She had given birth a few days before, but there had been no afterbirth; the placenta wouldn't budge. The family had traveled by mule and bus for two days to get to Missing. And as Gebrew, in his compassion, lifted the poor girl out of the gharry, she screamed. Gebrew, instrument of God, had inadvertently stepped on the trailing umbilical cord, causing the placenta to break free. The little girl was cured even before she crossed the threshold of the casualty room.

Harris shivered in a sleeveless cotton shirt, his eyeballs oscillating, his fingers tugging at his collar, then adjusting a pith helmet which Matron didn't realize he had with him.

Matron walked him through the children's ward, which was no more than a room painted bright lavender with infants on high beds with metal rails. The mothers camped out on the floor beside the beds. They jumped up at the sight of Matron and bowed. "That child has tetanus and will die. This one has meningitis, and if he lives he might well be deaf or blind. And its mother"—she said, affectionately putting her arm around a waiflike woman—"by staying at Missing night and day is neglecting her three other children. Lord, we've had a child back home fall into a well, get gored by a bull, and even kidnapped while the mother was here. The humane thing is to tell her to go home, to take the child home."

"Then why is she here?"

"Look at how anemic she is! We are feeding her. We give her the child's portions, which the child can't eat, as well as her portion, and I've asked them to give her an egg every day, and she is getting an iron injection and medicine for hookworm. In a few days we'll find her bus fare and then send her home with this child if he is alive. But at least she'll be healthier, better able to look after the other children . . . Now this child is awaiting surgery . . ."

In the male ward, which was long and narrow and held forty people, she kept up her recitation. The patients who could tried to sit up to greet them. One man was comatose, his mouth open, his eyes unseeing. Another sat leaning forward on a special pillow, struggling mightily to breathe. Two men, side by side, had bellies swollen to the size of ripe pregnancy.

"Rheumatic heart valve damage, nothing we can do . . . and these two fellows have cirrhosis," Matron explained.

Harris was struck by how little it took to nurture and sustain life. A huge chunk of bread in a chipped basin and a giant battered tin cup of sweetened tea—that was breakfast and lunch. Very often, as he could see, this feast was being shared with the family members squatting by the bed.

When they emerged from the ward, Matron stopped to catch her breath. "Do you know that at this moment we have funds for three days, that's all? Some nights I go to sleep with no idea of how we can open in the morning."

"What will you do?" Harris asked, but then he realized he knew the answer.

Matron smiled, her eyes almost disappearing as her cheeks pushed up, giving her a childlike quality. "That's right, Mr. Harris. I pray. Then I take it out of the building fund or whatever fund has money. The Lord knows my predicament, or so I tell myself. He must approve the transfer. What we are fighting isn't godlessness—this is the most godly country on earth. We aren't even fighting disease. It's poverty. *Money* for food, medicines . . . that helps. When we cannot cure or save a life, our patients can at least feel cared for. It should be a basic human right."

Harris's anxiety about the steering committee had all but gone.

"I'll confess, Mr. Harris, that as I get older, my prayers aren't about forgiveness. My prayers are for money to do His work." She reached out for his hand and held it in both of hers, patting it. "Do you know, dear man, that in my darkest moments, you have so often been the answer to my prayers?"

Matron felt she had said enough. It was a gamble. She had nothing to put on the table but the truth.

CHAPTER 15

Crookedness of
the Serpent

THE NEWBORNS SEEMED UNREAL to Ghosh, all noses and wrinkles, as if they'd been planted in Hema's house, a lab experiment gone awry. Ghosh tried to make appropriate noises and act interested, but he found himself resenting the attention they were getting.

It was five days since Sister Mary Joseph Praise's death. He had stopped by Hema's house in the early evening before setting out to look for Stone. He'd found his Almaz there, very much at home, immersed in the task of caring for the babies, barely registering his presence. The last few days, he had been forced to make his own coffee and heat his own bathwater. Matron, Sister Asqual, Rosina, and several nursing students were there, too, fussing over the newborns. Rosina, with nothing to occupy her now that Thomas Stone was gone, had also moved over to Hema's. No one noticed when he left Hema's bungalow.

He drove first to the Ghion and the Ras hotels, then to the police headquarters where he sought out a sergeant he knew. The man had no news for him. He drove through the Piazza from one end to the other, and then, after a beer at St. George's, decided it was time to go home. His plans to leave had solidified. He had an airline ticket to Rome, then on to Chicago, leaving in four weeks. By that time, perhaps things at Missing would have settled. He couldn't see himself staying on, not now, not with Stone gone and Sister dead. But he had yet to find the courage to tell Matron or Almaz—or Hema.

It was dark when he pulled into his carport. He saw Almaz squatting by the back wall, wrapped against the cold so only her eyes showed. She was waiting for him just as she had the night Sister Mary Joseph Praise had died.

"Oh God. What now?"

She came to the passenger door, yanked it open, and climbed in.

"Is it Stone?" he said. "What happened?"

"Where have you been? No, it's not Stone. One of the babies stopped breathing. Let's go to Dr. Hema's bungalow."

THE BLUE NIGHT-LIGHT made Hema's bedroom seem surreal, like a set for a movie. Hema was in a nightdress, her hair loose and flowing over her shoulders. He found it difficult to look away.

The two newborns were on the bed, their chests rising and falling evenly, eyes closed, and their faces peaceful.

Turning back to Hema, he saw she was trembling, her lips quivering. He put his hands out, palms up, asking what had happened. By way of an answer, she flew into his arms.

He held her.

In the years he had known her, he'd seen her happy, angry, sad, and even depressed but, underneath, always feisty. He had never seen her fearful; it was as if she'd become some other person.

He tried to lead her outside of the room, his arm still around her shoulder, but she resisted. "No," she whispered. "We can't leave."

"What's going on?"

"I happened to be looking at them just after I put them to bed. I saw Marion breathing evenly. But Shiva . . ." She sobbed now, as she pointed to the child with the dressing on his scalp. "I saw his stomach rise, then it went down as he exhaled . . . and then nothing. I watched as long as I could. 'Hema, you are imagining things,' I said. But I could see him turning blue, even in this light, especially when I compared his color with Marion's. I touched him, and his arms shot out as if he was falling, and he took a deep breath. His fingers curled around my finger. He was saying, *Don't leave me.* He was breathing again. Oh, my Shiva. If I hadn't been standing there . . . he'd be gone by now."

She sobbed into her hands, which rested on his chest. Ghosh held her, her tears making his shirt damp. He didn't know what to say. He hoped she didn't smell beer. In a moment, she pulled away, and they stood arm in arm, Almaz just behind them, gazing at Shiva.

Why had Hema taken on the naming of the babies? It felt premature. He couldn't get his lips around the names. Were the names negotiable? What if Thomas Stone showed up? And why name the child of a nun and an Englishman after a Hindu god? And for the other twin, also a boy, why Marion? Surely it was temporary, until Stone came to his senses, or the British Embassy or someone made arrangements. Hema was acting as if the kids were hers.

"Did it happen more than once?" he asked.

"Yes! Once more. About thirty minutes later. Just when I was about to turn away. He exhaled . . . and stopped. I made myself wait. Surely he has to breathe. I held back until I couldn't stand it any longer. When I touched him he started breathing as if he'd been waiting for that little push, as if he forgot. I've been here for the last three hours, too scared to even go to the loo. I didn't trust anyone else to watch, and besides I could not quite explain it to them . . . Thank God Almaz decided to stay to help me with the night feeds. I sent her to get you," Hema said.

"Go ahead," he said. "I'll watch them."

She was back in no time. "What do you think?" she said, leaning against his arm as she dabbed her eyes with a hankie. "Shouldn't you listen to his lungs? He wasn't coughing or struggling."

Ghosh, finger to chin, his eyes narrowing, studied the child quietly. After a long while he said, "I'll examine him thoroughly when he is awake. But I think I know what it is."

The way she looked at him made his heart swell. This wasn't the Hema who reacted to everything he said with skepticism. "In fact, I'm sure. Apnea of the premature. It's well described. You see, his brain is still immature, and the respiratory center, which triggers each breath, isn't fully developed. He 'forgets' to breathe every now and then."

"Are you sure it isn't something else?" She wasn't challenging him; like any mother, she wanted certainty from the doctor.

He nodded. "I'm sure. You were lucky. Usually apnea is fatal before anyone recognizes it."

"Don't say that. Oh God. What can we do, Ghosh?"

He was about to tell her that there was nothing one could do. Nothing at all. If the child was lucky, it might outgrow the apnea in a few weeks. The only choice was to put these preemies on machines that breathed for them till their lungs matured. Even in England and America this was rarely done. At Missing it was out of the question.

She waited for his pronouncement. She had suspended her own breathing.

"Here is what we do," he said, and she sighed. He was making this up. He didn't know if his plan would work. But he knew he did not have the heart to say there was nothing to be done.

"Get me a chair. One of those from the living room. Also give me some of your anklets and a pair of pliers. And some thread or twine. A clipboard or a notebook if you have one. And tell Almaz to make coffee. The strongest she can make and as much of it as she can make and tell her to fill up the thermos flask."

This new Hema, the adoptive mother of the twins, rose at once to do his bidding, never asking why or how. He watched her dance away.

"If I knew you were that agreeable I'd have asked for a cognac and a foot massage as well," he muttered to himself. "And if this doesn't work . . . at least I'll have my bags packed."

GHOSH SAT IN THE CHAIR, sipping coffee, a string wrapped around his finger, and the house silent around him. It was two in the morning. The other end of the string connected to one of Hema's anklets which he'd cut in half and looped around Shiva's foot. The tiny silver bells dangling from the anklet made a pleasant cymbal-like sound when the foot moved.

He had strapped his wristwatch to the arm of his chair. On the first page of an exercise book, he made vertical columns labeled with date and time. Shiva stirred in his sleep; the anklet sounding reassuringly. Earlier, they had fed the twins, adding one drop of coffee to Shiva's bottle. It was Ghosh's hope that caffeine, a nervous-system stimulant and irritant, would keep the respiratory center ticking. It had clearly made the infant more restless than his identical twin.

Hema slept on the sofa in the far corner of the living room, which was just beyond this bedroom. A floor lamp with a shade that they moved to Hema's room gave him light to see the page.

Ghosh studied the walls. A little girl in pigtails and a half sari stood between two adults. A framed picture of Prime Minister Jawaharlal Nehru, handsome and pensive, one finger on his cheek, hung opposite Ghosh's chair. He'd imagined Hema's bedroom would be neat, everything in its place. Instead, there were clothes spilling off the bed rail, a suitcase open on the floor, more clothes piled in the corner, and books and papers stacked on a chair. And just inside the bedroom door he noticed for the first time was a crate the size of a sideboard. She did it, he thought, as he leaned closer to read the writing on the outside. A Grundig, no less. The best money can buy. His own gramophone and radio had conked out a few months before.

Periodically he would glance at the child, make sure the little chest was moving. After what felt like half an hour, he yawned, looked at his watch, and was astonished to find that only seven minutes had passed. My God, this is going to be difficult, he thought. He finished his cup of coffee and poured a second.

He stood and circled the room. On one shelf was a bound set of books. GREAT WORLD CLASSICS SERIES was stamped in a gold imprint. He picked one volume and sat down. The book was beautifully bound, in a leathery cover, and had gold-trimmed pages that looked as if they had never been opened.

AT FOUR IN THE MORNING, he went to wake Hema. In sleep she looked like a little girl, both hands together and tucked under one cheek. He gently shook her, and she opened her eyes, saw him, and smiled. He held out the cup of coffee.

"My turn?" He nodded. She sat up. "Did he stop breathing?"

"Twice. There was no doubt about it."

"God. Oh God. I wasn't imagining it, was I? We're so lucky I saw that first one."

"Drink this, then wash your face and come to the bedroom."

When she returned he gave her the thread running to the anklet, the notebook with the pen clipped to it. "Whatever you do, don't lie on the bed. Stay in this chair. It's the only way to stay awake. I've been reading, which really helps. I look up at the end of every page. If I hear the anklet move, then I don't look up and I keep reading. When he stopped breathing, I tugged at the anklet and he started right back up. Little fellow just forgets to breathe."

"Why should he have to remember? Poor baby."

HEMA HAD HARDLY SETTLED in the chair when she heard a strange noise. It took her a second to realize that it was the sound of Ghosh snoring. She tiptoed to where he was on the sofa, dead to the world, looking like a big teddy bear. She covered him with the blanket which had slipped to the floor, and she returned to her vigil. The snoring reassured her. It told her she was not alone. She picked up the book Ghosh had been reading.

She'd bought the set of twelve books from a staffer at the British Embassy who was returning home. She was ashamed not to have read even one. Ghosh had put a bookmark on page ninety-two. Had he really come that far? Why did he pick this book? She turned to the first page:

Who that cares much to know the history of man, and how the mysterious mixture behaves under the varying experiments of Time, has not dwelt, at least briefly, on the life of Saint Theresa, has not smiled with some gentleness at the thought of the little girl walking forth one morning hand-in-hand with her still smaller brother, to go and seek martyrdom in the country of the Moors?

She read that opening sentence three times before she understood what it might be about. She looked at the title of the book. *Middlemarch*. Why couldn't the writer be clear? She read on, only because Ghosh had managed to keep reading. Little by little, she found herself immersed in the story.

THE NEXT MORNING, as Ghosh made rounds, he wondered if the Colonel made it back to his garrison in Gondar without incident. If the Colonel had been arrested, or hanged, would news ever reach Missing? *The Ethiopian Herald* never wrote about treason, as if it were treasonable to report treason.

After looking in on his patients, Ghosh unearthed an incubator from one of the storage sheds behind Matron's bungalow. Ghosh was Missing's de facto pediatrician. In the early years he'd fashioned an incubator for premature babies. After the Swedish government opened a pediatric hospital in Addis Ababa, Missing sent all the very premature babies there and put the incubator away.

Despite its delicate construction with glass on four sides and a tin base, the incubator was still intact. He had Gebrew hose it off, dust it for fleas, put it in the sunlight for a few hours, then rinse it again with hot water. Ghosh wiped it down with alcohol before setting it up in Hema's bedroom. No sooner had he stepped back to admire it than Almaz walked around it three times making *thew-thew* sounds, stopping short of actually spitting. "To ward off the evil eye," she explained in Amharic, wiping her lip with the back of her forearm.

"Remind me never to invite you into the operating theater," Ghosh said in English. "Hema?" he said, hoping she would weigh in. "Antisepsis? Lister? Pasteur? Are you no longer a believer?"

"You forget I am postpartum, man," she said. "Warding off spirits is much more important."

The twins lay swaddled next to each other like larvae, sharing the incubator, their skulls covered with monkey caps and only their wizened, newborn faces showing. No matter how far apart Hema put them, when she came to them again, they would be in a *V*, their heads touching, facing each other, just as they had been in the womb.

SOME NIGHTS as he took his shift by the sleeping infant, exhausted, fighting sleep, he talked to himself. "Why are you here? Would she do this for you?" The old resentments made his jaw tighten. "You silly bugger, you allowed yourself to succumb to her spell again?" Why did he lack the willpower to say what must be said?

He told himself that once the infant, this Shiva, was over its breathing problem, he would leave. Knowing Hema, when she no longer had to rely on him, things would be back to where they had always been. Since Harris's visit, it was unclear if the Houston Baptists would continue their support. Matron wouldn't give her opinion.

For two weeks he and Hema kept a vigil over Shiva, getting help in the daytime, but reserving the night for themselves. They had finished *Middlemarch* in a week and it had given them plenty to discuss. He picked Zola's *Three Cities Trilogy: Paris* next, and that they both found absorbing. Shiva's episodes of apnea decreased from more than twenty a day to two a day and then ceased. They extended their vigil into a third week, just to be on the safe side.

Hema's sofa was too small for a man of Ghosh's proportions, and seeing him scrunched up there, she felt grateful to him and conscious of his sacrifice. It would have surprised her to know how much he relished occupying the space that she'd just vacated, and covering himself with a blanket still scented with her dreams. The jingling of Shiva's ankle bracelet filtered into his sleep, and one night he dreamed that Hema was dancing for him. Naked. It was so vivid, so real, that the next morning, he hurried to Cook's Travel, waited till they opened, and canceled his ticket to America. He did it before he had any coffee—or a chance to second-guess himself.

MATRON WAS INCREASINGLY STOOPED, her face more weathered in the aftermath of Sister Mary Joseph Praise's death. She spent her evenings at Hema's—everybody did—but she didn't protest when Ghosh and Hema sent her back to her quarters by eight, accompanied by Koochooloo. That dog had become protective of Matron, and since the other two nameless dogs often followed Koochooloo, Matron had an entourage with her.

Two weeks after they buried Sister, Gebrew saw a barefoot coolie walk by with his right arm in a long cast, the elbow straight at his side. Worse still, the man was so sleepy he staggered and was in danger of breaking his head, not to mention his other arm. Gebrew felt terrible because it was he who had directed the coolie to the Russian hospital when he showed up at Missing with a fracture. The Russian doctors loved injecting barbiturates no matter what ailed you, and since their patients loved the needle, no one left the Russian hospital unsedated. Gebrew knew from his years at Missing that a broken forearm had to be cast in a neutral and functional position, with the elbow flexed to ninety degrees, the forearm midway between pronation and supination, even though he knew none of those terms. He escorted the unsteady coolie to the casualty room where, after Ghosh looked at the X-ray, the orderlies reapplied the cast. At that moment, though none of them quite realized it, Missing officially reopened for business.

Hema refused to leave the infants. She claimed she was no longer a doctor, but a mother. She was the kind of mother who was fearful for her children, who loved being with them and was unwilling to part from them. The two *mamithus*—Stone's Rosina and Ghosh's Almaz—took turns sleeping on a mattress in her kitchen, and were ready to help.

With Stone gone or dead, and Hema a full-time mother, once the gates opened, the burden on Ghosh was huge. Matron hired Bachelli to run the morning outpatient clinics where the great majority of Missing's patients were seen. This allowed Ghosh the freedom to operate when he could, and to concentrate on the patients admitted to the hospital.

Six weeks after Sister Mary Joseph Praise's death, the gravestone arrived, hauled up by donkey cart. Hema and Ghosh went to see it levered into place. The mason had carved a Coptic cross on the stone. Below it he had etched letters he copied from the paper Matron had given him:

ΣΙΣΤΕΡ ΜΑΡΨ JΟΣΕΠΗ ΠΡΑΙΣΕ
ΒΟΡΝ 1928, ΔΙΕΔ 1954
ΣΑFΕ ΙΝ ΑΡΜΣ ΟF JΕΣΥΣ

Matron arrived, short of breath and agitated. The three of them stood there, studying the strange lettering. The mason looked on, hoping for a commendation. Matron let out a sigh of exasperation.

"I don't suppose he can do much about that now," Matron said, and gave the man a nod. He gathered his crowbars and gunnysacks and led his animal away.

"I was thinking," Hema said, her voice hoarse. "That inscription should read, 'Died at the hands of a surgeon. Now safe in the arms of Jesus.' "

"Hema!" Matron protested. "Custody of the tongue."

"No, really," Hema said. "A rich man's faults are covered with money, but a surgeon's faults are covered with earth."

"Sister Mary Joseph Praise is covered in the soil of the land she came to love," Matron said, hoping to put a stop to this kind of talk.

"Put there by a surgeon," said Hema who had to have the last word.

"Who has now left the country," Matron said.

They turned to look at her, mouths open.

Matron said, apologetically, "I got a call from the British Consulate. That's why I was late. From what I can piece together, Stone went to the Kenyan border, then to Nairobi, don't ask me how. He's in bad shape. Drink, I presume. The man was crazed."

"He's not hurt or anything?" Ghosh said.

"As best as I can tell he's in one piece. I made a trunk call to Mr. Elihu Harris just now. Yes, I got Harris involved. They have a big mission in Kenya. If he sobers up, Harris thinks Stone could work there. Or if he doesn't want that, Eli can arrange for him to go to America."

"But what about his books, and his things?" Ghosh said. "Should we send them on to him?"

"I imagine he'll write for his books and specimens once he is settled," Matron said.

The news both annoyed and pleased Hema. It meant Stone had abandoned the children, and that he'd given up any claims on them. She wished he'd signed a paper to that effect. She still felt uneasy. A man who made his name at Missing, whose lover was buried at Missing, and whose children were being raised at Missing, might not be able to cut the Missing cord that easily. "The crookedness of the serpent is still straight enough to slide through the snake hole," Hema said.

"He's no serpent," Ghosh said sharply, contradicting Hema. She was too astonished to reply. "He is my friend," Ghosh continued in a tone that dared anyone to disagree. "Let's not forget what a valuable colleague he was all these years, the great service he gave to Missing, the lives he saved. He's no serpent." He spun on his heels and walked off.

Ghosh's words pricked Hema's conscience. She couldn't assume that he was to feel everything she felt. Not if she cared for him. Ghosh was his own man, had been all along.

She gazed at Ghosh's receding back and was frightened. She'd never worried particularly about Ghosh's feelings, but now, at the graveside, she felt like a young girl who, while drawing water at the well, meets a handsome stranger—a once-in-a-lifetime opportunity—but she ruins it by saying the wrong thing.

CHAPTER 16

Bride for a Year

THE MILK COW WAS HEMA'S FOLLY, but once the first cream-rich mouthful slid down her throat there was no going back, even if Ghosh had taken away the reason for a cow.

"Are you joking, Hema? You can't give *cow's* milk to newborn babies!"

"Who says so?" she said, but without conviction.

"*I* do," he said. "Besides, they've been thriving on formula for weeks. They are staying on formula."

After his sharp words at Sister's graveside, she'd felt a terrible premonition that he would leave Missing, but in the ensuing days he had proved true to her, returning to sleep on the sofa. The calm, methodical way he'd approached Shiva's problem was a side of him she hadn't appreciated. On the wall by the door he'd taped a paper that graphed the waning and disappearance of those terrifying episodes of apnea. Hema would never have had the confidence to say what he said one evening— that the night watch was over.

He'd been sleeping on the sofa since the day she summoned him, and now she didn't want him to leave—his snoring was a sound she'd come to depend on. But she couldn't resist arguing with him now and then; it was an old reflex. She thought of it as her way of being affectionate.

They didn't take the anklet off Shiva's foot, even though it was no longer needed. The sound had become part of Shiva, and to remove it felt akin to taking away his voice.

In the early morning a stone bell heralded the procession of cow, calf, and Asrat, the milkman, up the driveway. The cowbell was tonally related to the chime of Shiva's anklet. Asrat charged more for bringing the milk factory to the house, but by milking under Rosina's or Almaz's watchful eye, there was no question of the milk being watered down.

By the time Hema rose, the house was suffused with the scent of boiling milk. She took to adding more and more milk to her morning coffee. Soon when Hema heard the cowbell, her mouth watered, just as if she were one of Professor Pavlov's mutts. Her morning "coffee" grew to two tumblers, and she had another two glasses during the day, more milk than coffee, loving the way the buttery flavor lingered on her tongue. Unlike the buffalo milk of her childhood, this milk was made so very tasty by the highland grass on which the cow fed.

When Asrat, whose bovine equanimity Hema believed came from having his cows sleep inside his hut at night, said one morning, "If only madam would buy corn feed, the milk would be so thick a spoon would stand up in it," she didn't hesitate. Soon a coolie arrived with ten sacks on a handcart stamped ROCKEFELLER FOUNDATION and NOT FOR RESALE. "The best investment I've ever made," Hema said a few days later, smacking her lips like a schoolgirl. "Corn makes all the difference."

"Hardly a controlled experiment, given the bias you introduced by paying for the corn," Ghosh said.

Asrat tethered the animals behind the kitchen, the calf just out of reach of its mother's udders, while he delivered what milk remained to other homes. The cow and calf called to each other with such soothing and auspicious sounds. Hema remembered her mother saying, "A cow carries the universe in its body, Brahma in the horns, Agni in the brow, Indra in the head . . ."

The calf's call for its mother was nothing like the cry of her twins, but the emotion was identical. In her years as an obstetrician, Hema had never thought too much about a newborn's cry, never paused to consider the frequency that made a baby's tongue and lips quiver like a reed. It was such a helpless, urgent sound, but hitherto its importance lay in what it signaled: a successful labor, a live birth. Only when it was absent was it noteworthy. But now, when *her* newborns, her Shiva and Marion, cried, it was like no other earthly sound. It summoned her from sleep's catacombs and brought shushing noises to her throat as she rushed to the incubator. It was a *personal* call—her babies wanted her!

She remembered a phenomenon she'd experienced for years when she was about to fall asleep: a sense that someone was calling her name. Now she told herself it had been her unborn twins telling her they were coming.

There were other noises she became attuned to in her new-mother state. The *thwack* of wet cloth on the washing stone. The clothesline sagging with diapers (banners to fecundity) and raising a flapping alarm before a rain squall, sending Almaz and Rosina racing outside. The glass-harp notes of feeding bottles clinking together in the boiling water. Rosina's singing, her constant chatter. Almaz clanging pots and pans . . . these sounds were the chorale of Hema's contentment.

A Maharashtrian astrologer, on a tour of East Africa, came to the house over Ghosh's objections. Hema paid for him to read the children's fortunes. With his spectacles and fountain pens in his shirt pocket, he looked like a young railway clerk. After recording the exact time of the twins' births, he wanted the parents' birth dates. Hema gave hers and then volunteered Ghosh's, throwing Ghosh a warning look. The astrologer consulted his tables and his calculations filled one side of a foolscap paper. At last he said, "Impossible." He looked nervously at Hema, but avoided Ghosh's eyes. He capped his pen, put away his papers, and while an astonished Hema looked on, he made for the door. "Whatever is their destiny," he said, "you can be sure it's linked to the father."

Ghosh caught up with him at the gate. He declined Ghosh's offer of money. With a mournful expression he intoned, "Doctor *saab,* I'm afraid you cannot be the father." Ghosh pretended to be deeply troubled by this news. Ghosh reported back to Hema, but she wasn't half as amused as he was. It left her fearful, as if the man had somehow predicted Thomas Stone's return.

The next day Ghosh found Hema squatting, cupping rice flour in her fist and drawing a *rangoli*—an elaborate decorative pattern—on the wooden floor just outside her bedroom, taking pains that the lines were uninterrupted, so the evil spirits could not pass. Above the door frame to the bedroom, Hema hung a mask of a bearded devil with bloodshot eyes, his tongue sticking out—a further deflection of the evil eye. It became part of her morning ritual along with the playing of "Suprabhatam" on the Grundig, a version sung by M. S. Subbulakshmi. The chant's hiccuping syncopation evoked for Ghosh the sound of women sweeping the front yard around the banyan tree in the early mornings in Madras and the *dhobi* ringing his bicycle bell. "Suprabhatam" was what radio stations used to begin their daily broadcast, and as a student, Ghosh had heard the words of "Suprabhatam" on the lips of dying patients. It amused him that he had to come to Ethiopia to learn exactly what it was: an invocation and a wake-up call for Lord Venkateswara.

Ghosh noticed that Hema's bedroom closet was now a shrine dominated by the symbol of Shiva: a tall lingam. In addition to the little brass statues of Ganesh, Lakshmi, and Muruga, now came a sinister-looking ebony carving of the indecipherable Lord Venkateswara, as well as a ceramic Immaculate Heart of the Virgin Mary and a ceramic crucified Christ, blood welling out of the nail holes. Ghosh held his tongue.

Without fanfare and quite unexpectedly, Ghosh had become Missing's surgeon. Though he was no Thomas Stone, he had now handled several acute abdomens (his stomach fluttering just like the first time) and dealt with stab wounds and major fractures and even put in a chest tube for trauma. A woman in the labor and delivery room had suddenly developed airway obstruction. Ghosh ran in and cut high in the neck, opening the cricothyroid membrane; the aspirate sound of air rushing in was its own reward, as was the sight of the patient's lips turning from deep blue to pink. Later that day, under better lighting in the operating theater, he did his first thyroidectomy. Operating Theater 3 was now a familiar place, but still fraught with danger. Nothing was routine for him.

On the day the twins turned two months old, Ghosh was in midsurgery when the probationer poked her head in to say that Hema urgently needed him. Ghosh was removing a foot so destroyed by chronic infection that it had become a weeping, oozing stump. The boy had traveled alone from his village near Axum, a voyage of several days, to beg Ghosh to cut off the offending part. "It has stuck to my body for three years," he said, pointing to the foot that was four times the size of his other foot and shapeless, with toes barely visible.

Madura foot was found wherever people habitually walked barefoot, but the town of Madurai, not far from Madras, had the dubious honor of lending its name to this disease. No place ever came off well when a disease was named after it: Delhi belly, Baghdad blues, Turkey trots. Madura foot began when a field-worker stepped on a large thorn or nail. Their livelihood gave them no choice but to keep walking, and slowly a fungus overran the foot, invaded bone, tendon, and muscle. Nothing short of amputation would help.

Encouraged by the old surgical saw "Any idiot can amputate a leg," Ghosh had decided to proceed. If he hesitated, it was because the rest of the saying went "but it takes a skilled surgeon to save one." Still there was no saving this foot.

The boy was the first patient Ghosh had ever seen who sang and clapped his way into the theater, overjoyed at having surgery. Ghosh cut through skin above the ankle, leaving a flap at the back to cover the stump. He tied off the blood vessels and sawed through the bone and heard the thump of the foot landing in the bucket. It was at this point that the probationer delivered her summons.

Ghosh covered the wound with a damp sterile towel, and he ran home, tearing off his mask and cap, imagining the worst.

He burst into Hema's bedroom, breathless. "What is it?"

Hema, in a silk sari, had spread rice out on the floor. In Sanskrit letters, she'd spelled out the boys' names in the grains. Shiva was in her arms, and Rosina held Marion. Hema had assembled a few Indian women, who were glaring at him in disapproval.

"The post came," Hema said. "We forgot to do the *nama-karanum*, Ghosh. Naming ceremony. Should be on the eleventh day, but you can also do it on the sixteenth day. We have not done it on either of those two days, but in my mother's letter she says as long as I do it as soon as I get her aerogram we are all right."

"You made me leave an operation for this?" He was furious. It was on his lips to say, *How can you subscribe to all this witchcraft?*

"Look," Hema hissed, embarrassed by his behavior, "the father is supposed to whisper the child's name into its ear. If you don't want to do it, I'll call someone else."

That word—"father"—changed everything. He felt a thrill. He quickly whispered "Marion" and then "Shiva" into each tiny ear, kissed each child, then kissed Hema on the cheek before she could pull away, saying "Bye, Mama," scandalizing Hema's guests before he raced back to the theater to fashion the flap over the stump.

THE TWINS WEREN'T EASY to tell apart but for the anklet which Hema had kept on Shiva as a talisman. While Shiva was peaceful, quiet, Marion tended to furrow his eyebrows in concentration when Ghosh carried him, as if trying to reconcile the strange man with the curious sounds he made. Shiva was slightly smaller, and his skull still bore the marks of Stone's attempts at extraction; he fussed only when he heard Marion crying, as if to show solidarity.

By twelve weeks, the twins had gained weight, their cries were lusty, their movements vigorous. They clenched their fists against their chests, and now and then they stretched out their arms and focused on their hands with cross-eyed wonder.

If they didn't show awareness of each other, Hema believed it was because they thought they were one. When they were bottle-fed, one in

Rosina's arms, the other in Hema's or Ghosh's, it helped greatly for them to be within earshot, heads or limbs touching; if they took one twin to another room, they both became fussy.

At five months, the boys had a riot of black curly hair. They had Stone's close-set eyes, which made them appear hypervigilant, examining their surroundings like clinicians. Their irises, depending on the light, were a very light brown or a dark blue. The forehead, round and generous, and the perfect Cupid's bow of the lip was all Sister Mary Joseph Praise. They were, Hema thought, much more beautiful than Glaxo babies, and there were two of them. And they were hers.

To his delight, Ghosh had the magic touch when it came to putting them to sleep. He supported one child on each forearm, their cheeks against his shoulder while their feet rested on the shelf of his belly. He would circumnavigate Hema's living room, bobbing and swaying. For lack of lullabies, he reached into his repertoire of bawdy verse. One night Matron took Ghosh aside and said: "Your limericks are usurping my prayers." Ghosh pictured Matron on her knees reciting:

> *There was a man from Madras*
> *Whose balls were made out of brass*
> *In stormy weather*
> *They clanged together*
> *And sparks came out of his arse.*

"I'm sorry, Matron."

"It can hardly be good for them to hear these things at such a tender age."

GHOSH COULD BARELY REMEMBER what his life was like before the twins arrived. When they snuggled in his arms, smiled, or pressed their wet chins against him he felt his heart would burst with pride. Marion and Shiva; now he could not imagine any better names. Of late his shoulders ached and his hands were numb when the *mamithus* lifted the sleeping boys from his arms.

Since he started sleeping on Hema's sofa, he'd not had a twinge of discomfort when he peed.

Hema regained some of her old manner. At times he missed their sparring. Had he pursued her all these years precisely because she was so unattainable? What if she had agreed to marry him as soon as he arrived in Ethiopia? Would his passion have survived? Everyone needed an obsession, and in the last eight years, she'd given him his, and for that perhaps he should be grateful.

Many a night, after putting the boys to bed, he had to return to finish up at the hospital. Not one drop of beer had touched his lips since his first night on Hema's sofa. On Hema's narrow couch he slept peacefully and woke refreshed.

Living under the same roof, Ghosh discovered that Hema chewed khat. It began during the night vigils with Shiva and it had helped her through her shift. Her bookmark was soon ahead of his in *Middlemarch,* and she was on Zola before he was done. She tried to hide the khat from him, and when he mentioned it, he found it touching how flustered she became. "I don't know what you're talking about," she said.

So he didn't bring it up again, though he knew when he saw her knitting late into the night, or when she waited up for him and was chattier than Rosina, that she had probably had a little chew before he arrived. Adid, the always smiling merchant she had seen on the plane coming back from Aden and whose company they both enjoyed, brought her the leaves.

As for Ghosh, proximity to Hema was his drug. He brushed against her when he lowered the sleeping babies into the crib that replaced the incubator. He was encouraged when she didn't turn around and snap at him. He gazed at her while sipping his morning coffee as she wrote out shopping lists for him, or consulted with Almaz about the plans for the day. One day she saw him looking.

"What? I look horrible first thing in the morning. Is that it?"

"No. You look the opposite of horrible."

She blushed. "Shaddap," she said, but the glow in her face did not fade.

One evening at dinner, he said, more to himself than to her, "I wonder what has become of Thomas Stone."

Hema pushed her chair back and stood up. "Please. I don't want you to ever mention that man's name in this house."

There were tears in her eyes. And fear. He went to her. He could bear her anger, he could suffer it, but he couldn't bear to see her in distress. He grabbed her hands, pulled her toward him; she fought but finally gave in, as he murmured, "It is all right. I didn't mean to upset you. It's all right." *I'd sell my best friend down the river to be able to hold you like this.*

"What if he comes and claims them? You heard the astrologer." She was trembling. "Have you thought about that?"

"He won't," Ghosh said, but she heard the uncertainty in his voice. She marched to her bedroom. "Well, if he tries, it will be over my dead body, do you hear me? Over my dead body!"

ONE VERY COLD NIGHT when the twins were nine months old, and while the *mamithus* slept in their quarters, and when Matron had returned to hers, everything changed. There was no longer a reason for Ghosh to sleep on the couch, but neither of them had brought up the idea of his leaving.

Ghosh came in just before midnight, and he found Hema sitting at the dining table. He came up close to her so she could inspect his eyes and see if there was liquor on his breath—it was what he always did to tease her when he returned at this hour. She pushed him away.

He went in to look at the twins. When he came out he said, "I smell incense." He'd scolded her before for letting the twins breathe in any smoke.

"It's a hallucination. Maybe the gods are trying to reach you." She pretended to be absorbed in the task of putting his dinner on the table.

"Macaroni that Rosina prepared," she said, uncovering a bowl. "And Almaz left chicken curry for you. They are competing to feed you. God knows why."

Ghosh tucked his napkin into his shirt. "You call *me* godless? If you read your Vedas or your Gita, you'll remember a man went to the sage, Ramakrishna, saying, 'O Master, I don't know how to love God.'" Hema frowned. "And the sage asked him if there was anything he loved. He said, 'I love my little son.' And Ramakrishna said, '*There* is your love and service to God. In your love and service to that child.'"

"So where were you at this hour, Mr. Godly Man?"

"Doing a Cesarean section. I was in and out in fifteen minutes," Ghosh said. Hema did three Cesarean sections in the weeks after the birth of the twins: once to teach Ghosh, once to assist him as he did it, and the third time to stand by and watch. No woman would die at Missing or be sent elsewhere for want of a C-section. "The baby had the cord wrapped around its neck. Baby is fine. The mother is already asking for her boiled egg."

Watching Ghosh eat had become Hema's nightly pastime. His

appetites engaged him; he lived in the center of a flurry of ideas and projects that made piles around her sofa.

Her mind had been drifting, so she had to ask him to repeat what he said.

"I said I would be in the middle of my internship at Cook County Hospital now, had I gone. I was ready to leave Ethiopia, you know."

"Why? Because Stone left?"

"No, woman. Before that. Before the babies were born or Sister died. You see, I was convinced that you would come back from India a married woman."

To Hema this was so absurd, so unexpected, a reminder of an innocent time from so long ago, that she burst out laughing. Ghosh's consternation made it even funnier, and the safety pin that held the top of her blouse together flew into the air and landed in his plate. That was too much for her, and she clutched her breast and rose from her chair, doubled over.

Since her return from India and the tragedy of Sister's death, there had been few occasions for side-splitting humor. When she caught her breath she said, "That's what I like about you, Ghosh. I'd forgotten. You can make me laugh like no one else on earth." She sat back in her chair.

Ghosh had stopped eating. He pushed the plate away. He was clearly upset and she didn't know why. He wiped his lips with the napkin, his movements precise and deliberate. There was a quaver in his voice.

"What joke?" he said again. "My wanting to marry you all these years was a joke?"

She found it difficult to meet his gaze. She'd never told him what had gone through her mind when she thought her plane was crashing, and how her last earthly thought was about him. The smile on her face felt false and she couldn't sustain it. She looked away, but her eye caught the menacing mask nailed up over the bedroom door.

Ghosh dropped his head into his hands. His mood had turned from ebullient to despairing; she had pushed him past a breaking point. And all because she had laughed? Once again she felt uncertain around him, as she had that day at Sister Mary Joseph Praise's grave.

"It's time I moved back to my quarters," he said.

"No!" Hema said, so forcefully that they were both startled.

She pulled her chair closer to his. She peeled his hands from his head and held them. She studied the strange profile of her colleague, her unhandsome but beautiful friend of so many years who had allowed his fate to become so inextricably tangled with hers. He seemed intent on leaving. He wasn't looking to her for guidance.

She kissed his hand. He resisted. She moved even closer. She pulled his head to her bosom, which, without the safety pin, was more exposed than it had ever been in front of a man. She held him the way he had held her when he came running the night Shiva stopped breathing.

After a while she turned his face to hers. And before she could think about what she was doing, or why, and how this had happened, she kissed him, finding pleasure in the way his lips felt on hers. She saw now and was ashamed to see how selfishly she had dealt with him, made use of him all these years. She'd not done it consciously. Nevertheless, she'd treated him as if he existed for her pleasure.

It was her turn to sigh, and she led the stunned Ghosh to the second bedroom, which was used to iron clothes and as storage, a bedroom she should have given him long ago instead of leaving him on the sofa. They undressed in the dark, cleared the bed of the mountain of diapers, towels, saris, and other garments. They resumed their embrace under the covers. "Hema, what if you get pregnant?" he asked. "Ah, you don't understand," she said. "I'm thirty. I may have left it too late already."

To his shame, now that those magnificent orbs he had fantasized about were unfettered and in his hands, now that she was his from the fleshy chin pad to the dimples above her buttocks, the transformation of his member from floppy flesh to stiff bamboo did not happen. When Hema realized what was amiss, she said nothing. Her silence only increased his distress. Ghosh didn't know that Hema blamed herself, that she thought she had been overeager and that she had misread the signs and misunderstood the man. A hyena's coughing in the distance seemed to mock them both.

She stayed perfectly still, as if lying on a land mine. At some point she fell asleep. She awoke to a sensation of rising from underwater to be resurrected and reclaimed. And it was because Ghosh's mouth was around her left breast, trying to swallow it. He directed her movements, pushing her this way and that, and it made her think that even when he had been at his most passive, he had really been in charge.

The sight of his great block of a head and his lips resting where no man had been before brought forth a rush of blood to her cheeks, her chest, and deep in her pelvis. One of his hands held her other breast, shock waves surging through her, while his other hand caressed her inner thighs. She found her hands responding in kind, pulling his head to her, reaching for his broad back, wanting him to swallow her whole. And now she felt something unmistakable and promising against her thighs.

In that moment, witnessing his animal eagerness, she understood that she'd forever lost him as a plaything, as a companion. He was no longer the Ghosh she toyed with, the Ghosh who existed only as a reaction to her own existence. She felt ashamed for not having seen him this way before, ashamed for presuming to know the nature of this pleasure and thereby denying herself and denying him all these years. She pulled him in, welcomed him—colleague, fellow physician, stranger, friend, and lover. She gasped in regret for all the evenings they'd sat across from each other, baiting each other and throwing barbs (though, now that she thought about it, she did most of the baiting and throwing) when they could have been engaged in this astonishing congress.

IN THE EARLY MORNING she awoke, fed and changed the children, and when they went back to sleep, she returned to Ghosh. They began again, and it was as if it were the first time, the sensations unique and unimaginable, the headboard slapping against the wall advertising their passion to Almaz and Rosina who were just arriving in the kitchen, but she didn't care. They slept, and only when they heard the cowbell and the calf cry did they rise.

Ghosh stopped Hema as she was about to leave the room.

"Is marrying me still a laughing matter?"

"What are you saying?"

"Hema, will you marry me?"

He was unprepared for her response, and later he wondered how she could have been so ready with an answer, one that would never have occurred to him.

"Yes, but only for a year."

"What?"

"Face it. This situation with the children threw us together. I don't want you to feel obliged. I will marry you for a year. And then we are done."

"But that is absurd," Ghosh sputtered.

"We have the option to renew for another year. Or not."

"I know what I want, Hema. I want this forever. I have always wanted it forever and ever. I know that at the end of the year I will want to renew."

"Well *you* may know, my sweet man. But what if I don't? Now you have surgery scheduled this morning, no? Well, you can tell Matron that I'll start doing hysterectomies and other elective surgery again. And it's time you learned some gynecologic surgery, something other than just C-sections."

She glanced at him over her shoulder as she departed, and the coyness in her smile and the mischief in her eyes and her arched eyebrows, and the steep tilt of her neck, were those of a dancer sending a signal without words. Her message silenced him. Instead of a year or a lifetime, suddenly he could only think of nightfall, and though it was only twelve hours away, it felt like an eternity.

PART THREE

I will not cut for stone, even for patients in whom the disease is manifest; I will leave this operation to be performed by practitioners, specialists in this art . . .

Hippocratic Oath

Theirs is the stoneless fruit of love
Whose love is returned.

Tiruvalluvar, *The Kural*

CHAPTER 17

"Tizita"

I REMEMBER THE EARLY MORNINGS, sweeping into the kitchen in Ghosh's arms. He is counting under his breath, "*One*-two . . . onetwothree." We twirl, dip, lunge. For the longest time I will think that dancing is his occupation.

We execute a turn before the stove and arrive at the rear door, where Ghosh works the lock and shoots back the bolt with a flourish.

Almaz and Rosina step in, quickly shutting the door against the cold, and against Koochooloo, who is wagging her tail, awaiting breakfast. Both *mamithus* are wrapped like mummies, only their eyes showing in a crescent gap. They peel off layers, and the odors of cut grass, and then turned earth, then *berbere* and coal fires rise from them like steam.

I laugh uncontrollably in anticipation, tuck my chin into my body, because I know Rosina's fingers, which are like icicles, will soon stroke my cheek. The first time she did this, I was startled into laughter instead of tears, a mistake, because it has encouraged this ritual that I dread and anticipate every day.

AFTER BREAKFAST, Hema and Ghosh kiss Shiva and me good-bye. Tears. Despair. Clinging. But they leave anyway, off to the hospital.

Rosina places us in the double pram. Soon, with uplifted hands, I beg to be carried. I want higher ground. I want the adult view. She gives in. Shiva is content wherever he is placed, as long as no one tries to remove his anklet.

Rosina's forehead is a ball of chocolate. Her braided hair marches back in neat rows, then flies out in a fringe that reaches her shoulders. She is a bouncing, rocking, and humming being. Her twirls and turns are faster than Ghosh's. From my dizzy perch, her pleated dress makes gorgeous florets, and her pink plastic shoes flash in and out of sight.

Rosina talks nonstop. We are silent, speechless, but full of thoughts, impressions, all of them unspoken. Rosina's Amharic makes Almaz and Gebrew laugh because her guttural, throat-clearing syllables don't really exist in Amharic. It never dissuades her. Sometimes she breaks into Italian, particularly when she is being forceful, struggling to make a point. *Italinya* comes easily to her, and strangely its meaning is clear, even though no one else speaks it, such is the nature of that language. When she speaks to herself, or sings, it is in her Eritrean tongue—Tigrinya— and then her voice is unlocked, the words pouring out.

Almaz, who once served Ghosh in his quarters, is now the cook in his and Hema's joint household. She stands rooted like a baobab to her spot in front of the stove, a giantess compared with Rosina, and not given to sound other than deep sonorous sighs, or an occasional *"Ewunuth!"*— "You don't say!"—to keep Rosina or Gebrew's chatter going, not that either of them needs encouragement. Almaz is fairer than Rosina, and her hair is contained by a gauzy orange *shash* that forms a Phrygian helmet. While Rosina's teeth shine like headlights, Almaz rarely shows hers.

By MIDMORNING, when we return from our first Bungalow-to– Casualty-to–Women's Ward-to–Front Gate excursion, with Koochooloo as our bodyguard, the kitchen is alive. Steam rises in plumes as Almaz clangs lids on and off the pots. The silver weight on the pressure cooker jiggles and whistles. Almaz's sure hands chop onions, tomatoes, and fresh coriander, making hillocks that dwarf the tiny mounds of ginger and garlic. She keeps a palette of spices nearby: curry leaves, turmeric, dry coriander, cloves, cinnamon, mustard seed, chili powder, all in tiny stainless-steel bowls within a large mother platter. A mad alchemist, she throws a pinch of this, a fistful of that, then wets her fingers and flings that moisture into the mortar. She pounds with the pestle, the wet, crunchy *thunk, thunk* soon changes to the sound of stone on stone.

Mustard seeds explode in the hot oil. She holds a lid over the pan to fend off the missiles. *Rat-a-tat!* like hail on a tin roof. She adds the cumin seeds, which sizzle, darken, and crackle. A dry, fragrant smoke chases out the mustard scent. Only then are the onions added, handfuls of them, and now the sound is that of life being spawned in a primordial fire.

Rosina abruptly hands me to Almaz and hurries out the back door, her legs crossing like scissor blades. We don't know this, but Rosina is carrying the seed of revolution. She is pregnant with a baby girl: Genet. The three of us—Shiva, Genet, and me—are together from the start, she in utero while Shiva and I negotiate the world outside. The handoff to Almaz is unexpected.

I whimper on Almaz's shoulder, perilously close to the bubbling cauldrons.

Almaz puts down the stirring ladle and shifts me to her hip. Reaching into her blouse, grunting with effort, she fishes out her breast.

"Here it is," she says, putting it in my hands for safekeeping.

I am the recipient of many gifts, but this is the first one I remember. Each time it is given to me it is a surprise. When it is taken away, the slate is wiped clean. But here it is, warm and alive, eased out of its cloth bed, bestowed on me like a medal I don't deserve. Almaz, who hardly speaks, resumes stirring, humming a tune. It is as if the breast no more belongs to her than does her ladle.

Shiva in the pram puts down his wooden truck, which his saliva has digested to a soggy pulp. It is, unlike his anklet, separable from him if need be. In the presence of that magnificent one-eyed teat, Shiva lets the truck fall to the floor. Though I have possession of the breast, stroking it, palpating it, I am also his amanuensis.

A rapt Shiva spurs me on and sends silent instructions: *Throw it to me.* And when I cannot, he says, *Open it and see what is inside.* That, too, is impossible. I mold it, indent it, and watch it rebound.

Put it to your mouth, Shiva says because this is the first means by which he knows the world. I dismiss this idea as absurd.

The breast is everything Almaz is not: laughing, vibrant, an outgoing member of our household.

When I try to lift it, to examine it, that teat dwarfs my hands and spills out between my fingers. I wish to confirm how all its surfaces sweep up to the summit, the dark pap through which it breathes and sees the world. The breast comes down to my knees. Or perhaps it comes down to Almaz's knees. I can't be sure. It quivers like jelly. Steam condenses on its surface, dulling its sheen. It carries the scent of crushed ginger and cumin powder from Almaz's fingers. Years later, when I first kiss a woman's breast, I become ravenous.

A flash of light and a blast of crisp air announce Rosina's return. I am back in her arms, removed from the breast which vanishes as mysteriously as it has appeared, swallowed by Almaz's blouse.

. . .

IN THE LATE MORNING, the chill long gone and the mist burned away, we play on the lawn till our cheeks are red. Rosina feeds us. Hunger and drowsiness blend together perfectly like the rice and curry, yogurt and bananas, in our belly. It is an age of perfection, of simple appetites.

After lunch, Shiva and I fall asleep, arms around each other, breath on each other's face, heads touching. In that fugue state between wakefulness and dreaming, the song I hear is not Rosina's. It is "Tizita," which Almaz sang when I held her breast.

I WILL HEAR THAT SONG through all my years in Ethiopia. When I leave Addis Ababa as a young man, I will carry it with me on a cassette that has "Tizita" along with "Aqualung." Departure or imminent death will force you to define your true tastes. During my years of exile, as the battered cassette wears out, I'll meet Ethiopians abroad. My word of greeting in our shared language is a spark, a link to a community, a network: the phone number of Woizero (Mrs.) Menen who, for a modest fee, cooks *injera* and *wot* and serves you in her house if you call her the day before; the taxi driver Ato (Mr.) Girma, whose cousin works for Ethiopian Airlines and brings in *kibe*—Ethiopian butter—because without butter from cows that live at altitude and graze on high pastures, your *wot* will taste of Kroger or FoodMart or Land O'Lakes. For Meskel celebrations, if you want a sheep slaughtered in Brooklyn, call Yohannes, and in Boston try the Queen of Sheba's. In my years away from my birth land, living in America, I will see how Ethiopians are invisible to others, yet so visible to me. Through them I will easily find other recordings of "Tizita."

They are eager to share, to thrust that song in my hands, as if only "Tizita" explains the strange inertia that overcomes them; it explains how they were brilliant at home, the Jackson 5, the Temptations, and "Tizita" on their lips, a perfect Afro on their heads, bell-bottoms swishing above Double-O-Seven boots, and then the first foothold in America—behind the counter of a 7-Eleven, or breathing carbon monoxide fumes in a Kinney underground parking lot, or behind the counter of an airport newsstand or Marriott gift shop—has turned out to be a cement foot plant, a haven that they are fearful of leaving lest they suffer a fate worse than invisibility, namely extinction.

Getachew Kassa's slow version of "Tizita," a bright but haunting, sober lament on a backdrop of minor-chord arpeggios, is the best known. He has another version, with a fast Latin rhythm. Mahmoud Ahmed, Aster Aweke, Teddy Afro . . . every Ethiopian artist records a "Tizita." They record it in Addis Ababa, but also in exile in Khartoum (yes, Khartoum! which proves that even hell has a recording studio) and of course in Rome, Washington, D.C., Atlanta, Dallas, Boston, and New York. "Tizita" is the heart's anthem, the lament of the diaspora, reverberating up and down Eighteenth Street in the Adams Morgan section of Washington, D.C., where it pours out from Fasika's, Addis Ababa, Meskerem, Red Sea, and other Ethiopian eateries, drowning out the salsa or the ragas emanating from El Rincon and Queen of India.

There is a fast "Tizita," a slow "Tizita," an instrumental "Tizita" (which the Ashantis made so popular), a short and a long "Tizita" . . . there are as many versions as there are recording artists.

That first line . . . I hear it now.

Tizitash zeweter wode ene eye metah.
I can't help thinking about you.

CHAPTER 18

Sins of the Father

IN OUR HOUSEHOLD, you had to dive into the din and push to the front if you wanted to be heard. The foghorn voice was Ghosh's, echoing and tailing off into laughter. Hema was the songbird, but when provoked her voice was as sharp as Saladin's scimitar, which, according to my *Richard the Lion Hearted and the Crusades*, could divide a silk scarf allowed to float down onto the blade's edge. Almaz, our cook, may have been silent on the outside, but her lips moved constantly, whether in prayer or song, no one knew. Rosina took silence as a personal offense, and spoke into empty rooms and chattered into cupboards. Genet, almost six years of age, was showing signs of taking after her mother, telling herself stories about herself in a singsong voice, creating her own mythology.

Had ShivaMarion been delivered vaginally (impossible, given how our heads were connected), Shiva, presenting skull first, would have been the firstborn, the older twin. But when the Cesarean section reversed the natural birth order, I became the first to breathe—senior by a few seconds. I also became spokesperson for ShivaMarion.

Trailing after Hema and Ghosh in the Piazza, or threading between gharries and lorries into Motilal's Garments in the crowded Merkato of Addis Ababa, I never heard Hema say, "That blue shirt will look so good on Shiva," or "Those sandals are perfect for Marion." The arrival of Dr. Ghosh and Dr. Hema meant chairs were dragged out and dusted, and a boy sent running to return with warm Fanta or Coca-Cola and biscuits, despite all protests. Tape measures sized us, our cheeks were pinched by rough hands, and a small crowd gathered to gawk, as if ShivaMarion was a lion in the cages at Sidist Kilo. The upshot of all this would be that Hema and Ghosh purchased two of whatever piece of clothing it was they felt we needed. Ditto for cricket bats, fountain pens, and bicycles.

When people saw us and said, "Look! How sweet," did they really imagine that we had picked the matching outfits ourselves? I'll admit, the one time I tried to dress differently from Shiva, I felt uneasy as we stood before the mirror. It was as if my fly were undone—it just didn't feel right.

We—"The Twins"—were famous not just for dressing alike but for sprinting around at breakneck speed, but always in step, a four-legged being that knew only one way to get from A to B. When ShivaMarion was forced to walk, it was with arms locked around each other's shoulders, not really a walk but a trot, champions of the three-legged race before we knew there was such a thing. Seated, we shared a chair, seeing no sense in occupying two. We even used the loo together, directing a double jet into the porcelain void. Looking back, you could say we had some responsibility for people dealing with us as a collective.

Ask *The Twins* to come inside for dinner.

Boys, isn't it time for your bath?

ShivaMarion, do you want spaghetti or *injera* and *wot* tonight?

"You" or "Your" never meant one of us. When we replied to a question, no one cared which of us had spoken; an answer from one was an answer for The Twins.

Perhaps the adults believed that Shiva, my busy, industrious brother, was naturally parsimonious with his words. If the sound of the anklet which he insisted on wearing counted as speech, then Shiva was a terrible chatterbox, only silent when he muffled the tiny bells under his sock for school. Perhaps the adults believed I never gave Shiva much of a chance to speak (which was true), but no one wanted to tell me to shut up. In any case, in the hullabaloo of our bungalow, where the bridge crowd congregated twice a week, where a 78 rpm spun on the Grundig, and where Ghosh's lumbering tread rattled the dishes as he struggled to learn the rumba and the cha-cha-cha, two years went by before the adults fully registered that Shiva had stopped speaking.

WHEN WE WERE INFANTS, Shiva was considered the more delicate: it was his skull that Stone attempted to crush before Hema saved us. But then Shiva hit all his developmental milestones on time, lifting his head when I did and crawling when it was time to crawl. He said "Amma" and "Ghosh" on cue, and we both decided to walk when we were a month shy of one year of age. Hema and Ghosh were reassured. According to

Hema, we forgot how to walk within a few days of taking our first steps, because we had discovered how to run. Shiva spoke as much as he needed to well into his fourth year, but about that time he began to quietly hoard his words.

I hasten to say, Shiva laughed or cried at the appropriate times; he often acted as if he were about to say something just when I piped in; he punctuated my words with exclamations from his anklet and he sang *la-la-la* lustily with me in the bath. But when it came to actual words— he had no need for them. He read fluently, but refused to do so aloud. He could add and subtract big numbers at a glance, scribbling out the answer while I was still carrying the one over and counting fingers. He was constantly jotting notes to himself, or to others, leaving these around like droppings. He drew beautifully, but in the oddest places, like on cardboard cartons or the back of paper bags. What he loved to draw best at that stage was Veronica. We had an issue of Archie comics in the house—I bought it from Papadakis's bookstore; the three frames on page sixteen had to do with Veronica and Betty. Shiva could reproduce that page, complete with balloons, lettering, and crosshatch shading. It was as if he had a photograph stored in his head and could spill it onto paper whenever he wanted. He left nothing out, not even the page number, or the stain of the fly that had met its death on the margin of the original. I noticed that he always accentuated the curved line under Veronica's breast, particularly when compared with Betty's. I checked the source, and sure enough, the line was there, but Shiva's was thicker, darker. Sometimes he improvised and departed from the original image, rendering the breasts as pointed missiles about to launch, or else as pendulous balloons that hovered over the kneecaps.

Genet and I covered for Shiva's silence. I did it unconsciously; if I was talkative to excess, it was because I saw this as the necessary output for ShivaMarion. Of course, *I* had no problem communicating with Shiva. In the early morning, the shake of his anklet—*ching-ding*—said, *Marion, are you awake? Dish-ching* was *Time to get up.* Rubbing his skull on mine said, *Rise and shine, sleepyhead.* All one of us had to do was *think* of an action and the odds were the other would rise to carry it out.

It was Mrs. Garretty at school who made the discovery about Shiva's having given up speech. The Loomis Town & Country School catered to the merchants, diplomats, military advisers, doctors, teachers, representatives of the Economic Commission for Africa, WHO, UNESCO, Red Cross, UNICEF, and especially the newly forming OAU—the Organization of African Unity. The Emperor had offered the gift of Africa Hall, a stunning building, to the fledging OAU, a cunning move that would bring the organization's headquarters to Addis Ababa and already was boosting business for everyone from the bar girls to the Fiat, Peugeot, and Mercedes importers. The OAU kids could have gone to the Lycée Gebremariam, an imposing building that loomed over the steepest part of Churchill Road. But the envoys from the Francophone countries—Mali, Guinea, Cameroon, Ivory Coast, Senegal, Mauritius, and Madagascar—had an eye to the future, and so the cars with the Corps Diplomatiques plates carried *les enfants* past the lycée to Loomis Town & Country. For completeness, I must mention St. Joseph's, where, according to Matron, the Jesuits, those foot soldiers of Christ, believed in God and the Rod. But St. Joseph's was boys only, which ruled it out for us because of Genet.

Why not the rough-and-tumble of the government schools? If we'd gone there we might have been the only non-native children, and we would have been in a minority of kids with more than one pair of shoes and a home with running water and indoor plumbing. Hema and Ghosh felt their only choice was to send us to Loomis Town & Country, which was run by British expats.

Our teachers at LT&C had their A levels and the odd teaching certificate. It is astonishing how a black crepe robe worn over a coat or a blouse gives a Cockney punter or a Covent Garden flower girl the gravitas of an Oxford don. Accent be damned in Africa, as long as it's foreign and you have the right skin color.

Ritual. That was the balm to soothe the parents' disquiet about what they were getting for their money at LT&C. Gymkhana, Track and Field Day, the School Carnival, the Christmas Pageant, the School Play, Guy Fawkes Night, Founder's Day, and Graduation—we carried so many mimeographed notices home that they made Hema's head spin. We were assigned to Monday House, or Tuesday House, or Wednesday House, each with its colors, teams, and house masters. On Track and Field Day we competed for the glory of our house and for the Loomis Cup. Every morning in Assembly Hall, Mr. Loomis led us in Assembly Prayer, then a reading from the Revised Standard Version, and then we belted out the hymn from the blue hymnal while one teacher or another banged out the chords on the assembly piano.

I am convinced that one can buy in Harrods of London a kit that allows an enterprising Englishman to create a British school anywhere in the third world. It comes with black robes, preprinted report cards for

Michaelmas, Lent, and Easter terms, as well as hymnals, Prefect Badges, and a syllabus. *Assembly required.*

Unfortunately, the LT&C students' pass rates for the General Certificate of Education O levels were terrible when compared with the free government schools. There the Indian teachers were all degree holders whom the Emperor hired from the Christian state of Kerala, the place Sister Mary Joseph Praise hailed from. Ask an Ethiopian abroad if perchance they learned mathematics or physics from a teacher named Kurien, Koshy, Thomas, George, Varugese, Ninan, Mathews, Jacob, Judas, Chandy, Eapen, Pathros, or Paulos, and the odds are their eyes will light up. These teachers were brought up in the Orthodox ritual which St. Thomas carried to south India. But in their professional roles, the only ritual they cared about was engraving the multiplication and periodic tables as well as Newton's laws into the brains of their Ethiopian pupils, who were uniformly smart and who had a great aptitude for arithmetic.

My class teacher, Mrs. Garretty, called Hema and Ghosh at the end of a day when I stayed home from school with a fever. She knew us as the adorable Stone twins, those darling, dark-haired, light-eyed boys who dressed alike, who happily sang, ran, drew, jumped, clapped, and chattered to excess in her class. The day I stayed home, Shiva ran, drew, jumped, and clapped but never uttered a word and, when called on, would not or could not.

Hema went from disbelieving to blaming Mrs. Garretty. Then she blamed herself. She canceled the dancing lessons at Juventus Club, just when Ghosh had mastered the fox-trot and could circumnavigate a room. The turntable got its first rest in years. The bridge regulars shifted to Ghosh's old bungalow, which he had been using as an office and clinic for private patients.

Hema checked out Kipling, Ruskin, C. S. Lewis, Edgar Allan Poe, R. K. Narayan, and many others from the British Council and the United States Information Service libraries. In the evenings, the two of them took turns reading to us in the belief that great literature would stimulate and eventually produce speech in Shiva. In those pretelevision days, it was entertaining, except for C. S. Lewis, whose magical cupboards I didn't buy, and Ruskin, who neither Ghosh nor Hema could understand or read for long. But they persisted, hoping that at the very least Shiva might yell for them to stop, the way I did. They kept on even after we'd fallen sleep, because Hema believed one could prime the subconscious. If they had worried over Shiva's survival after birth, now they worried over lingering effects of the antiquated obstetric instruments that had been applied to his head. There was nothing they would not try to bring about speech.

Shiva remained silent.

ONE DAY, soon after we turned eight, we got home from school to find Hema had a blackboard installed in the dining room. She stood there, chalk at the ready, copies of *Bickham's Penmanship Made Easy (Young Clerks Assistant)* at each of our places, and a maniacal gleam in her eyes. On top of each book was a shiny new Pelikan pen, the Pelicano, every schoolkid's dream, along with cartridges—such a novelty.

A time would come when I would be glad to be known as a surgeon with good handwriting. My notes in the chart perhaps gave some intimation of similar skills with a knife (though I will say it is not a rule, and the converse isn't true: chicken-scratch scribbles aren't a sign of poor technique in the theater). One day I would grudgingly thank Hema for making us copy in the round and ornate styles:

> *Knowledge shall be promoted by frequent exercise*
> *Art polishes and improves nature*
> *Fortune is a fair but fickle mistress*
> *Yesterday misspent can't be recall'd*
> *Vanity makes beauty contemptible*
> *Wisdom is more valuable than riches.*

Shiva was already fingering his Pelicano. Genet said nothing. Her position in these matters was delicate.

I stood firm. I didn't trust Hema's motivation: guilt leads to righteous action, but rarely is it the *right* action. Besides, I had planned a special parade of my Dinky Toys in a weaving path I had carved out on a low embankment next to the house. Her timing was terrible.

"Why can't we go out and play? I don't want to do this," I said.

Hema's mouth tightened. She seemed to be considering not *what* I said, but my person, my obstinacy. Subconsciously, at least, she blamed me for Shiva. She saw me and even Genet as having camouflaged his silence in a blanket of chatter.

"Speak for yourself, Marion," she said.

"I did. Why can't we—I—go play?"

Shiva already had his cartridge loaded.

"Why? I'll tell you why. Because your school is nothing but play. *I* have to see to your *real* studies. Now, sit down, Marion!"

Genet quietly took her seat.

"No," I said. "This isn't fair. Besides, it won't help Shiva."

"Marion, before I twist your ear—"

"He won't speak till he is ready!" I shouted.

With that, I dashed out. I flew around one the corner of the house, gathering speed on the turn. At the second corner, I ran straight into Zemui's broad chest. My first thought was Hema had sent the military to get me.

"Cousin, where is the war?" Zemui said, smiling, peeling me free. His olive uniform was as crisp as ever, the belt, holster, and boots all brown and gleaming. As a reflex, he stomped his right foot and snapped a salute with enough vigor for his fingers to sail off.

Sergeant Zemui was the driver to a man who was now full colonel in the Imperial Bodyguard—Colonel Mebratu. Ghosh had saved his life in surgery years before. Colonel Mebratu was once under suspicion, but now he was in the Emperor's favor. He was both senior commander of the Imperial Bodyguard and liaison to the military attachés from Britain, India, Belgium, and America, all of whom had a presence in Ethiopia. The Colonel's job involved frequent diplomatic receptions and parties, not to mention the regular bridge nights at our place. Poor Zemui could only begin his long walk home to his wife and children when his boss's head was on the pillow and the staff car parked in the shed. The Colonel had assigned Zemui a motorcycle to make it easier for him to get back and forth. Since Zemui, who lived near Missing, didn't want to ruin his tires on the crude stone and shingle track that led to his shack, he got Ghosh's permission to park the bike under our carport. There his precious machine was sheltered from the elements and from vandals.

"Just the person I was hoping to see," Zemui said. "What's the matter, my little master?"

"Nothing," I said, suddenly embarrassed. My troubles seemed minor when talking to a soldier who'd just done his tour with the UN peacekeeping forces in the civil war in the Congo. "How come you're picking up your motorcycle so late?" I asked.

"The boss was at a party till four in the morning. When I got him home, the sun was coming up. He told me I could come back in the evening. Listen, come, sit down. I want you to read me this letter again."

He parked himself on the edge of the front porch, took the blue-and-red aerogram from his front pocket, and handed it to me. He took off his pith helmet to extract a half-smoked cigarette tucked carefully under one of the straps on the outside. The pith topee, in the manner of white explorers of old, was unique to the Imperial Bodyguard, recognizable at a distance.

"Zemui," I said, "can I read it later? Hema is after me. I talked back to her. She'll cut off my tongue if she catches me."

"Oh, that's serious. Of course we can do it later," Zemui said, springing up. He put the letter away, but I could sense his disappointment. "Do you think Darwin got my letter by now?"

"I am sure his letter is coming. Any day."

He saluted me and went on to the back of the house.

Darwin was a Canadian soldier who'd been wounded in Katanga; I'd read his letter to Zemui so often I knew it by heart. He said it was cold and snowing in Toronto. At times he was discouraged and he didn't know if he could ever get used to a wooden leg. "Are there women in Eytopia intrusted in a one-leg white man with a scard face? Ha-ha!" He did not have much, but if his pal Zemui ever needed anything, he, Darwin, would do it because he'd never forget how Zemui saved his life. I'd written back in English for Zemui, translating as best I could. I wondered how the two had conversed in the Congo. Zemui showed me a pinwheel gold pendant which he wore around his neck, a St. Bridget's cross. The wounded Darwin had pressed it on Zemui when they parted on the battlefield.

The sight of Rosina, peering back at me as Zemui walked toward her, made me start running again. I felt a vacuum where my brother should have been running next to me.

MY MOTHER'S GRAVE, with its halo of fresh cut apothecary blooms and its inscription of ΣAFE IN APMΣ OF JEΣUΣ, held no fascination for me. But in the autoclave room next to Operating Theater 3, I sensed her presence, a scent, a feel so linked to mine. That was where my feet took me. It wasn't the smartest choice as a place to hide.

I never understood Shiva's reluctance to visit this room. Perhaps he saw it as a betrayal of Hema, who had watched over his every breath, who had linked herself by a cord to his anklet. Coming here was one of the few things I did alone.

Seated in my mother's chair, the scent of Cuticura in the cardigan, I spoke to her, or perhaps I spoke to myself. I complained about injustice at home; I confessed my worst fear: that Hema and Ghosh might one day disappear, just as Stone and Sister were no longer in our lives. It was one reason I loitered around Missing's front gate—who was to say Thomas Stone might not come back? My fantasy was that on a sunny morning when the air was so crisp that you could hear it crackle, Gebrew would open Missing's gates, and instead of the stampede of patients, Thomas Stone would be standing there. The fact that I had no idea what he looked like, or what my mother looked like, was inconsequential to this fantasy. His eyes would fall on me. After a few seconds he would smile with pride.

I needed to believe that.

I RETURNED TO OUR BUNGALOW to face the music. There was music, all right, and the sight of Hema leading Genet and Shiva in dance. All three of them wore dance anklets, not Shiva's usual kind, but big leather thongs with four concentric rings of brass bells. They had moved the dining table against the wall. Indian classical music with a snappy tabla beat marked time. Hema had tucked her sari so that one loop ran between her legs, creating what looked like pantaloons. She'd taught Shiva and Genet a complex series of steps and poses in the time I'd been out. Arms in, arms out, arms together, pointing, dipping, drawing a bow, firing an imaginary arrow, the eyes looking this way and that, the feet sliding, a cymbal clash of anklets every time their heels thumped the floor. It hurt me to see this.

Shiva, Genet, and I had entered the world almost in unison. (Genet was a half step behind and a womb across from us, but she'd caught up.) As toddlers, we had freely traded milk bottles and pacifiers, much to Hema's dismay. Shiva's propensity to jump into buckets, puddles, or ditches full of water terrified the adults, who feared he'd drown. To keep him from deeper water, Matron purchased a Jolly Baby wading pool. Here the three of us splashed naked and posed for pictures that would embarrass us one day. Our first circus, our first matinee, our first dead body—we arrived at these milestones together. In our tree house, we'd picked at scabs until we found red, and then we took a blood oath that we Three Missketeers would stand together and admit no other.

Now, we'd arrived at another first: a separation. I stood outside, looking in. Hema beckoned me to join. She was no longer angry. Her forehead glinted with perspiration, strands of hair stuck to her cheeks. If she planned to punish me, perhaps she saw in my expression that it had already happened.

Genet, with an anklet, looked more feminine, more like a girl than the tomboy I knew. I never gave much thought to that sort of thing. In the games we played, she was like any boy. Now, as she danced, she was a step off, struggling; despite that she was graceful, extraordinarily so, as if the anklet had unlocked this quality in her. Even when she missed her cue, or bungled the turn, suddenly she was—and I couldn't help but notice—all girl.

My twin had no miscues. He'd learned the dance in a flash, I could see. He had a way of holding his chin high as if fearful that otherwise the curls he balanced on his head would slide off, and it made him seem taller, more upright than me. That mannerism of his was exaggerated in the dance. When Shiva was excited, his irises turned from brown to blue, and they were that way now as his heels hit the floor in unison with Hema's, and he matched her every dip and flourish. It was as if his anklet moved him, and that in copying the sound of Hema's anklets, the requisite movement of his body came about. I studied this lean, supple creature as if seeing him for the first time.

My brother who could draw anything from memory, who could juggle huge numbers in his head with ease, had now found a new vehicle for locomotion and a new language for his will to express itself, separate from me. I didn't want to join in. I was certain that I would look clumsy. I felt envious, almost as if I were a handicapped child, unable rather than unwilling to participate.

"Traitor," I said to Shiva, under my breath.

But he heard me; there was nothing wrong with his ears and he'd have known what I said even if I had said it only to myself.

My twin brother, my skull mate, this little dancing god skated away, averting his eyes.

CHAPTER 19

Giving Dogs Their Due

THE WEEK BEFORE Shiva gave up his anklet, we were all driving
into town when a motorcycle, siren wailing, went tearing by,
waving us off the street.

"All right, all right," Ghosh said, pulling to the side. "His Imperial
Majesty, Haile Selassie the First, Lion of Judah, needs the road."

We piled out onto Menelik II Avenue. Down the hill was Africa
Hall, which looked like a watercolor box standing on its side. Its pastel
panels were meant to mimic the colorful hems of the traditional *shama*.
Outside the new headquarters for the Organization for African Unity,
the flag of every country on the continent had its spot. The building
in its short existence had already been graced by the likes of Nasser,
Nkrumah, Obote, and Tubman.

The Emperor's Jubilee Palace was on the other side of the avenue. I
could see the mounted Imperial Bodyguard sentries, one on each side of
the palace gate. The Emperor's residence rose behind the lavish gardens
like a pale hallucination of Buckingham Palace. At night, the floodlit
building glowed ivory. Since it was that time of year, one of the pines in
the compound was strung with lights and became a giant Christmas
tree.

Pedestrians, gharries, cars—everything came to a stop. A barefoot
man with milky eyes took off his tattered hat to reveal a ring of curly gray
hairs. Three women in the black cloth of mourning, umbrellas over their
heads, also waited next to us. They were sweating from the effort of
walking uphill. One of these ladies sat on the curb. She eased off her
plastic shoe. Two young men stood back from the curb, looking dis-
pleased at having to interrupt their walk.

The seated woman said, "Maybe His Highness will give us a lift. Tell
him we can't afford the bus. My feet are killing me."

The old man glared, his lips moving as if working up the spittle to chastise her for such blasphemy.

Now a green Volkswagen with a siren and loudspeaker on top sped by. I never thought a Volkswagen could go that fast.

"I bet you His Majesty is in the new Lincoln," I said to Ghosh.

"The odds are against you."

It was 1963, the year Kennedy was assassinated. According to a schoolmate whose father was a member of Parliament, the Lincoln was President Kennedy's used car, but not the one in which he'd been shot. This one was covered and was spectacular, not for its curves but for its impossible length. A joke had circulated in town that for the Emperor to get from the Old Palace on top of the hill, where he conducted his official business, down to the Jubilee Palace, all he had to do was climb into the backseat and come out of the front.

Of the twenty-six cars at His Majesty's disposal, twenty were Rolls-Royces. One was a Christmas present from the Queen of England. I tried to imagine what else was under a monarch's Christmas tree.

A LAND ROVER PASSED BY—Imperial Bodyguard, not police—moving slowly, its tailgate open, men with machine guns across their thighs looking out. We heard a rumble that sounded like war drums; a phalanx of eight motorcycles emerged out of the ether, two abreast, the air shimmering around the engine's fins. The sun glinted off chrome headlights and crash bars. Despite their black uniforms, white helmets, and gloves, the riders reminded me of the wide-eyed, monkey-maned warriors who came out of the hills on horseback on the anniversary of Mussolini's fall, looking mean and hungry to kill again.

The ground shook as the Ducatis slid past, huge reserves of horsepower ready to be unleashed with a turn of the wrist.

His Majesty's green Rolls-Royce was polished to a mirrorlike finish. On a built-up seat, His Majesty looked out of windows specially constructed for monarchs to view and be viewed. In the wake of the motorcycles his car was all but silent save for a faint wheeze from the valves.

Ghosh muttered, "For the price of that, we could feed every child in the empire for a month."

The old man next to us was on his knees, and then as the Rolls reached us he kissed the asphalt.

I saw the Emperor clear as day, his little dog Lulu on his lap. The

Emperor looked directly at us, smiling as we bowed. He brought the palms of his hands together. Then he was past.

"Did you see that?" Hema said, excited. "Did you see the *namaste*?"

"In honor of you," Ghosh said. "He knows who you are."

"Don't be silly. It was the sari. Still, how sweet!"

"Is that all it takes to sway you? One *namaste*?"

"Stop it, Ghosh. I don't get involved in politics. I like the old man."

The Rolls turned toward the palace gate. The motorcyclists and the Land Rover pulled up just beyond the gate. The two guards on horseback, resplendent in their green trousers, white jackets, and white pith helmets, presented arms.

A lone policeman held back the usual cluster of petitioners who waited on one side of the gate. An old woman waving her paper must have caught the Emperor's eye. The Rolls stopped. I could see the little Chihuahua, its paws on the window and its head snapping back and forth: Lulu was barking. The old woman, bowing, thrust her paper to the window with both hands.

She seemed to be speaking. The Emperor was evidently listening. The old woman became more animated, gesturing with her hands, her body rocking, and now we could hear her clearly.

The car moved on, but the old lady wasn't done. She tried to run with the Rolls, fingers on the window. When she couldn't keep up, she yelled, *"Leba, leba"*—"Thief, thief." She looked around for a stone, finding none, took off her shoe and bounced it off the trunk before anyone could react.

I saw only the rise of the policeman's club and then she was slumped on the ground, like a sack. The palace gates swung shut. The motorcycle riders ran forward and began clubbing anyone near the gate, ignoring their shrieks. The old woman, motionless, nevertheless got a vicious kick to her ribs. The mounted sentries stared straight ahead, their mounts disciplined and still, only the horses' skin twitching.

We stood stunned. The two young men behind us snickered, and walked quickly away.

The woman next to us, her hands on her head, said, "How could they do that to a grandmother?" The old man, hat in hand, said nothing, but I could see he was shaken.

As we drove away, I saw the motorcycle riders had turned on the policeman, giving him a good thrashing. His mistake was not clubbing the old woman down before she opened her mouth and embarrassed them all.

. . .

THESE MANY YEARS LATER, even though I have witnessed so much violence, that image remains vivid. The unexpected clubbing of the old woman, seconds after the Emperor had greeted us so warmly, felt like a betrayal, and with it came the shock of knowing Hema and Ghosh were powerless to help.

In my mind, that bug-eyed Chihuahua was a party to the cruelty. She was the only creature permitted to walk before His Majesty. She ate and slept better than most of his subjects. From that day forth I had a new perception of the Emperor, and of Lulu. And I definitely didn't like that overweened dog.

IF LULU WAS THE CANINE Empress of Ethiopia, our Koochooloo and the two nameless dogs were the peasantry. A Persian dentist who'd worked briefly at Missing christened her "Koochooloo." To name a dog in Ethiopia is to save it. Missing's two nameless dogs had mangy coats that were so mud- and tar-stained that one could not be sure of the original color. During the long rains, when all other dogs sought shelter, these two stayed out rather than risk a boot to the head. It was quite possible that they were in fact a succession of nameless dogs who happened to visit in twos.

Sister Mary Joseph Praise fed Koochooloo when the Persian dentist disappeared. After her death, Almaz took over.

Koochooloo's eyes were expressive dark pearls. They hinted at a playfulness, a mischievousness, that life's disappointments hadn't quite snuffed out. Dogs aren't supposed to have eyebrows, I know, but I swear she had folds that could move independently. They conveyed apprehension, amusement, and even a befuddled look that reminded me of Stan of Laurel and Hardy fame—we saw their films at Cinema Adowa. There was no question of Koochooloo coming into our house. Cows were sacred; dogs were not.

We didn't know Koochooloo was pregnant until the day after New Year's. We hadn't seen her for two days and then, just before we left for school, we found her behind the woodpile in a crawl space. Our flashlight revealed her utter exhaustion. She could barely lift her head. The fur balls wriggling at her belly explained everything.

We ran to Hema and Ghosh and then to Matron to tell them the exciting news. We thought up names. In retrospect, the adults' lack of excitement should have warned us.

OUR TAXI DROPPED US at Missing's front gate after school. We had just crested the hill when we saw it, though at first we had no idea what we were seeing. The pups were in a large plastic bag whose mouth was tied with cord to the exhaust pipe of a taxi. We found out later that the driver had seen Gebrew making off with the litter, and he'd proposed a less messy means of getting rid of the pups than drowning them. Gebrew, always in awe of machinery, was too easily convinced.

Under our eyes the cabbie fired his engine, the bag ballooned out, and in a few seconds, the car stalled. Koochooloo, who that morning could hardly walk, tore around the wheels of the car, nipping at the smoke-filled bag. Inside it, her puppies, their snouts overblown when they pressed against the plastic, tumbled over one another looking for an exit. Koochooloo's expression was beyond grief. She was crazed and desperate. Patients and passersby found it entertaining. A small crowd had gathered.

I was numb, disbelieving. Was this some necessary ritual in the raising of puppies which I didn't know about? I took my cues from the adults standing around—that was a mistake. But inside, I felt just like Koochooloo.

Shiva took his cues from no one. He ran to the car and tried to untie the plastic bag from the exhaust pipe, burning his palms in the process. Then he was on his knees, ripping at the thick bag. Gebrew pulled him away, kicking and fighting. Only when Shiva saw that the puppies were quite still, a hillock of fur, only then did he stop.

I glanced at Genet and was shocked by her deadpan expression: it said she was well aware of the undercurrents of the world we lived in and had known well before us. Nothing surprised her.

How Koochooloo could forgive us and live on at Missing, I never understood. She knew nothing of Matron's quotas and edicts for Missing dogs. Just as we didn't know that several times in the past, Gebrew, under orders, had plucked Koochooloo's newborns from her teats and drowned them.

SHIVA HAD SCRAPED HIS KNEES and blistered his hands. Hema, Ghosh, and Matron rushed to meet us in Casualty.

Ghosh put Silvadene on Shiva's burns and dressed his knees. The grown-ups had nothing to say about the pups.

"Why did you let Gebrew do that?" I said. Ghosh didn't look up from the dressings. He was incapable of lying to us, but in this case he'd withheld knowledge of what would happen.

"Don't blame Gebrew," Matron said. "They were my instructions. I'm sorry. We just can't have packs of dogs roaming around Missing."

This didn't sound like an apology.

"Koochooloo will forget," Hema said soothingly. "Animals don't have that kind of memory, my loves."

"Will *you* forget if someone kills me or Marion?"

The adults looked at me. But I hadn't spoken. Moreover, I was a good eight feet away from where Shiva was getting bandaged. His irises had gone from brown to a steely blue, his pupils down to pinpoints, his chin thrust higher than ever, exposing his neck so that he was sighting down his nose at a world populated by people for whom he seemed to have the greatest disdain.

Will you *forget if someone kills me or Marion?*

Those words were formed in the voice box, shaped by the lips and tongue, of my heretofore silent brother. For his first spoken words in years, he'd crafted a sentence none of us would forget.

The adults looked at Shiva and then at me. I shook my head and pointed to Shiva.

Finally, Hema whispered, "Shiva . . . what did you say?"

"Will you forget about us tomorrow if someone kills us today?"

Hema reached for Shiva, wanting to hug him, tears of joy in her eyes. But Shiva drew back from her, drew back from all of them, as if they were murderers. He bent down, rolled down his sock, and snapped off the anklet, placing it on the table. That anklet had *never* come off except to be repaired, enlarged, and three or four times replaced by a new one. It was as if he'd cut off a finger and laid it on the table.

"Shiva," Matron said at last, "if we let Koochooloo have her litters, we'd have about sixty dogs around Missing by now."

"What happened to the other puppies?" Shiva asked, before I could.

Matron mumbled something about Gebrew having disposed of them humanely and that the car exhaust was ill-advised and not sanctioned, and Gebrew should have done it well before we came back from school. I was in step with him now.

Shiva touched my shoulder, and whispered in my ear.

"What did he say?" Hema asked.

"He said, when you all are so cruel, why should he speak? He says he doesn't think Sister Mary Joseph Praise or Thomas Stone would have done something like this. Maybe if they were here this would never have happened."

Hema sighed, as if she'd been waiting for one of us to bring their names up in just this way. "Darling," she said, in a voice like gravel, "you have no idea what they might do."

Shiva walked out. Ghosh and Matron had the stunned expression of people who had seen a ghost. Now they were the ones who were mute. How, I wondered, could these adults who cared so much whether my brother spoke or not, who cared for the poor, the sick, the motherless, who were as bothered as we were by the cruelty to the old woman outside the palace, be so indifferent to the cruelty we had witnessed?

I asked Matron later if she thought that the death of her pups left scars on Koochooloo's insides. Matron said she didn't know, but she did know that Missing couldn't afford to breed dogs, and three was the limit. And no, she didn't think there was a separate dog heaven, and frankly she did not know God's opinion on what was the right number of dogs for Missing, but He had given her some discretion on this matter and that was not something she wanted to debate with me.

AFTER THE KILLINGS, I saw in Koochooloo's eyes her disappointment in us as a race. She sought out places where she could curl up and not run into humans. We left food out for her, and if she ate, it was not when we were around.

For weeks, there was only one person for whom she would attempt to wag her tail, and that was Shiva.

When Shiva learned to dance Bharatnatyam (and became Hema's *sishya* and she was already talking about his *arangetram*—his debut), I first began to see him as separate from me. Now that he would talk and could express himself, ShivaMarion didn't always move or speak as one. In earlier years, our differences had complemented each other. But in the days after the death of the pups, I felt our identities slowly separating. My brother, my identical twin, was tuned to the distress of animals. As for the affairs of humans, for now at least, he was to leave that to me.

CHAPTER 20

Blind Man's Buff

M R. LOOMIS, headmaster of Loomis Town & Country, saw to it that our long holidays coincided with the long rains. That way, he could be in England in July and August, relaxing, spending our school fees, while we were stuck in Addis Ababa. Old hands in Addis referred to the monsoon months as "winter," which hopelessly confused new arrivals for whom July could only be summer.

It rained so much that it even rained in my dreams. I awoke happy that there was no school, but that incessant murmur on the tin roof immediately dampened the euphoria. This was the winter of my eleventh year, and when I went to bed at night, I prayed that the skies should open up on Mr. Loomis wherever he was, be it Brighton or Bournemouth. I hoped that a personal thundercloud trailed him every minute of that day.

SHIVA WAS UNAFFECTED BY COLD, fog, mist, or wetness, while I became morose and pessimistic. Outside our window, there was now a brown lake dotted with atolls of red mud. I lost faith that a lawn and flower bed could ever reappear out of that.

On Wednesdays Hema took us to the British Council and USIS libraries, where we returned books, checked out a new pile, loaded them in the car, then she dropped us off at the Empire Theater or Cinema Adowa for the matinee. We were free to read whatever we wanted, but Hema required of us a half-page journal entry to record new words we learned and the number of pages we had read. We were also to copy out a memorable idea or sentence to share at dinner.

I resented this winter curriculum, but it did bring Captain Horatio Hornblower sailing into my life. Matron, whose ability to read my soul I did not yet fully appreciate, asked me to borrow *A Ship of the Line* for her. I opened it out of curiosity and found I had sailed into a world more damp and wretched than my own, and strangely, I was happy to be there. Thanks to C. S. Forester, I was on a creaking ship on the other side of the world and in the head of Horatio Hornblower, a man who was like Ghosh and Hema—heroic in his professional role. But he was also like me—"unhappy and lonely." Of course, I wasn't *really* unhappy or lonely, but in the monsoon season it seemed necessary to think of myself that way. The unfairness of the Admiralty in London, the irony of Hornblower's seasickness, the tragedy of his returning from a long voyage to find his children mortally ill with smallpox . . . I had my equivalents, trivial as they were, for all these perils.

After hours of reading, I itched to be outdoors; I know Genet did, too. Shiva sketched and scribbled. Hema's calligraphy exercises catalyzed an unstoppable ink flow in Shiva's pen, but his medium was still paper bags, napkins, and end pages of books. He loved to sketch Zemui's BMW and had done so in every season. Veronica, if he drew her, now straddled a motorcycle.

On a Friday, after Ghosh and Hema left for work, the rain came down harder and there was now thunder and hail. The noise on the roof was deafening. I peeked out of the kitchen door and was met by the scent of sopping hide, and the sight of three donkeys sheltering under the roof overhang along with their overseer. If the wood the donkeys delivered was anywhere as wet as they were, it did not bode well for our stove. The animals stood still, resigned to their fate, half asleep, their skin twitching involuntarily.

When I went back to the living room, Genet yelled above the racket, *"Let's play blind man's buff!"*

"Sissy game," I said. "Stupid girls' game." But she was already hunting for a blindfold.

I never understood why blind man's buff was so popular at school, particularly in Genet's class. I'd seen the mob dancing just out of reach of "it," pushing or "buffing" the blind man till he (or she) captured a tormentor. The blind man had to name the captive or set the person free.

We modified the game for indoors: no buffing of the blind man. Instead, you hid by standing silent (though with the din on the roof you could be whistling and it wouldn't matter). You could hide anywhere but the kitchen, and not under or behind a barrier. Time was the object of the game: how fast could the blind man find the other two.

THAT MORNING, Genet went first. It took her fifteen minutes to find Shiva, and ten more to get me.

You would think after twenty-five minutes of standing there I would be bored. I wasn't. I was intrigued.

It took discipline to stand stock-still. I felt like the Invisible Man, one of my favorite comic book characters. The Invisible Man stood as the world moved around him, as his archenemy tried to find him.

Blindfolded, wearing white tights, her arms reaching in front of her, putting one foot out, then the other, Genet looked helpless, as if she were walking the plank on a pirate ship. She had the upright carriage and the balance of one who could do cartwheels with an arm tucked to her side, and who could walk on her hands with more grace than Ghosh on two feet. Barrettes made of yellow and silver beads were snug around her hair, which was parted in the middle and pulled up into two stalks. Genet wasn't vain about her dress. But when it came to headbands, combs, pins, and banana clamps, she was most particular. Of course, this trait might have been more Hema's or Rosina's or Almaz's doing: they were forever brushing her hair or braiding it into ponytails or rows. Hema sometimes put kohl inside Genet's lower lid. That black line highlighted her eyes, made them catch fire and flash like mirrors.

Girls matured faster than boys, so they said, and I believed it, because Genet acted older than ten. She distrusted the world and was more argumentative and always ready for combat; if I was too willing to defer to adults and assume they knew what they were doing, she was just the opposite, quite willing to think of them as fallible. But now, blindfolded, she had a vulnerability I'd never been aware of before; all her defenses seemed to reside in the high heat of her gaze.

Twice, Genet almost walked into me—as—Invisible Man, veering off at the last second. The third time, she was millimeters away, and the Invisible Man snorted to suppress a laugh. Her hands, sweeping like windmills, found me and nearly took my eyes out.

Then things turned strange.

When I wore the blindfold, I found Genet in thirty *seconds*, and Shiva in half that time. How? I followed my nose. I had no inkling such a thing was possible. I was "seeing" through olfaction. I heeded an instinct that only made itself known when my sight was gone.

Shiva, when it was his turn, found us just as quickly. Suddenly, we forgot about the rain.

When I blindfolded Genet again, it took her even longer than the first time. Her nose was no help. For half an hour, I watched her shuffle this way and that.

Frustrated, she whipped off the blindfold and accused us of moving and of being in collusion. On both counts we were innocent.

When Ghosh came home for lunch, Genet and I rushed to tell him about our game. "Wait! Stop!" he said. "I can't hear you when you speak over each other. Genet, you first. 'Begin at the beginning and go on until you come to the end: then stop.' Who said that?"

"You did," Genet said.

"The King in *Alice in Wonderland*," Shiva said, "page ninety-three. Chapter twelve. And you missed four words and two commas."

"I certainly did not!" Ghosh said, acting offended, but unable to conceal his surprise.

"You missed 'The King said, comma, very gravely, comma.' "

"Right you are . . . ," Ghosh said. "Now, tell me what happened, Genet."

She did and then begged him to referee. Ghosh stationed Genet here and there, and each time, blindfolded and sightless, I went straight to her. We blindfolded Ghosh at his request, but he was no better than Genet. We would have further "explored the phenomenon," as Ghosh put it, but he had to return to the hospital.

GENET'S FOREHEAD STAYED FURROWED all afternoon, her eyebrows meeting in a *V*. I felt the venom of her gaze on my face.

"What are you looking at?" she said.

"Is it against the law to look?"

"Yes."

I stuck my tongue out. She flew out of her chair and came at me. I expected that. We tumbled to the floor. I soon pinned her flat on her back, her arms above her head, straddling her, but it was far from an easy task.

"Get off me."

"Why? So you can have another shot?"

"Get off, I said."

"I will. But if you start again, I will do this." I dug my knee under her armpit and into her ribs. Her anger dissolved into screams and hysterical laughter. She begged me to stop. Knowing her and how quickly the fire could flare when you thought you had put it out, I gave her another dose to make sure. When I stepped off, I did not turn my back on her.

Genet could sprint faster than Shiva but could not quite beat me over a short distance. Her gait was so effortless, her feet barely touching the ground, that she could run all day. I wouldn't race her over anything longer than fifty yards. Climbing trees, playing soccer, wrestling, or sword fighting—in all these she was just about our equal.

But blind man's buff had found a difference.

DURING DINNER with Hema and Ghosh, Genet was quiet. The yellow and silver barrettes had given way to a vicious claw clamp and a knitting needle going across. When Hema asked, she reported on her Secret Seven book. She sat next to me and Shiva, fending off Almaz and Rosina, who bustled around, trying to add to our plates. The two of them always ate later in the kitchen.

After dinner, Genet said her good nights and retreated to Rosina's quarters behind our bungalow. I found Ghosh hunting through *Alice in Wonderland*. I looked over his shoulder as he found page ninety-three. Shiva was right, down to the two commas.

The rain stopped when we got into bed, precisely when it was too late to take advantage of the lull. The silence was both a relief and nerve-racking, because at any moment it would start back up.

Hema read to us in our bedroom, a nightly ritual that she had never interrupted once she began it in response to Shiva's silence. R. K. Narayan's *Man-eater of Malgudi* was our text the last few days. Ghosh sat on the other side of our bed, head bowed, listening. The book had started slowly and it had yet to pick up any pace. But perhaps that was the point. As we adjusted to the slow, the "boring" world of village India, it revealed itself to be interesting and even funny. Malgudi was populated by characters that resembled people we knew, imprisoned by habit, by profession, and by a most foolish and unreasonable belief that enslaved them; only they couldn't see it.

The sound of the phone ringing was foreign to Malgudi and it broke the thread of the story. Ghosh picked up the receiver. "Right away," he said, gazing at Hema. When he hung up he said, "Princess Turunesh is in labor. Six centimeters. Pains five minutes apart. Matron is with her in the private room."

"What does that mean, 'six centimeters'?" I asked.

Ghosh was about to answer, but Hema, already at the dresser, brushing her hair, said quickly, "Nothing, sweetie. The princess will have a baby soon. I have to go."

"I'll come with you," Ghosh said. He could assist if Hema opted for a Cesarean section.

I NEVER LIKED IT when they left at night. My dread wasn't intruders, but an anxiety about Hema and Ghosh, a fear that despite their best intentions, they might not come back. I never felt that way in the daytime. But at night, when they went dancing at Juventus or played bridge at Mrs. Reddy and Evangeline's house, I'd wait up for them, imagining the worst.

After they left, I padded into the living room in bare feet and pajamas. I worked the short-wave band on the Grundig.

Above the static, I heard the motorcycle. Halfway up our driveway, Sergeant Zemui would always cut the engine so as not to disturb us. Then in silence, save for the squeak of springs and the rattle of mudguards, he'd coast into the carport. The coda was the metallic *whump* of cycle rolling back onto its center stand.

I loved that ungainly BMW and the way its udderlike engine bulged out on either side of the frame. Shiva loved it, too. All machines have genders, and that BMW was a royal "she." For as long as I can recall I'd been hearing her low throb, a *lub-dub* sound in the early morning and at bedtime, as Zemui left for and returned from work. Whenever I heard the tramp of his heavy boots receding, I felt sorry for him. I pictured his lonely hike home, particularly during this season of mud and rain. Despite the long raincoat and a plastic hood for his pith helmet, it was impossible not to get soaked.

FIVE MINUTES LATER, I heard the kitchen door open. Genet came in wearing my hand-me-down pajamas.

Her anger from earlier wasn't there. In its place was something I rarely saw: sadness. Her hair was held back by a blue headband. She was listless, withdrawn, as if years, not minutes, had passed since I last saw her.

"Where's Shiva?" she asked, sitting across from me.

"In our room. Why?"

"Just asked. No reason."

"Hema and Ghosh had to go to the hospital," I said.

"I know. I heard them tell my mother."

"Are you all right?"

She shrugged. Her eyes looked through the glowing dial of the Grundig, to some planet beyond. There was a little fleck in the right iris, a puff of smoke around it, where a spark had penetrated. We were much younger, exploding cap-gun strips on the pavement, striking them with a heavy rock, when that happened. You could only see the blemish close up, and at certain angles. From a distance, the hint of asymmetry made her gaze seem dreamy.

A crackly Chinese station faded in and out, a woman's voice with sounds no throat should be able to produce. I thought it was funny, but Genet didn't smile.

"Marion? Will you play blind man's buff with me?" She asked in a sweet, gentle way. "Just one more time?"

I groaned.

"Please?"

The urgency in her voice surprised me. As if her future depended on this.

"Did you come back just for that reason? Shiva's already in bed."

She was silent, considering this, and then she said, "How about just you and me. Please, Marion?"

I was never good at saying no to Genet. I didn't think she would have any better luck finding me this time around than before. It would only make her more depressed. But if that was what she wanted . . .

OUTSIDE, the rain had scrubbed the sky free of stars; the black night leaked through the shutters into the house and under my blindfold.

"I've changed my mind," I said into the void.

She ignored me, tying a second knot to secure the blindfold. For good measure, she put an empty rice-flour sack over my head, rolling up the edges to leave my mouth uncovered.

"Did you hear me?" I said. "I don't want to do this, I never agreed to this."

"You cheated? You admit it?" The voice did not even sound like hers.

"I won't admit what is not true," I said.

A gust of wind rattled the windows. It was the bungalow's way of clearing its throat, warning us to cinch up for more rain.

She disappeared again, and when she returned I felt my hands being strapped against my sides with a piece of leather—Ghosh's belt. "That's so you won't remove the blindfold."

Now she grabbed me by my shoulders. She spun me around. Her

hands were paddles, slapping my chest, my shoulders, turning me like a top. When I yelled for her to stop she added a few more turns.

"Count to twenty. And don't peek."

I was still turning in that inner darkness, wondering why nausea had to be such a firm companion of vertigo. I crashed into something. A hard edge. The sofa. It caught me in the ribs, but it did keep me from falling. This wasn't fair, tying my hands, messing with my balance . . . She'd tricked me. If she wanted to disorient me, it had worked. "Cheater!" I yelled. "If you want to win so bad, just say you won, okay?"

A sharp sound on the tin roof made me jump. An acorn? I waited, but it didn't rattle down the slope. A thief checking to see if anyone was home? With my hands bound, I was doubly helpless. I sneezed. I waited for the second sneeze—they always came in twos. But not tonight. I cursed the musty sack.

"*Screw your courage to the sticking place!*" I shouted. I had no idea what that meant, but Ghosh said it a lot. It sounded vulgar and defiant, a good thing to repeat when you needed courage. My heart hammered in my chest. I needed courage.

The scent I had to follow wasn't as distinct as it had been in the morning. Not being able to reach in front of me and being saddled with a sack on my head were huge handicaps. "I'll find you," I yelled, "but then never again."

In the dining room, using my foot, I traced the sideboard, saying "Screw your courage to the sticking place" as my mantra. From there I went on down the corridor leading to the bedrooms.

I knew the spots where the narrow floorboards squeaked. There were many nights I'd stood outside Ghosh and Hema's room, listening, particularly when they seemed to be arguing. With them what you thought was a squabble could be just the opposite. I once heard Hema speak of me as "His father's son. Stubborn to a fault," and then she laughed. I was shocked. I didn't think of myself as stubborn, and I had no idea that I might be anything like the man I sometimes fantasized might come through the front gate. Hema never mentioned his name, and her tone of voice when she compared me to him suggested faint praise. Another night I overheard Hema say, "*Where? Exactly where? Under what circumstance?* Don't you think we could have looked at Sister's face, or *his* face, and known? *How did we not know?* They should have told us. Say something, Ghosh." I didn't get it. Ghosh was strangely silent.

Now, with the blindfold on, I could recall every word of theirs. Covering my eyes had opened up new channels in my memory, just as it had fired up my sense of smell. I felt I needed to ask Hema and Ghosh about this conversation. What were they talking about? But how could I? I couldn't tell them I'd been eavesdropping.

MY NOSE LED ME TO our bedroom. I turned in. I inched forward. I came to where the scent peaked. I was up against the dresser. Bending forward, my face touched flannel. Her pajamas. She'd piled them on top of my dresser. Like a tracker dog, I buried my nose in the cloth, shook my face in flannel and scattered the pajamas, sharpening my instrument.

"Very clever," I said. I knew Shiva was on his bed. He must have strapped on his big dancing anklet, because it sounded now, a noise that was his equivalent of a noncommittal grunt.

I retraced my steps. The kitchen was supposed to be off-limits, but that is where the trail led. But here, the scents of ginger, onions, cardamom, and cloves were like curtains that I had to claw through.

On an impulse, I knelt and put my nose to the tiles. What chance did bipedal man have, nose high up in the air, against a four-legged tracker whose nose was to the ground? Yes, there she was. The trail veered to the right.

Inching to the pantry, I knew that this game, born out of monsoon tedium, was no longer that. No rules now. Nothing would be the same after this. I knew. I may have been just eleven, but my consciousness felt as ripe as it would ever be. My body might grow and age and I would soon have more knowledge and experience, but all that was me, all that was Marion, the part that saw and registered the world and chronicled it in an inner ledger for posterity, was well seated inside my body and never more so than at that moment, robbed of eyes and hands.

I stood up as I entered the pantry. "I know you're there," I said. The echo gave me a fix on that long narrow room; I knew just where she was and I went to her.

Genet was in front of me. If my hands were free, I would've reached for her, tickled or pinched her. I heard a muffled sound. It could have been laughter, but I didn't think so. She was crying.

I wanted to console her. The urge to do so grew. It was a feral instinct, much like the one that led me to her.

I drew forward.

She pushed me away, but halfheartedly. The push was a plea for me *not* to leave.

I'd always assumed that Genet was content with her life. She ate at our table, went to school with us, and was part of the family. She didn't have a father, and we didn't have our real parents, and I assumed that, just like us, she felt lucky to have Hema and Ghosh. I saw us as equals, but in doing so, perhaps I glossed over the things she could not overlook. Our bedroom was bigger than her narrow and drafty one-room quarters. At night, if she wanted to visit the privy, Genet had to step out into the elements, passing the open shed where we stacked firewood. While Ghosh and Hema tucked us into bed, transported us to the magical world of Malgudi, then turned off the lights, Genet read to herself under the single naked bulb, trying to tune out the radio which Rosina played late into the night. There was one bed, and mother and daughter slept in it, but Genet would probably have relished her own bed. A charcoal brazier provided warmth. The smoke and incense that permeated her clothes embarrassed her. If we found her quarters cozy, she was ashamed of where she lived. In earlier years, we were as often in that room as we were in our house. But of late, though Rosina welcomed us, Genet didn't encourage us to come in.

Blindfolded, I suddenly saw all this so clearly. I understood her fierce competitiveness in a way I'd never appreciated.

One more step forward. I waited. The push or punch did not come. I inclined my head, used it as a probe to find her. Her ear and then her cheek brushed against mine. Wet. Her jerky breathing was hot against my neck. Slowly she settled her chin there.

The feral self stood dutiful and protective. *Watch and learn,* it said to me. Defend and comfort. I felt heroic.

My feet were close together. I had tilted forward to counter her weight. When she readjusted, I fell against her, sandwiching her against the pantry shelf. Our bodies were touching at the thighs, hips, and at the chest, our cheeks still together. I waited for her to push me back to the vertical, but she didn't.

How well we knew each other's bodies from wrestling, from pulling each other up to the tree house, and from earlier years, wading in our splash pool together. In the big packing cases stuffed with straw in which glassware was shipped to Missing, we played house and doctor. We were never self-conscious about our anatomical differences. But now, blindfolded, her face invisible to me and mine obscured by cloth, it was all new and unknown. I wasn't the Invisible Man. I was the blind man who could see, who is forgiven his clumsiness by the other qualities the blindness brings out.

Though my arms were pinned to my side, I could swivel my hands forward. I touched her hips. Her skin was cold. She didn't flinch. She needed my touch, my warmth. I pulled her to me.

She trembled.

She was naked.

I don't know how many minutes I stood there. It was precisely the comfort she seemed to need this night. If only she had known to ask, or I to give, we could've done away with the blindfold . . . Thank God for the blindfold.

She worked her hands into the gap between my arms and my trunk. She hugged me. It was an awkward, painful pose for me. Yet I didn't dare say a word for fear she'd let go.

The rain murmured gently on the tin roof.

After an eternity, she withdrew her arms. She took the rice bag off my face.

She undid my restraint, freeing my hands, and I heard the belt buckle clatter to the floor. But she left the blindfold on. If I'd wanted to, I could have taken it off.

I missed her embrace. I wanted to feel it again, now that my arms were free. I reached for her. Naked, she felt smaller, more delicate.

Something soft, fleshy touched my lips. I had never been kissed before. At the movies, Genet and I groaned and laughed when we saw the actors kiss. There was always one Italian movie in the triple feature, particularly at Cinema Adowa. It was either dubbed or had subtitles. It typically came before the short comic feature—the Chaplin or Laurel and Hardy—and it always had lots of kissing. Shiva studied those on-screen smooches with great seriousness, cocking his head. Genet and I didn't. Kissing was silly. Adults had no idea how stupid they looked.

Our lips were dry. A big nothing, just as I thought. Perhaps the kissing had the same purpose as the embrace. To give and get comfort. I tilted my head to one side, movie style, wondering if the sensation would get any better. I caught her lower lip between my lips. This was a new discovery, that the mouth could be this delicate tactile instrument, particularly in the absence of sight. Her tongue touched my lips and I wanted to snap my head back. I thought of the twenty-five-cent, one-hour sucker on which the three of us took turns. Now, slowly, our two mouths shared the candy without the candy. Not really pleasurable. Not disgusting either.

Genet's hands were on my face. They did that in the movies. I slid my right hand to her shoulders, then down her chest. I felt the hillocks on which her nipples sat, no different than mine. Her fingers slid down to touch my chest, where it should have been ticklish, but it was not. My hand swept over her belly, and then down farther, between her legs, running over a soft fissure, the absence, the empty space, more intriguing than what might have been present. Her hand, tentative like mine, slipped past my waistband, prospecting. When she held me, it felt *so* different than when I touched myself.

THE DOOR FROM THE OUTSIDE to the kitchen opened.

It had to be Rosina. Or perhaps it was Ghosh and Hema. The footsteps went on into the living room.

I stepped back. I pulled off the blindfold, blinking in the dark pantry, an alien landing on earth.

In the reflected light of the kitchen, Genet's eyes were moist, her face puffy and her lips swollen. She didn't want to meet my gaze. She preferred me blind. Her eyes were slanted, her nose rising to a quick point. Her forehead planed back, not at all like Rosina's rounded one. She looked like the bust of Queen Nefertiti in my *Dawn of History* book.

My blindfold was off but I still possessed a hyperacuity of the senses. I could see the future. Genet's face in that pantry was the face that most revealed her. It carried intimations of the woman she would grow up to be. I could see how those eyes would stay serene, beautiful, concealing the kind of restlessness and recklessness so evident tonight. Her cheekbones would push out, expressing the sheer force of her will, making her nose even sharper, further elongating her lovely eyes. The lower lip would outgrow the upper, the buds on her chest turn into fruit, and her legs would grow like tall vines. In a land of beautiful people, she would be most beautiful and exotic. Men—I knew this before I should have known—would perceive her disdain and would want her. *I* would want her most of all. She'd put up obstacles. I might never be as strong for her or as close to her as I was this night. Despite this knowledge, I'd keep trying.

I knew all this. I felt it, saw it. It entered my consciousness in a flash, but the proof was yet to come.

Rosina called Genet's name from somewhere in the house.

I picked up the belt. How we could both be so serene, I'll never know. I touched Genet on her shoulders, gently, carefully. The other moment of touch was long gone. Her eyes turned to me with what could be love or its opposite.

"I will always find you," I whispered.

"Maybe," she said, bringing her lips close to my ear. "But I might get better at hiding."

Rosina walked in and stopped, frozen at the sight of us.

"What are you two doing?" she said, in Amharic. She smiled out of habit, but her brows conveyed her puzzlement. "I've been looking all over for you. Where are your clothes? What is this?"

"A game," I said waving the blindfold and belt as if it answered her questions, but my throat was so dry I don't think any noise came out.

Genet brushed past me, heading back to the living room. Rosina grabbed her hand. "Where are your clothes, daughter?"

"Let go my hand."

"But why are you naked?"

Genet said nothing, her face defiant.

Rosina jerked her by the arm. "Why did you take them off?"

When Genet replied, her voice was cutting, spoiling for a fight. "Why do *you* take your clothes off for Zemui? When you send me out, is it not for you to get naked?"

Rosina's mouth froze in the open position. When she could speak, she said, "He is your father. He's my husband."

Genet's face showed no surprise. She laughed, a cruel, mocking sound, as if she'd heard these words before. I cringed for my nanny as Genet spoke. "Your *husband*? My *father*? You lie. My father would stay the night. My father would have us live with him in a real house." She was angry, tears spilling down her cheeks. "Your husband wouldn't have another wife and three children. Your husband wouldn't come home and send me out to play so he can play with you." She pulled her arm free and went to get her clothes.

ROSINA HAD FORGOTTEN I was there.

Innocence, the carefree days, hung over a chasm. She finally turned to me.

We studied each other as if we were looking at strangers. I'd gone into the pantry sightless. Now the blindfold was off. *Zemui was Genet's father.* Was I the only one not to know this? How stupid was I? Why had I never thought to ask? Did Shiva know? All the long hours the Colonel spent with us playing bridge . . . It made sense that Zemui was also around all that time. True, in a matrilineal society, one accepted these things and didn't ask about a father when none was present. But I *should* have asked. I saw it now. The signs were there. I was blind, and naïve and dumb. All the letters I had written for Zemui to Darwin inquiring about his family and conveying best wishes from his pal had given no clue that Genet was his child. All those written words, spoken words, were just the shimmering surface of a deep and swift river; to think of the nights I lay in bed, hearing that motorcycle, feeling sorry for Zemui trudging home in the rain, in the dark. Clearly, I wasn't the only one to feel compassion for him.

Rosina knew me so well, she could read the progression of my every thought. I hung my head: I'd slipped in the esteem of my beloved nanny. Out of the corner of my eye I saw that now her head was down, too, as if she'd failed me, as if she had never wanted me to know this side of her. I wanted to say, *About what you saw, it was a game . . .*

I said nothing.

Genet returned, clothed in the flannel pajamas. She left without a backward glance, and Rosina followed.

Shiva was in the dining room, just beyond the door to the kitchen.

I stayed in the pantry after shutting the door, and I stood facing the shelves. A scent lingered, an ozone generated by me and Genet, by our two wills.

I heard footsteps draw near and stop, and I knew that Shiva was on the other side of the door, just as he knew I was on this side. ShivaMarion couldn't hide much from Shiva or Marion. But I squeezed my eyes shut and turned invisible and carried myself to a place where I was completely alone and no one could share my thoughts.

CHAPTER 21

Knowing What You
Will Hear

IN THE DAYS THAT FOLLOWED, when Rosina ran her fingers
through my curls, or insisted she iron my shirt before we went out, it
was as if nothing had happened. But I saw these acts of hers differently. They were familiar, but also designed to have a hand on me at all
times, and thereby put her body between me and her daughter.

Something *had* transpired that night in the pantry, just as Rosina
feared. I'd leaned on a hidden panel, and much like in the comics, I'd
plunged through. The falling was unintentional, but now that I was on
the other side I wanted to stay. I wanted to be around Genet more than
ever, and Rosina knew it.

I saw a new dimension to Rosina—call it cunning. The same cunning
was in me as well, because I no longer felt safe telling her what I was
thinking. But my feelings were tough to hide. When I was with Genet, I
felt the blood rushing to my face. I had forgotten how to *be*.

For the rest of the holidays, Genet gravitated to Shiva. His presence
generated no awkwardness, while mine clearly did. I watched them put
on their practice record, clear the dining room, strap on their anklets,
and run through their complex routines in Bharatnatyam. I wasn't jealous. Shiva was my proxy, just as I had been his when Almaz had given
me her breast. If I could not be with Genet, wasn't Shiva's being with her
the next-best thing?

Perhaps my bloodhound instinct, my ability to find Genet by scent,
was no more than a party trick. But perhaps not. We never played blind
man's buff again. The very idea was disquieting.

·   ·   ·

I avoided Zemui when he came to pick up or drop off his motorcycle, or when Colonel Mebratu came to play bridge. The Colonel enjoyed driving his Peugeot, or his jeep, or his staff Mercedes, and the last time Zemui spotted me, he'd been riding shotgun and he waved and grinned.

When I finally did encounter Zemui, I wanted to be annoyed with him; he had something in common with Thomas Stone, though Zemui at least saw his daughter every day. But when Zemui shook my hand and excitedly pulled out a new Darwin letter, I found myself sitting down with him on the kitchen steps. I was tempted to say, *Why don't you ask your daughter to do this?* But I didn't because I understood something I had missed before—that Genet surely didn't make things easy for her father. I was reading and writing letters for Zemui because his daughter had refused.

On a Friday evening, the Colonel breezed into Missing and into Ghosh's old quarters bringing energy with him, as if not one man but a regiment in full colors had arrived, along with the marching band. Half an hour later, there were two tables going. The players—Hema, Ghosh, Adid, Babu, Evangeline, Mrs. Reddy, and a newcomer they brought— seemed to inhabit their bridge hands, becoming Pass and Three-No-Trumps, their faces flushed with concentration. Adid, the khat merchant and old friend of Hema's, owned a shop in the Merkato right next to Babu's and had brought him into the group. A burst of conversation like a collective sigh signaled the end of a round. I loved to observe them play.

The Colonel, just back from London, had a rare bottle of Glenfiddich for Ghosh, chocolates for us, and Chanel No. 5 perfume for Hema. The cigarettes in the ashtrays were Dunhill and 555—his contribution again. Though he wore a blazer and open shirt, his tucked-in chin and the shoulders drawn back made it seem he was still in uniform. If he left the party, I imagined the rest of them would slump over like toys whose spring had unwound.

Evangeline, an Anglo-Indian, a bridge regular, turned to Colonel Mebratu: "A little bird told me that we might soon be calling you Brigadier General. Is that true?"

Colonel Mebratu frowned. "Such vicious rumors. Such an incestuous community. And I fear, Evangeline, you are at the center of it. But in this case I must correct you, my dear. I am not *soon* to be called Brigadier General. As of yesterday, I *am* Brigadier General."

Well, there was no stopping them after that. Zemui and Gebrew made two runs for food from the Ras Hotel.

Much later that night, Mebratu and Ghosh palavered over cognac and cigars. "In Korea in '52 we were one of fifteen countries in the UN forces. I wasn't long out of command training when I went there. The other countries underestimated us. You see, they knew nothing about Ethiopian courage or the battle of Adowa or any of that. By God, we proved ourselves in Korea. By the time we got to the Congo, they knew what to expect. We had an Irish commander, then a Swedish commander, and in the third year, they made our own General Guebre commander of *all* the UN forces. You know, Ghosh, as a career military man that was my proudest moment. Even more than this promotion I got yesterday."

I'LL NEVER KNOW HOW, but Ghosh understood what I was going through after the pantry episode; perhaps he recognized that I was quarantined from Genet and that Shiva didn't share in that experience; perhaps he saw my confusion when Zemui was around. Maybe it was written on my face that I'd become aware of human complexity—that's a kinder word than "deceit." I was trying to decide where to peg my own truth, how much to reveal about myself—it helped to have such a steadfast father in Ghosh, never fickle, never prying, but knowing when I needed him. Had Hema learned what went on in the pantry, I'd hear about it two seconds later. But Ghosh, if he knew, was capable of keeping his peace, biding his time, hearing me out; he'd have even kept it secret from Hema if he didn't think it served any purpose to tell her.

One wet afternoon, when Genet and Shiva were having their dance lesson with Hema, Ghosh telephoned and asked me to meet him in Casualty. "I want you to feel a most unusual pulse." Ghosh was primarily a surgeon now, operating electively three days a week and doing the emergency cases as needed. But, as he often said at dinner, he was still an internist at heart and couldn't resist coming down to Casualty to see certain patients who presented a diagnostic puzzle, one that neither Adam nor Bachelli could crack.

I was grateful for Ghosh's call. I never had any interest in dancing, but it bothered me to see Genet enjoying something in which I had no part. I put on my gutta-percha boots and raincoat and dashed out with my umbrella.

Demisse was in his twenties, sitting on the examining stool in front of Ghosh, wearing only torn jodhpurs. I noticed at once the bobbing of his head, as if an eccentric flywheel turned within him. It was my first formal visit with a patient, and I was embarrassed. What would this barefoot farmhand think of a young boy entering the exam room? But he was thrilled to see me. Later I realized that patients felt privileged to be singled out in this fashion. Not only had they made it past Adam, not only had they seen the *tilik* doctor, the same big doctor whom the royalty came to see, but now they got a bonus—me.

Ghosh guided my fingers to Demisse's pulse at the wrist. It was easy to feel, unavoidable, a surging, slapping, powerful wave under my fingertips. Now I could see that his head bobbing happened in time with the pulse.

"Now feel mine," Ghosh said, holding out his wrist. It was harder to find, subtle.

He had me go back to Demisse's pulse.

"Describe it," Ghosh said.

"Big . . . strong. Like something alive under the skin, slapping," I said.

"Exactly! That is a classic *collapsing* or water hammer pulse. Its full name is the Corrigan's water hammer pulse."

He handed me a foot-long thin glass tube that I'd seen lying across his table. "Hold it up. Now turn it over." The tube was sealed at both ends and had a little water in it. When I flipped it, the water raced down to the bottom of the tube with an unexpected smacking sound and a shock. "There's a vacuum inside, you see," he said. "It's a toy that kids played with in Ireland. It's a water hammer. Dr. Corrigan was reminded of the toy when he first felt a pulse like Demisse's."

Ghosh had made the water hammer for me. He had sealed one end of a glass tube with a Bunsen flame. Then he put a few drops of water inside the tube through the open end. He heated the length of the tube above the liquid to drive the air out and quickly sealed the open end under the flame.

"Demisse's heart shoots blood out into the aorta. That's the big highway leading out of the heart," he said, making a sketch for me on paper. "A valve right here at the exit from the heart is supposed to close after the heart contracts, to keep the blood from falling back into the heart. His doesn't close well. So his heart squeezes blood out just fine, but half of that ejected blood falls right back into the heart between squeezes. *That's* what gives it the collapsing quality." How exciting to be able to touch a human being with one's fingertips and know all these things about them. I said as much to Ghosh, and from his expression you would think I'd said something profound.

He sent for me often during those holidays. Shiva came at times, but not if it interfered with his dance lesson or if he was in the middle of a drawing. I learned to recognize the slow, heaving, plateaulike pulse of a narrowed aortic valve. It was the opposite of a collapsing pulse. The small valve opening made that pulse both weak *and* prolonged. *Pulsus parvus et tardus,* Ghosh called it.

I loved those Latin words for their dignity, their foreignness, and the way my tongue had to wrap around them. I felt that in learning the special language of a scholarly order, I was amassing a kind of force. This was the pure and noble side of the world, uncorrupted by secrets and trickery. How extraordinary that a word could serve as a shorthand for an elaborate tale of disease. When I tried to explain this to Ghosh, he was excited.

"Yes! A treasure trove of words! That's what you find in medicine. Take the food metaphors we use to describe disease: the nutmeg liver, the sago spleen, the anchovy sauce sputum, or currant jelly stools. Why, if you consider just *fruits* alone you have the strawberry tongue of scarlet fever, which the next day becomes the raspberry tongue. Or how about the strawberry angioma, the watermelon stomach, the apple core lesion of cancer, the *peau d'orange* appearance of breast cancer . . . and that's just fruits! Don't get me started on the nonvegetarian stuff!"

One day I showed Ghosh the notebook in which I kept a written catalog of everything he had told me, and every pulse I had seen. Like a birder, I listed the ones I sought: *pulsus paradoxus, pulsus alternans, pulsus bisferiens* . . . and simple drawings of what they might look like. He wrote in the fly leaf: *Nam et ipsa scientia potestas est!* "That means 'Knowledge is power!' Oh, I do believe that, Marion."

We didn't stop at pulses. I went to Ghosh as often as I could. Fingernails, tongues, faces—soon my notebook was chock-full of drawings and new words. I found use at last for my penmanship: each figure was carefully labeled.

On a Friday evening, our last weekend before school started, I rode with Ghosh to see Farinachi, the toolmaker. Ghosh handed Farinachi two old stethoscopes and a drawing of his idea for a teaching stethoscope. Farinachi, a dour, stooped Sicilian, wore a vest under his leather apron. He studied the drawing carefully through a haze of cigar smoke, tracing the outline with a large forefinger. He had fashioned several contraptions for Ghosh, including the Ghosh Retractor, and the Ghosh Scalp Clip. Farinachi shrugged, as if to say if that was what Ghosh wanted, he would do it.

As we were driving back, Ghosh pulled out a present he'd wrapped for me. It was my very own brand-new stethoscope. "You don't have to wait for Farinachi. Now that you know your pulses, we're going to start listening to heart sounds." I was moved. It was the first gift I'd ever received that wasn't one of a pair. This was mine alone.

Looking back, I realize Ghosh saved me when he called me to feel Demisse's pulse. My mother was dead, and my father a ghost; increasingly I felt disconnected from Shiva and Hema, and guilty for feeling that way. Ghosh, in giving me the stethoscope, was saying, Marion, you can be you. It's okay. He invited me to a world that wasn't secret, but it was well hidden. You needed a guide. You had to know what to look for, but also *how* to look. You had to exert yourself to see this world. But if you did, if you had that kind of curiosity, if you had an innate interest in the welfare of your fellow human beings, and if you went through that door, a strange thing happened: you left your petty troubles on the threshold. It could be addictive.

CHAPTER 22

The School of Suffering

ONE MORNING toward the end of Michaelmas term, as Shiva, Genet, and I walked to Missing's gate, school satchels in hand, I saw a couple racing up the hill toward us, a child flopping lifeless in the man's arms. They were ready to drop, yet still trying to run up that incline when they had no breath to walk. But as long as they ran with the child in their arms, it was still alive to them, and there was hope.

Without a moment's hesitation, ShivaMarion raced to meet them. The parents' distress triggered this, gave us no time to debate our response, as a higher brain emerged, doing the deciding for us and guiding us to move as one organism if we knew what was best. I remember thinking, in the midst of that panic, how much I missed that state and how exhilarating it was to be ShivaMarion. Even as I grabbed the infant boy from the father (whose gait by now had become a weary shuffle) and raced away, Shiva's steady hand on my low back was my afterburner, and he matched my stride perfectly, ready to take over when I tired. I was conscious of the baby's skin, the way it chilled my hand, sucking the heat out of it as I ran—I knew I'd never again take being "warm-blooded" for granted, having now felt the alternative.

We handed the child over in Casualty and we waited outside, panting. When the parents caught up, we held the doors open for them. Minutes later we heard a scream, then loud protests, and ultimately the wailing that means the same in any language. It was all too familiar a sound.

There was another Missing sound that made my adrenaline flow: it was the shrieking, grating sound of Gebrew dragging the big gate open as fast as it would go. It always signaled a dire emergency.

A childhood at Missing imparted lessons about resilience, about fortitude, and about the fragility of life. I knew better than most children how little separated the world of health from that of disease, living flesh from the icy touch of the dead, the solid ground from treacherous bog.

I'd learned things about suffering that weren't taught to me by Ghosh: First, that white was the uniform of suffering, and cotton its fabric. Whether it was thin (a *shama* or *nettala*) or heavy as a blanket (in which case it was a *gabby*), it must keep the head warm and the mouth covered—no sun or wind should hit because these elements carried the *mitch,* the *birrd,* and other evil miasmas. Even the minister with the waistcoat and fob watch would, when he was ill, throw a *nettala* over his coat, cram eucalyptus leaf up his nose, take an extra dose of *kosso* for tapeworm, and then hurry over to be seen.

Day after day a white-robed mass flowed up our hill, gravity the current against which they swam. Those whose breath ran short as well as the crippled and the lame stopped at the halfway point to look up, to gaze past the tops of the flanking eucalyptus to where the African hawks soared against the blue sky.

Once they crested the hill, patients went to the registration desk to get their card. From there it was on to Adam, the man whom Ghosh called the World's Greatest One-Eyed Clinician. "Short of breath, are you?" Adam might say to a patient. "But still you managed to run up the hill and get the fourth card of the day?" In Adam's book, a number under ten on the outpatient card identified a hypochondriac more accurately than any test Ghosh might do.

From my spot observing the daily influx, I once saw a proud Eritrean woman carrying a heavy basket; inside was something large, sprouting, with a surface that was red, raw, and weeping. It was her breast. It had become so huge from cancer that this was the only way for her and her breast to come to Missing.

I drew such sights in my notebook. My sketches were nothing like Shiva's, but they served me well. A glance at them allowed me to recall the memory, even if it was not Shiva's photographic kind.

On page thirty-four I drew a child in profile, chubby-cheeked, healthy. But from the other side, his profile showed a chunk of his cheek, one nostril, and the eye missing, so that his glistening teeth and pink gum and the recess of the orbit were visible. I learned from Ghosh to call this ghastly sight *cancrum oris.* It came about from a trivial gum or tooth infection which spread because of malnutrition and neglect, often during an episode of measles or chicken pox. Once ignited, it progressed rapidly, usually causing death before the child could be brought to Missing.

Sometimes, the disease simply ran out of steam, or the body's defenses were finally able to contain the march, but at the expense of half the face. Death was perhaps a better fate than to live with the disfigurement. I watched Ghosh operate on this child. It was terrifying, and then I was in awe at what this man who sat down to dinner with us each night was capable of doing: rotate a flap of skin to cover the cheek, and another the hole in the nose. Further flaps and reconstruction he planned for a later surgery. Even so there was no restoring to normal the face, much less the soul, of a child so scarred. After the surgery, what Ghosh said to me was, "Don't be too impressed. I'm an accidental surgeon, son. I do all I can do. But your father . . . what he could have done to that face would have been as good as the best plastic surgeon alive. You see, your father was a *real* surgeon. I don't think I've seen anyone better." What made someone a *real* surgeon, I asked. Ghosh didn't hesitate: "*Passion* for his craft . . . and skill, dexterity. His hands were always 'quiet.' I mean he had no wasted movements, no dramatic gestures. It looked slow, routine, but when you looked at the clock you realized how fast it must have been. But even more important is the confidence once you make the first cut, the belief in yourself, which allows you to do more and get better results. I'm thankful I can do the simple things, the bread-and-butter operations. But I'm scared to death half the time."

He was being modest. But it was true that Ghosh was a different being in the outpatient department where he saw "consultations"—the patients Bachelli and Adam kept for him to render an opinion. Ghosh's real skill emerged with those who looked "normal" to my gaze. Hidden from us unschooled observers, a disease had left its traces. A woman who wove baskets said, "On St. Stefano's Day I passed urine on a barbed-wire fence . . ." Or this from a sad, distraught coolie: "The morning after the Wednesday fast, I accidentally stepped over the cast-off water from a prostitute's morning wash . . ." Ghosh listened, his eyes taking in the blister marks on the sternum which said the native healer had been consulted; he noted the thick speech and guessed that the uvula had probably been recently amputated on a second visit to the same charlatan. But Ghosh had an ear for what lay beneath those surface words, and a pointed question uncovered a story which matched with one in his repertoire of tales. Then it was time to look for the flesh signs, the bookmarks of the disease, and to palpate and percuss and listen with his stethoscope for clues left behind. He knew how that story ended; the patient only knew the beginning.

THERE IS ONE LAST SIGHTING at Missing—which had nothing to do with Ghosh—that I must describe because it happened during that period: it explained Shiva's life course, and why it veered away from my mine.

Late one morning as Shiva and I sat on the culvert by the side of Missing's hill, a frail, barefoot girl, no older than twelve, came stiff-legged up the hill. Prematurely stooped like an old woman, she leaned heavily on her giant of a father. His muddy, patched jodhpurs ballooned above bare feet and horned toenails. He could have taken the hill in twenty strides. Instead he took small steps to accommodate hers. They crept forward like snails, while other visitors sped up when they neared these two, as if father and daughter created an animating field. When she reached us, I understood why. An unspeakable scent of decay, putre-faction, and something else for which the words remain to be invented reached our nostrils. I saw no point in holding my breath or pinching my nose because the foulness invaded instantly, coloring our insides like a drop of India ink in a cup of water.

In the way that children understand their own, we knew her to be innocent of her terrible, overpowering odor. It was *of* her, but it wasn't hers. Worse than the odor (since she must have lived with it for more than a few days) was to see in her face the knowledge of how it repulsed and revolted others. No wonder she had fallen out of the habit of look-ing at human faces; the world was lost to her, and she to it.

When she paused to catch her breath, a slow puddle formed at her bare feet. Looking down the road, I could see the trail she left behind. I'll never forget her father's face. Under that peasant straw hat he burned with love for his daughter, and rage against the world that shunned her. His bloodshot eyes met every stare and even sought out those who tried not to look. He cursed their mothers, and cursed the gods they wor-shipped. He was deranged by a scent he could have escaped.

Did I say she met no one's gaze? No one's but Shiva's. A moment passed between them, a barely discernible easing of her features, as if Shiva had caressed her, reached out to comfort her. His lifted chin dipped for her, his eyes shaded to blue and his lips set firmly together. Her lids suddenly sparkled with liquid. The father who had blasphemed his way up the hill fell silent.

My brother, who once spoke with anklets and whose dance could be as complex as a honeybee's, didn't know he would dedicate his life to just such women, the outcasts of society; he would seek them at the Autobus Terra as they arrived from the provinces. He would pay touts to go to the furthermost villages and find them where they were hidden away, shunned by their husbands and families. He would have pamphlets distributed wherever the Coca-Cola truck went, which is to say wherever there were paved roads, asking for these women—girls, really—to come out of hiding, to come to him, so that he might cure them. He would become the world's expert . . .

But I am ahead of my story. Shiva's understanding of the medical condition behind that odor came later. That afternoon, one of many that I spent wondering about my future, Shiva had already sprung into action. With his eyes on her, he walked to them and led father and daughter to Hema. I look back now and I realize that in that act his career was already predetermined, and it was destined to differ vastly from mine.

CHAPTER 23

The Afterbird and Other Animals

THE RAINS HAD ENDED and we had been back in class fewer than two weeks when Hema woke us with what I took to be good news. "No school. We're keeping you home today," she said. Something about trouble in the city. Taxis wouldn't be running. I stopped listening after "no school."

It was a perfect day to be home. Meskel celebrations were to start, and already Missing's fields were carpeted with yellow. We'd lose the soccer ball in the daisies, we'd climb into the tree house . . . Then I remembered: with Genet under Rosina's watchful eye, it wouldn't be the same.

I pushed out the wooden shutters of my bedroom window and climbed onto the ledge. Sunshine flooded the room. By noon the temperature would reach seventy–five degrees, but for the moment I shivered in my bare feet. From my perch, I could see beyond Missing's east wall onto a quiet meandering road which descended and then disappeared, the hills rising just beyond, as if the road had gone underground before it emerged in the distance as a mere thread. It wasn't a road we traveled or even one that I knew how to get to, and yet it was a view I felt I owned. On the left side a fortresslike wall flanked the road, receding with it, struggling to stay vertical. Giant clusters of purple bougainvillea spilled over, brushing the white *shamas* of the few pedestrians. There was a quality to this pellucid first light and the vivid colors that made it impossible to imagine trouble.

In the dining room, I noticed the strained, preoccupied expression on Ghosh's face. He had his shirt, tie, and coat on. He'd been awake for hours, it seemed. Hema in her dressing gown was huddled next to him, twisting and untwisting a lock of her hair. I was surprised to see Genet there; her head jerked up when I came in, as if she didn't know I lived in the house. Rosina, who usually orchestrated our mornings, was nowhere to be seen. In the kitchen I found Almaz frozen by the stove; only when the egg began to smoke did she scoop it off the pan and onto my plate. I noticed the tears in her eyes.

"The Emperor," she said, when I pressed her. "How dare they do this to His Majesty? What thankless people! Don't they remember he saved us from the Italians? That he's God's chosen?"

She told me what she knew: While the Emperor was on a state visit to Liberia, a group of Imperial Bodyguard officers seized power during the night. They were led by our own Brigadier General Mebratu.

"And Zemui?"

"He is with them, of course!" she said, whispering, shaking her head in disappointment.

"Where is Rosina?"

She pointed with her chin in the direction of the servant's quarters.

Genet came into the kitchen, on her way to the back door. She looked frightened. I stopped her, and held her hand.

"Are you all right?" I noticed the gold chain and strange cross around her neck.

She nodded, then went out the back door. Almaz didn't look at her.

"It's true," Ghosh said, back in the dining room. He glanced at Hema, as if the two of them were trying to decide how much to divulge to us. What they couldn't hide was their anxiety.

The previous evening General Mebratu went to the Crown Prince's residence to tell him that others were plotting a coup against his father. At the General's urging, the Crown Prince summoned ministers loyal to the Emperor. When they came, General Mebratu arrested them all.

It was a brilliant ploy, but it unsettled me. I couldn't imagine Ethiopia without Haile Selassie at the helm—nobody could. The country and the man seemed to go together. General Mebratu was our hero, a dashing figure who could do no wrong. The Emperor had lost some of his glow for us. But I never expected this of the General—was this a betrayal, a dark side of his that had emerged? Or was he doing the right thing?

"How do you know all this?" I asked.

One of the prisoners, an old and frail minister, had had an asthma attack, and so Ghosh had been summoned to the Crown Prince's residence in the early morning. "The General doesn't want anyone dying if he can help it. He wants it to be peaceful."

"Does he want to be Emperor?" I asked.

Ghosh shook his head. "No, I don't think that's it at all. What he wants is for the poor to have food, to have land. That means taking it from the royals and from the Church."

"So is this a good thing he is doing, or a bad thing?" Shiva asked, looking up from the book he had brought to the table. That was Shiva: he hated ambiguity, and he wanted things cut and dried. Often when Shiva asked such a question, it was because he didn't see what was obvious to me. But in this case, it was a good question, one that I wanted to ask, too. "Isn't the Imperial Bodyguard supposed to defend the Emperor?" Shiva added.

Ghosh winced, as if Shiva's query hurt.

"This isn't my country, so who am I to judge? Mebratu has a good life. He didn't *have* to do this. I do think he's doing this for the people. Long ago he was under great suspicion, then he was the favorite son, and recently he was under suspicion again, and he felt he might be arrested very soon anyway."

Ghosh said that, as he left the Crown Prince's palace, Zemui had walked Ghosh to his car and given Ghosh something to give to Genet. It was the gold pendant Darwin Easton had taken off his own neck and given to Zemui—the St. Bridget's cross. He'd asked Ghosh to convey his love to her and to Rosina.

After Hema dressed, she and Ghosh left for the hospital. "Stay close to home, boys. You hear?" We were not to leave Missing property, no matter what.

I went to the gate. I met just three patients coming up the hill. No car or bus passed by Missing. I stood with Gebrew, staring out. The silence was eerie, not even the *clip-clop* of horseshoes or the jingle of harness bells to break the stillness. "When the four-legged taxis stay in their stables, you know things are serious," Gebrew said.

There were bars, a tailor's shop, and a radio repair shop in the two cinder-block buildings across from us; but there was no sign of life. Ignoring Hema and Ghosh's warnings, and over Gebrew's protests, I crossed the road to the tiny Arab souk, a plywood structure painted canary yellow that sat between the larger buildings. The window through which the souk usually conducted business was shuttered, but a child emerged through the door, which was barely cracked open, carrying a cone-shaped package made out of newspaper and wrapped in twine. Probably ten cents' worth of sugar for the morning tea. I slipped in. The air inside was thick with incense. If I leaned over the counter I could touch the back wall. The Arab souks all over Addis were like this, as if they'd come from the same womb. Dangling down from the ceiling, on clothespins attached to a string, were single-use packets of Tide, Bayer aspirin, Chiclets, and paracetamol. They twirled like party decorations. A meat hook hanging from the rafters held squares of newspaper, ready to use as wrapping. A roll of twine hung on another hook. Loose cigarettes sat in a jar on top of the counter, unopened cigarette packs stacked next to them. The shelves were stuffed with matchboxes, bottled sodas, Bic pens, pencil sharpeners, Vicks, Nivea Creme, notebooks, erasers, ink, candles, batteries, Coca-Cola, Fanta, Pepsi, sugar, tea, rice, bread, cooking oil, and much more. Mason jars full of *caramela* and cookies flanked the counter, leaving an opening in the middle over which I leaned. I saw Ali Osman, lace cap glued to his head, seated on the mat along with his wife, infant daughter, and two men. The floor space was hardly big enough for Ali and his family to sleep spooned against one another, knees bent, and now he had visitors. They sat around a pile of khat.

Ali was worried. "Marion, times like this are when foreigners like us can suffer," he said. It was strange to hear him use the word *ferengi* to describe himself, or me, because we were both born in this land.

I crossed back over to Gebrew and shared with him some stick candy I had bought.

Suddenly Rosina walked right past us. "Look after Genet," she called over her shoulder. I didn't know whether she meant me or Gebrew.

"Wait!" Gebrew said, but she didn't.

I ran after her and grabbed her hand. "Wait, Rosina. Where are you going? Please."

She spun on me as if to tell me off, but then her face softened. She was pale, and her eyes were puffy from crying. The skin was tight over her jaw, whether in fear or determination I couldn't tell.

"The boy is right. Don't go," Gebrew said.

"What would you have me do, priest? I haven't seen Zemui in a week. He's a simple fellow. I'm worried for him. He'll listen to me. I'll tell him he must be loyal to God, and the Emperor, before anything else." I was suddenly scared. I clung to Rosina. She pulled herself free, but gently. Out of habit, she pinched me on the cheek and ran her hand through my hair. She kissed me on the top of my head.

"Be reasonable," Gebrew said. "The Imperial Bodyguard headquarters is too far away. If he's with the General, then he's in the palace. You'll be walking right past the army headquarters and the Sixth Police Station. It will take you too long."

With a wave she was gone. Gebrew, whose eyes were perpetually weepy from trachoma, looked as if he might bawl. He perceived a danger far greater than anything I could imagine.

Ten minutes later, a jeep with a mounted machine gun appeared, followed by an armored car. They were Imperial Bodyguard soldiers, wearing grim expressions and also combat helmets in place of their usual pith helmets. Camouflage fatigues and ammo belts had replaced the regular olive-green drill. A voice came over a loudspeaker mounted on the armored truck: "People. Remain calm. His Majesty Crown Prince Asfa Wossen has taken over the government. He will be making an announcement at noon today. Listen to Radio Addis Ababa at noon. Radio Addis at noon. People. Remain calm . . ."

I wandered away from the gate and drifted over to the hospital. W. W. Gonad was sitting in the breezeway outside the blood bank, a transistor radio in his lap, and nurses and probationers sitting close to him. He looked excited, happy.

At noon in our bungalow we gathered around the Grundig and Rosina's transistor radio, one tuned to the BBC and the second to Radio Addis Ababa. Almaz stood to one side; Genet shared a chair with me. Hema took the clock down from the mantelpiece and wound it; the unguarded expression on her face showed the depth of her anxiety. Matron seemed the least concerned, blowing on a cup of dark coffee, smiling at me. A faceless, stentorian English voice said, "This is the BBC World Service."

At last, the announcer moved from a coal strike in Britain to what interested us. "Reports from Addis Ababa, the capital of Ethiopia, indicate that a bloodless coup has taken place while Emperor Haile Selassie was away on a state visit to Liberia. The Emperor has cut short his visit and abandoned his plans for a state visit to Brazil."

"Coup" was a new word for me. It implied something ancient and elegant, and yet the adjective "bloodless" implied that there had to be a "bloody" variety.

I confess that at that moment I was thrilled to hear our city, and even the Imperial Bodyguard, mentioned by the BBC. The British knew nothing of Missing, or the view of the road from my window. But now, we'd made them look in our direction. Years later, when Idi Amin said and did outrageous things, I understood that his motivation was to rattle the good people of Greenwich mean time, have them raise their heads from their tea and scones, and say, *Oh, yes. Africa.* For a fleeting moment they'd have the same awareness of us that we had of them.

But how was it that the BBC could look out from London and see what was happening to us? When we looked over the walls of Missing we saw nothing.

Well after noon, and long after the BBC broadcast, the martial music on Radio Addis Ababa ceased and, with a rustle of papers, a stuttering Crown Prince Asfa Wossen came on the air. What little I had seen of the portly, pale eldest son in the newspaper and in the flesh suggested a man who might scream at the sight of a mouse; he lacked the Emperor's charisma and bearing. The Crown Prince read a statement—and it was clear he was reading—in the high Amharic of officialdom, difficult for anyone but Almaz and Gebrew to understand. When he was done, Almaz left the dining room, upset. Minutes later—how did they do this?—the BBC aired a translation.

"The people of Ethiopia have waited for the day when poverty and backwardness would cease to be, but nothing has been achieved . . ."

The Crown Prince said his father had failed the country. It was time for new leadership. A new day was dawning. Long live Ethiopia.

"Those are General Mebratu's words," Ghosh said.

"More like his brother's," Hema said.

"They must have a gun to the Crown Prince's head," Matron said. "I don't hear any conviction in his voice."

"Well, then he should've refused to read it," I said. Everyone turned to look at me. Even Shiva lifted his head up from the book he was reading. "He should say, 'No, I won't read it. I would rather die than betray my father.'"

"Marion's right," Matron said, at last. "It doesn't say much about the Crown Prince's character."

"It's just a ploy, using the Crown Prince," Ghosh said. "They don't want to dump the monarchy right away. They want the public to get used to the idea of a change. Did you see how upset Almaz is at the idea of someone deposing the Emperor?"

"Why do they care about the public? They have the guns. The power," Hema said.

"They care about a civil war," Ghosh said. "The peasants worship the Emperor. Don't forget the Territorial Army, all those aging fighters who battled the Italians. Those irregulars are neither army nor Bodyguard, but they far outnumber them. They can come pouring into town."

"They might anyway," Matron said.

"Mebratu couldn't get the army, police, or air force's support ahead of time," Ghosh said. "I suppose the more people he involved before the coup, the more likely he'd have been betrayed. The General and his brother, Eskinder, were arguing when I got there this morning. Eskinder had wanted to trap all the army generals the previous night, using the same ruse that had trapped the other loyalists. But the General vetoed that."

"You saw the General when you went there?" I asked.

"I wish he hadn't," Hema said. "He has no business getting in the middle of this," she said looking cross.

Ghosh sighed. "I went as a physician, Hema, I told you. When I got there, Tsigue Debou, the head of the police, had thrown in his lot with Mebratu. He and Eskinder were pressing the General to attack the army headquarters before the army can get organized. But he refused. He was . . . emotional. These were his friends, his peers. He was sure that good men in the other services would throw their lot in with him. You know he took the time to see me to the door, he thanked me. He told me he was determined to avoid bloodshed."

THE REST OF THE DAY went by with the streets eerily silent. Very few patients came to Missing, and patients who could leave fled for home. We sat glued to the radio.

Genet stayed in her quarters alone. In the late afternoon, Hema sent me to fetch her. I led her back by the hand. She put on a brave front, but I knew she was worried and scared. That night, she slept on our sofa: there was no sign of Rosina.

The next day, the city was so quiet, and the only thing circulating was rumors. Only the bravest of shopkeepers opened his doors. Word was that the army was still wavering, undecided about whether to support the coup leaders or remain loyal to the Emperor.

At noon, Gebrew came to tell us that we should go to the gate. We got there in time to see a huge procession of university students carrying Ethiopian flags, their faces glowing with sweat and excitement. They were grouped under banners: COLLEGE OF ARTS AND SCIENCES, COL-LEGE OF ENGINEERING . . . Marshals with armbands kept order. To my amazement, there was W. W. Gonad marching under the banner of the School of Business. He gave us a sheepish grin, adjusted his tie, and marched on, trying to look like a member of the faculty. There must have been several thousand students and staff, and they chanted in one voice in Amharic:

> *My countrymen awake—history calls you*
> *No more slavery, let freedom reign anew*

Banners in English read: FOR EVERYONE, A BLOODLESS REVOLU-TION and LET US STAND PEACEFULLY WITH THE NEW GOVERNMENT OF THE PEOPLE.

The street was lined with wary onlookers who, like us, had been indoors much too long. Stray dogs gathered, barking at the marchers and adding to the noise. A pretty student in jeans put leaflets in our hands. Almaz pushed the paper away as if it were contaminated. "Hey, miss! Is this why they sent you to university?" Almaz called after her.

An old man with a beard waved his flyswatter as if he were trying to smack the students. "If you were studying, you shouldn't have time for this," he shouted. "Don't forget who built your university, who taught you to read!"

We learned later from W. W. Gonad that in the Merkato the Mus-lims and Eritrean shopkeepers received the students with cheers. But elsewhere in Addis, their reception by the public was cold, and when the procession turned to reach the army headquarters, where they had intended to convince the army to join the revolt, they were met at an intersection by an army platoon in combat gear. The young commander told the crowd that they had exactly one minute to disperse or he would give his soldiers orders to fire. The students tried to argue, but the sounds of rifle bolts pulling back convinced the marchers to retreat. That was when W. W. Gonad left the rally.

I was still pleased to be out of school, but the anxiety on the faces of the adults had rubbed off. Ghosh and Matron returned to the hospital to prepare for casualties. Hema had her Version Clinic that afternoon. Shiva, who till then had little interest in what was going on, was uneasy, as if he sensed something no one else did. Unusual for Shiva, he asked Hema if she would stay home and not to go to work.

"I don't want to leave, my love," she said, agonizing over what to do, "but I have Version Clinic."

"Take us with you," Shiva said. Then he added, "We practiced Bickham. See my paper? Just as you told us." His calligraphy was better than the examples of the ornate and round style in the book. "So please?"

"I really can't . . . ," Hema said. "I have to go to the labor room first before clinic."

"We'll go with you," Shiva said.

"No. I won't have you in the labor room." She could see the disappointment in Shiva's face. "I tell you what, you boys go to the Version Clinic and wait for me. Whatever you do, stay together."

This was the rarest of invitations. Unlike Ghosh, if Hema carried a stethoscope, she didn't bring it home. The white coat we glimpsed her wearing in the hospital stayed there. I rarely thought of Hema as a doctor because at home she was all mother. Ghosh constantly talked medicine, but Hema never did. We knew she went to Labor and Delivery and that she operated on Mondays and Wednesdays. From what we overheard, she was very good and in great demand, but the specifics were not mentionable to us. She wanted us to always know that her eyes were on us, and no doctoring would distract her from that vigilance. The Version Clinic was a good example. We'd heard of it for years, but we hadn't the least idea what went on there. According to the dictionary, one meaning of "version" was from the Latin, *versus*—"to turn."

Hema's departures in the night came with cryptic phrases, words stranger than "version" tossed over her shoulder: "eclampsia" or "postpartum hemorrhage" or, that most chilling term of all, the "Delayed Afterbird." That one wasn't even in the medical dictionary. And you never heard of the Afterbird except when it was Delayed. It was feared, and yet its arrival was necessary. Shiva and I looked for that Delayed Afterbird on the trees of Missing, or high up in the sky.

Shiva drew the Afterbird, and in his many renderings it was like a flying wing, an elongated triangle, sightless, legless, but beautiful, sleek, aerodynamic, and utterly mysterious. Could our mother's death be linked to the Delayed Afterbird? It would have been so easy to ask Hema. But the topic was off-limits. At least that was how Hema made it feel.

THE WOMEN'S CLINIC behind the main hospital building deviated from the whitewashed decor of Missing, because it had lime-green paint on the outer walls and blue banisters. A hygenia tree dropped orange blossoms on the steps. The soil underneath the tree was aflame with blue lobelia and pink clover. We found a gaggle of pregnant patients seated on the steps, their hair covered by *shashes*. While waiting, they'd tucked fresh blossoms behind their ears and stretched their legs out in front of them. Their white *shamas* glowed in the sun, and with bellies swollen, clutching their pink outpatient cards, they resembled a flock of lively geese. Some were barefoot, and those who weren't had eased off their plastic shoes. It was tense in the city, but looking at these woman, and hearing their laughter, their complaints about swollen ankles, husbands, or heartburn, you would never have known.

When they spotted us, they called us over to shake our hands, ask our names, our age, fuss with our hair, and remark on our similarity. They insisted that we sit with them, and I would have declined, except Shiva happily said yes. I sat there embarrassed, like a chick squished between hens. Shiva seemed to be in heaven.

So often we never truly see our own family and it is for others to tell us that they've grown taller or older. I confess, I mostly took Shiva's appearance for granted—he was my twin after all. But at that moment, I was seeing my brother anew: the large rounded forehead, the curls that piled up on his head, threatening to fall forward and obscure his sight, the equanimity around the brow and eyes, and his mannerism of putting his finger alongside his cheek just like the Nehru portrait on our wall at home. What was completely new was this smile which transformed my wombmate into a blue-eyed stranger, rendering a lightness to his being, so that were it not for the sturdy female arms draped over his shoulders, caresssing his hair, he would have floated off those steps.

A woman read a pink pamphlet that had been dropped over the Piazza and Merkato by an air force plane. She was the lone woman who could read, albeit slowly: "Message from His Holiness, Patriarch of the Church, Abuna Basilios," she said, and heads at once bowed, and hands made the sign of the cross, as if His Holiness were on the steps with them. "To my children, the Christians of Ethiopia and to the entire Ethiopian people. Yesterday, at about ten in the evening, the Imperial Bodyguard soldiers who were entrusted with the safety and welfare of the royal family committed crimes of treachery against their country . . ."

Seated in their midst, sweating in the sun, I shivered. I could see that the patriarch's words rang true for these ladies. He was speaking for God. This did not bode well for the man we so admired, General Mebratu.

The women turned naughty after that, mocking the Bodyguard and then men in general, laughing and carrying on as if they were at a wedding. Shiva was in rapture, grinning from ear to ear. His earlier apprehension had vanished. It was as if he'd found his ideal spot, surrounded by pregnant women. There was much about my brother I did not understand.

When Hema appeared, the women struggled to their feet, despite Hema's protests. A mother's pride showed in Hema's eyes to see us adopted by her patients.

THREE AT A TIME, the women mounted the examining tables. They pushed their skirts down just below their bellies and pulled their chemises up to expose their watermelon swellings. When one of the patients on the table waved to Shiva to come close and hold her hand, he stepped in, and I followed. Hema bit her tongue.

"All late third trimester," Hema said, after a while, without explaining what that meant. She used both hands to confirm that the baby's position was "something other than head down. A baby can't come out easily unless its head is pointing down to the mother's feet. That is why the Prenatal Clinic sent them here to Version Clinic," she said, mentioning another clinic which we knew she attended in this very room but on a different day.

She pulled out a strange, stunted version of a stethoscope—a fetoscope. The bell of the stethoscope had a U-shaped metal bracket on which she could rest her forehead, and then use the weight of her head to press the bell into the skin, leaving her hands free to stabilize the belly. She held up a finger like a conductor signaling for quiet. Conversation stopped, and the patients on the stretchers and the throng around the door held their breaths, till Hema raised up and said, "Galloping like a stallion!" A score of voices added, "Praise the saints!" Hema didn't offer to let us listen.

She got down to business. "With this hand I cup the baby's head. My other hand I put here where the baby's bottom is—how do I know?" She looked at Shiva as if his question was impertinent. Then she laughed. "Do you know how many thousands of babies I've felt this way, my son? I don't have to think. The head is this coconutlike hardness. The bottom is softer, not as distinct. My hands give me a picture," she said, outlining a shape in the air above the exposed belly. "The baby's back is to me.

Now watch." She set her feet, then using firm and steady pressure of her cupped hands, she pushed the head one way, the butt the other way, while also pushing her hands toward each other as if to keep the baby curled up. Something in the way her thumbs were aligned with the rest of her fingers, all held close together, reminded me of her Bharatnatyam dance gestures. "There! You see? An initial resistance, a stickiness, then it gives, and the baby tumbles over." I saw nothing. "Well, of course you didn't *see*. The baby's floating in water. Once I start the turn, the baby finishes the last quarter turn by itself. Now it's not a breech baby. It's a head presentation. Normal." She listened to the fetal heart again to be sure it was still strong.

In no time, Hema, possessed of the same bustling energy with which she dealt cards or drilled us on our spelling, was done. Only one baby refused to somersault.

"For all I know, this clinic could be the biggest waste of time. Ghosh wants me to do a study to see how many babies float back to where they were after version. You know how he talks. 'The unexamined practice is not worth practicing.'" She snorted, remembering something else. "I had a friend when I was a child, a neighbor boy by the name of Velu. He kept chickens. Now and then a hen would cluck in a peculiar way, and Velu knew, don't ask me how, that it meant an egg was stuck in a transverse position. He would reach in and turn it to vertical. The chicken stopped clucking, and the egg would pop out. Velu was obnoxious at your age. But I remember his trick with the chicken now, and I wonder if I underestimated him."

I didn't say a word for fear of breaking the spell. It was so rare to hear her think aloud like this.

"Between you and me, boys, I have no desire to publish a paper that might put me out of this business. I *enjoy* Version Clinic."

"Me, too," Shiva said.

"Whether it is India or here, the ladies are all the same," Hema said, gazing at the women milling around. No one had left. They waited for the tea, bread, and vitamin pill that would follow the clinic. They grinned back at Hema with sisterly affection—no, with adoration. "Look at them! All happy and radiant. In a few weeks, when labor starts, they'll be yelling, screaming, cursing their husbands. They'll turn into she-devils. You won't recognize them. But now they're like angels." She sighed. "A woman is never more a woman than in this state."

The problems of the city and the country had disappeared, at least for me and Shiva. How fortunate we were to have Hema and Ghosh as parents. What was there to fear?

"Ma," Shiva said, "Ghosh says pregnancy is a sexually transmitted disease."

"He says it knowing you will repeat it to me. That rascal. He shouldn't be telling you such things."

"Can you show us where the baby comes out?" Shiva said. I knew he was utterly serious, and I also knew that with those words he'd broken the spell. I was furious with him. Kids need a certain cunning when it comes to dealing with adults, and somehow Shiva had none. In the same mysterious fashion with which permanent teeth arrived, so also self-consciousness and embarrassment came to camouflage my guilt, while shame took root in my body as a price for curiosity.

"Okay. That's enough. Time for you chaps to go home," Hema said.

"Ma, what does the word 'sexual' mean?" Shiva said, as she pushed us out. I studied my twin. For once I was unsure of his intent: Was he teasing her, or was this just his unconventional way of thinking? Hema's response only added to my confusion: "I have to go to the wards for a short time. You boys don't leave the house." She shooed us off. Her tone was annoyed, and yet if I was not mistaken, she was trying very hard to hide a smile.

CHAPTER 24

Loving the Dying

I N A C O U N T R Y where you cannot describe the beauty of the land without using the word "sky," the sight of three jets streaking up in a steep climb was breathtaking.

I happened to be outside on the front lawn. The shock wave traveled through the earth to my feet and ran up my spine before I heard the explosion. I stood rooted there. Smoke rose in the distance. The stunned silence that followed was shattered by the screech of hundreds of birds, which took to the sky, and by the barking of every dog in the city.

I still wanted to believe that this—the jets, the bombs—was all part of some grand plan, the expected course of events, and that Hema and Ghosh understood what was going on, even if I didn't. Whatever this was, they could turn it around.

When Ghosh emerged from the house, running as fast as he could, and when he grabbed me, fear and concern in his eyes, the last of my illusions vanished. The adults weren't in charge. There were clues to that earlier, I suppose, but even when I had seen the old woman pummeled by the Emperor's guards, it suited me to believe that Hema and Ghosh still controlled the universe.

But fixing this was beyond their ability.

GHOSH, HEMA, AND ALMAZ dragged mattresses into the corridor. Our whitewashed *chikka* walls—packed mud and straw—offered little protection. In the corridor, the bullets would at least have to pass through two or three *chikka* walls. Bullets whined overhead, sounding close, while the pops and thuds sounded distant. Glass tinkled in the kitchen, and later we found a bullet had shattered a pane. I lay on the mattress, frozen, my body incapable of movement. I waited for someone to say, This is a colossal error that will soon be corrected, and you can go out and play again.

"I suppose we can assume the army and air force decided *not* to join the coup," Ghosh said, looking to see if this understatement got a response from Hema. It did.

Genet's lips were quivering. I could only imagine how worried she was: I felt a cold flutter in my belly whenever I thought about Rosina, gone for more than twenty-four hours now. I reached out, and Genet clutched my hand.

By dusk, the firing intensified, and it turned bitterly cold. Matron, fearless, went back and forth to the hospital, despite our pleas that she stay. When I had to go to the bathroom I crawled. I saw through the window the bright tracers crisscrossing the sky.

Gebrew locked and chained the main gate and withdrew from his sentry hut to the main hospital complex. The nurses and nursing students were bedded down in the nurses' dining room with W. W. Gonad as well as Adam, the hospital compounder, watching over them.

NEAR MIDNIGHT, there was a knock at our back door, and when Ghosh opened it, there stood Rosina! Genet, Shiva, and I swarmed all over her, hugging her. Through hot tears Genet screamed at her mother in Tigrinya for leaving her and making her worry.

Matron stood grinning just behind Rosina; some instinct had made Matron and Gebrew go down to the locked gate to check one last time. Huddled against it they found Rosina, sheltering from the wind.

As she gobbled down food, Rosina told us that things were much worse than she'd imagined. "I wanted to reach the upper part of town, but there was an army roadblock. I had to take a big detour, first this way, then that." A firefight around a villa forced her to take cover, and then army tanks and armored vehicles prevented her return. She spent the night on the porch of a shop at the Merkato, where others trapped by darkness had taken shelter. In the morning, she'd been unable to move from the Merkato because of roaming army platoons who ordered everyone off the street. It had taken her till nightfall to cover a distance of three miles. She confirmed our worst fears: the Imperial Bodyguard was under attack by the army, air force, and police. Pitched battles were being fought all over, but the army was steadily concentrating its efforts on General Mebratu's position.

Rosina snuck off to her quarters to wash and change clothes, and she returned with her mattress, and also with *caramela* for us. Genet still hadn't forgiven her, but she clung to her.

Matron sank down on the mattress and stretched out her feet. She reached under her sweater and pulled out a revolver, tucking it between mattress and wall.

"Matron!" Hema said.

"I know, Hema . . . I *didn't* buy this with the Baptist money, if that is what you are thinking."

"That's not what I was thinking at all," Hema said, looking at the gun as if it might explode.

"I promise you, this was a gift. I keep it in a place where no soul could find it. But you see, looters—that's what we need to worry about," Matron said. "This might stop them. I did buy two other guns. I've passed them out to W. W. Gonad and Adam."

Almaz carried in a basket of *injera* and lamb curry. We ate with our fingers from this communal dish. Then it was back to waiting, listening to the crackles and pops in the distance. I was too tense to read or do anything but lie there.

Shiva sat cross-legged. He carefully folded a sheet of paper, then tore it in half and then repeated the process again and again till he had a bunch of tiny squares. I knew he was just as shaken as I was by the turn of events. Watching his hands moving methodically, I felt as if I was keeping my mind and my hands busy. Now he put one paper square by itself, then counted and stacked three squares next to it, then seven, then eleven. I had to ask.

"Prime numbers," he said as if that explained anything. He rocked back and forth, his lips moving. I marveled at his gift for distancing himself from what was going on by dancing, or by drawing the motorcycle, or playing with prime numbers. He had so many ways of climbing into the tree house in his head, escaping the madness below, and pulling the ladder up behind him; I was envious.

But Shiva's escape was incomplete tonight; I knew, because in watching him, I felt no relief.

"Don't try," I said to Shiva. "Let's go to sleep."

He put his papers away at once.

Rosina and Genet were already fast asleep, both exhausted. Rosina's return was a great reprieve, but my greatest relief that night came when my head touched Shiva's, a sense of safety and completion, a home at the end of the world. Thank God that whatever happened we'd always have ShivaMarion to fall back on, I thought. Surely, we could always summon ShivaMarion when we needed to, though I guiltily remembered that we hadn't done so in a while. I nudged his ribs and he nudged back, and I could feel him smile without opening his eyes. I took reassurance from that, because earlier that day he'd been a stranger sitting on the Version Clinic steps, but now he was Shiva again. Together we had an unfair advantage on the rest of the world.

I awoke at some point to find everyone but Matron and Ghosh asleep. The gunfire came in intense bursts, but with unpredictable moments of quiet, so that I could hear Matron clearly as she spoke to Ghosh: "When the Emperor fled Addis in '36, just before the Italians marched in, it was chaos . . . I should have gone to the British Legation. One look at the Sikh infantrymen at the gate, with their turbans and beards and bayonets, and no looter was going to get near. Biggest mistake I made was not to go there."

"Why didn't you?"

"Embarrassment. I'd dined once with the ambassador and his wife. I felt so out of place. Thank God for John Melly. He was a young missionary doctor. He sat next to me. He talked about his faith, and his hopes to build a medical school here . . ." Her voice trailed off.

"You told me about him once," Ghosh said. "You loved him. You said one day you'd tell me all about it."

There was a long silence. I was tempted to open my eyes, but I knew that would break the spell.

Matron's voice sounded thick. "By staying here, I was responsible for John Melly's death. It wasn't Missing Hospital then. Surely, a hospital will be spared is what I thought anyway. But our own ward boy led a mob here. They snatched a young nursing assistant and raped her. I fled to the other end of the infirmary, where I found Dr. Sorkis. You never met him. A Hungarian. A terrible surgeon, a morose fellow. He operated like a technician. Disinterested. We'd had such a parade of short-time doctors till you and Hema and Stone arrived . . ." She sighed again. "On that night, though, Sorkis made all the difference in the world. He had a shotgun and a pistol. When the mob reached the infirmary, I pleaded through the closed door with Tesfaye—that was the ward boy's name— 'Don't be part of this evil, for the sake of God.' Oh, but he mocked me. 'There is no God, Matron,' he said. Said many other vile things.

"When they broke down a panel on the door, Dr. Sorkis fired first one barrel at eye level, and the second barrel at groin level. The sound deafened me. When my hearing came back, I heard men screaming in pain. Sorkis reloaded and went outside, firing the shotgun at knee level.

"I confess I felt pleasure to see them hobble away. Instead of fear, I felt anger. Tesfaye came charging again . . . I think he thought the rabble was still with him. Sorkis raised his pistol—this very one here—and he squeezed the trigger. Even before I heard the sound, I saw Tesfaye's teeth spray out and the back of his head pop. The fight went out of the rest.

"When the Italians marched into town the next morning, call me a traitor, Ghosh, but I for one welcomed them because the looting stopped. That's when I discovered that John Melly had tried to get me to safety. He stopped his truck to help a wounded man, and when he did, a drunken looter came right up to him and fired a pistol into Melly's chest. For no reason at all!

"I hurried to the legation when I heard. I nursed him round the clock. He suffered for two weeks, but his faith never wavered. It is one reason I never left Ethiopia. I felt I owed it to him. He'd ask me to sing 'Bunyan's Hymn' to him while I held his hand. I must have sung it a thousand times before he died.

> "He who would valiant be
> 'Gainst all disaster
> Let him in constancy
> Follow the Master.
> There's no discouragement
> Shall make him once relent
> His first avowed intent
> To be a Pilgrim."

What incredible discoveries one could make with one's eyes closed: I'd never heard Matron talk (let alone sing) about her past; in my mind it was as if she'd arrived into the world fully formed, in nun's garb, always running Missing. Her whispered tale, her confession of her fear, of love, of a killing, were more frightening than the gunfire in the distance. In that dark corridor, lit only by the intermittent glow of flares and artillery tracers which made dancing shadows on the wall, I pressed hard against Shiva's skull. What else did I not know? I wanted to sleep, but Matron's hymn, her quavering voice, still echoed in my ears.

CHAPTER 25

Anger as a
Form of Love

B Y THE NEXT EVENING, it was all over—the coup had failed. In three days, hundreds of Imperial Bodyguard soldiers had been killed, and many more had surrendered. I saw one man being dragged out of the cinder-block building across from Missing; he'd tried to get rid of his distinctive uniform, but the fact that he was wearing just a vest and boxers identified him as a rebel.

As the army tanks and armored cars closed in, General Mebratu and a small contingent of his men fled from the back of the Old Palace, heading north into the mountains under cover of darkness.

The morning after that, Emperor Haile Selassie the First, Conquering Lion of Judah, King of Kings, Descendant of Solomon, returned to Addis Ababa by plane. Word of his arrival spread like wildfire, and a dancing, ululating crowd lined the road as his motorcade went by. Throngs took to the street, arms linked, hopping in unison, springs in their feet, chanting his name long after he passed. Among them were Gebrew, W. W. Gonad, and Almaz; she reported that His Majesty's face had been full of love for his people, appreciation for their loyalty. "I saw him as clearly as I see you standing there," she said. "I swear he had tears in his eyes, God strike me down if I am lying." The university students who had marched through the streets a few days before were nowhere to be seen.

The mood in the city was celebratory. Shops were open. Taxis of both the horse-drawn and petrol variety were out with a vengeance. The sun was shining and it was a beautiful day in Addis Ababa.

In our bungalow, the mood was somber. I'd always thought of General Mebratu and Zemui as the "good guys," my heroes. The Emperor was far from a "bad guy," and the attempts of the coup leaders to make him one weren't convincing. Still, I wanted the General to succeed in what he'd started. The tide had turned, and the worst possible thing had happened: my heroes had become the "bad guys," and one didn't dare say otherwise.

Rosina and Genet suffered agonies, waiting for news, knowing that whatever it was, it wouldn't be good.

It sunk in for me that Zemui would probably never pick up his motorcycle again. Darwin would get no more letters from his friend. The bridge evenings with General Mebratu as the life of the party were almost certainly over.

The Emperor offered a huge reward for the capture of General Mebratu and his brother. The night after the Emperor's return there were gun battles in different neighborhoods as the last of the "rebels" were hunted down. I felt so sorry for the rank-and-file Imperial Body-guard men like the one I saw dragged away: his crime was to belong to the losing side, or perhaps even the wrong side. But all he'd done was follow orders; General Mebratu had determined his fate.

I didn't know what to think about our General anymore; the man we knew and admired seemed unrelated to the notorious and now hunted rebel who led the failed coup. Every time I heard small arms fire, I wondered if that was his and Zemui's last stand.

I AWOKE THE NEXT MORNING to loud wails from Rosina's quarters. I ran into Ghosh and Hema in the corridor, and we went rushing out in our pajamas.

Gebrew and two somber men stood outside Rosina's door. Her hysterical wailing was in Tigrinya, but its meaning would have been clear in any language.

We learned that General Mebratu's small group had escaped up into the Entoto Mountains and then circled back into the lowlands near the town of Nazareth. They were headed to Mount Zuquala, a dormant volcano, where they hoped to shelter on land belonging to the Mojo family.

In the end, it was peasants who betrayed the General with loud cries of *lulululu* when they stumbled on his group.

A police force soon surrounded General Mebratu. In that last firefight, running out of ammunition, the General disarmed a wounded policeman, then crawled to another wounded policeman to get his weapon. He called to Eskinder, his brother, to help, but instead Eskinder shot our beloved General in the face before putting the gun in his own mouth. I wondered if they had made a suicide pact. Or had Eskinder made a decision for the two of them? As for Zemui, father of Genet, friend of Darwin, he refused to surrender or to take his own life. He charged the forces that had him surrounded, and they gunned him down.

Eskinder's bullet had hit the General's cheek and ripped out his right eye, leaving it dangling, before lodging under the left eye. By some miracle the bullet did not enter the skull. The General was unconscious but alive. He was rushed to the military hospital in Addis Ababa, a distance of about one hundred kilometers.

WE SAT AROUND the dining table, the four of us, trying to block out the wailing from Rosina's. I could hear Genet's sobs from time to time. Though Hema had gone in and come out of Rosina's quarters, I couldn't bring myself to do so. Shiva had his hands over his ears, and his eyes were moist.

While we were still huddled at the table Mr. Loomis's office called. "Business as usual," Ghosh said, putting down the phone. Loomis Town & Country was open, and if we were Tuesday House, we had to remember to bring our sports gear.

Despite our misgivings, Ghosh convinced us that school would be better than listening to Rosina's wailing all day. He drove us there, Shiva and I sharing the front seat.

Near the National Bank a crowd spilled off the sidewalk, into the street, charged with a strange energy, heading toward us. We inched forward. Suddenly I saw directly in front of us, as clearly as if they were on a stage, three bodies strung up on makeshift gallows. Ghosh told us to look away, but it was too late. In their immobility, the corpses appeared to have been dangling there for centuries. Their heads were angled awkwardly, and their hands lashed behind their backs.

The crowd swarmed around our car. The festivities were apparently just over. One young man walking with two others slapped the hood of our car, the sound making me jump. He grinned, and whatever it was he said, it wasn't nice. Someone else slammed the roof above our heads, and then we felt our car rock back and forth.

I was sure the mob would string us up by our necks, too. I clutched the dashboard, a scream in my throat. Ghosh said, "Keep calm, boys! Smile, wave, show your teeth! Nod your head . . . make it look as if we came for the show." I don't know if I smiled, but I do know that I stifled that scream. Shiva and I grinned like monkeys and pretended we weren't frightened. We waved. Perhaps it was the sight of identical twins, or the sense that we were just as crazy inside the car as they were on the outside, but we heard laughter, and the thumps on the car were now more good-natured, less violent.

Ghosh kept nodding his head, a big smile on his face, waving, keeping up an agitated chatter, "I know, I know, you unkempt rascal, good morning to you, too, yes indeed, I have come to delight in this heathen spectacle . . . Let's hang *you*, by Jove, it certainly is most civilized of you to do this, thank you, thank you," and inching forward. I'd never seen him this way before, expressing such dangerous contempt and anger under a smiling and false exterior. At last we were through, the car moving freely. Looking back, I could see hands tugging at the leather shoes of the corpses.

Shiva and I had arms around each other in our ancient pose. We were badly shaken. In the school parking lot, Ghosh turned off the engine and held us to him. I wept for Zemui, for General Mebratu, shot in the eye, for Genet and Rosina, and at last for myself. To be in Ghosh's arms and against his chest was to find the safest haven in the world. He cleaned my face with one end of his kerchief and then used the other end on Shiva. "That was the bravest thing you might ever do in your lives. You kept your head. You screwed your courage to the sticking place. I'm proud of you. I tell you what—we'll go out of town this weekend. To the hot springs in Sodere, or Woliso. We'll swim and forget all about this."

He gave us each a final hug. "If I find Mekonnen, then he'll be here with his taxi the usual time. If I don't find him, I'll be here myself at four." When I was about to enter my classroom, I turned back to look. Ghosh was still standing there, waving.

Loomis Town & Country was abuzz. I heard boasts of what the other kids had seen and done. I felt no desire to contribute or listen.

THAT DAY, while we were in school, four men in a jeep came to visit Ghosh. They took him away as if he were a common criminal, his hands jacked up behind his back. They slapped him when he tried to protest. Hema learned this from W. W. Gonad, who told the men they were surely mistaken in taking away Missing's surgeon. For his impertinence W.W. got a boot in his stomach.

Hema refused to believe Ghosh was gone. She ran home, certain that she'd find him sunk into his armchair, his sockless feet up on the stool, reading a book. In anticipation of seeing him, in the certainty that he would be there, she was already furious with him.

She burst through the front door of our bungalow. "Do you see how dangerous it is for us to associate with the General? What have I been telling you? You could get us all killed!" Whenever she came at him like that, all her cylinders firing, it was Ghosh's habit to flourish an imaginary cape like a matador facing a charging bull. We found it funny, even if Hema never did.

But the house was quiet. No matador. She went from room to room, the jingle of her anklets echoing in the hallways. She imagined Ghosh with his arm twisted behind his back, being punched in the face, kicked in the genitals . . . She ran to the commode as her lunch came up. Later she lit incense, rang the bell, and vowed that she'd make pilgrimages to the shrines at Tirupati and Velankani if they released Ghosh alive.

Hema picked up the phone to tell Matron. But the line was dead. The phones had stopped working when the bombs fell, and ever since, they had only worked sporadically. She stood looking out of the kitchen window.

Ghosh's car was at the hospital. But even if she got in the car, where was she supposed to go? Where had they taken him? And if she went and they arrested her as well, then her sons would be left alone . . . It took a monumental effort of will for her to decide to wait for us.

Hema could hear a sobbing monologue from the servant's quarters— the voice was Rosina's, though it was hoarse and sounded nothing like her. It was addressed to Zemui, or to God, or to the men who killed her husband. It had begun that morning, and it had not reached its zenith.

Hema saw Genet emerge, red-eyed but composed, leading a wobbly Rosina. They were heading for the outhouse. They had no one to mourn with them other than Almaz and Gebrew, who at that moment were elsewhere. Hema felt that Genet had aged suddenly, that a hardness had crept into the little girl's face, and the sugar and spice and everything nice had died.

Hema splashed water on her cheeks. She took a deep breath. It was crucial that she stay calm for our sakes, she told herself.

She drank a glass of water that had passed through the purifier. She had just put the glass down when Almaz came running in. "Madam, don't drink the water. They are saying the rebels poisoned the water supply."

But it was too late because Hema felt her face burning and then came the worst belly cramps of her life.

CHAPTER 26

The Face of Suffering

WHEN GEBREW MET US at the gate and said men had come and snatched Ghosh from Missing, my childhood ended.

I was twelve years old, too old to cry, but I cried for the second time that day because it was all I knew to do.

I was not yet man enough to sweep into the house of whoever had taken Ghosh away and rescue him. The only skill I had was to keep going.

Shiva was ashen, silent. For a brief moment I felt immensely sad for him, my handsome brother who had reached the height of a teenager without shedding the rounded shoulders of boyhood. His eyes reflected my pain, and for that instant we were one organism, with no separation of flesh or consciousness. And we ran as one being, The Twins, up the hill, frantic to get home.

WE FOUND HEMA on the sofa, pale, sweaty, wet strands of hair sticking to her forehead. Almaz, her cheeks tear-stained, and looking nothing like the stoic Almaz we knew, was by Hema's side, holding a bucket.

"She drank the water," Almaz said before we could ask. "Don't drink the water."

"I'm all right," Hema said, but her words were hollow.

It wasn't all right. How could she say it was? My worst nightmare had come true: Ghosh gone, and now Hema mortally ill.

I buried my face in the darkness of her sari, my nostrils filled with her scent. I felt responsible for it all. The General's ill-fated rebellion, Zemui's death, the arrest of a man who was more father to me than any man can be, and, yes, even the poison in the water . . .

Just then the front door flew open, and Matron and Dr. Bachelli ran in. Bachelli carried his well-worn leather bag, his chest heaving. Matron, also gasping for breath, said, "Hema! There's nothing wrong with the water. It was just a rumor. It's all right."

Hema looked confused. "But . . . I've had cramps, nausea. I threw up."

"I drank it myself," Bachelli said. "There's nothing wrong with it. You will feel better in a few minutes."

Shiva looked at me.

A glimmer of hope.

Hema rose then, testing her limbs, her head. Later we found out that similar scenes were playing out all over the city. It was an early lesson in medicine. Sometimes, if you think you're sick, you will be.

If there was a God, he had just given us a huge reprieve. I wanted another. "Ma, what about Ghosh? Why did they take him? Will they hang him? What did he do? Is he hurt? Where did they take him?"

Matron sat us down on the sofa. Her bright handkerchief came out. "There, there, little loves. We'll sort this out. We all need to be strong, for Ghosh's sake. Panic does not serve us."

Almaz, silent till then, watching with her hands on her hips, interrupted to say in Amharic, "What are we waiting for? We have to go at once to Kerchele Prison. Let me get the food ready. And we need blankets. Clothes. Soap. Come on!"

THE VOLKSWAGEN FELT like a strange machine with Hema driving. Bachelli sat up front, and Almaz and Matron were in the backseat with us on their laps. We made our jerky way through the city.

I saw Addis Ababa anew. I had always thought it a beautiful city, with broad avenues in its heart, and many squares with monuments and fenced gardens around which traffic had to circle: Mexico Square, Patriot's Square, Menelik Square . . . Foreigners, whose only image of Ethiopia was that of starving people sitting in blinding dust, were disbelieving when they landed in the mist and chill of Addis Ababa at night and saw the boulevards and the tram-track lights of Churchill Road. They wondered if the plane had turned around in the night and they were in Brussels or Amsterdam.

But in the aftermath of the coup, in the light of Ghosh's arrest, the city looked different to me. The squares which commemorated the bloodshed of Adowa and the liberation from the Italians were now fitting places for a mob to conduct a lynching. As for the villas I had once admired—pink, mauve, tan, and hidden by bougainvillea—it was in these houses that men like the General or his counterparts in the army and police plotted the revolution and its betrayal. There was treachery in the streets, treachery in the villas. I could smell it. Perhaps it had always been there.

SOON WE WERE AT the green gates of the prison everyone called Kerchele, a corruption of the Italian word *carcere,* or incarcerate. Others called it the Alem Bekagne, an Amharic expression that meant "Good-bye, cruel world." The entrance was past a railway crossing on a busy trunk road. There was no pavement here, no shoulder, just asphalt falling abruptly off into dirt, dirt now stirred by the feet of hundreds of anxious relatives, who became our kin in suffering. They stood rooted in their helplessness, but they let us pass between them till we reached the sentry office.

Before Matron could ask, the man said without looking up, "I don't know if he or she is here, I don't know when I will know if he or she is here or not here, if you leave food or blankets or whatever, if he or she is here, they might get it, if not somebody else gets it. Write his name on a paper with whatever you are dropping off, and I will not answer any questions."

People leaned against the wall, and women stood under umbrellas unfurled out of habit even though the sun was behind clouds. Almaz found a spot to squat where she could observe the comings and goings, and then she did not budge.

An hour passed. My feet ached, but still we waited. We were the only foreigners there, and the crowd was sympathetic. One man, a lecturer at the university, said his father had been in this jail many years ago. "As a boy I would run the three miles from my house, once a day, to bring food. He was so thin, but each time he would feed me first and make me take back more than half the food. He knew that for him to eat, we had to starve. One day, when my older brother and mother came with food, they heard the dreaded words 'No need to bring food anymore.' That's how we knew my father was dead. And you know why they arrested my brother today? For no reason. He is a hardworking businessman. But he is the child of one of their old enemies. We are the first suspects. The old enemies and the children of enemies. God knows why they spared me. I was in the demonstration by the university students. But they took my brother instead. Because he is the oldest."

Bachelli took a taxi to the Juventus Club to see if he could get the Italian consul involved, and then he had to return to Missing. With one doctor arrested, and his wife waiting outside the jail, it all rested on the shoulders of the third doctor, namely Bachelli. He could keep things going, oversee the nurses and Adam, the compounder.

Shiva, Hema, Matron, and I returned to the car to rest our feet, to get warm, to huddle. After fifteen minutes we returned to stare at the gates. Back and forth we went, reluctant to leave, even though we were accomplishing nothing.

WHEN IT WAS QUITE DARK, a man with a *shama* covering his head, mouth, and upper torso walked by, just as we emerged from the car. But for his shiny boots and the fact that he'd come from the narrow lane on the side of the prison, he might have passed for just another man heading home. In his hand he swung a cloth showing the outline of a covered pot—his lunch or dinner. He stared at Matron. He paused behind the car, his back to the road as if he were taking a leak.

"Don't turn this way!" he said harshly, in Amharic. "The doctor is here."

"Is he all right?" Matron whispered.

He hesitated. "A little bruised. Yes, but he is fine."

"Please, I beg you," Hema broke in. I had never heard her beg anyone in my life. "He's my husband. What is going to happen next? Will they let him go? He had nothing to do with all this—"

The man hissed. A large family walked by. When they passed, he said, "Talking to you is enough for someone to accuse me. If I want to be safe, I must accuse someone. Like animals eating our young. It's a bad time. I'm talking to you because you saved my wife's life."

"Thank you. Is there anything we can do for you? For him—"

"Not tonight. In the morning at ten o'clock, be in this spot. No, be farther away. See that post with the streetlight? Be there and bring a blanket, money, and a dish just like this. The money is for him. Go home now."

I ran over to fetch Almaz, who had not left her spot, her voluminous skirts ringed around her like a circus tent, her white *gabby* wrapped around her head and shoulders, only her eyes showing. She wouldn't hear of leaving. She was going to stay the night. Nothing would persuade her. Reluctantly we left her, but only after we forced Almaz to put on Hema's sweater and then wrap herself with the *gabby*.

At home, mercifully the phones were working. Matron got the British and Indian embassies to promise to send their envoys in the morning. None of the royals would talk to Matron; if the Emperor's own son was under suspicion, so were his nieces, nephews, and grandchildren. We heard that there were rumblings of discontent among the junior army officers who felt their generals erred in not joining the coup; there must have been some truth to that, because that day the Emperor authorized a pay raise for all army officers. The word was that only the intense rivalry and jealousy between the senior army and Imperial Body-guard officers had saved His Majesty.

THAT NIGHT SHIVA and I slept with Hema in her bed. Ghosh's Bryl-creem scent was on the pillow. His books were piled on the nightstand with a pen wedged in *French's Index of Differential Diagnosis* to mark a page, and his reading glasses balanced precariously on the cover. His bedtime rituals of inspecting his profile and sucking his belly in and out ten times, of lying across the mattress for a few minutes so his head hung back over the edge—"antigravity" maneuvers, as he called them—were unexciting, but in his absence, their importance was revealed. "Another day in paradise" was his inevitable pronouncement when he settled his head on his pillow. Now I understood what that meant: the uneventful day was a precious gift. The three of us lay there and waited as if he'd just gone to the kitchen and would fill the doorway any second. Hema sobbed. She voiced our thoughts when she said, "Lord, I promise never to take that man for granted again."

Matron, who'd decided to sleep in our house, in the bed that belonged to me and Shiva, called out, "Hema, go to sleep now. Boys, say your prayers. Don't worry."

I prayed to all the deities in the room, from Muruga to the Bleeding Heart of Jesus.

IN THE EARLY MORNING Almaz was back. There'd been no news. "But I stood up whenever a car came and went. If the doctor was in the car, I wanted him to see me."

Hema and Matron planned to go to the arranged spot at ten o'clock, carrying food, blankets, and money. Then they'd make the rounds of the embassies and the royals. Hema convinced us to stay at home. "What if

Ghosh calls home? Someone needs to be here to take the message." Rosina and Genet were there, so we weren't completely alone. Almaz, after rejuvenating herself with bread and hot tea, insisted on going back to Kerchele with Hema and Matron.

By noon, they were still not back. Shiva, Genet, and I fixed sandwiches while Rosina looked on, distracted. She was red-eyed and hoarse. "Don't worry," she said, "Ghosh will be all right." Somehow her words weren't reassuring. Genet, pale and strangely listless, squeezed my hand.

KOOCHOOLOO WAS THE KIND OF MUTT who rarely made any noise. At Missing, barking at strangers would have been a never-ending proposition. So when I heard Koochooloo bark, I paid attention. Looking out of the living room window I saw a scruffy man in a green army jacket stroll up the driveway and disappear behind our house. Koochooloo turned rabid, unleashing a volley of deafening yelps. Her message was *A very dangerous man is at our doorstep.*

I ran to the kitchen where Rosina, Genet, and Shiva were already at the window. Koochooloo was just below us, loud as I had ever heard her. She moved forward, her neck disappearing in a collar of raised fur, her teeth bared. The man pulled open his heavy jacket and drew a revolver which was tucked in his pants. He had no belt, no holster, and no shirt, just a white vest. At the sight of the gun, Koochooloo fled. She was brave but not stupid.

"I know him," Rosina whispered. "Zemui gave him a ride a few times. He is army. He used to stand just outside the gate, hoping Zemui would come by. He was always flattering Zemui. 'Envy is behind flattery,' I told Zemui. Zemui would pretend not to see him, or he'd tell him he was going in another direction."

The army man tucked the gun back into his pants, then he walked over to the BMW and caressed the seat.

"See! What did I tell you?" Rosina said.

"Come out, please," he called, looking our way. "I know you're in there."

"Stay here," Rosina said, drawing a deep breath. "No. Don't stay. You all go by way of the front door and run to the hospital. Wait with W.W. Wait till I come for you." She threw the bolt back. "Lock the door behind me," she said, as she stepped out.

I cannot tell you why the three of us, instead of obeying her, simply opened the door again and followed her. It wasn't bravery. Perhaps the notion of running away felt more dangerous than staying with the one adult we could count on.

The intruder's eyes were bloodshot, and he looked as if he'd slept in his clothes, but his manner was jocular. The bulky camouflage jacket was big enough to swallow him, and yet his arms stuck out of the sleeves. He was missing his beret. He had a dark vertical furrow in the middle of his forehead, like a seam where the two halves of his face met. Despite the scraggly mustache, he looked too young for his uniform.

"This," he said, almost purring as he stroked the motorcycle tank, "belongs to . . . to the army now."

Rosina pulled her black *shama* over her hair, the gesture of a woman entering a church. She stood silent and obedient before him.

"Did you hear me, woman? This belongs to the army."

"I suppose it is true," she said, eyes downcast. "Perhaps the army will come and get it." Her tone was deferential, which was why her words took a few seconds to sink in. I wondered later why she chose to provoke him and put us at risk.

The soldier blinked. Then he exclaimed in a high-pitched voice, "*I* am the army!"

He grabbed her hand and yanked her to him.

"*I* am the army."

"Yes. This is the doctor's house. If you are taking anything, you should let him know."

"The doctor?" He laughed. "The doctor is in jail. I'll let him know when I see him again. I'll ask him why he hires an impertinent whore like you. We should hang you for sleeping with that traitor."

Rosina stared at the ground.

"Are you deaf, woman?"

"No, sir."

"Go on. Tell me one good thing about Zemui. *Tell me!*"

"He was the father of my child," Rosina said softly, refusing to look him in the face.

"A tragedy for that bastard child. Just tell me something more. Go on!"

"He did what he was told. He tried to be a good soldier, like you, sir."

"A good soldier, huh? Like me?" He turned to us, as if asking us to witness her impudence.

Then, so quickly that none of us saw it coming, he backhanded her. It was a tremendous blow, sending her reeling, and yet somehow she didn't fall. She held her *shama* to her face. I could see the blood. She brought her feet together and stood upright. Shiva and I instinctively clasped hands.

I felt something wet running down my shin. I wondered if he'd notice, but he was preoccupied with a nasty gash on the knuckle of his middle finger. I could see a flash of white, either sinew or tendon or a tooth fragment.

"The devil! You cut me, you gap-toothed bitch."

Out of the corner of my eye, I saw Genet moving. I knew that look on her face so well. She flew at him. He raised his foot, caught her in the chest, and pushed her off before she could get near him. He pulled out his gun again, cocked it, pointed it at Rosina. "Do it again, bastard child, and I'll kill your mother. Do you understand? Do you want to be an orphan? And you two," he said, addressing us, "stay out of my way. I could kill the lot of you right now and I'd get a medal."

We all recognized the plastic key chain that he pulled from his pocket. It was in the shape of the Congo. There was only one like it in our world, and it belonged to Zemui.

In getting the motorcycle off its stand, he almost fell over. After straddling the bike, he looked around for the lever and, finding it, he tried to kick-start the engine, but the bike was in gear, and so it lurched forward, almost toppling him again. When he got his balance, he looked to see if we'd noticed.

He tromped on the pedal, trying to find neutral. It was such a contrast to Zemui, who merely toed the lever and who handled the BMW as if it were featherlight. Zemui would prime the cylinders with a slow-motion stroke, followed by a brisk kick, and the motor would chug into life. Thinking of Zemui, who'd fought to the death rather than surrender, I felt ashamed. It made me want to act in a manner befitting the bike's true owner. I squeezed Shiva's hand. ShivaMarion was on the same page, I could tell, because he squeezed back.

The soldier flailed at the kick-start lever, as if he were stomping an enemy, his face getting flushed, sweat pouring off his brow. I smelled gas. He'd flooded the carburetor.

It was a cool day, the sun filtering through a few clouds and glinting off the chrome of the motorcycle. He paused to get his breath, then took off his jacket, slung it on the seat behind him. He shook out the hand with the bloody knuckle. He was a scrawny, thin fellow, I saw. Annoyed and humiliated by the engine resisting him, his lips drew back in a snarl. His frustration was dangerous.

"Let us push it for you. You flooded the engine and that's the only way to start it now." This from Shiva.

"When you get to the bottom of the hill, just put it in first gear," I said. "It'll start right away."

He looked over, surprised, as if he didn't know we were capable of speech, let alone in his mother tongue.

"Is that how he started it?"

He never ever flooded it, I wanted to say.

"Every time," I said. "Especially if he hadn't started it for a while."

He frowned. "Okay, you two help me push the motorcycle." He shoved his gun deeper into his waistband, behind his belt buckle. He tucked the jacket that he had thrown over the seat under his buttocks.

From the top of our driveway, the gravel road leading down to Casualty started off flat and then descended and seemed to disappear over a ledge, beyond which one could see the lower branches of trees that were just within the perimeter wall. Only when you were halfway down did you see how the road turned sharply, well before the ledge, and then went on to the roundabout near Casualty.

"Push!" he said. "Push, you bastards."

We did, and he helped by leaning forward and walking the machine. Soon he was rolling, licking his lips, happy. The bike weaved and the handlebars made wide excursions.

"Steady!" I called. ShivaMarion was pushing in unison, a three-legged trot that soon became a four-legged sprint.

"No problem," he shouted, putting his feet on the pedals. "Push!"

We gathered speed on the down slope now.

"Open the gas cock! Open the valve," Shiva called out.

"What? Oh, yes," he said and he took his right hand off the handlebars to feel for the petcock under the tank, precious seconds ticking away.

"It's on the other side!" I shouted.

He switched hands. He'd never find it and it didn't matter because there was enough fuel in the carburetor to take him at least a mile.

The bike was traveling at speed now, springs squeaking and mudguards rattling, its weight accelerating it down the hill, aided by our efforts. He'd taken his eyes off the road to find the petcock. By the time he looked up, ShivaMarion was running as fast as it could, adding every ounce of thrust possible to his progress. I saw his white-knuckled grip on the throttle, while his left hand was undecided whether to continue its search or return to the handlebars.

"Put it in gear, quick," I shouted, giving the bike a last desperate push.

"Full gas!" Shiva yelled.

He was slow in responding, first twisting the throttle all the way, then glancing down to stamp on the gear lever. For a heart-stopping moment when it slipped into first, the bike seized, the back wheel locking, we had failed . . .

And just when I thought that, the engine sputtered and roared to life, revving to its red line with a vengeance, as if it were saying, *I'll take it from here, boys*. It surged forward, the back tire spitting gravel at us, nearly throwing the rider off, which only made him cling harder, squeezing the throttle in a death grip instead of letting go.

A howl emerged as he saw what was ahead. He had only a few feet and a few seconds to negotiate the turn before the ledge. It is an axiom of motorcycling that you must always look in the direction you want to go and never at what you are trying to avoid. His gaze, I was sure, was fixed on the approaching precipice. The BMW roared ahead, still accelerating. I raced after him.

The front wheel hit the concrete curb at the ledge and stopped. The back wheel flew up in the air; but for the weight of that big engine, the motorcycle would have somersaulted over. Instead it was the rider who sailed past the handlebars, his howl now a scream. He flew in an arc, shooting over the ledge and then falling until his motion was arrested by a tree trunk. I heard a *whump*, an involuntary grunt as the air in his lungs was evicted. His momentum snapped his neck forward and smashed his face into the tree. He tumbled down and rolled another ten feet.

The BMW, after standing on its nose, fell back to the ground and onto its side; the engine stalled but the back wheel kept spinning. I had never heard such silence.

I CLAMBERED DOWN. I got to him first. I'd wanted this to happen, but now I felt terrible that it had. Amazingly, he was conscious, flat on his back, blinking, stunned, as blood trickled into his eyes and poured out of his nostrils and lips. There was no more army in him. His expression was that of a child whose reach had exceeded its grasp with disastrous results.

His foot lay twisted under him in a fashion that made me want to throw up. He moaned, clutching at his upper belly. His face was a bloody mess. It was a grotesque sight.

Neither his face nor his foot seemed to concern him as much as his belly. "Please," he said. His breath was short and he clawed at his belt.

His eyes found me.

"Please. Get it out."

For a moment I'd forgotten what he had done to Zemui or Rosina and Genet, or what he'd done to Ghosh. All I could see was his suffering, and I felt pity.

I looked up to see Rosina, her lip swollen and split, a front tooth missing.

"Please . . . ," he said again, clutching at his chest. "Get this out. For the love of St. Gabriel, get this out."

"I'm sorry," I said.

He kept rooting ineffectively, desperately, at his belly, and now I could see why. The pistol butt was digging into him—it had just about disappeared under his ribs on the left side.

"Watch out!" Rosina yelled. "He's trying to get his gun."

"No," I tried to say, "the gun handle has smashed in his lower ribs." I did hear myself say to him, "Hold on. I'll get it out!" I wrapped my hands around the handle of that gun and pulled with all my strength. He screamed. It would not budge. I changed my grip.

I felt a mule kick in my hand before I heard the shot.

Then the gun came sliding free in my hand, as if it had never been wedged there but had simply been sitting on his belly button.

I smelled burned clothing and cordite. I saw a red pit in his belly. I saw life slip out of his eyes as easily as a dew drop rolls off a rose petal.

I felt his pulse. It was a variety Ghosh had never shown me: the absent pulse.

ROSINA SENT GENET to fetch Gebrew.

He came running. He hadn't heard the shot. The bungalow was far enough removed and the gun so muffled by the man's belly that the sound had not carried.

"Hurry. Someone might come for him," Rosina said. "But first we must move the motorcycle." With all five of us heaving, we righted the BMW and managed to get it to the toolshed, just past the curve at the bottom of our driveway. Other than a ding on the tank, the bike looked no worse for wear. In the toolshed we rearranged the cords of firewood, the stacks of Bibles, the sawhorse, incubator, and other junk kept there, so that the bike was hidden from sight.

Returning to the body, we had little to say to one another. Gebrew and Shiva fetched the wheelbarrow, and with Rosina and Genet's help, they fed the body into its rusty cavity. I leaned against a tree, looking on. He lay in the wheelbarrow in the kind of unnatural posture only the dead achieve. Now with Rosina leading us, we pushed him through the trees on the perimeter trail, just inside of Missing's wall, until we reached the Drowning Soil. The hospital's old septic tank was located here, deep underground, and for years it had overflowed before it was taken out of use. USAID concrete, Rockefeller funds, and a Greek contractor named Achilles had built a new one. But the old tank's effluent had digested the land. A downy growth of moss served to deceive the eye; anything heavier than a pebble would sink. The odor, present at all times, kept trespassers away. Matron had barbed wire strung around it, and the sign in Amharic said DROWNING SOIL, which was the closest translation for "quicksand."

The smell was powerful. Pushing down the fence post so that the barbed wire was flat on the ground, Rosina and Gebrew got the wheelbarrow as far forward as they dared. I glared at Shiva. He was impassive, looking on. He could have been watching shoeshine boys at work—it was the opposite of what I felt. They were about to pitch the body forward when I said, "No!" I grabbed Rosina's hand, forcing her to set the wheelbarrow down. I was shaking, crying. "We can't do this. It is wrong. Rosina . . . Oh my God, what have I done—"

Rosina slapped me hard. Shiva put his hand on my shoulder, more to restrain me perhaps than to offer support. Rosina and Gebrew took the handles again, and they tipped the dead man out.

The mossy ground sagged like a mattress. The face on that body no longer belonged to the man who had terrorized us; it was a pathetic face, a human face, not that of a monster.

When the body finally disappeared, Rosina spat in its direction. She turned to me, the anger and bloodlust contorting her face. "What's wrong with you? Don't you know he would have killed us all for the fun of it? The only reason he didn't is he was even hungrier to steal Zemui's motorcycle. Don't feel anything but pride for what you did."

. . .

WE WALKED BACK in silence. When we were home, inside the kitchen, Rosina turned to us, her hands on her hips. "No one but us knows what happened," she said. "No one can know. Not Hema. Not Ghosh. Not Matron. No one at all. Shiva, you understand? Genet? Gebrew?"

She turned to me. "And you? Marion?"

I looked at my nanny, her face bloodied and the missing tooth making her look like a stranger. I steeled myself for more harsh words from her. Instead, she came over and held me in her arms. It was the hug a woman gives either her son or her hero. I held her tight. Her breath was hot in my ear as she said, "You are so brave." This was my consolation: all was well between me and Rosina. Genet came over and put her arms around me.

If this was what brave felt like—numb, dumb, with eyes that could see no farther than my bloody fingers, and a heart that raced and pined for the girl who hugged me—then I suppose I was brave.

CHAPTER 27

Answering Medicine

HANGING SEEMED TO BE THE FATE of anyone who'd been close to General Mebratu. What spared Ghosh thus far was that he was a citizen of India. That and the prayers of his family and his legions of friends. His imprisonment did more than suspend everything in my world; it took away any meaning life once had for me.

It was then, as we despaired, that I thought of Thomas Stone. Before the coup, I'd go for months without thinking of him. Having no picture of him, and no knowledge that he had authored a famous textbook (Hema, I learned later, had given away or removed every extant copy of *A Short Practice* at Missing), Thomas Stone seemed unreal to me, a ghost, an idea. It didn't seem possible that I might have been fathered by someone as white-skinned as Matron. An Indian mother was easier to imagine.

But now, as time stood still, this man whose face I couldn't picture was on my mind. I was his son. This was my moment of greatest need. When the army man came to steal the motorcycle and could have killed us, where was Stone? When I murdered the intruder—that was still how I saw it—where was Stone? When that death mask loomed in front of my eyelids at night, or when cold hands clutched at me from the shadows, where was Stone? Above all, when I needed to free the only father I ever had, where was Stone?

In those awful days which soon stretched out to two weeks, as we went back and forth from house to jail, to Indian Embassy, to Foreign Ministry, I was convinced that had I been a better son to Ghosh, if I'd been worthy of him, I might have spared him his present torture.

Perhaps it wasn't too late.

I could change. But what form should this change take?

I waited for a sign.

It came on a blustery morning when word of fresh hangings in the Merkato reached us. I set out hurriedly for the gate for no particular reason: wherever I was, I was ready to be somewhere else. On my way there, a mysterious sweet, fruity odor reached my nostrils. Simultaneously, a green Citroën, floating on its shocks, its back tires hidden by skirtlike fenders, wheezed into the portico of Casualty. A portly man slumped in the backseat was carried out by two younger men, and at once the scent got stronger. He had the café-au-lait skin and jowly features of the royal family, as if he'd been raised on clotted cream and scones in place of *injera* and *wot*. To me he looked asleep. His breathing was deep, loud, and sighing, like an overworked locomotive. With every exhalation he gave off that sweet emanation—it even had a color: red.

I knew I'd encountered this odor before. Where? How? I stood thinking outside Casualty as they carried him in, trying to solve this puzzle. I realized I was engaged in the kind of reflection, the kind of study of the world, which I so admired in Ghosh. I remembered how he'd conducted that experiment with blind man's buff—literally a blinded experiment—to validate my ability to find Genet by her scent.

Later Dr. Bachelli told me the man had diabetic coma—the fruity odor was characteristic. I went to Ghosh's office—his old bungalow—and read from his textbooks about the ketones that built up in the blood and caused that scent. Which led me to read about insulin. Then about the pancreas, diabetes . . . One thing led to another. It was perhaps the only time in the two weeks since Ghosh had gone to prison that I'd been able to think of anything else. I expected Ghosh's big books to be unreadable. But I found that the bricks and mortar of medicine (unlike, say, engineering) were words. You needed only words strung together to describe a structure, to explain how it worked, and to explain what went wrong. The words were unfamiliar, but I could look them up in the medical dictionary, write them down for future use.

Hardly two days later, I encountered the scent again at Missing's gate. This time an old woman stretched out on the bench of a gharry, propped there by her relatives, was the source. She had the same sighing, breathing, and not even the horse's strong scent could conceal the fruity odor. "Diabetic acidosis," I said to Adam, and he said it was possible. The blood and urine tests confirmed that I was right.

Somehow, life went on at Missing. Whether we had one doctor or four, the patients kept coming. The simple things—treating dehydration in infants, treating fevers, conducting normal deliveries—were routinely managed. But anything surgical had to be turned away. I hung around Casualty with Adam, or else I hid in Ghosh's old bungalow browsing through his textbooks. Time didn't speed up, nor did my fear for Ghosh diminish one bit, but at last I felt I had found something that was the equivalent of Shiva's drawing or his dancing, a passion that would keep disturbing thoughts at bay. What I was doing felt more serious than Shiva's pursuits; mine felt like an ancient alchemy that could cause the prison gates in Kerchele to spring open.

During that awful period with Ghosh in jail, Almaz holding vigil outside prison, and the Emperor so distrustful of everyone that Lulu had to sniff every morsel of His Majesty's food, my olfactory brain, the feral intelligence, came awake. It had always known odors, the variety of them, but now it was finding labels for the things it registered. The musty ammoniacal reek of liver failure came with yellow eyes and in the rainy season; the freshly baked bread scent of typhoid fever was year-round and then the eyes were anxious, porcelain white. The sewer breath of lung abscess, the grapelike odor of a *Pseudomonas*-infected burn, the stale urine scent of kidney failure, the old beer smell of scrofula—the list was huge.

One night after supper, Matron dozed on the sofa while Shiva drew intently at the dining table. Hema, who was pacing the room, stopped by my armchair. This was Ghosh's spot. I had my feet up and books piled next to me. I think she understood that I was preserving his space. Over my shoulder she saw the thick gynecology textbook of hers that I'd opened, purely by chance, to a picture of a woman's vulva distorted by a giant Bartholin's cyst. I made no attempt to hide what I was doing. I sensed Hema struggle to find an appropriate response. She put her hand on my hair and then the hand slipped down to my ear, and I thought she was going to twist my pinna (that's what I learned the fleshy part of the ear was called). I felt her indecision. She caressed my pinna and stroked my shoulder.

When she walked away I felt the weight of what she left unsaid. I wanted to call after her, *Ma! You have it all wrong.* But just as she kept her thoughts to herself, I was learning to do the same. This was what growing up was about: *hide* the corpse, *don't* bare your heart, *do* make assumptions about the motives of others. They're certainly doing all these things to you.

I'm sure Hema believed that a prurient interest in a woman's anatomy took me to that page in the textbook. And perhaps it did, but that wasn't all there was to it. Would she believe me if I said that those musty old books with their pen-and-ink drawings, their grainy photographs of people parts contorted and rendered grotesque by disease, held out a special promise? *Kelly's Obstetrics* and *Jeffcoate's Gynecology,* and *French's Index of Differential Diagnosis* (at least in my childish way of thinking), were maps of Missing, guides to the territory into which we were born. Where but in such books, where but in medicine, might our conjoined, matricidal, patrifugal, twisted fate be explained? Where else could I understand the urge in me (was it homicidal? I'd lie awake at night wondering) that did away with the army man, and then the simultaneous urge to keep it concealed and to confess? Maybe there were answers in great literature. But I discovered in Ghosh's absence, in the depths of my sorrow, that *the* answer, *all* answers, the explanation for good and evil, lay in medicine. I believed that. I was sure that only if I believed would Ghosh be freed.

On the third week of Ghosh's abduction, I walked to the front gate in the morning, just as St. Gabriel's sounded the hour, which was Gebrew's command to allow entrance. The narrow pedestrian opening permitted just one person at a time to come through. What prevented chaos and a stampede was the sight of Gebrew in his priest's garb.

Two men jostled each other, high stepping over the frame of the gate like hurdlers. "Behave yourselves, for God's sake," Gebrew admonished. Next came a woman who stepped over gingerly, as if getting out of a boat and onto the dock. As the patients took turns to peck like hens around the four points of Gebrew's handheld cross—once for the crucified Christ, then for Mary, then once for all the archangels and the saints, and then for the four living creatures of the Book of Revelation—and waited for Gebrew to touch it to their forehead, order was imposed. These visitors to Missing feared illness and death, but their fear of damnation was greater.

I studied the faces, each one an enigma, no two alike. I hoped that the next face would be Ghosh's.

I imagined the day my "real" father—Thomas Stone—would step through the gate. I imagined myself standing here. I'd be a doctor by then, and I might be in my green scrubs, taking a break between surgeries, or in my white coat with a shirt and tie beneath. Even though I had no photograph or memory of Stone to go by, I'd know it was him right away.

I knew what I'd say to him: *You're much too late. We went ahead with our lives without you.*

CHAPTER 28

The Good Doctor

I AWOKE WHILE IT WAS NOT YET DAYBREAK. I ran as fast as I could in the dark to the autoclave room. This was the thought that woke me up: What if Sister Mary Joseph Praise could intercede and free Ghosh? My "father" would never come, but what if my birth mother was just waiting to be asked? I hoped she wouldn't hold my long absence from her desk chair against me.

Seated, staring up at that print of the *Ecstasy of St. Teresa*, seeing only faint outlines as I hadn't put on the light, I felt as if I were in a confessional, but with no desire to confess. I was silent for ten minutes or so.

"You know for the longest time I assumed that *all* babies came in twos," I said. I was making conversation. I didn't want to get to Ghosh or the favor I sought right away. "Koochooloo's pups came in fours and sixes. At Mulu Farm we saw a sow with twice that number.

"We are identical twins, but the truth is we aren't exactly identical. No, not the way a one-birr note is identical with another birr note in all but the serial number. Shiva is actually my mirror image.

"I'm right-handed, and Shiva's left-handed. The swirl on the back of my head is on my left. Shiva's is on the right."

My hand went to my nose, again something I wasn't telling her. A month before the coup, I had a confrontation with Walid, who'd been teasing me over my name (such an easy target). I found myself flattened by a head butt—a *testa*—and the fight went out of me. *Testa*—Italian for "head"—some claim is an ancient Ethiopian martial art, but if so, there are no dojos, no belts, just lots of broken noses. The only defense against the "big knuckle" is to lower your head. Walid used his *testa* when I wasn't expecting it.

To my surprise, Shiva helped me up. Shiva was so tuned to the distress of animals and pregnant women, yet he could be blissfully unaware of the pain of other humans, especially if he was the cause. I watched in astonishment as Shiva confronted Walid. Walid's answer was another *testa*. Their frontal bones met with a sickening clash. When I could bear to look, I saw Shiva standing as if nothing had happened. The junior boys came running like vultures around carrion, because the fall of a bully makes big news. Walid was supine on the ground. He came to his feet and tried it again. The dull thud of their heads left me in mortal fear for Shiva. But Shiva hardly blinked while Walid was out cold with a big gash on his skull. When he eventually returned to school, he was a subdued figure.

That night Shiva allowed me to explore his head. Unlike me, he had a gentle peak at the vertex, and his frontal bones were very thick and as hard as steel. My topography was different. I had asked Ghosh why this might be, and he postulated that the instruments used on Shiva at birth might have caused the bones of his head to heal in this "exuberant" manner. Or else it might have had to do with the fact that we were *conjoined*. I was too proud to ask what exactly that meant.

A folio-size book in the British Council Library had pictures of Chang and Eng of Siam, the most famous Siamese twins. A few pages later was a portrait of the Indian Laloo, who toured the world as a circus freak. Laloo had a "parasitic twin emerging from his chest." Laloo stood in a loincloth, and from his bare chest sprouted two buttocks and a pair of legs. To me it looked as if the parasitic twin wasn't "emerging" from Laloo, but climbing back *into* him.

When I could unglue my eyes from the pictures, every word in that text was a revelation to me. I learned that when two embryos just happened to grow in the mother at the same time, the result was fraternal twins—they didn't look alike and they could be boy and girl. But if a *single* embryo in a mother happened to split very early on in its growth into two separate halves, the result was identical twins like me and Shiva. Conjoined twins, then, were identical twins where the early split of the fertilized egg into two halves was incomplete, so the two halves remained stuck to each other. The result could be like Chang and Eng, two individuals connected at the belly or some other spot. It could also result in unequal parts, like Laloo and his parasitic twin.

"Did you know that Shiva and I were *craniophagus*? Connected at the head?" I said to Sister Mary Joseph Praise. "They cut that connection at birth—they had to. It was bleeding."

I was silent for a long while, and I hoped she understood that I was being respectful. It was selfish for me to talk about our births when they coincided with her death. We had another long and awkward silence.

"Can you please get Ghosh out of jail?"

There, I said it.

I waited for a reply. In the ensuing quiet, I felt guilt and shame wash over me. I hadn't told her that I'd ripped out the page on Laloo and left the library with it; I'd said nothing about killing the army man and how I feared a terrible retribution some day.

There was something else I'd held back, something I understood only after seeing the pictures of Chang and Eng, and of Laloo: the fleshy tube between Shiva and me had been cut and it was long gone . . . but it *wasn't* gone—it still connected us. That picture of Laloo captured how I felt, as if pieces of me were still stuck to Shiva and parts of him were inside me. I was connected to Shiva for better or worse. The tube was still there.

What would it have been like if ShivaMarion walked around with heads fused, or—imagine this—sharing one trunk with two necks? Would I have wanted to make my way—our way—through the world in that fashion? Or would I have wanted doctors to try and separate us at all costs?

But no one had given us that choice. They'd separated us, sliced through the stalk that made us one. Who's to say that Shiva's being so different, his circumscribed, self-contained inner world that asked nothing of others, didn't come from that separation, or that my restlessness, my sense of being incomplete, didn't originate at that moment? And in the end, we were still one, bound to each other whether we liked it or not.

I left the autoclave room abruptly, without even a good-bye. How could I expect Sister to help me when I was holding back so much?

I didn't deserve her intercession.

So I was astonished when, an hour later, it came.

It took the form of a cryptic note on a Russian hospital prescription pad. It came to Gebrew from Teshome, his counterpart at the Russian hospital gates. Teshome said it was from a Russian doctor who had made Teshome swear to keep his identity a secret. On one side the doctor had scribbled: "Ghosh is fine. Absolutely no danger." On the back Ghosh had scrawled: "Boys, SCREW YOUR COURAGE TO THE STICK-ING PLACE! Thank Almaz and no need to wait. Matron please call in all favors. Hope lovely bride renews yearly contract. XXX G."

I went back to the autoclave room. I stood behind the chair like a penitent and I thanked Sister Mary Joseph Praise. I told her all. I held back nothing. I asked for her forgiveness—and for her to continue to help us free Ghosh.

I SAW ALMAZ ANEW, saw her quiet strength and determination in the nightly vigil she had held outside Kerchele Prison. Whatever she lacked in education she made up for in character and in loyalty.

But I'd lost all respect for the Emperor. Even Almaz, always a staunch royalist, had a crisis of faith.

No one really believed that Ghosh was a party to the coup. The problem was—and it was the same for hundreds of others who'd been rounded up—His Majesty Haile Selassie made all the decisions. His Majesty wouldn't delegate and His Majesty felt no haste.

Every afternoon we went to Kerchele to deliver the one meal we were allowed to bring, and to pick up the container bearing the previous day's meal. The relatives outside the prison were our family now. It was also the most fertile place to gather new information and plausible rumors. We heard that the Emperor took a morning walk in the palace garden, during which the Minister of Security , the Minister of State, and the Minister of the Pen came out to him one by one. They walked three paces behind him and reported on rumors and real events of the previous twenty-four hours. Each man worried whether the one who went before him had set a trap by mentioning something which he then failed to mention. Lulu, a royal diviner, peed on certain people's shoes, and the rumor mills were undecided if that was an indication that you were to be trusted or you were under suspicion—this was the sort of thing one learned by visiting Kerchele.

The next day, just twenty-four hours after my visit to Sister Mary Joseph Praise, we were allowed to see Ghosh.

The prison yard with its lawn and giant shade trees looked like a picnic spot. Under that green canopy, the prisoners stood like leafless saplings.

I spotted Ghosh at once. Shiva and I flung ourselves into his arms. It didn't register till we were in his embrace that his head had been shaved or that his face had become gaunt. What *did* register was that my chest stopped aching for the first time in over a month. The scent on his clothes, on his person, was a coarse, communal odor that made me sad, because it spoke of his degradation. We stood aside to allow Hema and Matron to get near him, but I kept a hand on him, frightened that he might vanish. Some men are improved by losing weight, but Ghosh, without his plump cheeks and jowls, looked diminished.

Almaz stood back, her face all but hidden by the tail of her *shama*, waiting. Ghosh freed himself from Hema and Matron, and he walked over to her. She bowed deeply, then bent as if to touch his feet, but Ghosh grabbed her arms before she could, and he pulled her up and kissed her hands. He embraced her. He said he'd been so happy to see her standing and waving when they would take him back and forth in the covered jeeps, even though he knew she didn't see him. Almaz, whose teeth I'd never noticed before, grinned from ear to ear, while tears ran down her face.

"The only suffering for me was worrying about all of you. You see, I didn't know if they'd arrested Hema as well. Or maybe even Matron. When I saw Almaz standing in the prison yard, holding that picture of the family in her hands in that frame, I understood she was saying you were all right. Almaz, you put my heart at ease."

None of us knew till then that Almaz's vigil had included the family picture, and that whenever a car came or left the prison, she'd stand up and hold that picture up and smile.

The minutes were ticking by and we pressed Ghosh to tell us all. I don't think he wanted to alarm us, but he couldn't lie. "The first night was the worst. I was put in that cage," he said, pointing to a grubby, low-slung shack that looked like a storeroom. "It's a tiny space. You can't stand up. That's where they put common criminals, murderers, along with vagrant boys, pickpockets. The air is terrible, and at night, they lock the door and then there's no air at all. This one fellow, a brute, rules the place, and he decides who sleeps where. The only place where you can get a little air is by the door, and in return for my wristwatch, he let me sleep there. If I spent another night there I thought I'd have died. No sheets, no blankets, sleeping on the cold ground. When the sun rose, I was scratching from lice.

"A major came directly from the palace with instructions to take me to the military hospital and give me everything I needed to care for General Mebratu. The Emperor didn't have much faith in the doctors who were caring for him. When this major saw where I'd spent the night, and saw that my face was swollen, and that I was limping, he was furious. He took me to the military hospital where I could shower, get deloused, and get a fresh set of clothes.

"At the military hospital, they showed me the General's X-rays, then took me to him. Who do I see there but Slava—Dr. Yaroslav from the Russian hospital. Slava was shaking badly and not looking good. As for Mebratu, he was in deep sleep, or else he was unconscious. Slava said the Ethiopian doctors wouldn't go near the General. They were terrified that if he died they'd suffer, and if they saved him they'd be suspected of being sympathizers. 'Slava,' I said, 'tell me he is sedated, and wasn't this way before you saw him.' Slava said the General had been wide awake, speaking, no weakness in hands and legs when he came in. 'I was against sedation,' Slava said. All this time, there was another Russian doctor with Slava, a youngish woman—Dr. Yekaterina. She said, 'Sedation is very good. He has head injury. We have to operate.' I said, 'Head injuries are only important because the head contains the brain. That bullet is not near the brain.' 'What you call this,' she says pointing to his eye. 'Comrade,' I said to her, 'I call it his orbit.' She didn't think much of me, and I didn't like the way she was disrespectful of Slava. Slava may be an alcoholic, but he was a pioneer in orthopedics before they banished him to Ethiopia. Slava mouths to me from behind her, 'KGB!' I called in the major. 'What are your instructions as far as my authority?' He said, 'Whatever you need. You are in charge. Those are my direct orders from His Majesty.' 'Good,' I said. 'Take this doctor back to Balcha Hospital. Don't let her come back. I need medicinal brandy, some smelling salts, and let's put two beds in this room for me and Slava.' I dosed General Mebratu with every antibiotic there was, and gave Slava the brandy and he stopped shaking. Then Slava and I debrided the General's eye, right at the bedside, cut away what was hanging without trying to do too much more. The General never stirred. I had no plans to take the bullet out.

"For the next two nights, I had Slava for company, and I slept in a regular bed. It was three days before that Communist sedation wore off. 'Slava, was that dose of sedative for a horse, by any chance?' I asked. 'No, but it was given by a nag named Yekaterina!' Slava said.

"When General Mebratu woke up, other than a slight headache and a nasal voice, he was in good shape. They wouldn't let me stay there anymore, and they sent Slava off. That's when I scribbled the note. When I came back here they put me in one of the proper cells with some decent chaps. They brought me back and forth once or twice a day, to dress the wound, but I wasn't allowed more than a few words with the General."

I'd already spotted two giant rats emerging in broad daylight from a gutter between two buildings. Ghosh was hiding things from us, but then we were hiding something from him.

From that day on, we were allowed twice-weekly visits. Now the only question was when he would be released.

First one, then another of Ghosh's VIP patients came by the house to pick up some comfort from home that Ghosh sought—a particular pen, more books, a paper in a certain stack. They'd bring with them a Latinate script in Ghosh's handwriting, a prescription for a compound mixture, and I'd lead them to Adam, the compounder.

In Ghosh's absence I understood what kind of doctor he was. These royals, or ministers or diplomats, weren't seriously ill, not to my eyes anyway. They didn't have the power to get him out of jail, but they had the power to get into prison to see Ghosh. He, by pulling down the lower eyelid and looking at the color of the conjunctivae, by asking them to protrude the tongue, and all the while with his finger on the pulse, managed to diagnose and reassure them. The modern designation "family practitioner" doesn't quite cover all the things he was.

THREE WEEKS AFTER we first saw Ghosh, General Mebratu was put on trial, a show for international observers. An underground newspaper carried reports of the trial, as did a few foreign papers. General Mebratu, proud and far from penitent, wouldn't renounce what he'd done. His bearing made a great impression on people who were allowed to attend. From the witness box he preached his message: land reform, political reform, and the end of entitlements that reduced peasants to slaves. Those who had fought to put down Mebratu's coup now wondered why they had opposed him. We heard that a core of junior officers plotted to spring the General from prison, but Mebratu vetoed this. The death of his troops weighed on him. The court sentenced him to hang. His last words in the courtroom were "I go to tell others the seed we planted has taken root."

ON THE EVENING of the forty-ninth day of Ghosh's captivity, a taxi drove up our driveway and swung around the back. I heard Almaz yell, and I tried to imagine what new calamity we were facing.

Getting out of the taxi, surveying our quarters as if he'd never seen them before, was our Ghosh. Gebrew, who'd ridden on the running board of the taxi from the gate, jumped off, clapping with glee, hopping in place. Genet and Rosina came out from their quarters. We danced around Ghosh. The air was filled with shrieks and with *lulululu*—the sound of Almaz's joy. Koochooloo was there, barking, wagging her tail, and howling, the two nameless dogs standing at a distance following her cue.

It was midnight when we went to bed, Shiva and me crowded in with Ghosh and Hema. It was far from comfortable, and yet I never slept better. I woke once and heard the sound of Ghosh's heavy snoring: it was the most reassuring sound on earth.

WE AWOKE EARLY the next morning, our mood still celebratory. Unbeknownst to us, at that moment General Mebratu, veteran of Korea and the Congo, graduate of Sandhurst and Fort Leavenworth, was taken to his execution.

They hung him in a clearing in the Merkato, perhaps because it was in the Merkato that the student procession and the idea of the coup had found its most vocal support. The executioner, we later learned, was the Emperor's aide-de-camp, a man General Mebratu had known for years. "If you ever loved a soldier, put that knot carefully," General Mebratu was reported to have said. When the noose was in position, and just as the truck was about to pull away, the General took a running jump off the back of the truck, sailing off into martyrdom.

We heard about it by late morning. That night in the stone villas, the barracks, and in *chikka* houses, junior officers who graduated from the Holeta Military Academy, or the Harar Military Academy, or the Air Force Academy in Debre Zeit, went to bed plotting to finish what General Mebratu had started.

With every passing day, General Mebratu's stature grew until he was unofficially canonized. His likeness appeared in anonymous leaflets, drawn in the cartoon style of the ancient Ethiopic icon painters, with an abundance of yellow, green, and red; they depicted a black Christ flanked by a black John the Baptist, and our own General Mebratu. All three had yellow halos around their heads and the River Jordan running over their feet. The text read, *For this is He that was spoken of by the prophet Esaias, saying: The voice of one crying in the wilderness. Prepare ye the way of the Lord, make His paths straight.*

CHAPTER 29

Abu Kassem's Slippers

Two DAYS AFTER the General's execution, the hospital staff, led by Adam and W. W. Gonad, had a welcome-back party for Ghosh. They bought a cow, hired a tent and a cook.

Adam slit the beast's throat. An overeager orderly with a yearning for *gored-gored*—raw beef—cut a thin and still quivering steak from the flank while the animal stood on glass legs. They strung the cow from a tree, made their cuts, and carried the meat to an outdoor table to be processed.

When I saw an army jeep come up our driveway, my blood turned cold. The cooks stood still as we watched a uniformed officer go into our bungalow. I sleepwalked toward the house. I was at the front door when the officer stepped out, Ghosh and Hema with him. Shiva was by my side.

"Boys," Ghosh said. "The motorcycle. Do you know who came to take it?" Ghosh was calm, unaware of any reason to be alarmed.

My first response was relief—they hadn't come for Ghosh! Then, when it sunk in why the man was here, came panic. The five of us had worked out the story: *A soldier came with the key. He drove the motorcycle away. We had no words with him.* We'd repeated the story to Hema the day the soldier went missing. As preoccupied as she was with Ghosh's arrest, she'd shrugged it off.

I was about to speak when I got a good look at the officer's face.

It was the intruder, the army man, the one who came to take the motorcycle.

It was his face. The same forehead and teeth, but a body that was not as lean and gangly. The spotless, pressed uniform, the beret tucked under his shoulder lapel, gave him the manner of a professional soldier, something which the intruder had lacked. I felt my face turning colors.

Rosina and Genet came walking rapidly around the corner of the house. Word had gotten out. There was a crowd around us.

"A soldier came with a key and he drove it away," Shiva said.

I nodded. "Yes."

The officer smiled. He leaned forward to me and said politely, in English, "Is there anything else you remember? Something you aren't telling me?"

Ghosh interrupted, saying, "Ah, here's Rosina." In Amharic, Ghosh said, "Rosina, this officer wants to know about Zemui's motorcycle."

Rosina made a deep bow. I was reminded of her politeness to the thief, and how her choice of words then had been inflammatory. I hoped she'd be prudent.

"Yes, sir. I was with the boys when he came—" She stopped and brought the edge of her *shama* to her mouth, her eyes popping. "Excuse me, sir. The man . . . he looked very much like you. When I saw your face . . . forgive me," and she made a little bow again. "He wasn't . . . he wasn't as polite as you. Dressed . . . not like you."

"We have the same mother," the officer said, with a wry smile. "It's true, he looks like me. What was he wearing?"

"Just the army jacket. No shirt. A white singlet underneath. Boots, trousers," Rosina said.

"Did he look all right to you?"

"He had his gun tucked here," she said, pointing to her midriff, "instead of in his . . ."

"Holster?" the brother offered.

"Yes. And he looked . . . his eyes red. He looked as if he might be . . ."

"Drunk?" the brother said softly. "Did you ask him why he wanted the motorcycle?"

"Please, sir. He had that gun," she said. "He seemed very angry. He had the key."

"What did he say to you?"

"He . . . said many things. He said he's taking the motorcycle. I said nothing." She'd departed from the script we had rehearsed, but it seemed to be working.

"Why? What has happened? What happened to the motorcycle?" Shiva said in English, his deadpan expression revealing nothing. I was astonished at Shiva's nerve.

"Well, that's what I don't know," the officer said. His English was excellent and his manner softened. "He wasn't supposed to take the motorcycle. The army wouldn't have let him keep it, anyway." He paused as if considering whether to say more. When he continued, it was to Ghosh and Hema that he directed his remarks. "He hasn't been seen since he came here. I'm posted in Dire Dawa, and I only found out he was AWOL two weeks ago. He told a woman he kept that he was going to pick up a motorcycle." He turned to me and Shiva. "So you saw him drive away?"

"I heard the sound," I said.

He nodded. "Doctor, do you mind if I take a quick look around . . ."

"By all means," Ghosh said.

I felt the sky pressing down on me as the officer and his driver went to the back of the house, and then walked down the gravel driveway. Had we come this far, with Ghosh free, only to have the army man send us back to hell? Genet glared at me, while Rosina squatted, applying a eucalyptus stick to her teeth. The two men walked to the ledge, then turned in the direction of the roundabout and disappeared from view. If on their return they went to the toolshed, we were doomed. The motorcycle was well hidden, but not to one who was intent on finding it.

After an eternity, they returned.

"Thank you, Doctor," the officer said, extending his hand to Ghosh. "I fear the worst. The day the Emperor returned, some of our soldiers got their hands on a lot of money. My brother had something to do with that. It's perhaps a good thing he disappeared."

Once the jeep was out of sight, Ghosh studied us for a moment. He sensed something amiss, but he didn't ask any questions. When Hema and Ghosh stepped back inside, I went to the corner of the house and I threw up. Genet and Shiva followed me. I waved them off. The gastrointestinal system has its own brain, its own conscience.

Inside the tent the folding chairs wobbled on the soft grass. Soon the tables sagged with beakers of *tej* and plates of food. The *kitfo*—coarsely ground raw meat mixed with *kibe* (a spiced and clarified butter)—was my favorite dish. We never served this at home, but from the time I was a baby, I'd eaten *kitfo* in Rosina's quarters, or in Gebrew's shack. On this day I had no appetite. The *injera* was stacked on the table like napkins. The *gored-gored* was the dish everyone went after: cubes of raw meat, which you dipped in a fiery red pepper sauce. The dishes kept coming: meatballs, meat curry, lentil curry, tongue, and kidney. What had been grazing under a tree that morning had, in short order, reached the table.

Ghosh sat on a dais in an armchair. One by one the nurses, nursing students, and the other Missing employees came to shake his hand and to praise the saints for allowing him to survive his ordeal.

Rosina didn't come out, but I found Genet in a corner of the tent. I sat by her. Dressed in black, pushing food around on her plate, she looked like a dour and distant cousin of the Genet I knew—she'd hardly left the house since Zemui's death. When an orderly came and greeted her, kissed her on her cheeks, she barely acknowledged him.

"When will you go back to school?" I said. "When will you start eating with us again?"

"They killed my father. Did you forget? I don't care about school." Then she hissed at me, "Tell the truth. You told Ghosh, didn't you?"

"I did not!"

"But you were thinking of telling him, weren't you? Tell the truth!"

She had me there. When I felt Ghosh's arms around me for the first time in that prison yard, a confession jumped to my lips. I had to suck it back and swallow.

"Since when did thinking become a crime? . . . Don't look at me that way," I said.

She took her plate and sat far away from me. Even if I didn't have great faith in myself, I wanted her to have more faith in me. It hurt that she no longer saw me as the hero who shot the intruder.

BY THE LATE AFTERNOON the tent came down, and now visitors from outside Missing arrived as word spread that Ghosh was free. For Evangeline and Mrs. Reddy, the moment was bittersweet because, though Ghosh was back, General Mebratu was gone forever. Evangeline kept saying, "So young. So young to be no more," dabbing at her eyes, while Mrs. Reddy comforted her, pulling Evangeline's head into her considerable bosom. The two brought a giant pot of chicken *biriyani* and the fiery mango pickle that was Ghosh's favorite. "It's your second honeymoon, sweetie," Evangeline said to Ghosh. She winked at Hema. Adid, their old friend, came carrying three live chickens roped together by their feet, handing them over to Almaz. He brushed feathers off his spotless white polyester shirt, which he wore over a flowing, plaid *ma'awis* that extended to his sandals. Behind him came Babu, who was General Mebratu's usual bridge partner, bearing a bottle of Pinch, the General's favorite. By nightfall, there was talk of pulling out the cards for old time's sake. At any moment I expected Zemui to drive up with General Mebratu.

The house got stuffy. I opened windows back and front. At one point Ghosh retreated to the bedroom to shed his sweater and Hema went with him. I followed and stood in the doorway. He went to the bathroom to brush his teeth. It was as if he couldn't get over the novelty of running water. Hema stood outside the bathroom looking at his reflection in the vanity.

"I've been thinking . . . ," I heard Ghosh say. "We've had a good innings. Maybe we should leave . . . before the next coup."

"What? Back to India?" Hema said.

"No . . . then the boys would have to learn Hindi or Tamil as a compulsory second language. It's too late for that. Don't forget why we left in the first place."

They didn't know I was listening.

"Lots of Indian teachers have gone from here to Zambia," Hema said.

"Or America? To the county of Cook?" he said and laughed.

"Persia? They say there are huge needs, just like this place. But they have tons of money to spend."

Zambia? Persia? Were they joking? This was my country they were talking about, the land of my birth. True, its potential for violence and mayhem had been proved. But it was still home. How much worse would it be to be tortured in a land that wasn't your own?

We've had a good innings.

Ghosh's words felt like a kick to my solar plexus: this was my country, but I realized it wasn't Hema's or Ghosh's. They weren't born here. Was this for them a job only good for as long as it lasted? I slipped away.

I stepped out to the lawn. I remember the air that night, and how it was so brisk that it could revive the dead. The fragrance of eucalyptus stoking a home fire, the smell of wet grass, of dung fuel, of tobacco, of swamp air, and the perfume of hundreds of roses—this was the scent of Missing. No, it was the scent of a continent.

Call me unwanted, call my birth a disaster, call me the bastard child of a disgraced nun and a disappeared father, call me a cold-blooded killer who lies to the brother of the man I killed, but that loamy soil that nurtured Matron's roses was in my flesh. I said *Ethyo-pya*, like a native. Let those born in other lands speak of *Eee-theee-op-eee-ya*, as if it were a compound name like Sharm el Sheikh, or Dar es Salaam or Rio de

Janeiro. The Entoto Mountains disappearing in darkness framed my horizon; if I left, those mountains would sink back to the ground, descend into nothingness; the mountains needed me to gaze at their tree-filled slopes, just as I needed them to be certain I was alive. The canopy of stars at night; that, too, was my birthright. A celestial gardener sowed *meskel* seeds so that when the rainy season ended, the daisies bloomed in welcome. Even the Drowning Soil, the foul-smelling quicksand behind Missing, which had swallowed a horse, a dog, a man, and God knows what else—I claimed that as well.

Light and dark.

The General and the Emperor.

Good and evil.

All possibilities resided within me, and they required me to be here. If I left, what would be left of me?

By eleven o'clock, Ghosh excused himself from the company in the living room and came back with us to our room. Hema followed.

Shiva said, "We haven't slept in this bed since you left."

Ghosh was touched. He lay in the center, and we huddled on either side. Hema sat at the foot of our bed.

"In prison, lights were out by eight o'clock. We'd each tell a story. That was our entertainment. I told stories from the books we read to you in this room. One of my cell mates, a merchant, Tawfiq—he would tell the Abu Kassem story."

It was a tale well known to children all over Africa: Abu Kassem, a miserly Baghdad merchant, had held on to his battered, much repaired pair of slippers even though they were objects of derision. At last, even he couldn't stomach the sight of them. But his every attempt to get rid of his slippers ended in disaster: when he tossed them out of his window they landed on the head of a pregnant woman who miscarried, and Abu Kassem was thrown in jail; when he dropped them in the canal, the slippers choked off the main drain and caused flooding, and off Abu Kassem went to jail . . .

"One night when Tawfiq finished, another prisoner, a quiet, dignified old man, said, 'Abu Kassem might as well build a special room for his slippers. Why try to lose them? He'll never escape.' The old man laughed, and he seemed happy when he said that. That night the old man died in his sleep.

"The next night, out of respect for the old man, we lay in silence. No story. I could hear men crying in the dark. This was always the low point for me. Ah, boys . . . I'd pretend you both were against me, just like this, and I would imagine Hema's face before me.

"The following night, we couldn't wait to talk about Abu Kassem. We all saw it the same way. The old man was right. The slippers in the story mean that everything you see and do and touch, every seed you sow, or don't sow, becomes part of your destiny . . . I met Hema in the septic ward at Government General Hospital in India, in Madras, and that brought me to this continent. Because of that, I got the biggest gift of my life—to be a father to you two. Because of that, I operated on General Mebratu, who became my friend. Because he was my friend, I went to prison. Because I was a doctor, I helped to save him, and they let me out. Because I saved him, they could hang him . . . You see what I am saying?"

I didn't, but he spoke with such passion I wasn't about to stop him.

"I never knew my father, and so I thought he was irrelevant to me. My sister felt his absence so strongly that it made her sour, and so no matter what she has, or will ever have, it won't be enough." He sighed. "I made up for his absence by hoarding knowledge, skills, seeking praise. What I finally understood in Kerchele is that neither my sister nor I realized that my father's absence *is* our slippers. In order to start to get rid of your slippers, you have to admit they are yours, and if you do, then they will get rid of themselves."

All these years and I hadn't known this about Ghosh, about his father dying when he was young. He was like us, fatherless, but at least we had him. Perhaps he'd been worse off than we were.

Ghosh sighed. "I hope one day you see this as clearly as I did in Kerchele. The key to your happiness is to own your slippers, own who you are, own how you look, own your family, own the talents you have, and own the ones you don't. If you keep saying your slippers aren't yours, then you'll die searching, you'll die bitter, always feeling you were promised more. *Not only our actions, but also our omissions, become our destiny.*"

AFTER GHOSH LEFT, I wondered if the army man was my pair of slippers. If so, they'd come back once already in the form of his brother. What form would they take next?

Just when my thoughts were coming in illogical sequences, a prelude to sleep, I felt someone lifting up the mosquito net. In the instant that I saw her, she was already sitting on my chest, pinning my arms down.

I could have thrown her off. But I didn't. I liked her body on mine and I liked the faint scent of charcoal and the frankincense that permeated her clothes. Maybe she'd come to make up to me for being so rude before. She could've climbed in through one of the open windows.

In the light from the hallway, I could see the fixed smile on her face.

"So, Marion? Did you tell Ghosh about the thief?"

"If you were hiding here, you already know."

Shiva, awake now, looked at the two of us, then rolled over, and closed his eyes.

"You almost told that officer, his brother."

"I didn't. I was just surprised . . . ," I said.

"We think you told Ghosh and Hema."

"Of course not. I wouldn't."

"Why wouldn't you?"

"You know why. If it gets out, they'll hang me."

"No, they will hang me and my mother for sure. You'll be to blame."

"I dream about his face."

"I do, too. And I kill him every night. I wish *I'd* shot him."

"It was an accident."

"If I'd killed him, I wouldn't call it an accident. If I'd killed him, we'd have no worries."

"Easy for you to say because you didn't kill him."

"My mother thinks you'll tell. We're worried about you."

"What? Well, you tell Rosina not to worry."

"It'll slip out one day and get us all killed."

"Okay, stop. If you know I'll tell, why talk to me? Get off me now."

She slid down so that her body was spread-eagled over mine. Her face hovered over me, and for one second I thought she was going to kiss me, which would have been very strange in the context of our exchange. I studied her eyes so close to mine, the blemish in the right iris, her breath on my face, sweet, pleasant. I could see the dangerous beauty she was going to turn into. I thought of the last time we were this close. In the pantry.

Her pupils dilated, her eyelids sagged down over the irises.

I felt something warm where her thighs were on top of mine, a spreading heat.

I felt fluid soak my pajamas. The air under the mosquito net filled with the scent of fresh urine. Now her eyes rolled up, showing only the whites, and she threw her head back. She shivered. Her neck was arched, the strap muscles taut. She looked down one last time. "That's so you don't ever forget your promise." She jumped off and was gone before I could think of reacting. I reared up now, ready to chase after her, to tear her to pieces.

Shiva held me back, whether from his desire to be a peacemaker or to protect her, I couldn't say. His eyes were downcast and they managed not to look at me. I stood shaking with anger as Shiva stripped the bed. My pajama bottom was soaked; Shiva had been spared. In the bathroom Shiva ran the tub and I got in. Shiva sat on the commode, quiet but keeping me company. We did not exhange a word. Back in the bedroom I was putting on fresh pajamas when Ghosh came in.

"I saw your light. What happened?"

"An accident," I said.

Shiva said nothing. The scent was unmistakable. I was ashamed. I could've told on Genet, but I didn't. I opened the window for a few minutes and then closed it.

Ghosh wiped down the mattress. He helped us flip it over. He brought fresh sheets, made the bed for us. I could tell that he was distressed.

"Go back to the guests," I said. "We're all right. Really."

"My boys, my boys," he said, sitting on the edge of the mattress. I know he thought I had wet the bed. "I can't imagine what you have been through."

That was true. He couldn't imagine. And we probably wouldn't know what he'd been through either.

He sighed. "I'll never leave you again."

I felt a twinge in my chest at those words, a desire to make him take them back. He'd spoken as if it were all in his hands to decide. As if he had forgotten about fate and slippers.

CHAPTER 30

Word for Words

SIXTY DAYS HAD PASSED since Zemui's death, and Genet was still confined to the house. Rosina, sinister with her missing tooth, was unsmiling and prickly like an Abyssinian boar.

"Enough," Gebrew told her on the Feast of St. Gabriel. "I'll melt a cross to get you a silver tooth. It's time to smile and to find white in your clothing. God wishes it. You are making His world gloomy. Even Zemui's legal wife has given up mourning."

"You call that harlot his wife?" she screamed at Gebrew. "That woman's legs swing open when a breeze comes through the door. Don't talk to me about her." The next day Rosina boiled up a big basin of black dye and into this she tossed all her remaining clothes as well as a good many of Genet's school clothes.

When Hema tried to get Genet to go back to LT&C, Rosina rebuffed her. "She's still in mourning."

Two days later, on a Saturday, I heard a *lululu* of celebration from Rosina's quarters as I was coming into the kitchen. I knocked. Rosina opened it just a crack, peering out at me with a hunter's eye, a blade in her hand.

"Is everything all right?"

"Fine, thank you," she said and closed the door, but not before I saw Genet, a towel pressed to her face, and bloody rags on the floor.

I couldn't keep this knowledge to myself. I told Hema and now she knocked on their door.

Rosina hesitated. "Come in if you must," she said, her manner surly. "We're all done."

The room was redolent of cloistered women. And frankincense and something else—the scent of fresh blood. It was difficult to breathe. The naked bulb hanging from the ceiling was off. "Close the door," Rosina snapped at me.

"Leave it open, Marion," Hema said. "And turn on the light."

A razor blade, a spirit lamp, and a bloody cloth were by Genet's bed.

Genet sat demure, her hands pressed to both sides of her face, her elbows resting on her knees. The posture of a thinker, but for the rags in each hand.

Hema pulled Genet's fingers away to reveal two deep vertical cuts, like the number II, just past the outer end of each eyebrow. A total of four cuts. The blood that welled up looked as dark as tar.

"Who did this?" Hema said, covering the wound and applying pressure.

The two occupants were silent. Rosina's eyes were locked on the far wall, a smirk on her face.

"I said, who did this?" Hema's voice was sharper than the razor that made the cuts.

Genet replied in English. "I wanted her to do it, Ma."

Rosina said something sharp to Genet in Tigrinya. I knew that short guttural phrase meant *Shut your mouth.*

Genet ignored her. "This is the sign of my people," she went on, "my father's tribe. If my father were alive he would have been so proud."

Hema opened her mouth as if considering what to say. Her face softened a bit. "Your father isn't alive, child. By the grace of God, you are."

Rosina frowned, not liking this much of an exchange in English.

"Come with me. Let me take care of that," Hema said more gently.

I knelt beside Genet. "Come with us, please?"

Genet glanced nervously at her mother, then hissed, "You'll only make it harder for me. I wanted these marks as much as she did. Please, please go."

GHOSH COUNSELED PATIENCE. "She isn't our daughter."

"You're wrong, Ghosh. She ate at our table. We send her to school at our expense. When something bad is happening to her, we can't say, 'She isn't our daughter.'"

I was stunned to hear what Hema said. It was noble. But if Hema saw Genet as my sister, this introduced complications as far as my feelings for Genet . . .

Ghosh said soothingly, "It's just to keep away the *buda*, the evil eye. Like the *pottu* on the forehead in India, darling."

"My *pottu* comes off, *darling*. No blood is shed."

. . .

A WEEK LATER, when Hema and Ghosh came home from work, they heard Rosina's wailing soliloquy, loud as ever, no different than when they'd left for work that morning. She bemoaned fate, God, the Emperor, and chastised Zemui for leaving her.

"That's it," Hema said. "The poor child will go mad. Are we going to stand by while that happens?"

Hema gathered Almaz, Gebrew, W.W., Ghosh, Shiva, and me. En masse we went to Rosina's door and pushed it open. Hema grabbed Genet by the arm and brought her into our house, leaving the rest of us to pacify Rosina who screamed to the world that her daughter was being abducted.

BEHIND THE CLOSED DOOR of Hema's bedroom, we could hear the sounds of Genet in the tub. Hema came out to get milk and asked Almaz to slice up papaya and pour lemon and sugar over it. Soon Almaz disappeared into the bedroom and stayed there.

An hour later, Hema and Genet emerged arm in arm. Genet was in a sequined yellow blouse and a glittering green skirt—parts of Hema's Bharatnatyam dance outfit. Her hair was pulled back off her forehead, and Hema had darkened her eyes with a kohl pencil. Genet stood regal, happy, her head high, her carriage that of a queen who'd been unshackled and restored to her throne. She was my queen, the one I wanted by my side. I was so proud, so drawn to her. How could she ever be my sister when she was already something else to me? Hema's glittering green sari matched Genet's colors. We almost missed the sight of Almaz, ducking away to the kitchen, her eyes darkened, her lips red, blush on her cheeks, and huge dangling earrings framing that strong face.

The five of us piled into the car, Genet in the backseat between me and Shiva. At the Merkato Hema got a new set of clothes for Genet. It was Christmas and Diwali and Meskel all rolled into one.

We finished up at Enrico's. Genet sat across from me, smiling at me as she licked her ice cream. Hesitantly at first, but then gathering speed, she chattered away. If she'd been brainwashed as Hema said, her brain was drying out.

I picked my moment, having scouted the obstacles under the table. I loved her so much, but I hadn't forgotten the indignity of her visit to my bed not two weeks before, and the wet present she left me. I loved the image of her hovering over me, a moment of such rare beauty. But I wanted to erase the wet part.

I kicked her shin savagely with my toe cap. She managed not to make a sound, but the pain showed in her face and in the tears that sprung to her eyes. "What's the matter?" Ghosh said.

She managed to say, "I ate my ice cream too fast."

"Ah! Ice-cream headache. Strange phenomenon. You know, that is something we ought to study, don't you think, Hema? Is it a migraine equivalent? Is everyone susceptible? What is its average duration? Are there complications?"

"Darling," Hema said, kissing him on the cheek, such a rare display of affection in a public place, "of all the things you've wanted to study, you've finally found one I'd love to study with you. I'm assuming it will involve lots of ice cream?"

In the car, Genet showed me the big welt on her shin. "Are you done?" she said, quietly.

"No, that was just a warm-up. I have to repay you in kind."

"You'll ruin my new clothes," she said coyly, leaning against me. The scars at the ends of both eyebrows were still angry at the edges. Hema saw them as barbaric, but I thought they looked beautiful. I put my arm around Genet. Shiva looked on, curious as to what I would do next. Those slashes next to her eyes made her look preternaturally wise, because they were at the spot where people developed wrinkles when they aged. She grinned, and the number iis were exaggerated. I felt my heart racing, powerless. Who was this beauty? Not my little sister. Not even my best friend. Sometimes my opponent. But always the love of my life.

"So," she said again, "seriously, are you done with your revenge?"

I sighed. "Yes, I'm done."

"Good," she said. She took my little finger and bent it back and would have snapped it if I didn't snatch it away.

GENET SLEPT IN A BED made up for her in our living room. The next morning, before we went to school, Hema sent for Rosina. Shiva, Genet, and I snuck into the corridor to listen. I peeked, and I saw Rosina standing before Hema the way she'd stood before the army man.

"I expect to see you back in the kitchen, helping Almaz. And from now on, in the daytime, the door and window to your quarters stay open. Let some light and air in there."

If Rosina was going to make claims on her daughter, this was the moment.

We held our breath.

She didn't say a word. She made a curt bow, and left.

WE FELL BACK into our school routine: loads of homework, then Hemawork, which included penmanship, current affairs discussions, vocabulary, and book reports. Cricket for me and Shiva, and dance for Shiva and Genet. Many an evening Gosh bowled to us on a makeshift pitch on our front lawn. For a large man he had a delicate touch with the bat and taught us how to sweep, to drive, and to square-cut.

Shiva was, as of that year, exempt from school assignments, the result of Hema and Ghosh negotiating with his teachers at Loomis Town & Country. Both sides were relieved. Shiva didn't have to write an essay on the battle of Hastings if he saw no point to it. Loomis Town & Country would collect Shiva's fees and let him attend class, since he wasn't disruptive. Shiva didn't mind the ritual of school. The teachers knew us and they understood Shiva as well as one could understand Shiva. But just like Mr. Bailey, newly arrived from Bristol, some teachers had to discover Shiva for themselves. Bailey was the only teacher in LT&C's history to have a degree, and therefore he felt obliged to set a very high standard. Two-thirds of us failed the first math test. "One of you scored a perfect one hundred. But he or she didn't write a name on the paper. The rest of you were miserable. *Sixty-six* percent of you failed," he exclaimed. "What do you think about that number? *Sixty-six!*"

For Shiva, rhetorical questions were a trap. He never asked a question to which he knew the answer. Shiva raised his hand. I cringed in my seat. Mr. Bailey's eyebrow went up, as if a chair in the corner which he'd managed to ignore for a few months had suddenly developed delusions that it was alive.

"You have something to say?"

"Sixty-six is my second-favorite number," Shiva said.

"Pray, why is it your second favorite?" said Bailey.

"Because if you take the numbers you can divide into sixty-six, including sixty-six, and add them up, what you have is a square."

Mr. Bailey couldn't resist. He wrote down 1, 2, 3, 6, 11, 22, 33, and 66—

all the numbers that went into 66—and then he totaled. What he got was 144, at which point both he and Shiva said, "Twelve squared!"

"That's what makes sixty-six special," Shiva said. "It's also true of three, twenty-two, sixty-six, seventy—their divisors add up to a square."

"Pray, tell us what's your favorite number," Bailey said, no sarcasm in his voice anymore, "since sixty-six is your second favorite?"

Shiva jumped up to the board, uninvited, and wrote: 10,213,223.

Bailey studied this for a long while, turning a bit red. Then he threw up his hands in a gesture that struck me as very ladylike. "And pray, why would this number interest us?"

"The first four numbers are your license plate." From Mr. Bailey's expression, I didn't think he was aware of this. "That's a coincidence," Shiva went on. "This number," Shiva said, tapping on the board with the chalk, getting as excited as Shiva allowed himself to get, "is the only number that describes itself when you read it. 'One zero, two ones, three twos, and two threes!" Then my brother laughed in delight, a sound so rare that our class was stunned. He brushed chalk off his hands, sat down, and he was done.

It was the only bit of mathematics that stayed with me from that year. As for the student who scored one hundred percent?—whoever it was had drawn a picture of Veronica on the test paper in lieu of a name.

I mulled over our fates, especially the good fortune that let him skip homework. I suppose I understood. Since Shiva *couldn't* do or *wouldn't* do what was required of him, he was no longer required to do it. Since I could, I had to.

Shiva went to Version Clinic whenever our school schedule allowed. He'd managed to make his way into one of Hema's surgeries, a Cesarean section, and now he was hooked. *Gray's Anatomy* became his Bible, and he drew at a frenetic pace, pages of his drawings littering our room. His subject was no longer just BMW parts or Veronica but sketches showing the vulva and uterus and uterine blood vessels. To control the proliferation of paper, Hema insisted he draw in exercise books, which he did, filling page after page. You rarely saw Shiva without his *Gray's* in his hand.

Perhaps as a reaction to Shiva, I'd seek out Ghosh after school. I knew his haunts: Operating Theater 3, Casualty, the post-op ward. My clinical education was gathering speed. Sometimes I assisted him with the vasectomies which he did in his old bungalow.

· · ·

GENET AND I SAT DOWN one evening, practicing our penmanship by copying out a page of aphorisms from *Bickham's* before beginning our homework. I looked up and was startled to see hot tears in her eyes. "If 'Virtue is its own reward,' " she said suddenly, "then my father should be alive, no? And if 'Truth needs no disguise,' why do we have to pretend that His Majesty isn't short or that his affection for his ugly dog is normal? You know he has a servant whose only job is to carry around thirty pillows of different sizes to place at His Majesty's feet, so that whatever throne he sits on his feet don't dangle in the air?"

"Come on, Genet. Don't talk that way," I said. "Unless you want to have your neck stretched." Even before the coup, it was heresy to speak against His Majesty. People went to the gallows for less. After the coup, you had to be ten times more careful.

"I don't care. I hate him. You can tell anyone you want." She stormed off.

WHEN THE SCHOOL TERM drew to a close, Rosina dropped a bombshell. She asked for leave to return to the north of the country, to Asmara, the heart of Eritrea. She wanted to take Genet with her to meet her family and to meet Zemui's parents. Hema feared she wouldn't return, and so she recruited Almaz and Gebrew to try to talk Rosina out of it, or have her go alone, but Rosina was adamant. In the end, Genet solved the problem. "No matter what," she told Hema, "I'll be back. But I do want to see my relatives."

When their taxi to the bus depot pulled away, Genet waved happily; she'd been so excited about the three-day journey, and she could talk of nothing else. But for me (and for Hema) it was heartbreaking. That very night, the wind picked up, the leaves were swishing and rustling, and by morning a squall arrived, heralding the long rains.

NOW THAT I WAS about to turn thirteen, I was aware that for Matron, Bachelli, and Ghosh, and for Missing Hospital, the rainy season meant the croup, diphtheria, and measles season. There was no letup in the work.

One morning, as I went down to the gate, umbrella in hand, I saw a woman coming up the hill to Missing, rivulets of water pouring off her umbrella. She looked frightened. I recognized her; she worked in one of the bars in the cinder-block buildings opposite Missing. Some mornings

I saw her looking much as she did now, a plain and pleasant face, wearing a homely cotton skirt and top. I'd also seen her at night, her hair teased out, wearing heels, jewelry, elegant clothes, and looking glamorous.

She asked me for directions. Her name was Tsige, I learned later. I heard the muted, glottic, honking cough coming from the infant slung to her back in a *shama*, papoose fashion. It was a sound like the cry of a gander, and for that reason, I bypassed Casualty and took Tsige directly to the croup room. The croup room was at other times the diarrhea/ dehydration room. A lab bench ran along the four walls, its surface covered with red rubber sheets. A curtain rod at head height circled the room and intravenous bottles were suspended from this. In a pinch, Missing could resuscitate up to sixteen or even twenty infants packed side by side on that bench.

The baby's eyes were screwed shut, the fingers curled, the tiny translucent nails leaving marks in the palm. The rise and fall of the little chest seemed too fast for a four-month-old. The nurse found a scalp vein and hooked up an intravenous drip. Ghosh arrived and quickly examined the little fellow. He let me listen with his stethoscope: it seemed impossible for such a tiny chest to be so full of squeaks, whistles, wheezes, and rattles. Over the left side, the heartbeat was so rapid I couldn't imagine how such a pace could be sustained. "You see these bowed legs, the lumpy bossing of the forehead?" Ghosh said. "And the hot-cross-bun pattern on the top of the skull? These are the stigmata of rickets."

"Stigmata" in my religion class at LT&C meant the nail wounds, the cuts from the crown of thorns, the gash made by the spear of Longinus in Christ's flesh. But Ghosh used the word to mean the flesh signs of a disease. In the Piazza he had once pointed out the stigmata of congenital syphilis in a listless boy who was squatting on the sidewalk: "Saddle nose, cloudy eyes, peg-shaped incisor teeth . . ." I read about the other stigmata of syphilis: mulberry molars, saber-shinned tibias, and deafness.

All the infants in the croup room appeared related because they *all* had the stigmata of rickets to a greater or lesser degree. They were wizened, bug-eyed, with big foreheads.

Ghosh put the child in the crude oxygen tent fashioned out of a plastic sheet. "The croup following measles, on top of malnutrition, on top of rickets," he said to me under his breath. "It's the cascade of catastrophes."

Ghosh took Tsige aside, his Amharic surprisingly fluent as he explained what was going on. He cautioned her to keep breast-feeding "no matter what you hear from anyone else." When Tsige said the child was hardly sucking, he said, "Still, it will comfort him because he will know you are there. You're a good mother. This is hard." Tsige tried to kiss Ghosh's hand when he left, but he'd have none of it.

"I'll try to check on this baby later," Ghosh said on his way out. "We have a vasectomy tonight. Dr. Cooper from the American Embassy is coming to learn. Would you bring over a sterilized vasectomy pack from the operating theater? And plug in the sterilizer in my quarters?"

I stayed in the croup room with Tsige, because I sensed that she had no one else. Her infant looked no better. I thought of the shops on Churchill Road and how I'd seen tourists stop there, thinking it was a flower shop or flower market, only to find that the "flowers" were wreaths. Then they noticed the shoe-box-size coffins, just for infants.

Tears streamed down Tsige's face—she could see her baby was the sickest one there. The other mothers withdrew as if she were bad luck. At one point I held her hand. I searched for words of comfort but realized I didn't need any. When her baby began grunting with each breath, Tsige cried on my shoulder. I wished Genet were with me—whatever she was doing in Asmara surely couldn't be as meaningful as this. Genet *said* she wanted to be a doctor—for a smart kid growing up at Missing, perhaps it seemed inevitable. And yet Genet had an aversion to the hospital and had no interest in following Ghosh or Hema around. Even if she were in Addis, I couldn't see her sitting here with Tsige.

AT THREE THAT AFTERNOON, Tsige's child died. It had been like watching a slow drowning. The effort of breathing ultimately proved too much for that tiny chest.

At once the staff nurse ran out in the rain to the main hospital, just as she'd been instructed to do. She gestured for me to follow, but I stayed put. A parent's grief needed a scapegoat, and parents were occasionally moved to violence, to exacting retribution on those who'd tried to help. I knew I had nothing to fear from Tsige.

Half an hour later, Tsige held the shrouded body in her arms, ready for his voyage home. Belatedly, the other mothers gathered around Tsige. They raised their mouths to the heavens, the veins on their necks forming cords. *Lulululululu,* they cried, hoping their lament might weave some protection around their infants.

I walked with Tsige to the gate. There she turned to me, her eyes full of pain. We held each other's gaze for what seemed like a long time. She bowed, then carried her bundle away. I felt so sad for her. Her baby's suffering had ended, but hers had just begun.

DR. COOPER ARRIVED promptly at eight that evening in an embassy staff car, just as the patient, a Polish gentlemen, pulled up in his Kombi.

Ghosh had learned the technique of vasectomy as an intern, and he'd learned directly from Jhaver in India, whom he spoke of as "the maestro of male nut clipping who is personally responsible for millions of people not being here." The operation was a novelty in Ethiopia, and now expatriate men, particularly Catholics, came to Ghosh in increasing numbers for an operation that was uncommon or unavailable in their countries.

"I have a proposition for you Dr. Cooper. I shall teach you the vasectomy, and once you are proficient, you can pay me back by doing a vasectomy on a VIP patient."

"Do I know him?" Cooper asked.

"You are talking to him," Ghosh said. "So you see I have a vested interest in seeing you are superbly trained. My assistant, Marion, will help me judge your skills. Marion, not a word to Hema—you either, Cooper—about my plans, please."

Cooper had a stiff brush cut and overlapping square teeth that looked like Chiclets. His American accent was sharp, jarring to the ear, but offset by the way he drawled out his words, by his relaxed, affable manner, as if he'd never had an unpleasant moment in his life and did not expect to.

"See one, do one, teach one. *Raaaiyt,* old buddy?" Cooper said.

"Indeed, yes," Ghosh said. "It is easy to do, but harder than it looks. Some preliminaries, Dr. Cooper. I tell the patient to use an enema the night before, because nothing makes them more tense than being constipated. Warm milk and honey mixed together and put into an enema bag held shoulder high is what I recommend."

"Does it work?"

"Does it work? Let me put it this way: if the patient happens to be drinking a whiskey and soda, it'll suck the glass right out of his hand."

"Gotcha," said Cooper.

"I also ask the patient to take a warm bath beforehand. It relaxes him." He added sotto voce, "And it improves my olfactory experience, you know?"

The patient hadn't said a word thus far. He was, Ghosh had told me, a consultant to the Economic Commission for Africa, an expert on population control who happened to be the father of five girls. He didn't mind all the attention.

"We can't finish if we don't start, so we better start, yes? Marion, the heater please?" I'd already turned on the electric heater under the table. "Here is the first caveat. If you don't want the scrotum to shrivel up, and the balls to retract to the armpit, the room has to be really warm. Now, the second caveat is relaxation. *Very* important. A barbiturate or narcotic might help. I recommend an ounce of Johnny Walker Red or Black. I'm not particular. A *wonderful* relaxant. And yes, you might give one to the patient, too."

Cooper's laugh rolled leisurely out of his mouth, like the great banks of clouds that spilled over the Entoto Mountains.

I hoped Cooper was paying attention. I'd seen it before: when the patient's private parts were first exposed, even when the room was warm, the scrotal skin—the dartos muscle—would wrinkle and shrink, and the cremaster muscle would tug the testis up. Then, after a good swallow of whiskey (by the patient), which was served only at this point and not before, the sac unfurled.

Both surgeons were gloved, and Ghosh cleaned the area thoroughly and then draped sterile towels to frame the field. "Another tip, Dr. Cooper. Even though it's a simple operation, mustn't allow any bleeding. Do you know what a *brinjal* looks like, Dr. Cooper?"

"I don't believe I do, no sir," Cooper said.

"Aubergine? . . . *Melanzana?* . . . Eggplant?"

Cooper recognized the last word.

"Well, if you don't meticulously control bleeding, you'll have an egg-plant. Or two. And you know what we call that complication, Cooper. We call it the bloody-*brinjal*-and-bugger-all. Which is also what they fed us for five years in my medical-school hostel."

I served the patient his Johnny Walker, which he downed in one gulp.

I loved assisting Ghosh. Ever since he treated me as if I were old enough to learn and understand, I took my role very seriously. I was thrilled to have Cooper there watching.

Ghosh, on the patient's right, rooted with his thumb and index finger at the top right of the scrotum, just where it joined the body. "You feel all the wiry things—lymph vessels, arteries, nerves, and whatnot? Well, the vas deferens is in that lot, and with practice you can tell it apart from all the other wires. It has the largest wall-to-lumen ratio of any tubular structure in the body, believe it or not. Here it is. A whiplike structure. Put your finger behind mine."

Cooper rooted around, and said, "Got it. The vas. Yup."

"Now, push the vas forward from the back with the tip of your index finger, fix it like this against the pulp of your finger so that it doesn't slip away."

Ghosh's instructions to Cooper were similar to what he said to me when I assisted him. He loved to teach, and in Cooper, he had the kind of student he deserved. If he dazzled Cooper with his polished delivery, it was because he'd practiced it on me. *Practicing* medicine and *teaching* medicine were completely connected for Ghosh. When there was no one to instruct, he suffered. But that was rare. He would happily teach a probationer, or even a family member—whoever happened to be around.

"I use Adrenalin with my local anesthetic to keep the bleeding minimal. And don't be stingy." He emptied a five-cc syringe of local into the tissue that his index finger pushed forward. "Any less than that and he'll have pain and the balls will go to the armpit. You'll have to call a chest surgeon to bring them down. Now . . . see how my index finger still has the vas stretched over it? I make a tiny cut in the scrotal skin. I keep pushing on the vas, pushing it forward . . . and . . . there! When I can see it in the wound, I use an Allis to grab the vas."

He pulled out a short length of pale, white, wormlike tissue. "I put a mosquito clip here and here . . . and then I cut between the clips. I remove a two-centimeter segment. Ideally you'd send it to pathology. That way if his wife gets pregnant a year from now, you can show the patient the pathology report and he'll know it's not because you didn't do your job but because a third party did his job better. I don't send it to pathology for the simple reason that we don't have a pathologist. But for a while, there was a pathologist at the American Embassy clinic in Beirut. I'd do the vasectomies for the American staff and send him these little pieces I cut out. The man did the pathology for all the American embassies in East and West Africa. He kept sending back reports that my specimens were inadequate: though he *thought* he saw some uroepithelial tissue, he couldn't be certain it was the vas. 'It's the vas,' I wrote to him each time. 'What other uroepithelial tissue could I have cut out? Call it the vas.' But he kept complaining: 'Cannot be certain. Not enough tissue.' It was starting to annoy me, you know? So finally, I sent him a pair of sheep's balls. I put them in formalin and sent them off in the same diplomatic pouch. With a note: 'Is this enough tissue?' Never had a problem with him after that."

Cooper hee-hawed, his mask sucking in and out.

"Now, I tie off the cut ends with catgut. And then I tell the patient, 'No communication with wife allowed for the next ninety days.' "

Ghosh turned to face the patient, and repeated the sentence. The patient nodded. "Okay, you can communicate, say 'Good morning, darling,' and all that, but no sex for three months." The patient grinned. "Okay, you can have sex, but you must wear a condom."

"I use interruptus," the patient said, speaking for the first time in a heavy East European accent.

"You use what? *Interruptus?* Pull and pray? Good God, man! No wonder you have five kids! It's noble of you to try to get off the train at an earlier station, but it's unreliable. No sir. Interrupt the interruptus, man, unless you want to reach your half dozen this year." The patient looked embarrassed. "You know what we call young men who use coitus interruptus?" Ghosh said.

The population expert shook his head.

"We call them Father! Daddy. Pater. Pappa. Père. No sir, I have done the interrupting for you. Give me three months and you can tell your missus that she is not to worry because you will be shooting blanks, and there will be no more interruptions and you will be staying for dessert, coffee, and cigars."

CHAPTER 31

The Dominion of the Flesh

WITH GENET AND ROSINA AWAY, our quarters felt empty. I missed Genet terribly. Hema and I both worried that we'd never see her again. She'd promised to call, and write, but three weeks had gone by and we'd yet to hear from her. That year, 1968, we had torrential rains; the Blue Nile and Awash had spilled their banks, causing flooding. The babbling brook behind Missing looked like a river. In Addis, the populace was bottled up indoors so that a lull in the rain released the scent of stifled humanity, dung fires, and clothes that refused to dry. The ivy raced up the drainpipes and found chinks in walls, while the tadpoles hurried into croaking frogs before their limbs were fully formed. No child I knew was ever tempted to turn its face to the sky and catch raindrops on the tongue, not when you lived and breathed water.

Now that Shiva and I were teenagers, looking ahead to our fourteenth birthday, I kept expecting something to feel different. I tried to stay busy, but all I could think about was Genet and what she might be up to in Asmara. I hoped she was homebound, miserable, and missing me. Without Genet as a witness, nothing I did was meaningful.

LATE ON A TUESDAY EVENING, I watched Ghosh in Operating Theater 3 as he removed a gallbladder. When he was done, we swung by the surgical ward to see Etien, a diplomat from Ivory Coast, a man we knew socially, who'd suddenly developed a bowel obstruction. In surgery, Ghosh had found an obstructing rectal cancer which he was forced to resect. It was a big and challenging operation, and I knew Ghosh was hopeful for a cure. But he was forced to create a colostomy on the belly wall. "Etien's very depressed," Ghosh said. "Not about the cancer, but over his colostomy. He can't accept the idea of waste coming out from an opening in his abdomen."

Etien had the sheet over his head. When Ghosh examined him, and then said the colostomy looked beautiful, tears welled up in Etien's big eyes. He wouldn't look down there. All he said was "Who will marry me now?"

Ghosh was surprisingly firm. "Etien, that's not the part of your body I cut off, the marrying part. You'll find a woman who loves you, and you'll explain it to her. If she loves you for yourself, you'll both be glad that you are alive." Ghosh's facial expression brooked no argument, but then he softened. "Etien, imagine if all humans were born with their anus on the belly and that's where *everyone's* waste emerged. Then imagine if someone said they were going to operate on you and reroute your bowel so it opened behind you, between your buttock cheeks, somewhere where you couldn't see it except in a mirror, and where you could hardly reach it or easily keep it clean . . ." It took a few seconds, but then Etien smiled. He dabbed his eyes. He ventured a glance down at his colostomy. It was a small step in the right direction.

Ghosh had one more patient to see. He told me to go on home so I wouldn't be late for dinner.

The rain began to come down hard and I had no umbrella. I walked under the sheltered walkways connecting the theater to Casualty and Casualty to the male ward. Where the walkway ended, I dashed across a short gap, leaping over a puddle to arrive at the nurses' quarters. I rarely explored this female warren. It looked deserted. If I went up the long outer balcony and down the stairs at the other end . . . well, I'd still get soaked, but I'd be fifty yards closer to home before I had to dash out into the rain. I hoped Adam's wife, the keeper of the virgins, with that big cross around her neck, didn't see me, because she would chase me out.

Upstairs, the doors of the individual nurses' rooms opened onto the shared veranda. They must have all been in the dining room, otherwise they would have been lined up against the veranda railing, teasing out their hair, painting their nails, sewing, and chatting.

I heard music from the corner room that had once been my mother's. I'd been up here a few times, but just like her grave, this wasn't a place where I felt her presence. The strangeness of the music, the beat, were what pulled me closer. Guitars and drums in a driving rhythm repeated a musical refrain first in one register, then another. Of late some Ethiopian music adopted a Western sound, with horns, snare drums, and a repeating electric guitar riff that took the place of the muffled strings of the *krar* and the hand clapping. But this wasn't Ethiopian music, and not just because the words were English (albeit an English I couldn't quite understand). This was radically different, like a new color in the rainbow.

The door was open a crack.

She stood barefoot in the center of the room, her back to me. A white slip exposed her shoulders and ended at the back of her knees. Her head went from side to side, and her long, straight hair, conked with chemicals, followed as if welded to her skull. Her hips were driven by the bass line, while her upraised right hand kept the melody. Her left hand must have been pressed to her belly, because the elbow jutted out like the handle of a teacup. The music had entered her; it lubricated her joints, softened her bones and flesh to produce this gyrating, fluid, and sensual movement.

She turned. Her eyes were closed and her face was tilted up. The lower lip was twisted, as if it had been split and had healed out of alignment.

I knew that lip, that faintly pockmarked face, though now the pocks textured the skin and exaggerated her cheekbones. It was the body I didn't recognize. She'd been a student probationer forever, until Matron, taking pity on her, gave her a new title, Staff Probationer, which transformed her. From being on the long-term plan, a perpetual student, she became an instructor for incoming probationers. In the classroom, with textbooks that she knew by heart, she could both drive facts into the probationers' heads and demonstrate that it was possible to keep them there, by the manner in which she regurgitated her material, never looking at the text.

Normally she wore her hair pulled off her forehead and neck and gathered into a top bun so tight that it arched her eyebrows. When she crowned this with the winged nurse's cap, it looked as if she'd inverted an ice-cream cone on her head.

Other than her precarious hairdo, I'd always thought of the Staff Probationer as plain. At school, I knew girls who were neither ugly nor beautiful but who saw themselves one way or the other, and that conviction made it come true. Heidi Enqvist was gorgeous, but alas not in her own eyes, and so she lacked the mystery and allure of Rita Vartanian, who despite her overbite and prominent nose managed to make Heidi envious.

The probationer was of the Heidi mold. I think that's why she made herself a willing prisoner of a stiff, starched uniform and adopted an unsmiling expression to go with it. The only identity she had was that of being in the nursing profession; in her own eyes, and in the light of the world, she thought she was nobody. I'd always felt the probationer's discomfort around us. But then she was shy around everybody.

But I could see now that there was more to her than nursing. The uniform concealed a body full of curves, like the figures Shiva used to draw, and the body moved in ways that would have made a harem dancer jealous.

Her eyes were closed. Were she to see me she'd be startled, embarrassed, and probably furious. I was about to step back when, to my surprise, she stepped forward and pulled me in by my hand, as if a phrase in the song was my cue. She kicked the door shut. The music was louder and more intense inside the room.

She had me taking little steps in time to the beat, moving my body this way and that. I was embarrassed at first. I wanted to laugh or say something clever, the way an adult would. But her expression and the throbbing beat made me feel anything but dancing would have been like talking in church. My steps became effortless. I imitated her, my shoulders moving in the opposite direction from my hips. My hands drew figures in the air. The trick was not to think. My body felt segmented, and each segment answered the call of a particular instrument. The pattern of our steps felt inevitable.

Just when I mastered that, she pulled me to her, my cheek against her neck, my chest against her breasts, separated from them by the thinnest of materials. I'd never danced before, certainly not like this. I breathed in her perfume and her sweat. She squeezed, taking my breath away, as if to make our two bodies one. She guided my arm so that it was around her, my hand over her sacrum, and I held her close. We never stopped moving. She led.

I anticipated her every step, clueless as to where that knowledge came from. We spun, then surged this way, then that, like one organism. I thought of Genet. Emboldened, I led and she followed. I pressed against the soft flesh where her legs came together only because she pressed, too, grinding her hips into me. Blood surged to my face, to my arms, into my stomach, my groin. The world had fallen away. I was in an elaborate dialogue with her.

The music wouldn't stop, and I never wanted it to stop, and just when

I thought that, it faded. The American announcer's lazy drawl was so unlike the crisp formal tones of the BBC. "Well, well," he said. "My, my. Umm, hmmm," as if he'd seen us carrying on. "Have you ever heard anything quite like that? This is the Rock of East Africa. East Africa's Big 14. Armed Forces Radio Service, Asmara." It wasn't a station that I knew existed. I knew of a huge American military presence, a listening post, I'd heard it called, just outside of Asmara in Kagnew. Who knew they had something *we* could listen to?

We were still pressed together, holding the world at bay. She gazed into my eyes, I didn't know if she was about to cry or laugh. All I knew was that I'd have cried with her, or laughed or got down on all fours and pretended to be Koochooloo if she asked.

"You're so beautiful," I said, surprising myself.

She gasped. My words seem to ripple through her. Had I said the wrong thing? Her lips quivered; her eyes shone. She was expressing joy. I'd said the right thing.

She lowered her face, brought that lip with the puckered scar and the bulges on either side close to mine. Her mouth overlapped mine, forming a seal. The silliest image entered my mind, and it was that of connecting one garden hose to another. What flowed across wasn't water, but her tongue. This time, unlike in the pantry with Genet, I received her tongue eagerly. It was so very exciting. I put my hand behind her head. I pressed my body to her, feeling every atom in me come to a point.

I pulled away once to look at her and say, "You're so beautiful," because it was a magical phrase, one I knew I should use often, but only if I believed it to be true. I don't know how long we were coupled by our mouths, but it came most naturally, as if I were satisfying a hunger. I didn't realize this potential existed in me. It carried me forward. Whatever was next, I didn't know, but my body knew. I trusted my body. I was ready.

Suddenly, she stepped away. She held me at arm's length. She sat on the edge of the bed. She was crying. Something had happened about which my body had failed to inform me. Or perhaps there was a rule, an etiquette, that I'd failed to observe. I eyed the door, measuring my escape.

"Can you ever forgive me?" she said. "Your mother shouldn't have died. Maybe if I told someone she was sick, they could've helped her."

This was astonishing. I could feel the hair on the back of my neck rise. I'd entirely forgotten this was my mother's room. I couldn't picture

Sister Mary Joseph Praise in here, certainly not with a poster of Venice on the wall, and on another wall a black-and-white poster of a white singer, his pelvis thrust forward at the microphone stand which he'd pulled toward him, his face contorted with the effort of singing. I looked back to the Staff Probationer.

"I didn't know how sick she was." She hiccuped through her tears, just like a baby.

"It's all right," I said, feeling as if someone else gave me those words.

"Say you forgive me."

"I will if you stop crying. Please."

"Say it."

"I forgive you."

She only cried louder. Someone would hear. I didn't think I was supposed to be in this room. And I certainly wasn't supposed to make her cry.

"I said it! I said I forgive you. Why are you still crying?"

"But I almost let you and your brother die. I was supposed to help you breathe when you came out. I was supposed to resuscitate you. But I forgot."

WHEN I FIRST CAME to this room, I was adrift, feeling as if a part of me was missing, all because Genet was away. Then I'd forgotten all that and found happiness, no, ecstasy, in the dance, a hint of what I wanted with Genet. And now I was adrift again, and confused. Paradise had seemed so close, and now I was clawing through fog. She grabbed my hand and pulled me to her, to the bed.

"You can do anything you want to me. Anytime," she said, tilting her head back, looking up at me as I stood over her.

What did she mean?

"Do what?" I said.

"Anything."

She let me go and she fell back on her bed. She was spread-eagled. She was ready. For whatever I might want to do.

Yes, there was something I wanted to do. If I were given free rein, dominion over her body, I knew I'd discover it by instinct. I had a general idea. I was nearly fourteen after all.

She was giving me license and still I waited.

She rolled over onto her belly, showing me her buttocks and peering at me over her shoulder. Her eyelids were puffy, her expression dreamy and faraway. She spun one hundred eighty degrees so her head faced me. She propped herself up on her elbows. Her breasts hung down, the nipples barely concealed. She followed my gaze to her cleavage.

I heard voices and footsteps outside. The other nurses and probationers were back from dinner.

I didn't want to leave. But the world had intruded. My hesitation doomed me. That and her uninvited confession.

"I want to dance with you again," I said, in a whisper.

"You can . . . ," she whispered, but as if that were the wrong answer.

"I do want to do . . . anything with you."

"Yes! That's what I want, too." She was kneeling on the bed now, brightening, smiling through her tears. "Come," she said, arms extended, beckoning.

"But nothing right now. I'll be back another day." I put my hand on the doorknob.

"But . . . how about anything now?" she said, loud enough for the world to hear.

I slipped out quickly, hoping that if anyone saw me, they'd think it perfectly normal for me to visit.

The rain hadn't let up. I let it beat on my head. I didn't mind. Rain was familiar. But this balancing on the edge of feelings so powerful they seemed capable of making me fly, this was a revelation. By the time I reached our quarters I was soaked. When I saw the door to Rosina and Genet's room, I longed for the padlock not to be there. I stood staring at that closed door.

It was at that moment, with raindrops smacking me on the fontanel, that I came to the decision that I must marry Genet. Yes, that was my destiny. What I felt with the probationer, I never wanted to feel with anyone but Genet. There were too many temptations out there, great forces ready to shake me free of my avowed intent. I wanted to succumb to temptation. But with just one woman, and that was Genet.

If I married her, I'd solve everything. It would keep Rosina from pulling away, it would make Hema, Ghosh, and Rosina happy, and they'd have both of us as their children. I could see us having kids of our own. We'd tear down the servant's quarters and build the twin to the main house, with a linking corridor, so we could all be under the same roof; we'd have a room, or maybe a suite, for Shiva. He'd be happy to have Genet as a sister-in-law. Since Shiva wasn't one to look back, to celebrate the past, it was all the more important for me to preserve the family, keep us as one.

I STEPPED INTO THE HOUSE, dripping water on the floor. In the bathroom I stripped naked and studied myself in the mirror, looking to see what the probationer saw. I was tall for my age, nearly six feet, and my skin was fair. I could perhaps have passed for someone of Mediterranean ancestry; my irises were brown—I never saw the hint of blue I could see in Shiva's. My expression seemed unduly earnest, particularly when my hair was damp. Once it dried, the curls would return and would have a life of their own, refusing to be corralled. This is what it means to arrive at manhood, I thought, hands on my hips, turning to admire my flanks, my buttocks.

I dressed and returned to the kitchen, breathing in the scents steaming out of the pots and snatching a piece of meat before Almaz could slap my hand away. She scolded me, but it was a sweet sound, as was the music from the living room with the heavy beat of a tabla, and the thump and thud of Hema and Shiva dancing, of Hema calling out instructions. I heard the rattle of the loose bumper on the Volkswagen as Ghosh came up the driveway. I felt ecstatic, as if I was at the epicenter of our family, missing only Genet and Rosina who surely would come back, and then our family would be whole.

I pushed out of my mind what the probationer said about what she'd done—or hadn't done—for my mother. There wasn't any point in dwelling in the pain of the past, not when the future could hold such pleasure. And as for my father? No, he wouldn't ever walk through those gates; I now knew that. Whatever Thomas Stone had, wherever he was at this moment, he had no idea what he'd given up in the exchange.

CHAPTER 32

A Time to Sow

G ENET AND ROSINA RETURNED two days before school began; they arrived with the clamor and excitement of the Indian circus coming to the Merkato. Their taxi from the bus station sagged on its springs, the roof carrier and trunk so laden with goods.

The first thing I noticed was Rosina's gold tooth and the grin that went with it. Genet, too, was transformed, radiant, wearing a traditional cotton skirt and tight bodice, with a matching *shama* around her shoulders. She shrieked with happiness as she leaped out to hug Hema, almost knocking her over. Then she rushed to Ghosh, then Shiva, then Almaz and me, and then back into Hema's arms. When Rosina hugged me, it was loving and affectionate; but her lengthy embrace of Shiva made me feel a stab of envy. Her absence allowed me to now see clearly what I'd overlooked before—that she favored Shiva. Was this a result of her seeing me in the pantry with her naked daughter? Or had she always had a soft spot for Shiva? And was I the only one to notice?

They were all talking over one another now. Rosina, one arm still around Shiva, allowed Gebrew to admire her gold tooth.

"Genet, darling, your hair!" Hema said, because it was braided into tight cornrows, like her mother's, each braid springing free at the back of her head where it was tied around a shiny disk. "You cut it?"

"I know! Don't you love it? And see my hands," she said. Her palms were orange with henna.

"But it's so . . . short. And you pierced your ears, darling!" Hema said. Blue hoops hung down from her lobes. "My God, girl," she said, holding Genet by the shoulders, "Look at you! You've grown taller and . . . fuller."

"Your tits are bigger," Shiva said.

"Shiva!" Hema and Ghosh said at the same time.

"Sorry," he said, surprised by their reaction. "I meant her breasts are bigger," he said.

"*Shiva!* That isn't the sort of thing you say to a woman," Hema said.

"I can't say it to a man," Shiva said, looking impatient.

"It's all right, Ma," Genet said. "And it's true. I'm a B, or maybe even a C!" she said looking down proudly at her breasts, which pointed up like stargazers.

Rosina could tell what was being discussed. *"Stai zitto!"* she said to Genet, her finger on her lips, which made Genet laugh.

"Madam," Rosina said to Hema in Amharic, "I've had my hands full with this girl. All the boys are chasing her. Does she have the sense to discourage them? No. And look how she dresses!" I was distressed to hear a trace of pride in her complaint.

Genet said, "I just love the clothes in Asmara. Oh! I brought postcards. *Dov'è la mia borsetta,* Mama? I want to show you. Oh, it's in the taxi . . . Hold on." She went headfirst through the open window of the taxi, treating us to a view of her panties. Rosina screamed at her in Tigrinya, to no avail.

Genet thrust postcards at us. "Oh, Asmara, you can't imagine what a beautiful city the Italians built so long ago. See?" It wasn't something to brag about: being colonized for so long *before* Ethiopia. The strange, colorful buildings were all angles, like something out of a geometry set.

HEMA AND GHOSH soon drifted back into the house. The taxi driver helped Gebrew unload wooden stools and a new bed into Rosina's quarters. The bed was made of hand-carved dark wood, a gift from Rosina's brother in Asmara, we learned.

I sat on the new bed, gazing at Genet. It felt as if she'd been away for years. I was tongue-tied. "So how was your winter, Marion?" If I was unsure of myself in front of her, she didn't know the meaning of shy.

I'd saved up things to tell her. I even had a script. But this tall beautiful girl—this *woman,* I should say—sitting next to me, so Eritrean and so enamored of things Italian, messed up my speech. The patients I'd seen, the books I'd read . . . none of this could compete with Asmara.

"Oh, nothing really," I said. "You know how it is here in the long rains."

"That's it? Nothing? No movies, no adventures? And . . . girlfriends?"

I was still smarting from Rosina's description of the boys chasing Genet in Asmara. It was a betrayal. Surely Genet had a role in that: What boy would bother you if you told him to get lost?

"Well," I said, "I don't know about girlfriends, but . . ."

Reluctantly at first, I told her about my visit to my mother's old room, but I recast my time with the probationer as something casual, portraying myself as the indifferent participant. However, the further I got into the story, the less I was able to sustain that tone.

Genet's eyes became as round as the hoops on her ears.

"So you did it with her?" she said.

"No!" I said.

She seemed disappointed, when I would have expected her to be jealous.

"For God's sake, Marion, why not?"

I shook my head. "I didn't because . . ."

"Because what? Spit it out," she said, poking my side, as if to help the words come out. "Who are you waiting for? The Queen of England? She's married you know."

"I didn't do it, because . . . I knew it would be wonderful, more than wonderful. I knew it would be fantastic—"

"What kind of explanation is that?" she said, rolling her eyes in frustration.

"But . . . I knew I wanted my first time to be with you."

There, I said it.

Genet looked at me for the longest time, her mouth open. I felt vulnerable. I held my breath hoping what came out of her mouth next wouldn't be mockery or amusement. Ridicule would destroy me.

She leaned over, her eyes soft, her expression loving and tender, and she took my chin in both her hands and shook it side to side as if I were a little baby.

"Ma che minchia?" Rosina asked, her hands on her hips, rudely interrupting us. I hadn't noticed her come back into the room.

Genet burst out laughing. Rosina didn't find it amusing, but Genet was losing her breath, keeling over. Rosina glared at her, then gave up, muttering to herself. This hysterical laughter of Genet's was something new.

When she could speak, Genet explained. " *'Ma che minchia?'* means 'What the fuck?' which *I* kept saying in Asmara. I learned it from my cousins. My mother threatened to slap me every time I said it. And now *she* says it, can you believe it? . . . So, Marion—*che minchia,* eh?"

. . . .

WE HAD DINNER together in the bungalow, Genet seated with us, while Rosina and Almaz ate in the kitchen.

It had become my practice to take over the Grundig once we'd eaten. Often I listened to the Rock of Africa till midnight when it went off the air. The music spoke to what I was feeling; in the tight structure of a twelve-bar blues or in Dylan's haunting ballads, order was imposed. Shiva sat with me most evenings. The music spoke to him, too.

Now the DJ came on, "Rock of East Africa, AFRS Asmara, where everyone is a mile and a half high. This is a Boone's Farm Saturday here at the base. The first shipment of Boone's Farm wine came in last night, and folks, if you missed it, I hate to tell you, but it's all gone, and so are some people here. Now let's listen to Bobby Vinton, 'My Heart Belongs Only to You.'"

I was pleased to find Genet knew nothing of this radio station. The cousins in Asmara couldn't be that cool if they never tuned in to this show.

The next song began without any introduction. I jumped up. "This is it!" I said to Genet. "This is the tune I was telling you about."

In all the evenings of listening to the radio, here for the first time was the song that I'd heard in the probationer's room.

I was shimmying and twisting to the music, blind to Hema's shocked expression and the stares of Ghosh and Genet. I cranked the volume up; Rosina and Almaz came out of the kitchen. They must have thought I was mad. This was out of character for me, but I couldn't stop myself, or I chose not to, and something told me this was the day for it.

Now Shiva stood up and joined me, and his dancing was smooth, silky, and so polished, as if all his lessons with Hema had been a way of biding time till he heard this song. That was all it took for Genet to jump in. I pulled Hema up from her chair, and soon she moved in time to the music. Ghosh needed no urging. I tried to pull Rosina in, but she and Almaz fled to the kitchen. The five of us in that living room danced till the very last note had sounded.

Chuck Berry.

That was the name of the artist. The song was "Sweet Little Sixteen"—so the announcer said.

When it was time for bed, Genet said she was going back to Rosina's quarters. Hema looked hurt. "I'll keep my mother company," Genet said. "I have my own bed now. There were six of us on the floor in Asmara. Having a bed for myself will be a real luxury."

The next day in the Piazza, I found the Chuck Berry 45 in a record shop. I realized from the dust jacket that "Sweet Little Sixteen" was a number one hit—but in 1958! I was crushed. The rest of the world had heard this song more than a decade before I knew it existed. When I thought of how I had danced to it the previous night, it felt like the dance of an ignoramus, like the awe of a peasant seeing the neon beer mug on top of the Olivetti Building.

ON THE EVE of the new school year, Hema and Ghosh took us with them to the Greek club for the annual gala to celebrate the end of "winter." Genet surprised me by saying she'd stay back and get her school clothes ready; she, Rosina, Gebrew, and Almaz planned a cozy dinner in Rosina's quarters.

The big band was made up of moonlighting musicians from the army, air force, and Imperial Bodyguard orchestras. They could play "Stardust," "Begin the Beguine," and "Tuxedo Junction" in their sleep. Chuck Berry wasn't in their repertoire.

The expatriate community, back from vacations, was out in force, looking tanned. I saw Mr. and Mrs. G——, who weren't really married, and the word was they'd abandoned their spouses and children in Portugal to be with each other; Mr. J——, a dashing Goan bachelor who was jailed briefly for a financial shenanigan, was in full form. The newly arriving expats would quickly learn their roles; they'd find that their foreignness trumped their training or talent—it was their most important asset. Soon they'd be regulars, smiling and dancing at this annual event.

I'd always thought the expatriates represented the best of culture and style of the "civilized" world. But I could see now that they were so far from Broadway or the West End or La Scala, that they probably were a decade behind the times, just as I'd been with Chuck Berry. I watched the ruddy, sweaty faces on the dance floor, the childlike brightness in their eyes; it made me sad and impatient.

Shiva danced first with Hema, then with women he knew from Hema and Ghosh's bridge circle, and then with anyone who looked keen to dance. Suddenly I didn't want to be there any longer; I left early, telling Hema and Ghosh I'd take a taxi home.

I thought of the probationer as I walked up the hill to our quarters. I'd been avoiding her. When her students were with her, she made no sign of recognition. When she saw me with Shiva, she greeted us without comment. The first time I ran into her alone, she stopped me, and said, "Are you Marion?" From her eyes I knew that nothing had changed, and that her door was still open to me. "No," I had said. "I'm Shiva." She never asked again.

I heard the murmur of the radio in Rosina's quarters, but their door was closed and in any case I wasn't looking for company.

I went to bed alone, went to bed with my thoughts—I felt older than my thirteen years.

I woke when Shiva came home. I watched him in the mirror. He was taller than I saw myself, and he had the narrow hips and the light tread of a dancer. He slipped off his coat and shirt. His hair was parted and combed to one side when he left the house, but now it was an unruly mass of thick curls. His lips were full, almost womanly, and there was a dreamy, prophetic quality to his face. When he was down to his underwear, he studied himself in the mirror. He held one arm up, and the other out. He was imagining a dance with a woman. He made a graceful turn and dip.

"You had a good time?" I said.

It stopped him in his tracks. His arms remained where they were. He looked at me in the mirror, which gave me goose bumps. "A good time was had by one and all," he said in a hoarse voice that I didn't recognize.

CHAPTER 33

A Form of Madness

THE TAXI DROPPED SHIVA and me across from Missing's gate, in front of the cinder-block buildings, just as the streetlights came on. At sixteen, I was captain, opening batsman, and wicketkeeper for our cricket eleven and Shiva was a middle-order batsman. As opener, my forté was whaling away at the ball and trying to weather the first salvo while demoralizing the bowlers, while Shiva's strength was to doggedly defend his wicket, anchoring the team, even if he scored few runs. After practice it was always dark when we came home.

I saw a woman framed by the bead curtains and silhouetted against the light of the bar, at the end of the building closest to Ali's souk.

"Hi! Wait for me," she called out. Her tight skirt and heels restricted her to mincing steps as she crossed the plank that forded the gutter. She hugged herself against the cold, smiling so that her eyes were reduced to slits.

"My, you have grown so tall! Do you remember me?" she said, looking uncertainly from me to Shiva. A jasmine scent reached my nostrils.

After her baby died, I'd seen Tsige many, many times but only at waving distance. She had worn black for a year. That rainy morning when she brought her baby to Missing, Tsige had looked quite plain. Hers was a simple, guileless face, but now with eyeliner, lipstick, hair in waves down to her shoulders, she was striking.

We touched cheeks like relatives, first one side, then the other, then back to the first side again. "Uh . . . this is . . . may I present my brother," I said.

"You work here?" Shiva said. Shiva was never tongue-tied around women.

"Not anymore," she said. "I own it now. I invite you to please come in."

"No . . . but . . . thank you," I stammered. "Our mother is expecting us."

"No, she's not," said Shiva.

"I hope you won't mind if I come another day," I said.

"Whenever you want, you are welcome. Both of you."

We stood in awkward silence. She still had my hand.

"Listen. I know it was a long time ago, but I never thanked you. Every time I see you I want to talk to you, but I don't want to embarrass you, and I felt ashamed . . . Today, when I saw you this close, I thought I'd do it."

"Oh no," I said, "it's I who worried that you were angry with me—with us. Maybe you blamed Missing for . . ."

"No, no, no. I'm to blame." The light dimmed in her eyes. "That's what happens when you listen to these stupid old women. 'Give him this,' 'Do that,' they told me. That morning I looked at my poor baby, and I realized all those *habesha* medicines had hurt him. When your father examined Teferi, I knew he could have helped if I had come days earlier. I'd made a horrible mistake by waiting. But . . ."

I remained silent, remembering her sadness and how she had cried on my shoulder.

"I hope God forgives me. I hope He gives me another chance." She spoke earnestly, her face reflecting her feelings, hiding nothing. "But listen, what I came to tell you is, may God and the saints watch over you and bless you for all the time you spent with us. Such a good doctor your father is. Are you going to be doctors?"

"Yes," Shiva and I said easily, speaking in unison. It was about the only thing I could say with confidence these days, and it was about the only thing Shiva and I seemed to agree on.

The light came back to her face.

As we walked to our bungalow, Shiva said, "Why didn't we go inside? She probably lives at the back. She would have let you sleep with her."

"What makes you think I have to sleep with every woman I see?" I'd turned on him with more venom than was needed. "I don't *want* to sleep with her. Besides, she's not that kind of woman," I said.

"Maybe not anymore. But she knows how."

"I've had my chances, you know. It's a choice." I told him about the probationer, as if to prove my point.

Shiva had nothing to say to that, and we walked in silence. He was getting under my skin. I didn't want to think about Tsige in that way; I didn't want to picture her sweet face and how she had to make her living. It was painful to imagine, and so I chose not to. But Shiva had no such qualms.

Shiva said, "One day we'll have sex with women. I think today is as good as any other day." He looked up as if to ascertain that the arrangement of the stars was auspicious.

I stopped him and grabbed his shirt. I tried to find reasons for my objection. What came out was lame.

"Are you forgetting Hema and Ghosh? You think it's something that will make them happy? People look up to them. We mustn't do anything to embarrass them."

"I think it's inevitable," Shiva said. "They do it, too. I'm sure they—"

"Stop!" I said. What a disturbing thought. But not so for Shiva.

THE VERY MONTH we turned sixteen, my voice cracked when I didn't want it to. I had blackheads pushing out as if I had swallowed a sack of mustard seeds. The clothes Hema bought me grew tight or short in three or four months. Hair appeared in strange places. Thoughts of the opposite sex, mainly of Genet, made it difficult for me to concentrate. It reassured me to see these physical changes mirrored in Shiva, but after our conversation about Tsige, I couldn't talk with him about the desire I was feeling or the restraint that had to come with it. Shiva felt no such need for restraint.

"Prison," I'd heard Ghosh laughingly tell Adid, "is the best thing for a marriage. If you can't send your spouse, then go yourself. It works wonders." Now that I knew what they were up to, I was deeply embarrassed, even shocked.

Despite our knowledge of the human body in the context of disease, Shiva and I were naïve for the longest time about sexual matters—or perhaps it was just me. Little did I know that our Ethiopian peers both at our school and at the government schools had long ago gone through their sexual initiation with a bar girl or a housemaid. They never suffered my years of foggy confusion, trying to imagine what was unimaginable.

I remember a story my classmate Gaby told me when I was twelve or thirteen, a story which he'd heard from a cousin who had emigrated to America, a story which we all believed for the longest time. "When you land in New York," the cousin had said, "a beautiful blond woman will engage you in conversation at the airport. Her perfume will drive you mad. Big breasts, miniskirt. She will introduce you to her brother. They'll offer you a ride into town in their convertible, and, of course, not to be rude, you accept. As you are driving, the man will say, 'Let's just drop by my house in Malibu and have a martini before we get you to Manhattan.' You pull in to their mansion. A house like you've never seen. As soon as you are inside, the man will pull out a gun and point it at you, and say 'Screw my sister or you will die.' "

So many nights I lay awake dreaming of this horrible, twisted, beautiful fate, wishing I could go to America only for this reason. *Brother, put away the gun, I will screw your sister for free,* became a line Gaby and I and our little gang said to one another, our secret phrase that signaled our fellowship in adolescent horniness, our simmering sexual heat. Even after we realized the story was absurd, a fairy tale, it still delighted us, and we loved to repeat that refrain.

A few weeks after Shiva and I had seen Tsige outside her bar, I encountered the Staff Probationer walking down to Missing's gate. There was no escaping her. Seeing her always provoked anxiety.

She was with her brood of probationers. She usually ignored me in that situation. But on this day she smiled and blood rushed to her face. I smiled back so as not be rude. She winked and came to me as her students walked on. "Thank you for last night. I hope the blood didn't scare you. Did that surprise you? I waited for you all these years. It was worth it." She brushed against me. "When are you coming next? I'll be counting the days."

She swung every bit of flesh that would swing as she shimmied after her students, as if Chuck Berry were strutting behind her, playing his guitar. She called over her shoulder, loud enough for the whole world to hear, "Next time please don't run off afterward like that, okay?"

I raced home. Of late, particularly on weekends, Shiva went off on his own and I hadn't given it much thought. I never imagined this is what he'd been up to.

Shiva, Genet, and Hema were at the dinner table, Rosina serving. Ghosh had gone to wash up. I hauled Shiva off to our room.

"She thinks it was me!" I wished I'd never told him about my dancing with the probationer. "Why didn't you ask me? I would have forbidden you to go. I *did* forbid you to go. What did you tell her? Did you pretend to be me?"

Shiva was puzzled by my anger. "No. I was me. I just knocked on her door. I said nothing. She did all the rest."

"My God! Just like that? You broke your virginity *and* hers?"

"It was my first time with her. And what makes you so sure about her, eh, older brother?" His words were like a punch in my gut. I'd never heard Shiva speak sarcastically to me, and it felt cutting, ugly. He went on as I stood speechless. "It's not *my* first time, anyway. I've been going to the Piazza every Sunday."

"What? How many times have you gone?"

"Twenty-one times."

I couldn't speak. I was stunned, embarrassed, disgusted, and terribly envious.

"The same woman?"

"No, twenty-one different women. Twenty-two if you count the probationer." He was standing there, chin pointing at me, one arm languidly set against the wall.

When I found a voice I said, "Well would you mind not going back to the Staff Probationer?"

"Why? Will you visit her?"

I no longer felt I had any authority over him, no credible experience with which to advise him. I felt very tired. "Never mind. But do me a favor; tell her who you are if you go back. And stay around and hold her and whisper sweet things in her ear when you are done. Tell her she's beautiful."

"Whisper what? Why?"

"Forget it."

"Marion, all women are beautiful," Shiva said. I looked up and realized that he spoke with conviction and not a trace of sarcasm. He wasn't embarrassed, or angry that I hauled him off, or the least bit upset. My conceit was that I thought I knew my brother. Yet all I really knew were his rituals. He loved his *Gray's Anatomy* and carried it around so much, it had pale indentations on the cover from his fingers. When Ghosh got Shiva a new edition of *Gray's,* my brother was insulted, as if Ghosh had brought him a stray puppy to replace his beloved Koochooloo, who was on her last legs. I knew Shiva's rituals, but not the logic behind them. Shiva *did* find women beautiful—I'd seen that from the first time we visited the Version Clinic. He never missed a clinic and ultimately wore Hema down until she taught him how to turn babies. There was nothing prurient about his interest in the Version Clinic or in obstetrics and gynecology. If the clinic day happened to fall on a holiday, or Hema decided to not have it for some reason, Shiva would still be there, seated on the steps of the locked building. Here I was telling him to be nice to the probationer, but he could argue that he'd given the probationer just what she'd wanted while I'd been anything but nice to her. Meanwhile, I was saving myself for one woman. My abstinence felt noble because it was so very difficult. I burned with my celibacy and I wanted it to impress Genet. How could it not?

It had been clear to me ever since that sunny Saturday three years before when Genet returned from her holiday in Asmara that puberty for her was all but complete. Her growth spurt that winter made everything longer: legs, fingers, even lashes. Her eyelids turned sleepy looking, and her eyes seemed even more widely spaced. After her return from Asmara, she'd begun to drive the household mad. According to *Nelson Textbook of Pediatrics,* breast buds and pubic hair were the first signs of puberty in girls. How strange that *Nelson* overlooked the first sign I noted, namely, a heady, mature scent that beckoned like a Siren. When she wore perfume, the two scents would mingle, and what emerged made me dizzy. All I could imagine was tearing off her clothes and drinking from the source.

Genet's changes galvanized Rosina—I could see that clearly. Hema and Rosina were allies, united by their desire to protect Genet from the predators, the boys. But the two mothers were never protective enough for my tastes, and they sabotaged their own efforts by buying her the kinds of clothes and accessories that made her more attractive to the opposite sex. The hounds—judging by how I felt—couldn't help sniffing at our doorstep, and what's more, Genet, by her own admission, was in heat.

THAT TERM, on a Thursday, Genet sent word that she wouldn't be riding back to school in our taxi. She said she'd come home on her own. As Shiva and I walked the last fifty yards up our driveway, a sleek black Mercedes-Benz dropped Genet off.

Shiva went on into the house, but I waited.

"I don't like you coming back with Rudy," I said to her. It was such an understatement—that luxurious car made me feel so inadequate and it made my blood boil. Rudy's father had the porcelain and bathroom fixture monopoly in Addis. There were perhaps two other kids in the school who drove their own cars. What rankled most was that Rudy had once been one of my best friends.

"You sound like my mother," Genet said, oblivious to my distress.

"Rudy is the crown prince of the toilets. He just wants to sleep with you."

"Don't you?" she said looking at me coyly, tilting her head.

"Yes. But I want to sleep *only* with you. And I love you. So it's different."

For all my shyness around women, I didn't have a problem telling Genet how I felt. Perhaps it was a mistake to show my hand so easily. It gave a shallow woman great power over you, but my faith insisted she couldn't be shallow, that such love, such commitment from me, would empower her, free her.

"Will you do it with me?" she asked.

"Of course I will. I dream of it every night. We only have to wait three more years, Genet, and we can get married. And then we will lose our virginity in this place," I said pulling out a much-folded picture I had torn out of *National Geographic*. It showed the Lake Palace in Udaipur, a gleaming white hotel in the middle of a pristine blue lake. "I want to marry in India," I said. I had visions of me, the groom, riding in on an elephant, a symbol of the desire and the frustration I had repressed— only an elephant (or a jumbo jet) would do. And beautiful Genet, bejeweled and dressed in a gold sari, jasmine all around . . . I could see every detail. I even had the perfume picked out for her—Motiya Bela made from jasmine flowers. "And this is the honeymoon suite." The flip side showed a room with a giant four-poster bed, with huge French doors beyond that opened out onto the lake. "Notice the bathroom with a claw-foot tub *and* a bidet." The crown prince of toilets could never top that.

Genet was surprised and touched by the photographs and the fact that I would be carrying that page in my wallet. My tigress fixed her gaze on me with new interest.

"Marion, you've really thought about this, haven't you?"

I described the white silk sheets on the bed, how the sheer cotton curtains would enclose it in the daytime, but at night, they'd be open, as would the doors to the veranda. "I'll cover the bed with rose petals, and when I undress you, I'm going to lick and kiss every inch of your body, starting with your toes . . ."

She moaned. She put a finger on my lips, her eyeballs rolling back in her head, showing me her throat. "My God, you better stop before I go crazy." She sighed. "But listen, Marion, what if I tell you that I don't want to get married? I don't want to wait. I want to be deflowered. *Now.* Not in three years."

"But what about Hema? Or your mother?"

"I don't want them to deflower me. I want you."

"That's not—"

A peal of laughter, for which I forgave her because it lifted my spirits. "I know what you mean, silly. What if *I* don't have your strength to resist? Some days I just want to do it. Don't you? Just to get it over with! Just to know." She sighed. "If you won't do it, maybe I should ask Shiva? Or Rudy?"

"Not that toilet prince. And Shiva . . . well, Shiva is no longer a virgin. He's done it already. Besides, I thought you loved me."

"What?" She clapped her hands in delight, and looked around for Shiva. "Shiva?" She was almost jumping for joy. She'd sidestepped the question of her love for me. She was too shy to profess it, I told myself. "Oh, Shiva, Shiva! We must get all the details from him. Shiva, no longer a virgin, you say? What are you and I waiting for, then?"

"I'm waiting for you and—"

"Oh, stop. You sound like a stupid romance novel. You sound like a girl, for God's sake! If you want first shot you better move fast, Marion." She seemed serious, no trace of humor in her face. She scared me when she spoke that way. "Otherwise, I have some others in mind. Your friend Gaby, or even the toilet prince, though his breath stinks of cheese." She burst out laughing again, enjoying my distress but also showing me that she was just joking, thank God.

I couldn't take much more teasing; it was hard to hear her mention the names of other suitors. I spied the stack of women's fashion magazines in her hands. "What's happened to you?" I demanded. I was angry now. I remembered the girl who had mastered *Bickham's Penmanship,* and who, after Zemui's death, had read books voraciously, anything that Hema fed her. "You used to be . . . serious," I said. Now her best friends were two beautiful Armenian sisters. The three of them went shopping together in the afternoons or to the movies where they observed actors whose dress and behavior they held to be the gold standard. They kept all the boys guessing. Genet's grades had once been so good that she skipped a grade and joined our class. But of late she rarely studied, and her grades were average. "What's going on, Genet? Don't you want to be a doctor?"

"Yes, Doctor, I want to be a doctor," she said coming very close to me.

"Doctor, I want you to give me a checkup." She held her arms apart, the book bag in one hand, the fashion magazines in her other hand. She brought her body close to mine and thrust her hips into me. "I hurt down here, Doctor."

Rosina jumped out of the front door of our quarters like a jack-in-the-box. Her sudden appearance was startling, and I admit it was comical, but I didn't think that the way Genet burst out laughing would please Rosina.

In a torrent of Tigrinya, with *italinya* thrown in, Rosina screamed at Genet and descended on us. Genet danced around me to stay out of Rosina's reach, finding even more humor in her mother chasing her. I understood Rosina's words here and there and guessed what she was saying: *Where are your brains and what do you think you were doing just now? Who is that boy with the car and do you know he only wants one thing? Why are you pressing against Marion as if you are a bar girl?* Each question provoked fresh laughter from Genet.

Rosina glared at me, as if I should answer for her daughter. This was the second time she'd caught Genet and me in a compromising position. She switched to Amharic as she grilled me. "You! Why didn't she come back with you and Shiva? And what were you two doing just now?"

"We're going to be doctors, don't you know, Mother?" Genet shouted in Amharic, tears in her eyes, barely able to speak. "I was teaching him how to examine a woman!"

Rosina's shocked face was Genet's reward, and she found this so hysterical that she dropped her magazines and her book bag, clutched at her stomach, and staggered away in the direction of their quarters. The two of us watched her sashay away, holding her sides. Rosina turned to me, hiding her dark confusion by putting on the stern look she'd use when Shiva or I had been naughty. But it felt artificial, more so now because, at six feet and one inch, I towered over my nanny. "What do you have to say for yourself, Marion?"

I hung my head, took two shuffling steps toward her. "I want to say . . . ," I said, and then I grabbed Rosina, lifted her up in the air, whirled her about while she beat on my shoulders. "I want to say that I am so happy to see you. And I want to marry your daughter!"

"Put me down. Put me down!"

I put her down, and she tried to slap me, but I jumped away.

"You're crazy, you know that?" Rosina said, trying to adjust her blouse, smoothing out her skirt, determined not to smile at all costs. "The evil spirits have gotten into all you children." She picked up the book bag and the magazines and retreated after Genet, shouting for her and me to hear, "You two just wait, I'm going to get a stick and line you evil children up and beat that devil out of you."

"Rosina, why talk to your future son-in-law that way?" I called after her.

She made to turn back and come after me, but I dodged away.

"Madness! Lunacy!" she said and stalked off, talking to herself.

I looked up to see Shiva standing in the big picture window, looking out. The wind in the eucalyptus trees stirred up the kind of dry rustling sound that could fool you into thinking it was a rain squall. But the sky was cloudless. Through the glass I could see Shiva studying me, his face flushed. Our eyes met, and his expression suggested he'd been laughing, that he probably saw and heard everything. I admired his pose, one hand in his pocket, knees locked, his weight on one leg—my brother was elegant even in the act of standing in place; it was a quality he shared with Genet. He rarely smiled, and there was, in the tautness of his upper lip, the hint of a leer. I grinned, holding nothing back. I felt good, pleased with myself. My brother could read my mind. My brother loved me, he loved Genet, and I loved them both. Yes, Rosina was right, madness all around at Missing, but only a madman would want to be anywhere else.

CHAPTER 34

A Time to Reap

THE MADNESS OF THAT EVENING came at a most inopportune time. It was my last year at LT&C and I was hell-bent on doing well in the school finals. My motivation was simple: a magnificent, ivory-colored hospital, five times as large as Missing, had been built on a rise looking down at Churchill Road and the post office and the Lycée Français. It was to be the teaching hospital of a new medical school to be staffed with the help of the British Council, Swissaid, and USAID. The teachers were distinguished physicians from these countries who had recently retired from long academic careers and accepted short assignments to Addis.

So while Rosina went after Genet, hauling the magazines and textbooks Genet had dropped, and certain to continue her fight, I wasted no time. I went inside, washed up, and then spread my books out on the dining table. Hema and Ghosh were playing bridge with a few others at Ghosh's old bungalow.

I ate as I studied. Every minute counted, as far as I was concerned. I'd mapped out how many days and hours and minutes remained before the school-leaving exam. If I wanted to sleep, play cricket, *and* get into medical school, I had no time to waste.

Genet arrived an hour later to study with me. I tried not to look up. Soon, Shiva joined us. He'd brought *Jeffcoate's Principles of Gynaecology* to the table, and it bristled with bookmarks. Shiva didn't read books as much as he disassembled and digested them, made them appendages of his body.

For Genet and me to get into medical school we had to get top grades in the school finals. Genet professed to be just as enamored with medicine as I was, but she was often late joining me at the study table, and she packed it in earlier than I did. Sometimes she didn't come at all. On two weeknights I took a taxi to Mr. Mammen's house, for tuition in math and organic chemistry. Genet came once, bristled at Mammen's ironclad discipline, and wouldn't go back, while I found his help to be priceless. On weekends I retreated to Ghosh's old quarters to study, leaving Ghosh and Hema free to turn the radio on or entertain without worrying about disturbing me. Genet could have joined me at Ghosh's quarters, but she rarely did.

Shiva didn't have any of our worries. He'd been lobbying to drop out of school altogether. He wanted to function as Hema's assistant—degrees and diplomas did not matter to him. Hema was blunt: if he wanted to work with her, he'd have to finish his final year, even if he didn't take the exams. Meanwhile, on his own he was learning everything he could about obstetrics and gynecology. I overheard Hema tell Ghosh that Shiva knew more than the average final-year medical student when it came to obstetrics and gynecology.

Shiva had appropriated the toolshed where we'd hidden the motor-cycle. He'd learned to weld from Farinachi, and he kept his torch and equipment in there. A month or so earlier, I'd stuck my head in the tool-shed and was surprised to see the back wall was visible, with no sign of the motorcycle, or the wood stacks, gunnysacks, and Bibles we'd used to conceal it.

"I took it apart," Shiva had said, when I asked. He pointed to the base of his heavy worktable—the square wooden plywood support concealed the engine block. The bike's frame he'd wrapped in oilcloth and tarp and buried under the table. The rest of the bike was stored in containers which ranged from matchboxes to stacked crates, neatly arranged on metal shelves he'd welded together.

"TELL ME ABOUT IT, Shiva," Genet whispered from behind her book, *Chemistry by Concept.* She'd lasted just ten minutes before breaking the silence and my concentration.

"Tell you about what?" Shiva said, not bothering to lower his voice.

"About your first time! What else? Why didn't you tell me before? I just heard from Marion that you're not a virgin."

Shiva's story, which I'd been too embarrassed and envious to ask about myself, was stunning in its simplicity.

"I went to the Piazza. Down the side street next to the Massawa Bak-ery, you know, where you see the rooms, one after the other? A woman in each doorway, different-colored lights?"

"How did you pick?"

"I didn't. I went to the first door. That was it," he said, smiling, and turning back to his work.

"No, it isn't *it!*" She snatched his book away. "What happened next?"

I pretended to be annoyed, but every cell in my brain was attentive. I was glad that Genet was doing the questioning.

"I asked how much. She said thirty. I said I had only ten. She said okay. She took off her clothes and lay on the bed—"

"*All* her clothes?" I blurted out. Shiva looked at me, surprised.

"All but her blouse, which she pulled up."

"A bra? What was she wearing?" Genet wanted to know.

"A little sweater, I think. A half-sleeve thing. And a miniskirt. Bare legs and high heels. No underwear. No bra. She stepped out of her heels, dropped her skirt, lifted her blouse, and lay down."

"Oh, God! Go on," said Genet.

"I took all my clothes off. I was ready. I told her it was my first time. She said, 'God help us.' I said I didn't think we needed God. I got on top of her, she helped me start—"

"Did it hurt her? Were you . . ."

"Erect. Yes. No, I don't think it hurt her. You know the vagina has walls that are expansible, they can accommodate a baby's head—"

"Okay, okay," Genet said. "Then what?"

"She started to move, showing me how till I understood. I did that till I experienced the ejaculatory response."

"What?" Genet said.

"The contraction of the vas and the seminal vesicles mixing with pro-static secretions—"

"He came," I explained. I'd learned the word from a scruffy little pamphlet authored by a T. N. Raman, a writer of purple prose. My class-mate Satish brought these pamphlets back from his holiday in Bombay. T. N. Raman was responsible for most everything Indian schoolboys learned (or misunderstood) about sex.

"Oh . . . and after that?" Genet said.

"Well, I got up, got dressed, and left."

"Did it hurt you?" I asked.

"No pain." From his unsmiling expression, he could have been talk-ing about getting an ice cream at Enrico's.

"That's it?" Genet asked. "Then you paid her?"

"No, I paid her first."

"What did she say when you were leaving?"

Shiva thought about that. "She said she liked my body, and she liked my skin. That next time she would give it to me . . . doggy style!"

"What did she mean, 'doggy style'?"

"I didn't know. I said, 'Why wait till next time? Show me now.' "

"You had money?"

"That's what she asked. 'You have money?' But I didn't. She let me do it anyway. From the back was what she called doggy style. This time I think she had her own . . . explosion."

"God," Genet said, groaning and sliding down in her chair, her face suffused with blood. "What's the matter with you, Marion? Where are you going?"

I had risen from my chair. The scent coming from Genet was overpowering, the air shimmering pink with it.

"What's the matter with me?" I was not as annoyed as I acted. "How am I supposed to study here, tell me? I can't believe you asked me that."

The matter with me was that I was terribly aroused, hearing Shiva's story, and now seeing the sultry look in Genet's eyes, her body in touching distance, smelling her in heat, and knowing she was willing. If I didn't leave, I was going to have my own explosion in my pants. I had to leave. I shoved my biology notes into my jacket.

I found Rosina standing too close to the kitchen door and now pretending some special interest in the stove. Even if she wasn't eavesdropping or lacked any sense of smell, she surely saw the pink cloud wafting out of the dining room. She avoided my eyes. Mother and daughter couldn't seem to escape each other, with Genet determined to act outrageously, and Rosina just as determined to respond, and it was difficult to say who initiated their battles. Rosina was my ally in one sense, because she kept Genet safe for me. But it annoyed me to see her hovering in this way.

"I'm going to the souk," I said gruffly.

"But you just sat down to study, Marion."

I glared at her, daring her to stop me.

I TOOK MY TIME walking down to the front gate. I bought a Coke but then gave it to Gebrew. I sat in his sentry hut. I didn't want to go home until my mind and my body were back to baseline. Gebrew's long story about a troublesome nephew helped the cause.

Eventually, I bid Gebrew good night, and I headed back. When I turned up from the roundabout to the road leading to our bungalow, I saw that there was a light on in the toolshed. Shiva worked late there many nights.

Whenever I came this way in the dark, I felt dread as I neared the spot where the army man went airborne. There was a crack in the concrete of the curb that commemorated that moment when the BMW's front wheel had been arrested.

The tree trunks creaked and groaned. The rustling of the leaves sounded ominous, like a hand sifting through coins. I fully expected to see the army man rise out of the darkness. After years of imagining him, I would find it almost a relief when he appeared. Shiva had no such qualms because he stayed in the toolshed late into the night. The passing years hadn't taken away from me the weight of what had happened at this spot; but the fear had become familiar. I understood what made people confess to murder years after the fact; they believed that it was the only way to cease tormenting themselves. I hurried past that turn in the road.

I heard music from Shiva's radio in the toolshed.

I was just past the toolshed, almost to our house, when I saw a figure come purposefully down the hill. It was pitch-dark, and now I heard a muttering sound—it was talking to itself. My heart was in my mouth, but what kept me from panic was that it sounded like a woman. Only when the figure was almost on me did I see that it was Rosina. Where could she be headed at this hour? She came up very close to me, studying my face the way she often did to be sure I was not Shiva. Then, before I registered her anger, she slapped me. She was all over me, cuffing me and pulling me down by my hair with her left hand while she slapped me with her right.

"I warned you!" she screamed.

"Rosina! What are you talking about?" I said, cowering.

This only infuriated her. I suppose I could easily have stopped her, or run, but I was too shocked to react. She slapped me again.

"Five minutes I leave you alone, and this is what happens! So clever, you pretending to go to the souk, and she to the bathroom."

When I asked her to explain, she swung at me, and this time I turned so her blow found the back of my head.

"I waited," she said. "I gave you the benefit of the doubt. Then I went looking for you. I saw her coming up the hill. You sent her out first, didn't you? If she gets pregnant, what happens?" Rosina hissed in my ear.

"It means she'll be a maid like me. All that English and studying books won't make any difference in her life."

"But, Rosina, I didn't—"

"Don't lie to me, my child. You were never good at lying. I saw you two looking at each other. I should have kept her home right then."

I stood silent, staring at her.

"You want proof? Is that it?" she yelled. "She reached to her waist and drew something out and flung it at me. A pair of women's panties. "*Her* blood . . . and your seed." I picked the garment off my face. In the dark I could see nothing. But I could smell blood, the scent of Genet . . . and I could smell semen. It was mine. I recognized my starchy scent. No one else shared that odor.

No one but my twin brother.

I HAD NO HEART, no energy, to do anything but to crawl into bed. I felt battered. I felt alone. Shiva came to bed much later. I waited to see if he would say anything. At some point he fell asleep while I lay there awake. In Ethiopia there was a method of divining guilt called *lebashai:* a little boy was drugged and taken to the scene of the crime and asked to point out the guilty party. Unfortunately, a hallucinating youngster's pointing finger too often stopped in front of an innocent who was then stoned to death or drowned. *Lebashai* was banned in the empire, but it still went on in the villages. That was how I felt: falsely accused by the pointing finger, but unable to defend myself.

What I *could* do was extract revenge. The guilty party slept next to me. I could have killed Shiva that night. I thought about it. I decided it would solve nothing. My world was already destroyed. My arms were dead. My brain was numb. My love had been turned into a mockery of love, into shit. I had no reason, no desire, to do anything anymore.

GENET DIDN'T GO to school the next day. Shiva left with Hema's reluctant permission to go with Mr. Farinachi to Akaki, to the textile factory where one of the giant dye machines had seized. Farinachi had been asked to manufacture a part, and he wanted Shiva to come and see the giant looms.

I stayed in bed. When Hema came to see why, I said I didn't feel well and wouldn't go to school. She took my pulse, looked at my throat. She was puzzled. When she tried to quiz me, I said, "Never mind, I'm going." That was easier than facing an interrogation.

I don't remember anything about that day in school. Ghosh and Hema had no idea what had transpired, but they knew *something* had happened. The door and window to Rosina's quarters were closed, and they could hear Rosina carrying on in there in a loud voice.

That evening Hema said there were three of Rosina's relatives— a woman and two men—visiting her. Hema pressed me as to what was going on. I couldn't believe that she didn't know or that Rosina didn't tell her. It appeared that no one was talking about what happened the previous night. I was sure Rosina would go to Hema and accuse me and I couldn't understand why so far she had not. Had Hema talked to Shiva, I suspect she would have found out everything. But no one thought to ask him.

Shiva returned just as we were finishing dinner, pleased with his excursion to Akaki. Neither Genet nor Rosina was at the table. Almaz said that mother and daughter were having a big fight and that Rosina's relatives had come to mediate.

Hema rose to go see what was happening, but Ghosh held her back. "Whatever it is, if you get in the middle it's only going to get more complicated." Shiva said nothing, eating his food.

I wasn't being noble by keeping quiet. I didn't think anyone would believe my side of the story. It was up to my brother or Genet to save me if they wanted to. I studied Shiva's face at the dining table. There was no sign that he was aware of the calamity he'd caused. No indication at all.

That night I told Shiva I was moving to a room in Ghosh's old quarters. I was going to sleep and study there. I wanted to be alone there, I announced, not looking at him.

He said nothing. It would be the first time in our lives that we did not occupy the same bed. If there were filaments and cords of yolk or flesh that kept our divided egg sticking together, I was taking a scalpel to them.

Saturday morning, when I came over for breakfast, it seemed to me that Shiva hadn't slept any better than I had. After breakfast, he left for Farinachi's.

I was about to go back to my room to study when Almaz burst into the dining room. "I think you better come, madam," she said, addressing Hema.

She led the charge to the servant's quarters; Hema, Ghosh, and I followed.

Rosina sat in a corner of the darkened room, looking sullen, defensive yet anxious. Genet lay on her bed, her face pale, sweat beading on her forehead, her eyes open, but unfocused and dull. The room held a raw, sour odor of fever.

"What happened here?" Hema asked, but Rosina wouldn't answer or meet Hema's gaze. Almaz turned on the light, and she moved to block my view, then lifted the blanket to show Hema.

Ghosh said, "Open the window, Marion," and he moved closer to look.

"My God," Hema said. Genet moaned in pain. Hema grabbed Rosina's shoulders. "Did you? Did you just . . . this poor girl?" Choking with fury, Hema shook her. But Rosina wouldn't look up. "You stupid woman!" Hema said. "Oh, God, God. Why?" Hema's eyes were those of a madwoman, uncomprehending, dangerous. I thought she might strangle Rosina. Instead, she pushed her away. "You've probably killed her, Rosina, do you know that?" There were tears coming down Rosina's chin, but her expression remained surly.

Ghosh scooped Genet in his arms, and she let out an unearthly moan as he lifted her off the bed. "The car," Ghosh said, and Almaz ran ahead to get the door. Hema followed. I lingered for a second in the doorway on the threshold of Genet's home. My nanny sat just the way she had when we came in. I thought of the day she'd taken a razor to scarify Genet's face and how her expression had been defiant, proud. But now, I saw shame and fear.

As I ran to join them in the car, Hema spun on her heel and thrust her face in mine. "I think you had something to do with this, Marion. I'm not a fool!"

She got in the car and slammed the door. They pulled away with Almaz cradling Genet in the back, Ghosh driving. I ran down our drive, cut behind the toolshed and across the field, and caught up with them as they took her into Casualty.

They poured fluids and antibiotics into Genet's veins. Then Hema took her to Operating Theater 3 for a more careful examination. When Hema came out, she was shaken but more composed, and quietly furious. She didn't seem to care if I heard her report to Ghosh and Matron. "Can you imagine Rosina paid to slice off the child's clitoris? Not just clitoris but also the labia minora and then sew the edges together with sewing thread! Good God, can you imagine the pain? I cut the sutures out. It is hugely infected. Now it's up to God."

Genet was wheeled to the single room reserved for VIPs. I remembered Ghosh telling me it was the room that General Mebratu had occupied after emergency surgery, shortly after we were born.

I sat on a chair by her bed. At one point, Genet squeezed my hand, whether consciously or reflexively, I couldn't be sure. I held it.

Hema sat across from me in an armchair, her elbows on her knees, head in her hands. We had nothing to say to each other. I was as angry with Hema as she was with me.

At one point, Hema lifted her head up and said, "The people who did this should all go to jail." It wasn't the first time she'd had to rescue a woman in Genet's situation. She was probably one of the world's experts in treating botched and infected female circumcisions. But now her face was clamped down in a bitterness I'd never seen before.

It was evening when Genet opened her eyes. She saw me, and she tried to say something. I asked her if she wanted water, and she nodded. I guided a straw to her mouth. She looked around to see if there was anyone else in the room.

"I'm sorry, Marion," she whispered, her eyes swimming with tears.

"Don't talk," I said. "It's all right." It wasn't, but that's what came to my mouth.

"I . . . should have waited," she said.

Why didn't you, I wanted to say. *I didn't get any of the pleasure, the honor of being your first lover, but I'm getting all the blame.*

She moaned when she tried to move, licking her lips. I gave her more water.

"My mother thinks it was you." Her voice was weak.

I nodded, but said nothing.

"When I told her it was Shiva," Genet said, "she slapped me. She kicked me and called me a liar. She didn't believe me. She thinks Shiva is a virgin." She tried to laugh, but grimaced and then coughed. When she could speak, she said, "Listen, I made my mother promise not to tell Hema."

I couldn't resist a sarcastic snicker. "Well, don't worry. She *will* tell Hema. She's probably telling her right now."

"No. She won't," Genet said. "That was our deal."

"What do you mean?"

"I agreed to let her do this to me, if she wouldn't . . . say anything. She's to keep quiet. Not a word to Hema. Not one word. And no more shouting at you."

I slumped back on hearing this. Genet allowed a strange woman to cut her privates with an unsterilized blade, and it was all to protect me? So now I was to blame for the circumcision? It was so absurd that I wanted to laugh, but I found I couldn't: the guilt had settled on me as if it knew that was its home and it would be welcome.

Shiva came in the evening, his face pale and drawn. "Here, sit here," I said before he could open his mouth. I didn't trust myself near him and I needed a break. "Stay with her till I come back. Hold her hand. She gets restless when I let go." There was nothing else I could say to him, now. I was beyond anger, and he was beyond sorrow.

GENET'S FEVER RAGED for three days. I sat by her bed day and night. Hema, Ghosh, and Matron were in and out all the time.

On the third day, Genet stopped making any urine. Ghosh was very worried, drawing blood himself, then Shiva or I would run to the lab, help W.W. line up our reagents and tubes and measure the blood urea nitrogen level: high, and getting higher.

Genet was never completely unconscious, just sleepy, confused at times, often moaning, and at one point horribly thirsty. She called for her mother once, but Rosina wasn't there. Almaz told me Rosina wouldn't leave her room, which was probably a good thing. The atmosphere in the hospital room was tense enough without the prospect of Hema attacking Rosina.

On the sixth day, Genet's kidneys began to produce urine, and then they produced it in huge amounts, filling up the catheter bag. Ghosh doubled and tripled her intravenous fluid rates, and encouraged her to drink to keep up with the loss. "Hopefully this means her kidneys are recovering," Ghosh said. "They just aren't able to concentrate the urine too well."

One morning, when I woke up in the chair and saw her face, the texture of the skin, the relaxation around the brow, I knew she was going to make it. She was skinny to begin with, and now the illness had consumed her, burned her down to just bones. Her color was returning; the sword that hung over her had lifted away. My shoulders began to unknot.

That afternoon I went to my room in Ghosh's quarters, and I fell into a black sleep. It was only when I woke up that I turned my attention to Shiva. Did he understand how he shattered my dreams? Did he see how he hurt Genet, hurt us all? I wanted to get through to him. The trouble was that I couldn't think of any other way than to pummel him with my fists until he felt the same degree of pain he had caused in me. I hated my brother. No one could stop me.

No one but Genet.

When she told me about her deal with Rosina, how she had agreed to be circumcised if Rosina said nothing to Hema, Genet hadn't finished what she had to say. Later that first night, she struggled to consciousness to ask something of me. She had made me swear to it. "Marion," she said, "punish me, but not Shiva. Attack me and cast me away, but leave Shiva alone."

"Why? I can't do that. Why spare him?"

"Marion, *I* made Shiva do what he did with me that night. *I* asked him." Her words were like kidney punches. "You know how Shiva is different . . . how he thinks in another way? Believe me, if I hadn't asked him, he would have read his book and I wouldn't be here."

Reluctantly, on that first night, I had given Genet my word that I wouldn't confront Shiva. I did so mainly because that night had looked as if it might well have been her last.

I never told Hema what had really happened, leaving her to imagine whatever it was she thought I had done.

Why, you might ask, did I keep my word? Why did I not change my mind when I saw that Genet would survive? Why didn't I tell Hema the truth? You see, I'd learned something about myself and about Genet during her battle to stay alive. I'd come so close to losing her, and it helped me understand that despite everything, I didn't want her to die. I might never forgive her. But I still loved her.

WHEN SHE WAS DISCHARGED from the hospital, I carried Genet from the car to the house. No one objected, and if they had I would have stood my ground. My unceasing vigil at Genet's bedside had earned a grudging acknowledgment from Hema; she didn't dare deny me.

As I carried her daughter into our house through the kitchen, Rosina watched from her doorway. Genet never looked in that direction. It was as if her mother and the room in which she had lived her life no longer existed. Rosina stood there, beseeching with her eyes, pleading for forgiveness. But a child's ability for reprisal is infinite, and can last a lifetime.

I carried Genet to our old room, Shiva's room, which would now be hers.

The plan was that Shiva and I would sleep in Ghosh's old quarters, but separately, he in the living room.

Half an hour later, when I went to get Genet's clothes from Rosina's quarters, she had locked herself in and wouldn't answer despite my knocking. I pushed on the wood in anger, and I could tell from the resistance that she'd barricaded the door or else she was leaning against it. A peculiar silence blanketed the atmosphere. I went to the window. The shutters were bolted, but now, with Almaz helping, I pulled on the flimsy slats till they snapped off. The wardrobe had been used to block the window. I scrambled onto the ledge and tried to shove the wardrobe aside with my hands, but I couldn't. I craned my neck to peer above it. What I saw made me set my back to the window frame, put both feet on the wardrobe, and topple it without a thought to its contents. It hit the ground with a terrific crash, the wood splintering, the mirror shattering, plates smashing. It brought everyone running.

I could see clearly now. We all could see. Hema, Ghosh, Shiva were behind me, and even Genet, hearing the commotion, had dragged herself there.

There is a mathematical precision to that scene as I remember it, but there are no angles in *Carr's Geometry* or any other text that quite describe the slant of that neck. And no pill in the pharmacopoeia that might erase the memory. Hanging from a rafter, her head tilted on her spine, her mouth open and the tongue looking as if it had been yanked out of her throat, was Rosina.

CHAPTER 35

One Fever from Another

T HE MOSSY STONE WALLS and the massive gate of Empress
Menen School gave it the look of an ancient fortress. In her
white socks, light blue blouse, dark blue skirt, and with no headbands, clips, or earrings, Genet was just one of the girls, blending in. Her
only adornment was the St. Bridget's cross hanging from her neck.
She didn't want to stand out. Her old vivacious self had died along with
the corpse we took down from the rafter and buried in Gulele Cemetery.

My new ritual was to come on Saturday evenings to see Genet. She
was just up the hill from the palace where General Mebratu (with Zemui
at his side) took hostages and tried to bring about a new order.

Genet could have come home on weekends, but she said Missing
evoked painful memories. She insisted she was happy at Empress Menen.
The Indian teachers were strict but very good. Sheltered from society
and from us, she worked very hard.

We entered university together for our premedical course, and the
following year we entered medical school. Now out of uniform and in
regular clothes, her dress and manner remained reserved and subdued.
Each time I went to visit Genet in the Mekane Yesus Hostel opposite
the university, I'd pray that this would be the day when the locked door
to her heart opened and I might see traces of the old Genet. She was
appreciative for the tiffin carrier of food Almaz and Hema sent for her,
but the barrier she put up around herself remained.

I still loved her.

I wished I didn't.

We entered the Haile Selassie the First School of Medicine in 1974—
only the third class to be admitted. Genet and I were paired as dissection
partners on a cadaver, which was fortunate for her. Anyone else would
have taken offense at her frequent absences and her failing to carry her

load. I didn't think she was lazy. There was no good reason for this; something was brewing, and for once I had no clue.

OUR BASIC SCIENCE TEACHERS were very good, a mix of British and Swiss professors and a few Ethiopian physicians who graduated from the American University of Beirut and then took postgraduate training in England or America. There was one Indian: our own Ghosh. Ghosh had a title: not Assistant Professor, or Associate Professor, or *Clinical* Associate Professor (implying an honorary, unpaid designation), but Professor of Medicine and Adjunct Professor of Surgery.

I don't think any of us, not even Hema, realized the extent of Ghosh's scholarship during his twenty-eight years in Ethiopia. But Sir Ian Hill, dean of the new medical school, certainly did. Ghosh had forty-one published papers and a textbook chapter to his name. An initial interest in sexually transmitted illness had given way to major scholarship on relapsing fever, for which he was the world's expert, because the louse-borne variety of this disease was endemic to Ethiopia, and because no living person had observed the disease as closely.

I learned about relapsing fever as a schoolboy when Ali of the souk opposite Missing brought his brother, Saleem, to the hospital and asked me to intercede. Saleem burned with fever and was delirious. Ghosh said later that Saleem's story was typical: He'd arrived in Addis Ababa from his village with his life's belongings in a cloth strung over his shoulder. Ali found his brother a toehold in the seething, swarming docks of the Merkato, where, monsoon or not, he hauled sacks off the trucks and into the godowns. At night he slept cheek by jowl with ten others in a flophouse. In the rainy season, there was little opportunity to wash clothes because they would take days to dry. Saleem's living conditions were unfit for humans, but ideal for lice. While scratching his skin he must have crushed a louse, its blood entering his body through the scratch. Coming from the village, he had no immunity to this urban disease.

In Casualty, Saleem lay on the ground too weak to sit or stand, semiconscious. Adam, our one-eyed compounder, bent over the patient, and with one swift move made the diagnosis.

Years later Ghosh showed me the correspondence he had with the editor of the *New England Journal of Medicine*, who was about to publish Ghosh's seminal series of cases of relapsing fever. The editor felt "Adam's sign" was pretentious. Ghosh defended the honor of his uneducated compounder at the risk of not being published in that prestigious journal.

> *Dear Dr. Giles,*
> *. . . in Ethiopia we classify hernias as "below the knee" and "above the knee," not "direct" or "indirect." It's another order of magnitude, sir. Our casualty room often has as many as five patients prostrate on the floor with fever. The clinician asks: Is this malaria? Is it typhoid? Or is it relapsing fever? There is no rash to help sort this out (the "rose spots" of typhoid are invisible in our population), though I will grant you that typhoid causes a bronchitis and a slow pulse, and people with malaria often have giant spleens. I would be remiss in publishing a paper on relapsing fever without providing the clinician a practical way to make the diagnosis, particularly in settings where blood and serum tests are hard to come by. The clinician has only to grab the patient's thigh, squeeze the quadriceps muscle, squeeze it hard: Patients with relapsing fever will jump up because of the otherwise silent muscle inflammation and tenderness that is part of this disease. Not only is this a good diagnostic sign, but it can raise Lazarus. This sign was first noted by Adam, and is deserving of the eponym "Adam's sign."*

I could testify to Adam's sign—Saleem yelled and leaped to his feet when Adam mashed. The editor wrote back. He was pleased with all the other revisions but Adam's sign remained a sticking point. Ghosh held his ground.

> *Dear Dr. Giles,*
> *. . . there is a Chvostek's sign, a Boas's sign, a Courvoisier's sign, a Quincke's sign—no limit it seems to white men naming things after themselves. Surely, the world is ready for an eponym honoring a humble compounder who has seen more relapsing fever with one eye than you or I will ever see with two.*

Ghosh, working in an obscure African hospital, far from the academic mainstream, had his way. The paper was published in the prestigious journal, and no doubt led to his being invited to write a chapter in *Harrison's Principles of Internal Medicine,* the bible of senior medical students. Now, here he was, a professor. Hema bought our new professor two beautiful pin-striped suits, one black and the other blue. Also a tweed coat with leather elbow patches, as if to put "Professor" in quotes. The bow tie was his idea. In all things, especially when it cost little and did no harm to others, Ghosh was his own man. The bow tie told the world how pleased he was to be alive and how much he celebrated his profession, which he called "my romantic and passionate pursuit." The way Ghosh practiced his profession, the way he lived his life, it was all that.

CHAPTER 36

Prognostic Signs

LIFE IS FULL OF SIGNS. The trick is to know how to read them. Ghosh called this heuristics, a method for solving a problem for which no formula exists.

> Red sky in the morning, sailors take warning.
> Pus somewhere and Pus nowhere means Pus in the belly.
> Low platelets in a woman is lupus until proven otherwise.
> Beware of a man with a glass eye and a big liver . . .

Across the outpatient department, Ghosh would spot a breathless young woman, her cheeks flushed, contradicting her general pallor. He'd suspect narrowing of the mitral valve of the heart, though he'd be hard-pressed to explain exactly why. It would make him listen carefully for the soft, rumbling murmur of mitral stenosis, a devilish murmur which, as he said, "you'll only hear if you know it's there," and then it was only audible with the bell of the stethoscope lightly applied over the apex of the heart after exercise.

I'd developed my own heuristics, my mix of reason, intuition, facial appearance, and scent. These were things not in any book. The army soldier who'd tried to steal the motorcycle had an odor at the moment of his demise, and so, too, had Rosina, and the two odors were identical—they spoke of sudden death.

But I didn't trust my nose when I should have, when it picked up signals from Ghosh that put my nerves on edge. I wrote it off as being a function of his new job as a professor, a side effect of his new suits and new environment. When I was around him it was easy to be reassured. He'd always been upbeat, a happy soul. But now he was even more jovial. He'd found his best self. For a man who prided himself on "the three Ls: Loving, Learning, and Legacy," he'd excelled in all three.

On the anniversary of Hema and Ghosh's marriage, I woke myself at 4:00 a.m. to study. Two hours later, I walked over from Ghosh's old bungalow to the main house. Shiva had moved back to our boyhood room. It was still dark outside. I planned to creep into Shiva's room to see if a shirt I was missing had been laundered and hung in his closet. I came in as Almaz arrived. I hugged her and then waited as she made the sign of the cross on my forehead and murmured a prayer.

Hema was still sleeping. The hallway bathroom door stood open, steam coming out. Ghosh stood in front of the washbasin, a towel around his waist, leaning heavily on the sink. It was early for him. I wondered why he was using this bathroom. So as not to wake Hema? I could hear his labored breathing before I saw him and, certainly, before he saw me. The effort of bathing had winded him. In his reflection in the mirror, I saw his unguarded self. I saw terrible fatigue; I saw sadness and apprehension. Then he saw me. By the time he'd turned around, the mask of joviality which had fallen into the sink had been slapped back on, not a seam showing.

"What's wrong?" I asked. I felt my stomach flutter. The scent was there. It had to be connected to what I just saw.

"Not a thing. Scary, isn't it?" He paused to take a breath. "My beautiful wife is sleeping like an angel. My sons make me so proud . . . Tonight I'm going to take my wife dancing and I'll ask her to extend our marriage contract for another year. The only thing wrong is that a sinner like me doesn't deserve such blessings."

Hema came out to the hallway, shaking sleep from her hair. Ghosh flashed me an anxious look.

He turned back to the mirror, whistling as he slapped on cologne. His eyes pleaded with me not to alarm Hema. The effort of holding his arms up made his "Saints Come Marching In" full of staccato notes and pauses. I got my shirt and left.

I had an early morning class, an important one. But I followed my instinct, my intuition—my nose. I dressed and then hid myself behind Shiva's toolshed. Soon, the Volkswagen appeared out of the mist, with just Ghosh in it. I followed on foot.

I got to Casualty in time to see him enter Matron's office. Not only was Matron there at this early hour, she was waiting. I stood there considering what this meant, when Adam appeared carrying a bottle of blood. Matron's door opened for him. Adam emerged moments later empty-handed. He was startled to see me, and he tried to close the door behind him, but I had a foot there.

Ghosh was on a lounge chair, his feet up, a pillow behind his head, smiling. Bach's "Gloria" chorus sounded on Matron's ancient phonograph. Matron bent over his arm, taping the needle that carried blood into his vein in place. They looked up, thinking perhaps it was Adam returning for something.

Ghosh's lips moved.

"Son, you know I—"

"Don't bother to lie to me," I said.

He looked to Matron, as if for a cue. She sighed. "This is fate, Ghosh. I always thought Marion should know."

I'll never forget the stillness, the hesitation, and a trace of something I'd never before seen on Ghosh's face: cunning. Then it gave in to resignation and a faraway look. For a moment I saw the world through his eyes, his intellect, his sweeping vision that took in Hippocrates, Pavlov, Freud, and Marie Curie, the discovery of streptomycin and penicillin, Landsteiner's blood groups; a vision that recalled the septic ward where he wooed Hema, and Theater 3 where he was the reluctant surgeon; a vision that recapitulated our birth and looked to the future, looked past his life to the end of mine and beyond. And then and only then did it settle, gather, and focus, on the now, on a moment when the love was so palpable between father and son that the thought that it might end, and this memory be its only legacy, was unacceptable.

"All right, Marion, you budding clinician. What do you think it might be?" He loved the Socratic Method. Only this time, he was the patient, and it was my heuristic I would invoke.

I'd noticed his pallor before, but I'd refused to let it register. Now I remembered that I'd seen bruises on his arms and legs for the past few months—bruises for which he always had explanations. Was it just a week ago he had the paper cut on his finger? It happened in front of my eyes, and it bled for a while; when I saw him a few hours later, the wound was still oozing. How had I managed to dismiss that? I remembered, too, his hours exposed to radiation from the Old Koot, the ancient X-ray machine which, despite everyone's protests, he'd continued to use until Missing finally got a new machine. The Koot was broken apart with hammers and the pieces hauled to the Drowning Soil. There it would keep the army man company, while making his bones glow.

"A blood cancer? A leukemia?" I said, hating the sound of those ugly words on my lips. Ghosh's disease was only born, it only came to life, the moment I named it, and now it couldn't go away.

He beamed, turned to Matron, raising his eyebrows. "Can you believe this, Matron? My son, the clinician."

Then his voice lost its ebullience; he spoke in a manner in which pretense had fallen off like leaves after a frost.

"Whatever happens, Marion, you mustn't let Hema know. I had my slides sent off about two years ago through Eli Harris to Dr. Maxwell Wintrobe in Salt Lake City, Utah, USA. He's a fabulous hematologist. I love his textbook. He personally wrote me back. What I have is like an active volcano, rumbling and spitting. Not quite a leukemia, but brewing into one; it's called 'myeloid metaplasia,' " he said, pronouncing it carefully as if it were something delicate and exquisitely wrought. "Remember the term, Marion. It's an interesting disease. I still have many years left, I'm sure. The only troublesome symptom I have now is anemia. These blood transfusions are my oil changes. I'm going dancing tonight with Hema. It's our big day, you know. I wanted more gumption."

"Why won't you let Ma know? Why didn't you let me know?"

Ghosh shook his head. "Hema will go crazy . . . She'll, she shouldn't, she can't . . . Don't look at me that way, my son, I'm not being noble, I promise you."

"Then I don't understand."

"You didn't know about my diagnosis these last two years, did you? If you had known, it would've changed your relationship with me. Don't you think?" He grinned, and he ruffled my hair. "You know what's given me the greatest pleasure in my life? It's been our bungalow, the normalcy of it, the ordinariness of my waking, Almaz rattling in the kitchen, my work. My classes, my rounds with the senior students. Seeing you and Shiva at dinner, then going to sleep with my wife." He stopped there, silent for a long time as he thought of Hema. "I want my days to be that way. I don't want everyone to stop being normal. You know what I mean? To have all that ruined." He smiled. "When things get more severe, if it ever comes to that, I'll tell your ma. I promise."

He looked at me intently. "You'll keep this a secret? Please? It's what you can do for me. A gift, if you like. Give me as many normal days as I can possibly have. And you mustn't tell your brother either. That might be hardest for you. I know you two have had a . . . rift. But you understand Shiva better than anyone. I know you care enough for him to protect him from this news getting to him prematurely."

I gave him my word.

ABOUT THE NEXT FEW MONTHS, I remember very little, except that Ghosh's wisdom was revealed. It had been a blessing not to know for the last two years. Now that I knew, there was no turning back time or erasing that knowledge; it was as if he were back in jail again and, in a way, so was I. I read everything I could about myeloid metaplasia (how I hated that term which he loved). His bone marrow was quiet when I first learned of his diagnosis. But then the disease became more active, the volcano started rumbling, oozing lava, spitting telltale traces of sulfurous gas when the wind was right.

I spent as much time as I could with Ghosh. I wanted every bit of wisdom he could impart to me. All sons should write down every word of what their fathers have to say to them. I tried. Why did it take an illness for me to recognize the value of time with him? It seems we humans never learn. And so we relearn the lesson every generation and then want to write epistles. We proselytize to our friends and shake them by the shoulders and tell them, "Seize the day! What matters is *this* moment!" Most of us can't go back and make restitution. We can't do a thing about our should haves and our could haves. But a few lucky men like Ghosh never have such worries; there was no restitution he needed to make, no moment he failed to seize.

Now and then Ghosh would grin and wink at me across the room. He was teaching me how to die, just as he'd taught me how to live.

SHIVA AND HEMA went about their days ignorant of Ghosh's condition. They were caught up in their own excitement. Shiva had coaxed Hema into a major commitment to treating women with vesiculovaginal fistula, or "fistula" for short. It wasn't a condition that Hema (or any gynecologic surgeon) relished seeing because it was difficult to cure.

Now I can explain why that little girl whom we'd seen when we were young children—the one who came walking up the hill with her father, her head bowed with shame, dribbling urine at every step, carrying about her an unspeakable odor—had such a profound influence on Shiva's life.

Unbeknownst to Shiva and me, Hema had operated on her three times. The repair broke down the first two times; the last one held. We never got to see her leave Missing, but we had Hema's word that she was cured and had left happy. The mental scars, though, would never heal. We understood little at the time of what ailed her; it wasn't a subject Hema would speak about to us. But now, Shiva and I knew. In all likelihood, perhaps before she was a teen, the girl was married off to a man who could have been as old as her father. The painful consummation of her marriage (more traumatic if circumcision had left scar tissue at the entrance to the vagina for the husband to batter down) would have terrified her. She may even have been too young to connect this act with becoming pregnant, but soon she was swollen with child. When labor began, the baby's head jammed against her pelvic bones, the pelvic inlet already narrowed by rickets. In a developed country or a big city, she might have had a Cesarean section as soon as her contractions started. But in a remote village, without the help of anyone but her mother-in-law, she would suffer for days, her uterus trying to do the impossible, but succeeding only in ramming the baby's head against the bladder and the cervix, crushing those tissues against the unyielding bony pelvis. The baby soon died inside the womb and the mother's death would follow shortly, most often due to a ruptured uterus or infection and septicemia. It was the rare family who managed to transport the mother to a health center. There the lifeless fetus could be removed piecemeal, by first crushing the skull and then pulling the rest out.

During her convalescence from that dreadful labor, the dead and gangrenous tissues inside her birth passage eventually sloughed off, leaving her with a jagged hole between bladder and vagina. Instead of urine passing from bladder to urethra to emerge just under the clitoris (and only when she chose to void), the bladder now constantly leaked its contents directly into the vagina and down her legs. She was never dry, her clothes always soaked, and she dribbled all day. The bladder and its urine quickly became infected and foul-smelling. In no time her labia, her thighs, became wet and macerated and oozed pus. This must have been when her husband cast her off, and her father came to the rescue.

Fistulas have been described since antiquity. But it wasn't till 1849 in Montgomery, Alabama, that Dr. Marion Sims, my namesake, first succeeded in repairing a vaginal fistula. His first patients were Anarcha, Betsy, and Lucy, three slave women who had been cast out by their families and their owners because of this condition. Sims operated on them—willing subjects we are told—in an attempt to cure the fistula. Ether had just been discovered but wasn't in widespread use, so his patients were wide awake. Sims closed the gaping hole between bladder and vagina with silk and thought he had cured them. But a week later, he found pinhole openings along the line of his repair through which urine was leaking. He kept trying. He operated on Anarcha some thirty times. He learned from each failure, modified his technique until he ultimately got it right.

When Hema operated on the girl we'd seen, she used the principles of repair established by Marion Sims. She first put a catheter through the urethra into the bladder to divert the urine away from the fistula to allow the wet, macerated tissues to dry and heal. A week later, Hema operated vaginally, using the bent pewter spoon the Alabama surgeon had fashioned—the Sims speculum, we now call it—which allowed for good exposure and made vaginal surgery possible. She had to carefully dissect out the edges of the fistula, trying to find what had once been discrete layers of bladder lining, bladder wall, then vaginal wall and vaginal lining. Once she had trimmed the edges, she made her repair, layer by layer. Sims, after many failures, had a jeweler fashion a thin silver wire which he used to close the surgical wound. Silver elicited the least inflammatory reaction from the tissues, inflammation being the reason a repair would break down. Hema used chromic catgut.

At dinner, a month after I'd learned of Ghosh's blood disorder, Hema shared with us that she and Shiva had operated on fifteen successive fistula patients with not one recurrence. "I owe this to Shiva," she said. "He convinced me to take more time preparing the women for surgery. So now, we admit the patients and feed them eggs, meat, milk, and vitamins for two weeks. We treat with antibiotics till the urine is clear and use zinc oxide paste on their thighs and vulva. It was Shiva's idea to deworm them and correct iron deficiency anemia before surgery. We work on strengthening their legs, getting them moving." She looked at Shiva with pride. "I am embarrassed to say, he's seen and understood their needs better than I have after all these years. Like the idea of physical therapy—"

"Can't get them to walk after surgery if they won't walk before," Shiva said.

On four of their patients the hole into the bladder was so large, so scarred down and shrunk back, that it was impossible to pull the edges together. In these patients, Hema and Shiva had learned to expose a narrow but thick "steak" of flesh under the labia and, while keeping it connected at one end to its blood supply, tunnel its free end up and pull it into the vagina and use it as a live patch in the fistula.

"Matron has a donor who wants to support nothing but fistula surgery," Shiva said. "We're getting one thousand American dollars every month." I found it difficult to look at him, let alone congratulate him.

I STOPPED FRETTING over Genet. When she failed two of the four courses the first year and had to repeat both semesters, I was too distracted by Ghosh's illness to care. She wasn't having a good time and living it up. Instead she'd lost her desire, lost sight of her target if she'd ever had one. All it took was one week of not studying, missing class, to get impossibly behind, so hectic was the pace of the first year of medical school.

Halfway through my second year, I learned that Genet had again missed a few anatomy lab sessions. I felt obliged to check on her.

At Mekane Yesus Hostel, the door to her room was open. Her visitor's back was to me; neither of them saw me at first. Genet shared the room with another girl who wasn't there. The tiny room which had once been so neat was now cluttered and messy. The room held a bunk bed and a small table for two. When he was alive, Genet acted as if Zemui annoyed her. Her brave and loyal father had died in a hail of bullets, and now she had his picture on the ceiling, inches from her face when she lay on the top bunk.

Her visitor's coarse features and his gruff manner made him stand out. I knew him as a student firebrand, organizing others for curricular reform, or collecting signatures to oust an unpopular warden. But he was Eritrean first, just like Genet. The liberation of Eritrea was almost certainly his most important cause, but it was the one he'd have to keep secret. He was speaking to Genet in Tigrinya, but I heard a few English words: "hegemony" and "proletariat." He stopped in midsentence when he sensed me in the doorway. His bovine eyes gave me a look that said, *You will never be one of us.*

I deliberately spoke to Genet in Amharic, so her guest would see that I spoke it better than he did. He muttered something to her in Tigrinya and stalked off.

"Who are these radical friends of yours, Genet?"

"What radicals? I'm just hanging around with Eritreans."

"The secret police have informers on this floor," I said. "They'll link you with the Eritrean People's Liberation Front."

She shrugged. "Do you know the EPLF is making great gains, Marion? You can't know that. It's not in the *Ethiopian Herald.* But I doubt you're here to discuss politics?"

In the past I might have been wounded by her manner. "Hema says hello. And Ghosh says he wants to see you for dinner one of these evenings . . . Genet, I'm worried about your dissections. There is no one to do your labs for you this year. If you don't show, you'll fail, no matter what. *Come on,* Genet."

Her face, so interested and animated when the other man was there, had now become sullen.

"Thank you," she said icily.

I wanted badly to tell her that Ghosh was ill, to shake her out of her self-absorption. And yet I sat there feeling the witchcraft of her presence. It kept me coming after her and it made me tell myself I still loved her, no matter how she acted, even when our lives were so clearly drifting apart.

IN MY FINAL YEAR of medical school, during my surgery rotations, Ghosh's volcano erupted. I came home to a look on Hema's face that told me she knew. I steeled myself for her tirade. She hugged me instead.

Ghosh had thrown up blood, and also developed a major nosebleed. He'd tried to conceal it but failed. He was resting comfortably in the bedroom. I peeked in on him, then came out and sat with Hema at the dining table. Almaz, red-eyed, brought me tea.

"I suppose I'm glad he didn't tell me," Hema said. I could see from her swollen eyelids that she'd spent the afternoon crying. "Particularly when there's nothing to do for it. I've been able to enjoy the best of him. Such perfect days, without knowing any of this." She fingered the diamond ring on her finger, a present that he'd given her the last time they renewed their yearly vows. "Had I known . . . maybe we could have taken a trip to America. I asked him about that. He said he preferred to be here. The first sight of me every morning is all he wants! *Ayoh,* he is such a romantic chap, even now. It's funny, but a few months ago, I actually felt that things were so good that something bad had to happen. The signs were all in front of me. But I wasn't paying attention."

"Me, too," I said.

I found Almaz weeping in the kitchen, and Gebrew, tears in his eyes, his tiny Bible in his hand, rocking and reciting verses to console her. When they saw me, Gebrew said, "We shall fast for him. Our prayers have been lacking."

Almaz nodded, and though she let me hug her and try to reassure her, she was agitated. "We have not been prayerful," she said. "That is why such a thing comes on us."

I ASKED GEBREW if he'd seen Shiva, and he said Shiva had been gone all day, but if he was back, he might be in his workshop. Gebrew walked down with me to the toolshed.

"Are you still wearing your scroll?" Gebrew asked, referring to the thin strip of sheep's hide on which he'd drawn an eye, an eight-pointed star, a ring, and a queen and copied a verse in fine script. He had rolled the scroll tight and eased it into an empty bullet casing. On the metal he scratched out a cross and my name.

"Yes, it's always with me," I said, which was sort of true because I carried this phylactery in my briefcase.

"I should have made one for Dr. Ghosh and perhaps this would not happen."

I marveled at my faithful friend. To become a priest in Ethiopia, it was enough for the archbishop in Addis Ababa to blow his breath into a cloth bag which was then carried to the provinces and opened in a church yard, allowing for the mass ordination of hundreds. The more priests the merrier, from the standpoint of the Ethiopian Orthodox Church.

But having thousands and thousands of priests had its problems for God-fearing people like Almaz. A small number of these men were drunkards and cadgers for whom priesthood was a means of avoiding starvation while satisfying their other appetites. The worst reprobate priest who held out his cross obliged Almaz to stop and kiss its four points. I met her one day looking distressed, her clothes in disarray. She told me she'd beaten off a priest's advances with her umbrella, and others had come to her assistance and pummeled the man. "Marion, when I'm dying, go to the Merkato and get me *two* priests," she said to me then. "That way, just like Christ, I can die with a thief on either side of me."

But Gebrew was different. Almaz was sure God approved of Gebrew. He spent hours with his nose buried in his prayer books, leaning on his *makaturia*—his praying stick—beads clicking through his fingers. Even when he shed his priest garb to cut the grass, to run errands, to be Missing's watchman and gatekeeper, his turban stayed on and his lips never stopped moving. "Please make Ghosh a scroll," I said to Gebrew. "Have faith. Maybe it is not too late."

. . .

SHIVA HAD JUST COME BACK. I hadn't been in that toolshed for ages, and I was unprepared for the extreme clutter. Parts of engines and electrical boxes covered the floor. The narrowest of paths led to where his tank and welding equipment stood along with scraps of metal. Shiva had shored up the walls and ceiling of the shed with a welded metal scaffold, and from this his tools hung on wire holsters. He was hidden at his desk behind a mountain of books and papers. I made my way there. He was sketching a design for a frame of some kind, an apparatus he said would allow better exposure during fistula surgery. He put his pencil down and waited. He'd known nothing about what had transpired in the bungalow earlier. I told him the truth about Ghosh.

He listened but said nothing. Though he turned a little pale, his face otherwise gave away very little. He closed his eyes. He had climbed into his tree house and pulled up the ladder. He had no questions. I waited. Not even this news could break down the walls between us, I saw.

I needed him. I had carried Ghosh's secret alone, and now I was ready to spread the burden. I needed his strength for the days that were to come, but I didn't want to admit it. What was Shiva thinking? Did he feel anything at all? I left after a while, disgusted that those eyes would not open, convinced I couldn't count on him.

But Shiva surprised me. That night and for two more nights Shiva slept in the corridor outside Ghosh and Hema's bedroom with just a blanket wrapped under and over him. It was his way of expressing his love for Ghosh, of staying close. Ghosh was moved to tears seeing Shiva curled up there the next morning. I felt something around my heart break down and shatter when Hema told me. On the fourth night, as Ghosh's condition worsened, I decided to leave Ghosh's old bungalow and return to the bed I used to share with Shiva. I convinced Shiva not to sleep on the floor in the corridor. We slept awkwardly, on the edges of the mattress, getting up several times in the night to check on Ghosh. By morning, our heads were touching.

SHIVA AND I HAD the same blood group as Ghosh. With Adam's help, I'd been stockpiling my blood for this moment. Now, Shiva gave his. But blood was no longer sufficient, and it had caused a dangerous iron overload. Ghosh's platelets weren't working; he was oozing from his gums as well as losing blood in his bowel. He became progressively weaker.

Ghosh didn't want to move to the hospital. Soon the anemia left him short of breath, and he could no longer lie flat. We moved him from his marital bed of more than twenty years to his favorite armchair in the living room, his legs up on the footstool.

Quietly, systematically, he sought time with everyone he loved. He sent for Babu, Adid, Evangeline, and Mrs. Reddy and the other bridge players; I heard them laughing and reminiscing, though it wasn't all laughter. His cricket team surprised him when they arrived dressed in their whites to honor their captain. They regaled him with exaggerated stories of his past exploits.

Then it reached the point that he was breathing oxygen through a face mask that sat loosely over his chin. It was my turn to have *the* conversation with Ghosh. I'd been dreading the moment, resisting its implication.

"You're avoiding me, Marion," he said. "We must start. We can't finish unless we start, right?"

I would never have predicted what he'd say next.

"I don't want you to feel responsible for the entire family. Hema is very capable. Matron, even though she is getting old, is tough and resourceful. I am saying this to you because I want you to take your medical career to great heights. Don't feel bound by duty to Shiva or Hema or Matron to stay here. Or to Genet," he added, frowning slightly as he mentioned her name. He leaned forward to grab my hand, to make sure I understood how serious he was. "I wanted to go to America so badly. All these years I've read *Harrison's* and the other textbooks . . . and the things they do, the tests they order . . . it's like reading fiction, you know? Money's no object. A menu without prices. But if you get there, it won't be fiction. It'll be true." His eyes turned dreamy as he imagined what it was like.

"*We* stopped you from going, didn't we? Me and Shiva. Our birth?"

"Don't be silly. Can you imagine me giving up this?" he said sweeping his hand to indicate family, Missing, the home he'd made out of a bungalow. "I've been blessed. My genius was to know long ago that money alone wouldn't make me happy. Or maybe that's my excuse for not leaving you a huge fortune! I certainly *could* have made more money if that had been my goal. But one thing I won't have is regrets. My VIP patients often regret so many things on their deathbeds. They regret the bitterness they'll leave in people's hearts. They realize that no money, no church service, no eulogy, no funeral procession no matter how elaborate, can remove the legacy of a mean spirit.

"Of course, you and I have seen countless deaths among the poor. Their only regret surely is being born poor, suffering from birth to death. You know, in the Book of Job, Job says to God, 'You should've taken me straight from the womb to the tomb! Why the in-between part, why *life*, if it was just to suffer?' Something like that. For the poor, death is at least the end of suffering." He laughed as if he liked what he just said. His fingers automatically went up to his pajama pocket, then to the back of his ear searching for a pen, because the old Ghosh would have jotted that down. But there was no pen and no more need to write anything down.

"I haven't suffered. Well, maybe briefly. Only when my darling Hema made me pursue her for years. That was suffering!" The smile said it was a kind of suffering he wouldn't have traded for fame or fortune.

"Shiva will thrive with Hema. Hema needs him to keep her occupied. Hema's instinct will be to retreat to India. She'll make a lot of noise about that. It won't happen. Shiva will refuse. So she'll stay here in Addis. What I am saying is that it's not your worry. You understand?"

I nodded, without much conviction.

"I do have one small regret," Ghosh said. "But it's something you can help me with. It has to do with your father."

"You're the only father I've ever had," I said quickly. "I wish Thomas Stone had this leukemia instead of you. I wouldn't care one bit if he died!"

He waited before answering, swallowing hard. "Marion, it means everything to me that you consider me your father. I couldn't be prouder of you, of who you've become. But I bring up Thomas Stone for selfish reasons. As I said, it's one of *my* regrets.

"You see, I was as close a friend to your father as he was capable of having. You have to picture how it was then, Marion. He was the only other male physician here at Missing. We were so different, nothing in common, or so I thought, when I met him. But I found that he loved medicine in the same sort of way that I love medicine. He was dedicated. His passion for medicine . . . it was as if he came from another planet, *my* planet. We had a special bond."

His eyes drifted off to the window, perhaps recalling those times. I waited. Eventually he turned to me and squeezed my hand.

"Marion, your father was deeply wounded by something, God knows what. His parents died when he was a child. We never talked about things like that. But here, working alongside Sister Mary Joseph Praise, all of us working together, he was sheltered. He was as happy as such a man can be. I felt protective of him. He knew surgery well, but he had *no* understanding of life."

"You mean he was like Shiva?"

He paused to consider this. "No. Very different. Shiva's content! Look at him. Shiva has no need for friendship or social support or approval—Shiva lives in this moment. Thomas Stone wasn't like that; he had all the needs the rest of us have. But he was scared. He denied himself his needs, and he denied himself his past."

"Scared of what?" I found all this hard to swallow. "Matron told me once that he threw instruments when he got upset. She said he had a temper, that he was fearless."

"Oh, fearless in surgery, I suppose. But even that might not be true. A good surgeon *must* be fearful and he was a good surgeon, the best, never foolhardy, and appropriately fearful. Well . . . a few lapses of judgment, but then he was human. But when it came to relationships he was . . . terrified. He was frightened that if he got close to anyone they'd hurt him. Or perhaps he'd hurt them."

I was resisting this construction of Stone that was so different from what I'd made up all these years. Finally, I asked, "What do you want from me?"

"Now that my time is coming, Marion . . . I want to let Thomas Stone know that whatever happened I always considered myself his friend."

"Why don't you write to him?"

"I can't. I never could. Hema hasn't forgiven him for leaving. She was happy he left—she wanted you two from the moment you were born. But still, she wouldn't forgive him for leaving. And then, once he left, she was terrified—always—that he might come back and claim you. I had to promise her, swear to her, that I wouldn't write him or communicate with him in any form." He looked at me, and said with quiet pride, "I kept my word, Marion."

"Good. I'm glad."

I'd harbored such curiosity about Thomas Stone when I was younger. I had fantasized about his return. Now I resisted Ghosh, and I wasn't quite sure why.

Ghosh went on, "But I fully expected Stone to contact me. I was disappointed as the years went on that he didn't. Marion, he is filled with shame and he assumes that I have no desire to see him. That I hate him."

"How do you know?"

"I've no way of knowing this for sure. I suspect that to this day he sees himself as an albatross. Call it clinical intuition if you like. The truth is that you were better off with us than with him. Try as he might, I don't know that he could have created what we have here, a family. So I don't want you to hate that man. The cross he carries is huge."

"Why tell me this now?" I said. "I stopped thinking about him after you came out from jail. He was never there when we needed him. Why should I waste my time thinking about him?"

"For my sake. I told you, this is for *me*. My one regret. It's not about you. But only you can help me."

I said nothing.

"Let me see if I can explain . . ." He looked up at the ceiling for a few seconds. "Marion, there'll be something incomplete about my life if I don't let him know that I still consider him a brother." His eyes became wet. "And that whatever his reasons are for being silent all these years, I still . . . love him. *I* can't see him, I can't tell him this. But you can. I won't live to see it, but that's what I want. Do it without hurting Hema's feelings. Do it for me. Complete what is incomplete."

"Are you going to tell Shiva this?"

"If I tell Shiva that it's my dying wish, he'd do it. But Shiva may not know *how* to do it, how to . . . heal him. It requires more than delivering a message." He hesitated. "Speaking of Shiva: what I also need to tell you about Shiva is that whatever he did to you, please forgive him."

He stunned me there. Had he planned to say that? Was it an afterthought? I didn't think Ghosh knew the depths of my hurt, my bitterness toward Shiva, but I'd underestimated him. Still, what happened between me and Shiva wasn't a subject I wanted to bring up with Ghosh; it was too painful, too personal.

"I'll do my best about Thomas Stone. For you. But I can't believe this is what you want. You're forgetting this is the man who caused my mother's death . . . A nun's death. A nun he got pregnant. And then he abandoned his children. And to this day no one seems to know how any of it happened."

As my voice rose and quavered, Ghosh said nothing, but looked at me steadily till my shoulders collapsed and I gave in. I'd do what he asked.

WHEN THE END CAME a week later he was still in that chair, all of us with him, me and Shiva holding his left hand, Matron holding his right. Almaz, who had become so lean from rigorous fasting, squatted behind his chair with her hand on his shoulder; Hema sat on the arm of the chair, so Ghosh's head could rest against her body. Genet was not to be found. She wasn't in her hostel when Gebrew was sent in a cab to bring her to Missing. Gebrew stood next to Almaz, praying.

Ghosh's breathing was labored, but Hema gave him morphine—he'd taught her that, she said. Morphine "disconnects the head from the brain," so although the breathlessness was unchanging, the anxiety would be gone.

He opened his eyes once, startled. He looked at Hema, then at us. He smiled and closed his eyes. I like to think in that last gaze he saw a tableau of his family, his real flesh and blood, because our blood was now in his veins. I like to think in seeing us he felt his highest purpose was served.

And that is how he passed from this life to the next, without fanfare, with characteristic simplicity, fearless, opening his eyes that last time to make sure we were fine before he went on.

When his chest stopped moving, my sorrow was mixed with relief: I'd been matching every breath of his with mine for days. I know Hema felt the same way as she laid her head on his and wept, her arms still cradling him.

WITH GHOSH'S DEATH came a new understanding of the word "loss." I'd lost my birth mother and father, lost the General, lost Zemui, lost Rosina. But I only knew real loss when I lost Ghosh. The hand that patted me and put me to sleep, the lips that trumpeted bedtime songs, the fingers that guided mine to percuss a chest, to feel an enlarged liver or spleen, the heart that coaxed my ears to understand the hearts of others, was now stilled.

At the moment he died I felt the mantle of responsibility pass from him to me. He'd anticipated that. I remembered his advice to wear that mantle lightly. He'd handed me the professional baton, wanted me to be the kind of doctor who would surpass him, and then pass on that same knowledge to my children and to their children, a chain. "I shall not break the chain," I said, hoping Ghosh could hear me.

Freud, I knew, wrote that one only became a man the day one's father died.

When Ghosh died, I stopped being a son.

I was a man.

CHAPTER 37

Exodus

WHEN I LEFT ETHIOPIA two years after Ghosh died, it had nothing to do with Ghosh's deathbed wishes. It wasn't about finding Thomas Stone and healing his pain. It wasn't because the Emperor had been deposed by a creeping military rebellion, or that the armed forces "committee" that took power had been reduced by infighting and murder to one mad dictator, an army sergeant, a man named Mengistu, who'd eventually make Stalin look like an angel.

Rather, I left on Wednesday, January 10, 1979, the day news spread through the city like influenza that four Eritrean guerrillas posing as passengers had commandeered an Ethiopian Airlines Boeing 707 and forced it to fly to Khartoum, Sudan. One of the four was Genet. That morning she'd been a medical student, albeit one who had fallen three years behind. By evening, she was a liberation fighter.

I was a doctor at long last, an intern finishing up my last rotation. I'd done three months each in internal medicine, surgery, obstetrics and gynecology, and now all that remained was a month of pediatrics.

Hema tracked me down by telephone in the early evening. She'd heard the news about Genet.

"Marion, come home at once."

The tone of her voice made the air around me go still.

"Ma, are you okay? We can't help her. They may come to talk to us. You are her guardian."

Since Ghosh's death, without the buffer of his presence, I'd become closer to Hema. She sought my advice, and I looked for time to spend with her. I felt Ghosh's hand in that.

"Marion, my love, it's not about Genet . . . Adid just called. The secret police are searching for a co-conspirator named Marion Praise Stone. They may be on their way there."

Thank God for Adid's source, a Muslim in Security with a soft spot for Missing. Genet's roommate, a tiny waif of a girl who I am sure had no knowledge of the plot, spit out my name within an hour of the hijack. People will say anything when their fingernails are being ripped out.

Visions of Ghosh, his head shaved, in the Kerchele Prison yard, flashed through my mind. But the old Kerchele was a country club compared with what it was now: an overcrowded torture college, a butcher shop where enemies of the state came to their ends. Bodies and body parts were carried out in trucks every night and posed throughout the city, a macabre public arts program that served to educate and edify. *Portrait of the Artist as a Dead Man. Headless Woman Pointing Out Orion. Traitor Holding Head in His Hands. Dead Man with Penis in His Mouth.* The unifying message was clear: *You're Dead If You Think of Crossing Us.*

The Sergeant-President, an uncouth, barbaric man, had only one thing in common with the Emperor: he'd never let Eritrea secede. He launched a full-scale military offensive, bombing Eritrean villages where rebels mingled with civilians, putting the Eritrean homeland under siege. But of course, this only served to give new energy to the Eritrean People's Liberation Front.

Meanwhile, the Oromo tribes were pressing for freedom. The Tigres (who spoke a language similar to that of the Eritreans) had formed their own liberation front. The royalists around Addis Ababa, who believed in the Emperor and the monarchy, had set off bombs in government offices in the capital. The university students, once great fans of the military "committee," were now split into those pushing for democracy and those who felt nothing short of an Albanian-style Marxism would do. Neighboring Somalia decided this was the time to press its claims on disputed territory in the Ogaden Desert that even the vultures did not want. Who said being a dictator is easy? The Sergeant-President had his hands full.

WITHOUT A WORD TO ANYONE, I slipped out of the back of the Ethio-Swedish Pediatric Hospital, leaving my car parked in its spot. I took a taxi home. I couldn't believe this was happening. What had Genet accomplished? Hijacking an Ethiopian Airlines plane was all about publicity. Yes, BBC would pay attention. It would further embarrass the Sergeant-President, but he was doing a fine job of that without any outside help. Even if Genet's act hadn't put me in danger, I'd have resented the hijack. Ethiopian Airlines was a symbol of our national pride. Foreigners raved about EA's wonderful service, its skilled pilots. Jet flights from Rome, London, Frankfurt, Nairobi, Cairo, and Bombay to Addis made it easy for tourists to visit. Then EA's regional service of DC-3s flew a daily looping, hopscotch route so that you could leave the Hilton Addis Ababa in the morning, see the castles in Gondar, the ancient obelisks in Axum, the rock-hewn churches of Lalibela, and be back in the Hilton lounge in Addis just when the good-time girls were drifting in trailing perfume, and the Velvet Ashantis were playing their theme song, a version of "Walk—Don't Run" by the Ventures.

Ethiopian Airlines had for years been a target for the Eritrean People's Liberation Front. But even in the Emperor's time, crack security men on board disguised as passengers ensured a near-perfect safety record until Genet's flight. On one occasion, seven Eritrean hijackers stood up and announced their intentions. The two security men picked off five of the hijackers as easily as if they were shooting tin cans off a fence at ten paces. They overpowered the sixth. The seventh locked herself up in the bathroom and exploded a grenade. The pilot landed the crippled, rudderless plane despite a gaping hole in the tail section. On another occasion, the security force overpowered a hijacker and strapped him into a first-class seat. Instead of shooting him, they bibbed him with towels and slit his throat.

That January afternoon, Genet and her pals seized the plane without a fight. Word was they had help on the inside. The security men may have turned.

As my taxi drove through the Merkato, I took in the familiar sights. Could this be the last time I passed this way, the last time I smelled the hops from the St. George's brewery on this road? A woman with her hair in cornrows, Eritrean style, flagged my taxi down. "Lideta, please," she said, naming her destination.

"Lideta, is it?" the driver said. "Why don't you take a plane, sweetheart?" Her face fell, then turned hard. She didn't bother to argue. She just turned away.

"Those bastards better lay low tonight," the driver said to me, since I clearly wasn't one of them. "Look," he said, waving his hand at the pedestrians on both sides. "They're everywhere." There were thousands of Eritreans in Addis Ababa—people like the Staff Probationer, like Genet. They were administrators, teachers, university faculty, students, government workers, and officers in the armed forces, executives in telecommunications, waterworks, and public health, and legions of others who were just common folk. "They drink our milk and eat our bread. But in their homes tonight, you know they're butchering a sheep."

Since the military took power, many Eritreans I knew, including some physicians and medical students, had gone underground to join the Eritrean People's Liberation Front.

The news in the capital was that the situation in the north of Ethiopia around Asmara had turned against the Sergeant-President. The Eritrean guerrillas ambushed military convoys at night and disappeared in daylight. I'd seen grainy photos of these fighters. Dressed in their trademark sandals, khaki shorts and shirts, they had the daring, the conviction, and the passion of patriots fighting their occupiers. The conscripted Ethiopian soldiers in their jeeps and tanks, weighted down with helmets, combat boots, jackets, and weaponry, were confined to the main roads. How could they find an enemy they couldn't see, in a countryside where they didn't speak the language and couldn't tell civilians and sympathizers from guerrillas?

As my taxi approached Missing's gates, I saw Tsige stepping out of her Fiat 850 in front of her bar. She'd prospered these last few years, buying out the business next door, adding a kitchen, a full restaurant, and hiring more bar girls to serve customers. Upgrades to the furniture, two foosball machines, and a new television set made her bar the equal of the best in the Piazza. Tsige owned one taxi, and when we last spoke she'd told me she was looking for a second. She never failed to encourage me, to tell me how proud she was of me and that she prayed for me every day. Now, as I saw her lovely stockinged leg emerge from the car, I had a great urge to stop and say good-bye, but I couldn't. This was her land, too, and I hoped that unlike me she'd never have a need to flee.

MISSING'S MAIN GATE was wide open. This was Hema's prearranged signal that the coast was clear for me to come home.

When you have just minutes to leave the house in which you've spent all your twenty-five years, what do you take with you?

Hema had my diplomas, certificates, passport, a few clothes, money, bread, cheese, and water packed in a roomy Air India shoulder bag. I wore sneakers and layers of clothes against the cold. I threw in a cassette which I knew had both the slow and fast "Tizita" on it, but left the cassette player behind. I contemplated taking *Harrison's Principles of Internal Medicine,* or *Schwartz's Principles of Surgery,* but with each book weighing about five pounds, I didn't.

We left on foot, a small convoy heading to the side wall of Missing, but first I insisted we go by the grove where Ghosh and Sister Mary Joseph Praise were buried. I walked with my arm around Hema. Shiva assisted Matron. Almaz and Gebrew had gone ahead. I felt Hema's body trembling.

At Ghosh's grave, I took leave of him. I imagined how he would have tried to cheer me up, make me look at the bright side—*You always wanted to travel! Here's your chance. Be careful! Travel expands the mind and loosens the bowels.* I kissed the marble headstone and turned away. I didn't dwell at my birth mother's grave. If I wanted to say good-bye to her, this wasn't the place. I hadn't visited the autoclave room for more than two years. I felt a pang of guilt, but it was too late to go there now.

At the wall, Hema held me. She laid her head on my chest, and the tears were flowing freely, in a way that I'd only seen at Ghosh's death. She couldn't speak.

Matron, a rock of faith in moments of crisis, kissed me on the forehead and said simply, "Go with God." Almaz and Gebrew prayed over me. Almaz handed me a kerchief tied around a couple of boiled eggs. Gebrew gave me a tiny scroll that I was to swallow for protection— I popped it into my mouth.

If my eyes were dry, it was because I couldn't believe this was happening. As I looked at my send-off party, I felt such hatred for Genet. Perhaps Eritreans in Addis were slaughtering sheep and toasting her tonight, but I wished she could see this snapshot of our family as it was torn apart, all because of her.

It was time to say good-bye to Shiva. I'd forgotten what it felt like to hold him, what a perfect fit his body was to mine, two halves of a single being. Ever since Genet's mutilation, we'd slept separately except for a brief period around Ghosh's death. Once Ghosh died, I returned to his old quarters, leaving Shiva in our childhood room. Only now did I recognize the severity of the penance I'd enforced by sleeping apart. Our arms were like magnets, refusing to disengage.

I pulled my head back and studied his face. I saw disbelief and a bottomless sadness. I was strangely pleased, flattered to get such a reaction from him. I'd seen this only twice before: on the day of Ghosh's arrest and on the day of Ghosh's death. Our parting at Missing's wall was a kind of death, his expression said. And if it was so for him, it was for me, too. Or should have been.

There was a time, ages ago, it seemed, when we could read each other's thoughts. I wondered if he could read mine. I'd postponed this moment, this reckoning with him. It was the deal I'd made with Genet, but I felt no need to honor that now. Now, my mind expressed itself.

Shiva, do you see how deflowering Genet, a biological act as far as you were concerned, led to all this? It led Rosina to kill herself, led Genet to stray from us? It led to this moment where I hate the woman I hoped to marry? Even now Hema thinks that I set all this in motion, that I did something to Genet.

Do you see how you betrayed me?

This good-bye is like cutting off my body.

I love you as I love myself—that is inevitable.

But I can't forgive you. Perhaps in time, and only because that's what Ghosh wanted. In time, Shiva, but not now.

We stood at the foot of the ladder which Gebrew had placed against Missing's east wall.

Shiva handed me a cloth bag. In the darkness it was impossible to see, but I thought I recognized the shape and the color of his dog-eared copy of *Gray's Anatomy* and below that a pristine copy of some other heavy book. I was about to remonstrate. I bit my tongue. In giving me his *Gray's*, Shiva sacrificed a piece of himself, the most valuable thing he owned that was removable and portable.

"Thank you, Shiva," I said, hoping it didn't sound sarcastic. I now had two bags instead of one.

Gebrew slung burlap sacks on top of the bottle shards that crested the wall. I climbed over. On the other side was the road that I'd always seen from my bedroom window but never explored. It was a view that I thought of as pastoral, idyllic, a road disappearing into the mist and mountains to a land of no worries. Tonight it looked sinister.

"Good-bye," I called one last time, touching my hand to that moist wall, the living, breathing exoskeleton of Missing. Inside, a chorus of voices so dear to me, they who were the beating heart of Missing, called out, wished me Godspeed.

A hundred yards away, a truck sat idling. It carried stacks of retreaded tires. The driver helped me climb onto the bed, where a tarp had been strung over and under tires to make a small cave. Adid had water, biscuits, and a pile of blankets placed there. He had arranged my escape but under the aegis of the Eritrean People's Liberation Front. The EPLF had become the common path to leave Ethiopia, particularly if you planned to do it from the north and if you were willing to pay.

The less said about my cold, bumpy, seven-hour ride to Dessie, the better. After a night in a Dessie warehouse, where I slept on a regular bed, and a second night where we rested in Mekele, on the third day of out northern journey we reached Asmara, the heart of Eritrea. The city Genet had loved so much was under occupation. The Ethiopian army was visible in force, tanks and armored cars parked at key junctions, checkpoints everywhere. We were never searched, since the driver's papers showed the tires we carried were to supply the Ethiopian army.

I was taken to a safe house, a cozy cottage surrounded by bougainvillea, where I was to wait until we could make the trek out of Asmara and into the countryside. The furniture was just a mattress on the living room floor. I couldn't venture out to the garden. I thought I'd be in the safe house for a night or two, but the wait stretched out to two weeks. My Eritrean guide, Luke, brought me food once a day. He was younger than me, a fellow of few words, a college student in Addis before he went underground. He suggested I walk as much as I could in the house to strengthen my legs. "These are the wheels of the EPLF," he said, smiling, tapping his thighs.

There were two surprises in my meager luggage. What I thought was a cardboard base at the bottom of the Air India bag that Hema packed was instead a framed picture. It was the print of St. Teresa that Sister Mary Joseph Praise had put up in the autoclave room. Hema's note taped to the glass explained:

> *Ghosh had this framed in the last month of his life. In his will he said that if you ever left the country, he wanted this picture to go with you. Marion, since I can't go with you, may my Ghosh, Sister Mary, and St. Teresa all watch over you.*

I caressed the frame, which Ghosh's hands must have touched. I wondered why he'd taken so much trouble, but I was pleased. It was my talisman for protection. I had not said good-bye to her in the autoclave room, and it turned out I didn't need to, because she was coming with me.

The second surprise was the book under Shiva's precious *Gray's Anatomy*. It was Thomas Stone's textbook, *The Expedient Operator: A Short Practice of Tropical Surgery*. I'd never known such a book existed. (Later I learned that it went out of print a few years after our birth.) I turned the pages, curious, wondering why I'd never seen this before and how it came to be in Shiva's possession. And then, suddenly, there he was in a photograph that occupied three-fourths of the page, staring out at me, a faint smile on his lips: Thomas Stone, MBBS, FRCS. I had to close the book. I rose and got some water, took my time. I wanted to compose myself and look at him on my own terms. When I opened the page again, I noticed the fingers, nine of them, instead of ten. I had to admit the similarity to Shiva and therefore to me. It was in the deep-set eyes, in the gaze. Our jaws were not as square as his and our foreheads were broader. I wondered why Shiva had put it in my hands.

The book looked brand-new, as if it had hardly been opened. A bookmark placed on the copyright page said, "Compliments of the Publisher." The bookmark had been pressed between the pages for so long that when I peeled it off a pale rectangular outline remained.

On the back of the bookmark was written:

September 19, 1954
The Second Edition. The packet came addressed to me. But I
am sure the publisher meant it for you. Congratulations. Also,
I am enclosing a letter to you from me. Please read at once.
SMP.

My mother had penned this note a day before our birth and her death. Her clear writing, the even letters, retained a schoolgirl's innocence. How long had Shiva posessed the book and bookmark? Why give it to me? Was it so that I'd have something from my mother?

To get in shape, I'd pace around the house, hauling the bag with books on my shoulder. I read Stone's textbook during those two weeks. At first I resisted it, telling myself it was dated. But he had a way of conveying his surgical experience in the context of scientific principles that made it quite readable. I studied the bookmark often, rereading my mother's words. What was in the letter she had left for Stone? What would she have been saying to him just one day before we, her identical twin boys, would arrive? I copied her writing, imitating the loops.

One day when Luke brought my food, he said we'd leave that night. I packed one last time. The two books had to go with me; I couldn't abandon either one, though my Air India bag was still very heavy.

We set out after curfew. "That's why we waited," Luke said, pointing skyward. "When there's no moon it is safer."

He led me down narrow paths between houses, and then along irrigation ditches, and soon we were away from the residential areas. We crossed fields in the pitch-dark. I sensed hills in the distance. Within an hour, my shoulder hurt from the bag, even though I positioned it in different ways. Luke insisted on transferring some items from my bag to his knapsack. He looked shocked at the sight of the books, but said nothing. He took the *Gray's*.

We walked for hours, stopping only once. At last, we were in the foothills, climbing. At four-thirty in the morning, we heard a soft whistle. We met up with a troop of eleven fighters. They greeted us in their trademark fashion: shaking hands while bumping shoulders back and forth, saying, *"Kamela-hai"* or "Salaam." There were four women, sporting Afros just like the men. I was shocked to recognize one of the fighters: it was the firebrand, the student with the bovine eyes whom I had encountered in Genet's hostel room. On that occasion he'd stormed out contemptuously. Now, recognizing me, he sported a lopsided grin. He shook my hand with both his. His name was Tsahai.

The fighters were exhausted, but uncomplaining, their legs white with dust. They carried a heavy gun which they had dismantled into several large pieces.

Tsahai brought something over to me. "High-protein field bread," he said. It was a ration which was of the fighters' own invention, but it tasted like cardboard. He rubbed his right knee as he spoke, and it looked to me as if it was swollen with fluid. If it was sore, he said nothing about it.

We avoided the topic of Genet. Instead he described how earlier that night they'd ambushed an Ethiopian army convoy as it tried a rare night patrol. "Their soldiers are scared of the dark. They don't want to fight and they don't want to be here. Morale is terrible. When we shot the lead vehicle, the soldiers jumped out, forgetting to shoot, just running for cover. We had the high ground on both sides. Right away they screamed that they were surrendering, even though their officer was ordering them to keep fighting. We took their uniforms and sent them on foot back to the garrison."

Tsahai and his comrades had siphoned gas from the trucks, then hid the one working vehicle in the bush, stuffed with uniforms, ammunition, and weapons to be retrieved at another time. The real prize was the heavy gun and shells which they brought with them, everything carried on foot.

. . .

WE SET OFF after fifteen minutes. Before daybreak we reached a well-hidden, tiny bunker carved out of the side of a hill. I didn't think I was capable of walking as far as I had. It helped that my fellow walkers carried five times my load without complaint.

Luke and I stayed in the bunker. The others hurried on to a forward position, risking daylight and being spotted by the roaming MiG fighters because there was some urgency to reassemble the gun.

I slept until Luke woke me. My legs felt as if a wall had collapsed on them. "Take this," he said, giving me two pills and a tin mug of tea. "It's our own painkiller, paracetamol, manufactured in our pharmacy."

I was too tired to do anything but swallow. He made me eat some more of the bread, and I slept again. I awoke with less pain, but so stiff I could hardly get off the floor. I took two more of the paracetamol pills.

Five fighters arrived to escort us onward when it turned dark. One of them had a partially withered leg: polio, I knew. Seeing his swinging, awkward gait, his gun serving as a counterbalance, made it impossible for me to think of my own discomfort.

The second march was half as long as the first, and gradually my legs loosened. We arrived long before dawn at some scruffy hills. A narrow trail led to a cave, its entrance completely hidden by brush and by natural rock. Wooden logs framed the opening. A steep wooden ramp went down to more rooms, deep within. The trail on the outside led to other caves up and down the hill, all the openings cleverly concealed.

I was taken inside to a stall. I removed my shoes, and fell asleep on a straw pallet. It felt luxurious. I slept till late afternoon. Luke walked me around. I was stiff again, but he seemed fine. The base was empty of fighters because of a major operation going on elsewhere.

I suppose I should have admired these fighters, who could flit through the dust like sandflies. I should've admired their resourcefulness, their ability to manufacture their own intravenous fluid, their own sulfa, penicillin, and paracetamol tablets stamped out by a handpress. Hidden in these caves and invisible from the air or ground was an operating theater, a prosthetic limb center, hospital wards, and a school. The degree of sophistication in those surroundings was even more impressive for being so spartan. The quiet discipline, the recognition that the tasks of cooking, caring for children, sweeping the floors were as important as any other, convinced me that they would one day prevail and have their freedom.

I watched a fighter relaxing outside the bunker. The sun filtering through the acacia tree formed a changing mosaic of light on her face and on the rifle across her lap. She hummed to herself as she scanned the skies with binoculars, looking for MiGs, which were flown by the Russian or Cuban "advisers" to Ethiopia. America had long supported the Emperor, but it withdrew its support of Sergeant-President Mengistu's regime, halting weapons and parts sales. The Eastern Bloc stepped in to fill the void.

The fighter, who was about our age, reminded me of Genet in the way she arranged her limbs, in the ease with which she occupied her body. Despite the lethal weapon in her hand, her movements were delicate. She wore no makeup, and her feet were dusty and callous. Seeing her I was grateful for one thing: my Genet dream was gone forever and good riddance. I'd been so stupid to sustain a one-sided fantasy for so long. The honeymoon in Udaipur, our own little bungalow at Missing, raising our babies, setting off to the hospital in the morning, doctors working side by side . . . It would never happen. I never wanted to see her again. And I probably never would. She was surely in Khartoum, still basking in the glory of her daring operation. There was no going back to Addis for her either. Soon she would join these fighters, live in these bunkers, and fight alongside them. I hoped I would be long gone by then. I resented having to be in their camp at all, even more having to turn to her comrades for help.

That night I woke to the sounds of MiGs overhead and bombs dropping far away, but close enough for us to hear the rumble. Also the fainter thuds of artillery. No lights were allowed anywhere near the mouth of the cave.

Luke said that a massive raid had just been completed on a weapons and fuel depot. It had included Tsahai and the group of fighters we met on the first night. They had penetrated using a stolen army truck. Once inside, they set charges, but their comrades outside had been surprised by a reinforcement convoy that attacked them from the rear. It had not gone exactly as planned. Nine guerrillas including Tsahai were dead and many more wounded. The Ethiopians' losses were much larger and the fuel depot partially destroyed. Our casualties would arrive at the cave by early morning.

I woke to voices, the activity and urgency unmistakable. I heard moans and sharp cries of pain. Luke took me to the surgical ward.

"Hello, Marion," a voice said. I turned to see Solomon, who'd been my senior in medical school. He'd gone underground as soon as he finished his internship. I remembered him as a chubby, well-fed intern. The man before me had hollow cheeks and was as lean as a stick.

I followed Solomon, stooping down in a low-ceilinged tunnel where stretchers were arranged in pairs on the floor, triaged so that those most in need of surgery were closest to the operating theater at the end of the tunnel. The entrance to the theater was a cloth curtain.

The wounds were ghastly. One barely conscious man whispered last instructions into the ear of a friend, who hovered over him, writing furiously. Intravenous fluid and blood bottles dangled from hooks embedded in the cave walls. The attendants worked squatting next to the stretchers.

Solomon said he'd gone close to the battlefront for this mission. "Usually I stay here. We resuscitate at the battlefield. Intravenous fluid, control bleeding, antibiotics, even some field surgery. We can prevent shock just like the Americans in Vietnam. Only we don't have their helicopters." He slapped his thighs. "These are our helicopters. We carry our wounded by stretcher." He scanned the room. "That man over there needs a chest tube," he said, indicating with his head. "Please do it. Tumsghi will help you. I'll go ahead to the theater. That comrade cannot wait." He pointed to a pale soldier lying near the curtain with a bloody pad over his abdomen. He was conscious, but barely, breathing rapidly.

The fighter who needed the chest tube whispered "Salaam" when I squatted by him. The bullet had entered his triceps, then his chest, and miraculously missed the great vessels, the heart, and the spine. When I tapped with my bunched fingers above his right nipple it was dull, quite unlike the boxy, resonant note on the left. Blood had collected around the lung in the pleural space, compressing the right lung against the left lung and the heart in the confined cavity of the chest. Working just behind his right armpit, I injected lidocaine and anesthetized the skin, then the edge of the rib and deeper into the pleura, before making an inch-long cut with a scalpel. I pushed a closed hemostat into my incision till I felt it pop through the resistance of the pleura. I put my gloved finger into the hole, sweeping around to ensure space for the chest tube—a rubber hose with openings at side and tip—which I fed into the hole. Tumsghi connected the other end to a drainage bottle with water in it, so that the tube emerged under the water level. This crude underwater seal prevented air going back into the chest. Already dark blood was emerging, and the soldier's breathing improved. He said something in Tigrinya and pulled off his oxygen. Tumsghi said, "He wants you to give his oxygen to someone else."

I joined Solomon in the operating theater in time to see his patient come off the table. The man's chest didn't move. There was about a five-second silence. One of the women, fighting back tears, knelt and covered his face.

"Some things are beyond us," Solomon said quietly. "He had a laceration to the liver. I tried mattress sutures. But he also had a tear to the inferior vena cava where it goes behind the liver. It kept oozing. I couldn't stop it unless I clamped the inferior vena cava, which would kill him. You remember Professor Asrat used to say that injuries to the vena cava behind the liver are when the surgeon sees God? He used to say things like that that I didn't understand. I understand now."

The next patient had a belly wound. Solomon systematically sorted out what to me looked like an impossible and dirty mess. He pulled out the small bowel, identified several perforations which he oversewed. The spleen was ruptured and so this was removed. The sigmoid colon had a ragged tear. He cut out the segment, and then brought the two open ends to the skin in a double-barrel colostomy. We irrigated the abdomen vigorously, left drains in place, and did a sponge count. The field looked so neat compared with its condition when we started. Solomon must have read my mind. He held up his hands to show me his stubby fingers and his hammer thumbs: "I wanted to be a psychiatrist." Over the eight hours, that was the only time I saw him smile behind the mask.

We amputated five limbs. The last two procedures we performed were burr holes in the skulls of two comatose patients. We used a modified carpenter's drill. In the first we were rewarded by blood welling out from just under the dura where it had collected, pressing on the brain. The other patient was agonal, his pupils fixed and dilated. The burr hole produced nothing. The bleeding was deep inside the brain.

Two days later, I took leave of Solomon. There were dark rings under his eyes and he looked ready to fall over. There was no questioning his purpose or dedication. Solomon said, "Go and good luck to you. This isn't your fight. I'd go if I were in your shoes. Tell the world about us."

This isn't your fight. I thought about that as I trekked to the border with two escorts. What did Solomon mean? Did he see me as being on the Ethiopian side, on the side of the occupiers? No, I think he saw me as an expatriate, someone without a stake in this war. Despite being born in the same compound as Genet, despite speaking Amharic like a native, and going to medical school with him, to Solomon I was a *ferengi*— a foreigner. Perhaps he was right, even though I was loath to admit it. If I were a patriotic Ethiopian, would I not have gone underground and joined the royalists, or others who were trying to topple Sergeant Mengistu? If I cared about my country, shouldn't I have been willing to die for it?

We crossed the Sudan border by early evening. I took a bus to Port Sudan, and then Sudan Airways to Khartoum. In Khartoum I was able to call a number Adid had provided to let Hema know I was safe. Two days in sweltering Khartoum felt like two years, but at last I flew to Kenya.

IN NAIROBI, Mr. Eli Harris, whose Houston church had been the pillar of Missing's support for years, had arranged room for me at a mission clinic. Matron and Harris had made these arrangements by cable. I found the work in the small outpatient clinic difficult, as I was certain that many things were getting lost in translation. In my free time, I studied for the exams that I had to take to begin postgraduate training in America.

Nairobi was lush and green like Addis Ababa, the grass pushing up between pavement tiles as if the jungle seethed underneath the city, ready to take over. Nairobi's infrastructure and sophistication dwarfed that of Addis. One could thank the years of British rule for that, and, though Kenya was independent, many Brits lived on there. And Indians: in some parts of Nairobi you could imagine you were in Baroda or Ahmedabad with sari emporiums ten to a street, *chat* shops everywhere, the pungent scent of masala in the air, and Gujarati the only language spoken.

At first I spent my evenings in the bars, drowning my sorrows and listening to *benga* music and soukous. The jazzy Congolese and Brazilian rhythms were uplifting, full of optimism, but when I retired to my room, afloat in beer, my melancholia was always worse. Other than the music, Kenyan culture made no impact on me. The fault was mine. I resisted the place. Thomas Stone had come to Nairobi when he fled Ethiopia with his demons chasing him. It was another reason I was disinclined to stay.

I called Hema on a schedule, dialing different friends' houses every Tuesday night. Things were no better, she said. Were I to come back, I'd still be in danger.

So I stayed in my room and studied every waking minute. I passed the American medical equivalency exams two months later, and immediately presented myself to the American Embassy for my visa. Again, Harris had eased my way.

I was righteous: if my country was willing to torture me on suspicion, if it didn't want my services as a physician, then I disowned my country. But the truth is that by this time I knew that I wouldn't return to Ethiopia, even if things were suddenly rosy again.

I wanted out of Africa.

I began to think that Genet had done me a favor after all.

PART FOUR

The intellect of man is forced to choose
perfection of the life, or of the work,
And if it take the second must refuse
A heavenly mansion, raging in the dark.

William Yeats, "The Choice"

CHAPTER 38

Welcome Wagon

C APTAIN GETACHEW SELASSIE—no relation to the Emperor—piloted the East African Airways 707 that flew me out of Nairobi. I heard his calm voice twice during the abbreviated night. I had a new respect for his line of work, which brought him closer to God than any cleric. He was the first of three pilots who carried me through nine time zones.

Rome.

London.

New York.

THE RITUAL OF IMMIGRATION and baggage claim at Kennedy Airport went by so quickly that I wondered if I'd missed it. Where were the armed soldiers? The dogs? The long lines? The body searches? Where were the tables where your luggage was laid open and a knife taken to the lining? I passed into marbled hallways, up and then down escalators and into a cavernous receiving area which, even with two planes disgorging passengers, looked half empty. There was no one to herd us from one spot to the next.

Before I knew it, I was out of the sterile, hushed incubator of Customs. The automatic doors swished shut behind me as if to seal out the contamination of the cacophonous crowd outside, held back by a metal barrier.

A Ghanaian woman, whose flowered gown and headcloth had made her look so regal when she boarded in Nairobi, walked out from Customs beside me. We were both exhausted, dazed, unprepared for the sea of faces scrutinizing us. We stood there, manila X-ray folders (a requirement for immigration which no one checked) clutched awkwardly, baggage straps crisscrossing our chests, wide-eyed like animals coming off the Ark.

What struck me first was that the locals were of all colors and shapes, not the sea of white faces I had expected. Their lewd, inquisitive gazes traveled over us. In the cross fire of bewildering new scents, I picked up the Ghanaian woman's fear. She pressed close to me. Men in black suits held up signs on which they had printed names. Their gazes were flat, like overseers taking the measure of the Ghanaian woman's pelvis, noting the gap between her first and second toe which everyone knows is the only reliable gauge of fecundity. I had a vision of the Middle Passage, of blacks shuffling down the gangplank, shackles clinking while a hundred pairs of eyes probed their flanks, their biceps, and studied the exposed flesh for yaws, which was the Old World syphilis. As for me, I was nobody, her eunuch. She dropped her bag, she was so rattled.

It was while bending down to help her that I saw the sign in the hand of a swarthy brown-eyed man. He held it at waist level, as if he didn't want to be identified with the liveried sign holders. His bush shirt hung out over baggy white pajama pants. Brown sandals on sockless feet completed his outfit. The letters on his sign could have spelled MARVIN or MARMEN or MARTIN. The second word was STONE.

"Is that supposed to say 'Marion'?" I asked.

He surveyed me from top to bottom, and then he looked away as if I weren't worth a reply. The Ghanaian woman gave a cry of recognition and rushed away to family.

"Excuse me," I said, stepping into the man's line of sight. "I'm Marion Stone. For Our Lady of Perpetual Succour?"

"Marion is girl!" he said, his accent guttural and raw.

"Not this one," I said. "I'm named after Marion Sims, famous gynecologist?"

There was (according to the *Encyclopaedia Britannica*) a statue of Marion Sims in Central Park, at 103rd Street and Fifth Avenue. For all I knew, it was a landmark for taxis. Though Sims started off in Alabama, his success with fistula surgery brought him to New York City, where he opened the Woman's Hospital and then a cancer hospital, which later was named Memorial Sloan-Kettering.

"Gynecology should be woman!" he rasped, as if I'd broken a fundamental rule.

"Well, Sims wasn't and neither am I."

"You are not gynecologist?"

"No, I meant I'm not a woman. And yes, I'm not a gynecologist."

He was confused. *"Kis oomak,"* he said, at last. I knew enough Arabic to understand that he'd just invoked a gynecological term that made reference to my mother.

THE BLACK-SUITED DRIVERS led their passengers to sleek black cars, but my man led me to a big yellow taxi. In no time we were driving out of Kennedy Airport, heading to the Bronx. We merged at what I thought was dangerous speed onto a freeway and into the slipstream of racing vehicles. "Marion, jet travel has damaged your eardrums," I said to myself, because the silence was unreal. In Africa, cars ran not on petrol but on the squawk and blare of their horns. Not so here: the cars were near silent, like a school of fish. All I heard was the *whish* of rubber on concrete or asphalt.

Superorganism. A biologist coined that word for our giant African ant colonies, claiming that consciousness and intelligence resided not in the individual ant but in the collective ant mind. The trail of red taillights stretching to the horizon as day broke around us made me think of that term. Order and purpose must reside somewhere other than within each vehicle. That morning I heard the hum, the respiration, of the superorganism. It's a sound I believe that only the new immigrant hears, but not for long. By the time I learned to say "Six-inch number seven on rye with Swiss hold the lettuce," the sound, too, was gone. It became part of what the mind would label silence. You were now subsumed into the superorganism.

The silhouette of this most famous city—the twin exclamation marks at one end, King Kong's climbing toy in the middle—was familiar. Charles Bronson, Gene Hackman, Clint Eastwood, the Empire Theater, and Cinema Adowa had seen to that. My hubris was to think I understood America from such movies. But the real hubris I could see now was America's and it was hubris of scale. I saw it in the steel bridges stretching out over water; I saw it in the freeways looping over one another like tangled tapeworms. Hubris was my taxi's speedometer, wider than the steering wheel, as if Dali had grabbed the round gauge and pulled its ears. Hubris was the needle now showing seventy *miles* per hour, or well over one hundred and ten kilometers per hour, a speed unimaginable in our faithful Volkswagen—even if we'd found a suitable road.

What human language captures the dislocation, the acute insufficiency of being in the presence of the superorganism, the sinking, shrinking feeling at this display of industrial steel and light and might? It was as if nothing I'd ever done in my life prior to this counted. As if my past life was revealed to be a waste, a gesture in slow motion, because what I considered scarce and precious was in fact plentiful and cheap, and what I counted as rapid progress turned out to be glacially slow.

The observer, that old record keeper, the chronicler of events, made his appearance in that taxi. The hands of my clock turned elastic while I imprinted these feelings in memory. *You must remember this.* It was all I had, all I've ever had, the only currency, the only proof that I was alive.

Memory.

I WAS ALONE in my hemisection of Mr. K. L. Hamid's cab, my luggage next to me, and a scratched Plexiglas partition between us. Two strangers, isolated and distant, in a car so broad that the backseat alone could have held five humans and two sheep.

My muscles were tense because of our speed, worrying about a child drying cow patties on the hot tarmac or the cow or goat that surely would wander into the road. But I saw no animals, no humans except in cars.

Hamid's bullet-shaped head was covered with tight black swirls. On the laminated license next to the meter, the camera had caught his shock and surprise. The whites of his eyes showed. I convinced myself it was a picture taken on the day *he* landed in America, the day he saw and felt what I saw.

Which was why Hamid's discourtesy so wounded me. He wouldn't look my way. Perhaps when one has driven a taxi for a long time, the passenger becomes an object defined by destination and nothing else, just as (if one isn't careful) patients can become the "diabetic foot in bed two" or the "myocardial infarction in bed three."

Did Hamid think that if he looked I'd want his reassurance? Did he think I'd seek his explanation of every sight along the way so as to assuage my fears? He would have been right.

In that case, I said to myself, Hamid's silence must be instructive! An admonishment of sorts, the gentle warning of one who arrived on an earlier ship: *You there! Listen! Independence and resilience. This is what the new immigrant needs. Don't get fooled by all this activity. Don't invoke the superorganism. No, no. One functions alone in America. Begin now.* That was his message. That was the point of his rudeness: *Find your backbone, or be swallowed whole.*

I smiled now, relaxing, letting the scenery rush by. It was exhilarating to have arrived at this insight. I slapped the seat. I voiced my thoughts.

"Yes, Hamid. Screw your courage to the sticking place," I said aloud, invoking Ghosh, who never got to see what I was seeing, never heard the superorganism. How joyfully he would have embraced this experience.

Hamid jerked back at the sound of my voice. He glanced at me in the mirror, then away, then back again. Eye contact for the first time! Only now did he seem to acknowledge he was carrying something other than a sack of potatoes.

"Thank you, Hamid!" I said.

"What? What you say?"

"I said, 'thank you.' "

"No, before that!"

"Oh, that. It's Macbeth," I said, leaning forward to the Plexiglas, overeager for conversation. "*Lady* Macbeth, actually. My father used to say that to us all the time. 'Screw your courage to the sticking place.' "

He was silent, his gaze flitting from road to rearview mirror. Finally he burst out.

"You insult me?"

"Beg your pardon? No. No! I was merely talking to myself. It is as—"

"*Screw me?* Screw you!" he said.

My mouth fell open. Was it possible to be so completely misunderstood? His face in the mirror said indeed it was. I sank my neck back and shook my head in resignation. I had to laugh. To think that Ghosh—or Lady Macbeth—would be so misinterpreted.

Hamid still glared at me. I winked at him.

I saw him reach into the glove compartment. He pulled out a gun. He brandished it, showing me its different aspects through the dirty Plexiglas, as if he were trying to hawk it to me, or prove to me that it was in fact a gun, not a cheap plastic toy, which is what it looked like.

"You think I joke?" he said, a wicked energy taking over his face, as if the object in his hand made him not a joker but a philosopher.

I didn't mean to add fuel to the fire. I don't see myself as foolhardy or brave. But I found this little revolver pathetic and I simply didn't believe, indeed I was certain, he couldn't possibly use it. It was hilarious. I *knew* guns. I'd made a crater in a man's belly with one twice that size. I had buried gun and owner in a swamp (from which he still threatened to rise every night). Just four months ago, I had operated on rebels felled by guns. *This* popgun of his on this day, in the context of America, where cars stayed in lanes, where Customs never opened your bags, seemed like a prop, a cosmic joke. Could I not have had a proper *American* driver? Failing that, at least a gun that Dirty Harry wouldn't have been embarrassed to hold? Why escape Addis, flee Asmara, get out of Khartoum, and abandon Nairobi, only to face this?

Being the firstborn gives you great patience. But you reach a point where after trying and trying you say, *Patience be damned. Let them suffer their distorted worldview.* Your job is to preserve yourself, not to descend into their hole. It's a relief when you arrive at this place, the point of absurdity, because then you are free, you know you owe them nothing. I'd reached that point with Hamid. My body was shaking with laughter. Fatigue, jet lag, and disorientation contributed to my finding this so funny.

Hamid's use of the verb "screw" was quite different from screwing one's courage to the sticking place. His saying that word made me think of that story which had circulated when I had more pimples than common sense, more curiosity than sound sexual knowledge. It was the myth of the beautiful blonde and her brother whom one might meet at the airport when landing in America. They offered you a ride, took you home for a drink, at which point the brother brandished a weapon and said, "Screw my sister or you will die!" Long after I knew the story to be ridiculous, it retained its charm as a comic fantasy. *Screw my sister or you will die!* Here I was, well after the tale had slipped my mind, newly landed in America, and, sure enough, a man brandished a gun. I wished I could have shared the moment with Gaby, the schoolmate who first reported the story to me. A perverse impulse in me made me now repeat the phrase we schoolboys loved to say to each other, a challenge, a veiled threat, even though I was laughing hard: "Brother, put away the gun, I'll screw your sister for free." I don't know if he picked up the change in my tone and mood, or even if he heard me. Perhaps he just decided that my kind of lunacy wasn't to be toyed with. In any case, he had a change of heart.

THE WROUGHT-IRON GATES of Our Lady of Perpetual Succour were wide open. Dr. Abramovitz, the chief of surgery, was supposed to interview me at 10:00 a.m. My plan was to finish my interview, take another taxi to Queens, and *then* look for a hotel in which to get over my jet lag. I had interviews lined up in the next few days in Queens, Jersey City, Newark, and Coney Island.

A man with LOUIS embroidered on his blue overalls approached just as Hamid's taxi pulled out of the gate.

"Lou Pomeranz, Chief Caretaker of Our Lady of Perpetual Succour," he said, gripping my hand. A soft pack of Salems showed in his breast pocket. He was barrel-chested and top-heavy. "Do you play cricket?"

"Yes."

"Batsman or bowler?"

"Wicketkeeper and opening batsman." That was Ghosh's legacy to me.

"Good! Welcome to Our Lady. I hope you'll be happy," Mr. Pomeranz said. He thrust a sheaf of papers at me. "Here's your contract. I'll show you to the interns' quarters and you can sign. This silver key is for the main door. The gold key is for your room. This is your temporary identification badge. When Personnel take your mug shot, you'll get a permanent badge."

He took off with my suitcase and I followed. "But . . . ," I said, juggling the stuff in my hands to reach for the letter in my coat pocket. I showed it to him. "I don't want to mislead you. I am only here for my interview with Dr. Abramovitz."

"Popsy?" He chuckled. "Naw! Popsy don't interview no one. You see the signature?" He tapped on my letter as if it were a piece of wood. "That's really Sister Magda's writing." He looked back at me and grinned. "Interview? Forget about it. Taxi was prepaid. Cost you an arm and a leg otherwise. You're hired. I gave you the contract, didn't I? Yerhired!"

I didn't know what to say. It was Mr. Eli Harris of the Houston Baptists who suggested I apply to specific hospitals in New York and New Jersey for an internship in surgery. Eli Harris clearly knew what he was doing, because as soon as I applied, a telegram had arrived in Nairobi from Popsy (or perhaps it was from Sister Magda) inviting me to interview. A letter and brochure followed. Every hospital Harris suggested had also replied promptly, within a few days.

"Mr. Pomeranz. Are you sure I am hired? Your internship must be competitive. Surely many American medical students apply to be interns here?"

Louis stopped in his tracks to look at me. He laughed. "Ha! That's a good one, Doc. American medical students? I wouldn't know what they look like."

We rounded a dry fountain, streaked with pigeon droppings. It resembled the magnificent one depicted in the brochure, but the bronze monsignor who was the centerpiece leaned precariously forward. The monsignor's features were worn down like the sphinx's. Also not in the brochure was the iron rod wedged between the rim of the fountain and the monsignor's waist to keep him from falling over. It looked as if the monsignor was using his blessedly long phallus for support.

"Mr. Pomeranz—"

"I know. It does look like his pecker," he said, wheezing. "We're going to get around to it."

"That wasn't what—"

"Call me Louis."

"Louis . . . are you sure you have the right person? Marion? Marion Stone?"

He stopped. "Doc, take a look at the contract, wouldja?"

My name was on the top line.

"If that's who you are, that's who I was expecting."

A thought clouded his face. "You passed your ECFMG, didn't ya?"

The exam of the ECFMG—Educational Commission for Foreign Medical Graduates—established that I had the knowledge and credentials to pursue postgraduate training in America.

"Yes, I passed."

"So what gives? . . . Wait a minute. Wait just a minute. Don't tell me those bastards in Coney Island or Jersey got to you? Did they mail you a contract? Sons of bitches! I've been telling Sister Magda we should be doing that. Send out a contract sight unseen. The taxi was her idea, but it's not enough." He came up close to me. "Doc, let me tell you about those places. They're terrible." Louis was short of breath, his nostrils flaring. His rheumy eyes narrowed. "I'll tell you what," he said. "Give you the corner room in the interns' quarters. Has a small balcony. How's that?"

"No, no, you see—"

"Was it the Lincoln-Misericordia folks? Harlem? Newark? You shopping around to get the best deal?"

"No, I assure you—"

"Look, Doc, let's not play games. You just tell me yes or no, do you want an internship here?" His hands were on his hips, his chest heaving up and down.

"No, I mean yes . . . I *do* have interviews in other places . . . This is my first stop. But frankly . . . I thought it would be difficult to get an internship . . . I'd love to . . . *Yes!*"

"Good! Then sign the bleeding contract, for the love of Mary, and I'm not even Catholic."

I signed, standing by the fountain.

"Welcome to Our Lady, Doctor," Louis said, relieved, grabbing the contract and shaking my hand. He gestured expansively at the buildings around us. "This is the only place I've worked. My first job when I left the service . . . and probably my last. I've seen docs like you come and go. Oh, yeah. From Bombay, Poona, Jaipur, Ahmedabad, Karachi, you name it. Never had one from Africa before. I thought you'd look different. Let me tell you, we worked them all hard. But they gave us their best. They learned a lot here. I love 'em all. Love their food. They even got me to love cricket. I'm nuts about it. Listen, baseball has nothing on cricket. My boys are out there now," he said, pointing over the walls. "Raking in the dough in Kentucky or South Dakota—wherever they need docs bad. Dr. Singh sent me a plane ticket to fly to El Paso for his daughter's wedding. He comes to see me if he's in New York. We have an Old Boys Eleven that plays us every year. The Old Boys built us a new cricket pitch and batting nets. They're proud to be 'Pee Esses'—Perpetual Suckers is what we call our alums. They'll drive up here in fancy cars. I tell them, 'Don't put on airs for me. I remember when you didn't know your ass from your elbow. I remember when we could hardly understand a word you said. Now look at you!' "

I was impressed by what I could see of Our Lady of Perpetual Succour. The hospital was L-shaped, the long limb seven stories high, overlooking the street, a wall separating it from the sidewalk. The short limb was newer and just four stories high with a helicopter parked on top. The tiled roof of the older section sagged between the chimneys while the middle floors pushed out gently like love handles. The decorative grille under the eaves had oxidized to a bile green, old corrosion ran down the brick like mascara, parallel to the drainpipes. A lone gargoyle jutted out on one side of the entrance, its twin on the other side reduced to a faceless nub. But for me, fresh from Africa, these were not signs of decay, merely the dusting of history.

"It's grand," I said to Mr. Pomeranz.

"It's not much, but it's home," Mr. Pomeranz said, gazing at the building with obvious affection.

Undoubtedly, there were other hospitals that were newer and bigger, at least as depicted in their brochures. But you couldn't trust a brochure, I was discovering.

Fifty yards to the side of the hospital stood the two-story house staff quarters to which he led me. On the glass door to its lobby, someone had taped a handwritten sign in thick black felt-tip pen on yellow legal paper.

India Versus Australia, 2nd Test At Brisbane
Special Cable Viewing In B. C. Gandhi's Room

(Pakistanis, Sri Lankans, Bangladeshis, and West Indians welcome,
but if you cheer for Australia management reserves the right to eject you.)

Friday Night, July 11, 1980, 7 p.m.

($10 a person and bring drink and **non-veg** dish, repeat, non-veg dish only.
If it didn't move before it was cooked, we don't want it!!!
Single ladies free and chairs provided.
If you bring spouse, $10 extra and bring your own chair.)

B. C. Gandhinesan M.D.,
Captain Our Lady's Eleven,
Cricket Commissioner, Our Lady of Perpetual Succour

In the lobby I registered coriander, cumin—the familiar scents of Almaz's kitchen. On the stairs I inhaled the very brand of incense that Hema lit each morning. I heard the faint drone on the second-floor landing of "Suprabhatam" sung by M. S. Subbulakshmi and the sound of a bell being rung, as someone in some other room did their *puja*. I felt a twinge of homesickness. We paused for Mr. Pomeranz to get his breath. "We had to put industrial-size fans in the hoods above the cooking stoves on both floors. Had to! When they start cooking that *masala*, forget about it!"

A tall, good-looking Indian man with long hair still wet from the shower came bounding down the stairs. He had big strong teeth, a winning smile, and an aftershave that smelled simply wonderful. (I found out later it was Brut.)

"B. C. Gandhinesan," he said sticking out his hand.

"Marion Stone."

"Excellent! Call me B.C. or Gandhi," he said squeezing my hand. "Or call me Captain. Do you—?"

"Wicketkeeper," Pomeranz said, triumphantly. "And opening batsman."

B. C. Gandhi struck his forehead and staggered back. "God is great! Wonderful! Can you keep wickets for a pace bowler? A genuine fast bowler?"

"That's the kind I like best," I said.

"Smashing! I'm a fourth-year resident. Chief Resident–to–be next year. Deepak is our Chief Resident. I'm also captain of Our Lady's First Eleven. Winners of the interhospital trophy for two years. Until those *chutyas* from a residency program I shall not name brought in a batsman from Hyderabad last year. Test-level player. I lost big money on that. It took me all year to get out of debt."

"Jerks," Louis said, his face dark, referring I think to the other program. "They should have forfeited that last game."

"Turned out their star's a batsman all right, but not really a doctor," B.C. said. "The bugger was a photocopy expert. But on paper, by the statutes of New York, he was a doctor when we played, Lou. So we don't get our money back."

"Cocksuckers," Lou said. "They killed us."

"This year we have our own secret weapon," B.C. said to me, a consoling arm around Lou. "I personally flew to Trinidad with one of our Old Boys to recruit him. You'll meet him soon. Nestor. Tall, strong fellow. Six foot four. Fast bowler, new-ball bowler, seam bowler, body-line bowler. But none of us can keep wickets for him—ferocious pace. Now, with you, we will kill those *chutyas,* and the trophy will be ours. Go get some rest, Marion. We shall see you at batting practice in twenty-four hours."

CHAPTER 39

The Cure for
What Ails Thee

"PATIENT IS UNDER. What are we waiting for? Who is doing the case?" Dr. Ronaldo asked.

"I am," I said.

Ronaldo spun a dial on the anesthesia cart, as if this news mandated a change in the gas mixture.

"Deepak is supervising me," I offered, but Ronaldo ignored this.

Sister Ruth, the scrub nurse, unfolding her tray, shook her head. "I'm afraid not. Popsy just called. He wants to operate. Marion, you'd better come over to this side."

"Popsy! God help us," Dr. Ronaldo said, slapping his palm to his cheek. "Take the clock down. Call my wife, tell her I'll be late for dinner."

I picked up the scent of Brut and then Winston tobacco, and seconds later B. C. Gandhi was at my shoulder. He must have had a last drag in the locker room.

"I know. I heard," he said before I could say anything. "I'm doing that gallbladder in the next room. Listen, Marion. In case Deepak doesn't get here before Popsy, your job is to contaminate the old man as soon as he picks up the scalpel."

"What? How?"

"I don't know. Scratch your butt and touch his glove. You're a smart bugger. You'll think of something. Just don't let him get past skin, okay?" Gandhi walked off.

"Is he serious?" I asked.

Ronaldo said, "Gandhi is never serious. But he is right. Contaminate him."

I turned to Sister Ruth, hoping she could help.

"Pray for the intercession of Our Lady," she said. "And contaminate him."

IT WAS THE TWELFTH WEEK of my surgery internship at Our Lady of Perpetual Succour.

Little did I know that the thirty-minute drive from the airport to the Bronx would be the only glimpse of America I would have for three months.

After just a week in the hospital, I felt I'd left America for another country. My world was a land of fluorescent lights where day and night were the same, and where more than half the citizens spoke Spanish. When they spoke English it wasn't what I expected in the land of George Washington and Abraham Lincoln. The bloodlines from the *Mayflower* hadn't trickled down to this zip code.

Three months at Our Lady of Perpetual Succour had gone by at lightning speed. We were severely shorthanded, compared with the norm in other American hospitals, but I didn't know the norm. At Missing, there were only four or five doctors at the best of times; here we had three times that number of physicians in surgery alone. But at Our Lady of Perpetual Succour, we saw more patients. We kept so many complicated trauma patients alive on ventilators in the ICU, generated so many lab tests and so much paperwork, that the experience was completely different from Missing, where Ghosh or Hema rarely made more than a cryptic entry in the chart, leaving the rest to the nurses. I learned those quiet, long American cars, those floating living rooms on wheels, caused monstrous injuries when they crashed. The ambulance crews brought the victims to us before the tires on the wreck stopped spinning. They salvaged people we'd never see in Missing, because no one would have tried to bring them to a hospital. Judging someone to be beyond help never crossed the minds of police, firemen, or doctors here.

AT OUR LADY, we pulled every-other-night call. I had no time to be homesick. My typical day started in the early morning, when I made rounds with my team leader, B. C. Gandhi. Then my team and the other surgical teams came together to make formal rounds with Deepak Jesudass, the Chief Resident, at 6:30 a.m. On operating days, which were

Tuesdays and Fridays, we interns manned the wards and the emergency room. We worked till early evening. Then if I was on call, I simply worked on through the night admitting patients from the emergency room while caring for my existing patients and those of the interns who were not on call. Our chances to assist or even to operate as interns came when we were on call. It was rare to get any sleep on call nights. I didn't even try. The next day we kept going till the late afternoon, when I was finally off. For my off night all I could do was fall on the bed in my quarters and sink into a deep sleep. The next morning, the cycle started again. My senior resident, B. C. Gandhi, asked me late one night when we were both punch-drunk from lack of sleep, "Do you know the *disadvantage* of every-other-night call?" It was an imponderable question. I shook my head. He smiled and said, "You miss half the interesting patients."

The schedule was brutal, dehumanizing, exhausting.

I loved it.

At midnight, when the corridors became deserted, there were places in the hospital where the lights dimmed and where I could see traces of Our Lady of Perpetual Succour's past glory; it showed in the gold filigree work above the archways, in the high ceilings of the old maternity wing, in the marble floor of the administrative foyer, and the stained-wood cupola of the chapel. Once the pride of a rich Catholic community, and then a middle-class Jewish community, Our Lady of Perpetual Succour went the way of the neighborhood: it became poor in catering to the poor. B. C. Gandhi explained it to me: "The poorest in America are the sickest. Poor people can't afford preventive care or insurance. The poor don't see doctors. They show up at our doorstep when things are advanced."

"Who pays for all this, then?" I asked.

"The government pays with Medicaid and Medicare, from your taxes."

"How come we can afford a helicopter and a helipad if we're so poor?" The bull's-eye atop the newer four-story part of Our Lady, with the blue flashing perimeter lights and the shiny helicopter that came and went, seemed incongruous for our setting.

"*Salah,* you don't know about our claim to fame? Our number one industry? Sometimes I forget you just got off the boat. Man, that helipad was paid for by hospitals that are the opposite of ours. The helicopter is really theirs, not ours. Rich hospitals. Taking care of the wealthy, the insured. Even if some of them take care of the poor, they have a big university or a university private practice to underwrite their costs. *That* kind of 'taking care of the poor' is noble."

"And our kind of taking care?"

"Shameful. The work of untouchables. Those rich hospitals up and down the East Coast got together and paid for our helipad so they can fly here. Why? Ischemia time! You see, what we have here in our neighborhood is an abundance of guns, ABMs, and ALMs—Angry Black Males, Angry Latin Males, and actually angry males of all stripes, not to mention jealous females. The man on the street is more likely to carry a gun than a pen. Bang! Bang! Chitty! Chitty! And so we wind up with too many GPO patients—Good for Parts Only. Young, otherwise healthy, but brain-dead. Pristine hearts, livers, and whatnot. Under warranty to keep going long after your pecker droops. Great organs. Great for transplant. Transplants which we can't do. But we can keep them alive till the vultures get here. They get the organ and run. Next time you hear the *whup-whup-whup*, don't think helicopter blades. Think *paysa,* moola, *dinero*! Heart transplant costs, what, half a million dollars? Kidneys a hundred thousand or more?"

"That's how much they pay us?"

"*Us?* They don't pay us a fucking cent! That's how much *they* make. They come, cut, and take, show us the middle finger, and ride off in their whirlybird leaving us on our camels. Next time you hear the helicopter, come see what masters of medicine, the sahibs, look like."

I *had* seen them more than once, their white coats emblazoned with vivid university logos on breast and shoulder, and the same icons on ice chests, on the igloos on wheels, and even on the helicopter. I saw in their faces the same variety of fatigue that I experienced, but theirs somehow seemed more noble.

DR. RONALDO CROSSED and uncrossed his arms, looking at the clock, then the door, for any sign of Popsy. I draped the sterile towels to outline a perfect rectangle, the portal to Hugh Walters Jr.'s abdomen.

Mr. Walters, a graying gentleman, showed up in our emergency room the week before. That particular night, stretchers spilled out of the ER's trauma bays into hallways. Alcohol had leached out of the lungs, out of skin pores, out of the secretions of enough men and women to make the place smell like a cocktail lounge. There were two inebriated men vomiting blood, competing to see who could be louder. When Mr. Walters arrived, also vomiting blood, I unfairly assumed he was one of their kin, related through alcohol and cirrhosis. I assumed that his bleeding came from wormlike varicose veins blooming in his stomach from the scarring in the liver. Over the course of the next twenty-four hours, I slipped a gastroscope down each bleeder's throat and peered into the stomach. Unlike the other two, Mr. Walters had none of the angry redness of alcoholic gastritis, and no bleeding varicose veins to suggest cirrhosis. What he did have was a large oozing gastric ulcer. I took biopsies through the scope.

A few hours after the endoscopy, Mr. Walters, in a quiet dignified voice, again assured me that alcohol had never crossed his lips, and this time I believed him. He was a man of the cloth. He taught junior high school for a living. I chastised myself for lumping him in with the other two stomach bleeders. We started intense therapy to heal his ulcer.

Mr. Walters, I found, knew about my birth land. "When Kennedy died, I watched that funeral on TV. Your Emperor Haile Selassie came all the way. He was the shortest man there. But also the biggest man there. The only Emperor. The *only* Emperor. He was in the first row of dignitaries walking behind that coffin. He made me proud to be *bl–ack*." When Mr. Walters said the word, he gave it a weight and a heft.

Mr. Walters read the *New York Times* every day. That and a Bible were a constant at his bedside. "I could never afford college. Just Bible school. I tell my students, 'If you read this newspaper every day for a year, you'll have the vocabulary of a Ph.D. and you will know more than any college graduate. I guarantee you.' "

"Do they listen?"

He held up a finger. "Every year *one* does," he said, grinning. "But that one makes it worthwhile. Even Jesus only did twelve. I try to get one a year."

Despite antacids and H_2 blockers, Mr. Walters's ulcer was still bleeding. His stools remained the consistency and color of tar, a sure sign of blood being acted on by stomach acid. Five days after his admission, our troop had gathered at his bed during evening sign-out rounds.

Deepak Jesudass, our Chief Resident, sat on the edge of Mr. Walters's bed. "Mr. Walters, we have to operate tomorrow. Your ulcer is still bleeding. It isn't showing signs of stopping." He sketched out on a piece of paper what a partial gastrectomy would look like—removal of the acid-producing area of his stomach. I admired Deepak's quiet careful manner, his way of being with patients that made them feel they were the focus of all his attention and that there was nowhere else he had to be. Most of all I admired his wonderful, very British accent, which seemed doubly exotic in that it came from a South Asian man. It was the result of his having lived in Britain for years. Deepak inspired confidence in patients.

As Deepak spoke, B. C. Gandhi looked at me and rolled his eyes. He was reminding me of something he'd told me just the previous night. "You can be a cretin, but if you have the Queen's accent, next thing you know you are on Johnny Carson and he'll laugh at anything you say."

B.C. was being facetious, but on the sitcoms I caught while going in and out of patients' rooms, I had so far seen a black but *very* British butler serving a black American family; an eccentric Englishman who was the neighbor to a rich black family on the Upper East Side of Manhattan; and a rich British widower with a pretty Brooklyn nanny.

Mr. Walters had hung on Deepak's every word. At last he'd said, "I have faith in you. But for you-all, there wouldn't be any doctors here. I have faith in someone else, too," he said, pointing to the ceiling.

The day of surgery, I rose at four-thirty to review the steps of the operation in my *Zollinger's Surgical Atlas*. Deepak had let me know that it was my case, and I would stand on the right while he assisted me. I was thrilled and nervous. It would be my first time to work directly with the Chief Resident.

But Popsy had ruined our plans. I stood on the patient's left, awaiting the legendary Dr. Abramovitz. I had yet to meet him. There was no sign of Deepak.

AND SUDDENLY POPSY WAS THERE, his head perilously close to the operative lights. He had a deeply furrowed face, kind blue eyes, the pupils rimmed with gray but retaining a curious, little-boy quality. His mask hung just under his nose, wire-brush hairs poking out from his nostrils. He held out his gloved hand for the knife. Sister Ruth hesitated, glancing at me before putting it in his palm.

Popsy made a sound in his throat. The scalpel quivered in his fingers. Sister Ruth nudged me. Before I could do anything, Popsy made his incision. It was bold. *Very* bold. I dabbed and I clamped tiny bleeding vessels, and when Popsy didn't move to tie them off, I did. Popsy handled the forceps to pick up the peritoneum. He couldn't get purchase on the tissue.

For good reason. In one spot his skin incision had cut through fascia and peritoneum. Liquid matter, looking suspiciously like bowel content, welled into the wound. Ronaldo peered over the anesthesia screen and his eyebrows disappeared under his surgical cap.

Popsy tried again with the forceps, but the instrument slipped from his fingers and clattered to the floor. He brought his hand up, minus the forceps. "I touched the side of the table . . ." He was looking at me, as if I might dispute his account. "I've contaminated myself."

"I think you did," Sister Ruth said hastily when she saw that I was tongue-tied.

"You did, sir," Ronaldo said.

But Popsy still looked at me.

"Yes, sir," I stammered.

"Carry on," he said. He shuffled out of the room.

"Popsy, what did you do?" Deepak muttered under his mask as he brought out the injured loop of small intestine. I stayed on the left side of the table. "They say there are old surgeons, and bold surgeons, but no old-bold surgeons. But whoever said that never met Popsy. Fortunately it's a small-bowel tear and we can just stitch it over."

"I tried to—" I stammered.

"We have a bigger problem," Deepak said. He pointed to what looked like a small barnacle on the surface of the bowel. Once I saw that first one, I saw them everywhere, even on the apron of fat that covered the bowel. The liver was misshapen, with three ominous bumps within making it look like a hippo's head.

"Poor man," Deepak said. "Feel his stomach." The stomach wall was rock hard. "Marion, you biopsied the ulcer when you 'scoped him, right?"

"Yes. The report said benign," I said.

"But this was a large ulcer on the greater curvature?"

"Yes."

"And which ulcers in the stomach are more likely to be malignant?"

"Those on the greater curvature."

"So your suspicion for malignancy was high, right? Did you look at the slides with the pathologist?"

"No, sir," I said, dropping my eyes.

"I see. You trusted the pathologist to read the biopsies for you?"

I said nothing.

Deepak's voice wasn't raised. He could have been talking about the weather. Dr. Ronaldo couldn't hear him.

Deepak explored the pelvis, swept with his fingers to those places we could not see. Finally he said, almost under his breath, "Marion, when it's *your* patient and you are basing your surgery on a biopsy, be sure to look at the slides with the pathologist. Particularly if the result isn't what you expect. Don't go by the report."

I felt terrible for Mr. Walters. I could have spared him this operation, spared him Popsy. In retrospect, Mr. Walters's liver function tests were marginally off, and that should have been a clue.

Deepak repaired the hole in the bowel. Fortunately, there was just one. He oversewed the bleeding ulcer in the stomach; it would in time bleed again. We washed out the abdominal cavity with several liters of saline, pouring it in, then suctioning it out.

"Okay, come to this side, Marion. I want you to close."

I worked steadily under his eagle eye.

"Stop," Deepak said. He cut away the knot I had tied. "I know you have probably done a lot of surgery in Africa. But practice doesn't make perfect if you repeat a bad practice. Let me ask you something, Marion . . . Do you want to be a good surgeon?"

I nodded.

"The answer isn't an automatic yes. Ask Sister Ruth. In my time here, I've asked that question of a few others." I could feel my ears turning red. "They say yes, but some should have said no. They didn't know themselves. You see, you can be a bad surgeon, and as a rule you will make more money. Marion, I must ask you again, do you really want to be a *good* surgeon?"

I looked up.

"I guess I should ask what does it involve?"

"Good. You *should* ask. To be a good surgeon, you need to *commit* to being a good surgeon. It's as simple as that. You need to be meticulous in the small things, not just in the operating room, but outside. A good surgeon would want to redo this knot. You're going to tie thousands of knots in your lifetime. If you tie each one as well as humanly possible, you'll experience fewer complications. I want to see even tension on both limbs. The last thing you want is for Mr. Walters to have a burst abdomen when he gets post-op bloating. That knot, done well, may allow him to go home and get things in order. Done poorly it could keep him in hospital with one complication after another till he dies. The big things in surgery depend on the little things."

That afternoon we sat in the cramped office of Dr. Ramuna, the pathologist. She found cancer in the edge of one of the six biopsies I had taken days ago. A stern lady, Dr. Ramuna had a way of pursing her lips that reminded me of Hema. She was unfazed about having missed the cancer the first time. She pointed to the teetering stack of cardboard slide trays by her microscope—biopsies waiting to be read. "I'm doing the work of four pathologists, but I'm only here half-time. Our Lady can't afford more than that. But they don't give me half the work. I can't spend enough time with each specimen. Of course I missed it! No one comes down here to go over slides with me, other than you, Deepak. They call. 'Have you read this specimen yet? Have you read that specimen?' If it matters to you, come down, I say. Give me good clinical information and I can do a better job of interpreting what I see."

I KEPT VIGIL over Mr. Walters. We had passed a tube through his nose into his stomach and connected it to wall suction, to keep his gut empty for the next few days. He was miserable with the tube and hardly spoke.

On the third post-op day I took out the nasogastric tube. He sat up, smiled for the first time, taking a deep breath through his nose.

"That tube is the Devil's own instrument. If you gave me all of Haile Selassie's riches, I'd still say no to that tube."

I took my own deep breath. I sat on the edge of his bed. I held his hand. "Mr. Walters, I'm afraid I have some bad news. We found something unexpected in your belly." This was the first time in America that I had to give someone news of a fatal illness, but it felt like the first time ever. It was as if in Ethiopia, and even in Nairobi, people assumed that all illness—even a trivial or imagined one—was fatal; they expected death. The news to convey in Africa was that you'd kept death at bay. Those things that you couldn't do, and those diseases you couldn't reverse, were left unspoken. It was understood. I don't recall an equivalent word for "prognosis" in Amharic, and I'd never tried to speak to a patient about five-year survival or anything like that. In America, my initial impression was that death or the possibility of it always seemed to come as a surprise, as if we took it for granted that we were immortal, and that death was just an option.

Mr. Walters's expression went from joy over the tube being out, to shock, and finally sadness. A single tear trickled down his cheek. My gaze turned foggy. My beeper went off, but I ignored it.

I don't think you can be a physician and not see yourself reflected in your patient's illness. How would I deal with the kind of news I'd given Mr. Walters?

After a few minutes, he wiped his face with his sleeve. A smile cracked his features. He patted my hand.

"Death is the cure of all disease, isn't it? No one is prepared for news like this, no matter what. I'm sixty-five years old. An old man. I have had a good life. I want to meet my Lord and Savior." A mischievous light flashed in his eye. "But not just yet," he said, holding up a finger and laughing, a slow metronomic sound, *heh-heh-heh* . . .

I found myself smiling with him.

"We always want more, *heh-heh-heh*," he said. "Ain't that the truth, Dr. Stone? Lord, I'm a-coming. Not just yet. I'll be right there, now. You go on, Lord. I'll catch up with you."

I admired Mr. Walters. I wanted to learn to be this way, to possess his steady rhythm, to have that inner beat playing quietly inside me.

"You see, young Dr. Marion, that's what makes us human. We always want more." He clasped my hand now, as if *he* was ministering to me, as if *I* had come to sit on his bed for reassurance, courage, and faith. "Now you go on. I know you're busy. Everything's just fine. Just fine. I just got to think this one out."

I left him smiling at me, as if I had given him the greatest gift one man could ever give another.

CHAPTER 40

Salt and Pepper

A FTER LEAVING MR. WALTERS'S ROOM, I sat on the park bench by the house staff quarters. How unfair to Mr. Walters that his darkest day should be so impossibly beautiful. The trees of Our Lady turned colors I had never seen in Africa. And then they blessed the ground below with a fiery red, orange, and yellow carpet, which crunched underfoot and released a dry but sweet fragrance.

The laughter and shrieks coming from inside our building, from the patio, felt sacrilegious. B. C. Gandhi had christened our quarters "Our Mistress of Perpetual Fornication." There were days when I felt I lived in Sodom.

When it turned chilly, I went inside. I caught a glimpse of the roaring wood fire in the cast-iron pot on the patio, and the scent of tobacco and something more pungent. Nestor, our Carribean fast bowler and my fellow intern, had a herb garden at the back of our building. The summer we arrived he grew a bumper crop of curry leaves, tomatoes, sage—and cannabis.

Beyond the herb garden the meadow sloped down to a brick fence topped with razor wire. It separated us from a housing project named Friendship by the city authorities twenty years ago. It was now called Battleship by one and all. At night we heard the pop of handguns from Battleship and saw comet streaks, messages from earth to sky.

On Mondays we gathered at the nurses' quarters for a communal dinner at their invitation. But on this day it was their turn to visit us. I joined the crowd.

"How did it go?" B.C. said, coming over, putting his arm around my shoulders. I told him about my conversation with Mr. Walters.

B.C. listened quietly, and then said, "What a good man he is! What courage. You know, we've been lucky with Mr. Walters, particularly since he's a zero-to-one dirtballer. What's a dirt ball? The hard, stinky concretion that forms in the belly button. A patient with four dirt balls is often an alcoholic. He's had one or two heart attacks. Beats his wife. He's been shot a couple of times. He has diabetes. Kidney function is borderline. You try a BFO for a Triple A, guess what happens?"

"BFO" was Big Fucking Operation, and "Triple A" was Abdominal Aortic Aneurysm. B.C. loved acronyms and claimed to have invented a good many of them. A patient near death was CTD—Circling The Drain.

"A four dirtballer? . . . I guess he does terribly with a big operation?" I offered.

"No! Just the opposite. You see, he's already demonstrated his capacity to survive. Heart attacks, strokes, stabbings, falls off buildings—his protoplasm is resilient. Lots of collateral vessels, backup mechanisms. He waltzes out of the recovery room, farts the first night, pees on the floor trying to get to the bathroom, and does great despite the bourbon the family sneaks in to add flavor to the ice chips, which are all he's supposed to eat.

"The zero-to-one dirtballers are the ones to watch out for. They are your preachers or doctors. Men like Walters. They live good clean lives, stay married to the same woman, raise their kids, go to church on Sundays, watch their blood pressure, don't eat ice cream. You try a BFO for a Triple A and you will be CDSCWP."

Canoeing Down Shit Creek Without a Paddle.

"As soon as the anesthesiologist brings the mask near their face, your zero dirtballer has a heart attack on the goddamn table. If you manage to operate, the kidneys conk out or the wound breaks down. Or they get confused, and before you can call the Freud Squad they've jumped out of the window. So you see, your Mr. Walters was lucky."

Deepak took a drag on a cigar-size joint that Nestor passed to him. He handed it to me. "Here," he said, holding the smoke in, and speaking in a clipped voice. "The point is . . . clean living will kill you, my friend."

The cannabis did nothing for my fatigue. Soon I felt my face and body turn to wax. I stared into the sky above Battleship. The sounds—good-natured yelling, screams, the throb of a boom box, the clang of a basketball rattling the metal rim, the squeal of tires—were a symphony. They matched the chiaroscuro designs on the brick wall. I felt I could see into Battleship and that I was watching the lives of the hundreds of Americans living there, families who got their medical care from us. I felt like a visionary.

"Doesn't it seem strange," I said, after a long while, struggling to frame my question so it wouldn't sound silly, "doesn't it seem strange that . . . here we all are, foreign doctors—"

"You mean *Indian* doctors," Gandhi said. "You're half Indian, but luckily for you it's the pretty half. Even Nestor here has an Indian father, he just doesn't know it."

Nestor threw a bottle cap at Gandhi.

"Yes, well, doesn't it seem strange," I went on, "that here we are, a hospital full of *Indian* doctors and on the other side of that wall are the patients we are taking care of. *American* patients, but not representative of—"

"You mean *black* patients, mon," Nestor said in his lilting accent. "And you mean Puerto Ricans."

"Yes . . . but what I am getting at is where are the *other* American patients? Where are the other American doctors for that matter?"

"You mean where are the white patients? Where are the white doctors, mon?"

"Yes!" I said. "Precisely!"

"Look here, Marion," Gandhi said. "You mean to say you hadn't noticed this fact till just this moment?"

"No . . . I mean, yes, I have. Don't be silly. But my question is, are all hospitals in America like this?"

"My goodness, Marion, you do understand why you are here and not at the Mass General?"

"Because . . . I didn't apply there."

I was unprepared for the laughter that greeted me. Just when I thought I was on to something profound.

Nestor got up and jogged in place. He chanted, "Heenot not apply there! Heenot not apply there!" The cannabis seemed to facilitate their hysterical giggles, but it was doing nothing for me. I was getting angry. I rose to leave.

Gandhi grabbed my arm. "Marion, sit down. Wait. Of course you didn't apply," he said soothingly. "You didn't want to waste your time on the Massachusetts General Hospital."

I still didn't get it.

"See here," he said, taking a saltshaker and pepper shaker and putting them side by side. "This pepper shaker is *our* kind of hospital. Call it a—"

"Call it a shit hole, mon," said Nestor.

"No, no. Let's call it an Ellis Island hospital. Such hospitals are always in places where the poor live. The neighborhood is dangerous. Typically such hospitals are *not* part of a medical school. Got it? Now take this saltshaker. That is a Mayflower hospital, a flagship hospital, the teaching hospital for a big medical school. All the medical students and interns are in super white coats with badges that say SUPER MAYFLOWER DOCTOR. Even if they take care of the poor, it's honorable, like being in the Peace Corps, you know? Every American medical student dreams of an internship in a Mayflower hospital. Their worst nightmare is coming to an Ellis Island hospital. Here's the problem—who is going to work in hospitals like ours when there is a bad neighborhood, no medical school, no prestige? No matter how much the hospital or even the government is willing to pay, they won't find full-time doctors to work here.

"So Medicare decided *to pay* hospitals like ours for internship and residency *training* programs, get it? It's a win-win, as they say—the hospital gets patients cared for by interns and residents around the clock, people like us who live on site, and whose stipend is a bloody fraction of what the hospital would pay full-time physicians. And Medicare delivers health care to the poor.

"But when Medicare came up with this scheme, it created a new problem. Where do you get your interns to fill all these new positions? There are many more internship positions available than there are graduating American medical students. American students have their pick, and let me tell you, they don't want to come and be interns here. Not when they can go to a Mayflower hospital. So every year, Our Lady and all the Ellis Island hospitals look for foreign interns. You are one of hundreds who came as part of this annual migration that keeps hospitals like ours going."

B.C. sat back in his chair. "Whatever America needs, the world will supply. Cocaine? Colombia steps to the plate. Shortage of farmworkers, corn detasselers? Thank God for Mexico. Baseball players? Viva Dominica. Need more interns? India, Philippines *zindabad!*"

I felt stupid for not having seen this before. "So the hospitals where I was going to interview," I said. "In Coney Island, Queens—"

"All Ellis Island hospitals. Just like us. *All* the house staff are foreigners and so are many of the attending physicians. Some are all Indian. Some have more of a Persian flavor. Others are all Pakistani or all Filipino. That's the power of word of mouth. You bring your cousin who brings his classmate and so on. And when we finish training here, where do we go, Marion?"

I shook my head. I didn't know.

"*Anywhere.* That's the answer. We go to the small towns that need us. Like Toejam, Texas, or Armpit, Alaska. The kinds of places American doctors won't go and practice."

"Why not?"

"Because, *salah,* in those villages there's no symphony! No culture! No pro-ball team! How is an American doctor supposed to live there?"

"Is that where you will go, B.C.? To a small town?" I said.

"Are you kidding? You expect me to live without a symphony? Without the Mets or the Yankees? No, sir. Gandhi is staying in New York. I am Bombay born and Bombay bred, and what is New York but Mumbai Lite? I'll have my office on Park Avenue. You see, there is a crisis in health care on Park Avenue. The citizens are suffering because their breasts are too small or their nose is too big, or they have a roll around the belly. Who will be there for them?"

"You will?"

"Fucking right, boys and girls. Hold on, ladies, hold on! Gandhi is coming. B.C. will make it smaller, bigger, softer, cuter, whatever you want, but always better."

He held his beer aloft. "A toast! Ladies and gentlemen. *May no American venture out of this world without a foreign physician at his or her side, just as I am sure there are none who venture in.*"

CHAPTER 41

One Knot at a Time

ONE AFTERNOON, in my ninth month at Our Lady of Perpetual Succour, as we were on our way to the operating room, a bailiff served Deepak Jesudass with papers. My Chief Resident took them without comment, and we went on with our work. Well after midnight, as we sat in the locker room outside the theater and smoked, he smiled at me and said, "Anyone else would have asked me what the papers were about."

"You'll tell me if it concerns me," I said.

Deepak was perhaps thirty-seven when I met him. He had a youthful face and boyish shoulders that belied the bags under his eyes and the gray streaks in his hair. Had you seen us all in the cafeteria, you would have guessed B. C. Gandhi was the Chief Resident, because B.C. looked the part. But when I reflect back on my surgical training, I'm indebted to a small, dark man, a self-effacing surgeon whom the world might never celebrate. In the operating room, Deepak was patient, forceful, brilliant, creative, painstaking, and decisive—a true artisan.

"Don't stutter with that needle holder." "Self-discipline with those hands, Marion. Do each step just once, no wasted motion." When I learned to cross my hands the way he suggested to get equal tension on both limbs of the knot, a new problem arose: "Keep your elbows in, unless you're trying to fly." I redid more knots than I tied when I was with him. I took down entire suture lines and started again till he was satisfied. I gave new thought to light and exposure. "Working in the dark is for moles. We are surgeons." His advice was sometimes counterintuitive: "When you are driving, you look to see where you are going, but when you are making an incision, you look to see where you have been."

Deepak was from Mysore in southern India. That night in the locker room, he told me what I don't think he had told anyone else at Our Lady. When he graduated from medical school, his parents hastily arranged a marriage to a British-born Indian girl living in Birmingham; she'd been a reluctant bride, bullied into marriage by her parents who didn't like the crowd she was hanging around with. She flew down with her family a few days before the wedding and left the day after, because she was attending college. It took six months for Deepak to get his visa and join her at her parents' home. He found that if he opened his mouth he embarrassed her. She didn't want him near her in public or private. He left the house after a few weeks and found a house-officer position (equivalent to the internship in America) in Scotland. After a year he advanced to registrar, then to senior registrar. He passed the difficult exams to become a Fellow of the Royal College of Surgeons, the magic letters FRCS behind his name.

"I could have gone back to Mysore. With my FRCS up on a board, I would have done very well. But I pictured all the people who'd come to my wedding. I didn't want to face them . . . I just couldn't."

The next step for him in England would have been to be a surgical consultant appointed to a hospital. "There aren't many consultant jobs. Someone has to die for an opening to come up." After six years of working as a senior registrar, a consultant's understudy, doing all the emergency cases, Deepak decided to come to America.

"It meant starting all over again, because here you don't get credit for postgraduate training anywhere else. At my age, and after all the years of training, I wondered if I had it in me."

The American system of surgical training was different: after a year of internship and then four years as a surgical resident with ever increasing responsibilities (the last year as Chief Resident), one was allowed to sit for the exam to become a board-certified surgeon, a consultant.

"I did my internship in a prestigious place in Philadelphia. I worked hard for them . . ." He closed his eyes and shook his head at the memory. "When my father died, I didn't even tell them. I didn't even try to take one day off for that. I was promoted to second year, even though I was performing at a much higher level, and they actually used me almost like a Chief Resident. But they bumped me after the third year. One of my attending physicians who went to bat for me wound up resigning over this. He was so incensed.

"I could have gone into urology or plastic. That's what people often do if they're bumped at that stage. Many foreign graduates give up and wind up in psychiatry or something. But I love general surgery. The same guy who went to bat for me got me into another hospital, this time in Chicago, with the promise that I'd be promoted if I repeated my third year. I worked even harder—and got bumped again." He laughed at my expression of incredulity. "It helps to be me, I suppose. To not expect too much. To love surgery for its own sake. But I was lucky. One of the attending physicians in Chicago went out on a limb for me. He called Popsy, and he arranged for me to come here as a fourth-year resident. That's the funny thing about America—the *blessed* thing. As many people as there are to hold you back, there are angels whose humanity makes up for all the others. I've had my share of angels. Popsy was one of those."

Popsy made Deepak Chief Resident overnight, but with the proviso that he be Chief Resident for two years. Deepak was in his last year of training when I arrived.

"So you will be done the same day I finish my internship?"

His silence made me anxious.

Slowly he shook his head.

"We got notice today of a site visit soon from the people who accredit our residency training program. If they don't like what they see, they can shut us down. We've got too few interns. And too few resident physicians at every level for the patient volume we handle. Not to mention too few faculty."

"How did this happen?"

"Our competition is sweetening the pot. We were lucky to get you and Nestor and Rahul. We need more interns, more full-time faculty. Popsy just isn't as influential as he once was to attract good faculty. At this point, it's only Popsy's credentials and academic history that give our program accreditation. On paper, Popsy is golden. If Popsy steps down, or word gets out that he has early dementia, the house of cards falls."

I must have looked concerned because he said, "Don't worry. You'll be able to find another slot and get credit for this year."

"Is that what it is about—the bailiff serving you papers?"

"Oh, that's my so-called wife. Now she thinks I must be making a lot of money so she is filing in New York for spousal support. I have a lawyer who tells me that I have nothing to worry about. I owe her nothing."

"What about you, Deepak? What will you do if this place closes?"

"I don't know, Marion. I can't go through this again. Can't keep assisting someone who is my 'senior' but is butchering the case and doesn't have the sense to ask me to help. Maybe I'll just keep on working here. Sister Magda says the hospital will employ me. I'll live here, just like Popsy lives here. I'll operate. The hospital doesn't care if I am board certified or not, particularly if the residency program closes. Our Lady needs a surgeon. I'll be another Popsy. Believe it or not, Popsy, till his breakdown, was a super surgeon," Deepak said. "What's more important, he was a fine man. Truly color-blind."

After Mr. Walters's surgery, Deepak had spread the word that Popsy was not to operate anymore at any cost.

"Is there anything we can do to keep them from shutting us down?" I asked Deepak.

"Pray," he said.

CHAPTER 42

Bloodlines

I PRAYED, BUT IT DIDN'T HELP. With two months to go to finish my internship and for Deepak to finish his Chief Residency, our program was placed on probation. I worried about my fate. It was bad enough that we might be closed down, but it would be worse not to get credit for the year I'd put in. I felt terrible for Deepak, who had come so close to finishing his Chief Resident year. Until our appeal was heard, though, and the final order came to shut us down, there was little to do but plod on.

On a Friday evening, I was summoned to the trauma room, and I reached there just as the ambulance roared in. The crew slid out a stretcher, snapped its wheels down, then raced in with it as if it were a battering ram. The glass doors parted just in time. I thought of these things as minor miracles, everyday efficiencies that were such a contrast to what I'd known in Africa. I jogged alongside. After almost a year at Our Lady, I'd done this many times, but the adrenaline still surged.

"John Doe, MVA, barely breathing at the scene," one of the men pushing the stretcher said. "Ran a red light, got broadsided by a van on driver's side. No seatbelt—went airborne through windshield . . . Then, if you can believe this, his own car, spinning around, slammed into his body. Fly ball to centerfield . . . Kid you not. Eyewitnesses. He landed on the pavement. No obvious neck injuries. Left ankle shattered . . . bruises on chest and belly." I saw a handsome black male, clean-cut and no older than twenty.

The ambulance crew had two bags of intravenous saline going wide open. They had drawn blood, and now they handed over the red-, blue-, and lavender-topped tubes to the lab technician, who would begin typing and cross matching for blood before we'd even cut off the patient's clothes.

"There's more to this," the ambulance driver said. "Reason he ran the red light is because he was in a gunfight with gangbangers. One of them got shot in the head. An ambulance is on its way with that guy. Don't worry . . . it ain't no emergency. They had to scoop parts of his brain off the sidewalk—kindergarten through fifth grade from the looks of it. This guy," he said, pointing to our patient, "did the shooting."

Our patient's skull was intact, but he was unconscious. The part buzzed into his short hair was as straight as if it had been applied with a ruler. It was one of the strange things one noticed at such times. His pupils constricted briskly to the light I shone at them, a crude but reassuring sign that his brain was all right. His pulse was thready and racing under my fingers. The monitor read one hundred sixty beats a minute.

A nurse called out the pressure. "Eighty over nothing." A few seconds later she said, "Fifty over zero."

Fluids were pouring in, blood was on its way. There was a bruise over the lower right ribs. His belly was tense and it seemed to be swelling under my eyes.

"No pressure," the nurse announced just as the X-ray technician arrived with the portable machine.

"No time for this. He's exsanguinating," I said. "Let's take him to the operating room. It's his only chance."

Nobody moved.

"*Now!*" I said, giving the stretcher a push. "Call my backup, let them know."

In the operating room, I scrubbed for just thirty seconds, while Dr. Ronaldo, the anesthetist, adjusted the tracheal tube. Ronaldo looked at me and shook his head.

I pulled on my gloves while looking at what the scrub nurse had laid out.

"Forget sponges. Let's get lap packs. Open them out. We won't have time to unfold them. There is going to be so much blood. We'll need big basins to hold the clots."

The patient's belly was more tense than it had been downstairs.

Ronaldo, peering crocodilelike above his mask, shrugged when I looked at him for the signal to start.

"Get ready," I said to Ronaldo, " 'cause when I open, the pressure is going to bottom out."

"What pressure?" Ronaldo said. "No pressure."

For now, the blood expanding the belly was serving as a compress, tamping off the bleeding vessel wherever it was. But the moment I opened the belly, the geyser would open again. I layered pads all around. I poured Betadine over the skin, swabbed it off, said a prayer, and cut.

Blood welled out, spilled over the edge of the wound like a storm surge. Despite all the pads, despite my suction hose sucking greedily, the blood lapped over the drapes, onto the table, and splashed to the floor. I felt it soak through my gown, felt it on my thighs, in my socks, my feet squishing in my shoes.

"More packs!" I'd tried to warn the nurses, but we were still unprepared for the torrent.

I reached in with my hand, displacing a second wave of blood as I grabbed the small bowel. With two hands now, I pulled loops out, fed them onto a towel by the side of the incision. In seconds I had effectively disemboweled the patient.

Deepak appeared across from me, scrubbed and ready. I clasped my hands together, stepped back to cross to the other side of the table, but he shook his head.

"Stay there," he said. He grabbed a retractor and pulled so I could see under the diaphragm.

I stuffed the lap packs all around the liver. Then I did the same on the left side, in the vicinity of the spleen. With cupped fingers, I scooped out the big clots that remained in the abdominal cavity. I jammed more packs all over the abdomen and into the pelvis, until everything was wedged tight. No blood vessel was pumping that I could see.

We could stop and take a breath.

"Are we catching up on blood?" I asked Ronaldo.

"We never catch up," he said. When I kept staring at him, he shrugged; he nodded at his dials as if to say things were no worse than when we began—that's what I hoped he had said.

Now I carefully removed the packs, starting with the spots where the bleeder was least likely to be. The pelvis was clean—no gusher there. Off came the pack around the spleen. If the patient's belly was a room, the furniture—the most movable, central structures—had been pulled out so we had a good view to the rear. If there was a bleed from a torn aorta or its branches, then this back wall of the abdomen—the retroperitoneum—would have shown a big ugly swelling, a hematoma. But that was clean, too.

I had a premonition that we would find the bleeder behind the liver. A place full of shadows, hard to see or fix. This was where the inferior vena cava, the largest vein in the body, carried blood back from the lower limbs and trunk, running through and behind the liver on its way to the heart. While coursing through the liver, it picked up the stumpy, taut hepatic veins that drained that organ.

I took the pack away from the liver. Nothing.

I gently pulled the liver forward, to look at its dark side.

An angry gush of blood filled the empty bowl of the abdomen. I hastily pushed the liver back, and the pumping ceased. Things were all right as long as we didn't touch the liver. What was it that Solomon, operating in the bush, had called this? *The injury in which the surgeon sees God.*

"Okay," Deepak said, "let's leave it like that."

"What now?"

"He's oozing from the skin incision and from all the IV sites. His blood isn't clotting." Deepak had a soft voice, and I had to lean over to hear him. "It's inevitable with this much trauma. We open them up, pour fluids into them, and the body temperature drops . . . We have diluted the clotting system so it stops working. Let's pack around the liver and get out. Put him in ICU where we can warm him up, give him more fresh frozen plasma and blood. In a couple of hours, if he's alive, if he is more stable, we can come back."

I sandbagged the liver and fed the small bowel back into the wound. Instead of suturing the skin, we used towel clips to hold the wound edges together.

"The transplant teams will be here to harvest the corneas, heart, lungs, liver, and kidneys from the man he shot," Deepak said. "This theater is bigger, and I'll let them have it."

IN THE INTENSIVE CARE UNIT, two hours later, the oozing from the puncture wounds ceased. The cluster of poles and machinery around the bed made it tricky to get near Shane Johnson Jr.—that was his name. His family was in the waiting room, trying to fathom the unfathomable. Fresh frozen plasma, warmed blood, and fluids had given Junior a recordable blood pressure and a respectable temperature. He was alive, but just barely.

"Okay," Deepak said after reassessing the patient, and looking at the clock. "Let's go take another look."

This time we were in the smaller operating room. Ronaldo was still all gloom. Junior's face and limbs were puffy, his capillaries leaking out what was being poured into him. But we still had to pour fluid in to keep a blood pressure—it was like keeping a bucket full despite the holes in its side.

Deepak insisted that I be on the patient's right again. It took just seconds to remove the drapes, swab his skin, and pop open the towel clips that held the skin edges together. I removed the packs.

Deepak guided my fingers to the stalk of vessels that led into the liver. "Okay," he said. "Squeeze there." This was the Pringle maneuver. I squeezed, choking off the blood supply to the liver, while Deepak removed the last pad and lifted the liver forward. Blood gushed out at once, turning the dry clean field into a sopping red mess.

"Okay, you can let go," he said, pushing the liver back. "That's what I was afraid of. The vena cava is torn for sure. That's why, even with the Pringle maneuver, it still bleeds."

In some people, the inferior vena cava barely indents the back of the liver. In our patient, the vena cava was swathed by liver like a pig in a blanket. When Junior went airborne, then hit the pavement, his liver kept traveling; its momentum tore the short veins that anchored it to the vena cava, leaving a jagged rent.

Deepak asked for a suture on a long needle holder. At his signal I pulled the liver forward, and he tried to put the needle in one end of the tear. But before he could even see it, the field was awash with blood.

"God," I said, violating a cardinal rule about keeping quiet when assisting, "how do we fix this?"

Deepak said, "Oh, it's easy to repair the cava—it's just that the liver is in the way." It took me a second to realize this was as close as Deepak came to joking during surgery.

He was silent for a good while, almost in a trance, and I tried not to make a sound. At last, like a priest finishing a prayer, he moved. "Okay," he said. "It's a long shot. Let's switch sides."

I was unprepared for what followed. All I could do was marvel and be the best second pair of hands that I could be. Deepak swabbed Junior's chest, then cut vertically down over the breastbone from top to bottom, then ran an electric saw in the same groove. The smell of burning flesh and bone hung in the air. Suddenly the chest popped open like an over-stuffed suitcase.

I didn't ask what he was doing. He didn't explain. My exposure to chest surgery had consisted mostly of draining fluid collections outside the lung or, rarely, watching Deepak resect a cancerous lobe. Three times during my internship we had cracked the chest and oversewn a stab injury to the heart. One of the three survived. This was one of the deficits in our program, one of the reasons we were being shut down: we had to ship off much of the thoracic surgery, not to mention much of the urology and plastic surgery, to other hospitals.

Junior's heart, a fleshy, yellow-streaked mass covered by the pericardial sac, was exposed, pumping away, as it had done for all his nineteen years. It had never been more threatened. Deepak cut open the pericardium.

I was aware of activity in the operating room behind me and in the scrub area that was shared. At one point, I looked around, and through the three sets of windows, I saw a crowd of white faces around the other operating table.

Deepak put a purse-string suture around the right atrium, the upper chamber of the heart that received blood from the vena cava. He took a chest tube and cut side holes in it with scissors. Now he made a nick in the atrium of the heart, in the center of his purse-string suture. Then he slid his newly fashioned tube into the atrium, using the purse string to cinch the tissue around the tube which he pushed down through the orifice of the inferior vena cava, and down to where our problem was.

"Tell me when it reaches the level of the renal veins," he said.

I saw the inferior vena cava distend, like a garden hose filling with water. "Now," I said.

"The tube serves as a stent for the inferior vena cava," Deepak said, leaning over to look from below. "It's also a crude bypass so blood from the trunk can return to the heart while we make the repair. Now . . . let's see if we can fix this."

He adjusted the overhead lights. When I lifted the liver, the bleeding was much less than before, and what's more, the torn edges of the vein were visible on the backdrop of the tube. Deepak grabbed one edge of the tear with long forceps and passed the curved needle through and then grabbed the other edge, passed the needle through that and out, and tied a knot. I let the liver back down. It was a laborious process: lift, grab, pass needle, mop, pass needle to other side, mop, tie, relax the pull on liver.

At some point, just as were nearing completion, I sensed someone at my shoulder. Deepak glanced up but did not say anything.

"Is that a Shrock shunt, son?" a voice behind me said. It was a male voice, polite enough, conscious that it was a delicate moment to intrude, but with the authority of one who is entitled to ask.

Deepak looked up again, then back to his work. "Yes, sir," he said.

"How big was the tear?"

Deepak pulled up the liver and adjusted the overhead light so the visitor could see. "It was three-quarters of the way around the cava." The tube he'd pushed down from the heart made a lovely internal splint for the vein, and running across it like a crease was the first part of Deepak's neat repair. It was a beautiful sight, order restored from chaos.

"Very impressive," the voice said. There was no sarcasm, just genuine admiration. I stepped back so the visitor could have a better look, and when I did, he leaned in. "Very, very nice. I'd put some gel foam around the raw area of the liver. Were you planning to leave some drains?"

"Yes, sir."

"I'm assuming you are the attending physician?" the voice said.

"No, I'm the Chief Resident. My name is Deepak."

"Where is your attending?"

Deepak met the speaker's eyes, and said nothing.

"I see. Not one to get out bed for this sort of thing. Do you ever see him?"

As if in reply, Ronaldo snorted and turned to his dials, feigning disinterest. The visitor looked to Ronaldo and seemed about to bite his head off, but then remembering this wasn't his theater, he didn't.

"And how many Shrock shunts have you done before, Deepak?"

"This is my sixth."

"Really? In what period of time."

"In two years here . . . Unfortunately we see a lot of trauma."

"Unfortunate, yes. But fortunate for us. We are not ungrateful . . . Still, six Shrocks, did you say? Remarkable. How have they done?"

"One died, but a week after the surgery. He was walking, eating. Probably a pulmonary embolus."

"Did you get an autopsy?"

"Partial. The family allowed us to reopen the belly. The repair to the cava looked good. We took photographs."

"And the others?"

"Second, third, and fifth are alive and well, six months after the operation. Fourth died on the table before I got this far. I had just opened the heart."

"Do you count that one?"

"I should. 'Intention to treat'... that counts."

"Good man. You should count it. Most surgeons wouldn't. And your sixth?"

"This is him," Deepak said.

"Right. Well, that's better than my experience. I've done four. That's over six years. They all died. Two on the table, two so close after surgery that it was as good as dying on the table. They weren't all trauma like this. Two were tears from someone trying to remove an adherent cancerous mass. You ought to write up your experience."

Deepak cleared his throat. "With all due respect, sir. I have. No one will publish a report from Our Lady—"

"Nonsense. What is your full name?"

"Deepak Jesudass, sir. This is my intern—"

"I tell you what, write up this case and add him to your series, and then let me take a look at your paper. If it's good, I'll see that it gets published. I'll send it to the editor of the *American Journal of Surgery*. I'll check with you to see how this patient does. Good luck. By the way, my name is—"

"I know who you are, sir. Thank you."

The visitor must have been walking away when Deepak said, "Sir?... If you were to... never mind."

"What is it, man? I have a cadaver organ that I should have in the air by now. I just stopped to admire your work."

"If you were to show us how to harvest the liver... we could start it for you, save you time."

I tried to turn around to look, but because I was holding a retractor, I couldn't.

"I don't trust anyone else to do it," the voice said. "That's why I do it myself. My chief residents don't have the skill... Smart boys, but they don't get the volume you have in a place like this."

"We get the volume. And they are shutting us down."

"What? I had heard some such rumor. I heard Popsy... True?"

Deepak just nodded.

"This is your fifth year?" the voice said.

"Seventh. Eighth. Tenth. Depends how you count, sir." He didn't mention his training in England.

He didn't need to, because the visitor said, "I hear a Scotch inflection. Were you in Scotland? Took your FRCS?"

"Yes."

"Glasgow?"

"Edinburgh. I worked in Fife. All over there," Deepak said.

There was a profound silence. The man behind me hadn't moved. He seemed to be considering this.

"What will you do if they shut down?"

Deepak dropped his eyes. "I'll just keep working. Probably here. I love surgery . . ."

After an eternity the voice said, "Deepak Jesudass, with a *J*?" And then he spelled it out. "Did I get that right? Come see me in Boston, Dr. Jesudass. We'll pay your fare. I'll arrange for you to come up to my dog lab. We'll get you going. If anyone can harvest for me, you probably can. When you come up we'll visit at length. Have to run now. Good work, Deepak."

We heard the door swing behind him.

We worked in silence. At last, Deepak said, "He heard my name just once . . . and he was able to repeat it." Deepak's repair was done. He was closing up now, as carefully and efficiently as he had opened. He asked for gel foam from the scrub nurse. "In all my years here, no one's been able to remember my name when I'm introduced. No one has bothered. They usually see us as types, not as individuals."

His shoulders were straighter, his eyes bright and glowing. I'd never seen my Chief Resident like this. I was happy for him, and proud.

"Who was that?" I said, at last unable to contain my curiosity.

"Call me old-fashioned," Deepak said, "but I've always believed that hard work pays off. My version of the Beatitudes. Do the right thing, put up with unfairness, selfishness, stay true to yourself . . . one day it all works out. Of course, I don't know that people who wronged you suffer or get their just deserts. I don't think it works *that* way. But I *do* think one day you get your reward."

"Did you know him?" I said again.

Deepak sidestepped my question and turned to the circulating nurse. "Did that particular team come for liver or heart?"

"Liver. Another team took the heart and ran."

Deepak smiled and turned to me. "Marion, I'm not a hundred percent sure, because of his mask; had I seen his fingers I could have been certain. But I have a pretty good idea. You just met one of the foremost liver surgeons in the world, a pioneer of liver transplants.

"What's his name?"

"Thomas Stone."

CHAPTER 43

Grand Rounds

I BELIEVE IN BLACK HOLES. I believe that as the universe empties into nothingness, past and future will smack together in the last swirl around the drain. I believe this is how Thomas Stone materialized in my life. If that's not the explanation, then I must invoke a disinterested God who leaves us to our own devices, neither causing nor preventing tornadoes or pestilence, but a God who will now and then stick his thumb on the spinning wheel so that a father who put a continent between himself and his sons should find himself in the same room as one of them.

As a child I'd longed for Thomas Stone or at least the idea of him. So many mornings I waited for him at the gates of Missing. I saw that vigil now as necessary, a prerequisite for my insides to harden and cure just like the willow of a cricket bat must cure to be ready for a lifetime of knocks. That was the lesson at Missing's gates: the world does not owe you and neither does your father.

I hadn't forgotten what Ghosh asked of me. Let's just say I'd set it aside. I didn't feel guilty about not following through; I never had time to seek out Thomas Stone, and moreover, wherever he was, I never felt as if I was in *his* America. I was on an island, a protectorate, a territory that America claimed only in name. In carrying his textbook with me from Addis to Sudan and Kenya and then to America, I had developed a grudging respect for the author. I told myself that the book was my touchstone to Sister Mary Joseph Praise: I saw her hand in the line drawings and I carried the bookmark with her handwriting in my wallet. I'd discovered Thomas Stone in the text, just as he must have discovered himself in the discipline of making notes in a landscape of disease and poverty, overcoming his fatigue to fill exercise books with his observations. I was convinced that it was the accumulation of these journals that he pulled together to form a textbook. In doing so, he made his knowledge incarnate.

But when that writer, the sole living author of my DNA, stood peering over my shoulder, it was flesh that became incarnate, flesh of my flesh, with a scent that I should have recognized as kin and a voice that was my inheritance. When he leaned over the patient's belly to see our handiwork, cocked his skull on the atlas and axis vertebrae just so, tucked his arms to his chest, his scapulae gliding out, making himself small so as not to contaminate our field—those movements were echoes of my own.

Surely Thomas Stone sensed some disturbance in the universe and that is why he appeared in our theater. I confess when I didn't know who he was, I felt nothing: no aura, no tingling, nothing other than pride in the miracle Deepak had performed with PVC tube and the uncommon skill in his hands, a skill that the stranger appreciated. When I learned our visitor was Thomas Stone, I was unprepared. Should my first reaction have been anger? Righteousness? I had missed my chance to react while he was there. But now, for the first time since childhood, I wanted to do more than study his nine-fingered portrait. I wanted to know about the living, breathing surgeon who had stood next to me.

In the days that followed, I looked up Thomas Stone in *Index Medicus* in our library, pulling down one by one the oversize volumes, beginning with 1954, the year of my birth. I wanted to know about the post–*Short Practice* Stone; I wanted to see what scholarly contributions he had made after leaving the tropics. Ours was a small library, but Popsy had donated his collection of surgical journals dating back to the fifties. I found most of the papers listed in *Index Medicus*.

In my notebook I plotted out Thomas Stone's scientific career as reflected in his published work. In America his interest was liver surgery, and his career was interwoven with the history of transplantation, with the audacious idea of taking an organ from Peter to save the life of Paul. The story began well before Stone, of course, with Sir Peter Medawar and Sir Macfarlane Burnet in the 1940s, who showed us how the immune system recognizes "self" from foreign tissues and rejects and destroys the latter. Two months before our birth, Thomas Stone published a letter to the editor of the *British Medical Journal* describing the extraordinary length and redundancy of the colon of many Ethiopians, which he believed explained why it so readily twisted on itself—a condition called sigmoid volvulus. By 1967, when Christian Barnard in Cape Town's Groote Schuur Hospital replaced Lewis Washkansky's scarred and diseased heart with the heart of young Denise Darvall, killed in a car wreck, my father, now in Boston, had become interested in liver resection. His research question was, how much liver could you cut away and still leave enough behind to sustain life?

The transplant field in America was led by a brilliant surgeon—another Thomas, this one with the last name of Starzl. Working in Colorado, Starzl did the first human liver transplants in '63 and '64, but neither patient survived. Thomas Stone of Boston, the footnotes will show, also tried and failed in '65. Despite increasing public criticism, Starzl didn't give up. He performed the first successful liver transplant in 1967. Soon others, Thomas Stone included, managed the same feat. It was still very high risk, but by publishing their experience with such tricks as bypassing portal blood to the superior vena cava during the long surgery, or using the "University of Wisconsin solution" to better preserve cadaver livers, results were improving. The problem was no longer technical, even though this was the most technically difficult operation anyone could perform, the equivalent of a pianist playing Rachmaninoff's "Rhapsody on a Theme by Paganini," except that one dare not miss a note or fluff a phrase. The operation lasted ten, sometimes twenty, hours. Starzl showed it could be done. The two new hurdles were finding sufficient organs to transplant, and of course the problem of rejection of the transplant by the immune system.

In 1980, the year of my internship, Starzl turned his attention increasingly to rejection, focusing on a promising new drug that Sir Roy Calne's group at Cambridge discovered—cyclosporine.

THOMAS STONE TOOK a different approach; he focused on the problem of the shortage of organs and pursued a solution that most others considered a dead end: removing *part* of a liver from a living healthy parent and giving that to a child whose liver was failing. At least in dogs, he found the liver grew in size to compensate for its loss, while the transplanted segment of liver sustained the recipient. But splitting the donor's liver introduced complications such as bile leaks and clots in the hepatic artery that feeds the liver. It also put a healthy donor's life in real jeopardy, as the liver, unlike the kidney, is unpaired. Even more promising and immediately useful was Stone's work using animal liver cells, trying to strip the cells of those surface antigens which made humans cells recognize them as foreign, and then grow them in sheets on a membrane and use them as a sort of artificial liver—a dialysis type of solution.

As I read about transplants, I was excited. It was clearly one of the most compelling stories in American medicine.

JUNIOR WAS THE CENTER of attention in our ICU. He was deeply sedated, eyeballs roving under closed lids. The kind of trauma he'd been through resulted in "shock" lung, or Da Nang lung (recognized in GIs who were resuscitated on the battlefield, only to develop this strange lung stiffness), along with kidney shutdown. According to B. C. Gandhi's rules, if you had more than seven tubes in you, you were as good as dead. Junior had nine. But one by one, over the weeks, the tubes came out and he got better. It required meticulous nursing care, and Deepak and me poring over his daily flowcharts, anticipating his needs, and intervening with ongoing problems. J.R., as his family called him, left the ICU for a regular room after forty-three days. A week later, smiling sheepishly, he walked out on his own steam with the ICU and trauma teams lined up on either side of the hospital entrance to cheer. If he'd shot someone, the witnesses had all vanished, and the police had lost interest, so J.R. was going home. I think it was the sight of J.R. walking out of the hospital that set me on course as a trauma surgeon. His kind of recovery was by no means a rule in trauma surgery, but it happened often enough, particularly in those who were young and previously healthy, that it made the heroic efforts worthwhile. The mind was fragile, fickle, but the human body was resilient.

AS INTERNS we were allowed to attend one national conference, all expenses paid. I chose a liver transplant conference in May in Boston. I arrived on a lovely spring day. Boston's downtown fit every notion I had of what colonial America was like, and it felt steeped in history, completely different from my section of the Bronx. I told myself that it was coincidence that the conference was in Boston, walking distance from where Thomas Stone worked. I told myself I wasn't there to meet Thomas Stone, but to hear the keynote speaker, Thomas Starzl. As for Thomas Stone's plenary session—I was undecided about attending.

The morning of the conference I could no longer lie to myself. I skipped the transplant meeting and walked the six blocks to the hospital in which Thomas Stone had worked all these years. After wearing scrubs for almost a year, my suit and tie felt strange, as if I were in fancy dress.

"Send them to Mecca" was an expression we used when we dispatched patients to places that offered what Our Lady of Perpetual Succour could not. It was a common medical expression in hospitals all over America, when sending patients to any of the top referral places in the country—I'd even seen it in letters to the editor in the medical journals. Now I was going to Mecca.

"MECCA" CONSISTED OF a spanking-new hospital tower, weirdly shaped and shining as if it were made of platinum. It was the kind of structure architects compete to build. From a patient's perspective, it didn't look welcoming. The tower hid the older brick sections of the hospital, whose architecture felt authentic and aligned with the neighborhood.

"Good morning, sir," a young man in a purple jacket said to me. I glared at him, thinking he was being sarcastic. Then I realized that he and two others stood there ready to park cars and assist patients into wheelchairs.

The revolving doors led to a glass-walled atrium, the ceiling extending up at least three stories and accommodating a real tree. A grand piano played itself by some mysterious mechanism. Around it were plush leather chairs, lamps. Beyond this was a waterfall trickling gently over a slab of granite. Then a reception desk where a concierge, one of three, looked up, smiling, eager to help. I followed the blue line on the floor to the elevators of Tower A, which took me to the Department of Surgery on the eighteenth floor, just as she said it would, but I made no promise about having a nice day. I found it difficult to believe I was in a hospital.

When I emerged from the elevators I was met by five men and one woman of my age, all dressed in dark suits, chests labeled with visitor tags exactly like mine. "We're supposed to wait here," the woman said to me, helpfully.

Just then a young man, a white coat covering his blue scrubs, approached. "Sorry I'm late," he said, not sounding sorry at all. "Welcome to the Department of Surgery. My name's Matthew." He grinned at us. "God, a year ago I was in your shoes, interviewing for my internship. Time flies! Love the suits! Okay, we have about twenty minutes before morbidity and mortality conference. I'll give you a quick tour of the Department of Surgery. After M&M you'll have lunch with the house staff, then your individual interviews begin, and then the grand tour of the hospital. When I get you to the conference room, I'll break off. One of my patients is being presented at M&M. I have to go strap on the body armor."

In the year I'd been at Our Lady of Perpetual Succour, I had yet to take any potential intern recruits around. Indeed, I'd never seen anyone come to be interviewed. At Mecca this was a weekly event. I tagged along.

The individual on-call rooms had a television on the wall, a fridge, a nice desk, and an attached bathroom; it was a far cry from Our Lady's solitary on-call room crammed with bunk beds, with just one phone and interns from all the specialties expected to bed there; I never used it. Next, Matthew showed us the "small" conference room where the Mecca surgical team held their morning report. It looked like a corporate boardroom with high-backed leather chairs around a long table. Oil portraits of the past chairmen of surgery stared down from the walls, a who's who of surgery.

"Check this out," Matthew said, pushing a button. Screens came down behind the curtains to black out the room, and a projector rose out of what I took to be a coffee table. Constance, the woman in our group, rolled her eyes as if she thought this was so gauche.

When we arrived at the auditorium where morbidity and mortality conference was to be held, Matthew excused himself. "I have to change out of scrubs. Dr. Stone is a stickler for that. He doesn't even like scrubs on rounds."

The auditorium was a small version of the Cinema Adowa in Addis, only with better seats, upholstered in a nubby beige fabric that felt smooth to the touch. A steep incline made the view from the back excellent, and this is where we prospective interns sat. A bank of motorized X-ray viewing panels was built into one side of the wall behind the podium. A resident stood loading films, stepping on a pedal to advance panels.

Constance sat next to me. A gaggle of medical students in short white coats filed in and joined us in the back. I'd forgotten about the existence of medical students. How nice it would be at Our Lady of Perpetual Succour to have someone below me on the food chain. The residents wore longer coats, and their expressions were not as carefree as the students'. The attending physicians wore the longest coats and were the last to come in. We interviewees in our dark suits stood out like penguins at a polar bear convention. In all my time at Our Lady, we never had this kind of an assembly. Deepak got us together regularly for coaching sessions, but one sensed a tradition in this room, a way of doing things that had not changed for decades.

"So what school are you from?" Constance asked. I'd overheard her say she trained in Boston, but it wasn't at this institution.

"I went to school in Ethiopia," I said. If she could have moved one seat over, she probably would have.

Thomas Stone didn't look at the crowd when he walked in; he assumed their presence. He was taller than I'd realized from seeing him in the theater, almost as tall as Shiva or me. The room turned quiet. His hands were in the pockets of his white coat. The way he slid into his seat, the ease and fluidity of that motion, reminded me of Shiva. He was alone in the front row. I was well behind him but off to one side, so I could see his profile. This was my first good look at my father. I felt my body grow warm; it wasn't possible to study him dispassionately, clinically. My mind was racing, my heart pounding—I worried that I was giving away my presence. I looked away to try and calm down. When I looked back, Stone was studying a paper in his hand—it was hard to tell he was missing a finger. His hair was quite gray at the temples, but still dark brown on top. His masseter muscles stood out, outlining his jaw, as if he habitually clenched his teeth. The one eye socket that I could see was a recessed dark hollow on his face. I noticed that he kept his head exceptionally still.

I CAN'T TELL YOU MUCH about the case being discussed or exactly what transpired. While I looked at Thomas Stone and sat next to the supercilious Constance, a slow fuse burned inside me and it was about to ignite. I was ready to hurl furniture, activate the ceiling sprinklers, scream obscenities, and disrupt this orderly meeting. I felt an impending loss of control. At one point I had to grab the arms of my chair as my rage peaked, and then gradually subsided.

"It was my fault," Thomas Stone said, turning to face me. For a moment, I thought he was clairvoyant. He had heard me. Earlier, Matthew, our escort and the presenter of the case, came under harsh criticism from different quarters of the room. Matthew was only the messenger, but since his attending physician and the Chief Resident didn't come to his defense, he took the brunt of the attack. The snapping jaws were silenced when Thomas Stone stood up.

"Yes, it was my fault. Without a doubt we can do better surgically. I am installing a video camera in the two trauma bays. I want us to review the video after every major trauma that comes in. Were we standing in the right place? Did we take three steps to reach for an endotracheal tube when it should have been at hand? Did someone have to ask for something that should have been there? Did we distract each other with what we said? Who didn't need to be there? Is there a better way? That is always the challenge." He pulled out a piece of paper from his pocket and unfolded it.

"I take responsibility also for something addressed in this letter."

His accent was faintly British, the years in America having softened it, but without accruing any jarring American inflections. The day he spoke to Deepak over my shoulder in the operating room at Our Lady, I hadn't registered a particular accent. "This letter came to me from the deceased patient's mother. I want to make sure that this does not happen again. Here is what she says: 'Dr. Stone— My son's terrible death is not something I will ever get over, but perhaps in time it will be less painful. But I cannot get over one image, a last image that could have been different. Before I was asked to leave the room in a very rough manner, I must tell you that I saw my son was terrified and there was no one who addressed his fear. The only person who tried was a nurse. She held my son's hand and said, "Don't worry, it will be all right." Everyone else ignored him. Sure, the doctors were busy with his body. It would have been merciful if he had been unconscious. They had important things to do. They cared only about his chest and belly. Not about the little boy who was in fear. Yes, he was a man, but at such a vulnerable moment, he was reduced to a little boy. I saw no sign of the slightest bit of human kindness. My son and I were irritants. Your team would have preferred for me to be gone and for him to be quiet. Eventually they got their wish. Dr. Stone, as head of surgery, perhaps as a parent yourself, do you not feel some obligation to have your staff comfort the patient? Would the patient not be better off with less anxiety, less fright? My son's last conscious memory will be of people ignoring him. My last memory of him will be of my little boy, watching in terror as his mother is escorted out of the room. It is the graven image I will carry to my own deathbed. The fact that people were attentive to his body does not compensate for their ignoring his being.'"

Thomas Stone folded the letter and put it away in his breast pocket. There was a rustle in the auditorium, a murmur, an uncomfortable shifting of body weight. I sensed a willingness in the room to shrug off the letter, to scoff at what it said, but Stone's demeanor made it necessary to conceal that urge. Stone stood there, silent, looking out, as if considering the letter's context himself, unaware of his audience. No one spoke. As the moment stretched on, even the smallest noises were stilled until there was only the hum of the air-conditioning. Thomas Stone's expression was reflective, certainly not angry. Now, as if waking up, he searched the room for a reaction, seeing if the writer struck a chord. The scoffers had reconsidered their position.

When Stone finally spoke, it was in a quiet voice that was firm and commanded attention. He asked a question.

I knew the answer because it was in his book, a book I'd read carefully and more than once in my voyage out of Ethiopia and during my stay in Kenya.

"What treatment in an emergency is administered by ear?"

Surely with about two hundred people in the room, at least fifty would know the answer.

No one spoke.

He waited. The discomfort grew even more acute. I could sense Constance stiffening next to me.

Thomas Stone spread his feet and put his hands behind his back. He appeared willing to stand there all day. He raised his eyebrows. Waiting. The students sitting to my left were too scared to blink.

Stone looked over to me, surprised to see a response from the row of dark suits. I felt his eyes bore into mine. It was only the second time he registered my being in this world; the first was when I was born. This time, I only had to raise my hand.

"Yes?" he said. "Tell us, please, what treatment in an emergency is administered by ear?"

All eyes were on me. I was in no hurry. None at all.

Then my sight turned misty as I thought of Ghosh and the sacrifice he'd made for us. Though he died of leukemia, it now felt to me as if he'd given up his life from the time we were infants so that Shiva and I should have ours. When he died, it was as if a second umbilical cord had been severed. I thought of Hema, widowed, now laboring alone with Shiva at Missing, writing to me to say that her heart was breaking not to have me there, and would I forgive her for not giving me the attention and love I deserved? And all through those years, Thomas Stone probably never missed an M&M conference, never had a day of discomfort over Shiva, or over me. I thought of Matron, holding Missing together, an active and loving godmother to two boys, an anchor in our lives, and I thought of Gebrew, Almaz, and Rosina, who had stepped in to fill the void of this man's absence.

How unjust it was that Thomas Stone's reward for his failings, for his selfishness, should be to preside in that chair and command the respect, the awe, and the admiration of the likes of Constance and others in this room. Surely you couldn't be a good doctor *and* a terrible human being— surely the laws of man, if not of God, didn't allow it.

I met his gaze and I did not blink. "Words of comfort," I said to my father.

The intervening years lay compressed between us as if by bookends. The others in the room looked from my face to his, distressed, uncertain if mine was the right answer. But no one else existed for me or for him.

"Thank you," he said, his voice altered. "Words of comfort."

He left the room, but looked back at me once when he reached the door.

I FOUND WHERE HE LIVED by accident. An elegant condominium complex across the river would have been my guess. But at the base of Tower A, I saw a glass door leading to the outside. Across the street was the lobby to another building. I saw Thomas Stone enter and a doorman greet him. I waited. A few minutes later he emerged, without his white coat and with a yellow-and-black box in his hand—a slide carousel. He was on his way to the transplant conference. I gave him half an hour, and then I went up to the doorman. I flashed my badge. "I'm Marion Stone. Dr. Stone forgot some slides he needed for a talk he is giving. He sent me to pick them up."

He was about to quiz me, deny me, but then he cocked his head. "You a relative?"

"I'm his son."

"By God you are!" he said, coming closer to look into my eyes, as if that was where the similarity resided. He beamed as if the news vindicated him. As if it gave Thomas Stone a human dimension, a redeeming quality.

"By God you are!" He slapped his thigh in delight. "And not a word to us all this time."

"He never knew till this year," I said, winking.

"Joseph and Mary! Get out of here!"

I smiled and looked at my watch.

"You know where it is?" he said.

"Fourth floor?"

"Four-oh-nine."

I ENTERED HIS HOUSE using my penknife and the sort of ancillary surgical skills only a B. C. Gandhi can teach you.

It was a one-bedroom apartment.

The living-dining room had nothing to justify that label. A large worktable like a draftsman's desk occupied most of that area, with two side tables at its ends to form a U. There were papers in neat stacks on the side tables. Sectional bookcases covered three walls and were full of books and papers. They weren't arranged for display but for access.

The coffeepot in the kitchen was collecting dust. The stove appeared never to have been used. A toaster on the counter had a trace of crumbs on the top. The refrigerator held only a carton of orange juice, a stick of butter, and a half loaf of bread.

His bedroom was dark, the curtains drawn. There were no books or papers here. Only an army cot, a blanket folded neatly at its foot, as if he were camping for one night.

A single framed snapshot sat on the mantelpiece above the electric fireplace. The airbrush technique of the 1920s gave mother and son alabaster skin. They were posed like Madonna and Child. The boy was perhaps three, ensconced in the lap of the woman who must have been my grandmother—a presence in the world I realized I'd never once thought about.

Next to the picture was a glass cylinder, filled with murky fluid. Closer inspection revealed a human finger floating in the liquid.

I had come there wanting to . . . to do damage.

That picture made me change my mind.

Instead, I opened all the kitchen cabinets and left the doors ajar. I pulled down the oven door. I opened both sides of the fridge. I took the top off the juice container. I opened the bathroom cabinets. I unscrewed toothpaste, shampoo, and conditioner, setting the tops carefully along-side the bottles. I opened anything that had a lid or a cover. I left open wardrobe, chest of drawers, filing cabinet, ink bottle, medicine bottles. I opened the windows.

In the center of his desk I placed the bookmark with Sister Mary Joseph Praise's writing on it.

September 19, 1954
The Second Edition. The packet came addressed to me. But I
am sure the publisher meant it for you. Congratulations. Also,
I am enclosing a letter to you from me. Please read at once.
SMJP

I felt certain he had the letter my mother referred to. Now, in his home, I asked myself again: Where was it . . . and what did it say? I was tempted to ransack the place to find it but that would have spoiled what I had created.

I twisted open the formalin bottle, fished out his finger, shook it free of fluid, and put it next to the bookmark. I studied what I'd done. I changed my mind about the finger. I put it back in the formalin bottle, capped it, and took it with me. It was only fair. After all, I'd left him something of mine.

I propped the door open on my way out.

CHAPTER 44

Begin at the Beginning

It was two weeks later on a Sunday that I heard the knock on my door. We had beaten our archrivals from Coney Island at a limited overs match on their turf, coming away with the interhospital cricket trophy. Nestor had taken six wickets for twenty-five runs in a torrid spell of pace bowling, and four of those were by catches I took standing well behind the wicket. I had slipped away from the festivities in B. C. Gandhi's room, my fingers sore despite the keeper's gloves and my knees aching. I planned an early night.

"Come in," I said.

He scanned the dark room, getting his bearings. If he saw the shadow of my bed, he didn't see me because he looked away, to the light leaking from under the bathroom door. Then to the curtained window. When he looked back I was sitting up. It gave him a start.

He shut the door and stood there, a man who had walked into his past.

I waited. I hadn't invited him here. The seconds ticked away and he showed no inclination to speak. I had to give him this: he tracked me down, he figured it out. Perhaps he did register my presence in the operating room the day he peeked over my shoulder. Perhaps in the auditorium when I answered his question he saw in my face features of my mother or of himself. How strange to spot a son you've never seen or thought of till the day he appears at morbidity and mortality conference and gives new meaning to that activity.

"You might as well sit," I said. I didn't offer to turn on the light.

There was a chair beyond my bed. He walked forward quickly like a blind man who'd risk bumping into something rather than seem hesitant or ask for help. He sat down hard.

I didn't think he could see my face. I studied his. As his eyes adjusted, he looked at my possessions. I had more things than he did. If you didn't count books. I saw him linger on the framed print of the *Ecstasy of St. Teresa*—he must have recognized at once where that came from. Oh yes, and the finger in the jar. He knew he was in the right room.

The minutes passed. It was ten at night.

"Mind if I smoke?" he said at last.

"You don't smoke." I hadn't picked up the smell of cigarettes in his condo. Just his scent, which my nostrils registered again.

"I do now . . . When did you start?"

His nose was pretty good. I took my time answering.

"Since coming here. It's a prerequisite for surgical training. Go ahead."

He fumbled in his shirt pocket and brought out two cigarettes. I thought of Ali and his little souk, the only place I knew where you could buy loose smokes. In America you bought them in cartons or by the truckload.

He held a cigarette out to me. I stared at it. He was about to withdraw his hand when I took it. He flicked his lighter and stood to meet me as I swung my feet over the side of the bed.

His fingers shielded the fire, a nine-fingered sepulchre. I bowed to the flame and drew till my tip glowed.

Thank you, Father.

I sat back on the bed. He found an old Styrofoam cup in arm's reach. I took a thoughtful draw, passing judgment on his cigarette. It was a Rothmans, a throwback to his Ethiopia days, or, lest I forget, his British days. Rothmans was also what we puffed at Our Lady, courtesy of B. C. Gandhi, who got cartons at deep discount from Canal Street.

The smoke made sinuous shapes in the shaft of light leaking past the bathroom door. I remembered our kitchen at Missing and how the dust motes dancing in the morning rays formed their own galaxy. When I was a child, that sight had hinted at the wonderful and frightening complexity of the universe, of how the closer one looked the more one saw revealed, and one's imagination was the only limit.

"I don't expect you to understand," he said, and for a moment I thought he was talking about the dust motes. The sound of his voice irritated me. Who gave him permission to speak? In my room?

"Then let's not talk about it."

More silence.

He cracked first. "How do you like surgery?"

Did I really want to answer him? By answering, was I conceding something? I had to think about this for a few minutes. Let him sweat.

"How do I like surgery? Hmmm . . . I am lucky to have Deepak. He takes great pains with me. The basics, good habits. I think it is so important . . ." I clammed up then. I felt I had said too much. I detected in my tone a need for his approval, his affirmation—that was the last thing I wanted. I thought of Ghosh who became an accidental surgeon because of Stone's departure. He had no one to teach him. Ah, Ghosh! Ghosh's dying wish was that—

"I know some of the people Deepak trained with," Stone said, interrupting my train of thought. Ghosh's message to him could wait. This wasn't the time. I wasn't in the mood.

"Oh, really?"

"I made inquiries about him. You are lucky."

"But *Deepak* isn't lucky. He is going to get screwed all over again. In fact, we all are."

"Maybe not," he said.

I didn't pursue this. No favors, please. I wanted nothing from him. He squirmed in his chair, but not from discomfort. It was what he was holding back, waiting for me to ask. I would not give him the pleasure.

"I had a Deepak in my life," he said. "All it takes is one. Mine was a Dr. Braithwaite. A stickler for the right way. I appreciate him more now than I did then. Despite him, after all these years, I find it extraordinarily difficult to . . ."

The words had dried up on his tongue. This was such an effort, a physical trial for him to converse. He wasn't a man who ever spoke like this, I didn't think. Sharing his inner thoughts wasn't something he had practiced. Not even with himself. I gave him lots of time.

"What? You find it extraordinarily difficult to . . . what?"

I should have just told him to leave. Here I was *conversing*, helping him along.

"I find it difficult to operate. Particularly elective surgery. I have anxieties." He spoke slowly, drawing out his words. "No one knows. Even if I'm doing a hernia or a hydrocele . . . in fact the simpler the operation, the more likely this is to happen . . . I have to look up the surgical anatomy, go over all the steps in an operative book, even though after all these years I don't need to. I'm terrified I will forget. Or that my mind will go blank . . . Sometimes I throw up in the lounge. I feel sick, dizzy. It has never stopped. It made me consider giving up surgery. It's worse if it's someone I know, a hospital employee brings his mother . . ."

I thought of the surgical anatomy atlas I had seen in his condominium, a big folio book, and next to it an operative anatomy atlas, both open on his desk as if they were the last things he looked at before he left his apartment.

"What about the day I . . . the day of your morbidity and mortality conference?"

"Exactly. Early that morning I had to do a simple breast lump excision, and if the biopsy was positive, then a mastectomy and axillary node dissection. I've done hundreds of them. Maybe more. But this was one of our nurses. Someone putting faith in me."

"So what happened?"

"I walked into the theater, feeling as if I were about to faint. No one knows, of course. The mask helps. But as soon as I make the incision, it all vanishes. Then it feels silly to have been so anxious. Ridiculous. It'll never happen again, I tell myself. But it does."

"Did it ever happen in Ethiopia?"

He shook his head. "I think it was because I knew I was the only choice the patient had. There were no other options. Two other surgeons in the whole city. Here there are so many surgeons."

"Or maybe those lives weren't as valuable. Natives, right? Who cares? The alternative was death anyway, so why worry? Just like you come and take organs from our patients at Our Lady."

He flinched. I sensed that no one ever talked to him in this manner. We hadn't agreed to any rules. If he didn't like it, he could just leave. He had come to Our Lady. This wasn't Mecca.

He clamped his lips together. "I don't expect you to understand," he said.

I knew he wasn't talking about his surgical anxieties.

He patted his pockets. He didn't find what he was looking for. So he just sat there and blinked, waiting for more punishment.

He slumped down in the chair. He had crossed his legs, and hooked his free foot under the calf of the other, like a twisted vine. "You see . . . *Mar-ion*—" He wasn't used to saying my name. "I . . . It is not as if everything can be explained by logic."

Now he uncrossed his legs and leaned forward. "I can't give you a neat explanation about why . . . I did what I did, because I don't understand it myself. Even after all these years . . ."

Which "it" was he talking about? I had my daggers lined up, and my lances and mace ready just behind them. I thought of all kinds of clever things to say: *Save your breath.* Or, *I understand all right. You took the path less traveled. You bailed out. What else is there to understand?* But perhaps he meant the "it" of impregnating my mother.

"Ghosh said you didn't know how *it* happened. That it was a mystery to you."

"Yes!" he said, relieved, but then I sensed he was blushing. "He said that? Yes, it was."

"Like Joseph? Clueless about Mary and the baby? *Babies,* in your case."

". . . Yes." He crossed his legs.

"Maybe you don't think you are my father."

"No, it's not that. I *am* your father. I—"

"*No, you're not!* Ghosh was my father. He raised me. He taught me everything from riding a bike to hitting a square drive off the back foot. He gave me my love for medicine. He raised me and Shiva. I am here because of Ghosh. A greater man never lived."

I had baited the trap, lured him in. But I was the one who snapped.

" 'Lived' . . . ?" he said, leaning forward, the foot no longer wagging.

"Ghosh is dead."

His features turned leaden, then pale.

I let him ruminate on that. I'm sure he wanted to know how, why, but he couldn't ask. The news had stopped him cold, saddened him, I could see. Good. I was touched. But I wasn't done kicking him. I was impressed that he took it, waited for more.

"So you are off the hook," I said. "I had a father."

He sighed. "I don't expect you to understand," he said again.

"Tell me anyway."

"Where shall I start?"

" 'Begin at the beginning and go on until you come to the end,' the King said, very gravely, 'then stop.' Do you know who said that?"

I was enjoying myself. The famous Thomas Stone being grilled, getting screwed, getting a dose of his own medicine. Sure, he could rattle off the branches of the external carotid artery, or the boundaries of the foramen of Winslow, but did he know his Lewis Carroll? Did he know his *Alice in Wonderland*?

He surprised me with his answer. It was wrong but it was right.

"Ghosh," he said, and the air went out of his lungs.

CHAPTER 45

A Matter of Time

WHEN THOMAS STONE WAS A CHILD, he asked the *maali*—the gardener—where little boys came from. The *maali*, a dark man with muddy eyes and acid breath from the previous night's arrack, said, "You came with the evening tide, of course! I found you. You were succulent and pink with one long fin and no scales. Such fish they say only exist in Ceylon, but there you were. I almost ate you, but I wasn't hungry. I cut off the fin with this very sickle and brought you to your mother."

"I don't believe you. My mother and I must have washed in from the sea together. We were one large fish. I was in her belly and came out," the little boy said, walking away. The *maali* could coax roses out of the earth where their neighbors failed. But Hilda Stone would have fired him for telling such tales to her only child.

The little boy's home was just outside the rock walls of Fort St. George in Madras, India. The spire of St. Mary's poked up from behind the incomplete battlements. Its quaint, well-tended cemetery was his playground, a place where more than five generations of English men, women, and babies were buried, taken by typhoid, malaria, *kala azar*, and rarely old age.

Fort St. George was the first home of the East India Company. St. Mary's, built in 1680, was the first Anglican church in India (but by no means the first church, that being the one built in A.D. 54 by St. Thomas the Apostle, who landed on the Kerala coast). A plaque inside St. Mary's commemorated the marriage of Lord Clive, and another that of Governor Elihu Yale, who later founded a university in America. But the little boy saw no plaque to commemorate the marriage of Hilda Masters of Fife, tutor and governess, to Justifus Stone, civil servant in the British Raj and almost two decades her senior.

Thomas thought every child grew up as he did—in sight of the Indian Ocean, hearing the fearsome-sounding waves crashing around Fort St. George. And he assumed that all fathers were like his, crashing into furniture and making alarming sounds at night.

Justifus Kaye Stone's voice rumbled down from a height, and his bottle-brush mustache kept little boys at bay. District collectors in the Indian Civil Service were demigods, with secretaries and peons hovering around them like flies around overripe mangoes. Collectors went on tours for weeks at a time, holding court in each city. When Justifus Stone *was* home, despite his noisy presence, he was somehow not there. Thomas understood (in that way that children do, even though they lack words to express themselves) that Justifus was a self-centered man and neglectful of his wife. Perhaps this was why Hilda turned to religion. To imagine Christ's suffering allowed her to live with hers.

Blessed are the meek.

Blessed are the peacemakers.

Blessed the young governess who marries a DC hoping to clear his yellow-tinged skin of quinine and cure his taste for gin and native women, for hers is the kingdom of heaven.

Hilda's blessing came in the form of her blue-eyed, towheaded boy whose feet she hardly let touch the ground, even when he was old enough to walk.

The little boy's ayah, Sebestie, had nothing to do other than join in the play, since it was Hilda who let him ride on her back pretending he was Jim Corbett, the big-game hunter, and she the elephant carrying him to the tiger blind. Hilda drew red-chalk wickets on the whitewashed walls and bowled to him with a tennis ball. She sang hymns to him, and fanned him when it was too humid to fall asleep. The bell-like clarity of her voice caused somnolent lizards on the wall to snap to attention. Her brown hair, parted in the center, fell from a steepled head. Regardless of how she restrained it, a frizzy halo framed her face.

In the middle of the night he reached for her and she was there. But on the nights Justifus Stone was home, the little boy slept poorly, fearful for his mother because those were the only times she left his bed. He kept vigil with his cricket bat outside the closed bedroom door, prepared to break in if the noises did not subside. They always did and only then would he retreat to his room. In the morning, when he opened his eyes, she would be back in his bed, awake and peering out through her fringe of hair.

Every child should have a mother of such even temperament, her rare displeasure evidenced so gently that the effect was lasting. Thomas lived to please his mother and he was earnest in his pleasing. It was as if they both knew, though they could not have known, that life was short, the moment fleeting.

HE WAS EIGHT when Hilda had to excuse herself from the St. Mary's choir. A cough that at first was like distant artillery soon sounded like nails rattling in a paper bag. Dr. Winthrop, an overdressed man who did not converse as much as make pronouncements, said mother and son were to sleep apart, "for the child's betterment."

The little boy heard her nightly paroxysms from the other room and covered his ears with the pillows. "Undoubtedly consumption," Dr. Winthrop said to Thomas one day, using a delicate word for tuberculosis as he put away his stethoscope and thermometer. "It has turned dry. The sicca form of phthisis, you know." He talked to the little boy as if to a colleague and shook his hand with gravity. When would she get better? "Rest and diet and hydrotherapy," said the doctor. "Some of the time—let's say, much of the time—it becomes quiescent. After all, it's not up to us, is it, Master Stone?" When Thomas asked, Please, sir, whom might it be up to, Winthrop raised his eyes to the ceiling. It was only later that the little boy understood the doctor did not mean Justifus, whose heavy tread shook the chandelier. He meant God.

One morning Thomas awoke dreaming of horse-drawn carriages, and with the thunder of hooves echoing in his ears. He discovered that in the night his mother had coughed up blood, lots of it, and Winthrop had been summoned. They bundled her off, not letting her kiss her son's brow. She traveled to Coimbatore, and from there the narrow-gauge toy train took her up the mountain to a hill station sitting just below Ooty. Dr. Ross had built a sanatorium in the Nilgiri Hills fashioned after Trudeau's famed Saranac Lake in New York. The white cottages around the hospital were replicas of those at Saranac, with the same airy porches and trundle beds.

Thomas wept himself to sleep on Sebestie's bony chest. He was angry with Hilda for getting sick, for having fostered such a closeness with him so as to make this separation unbearable. He was not like his schoolmates who loved their ayahs more than their parents and cared nothing about long separations. Overnight, Sebestie blossomed into a surrogate mother, but Thomas was wary of giving her his love. For then she, too, might disappear.

Before school Thomas visited St. Mary's and recited fifty Our-Father-Hail-Marys and did the same on his way back. He was on his knees so often that boggy sacs formed under his kneecaps. Around his neck he fastened with twine the heavy crucifix that had been on her wall, hiding it under his school uniform, where it gouged the skin over his breastbone and the twine cut into his neck. Not having a firstborn or a ram or ewe, he sacrificed his Don Bradman signature cricket bat, smashed it on the washing stone. He fasted till he was dizzy. He cut his forearm with a razor, spilling blood onto the shrine for the Virgin Mary that he built in his room. Sebestie took him to the Mambalam Temple and even to the tiny pavement temple behind their house. If it was up to God, He did not seem to listen.

Meanwhile his father never missed a stop on his circuit: Vellore, Madurai, Tuticorin, and parts in between. When Justifus Stone was home, he barely had time to remove his pith helmet or unpack his bags before he was off again. Justifus called his son the Archbishop of Canterbury, and if these were words of reassurance, they did nothing for Thomas. He spoke to his son as if he were addressing multitudes. At night Thomas could hear his uneven footsteps like those of a giant in a bedroom of Lilliputian dimensions who could not help knocking over furniture. It was a relief when Justifus went out on tour again.

A YEAR PASSED with Thomas living all but parentless in the big house, along with Sebestie, Durai (the cook), the *maali*, Sethuma (who washed clothes and swabbed the tile floors), and an untouchable who came once a week to clean the toilets—that was his family.

On Christmas Day, son and backslapping father came together for dinner; his father's clerk, Andrew Fothergill, was their sole guest. "Well, what a feast! Good to have you all. Fine repast, just fine. Eat, do eat"—this when it was just the three of them at the table, with Durai waiting behind the kitchen door. "We can't let them get away with it all. There is money to be made in coir. Rope, you know, or matting. We deserve, we earned it, I'll say, and by golly we are going to have it," and on he went, barely stopping to swallow, the crumbs spraying from his lips. Fothergill tried valiantly to connect Justifus's thoughts, to give his superior's scattered remarks a spine, a thread of meaning. Justifus began to rub one thigh, then the other, fidgeting, glancing down with irritation as if the dog were underfoot, but of course she never came into the house when Justifus was around. By the time pudding was served the leg rubbing was so furious that Thomas had to ask, Please, sir, what is wrong.

"I have fur on me legs, son. Keeps me from feeling, it does. Ruddy nuisance." His father struggled to rise, almost upsetting the table in the process. He stumbled out, grabbing sideboard and wall, his feet sticking like magnets to the floor. Thomas remembered Fothergill's look of consolation as the boy saw the guest to the door.

> *Jan. 20,*
> *My darling son,*
> *My temperatures were 36.7, 37.2. 37.8, 37.3. I threw out the 38.6 because I didn't believe it. They roll our beds out to the porch, and back in at night. In and out. I'm not even allowed to go the lavatory. TOTAL BED REST, though the huge effort this requires seems to be against the idea of rest. I find it difficult to believe that on this porch, with the mist outside and the air so cold, that a body can generate a temperature over 36 degrees. No wonder we are called warm-blooded animals.*

She had circled a splotch on the page and captioned it with "My tears, as I cry for you, my darling boy." In each letter Hilda told him that he must be brave, and be patient.

TIME FOR THOMAS was no longer divided by days and nights or seasons. Time was a seamless yearning for his mother.

> *They say I have not made any great improvement but that I should be glad I am no worse . . .*

He went through the motions at school. She exhorted him to pray, told him that she prayed every hour and that God listened and prayer never failed. He prayed constantly, convinced that at the very least the prayers kept her alive.

> *I know God did not mean to keep us apart, and soon he will bring us back together.*

ONE DAY, Thomas woke to find his pillow moist. When Sebestie lit the lamp, there was the mark of the beast: a fine red spray on his pillow, a strangely beautiful pattern. Sebestie wept, but he was overjoyed. He knew this meant he would see his mother again. Why didn't he think of this sooner?

Two barefoot stretcher bearers in crisp white drill met his train in Ooty. They took him directly to Hilda's cottage. He climbed into her narrow cot, into her arms. He was eleven years old. "Your coming is the best and worst present I could ever have," she said.

Gray and shrunk to her bones, she was a shadow of the mother he once knew. Her playfulness was gone, but then so was the reciprocity it might have found in this gangly son of hers whose eyes were haunted and ringed by worry lines. They sat side by side on the porch of their cottage, their fingers intertwined like dried roots. In the early morning they watched the tea pickers float by on the footpath, their feet hidden in the mist, their lunch pails creaking with every step. During the day only the nurses interrupted their solitude to take their temperatures and to bring tiffin and medications. By dusk, when they saw the tea pickers head home, it was time for sleep.

Since Hilda had no wind, he read to her. She wept with pride at his precocious fluency. The cane-bottomed lounge chairs had large armrests and a writing palette made of the same teak. Here they penned letters to each other, put them into envelopes, and sealed them; after lunch they exchanged envelopes, tore them open, and read their letters. They prayed at least three times a day. In the most bitter cold they remained outside, bundled up.

At first Thomas was light-headed from the altitude. He grew stronger. His cough lessened. But nothing—not fresh air, or milk, meat, or eggs or the tonics that were forced on her—helped Hilda. Her cough was different. It was a honking, bleating sound. He noticed that she had an exquisitely painful swelling at her breastbone, pushing up under her blouse. He was embarrassed to ask about it, and careful not to let his head rest there. Once, when she was undressing, he caught a glimpse. It was as big as a robin's egg but of a darker color. He assumed it was the consumption, the phthisis, the tubercle bacillus, the Koch's agent, TB, the mycobacterium—whatever name it had, it was a treacherous enemy ripening within her.

. . .

ONE EVENING as they lay next to each other, their beds pulled together, and as he read to her from the daily worship book, she exclaimed in surprise. He looked back at the sentence to see if he had missed a word. He looked up to see blood staining her white nightgown and spreading out as if she had been shot.

As long as he lived he would remember that in the awful moment when she realized she was dying, and when her eyes sought his, her first thought, her only thought, was about abandoning her son.

For a second Thomas was paralyzed. Then he jumped up and pulled aside the soggy blouse. A red geyser shot up from her chest and arced to the ceiling, then fell to earth. In the next instant it did it again. And again. A pulsing obscene blood fountain, timed to every beat of her heart, kept striking the ceiling, showering him, the bed, and her face with blood, soaking the pages of the open book.

He recoiled from the monstrous sight, this eruption from his mother's chest which painted everything around it red. When it occurred to him to try to staunch it with the bedsheet, the jet was already dropping in height, as if the tank were empty. Hilda lay soaked in her blood, her face white as porcelain and flecked with scarlet. She was gone.

Thomas cradled her soggy head, his tears falling on her face. When Dr. Ross arrived, a white coat thrown over his pajamas, he said to Thomas, "It was inevitable. That aneurysm has been ticking in her chest for over a year. It was just a matter of time." He reassured Thomas that the blood was not infective—the thought had not crossed the boy's mind.

ALONE, TRULY ALONE, Thomas developed fever, and a cough. He refused to be moved from the cottage to the infirmary; the cottage was the last thing on earth to connect him to his mother. He let them take him for an X-ray. Later he watched Muthukrishnan, the compounder, arrive with a pushcart carrying the bulky pneumothorax apparatus in its polished wooden case. Muthu squatted on the balcony and, after wiping his face with a towel, he opened the wings of the fancy box and began unpacking the large bottles, manometers, and tubing. Dr. Ross, himself once a consumptive, soon cycled up. "The X-ray was no good, lad. No good at all," Ross said.

It is just a matter of time, Thomas thought. He looked forward to joining his mother.

He didn't flinch as the needle went between his ribs posteriorly and into the pleural space that lined the lung, a space that was normally a vacuum, Ross explained. "Now we measure pressures." He maneuvered the needle while Muthu fiddled with the two bottles, raising and lowering them on Ross's command. "This is 'artificial pneumothorax.' Fancy way of saying we put air in that vacuum that lines your chest to collapse the infected part of the lung, lad. Those Koch bacteria need their oxygen to thrive, and we won't give it to them, will we?"

Facedown, from the depths of his illness, Thomas thought this reasoning was illogical: What about *my* oxygen, Dr. Ross? But he said nothing.

For twenty-four hours Thomas had to lie prone, propped in position by sandbags. Muthu came by many times a day to check on him. Muthu noted the sudden fever and the chills. The artificial pneumothorax had introduced other bacteria into the pleural space around the lung. He heard Ross's voice from afar. "Empyema, my boy. That's what we call pus collecting around the lung. Doesn't happen that often in my hands, but it does happen. I am so sorry. Alas, the pus is too thick to come out with a needle," Ross said.

For the operation they took him to a tiled room with high windows. It seemed bare but for a narrow raised table in the middle, over which was suspended a giant dish light resembling the compound eye of an insect. The place left a strong impression on the boy. It was otherworldly, hallowed ground, but still secular. The name "theater" was fitting.

Ross cut into the skin, under local anesthesia, just to the outside of the left nipple, then exposed three adjacent ribs and cut out short segments from them, thereby unroofing, or "saucerizing," the empyema cavity. The pus had no place to collect. Despite the anesthesia, Thomas had moments of excruciating pain.

When he could speak, Thomas asked, "Won't an opening like that destroy the vacuum in the pleural space? Won't it cause air to rush in and the whole lung to collapse?"

"Brilliant question, lad," Ross said, delighted. "It *would* collapse in anybody else. But the infection, the empyema, has stiffened the lining of your lung, made it thick and inflexible, like a scab. So in your case, the lung won't collapse back."

For a week, pus oozed out onto gauze padding strapped over the hole.

When it slowed to a trickle, Ross stuffed the wound with gauze tape, to cause it to "heal by secondary intention." During dressing changes, Thomas studied his crater with a mirror, taking perverse pride in what it produced and the day-to-day changes as his body made repairs.

Ross was a short, cheerful man with the roundest and most forgettable of faces and the bow legs of a jockey. He always warmed the chest piece of his stethoscope in his chubby hands before letting the metal touch Thomas's skin. He percussed Thomas's chest, sounding it out skillfully. Ross pulled out the gauze and they peered into the crater. "You see the red, pebbly-looking base, Thomas? We call that granulation tissue. It will slowly fill up the wound and allow skin to form over it." And that was exactly what happened. At one point the granulation tissue grew excessively, pouching out like a strawberry. "Proud flesh," Ross called it. Holding a crystal of copper sulfate in his forceps, he rubbed it over the proud flesh, burning it back.

One day Ross brought him Metchnikoff's *Immunity in Infectious Diseases* along with Osler's *Principles and Practice of Medicine*. Metchnikoff was hard going, but Thomas liked the drawings of white cells eating bacteria. Osler was surprisingly readable.

In a life that was merely a prelude to death, Thomas found he looked forward to Ross's visit, to the short man's daily rituals. And yet he held back his affection for the doctor, because that was a recipe for loss. "I'm not going away, lad," Ross said one day. "And since you are staying, why don't you join us on rounds." Ross turned and left, not waiting for an answer.

WHEN ROSS PRONOUNCED him healed, Thomas had been at the sanatorium for a year and a half. During that time he never saw his father. Fothergill came twice, saying Justifus Stone was too ill to travel. Thomas asked Ross about the illness from which his father suffered. Ross said, "It's not tuberculosis, but something else."

"To do with his legs?"

Ross tousled Thomas's hair. "Something punky, lad. Unfortunate, it is. He is bedridden. You'll learn in medical school," he said.

It was the first time Ross had ever uttered the words "medical school" to Thomas. Thomas couldn't control the fluttering in his heart, as if a door had cracked open in his coal cellar, bringing in light, promising a future when he had visualized none.

ROSS, NOW OFFICIALLY THOMAS'S GUARDIAN, decided Thomas should go to boarding school in England. Thomas didn't even consider going to see his father in the infirmary in Madras before he sailed.

Two terms had gone by when Ross wrote to say that Justifus had died. A modest inheritance under Ross's guardianship would allow him to finish schooling and go to university.

Ross had led Thomas in the direction of medical school as if it were inevitable. Thomas had no reason to resist. Life thus far had convinced him of his aptitude for two things: sickness and suffering.

In medical school in Edinburgh, he lost himself in his studies, finding a stability and a sanctity missing before. He had no need to lift his head from his books, no desire to go anywhere but for classes or demonstrations. When his eyes tired, he went diffidently to the infirmary, hoping no one would throw him out. He got to know a house officer here, a senior student there, and before long, and well before his class had reached the clinical years, he was being pointed to interesting patients.

The hospital porter nicknamed him "the Lurker," and Thomas didn't mind. In the organized chaos of the hospital, in the labyrinth of corridors, in the stink and confinement of its walls, he found both order and refuge; he found home. Misery and suffering were his closest kin.

A drunk named Jones looked eerily like his father; Thomas realized it was the waxy complexion, the swollen parotids, the loss of the outer third of the eyebrows, and the puffy eyelids of alcoholism that gave both men a leonine appearance. Now that he was trained to see, he put together the other clues he recalled: red palms, the starburst of capillaries on cheek and neck, the womanly breasts, and the absence of armpit hair. His father had cirrhosis. Perhaps that was the "punky" thing that Ross had been too polite to mention.

IT WAS SLEETING on a bitter cold evening in the Founders' Library when the final piece came together, and when it did, Thomas slammed his book shut, alarming Mrs. Pincus, the librarian. The young man, who practically lived in the study carrel farthest from the fireplace, suddenly ran out into the spitting snow, hatless and distraught.

Thomas negotiated the long corridor leading to his room in the pitch-dark. Walking in the dark was something his father could not have done. The signals coming up from Thomas's toe and ankle and knee told him where he was in space, but in Justifus Stone those messages had been blocked in his spinal cord. His father's stamping, crashing gait, always worse at night when he no longer could see where his feet were planted—that was from syphilis of the spinal cord, or *tabes dorsalis*. No child should possess such knowledge of a parent.

The meandering conversation, the boastful tales at the dinner table, the delusions of grandeur—that was syphilis of the brain, not just the spinal cord.

Once in his room, Thomas stripped before the wardrobe mirror. With a second handheld mirror he examined every inch of his skin. No syphilids. No gumma on his skin. He listened to his heart but heard nothing unusual. He'd been spared congenital syphilis. But then he realized that his fear was absurd because congenital syphilis had to come through the placenta to him, it had to come from his mother. Absurd for him to worry. What his mother had was tuberculosis. Pure as the Virgin, his mother could never have had . . .

He cried out suddenly, the anguish of a child whose final illusion is stripped away. He understood at last.

It had been under his nose all this time. Tuberculosis didn't cause aneurysms like the one that killed her, but syphilis did. "Mother. Poor Mother," he cried, grieving for her all over again. His father had murdered Hilda with his unbridled lust. She might have recovered from her TB, but she probably never knew she had syphilis until that aneurysm blossomed and began eroding painfully through the breastbone when she was at the sanatorium. Ross would have told her what it was. She knew. By that point neither salvarsan nor even penicillin, had it been available, would have been of any use.

WHEN THOMAS STONE BOUGHT his own cadaver in his final year of medical school, it was unheard-of, but did not surprise anyone. He was planning a second complete dissection, searching for mastery of the human body.

"Is Stone around?" was a common question in the casualty room, because he was the medical student who was more constant than Hogan or the other porters, always willing to stitch up a laceration, or pass a stomach tube, or run to the blood bank. He was the happiest of students when asked to scrub in and hold a retractor during emergency surgery.

One night, Dr. Braithwaite, Senior Consultant Surgeon and Chief Examiner for the Royal College of Surgeons, came in to see a patient with a high stab wound to the abdomen. Braithwaite was a legend for having pioneered a new operation for esophageal cancer, a notoriously difficult condition to cure. The patient, already inebriated, was terrified, abusive, and combative. Braithwaite, a compact man with silver hair, wore a blue three-piece suit that was the same shade as his blue eyes; he dismissed the porters restraining the patient and he put his hand gently on the man's shoulder and said, "Don't worry. It is going to be all right." He kept his hand there, and the patient, staring at the elegant doctor, quieted down and stayed that way during the brief interview. Then Braithwaite examined him quickly and efficiently. When he was done, Braithwaite addressed his patient as if he were a peer, someone he might see later in the day at his club. "I'm glad to tell you that the knife spared your big blood vessels. I am confident you are going to do very well, so I want you not to worry. I'll operate, to repair whatever is cut or torn. We are going to take you to the operating theater now. Everything is going to be fine." The docile patient extended a grubby hand of thanks.

When they were out of earshot of the patient, Braithwaite asked the entourage of registrars and house-officers, "What treatment is offered by ear in an emergency?"

This was an old saw, particularly in Edinburgh. Still, the old saws were not well known anymore, a matter that distressed Braithwaite greatly. He saw it as emblematic of a slackness in the new generation of trainees, and it was sad that only one person knew the answer. And that too a medical student, of all people.

"Words of comfort, sir."

"Very good. You can come and assist me in surgery if you like, Mr. . . ."

"Stone, sir. Thomas Stone."

During the surgery Braithwaite found Thomas knew how to stay out of the way. When Braithwaite asked him to cut a ligature, Stone slid his scissors down to the knot and then turned the scissors at a forty-five-degree angle and cut, so there was no danger to the knot. Indeed, Stone so clearly understood his role that when the senior registrar showed up to assist, Braithwaite waved him off.

Braithwaite pointed to a vein coursing over the pylorus. He asked Thomas what it was.

"The pyloric vein of Mayo, sir . . . ," Thomas said, and appeared about to add something. Braithwaite waited, but Thomas was done.

"Yes, that's what it's called, though I think that vein was there long before Mayo spotted it, don't you think? Why do you think he took the trouble to name it?"

"I believe it was as a useful landmark to identify the *pre*pyloric from the pyloric area when operating on an infant with pyloric stenosis."

"That's right," Braithwaite said. "They should really call it the pre-pyloric vein."

"That would be better, sir. Because the right gastric vein is also referred to in some books as the 'pyloric vein.' Which is very confusing."

"Indeed, it is, Stone," Braithwaite said, surprised that this student had picked up on something that even surgeons with a special interest in the stomach might not know. "If we have to give it an eponym, maybe call it the vein of Mayo if we must, or even the vein of Laterjet, which seems to me much the same thing. Just don't call it pyloric."

Braithwaite's questions became more difficult, but he found the young man's knowledge of surgical anatomy to be shockingly good.

He let Thomas close the skin, and he was gratified to see him use both hands and take his time. There was room for improvement, but this was clearly a student who'd spent many waking hours tying knots one-handed and two-handed. Stone had the good sense to stick to a two-handed knot, tied well and with care, rather than showing off to Braithwaite with one-handed knots.

The next morning, when Braithwaite returned, he found Stone asleep in a chair at the bedside in the recovery room, having kept an all-night vigil on the patient. He did not wake him.

At year's end, after passing his final exams, when Thomas was appointed to the coveted position of Braithwaite's house officer, Shawn Grogan, a bright and well-connected medical student, found the courage to ask Braithwaite what he might have done to be selected instead of Stone.

"It's quite simple, Grogan," Braithwaite said. "All you have to do is know your anatomy inside out, never leave the hospital, and prefer surgery over sleep, women, and grog." Grogan became a pathologist, famous as a teacher in his own right, and famous for his extraordinary girth.

During the war, Thomas was commissioned. He traveled with Braithwaite to a field hospital in Europe. In 1946, he returned to Scotland, became a junior registrar, then a senior registrar. He'd skipped a real childhood and gone directly to doctorhood.

Ross came to Scotland on a rare visit. He told Thomas how proud he was of him. "You're my consolation for never having married. That wasn't by choice, by the way—not being married. 'Perfection of the life or of the work'—I could only do the one. I hope you don't make that mistake."

Ross planned to retire near the sanatorium, to play rummy at the Ooty Club every night, to catch up on a lifetime of reading, and to learn to play golf with the retired officers who lived there. But just as he did, a cancer made itself known in Ross's good lung. Thomas returned to India at once. He stayed with Ross for the next six months, during which time the cancer spread to his brain. Ross died peacefully, Thomas at his side, the faithful Muthu, old and gray, on the other side, with the many nurses and attenders who had worked with Ross holding vigil.

The funeral brought Europeans and Indians from as far away as Bombay and Calcutta to pay tribute. Ross was buried in the same cemetery where many of his patients rested. "They are heroes, one and all, all those who sleep in this cemetery," said the Reverend Duncan at the graveside service. "But no greater hero, and no humbler a man, and no better servant of God is buried here than George Edwin Ross."

THOMAS TOOK AN APPOINTMENT as a consultant surgeon in the Government General Hospital, Madras. But after independence in 1947, things were not the same. Indians now ran the Indian Medical Service, and they were not excited by Englishmen who wanted to stay on, though many did. Thomas knew he had to leave; if it had ever been his land, it no longer was. And that was how, in response to a notice from Matron in the *Lancet*, he made his voyage on the *Calangute* to Aden. It was on that ship that Sister Mary Joseph Praise literally fell into his arms and entered his life.

Thomas Stone believed there existed within him the seeds for harshness, for betrayal, for selfishness, and for violence—after all, he was his father's son. He believed the only virtues passed down to him were the virtues of his profession, and they came through books and by apprenticeship. The only suffering that interested him was that of the flesh. For the heartache and the grief of his own loss, he had found the cure and he'd found it by himself. Ross had it wrong, or so Thomas thought: perfection of the life *came* from perfection of the work. Thomas stumbled on an address by Sir William Osler to graduating medical students in which the man articulated this very thesis:

The master-word is *Work,* a little one, as I have said, but fraught with momentous sequences if you can but write it on the tablets of your hearts, and bind it upon your foreheads.

"The master-word is *Work.*" Stone bound it to his forehead. He wrote it on the tablet of his heart. He woke to it and fought sleep for it. Work was his meat, his drink, his wife, his child, his politics, his religion. He thought work was his salvation, until the day he found himself seated in Our Lady of Perpetual Succour, in the room of a child he had abandoned; only then did he admit to his son how completely work had failed him.

CHAPTER 46

Room with a View

H E STOPPED TALKING at this point. In the silence that followed, it seemed to me he was debating what to tell me next. When he resumed, I thought at first that he had leapfrogged over his years at Missing, dismissed the existence of my mother, and I nearly said something rude to interrupt him, but I'm glad I didn't, because what followed was all about her . . .

THE OAKS AND MAPLES outside the window of his room are wild men with their heads on fire. He shuts his eyes, but the view inside his eyelids is the same nightmare. His nerves are lancinating cables under his skin that send jolts of electricity to his muscles. He is so tremulous that when he brings a glass of water to his lips, he has spilled most of it before he can take a sip. He pukes his insides out, till he imagines the lining of his stomach is smooth and shiny like a copper pot. But the impulse to run is gone. He has put one or perhaps two oceans between him and the place he flees.

Eli Harris and another man, a doctor perhaps, judging by his detachment, leave him tincture of paregoric in a tiny bottle by the bedside. Thomas fails to see it at first, imagining that the peculiar scent of aniseed and camphor is a hallucination. But once he spies the bottle he drinks it as if it holds redemption. The antiseptic odor fills the room, and then it comes off his breath. It is the tiny amount of opium in paregoric that gives him some ease, or so he tells himself. Surely it isn't the alcohol base of the tincture. He is done with alcohol.

The only two women he has ever loved have died, and though one death occurred years before the other, they became superimposed in his brain. It made him lose his mind. He fled. He ran without knowing where to or what from. He has now run far enough. He has no memory of how he arrived in New Jersey from Kenya, except that he has a benefactor, Eli Harris.

A week passes, measured not in days, but in cold sweats and night terrors. It is two weeks before the agitation and the shakes ease, and before the ugly little invertebrates begin a retreat. For so long they have been on his skin and on the edge of his sheets, scurrying to the periphery of his vision when he turns to look at them. Now they retreat to the chitinous underworld from where they came.

There is bread and cheese by his bed, sitting on a newspaper that is two days old. The paregoric bottle is empty. A pitcher of water has been refilled. When at last he feels it safe to take his chair to the window, the leaves have gone from carrot to brick to crimson and every hue in between, a palette beyond the imagination of any painter. He sits there like a statue, grateful for being able to sit, to see things for what they are. Leaves spiral down, each descent unique and never to be repeated. A million voyagers leave their invisible trails in the air.

One morning he is steady enough to go downstairs. A sparrow hops on the warped wood of the porch, the varnish flaking under its feet. Stone sees the ginger kitten inching forward from the wisteria, its shoulder blades gliding like pistons under its fur. He wonders if he is hallucinating. The kitten's unblinking eyes are locked on its prey. The bird tilts its head like a coquettish woman to regard man and beast.

Just when Thomas thinks the tension is unbearable, the kitten pounces, but the sparrow hops easily to the railing and out of reach. Thomas feels something crack inside, releasing him from the torpor that stifled his movements and slowed his thoughts. He has emerged to a world where a sparrow's fate and that of a man can be decided in the blink of a cat's eye, such is the true measure of time.

HE KNOWS THE CEILING in his bedroom better than he knows his body. He has studied the molding. The decorative grooves are even in depth and width. He sees the handiwork of a craftsman. A clumsy amateur later subdivided the house with plywood partitions and with prefabricated doors. But the master's imprint is there to see.

At first he credits the paregoric for the curious phenomenon, but it continues after the paregoric is long gone: like a cinema projectionist he watches his life play out on the screen of the blank ceiling, or sometimes in the light playing on his window. He cannot control the content or order of the reels. What he can do is observe dispassionately, separate emotions from event, and judge the actor who plays him.

AN EARLY WINTER STORM comes over Ocean City and reaches inland by afternoon, first with freezing rain, crackling on the window, and then snow so heavy that when he stands outside it weighs down his eyelashes. It blankets northern New Jersey, five to six inches in as many hours. It shuts down interstates, airports, schools, and all commerce, but he knows nothing of this as he retreats to his room. Ice forms around the edges of his window, leaving a narrow prism through which to look onto a still and ghostly world. It is on this evening that he witnesses a scene from his life which makes him want to end it. He is seated on his bed, staring through that narrow breach in the frosted window. His mind is motionless and hushed like the landscape outside. The only thing that stirs is the ebb and flow of his breath, but even that seems to cease.

Then suddenly, he feels a quickening, as if the wearing away of brain cells has unroofed a lacuna of memory.

What spews out that winter's night is a vivid, colorful, and specific memory of Sister Mary Joseph Praise.

He is simply the observer, a man watching a bird, unaware of the feral cat lurking in the wisteria. This is what he sees, what he remembers:

Addis Ababa.

Missing Hospital.

Work.

He sees himself in the rhythm of operating, of clinics, of writing, forcing himself to sleep, his days full and satisfying. The weeks and months roll by. The master word. Work. And suddenly the machinery seizes . . .

(He thinks of this as his "Missing Period." He prefers that to "breakdown.")

It always begins the same way. He wakes from sleep in his quarters at Missing, wakes in terror, unable to breathe, as if he is about to die, as if the next breath will trigger the explosion. Though he is awake, the tentacles of dream and nightmare won't let go. A terrifying spatial distortion is the hallmark of this state. His bedroom in his quarters begins to shrink. His pen, the doorknob, his pillow—ordinary objects that normally do not merit a second glance—balloon in size. They become colossal and threaten to impale him, to suffocate him. He has no control over this state. He cannot turn it off by sitting up or moving around. He becomes neither child nor man, does not know where he is, or what scene he is reliving, but he is terrified.

Alcohol is not the antidote. It does not break the spell, yet it dulls the terror. It comes with a price: instead of straddling the line between wakefulness and nightmare, he crosses over. He roams in a world of familiar objects turned into symbols; he traipses through scenes of his childhood and through hell's portals. He hears a nonstop dialogue, like cricket commentary on the radio. That is the backdrop to these night terrors in Ethiopia. The commentator's voice is indistinct—sometimes it sounds like his own voice. As he drinks, he loses his fear but not his sorrow. He who has no tears in his waking now weeps like a child. He sees Ghosh—probably the real Ghosh, not a dream figure—standing before him, concerned, the Ghosh lips moving but the words drowned out by the commentator.

Then *she* is there. He cannot hear her words, but her presence is reassuring, and ultimately, only she stays, only she keeps vigil. She must have been asleep when she was summoned, because she wears a head scarf and a dressing gown. She holds him to her when a new wave of tears appears, and she cries with him, trying to rescue him from his nightmare but, in the process, she gets sucked in. (Every time he recalls this, there is a stirring in him.) In their work together, they share an intimacy that involves the body of another who lays between them, unconscious, naked, and exposed. But this weeping in her arms is shockingly different from their gowned forearms brushing or heads bumping during surgery. Separated as they are by an operating table for so many hours a day, when she holds him, the absence of the table, or of the mask, or the gloves, is startling. He feels like a newborn placed against its mother's naked belly. She whispers in his ear. What does she say? How he wishes he could remember. It sounds improvised, not a formal prayer. It succeeds in blunting the commentator's voice.

He remembers her blouse, damp with his tears—no, both their tears.

He remembers clinging to her, pressing his face to her bosom, sleeping, waking, clinging, weeping, sleeping again. She asks again and again, *What is it? What is it that has come over you?* For hours, days, who knows how long, she stays with him as he holds on for dear life, the storm raging, battering him, trying to pry him out of her grasp.

He remembers a lull, a startling silence which is a change in the pattern. Her blouse has opened.

Like a surgeon working to develop a tissue plane under the incision, he wills the blouse to open farther, and perhaps his nose, his cheeks, help it along. Her nipples stir from the coins on which they lie, and now her breasts escape her blouse to meet his lips. Her face must be a mirror of his because what he sees in it is fear coupled with desire.

She hovers over him, naked, her breasts full and reassuring, tears of relief on both their faces, their kisses devouring each other to make up for time lost. Then he is above her, and she looks up at him as if he is the Savior. When he enters her, he is anchoring himself to her goodness, a goodness and innocence he lost so young, from which he has drifted away, and which he vows never to let go . . .

Sitting on his bed in his New Jersey exile, the world outside muted in a canopy of snow, his heart is racing, a dangerous tachycardia, his shirt soaked with sweat despite the cold. There is a dull ache under his breastbone. How he wishes that he could recall the exact feel of her lips, of her breasts.

But he recalls *this* (and he prays it is a true image):

He recalls how he loses himself in her, pulling her like a soft lamb coat over him. She settles on him, smothers him like nightfall over a meadow. In their coming together they thwart the demons, his and hers, and when his cry of release comes it punctuates her soft exclamations. Order is restored. Proportion returns. Sleep comes as a blessing.

HIS CURSE IS THIS (and he weeps in New Jersey at the recollection, he beats his head with his hand): when he wakes from his Missing Period, he senses only a perturbation in space, a gap in time, a deep embarrassment and shame, the reason for which he cannot recall, but which he can only heal by throwing himself into his work anew. He has blocked out what came before.

How cruel it is that this memory should surface in a winter storm so long after she is dead. How cruel to have this fleeting, fragmented vision, seen through an ice-crusted window, then to wonder if it is real, or if it is the perturbation of a brain undone by alcohol. He has reassembled the memory like a shattered relic, and it is finally whole; and still he has doubts. He will never see her more clearly than that night at 529 Maple. When he recalls it in later years, he will wonder if he is distorting it, embellishing it, because each time he consciously recalls her, *that* forms a new memory, a new imprint to be stacked on top of the previous one. He fears that too much handling will make it crumble.

"You saved my life," he says aloud to Sister Mary Joseph Praise, seated on his small bed in New Jersey. "And my stupidity, my indecision, my panic, caused you to lose yours." Though it is much too late to say it to her, he knows it must be said, and though he is a nonbeliever, he hopes that somehow she is listening. "I cannot love any human being more than I love you." What he cannot bring himself to mention is the children; he feels he can do even less for them than he can do for Sister Mary Joseph Praise; they exist, two boys, twins, he knows, he remembers, in a universe even more removed than the one in which Sister resides.

But it is too late to say all this to Sister Mary Joseph Praise. Even this memory of her, beautiful and erotic, cannot arouse him or fill him with joy. Instead, when he sees her nakedness, his engorgement, the miscibility of their parts, what he feels is a violent jealousy, as if another person occupies his naked body and straddles the woman he loves, an *illusion des soises*—*That is me, but it is not me.* His thrusting body, the dark triangles of his shoulder blades, the hollows and dimples of the low back, only foretell death and destruction. They are an augury to a terrible end because this carnal pleasure will doom Mary, though she does not know it as yet, but he, watching the scene, does. His punishment is even worse: he must live.

CHAPTER 47

Missing Letters

THOMAS STONE STAYED IN MY ROOM past midnight. At some point he became one with the dark shadows, his voice filling my space as if no other words had ever been spoken there. I didn't interrupt him. I forgot he was there. I was inhabiting his story, lighting a candle in St. Mary's Church in Fort St. George, Madras, holding my own in an English boarding school, seeing how an unroofing of memory might lead to a vision of Mary. And if visions could happen in Fatima and Lourdes and Guadalupe, who was I to doubt that a secular vision of my mother had not appeared to him in a frost-rimmed rooming house window, just as I had seen and felt her in the autoclave room as a young boy? His voice walked me into a past that preceded my birth, but it was still mine as much as the color of my eyes or the length of my index finger.

I became conscious of Thomas Stone only when he was done; I saw a man under the spell of his own tale, a snake charmer whose serpent has become his turban. The silence afterward was terrible.

THOMAS STONE SAVED our surgery program.

He did it by making Our Lady of Perpetual Succour an affiliate of Mecca in Boston. All it took was his affixing his signature to a letter saying it was so. But Our Lady of Perpetual Succour was no mere paper affiliate of Mecca. Each month, four medical students and two surgical residents came down from Mecca to do a rotation with us. "A safari to see the natives killing each other, and to catch a few Broadway shows," is how B. C. Gandhi put it when he heard about the plan. But each of us also had opportunities to do specialty rotations up in Boston.

I finished my internship and began my second year of residency. The most important result of our affiliation with Mecca was that it allowed Deepak, the Wandering Jew of surgery (as B.C. referred to him), to finish. He was now a board-certified surgeon and could have gone anywhere to set up practice. Instead, he stayed on at Our Lady with the title of Director of Surgical Training; he was also appointed Clinical Assistant Professor at Mecca. I had never seen Deepak happier. Thomas Stone, true to his word, paved the way for publication of Deepak's study on injuries to the vena cava. That paper in the *American Journal of Surgery* became a classic, one that everyone quoted when discussing liver injuries. Though Deepak was getting a consultant's salary, he continued to live in the house-staff quarters. Courtesy of the Mecca surgical residents who came down to the Bronx for rotations, we had more manpower and Deepak got more sleep. In an unused basement space, Deepak researched the effects of different interruptions to the blood supply of pig and cow livers.

Popsy's dementia no longer needed to be concealed. He roamed safely throughout Our Lady, wearing scrubs, and with a mask dangling from his neck. He was turned away every time he wandered into the operating room, or tried to leave the premises, but he didn't seem to mind. He would sometimes stop people and declare, "I contaminated myself."

LATE ON A FRIDAY EVENING, a few months after Thomas Stone's first visit to my room, I heard a knock at my door. There he stood, tentative, embarrassed, and unsure what his reception would be.

My father's long confessional had changed things for me; it had been much easier to stay angry with him, to trash his apartment and violate his space, before I heard his story. Now his presence felt awkward and I didn't invite him in.

"I can't stay but I wondered . . . want to ask if . . . would you care to join me for dinner at an Ethiopian restaurant in Manhattan tomorrow, Saturday? . . . Here's the address—about seven?"

This was the last thing I expected from him. If he'd invited me to go to the Met, or to dine at the Waldorf-Astoria, I would have declined without any hesitation. But when he said "Ethiopian restaurant," it conjured up the sour taste of *injera* and a fiery *wot* and my mouth began watering and my tongue stopped working. I nodded, even though I really didn't want to be around him. But we had unfinished business.

On Saturday I emerged from the subway and I saw Thomas Stone at a distance standing outside the Meskerem in Greenwich Village. Though he'd been in America more than twenty years, he looked out of place. He had no interest in the menu displayed outside, and he did not notice the students pouring out from a New York University building, instrument cases in their hands, their hair, clothing, and multiple ear piercings setting them apart from other pedestrians. When he saw me he was visibly relieved.

Meskerem was small, with dark red curtains and walls that recalled the inside of a *chikka* hut. The aroma of coffee beans roasted over charcoal and the peppery smell of *berbere* made it feel a world away from Manhattan. We sat on rough-hewn, three-legged wooden stools, low to the ground, with a woven basket table between us. A long mirror behind Thomas Stone allowed me to see both the back of his head and people entering or leaving the restaurant. The posters thumbtacked to the walls showed the castles of Gondar, a portrait of a smiling Tigre woman with strong perfect teeth, a close-up of the wrinkled face of an Ethiopian priest, and an aerial view of Churchill Road, each with the same caption: THIRTEEN MONTHS OF SUNSHINE. Every Ethiopian restaurant I subsequently visited in America relied heavily on the same Ethiopian Airlines calendar for decor.

The waitress, a short, bright-eyed Amhara, brought us menus. Her name was Anna. She almost dropped her pencil when I said in Amharic that I'd brought my own knife and I was so hungry that if she pointed me to where the cow was tethered, I'd get started. When she brought our food out on a circular tray, Thomas Stone looked surprised, as if he'd forgotten that we would eat with our fingers off a common plate. To his dismay, Anna (who hailed from the neighborhood of Kebena in Addis, not that far away from Missing) gave me *gursha*—she tore off a piece of *injera,* dipped it in curry, and fed me with her fingers. Thomas Stone hastily rose and asked for the restroom, lest she turn to him.

"Blessed St. Gabriel," Anna said, watching him leave. "I scared your friend with our *habesha* customs."

"He should know. He lived in Addis for seven years."

"No! Really?"

"Please don't take offense."

"It's nothing," she said, smiling. "I know that type of *ferengi.* Spend years there, but they look through us. But don't worry. You make up for it, and you're better looking."

I could have taken up for him. I could have said he was my father. I smiled. I'm sure I blushed. I said nothing.

When Thomas Stone returned, he made a halfhearted effort to eat. Inevitably, one of the songs that cycled through the ceiling speakers was "Tizita." I studied his face to see if it meant anything to him. It didn't.

The mark of a native is that your fingers are never stained by the curry; you use the *injera* as your tongs, as a barrier, while you pick up a piece of chicken or beef sopped in the sauce. Thomas Stone's nails were red.

Tilahoun singing "Tizita," the cocoonlike atmosphere, and the frankincense brought memories bubbling to the surface. I thought of mornings at Missing and how the mist had body and weight as if it were a third element after earth and sky, but then it vanished when the sun was high; I remembered Rosina's songs, Gebrew's chants, and Almaz's magical teat; I recalled the sight of a younger Hema and Ghosh leaving for work, as we waved through the kitchen window; I could see those halcyon days, shiny like a new coin, glinting in sunlight.

"Do you plan to finish your next four years of residency at Our Lady?" Thomas Stone said, abruptly, breaking into my reverie. "If you were interested in moving to Boston . . ." So much for his perceptiveness. Just when I was ready to talk about the past, he wanted to know about my future.

"I don't want to leave Our Lady. The hospital is my Missing equivalent. I never wanted to leave Missing or Addis, but I had to. Now I don't want to leave Our Lady."

Any other man would have asked me why I had to leave Missing. That was my fault—had he posed the question, I might not have answered. And perhaps he knew that.

As she cleared our plates, Anna said to Thomas Stone in English, "How did you like the food?"

"It was good," he said, barely glancing at her. He reddened as she and I studied him. "Thank you," he added, as if he hoped that would help get rid of her. She took two packaged towelettes out from her apron pocket and put them on the table.

I said to Anna, "Honestly, it was good, but you could make the *wot* hotter."

"Of course we can," she said in Amharic, a little taken aback by the implied criticism. "But then people like him won't be able to touch the food. Also we use local butter, so even if we make it hotter, it won't taste the same as home. Only someone like you would know the difference."

"You mean there is no place to get real *habesha* food? The real thing? With all these Ethiopians in New York?"

She shook her head. "Not here. If you ever visit Boston, go see the Queen of Sheba. She's in Roxbury. She is famous. The house is like our embassy. Upstairs, in one room, they sell groceries, and downstairs they serve home food. Cooked with true Ethiopian butter. The Ethiopian Airlines crew bring it just for her. All the Ethiopian taxi drivers eat there. You won't see anybody but Ethiopians there."

THOMAS STONE HAD WATCHED this exchange, his face blank. When Anna left, he reached into his pocket. I thought he was reaching for his billfold. Instead, he pulled out the bookmark I had left in his room, the one on which Sister Mary Joseph Praise had written her note to him.

I dried my hands carefully and took it from him. I realized that I had missed it; it felt as if it shouldn't be here on a basket table but in a bank vault. It had been my talisman on a harrowing journey, an escape from Ethiopia which he knew nothing about. I read her last lines—"Also, I am enclosing a letter to you from me. Please read at once. SMJP"—and then I looked up.

Thomas Stone fidgeted in his seat. He swallowed hard, leaning on the basket table.

"Marion. This bookmark . . . was in the textbook, I presume?"

"Yes, it was. I have the textbook."

He grew stiff, his hands trapped under his thighs as if an electric current were running through him. "Would you . . . Can I ask if . . . Do you have . . . Was there a letter?"

He looked helpless, sitting so low to the ground, like a parent visiting kindergarten, his knees under his chin.

"I thought *you* had the letter," I said.

"No!" he said, so emphatically that Anna looked over at us.

"I'm sorry," I said, though I wasn't sure what I was sorry for. "I assumed that you took the letter when you left. That you left the book with the bookmark in it."

His face, so expectant a moment ago, collapsed.

"I took almost nothing," he said. "I walked out of Missing with the clothes I had on and one or two things from the office. I never went back."

"I know," I said.

He cringed when I said those words. No wonder he was reluctant to probe my past. No blade can puncture the human heart like the well-chosen words of a spiteful son. But did he really think of me this way? As a son? "But you took the finger with you?" I went on.

"Yes . . . that's all I took. It was in her room. I went back there." He looked up.

I said, "I'm sorry. I wish I had the letter."

"And the bookmark?" he said. "How did you get it?"

I sighed. Anna served us coffee. The small cup with no handle felt inadequate for my task of trying to cover a lifetime for this man. "I had to leave Ethiopia in haste. The authorities were looking for me . . . It's a long story. They thought I was involved in the hijacking of an Ethiopian Airlines plane. They thought I was a sympathizer for the Eritrean cause. Ridiculous, right? You remember your maid, Rosina? One of the hijackers was Rosina's daughter, Genet. Rosina is dead, by the way. Hanged herself."

It was more than he could digest.

"Rosina and Genet . . . ," I began. "Suffice it to say, I had an hour to get out of town. As I was leaving, climbing over Missing's wall, I said my good-byes to Hema, Matron, Gebrew, Almaz, and to Shiva, my brother . . ." I stopped. I had hit a roadblock. "Shiva, your other son . . . ?"

Stone swallowed. This was proving impossible. And yet he needed to know, particularly if it was painful.

"My son . . . ," he said, trying out the word.

"Your son. You want to see what he looks like?" He nodded, expecting me to pull out a wallet. "Look at that mirror behind you."

He hesitated as if this might be a joke, a trick. But he turned, and our eyes met in the mirror, startling me, because it was suddenly more intimate than I'd expected. "Shiva and I are mirror images."

"What is he like?" he asked without turning around.

I sighed. I shook my head. I dropped my gaze. He turned back to me.

"Shiva is . . . very different. A genius, I would say. But not in the usual way. Impatient with school. He'd never answer an exam question in a way that might make him pass, not because he didn't know . . . He has never understood the need to subscribe to convention. But he knows more medicine, certainly more gynecology, than I do. He works with

Hema doing fistula work. He's a brilliant surgeon. Trained, but by Hema. No medical school." None of this would have been difficult for Stone to discover on his own had he been interested. He was interested now.

"I was very close to Shiva when we were little boys."

Stone's eyes were unblinking. I couldn't tell him the details of what had happened since. I had told no one. Only Genet and Shiva knew the truth.

"He and Genet did something to hurt me that I cannot forgive . . ."

"Something related to the hijacking?"

"No, no. It happened long before. Anyway, I was and still am very angry with him. But he *is* my brother—my twin—and so when I had one hour to leave the city, when the time came to say good-bye to Shiva— well, it was very painful for both of us." Suddenly I found myself fighting for composure. It was terribly important for me not to cry in front of Thomas Stone. I pinched the inside of my thigh. "As I was saying good-bye to Shiva, he handed me two books. One was his *Gray's Anatomy*. That was his most valued possession. He dragged it around like a blanket.

"And the second was your book, with that bookmark inside. I didn't know how he got it, or how long he had it. I didn't even know you had written a book. The book was hardly opened. I don't think Shiva ever read it, certainly not like he devoured his *Gray's*. He probably saw and read the bookmark. But you have to know Shiva. He wouldn't be curious about the bookmark or the letter she referred to. Shiva lives in the now. I don't know just how he got the book or why he wanted to give it to me."

Stone remained silent, his gaze on the empty basket between us, as if it stood in for all that was unknown about his past, our past. His look of pain was so intense, it pierced me. "I can ask him," I offered. I wanted to know just as much as Thomas Stone did. "I will ask him," I said.

Thomas Stone was a world away. When he lifted his gaze, I understood the depths of his sorrow; I saw it in a darkening of his iris, even though that delicate structure should not change color. I could see that the almost mystical aura of this legendary surgeon—the single-mindedness, the dedication, the skill—was mere surface. The surgical persona was something he had crafted to protect himself. But what he had created was a prison. Anytime he strayed from the professional to the personal, he knew what to expect: pain.

When he spoke, his voice sounded tired, old. "And here I thought you had it, and you thought I . . ."

"What do you think is in the letter?"

"How I wish I knew," he said abruptly. "I'd give my right arm . . ."

It had been a few months since I met Thomas Stone. The anger I felt obliged to have had subsided. The story he told me of his childhood, his mother's death—it should have been enough to forgive him, but I didn't think I was ready for that. I hadn't forgiven Shiva, so why forgive Thomas Stone? Even if I *had* forgiven him, a perverse streak in me refused to let him know that. But I had unfinished business with him.

"There's something I have to tell you," I said. I never thought I would be ashamed in front of this man. "Something I was charged to tell you by Ghosh." Ghosh's wish had seemed irrational to me at the time. But now, looking into that hard, craggy face, I understood why Ghosh had wanted me to reach out to Stone. Ghosh knew Thomas, but Ghosh had overestimated my maturity.

"Ghosh had a dying wish which I promised to fulfill. But I didn't. I ignored it. I hope you—and he—will forgive me. Ghosh told me that he felt his life would be incomplete without my doing this . . . His wish was for me to come and find you. To let you know that he considered you a brother."

This was hard, both because I could recall Ghosh's labored breathing, could recall Ghosh's every word, and because I was now seeing the effect these words had on Thomas Stone. Other than his mother, and Dr. Ross in the sanatorium, who had ever expressed love for him? Sister Mary Joseph Praise perhaps, but did she ever get to tell him, and if she did, did he hear?

"Ghosh was disappointed that you never contacted him. But he wanted you to know that whatever your reason was for being silent all those years, it was all right with him." Ghosh had felt it was shame that kept Thomas from looking back. He was right, because it was shame that colored his face now.

"I'm so sorry," Stone said. I don't know whether he was speaking to me, or Ghosh, or the universe. It wasn't enough, but it was about time.

If there were other people in the restaurant, I was no longer aware of them. If there was music playing, I couldn't hear it.

I studied my father as I might study some specimen set before me: I saw the smile that struggled for purchase on his face and failed, and then I saw the haunted and hunted look that came in its wake. God help us if such a man had tried to raise us, if he had taken us away from Ethiopia. With all the sorrow and loss I'd experienced, I'd never have traded my past at Missing for a life in Boston with him. I should have thanked

Thomas Stone for leaving Ethiopia. The love he felt for Sister Mary Joseph Praise had come too late. She was the mystery, the great regret that he would take to his grave—and he would regret nothing more than not knowing what she said in that letter.

"I'll write to Shiva," I said. "I'll ask about the letter."

I suppose I understood Thomas Stone's shutting people out. After Genet's betrayal, I never wanted to have such strong feelings for a woman again. Not unless I had a written guarantee. I'd encountered a medical student from Mecca, a saint compared with my first love; she was kind, generous, beautiful, and seemed to transcend herself, as if her existence was secondary to her interest in the world and the things in it, including me. My belated and muted response must have pushed her away, lost me any chance of a future with her. Did I feel sad? Yes. And stupid? Yes, but I also felt relieved. By losing her, I was protected from her and she from me. I had that in common with this man sitting before me. I thought of a watch that had stopped ticking, and how it showed the correct time twice a day. He paid. I rose with him. At the door of the restaurant, our hands in our pockets, I waited.

" 'Call no man happy until he dies,' " he said. Before I could tell if that was a smile or an expression of sadness on his face, he nodded and walked away.

CHAPTER 48

Five Fingers

J UST AFTER MIDNIGHT on the first Sunday of every month, I would ring Hema at her bungalow. It was seven o'clock, Monday morning, Addis time. The rates were best at this hour, but since Almaz, Gebrew, and sometimes Matron came on before Hema, it could still be a long and expensive call. Ever since Hema delivered Mengistu's—sorry, *Comrade* Mengistu's—child, we no longer worried about the secret police eavesdropping on us; besides, they were preoccupied with real enemies. Mengistu Haile Mariam, Strength of Mary, Secretary General of the Council of Peasants and Workers, Chairman of the Military Council of Socialist Ethiopia, President-for-Life of the Armed Forces of the Democratic Peoples of Ethiopia, General in Command of the Bureau for Armed Struggle Against Imperial Aggression in Tigre and Eritrea, had adopted an Albanian style of Marxism. The upper and middle classes and even the working poor had their houses confiscated and land taken away. But favors to Mengistu and particularly favors to his wife weren't forgotten; Missing's medicines and supplies were not held up in the Customs godown, and there were no palms to grease.

As I dialed Hema's number that Sunday, I pictured my Missing family watching the clock, coffee cups in their hands, waiting for the phone to ring from a continent none of them had seen. Almaz picked up the receiver, with Gebrew leaning in, both of them suddenly shy and self-conscious. Their side of the conversation consisted of repeated *Ende-menneh? Dehna-ne-woy?*—How-are-you? Are-you-well, then?—until these godparents of mine were satisfied that their *lij*, their child, was all right. They told me they kept me in their prayers, fasted for me. "Pray that I'll see you soon and may God take care of you and your health," I said. Matron was just the opposite, chatty and spontaneous, as if we had run into each other in the corridor outside her office.

I had reported to Hema my first sighting of Thomas Stone. She'd listened without comment, and she must have smiled when she heard of her son breaking and entering Thomas Stone's apartment. I didn't censor information for her benefit; surely, Thomas Stone was no longer the threat he'd once been to her when we were minors. When I had told her about placing the bookmark on Stone's desk as my calling card, I had read from Hema's silence that she'd known nothing about Shiva's having *The Expedient Operator: A Short Practice of Tropical Surgery.* I surmised from that and later confirmed from Matron that Hema had made every attempt to banish the book from Missing; she'd never wanted me or Shiva to see his work, much less a picture of him.

"I had dinner with Thomas Stone, Ma," I said when she came on the line. "I ate *injera* for the first time in well over a year." She was miffed to learn that Ghosh had a message for Stone—I read that in the fact that she said nothing. When I told her just what Ghosh had wanted me to say to Stone, I heard a vigorous honk on her kerchief. The message said more about Ghosh and his selflessness than it did about Thomas Stone. I asked if she knew about the bookmark or a letter that accompanied it. She didn't.

"Maybe Shiva knows," I said. "Can I speak to him?"

She called out his name, a summons I had heard so many times since I was a child. I heard Shiva's reply, and could judge from its echo that it had come from our childhood room. While I waited, I heard Hema asking Matron about the bookmark; her "No!" told me it was news to her.

THE TELEPHONE WAS NEVER a comfortable instrument in Shiva's hands. He was fine, the fistula work was going very well, and no, he knew nothing about any missing letter.

"Do you remember the bookmark, Shiva, and the reference to a letter?" I asked.

"Yes."

"But you're saying there was no letter in the book?"

"No letter."

"How did you get the book, Shiva?"

"Ghosh gave it to me."

"When?"

"When he was dying. He wanted to talk with me about many things. This was one. He said he'd taken the book from Thomas Stone's quarters on the day we were born. He had kept it. He wanted me to have it."

"Was that the first time you'd seen the textbook or seen a picture of Thomas Stone?"

"Yes."

"Did Ghosh mention a letter from Sister Mary—our mother—to Stone?"

"No, he didn't."

"Did he say why he wanted you to have the book?"

"No."

"When you saw the bookmark and the reference to the letter, did you go back and ask him?"

"No."

I sighed. I could have stopped there, but I had come this far. "Why not?" I asked.

"If he wanted me to have the letter, he would have given it to me."

"Why did you give me the book, Shiva?"

"I wanted you to have it."

There was no annoyance in Shiva's voice; his tone was no different than when we began—I wondered if he'd picked up the irritation in mine. Shiva was right: there either was no letter, or Ghosh had the letter and had his reasons for destroying it.

I was about to say good-bye. I knew better than to expect my brother to ask about my health or my welfare. But he took me aback by saying, "How are your operating theaters?" He wanted to know about the layout, how far away the autoclave and the locker rooms were, and was there a sink outside each room, or one common scrubbing area. I gave him a detailed picture. When I was done, I waited. Once again, he surprised me: "When are you coming home, Marion?"

"Well, Shiva . . . I have four more years of residency."

Was this his way of saying he was sorry for everything that had happened? That he missed me? Did I want that from him? I wasn't sure, so all I added was, "I don't know if it is safe for me to come, but if it is, I'd love to come a year or so from now . . . Why don't you come visit here?"

"Will I be able to see your operating theaters?"

"Sure. We call them operating rooms here, not theaters. But I can arrange for you to see them."

"Okay. I'll be there."

Hema came back on the line. She was in a chatty mood, reluctant to let me go. Listening to her lilting voice, I was transported back to Missing Mean Time, as if I were sitting by the phone under Nehru's photograph and looking across the room at the portrait of Ghosh which consecrated the spot where he spent so many hours listening to the Grundig.

When I hung up I felt despair: I was back in the Bronx, my walls bare but for the framed *Ecstasy of St. Teresa*. My beeper, silent till then, went off. In answering its summons, I slipped the yoke back around my neck; indeed, I welcomed my slavish existence as a surgical resident, the never-ending work, the crises that kept me in the present, the immersion in blood, pus, and tears—the fluids in which one dissolved all traces of self. In working myself ragged, I felt integrated, I felt *American,* and I rarely had time to think of home. Then in four weeks, it was time to dial Missing again. Were these phone calls just as difficult for Hema? I wondered.

In a letter after our call, Hema said that she'd checked with Bachelli, Almaz, and even W. W. Gonad to see if they had heard of Ghosh or Sister leaving a letter behind, but no one had. She told me that Shiva's application for an exit visa to come visit me was held up by the government; he was asked to provide affidavits to show he had no debts in Ethiopia, and moreover that *I* had no debts for which he might be responsible. She said she would remind Shiva to work on the visa. Reading between the lines, I knew and she knew that Shiva had lost interest.

I wrote to Thomas Stone to let him know that the whereabouts of Sister Mary Joseph Praise's letter remained a mystery. He never wrote back to me thanking me for my troubles.

OVER THE NEXT FOUR YEARS, I saw Thomas Stone now and then when he came to conduct conferences or bedside teaching rounds; he was impressive, as I knew he would be, masterful, serious, and in command of his subject. He had the kind of perspective that could only come from careful study of the literature of surgery and from living it for many years. I much preferred being around him in that fashion than having a dinner with him. Perhaps he felt the same way, because he didn't call or visit again.

I went up to Boston for three separate, month-long rotations: plastic surgery, urology, and transplant, and the work was engrossing, challenging, so that each time my anxieties about being there and near him were forgotten. I worked with him in that last rotation, which was busier than I'd ever imagined. He suggested once during that time that we have a meal, but I begged off because my work in the transplant intensive care unit simply did not allow me to get away before nine in the evening, even on my nights off. I think he was relieved.

By 1986 I had finished my year as Chief Resident, which was also my fifth year of training, and I stayed on as an assistant to Deepak as I prepared to take my board exam. Grudgingly, I'd come to admire the long, arduous American system of surgical training; it was easier to admire when you were about done with it. I felt technically competent to do all the major operations of general surgery, and I knew my limits. There wasn't much I hadn't seen at Our Lady. More important, I was confident about caring for patients before and after surgery, and in the intensive care settings.

ALSO IN 1986, my brother became famous; it was Deepak who showed me the feature article in the *New York Times*. What a shock it was to see Shiva's picture, to see in it my reflection, but with shorter hair, almost a crew cut, and without the gray that had completely taken over my sideburns and temples. The image brought immediate bitterness, the recollection of the pain of betrayal. And yes, envy. Shiva had taken the first and only girl I loved and spoiled her for me. Now, he was making headlines in my backyard, in my newspaper. I'd followed all the rules, and tried to do the right thing while he ignored all the rules, and here we were. Could an equitable God have allowed such a thing? I confess, it was a while before I could read the article.

According to the *Times*, Shiva was the world's expert and the leading advocate for women with vaginal fistula. He was the genius behind a WHO fistula-prevention campaign that was a "far cry from the usual Western approach to these issues." The *Times* reproduced the colorful "Five Failings That Lead to Fistula" poster: it showed a hand, the fingers splayed out. Peering at the photograph, I could see that it was Shiva's hand. In the palm was a seated woman in a posture of dejection—was the model the Staff Probationer?

The poster was distributed all over Africa and Asia and printed in forty languages. Village midwives were taught to count off on one hand the Five Failings. The first was being married off too young, child brides; the second was nonexistent prenatal care; the third was waiting too long to admit that labor had stalled (by which time the baby's head was jammed halfway down the birth passage and doing its damage) and a Cesarean section was needed; the fourth failing was too few and too distant health centers where a C-section could be done. Presuming the mother lived (the baby never did), the final failing was that of the husband and in-laws who cast out the woman because of the dribbling, odiferous fistula from bladder to vagina, or from rectum to vagina, or both. Suicide was a common ending to such a story.

"Somehow women with fistula find their way to Shiva Praise Stone," the article said. "They come by bus, as far as they can before the other passengers kick them off. They come on foot, or by donkey. They come often with a piece of paper in their hand that simply says in Amharic, 'MISSING' or 'FISTULA HOSPITAL' or 'CUTTING FOR STONE.' "

Shiva Stone was not a physician, "but a skilled layperson, initiated into this field by his gynecologist mother."

When I next spoke to Hema, I asked her to congratulate Shiva for me. "Ma," I said, "you should have gotten more recognition in that story. Without you, Shiva couldn't be doing what he does."

"No, Marion. This is really all his doing. Fistula surgery wasn't something I relished. It suits someone as single-minded as Shiva. It needs constant attention, before, during, and after surgery. You should see the hours he spends thinking over each case, anticipating every problem. He can see the fistula in three dimensions." Shiva had fashioned new instruments in his workshop and invented new techniques. The article had mentioned Matron's fund-raising efforts and the desperate needs, and the article brought donations pouring in. Matron had in mind a new Missing building devoted to women with fistula. "Shiva has had the plans drawn out for years. It will be in the shape of a V with the wings converging on Operating Theater 3." Theater 3 was to be overhauled and remodeled, making two operating rooms with a shared scrub area in the middle.

I reread the *Times* article late that night. I felt a hollow sensation in my belly this time as I went through it again. The writer's unabashed admiration for Shiva came through, and one sensed she had abandoned her reserve, her usual dispassionate tone, because the man more than the subject so moved her. She ended with a quote from my brother: "What I do is simple. I repair holes," said Shiva Praise Stone.

Yes, but you make them, too, Shiva.

I HAD MY OWN SUCCESS, albeit a quieter one: I passed the written exam of the American Board of Surgery. A few months after that, I was assigned to take my oral exams in Boston at the Copley Plaza Hotel. After a grueling hour and a half in front of two examiners, I was done. I knew I did well.

Outside, the day was glorious. The monolith of gray stone that was the Church of Christian Scientists stood serene at the end of a long reflecting pool and framed against a blue sky. For five years I had spent my nights and days in the hospital, not seeing the sky, not feeling the sun on my face. I felt the urge to wade through the water fully clothed, or to let out a victory whoop. I contented myself instead with an ice-cream cone, which I enjoyed while sitting by the reflecting pool.

I planned to head to the airport, take the shuttle back to New York. But seeing that my driver was so obviously Ethiopian, and having greeted him in our language, I had another idea. Yes, of course he knew the Queen of Sheba's in Roxbury, and it would be an honor for him to take me there.

"My name is Mesfin," he said, grinning at me in the rearview mirror. "Who are you? What do you do?"

"My name is Stone," I said, putting my seat belt on, although I wasn't worried; nothing bad could happen to me on this day. "I'm a surgeon."

CHAPTER 49

Queen's Move

THE STREET HAD A JUNKYARD at the corner with high walls and barbed wire so reminiscent of Kerchele Prison. A massive dog, chained and asleep, was visible through the gate. Then came a string of vacant lots where ashes and soot outlined whatever had stood there. Mesfin seemed to be pointing the cab to the sole house at the end of the street that survived the blight that had felled the others. Its driveway began in the middle of the road, as if the paving machine had run out of asphalt when it got this far and so the owner took things into her own hands. The split-level house had yellow shingles. The steps, the railings, the pillars, the doors, the decks, and even the drains were painted the same canary yellow. A column of (unpainted) wheel hubs shored up a corner of the sagging front veranda. There were four taxis parked outside, all yellow.

The smell of fermenting honey elicited a Pavlovian response from my taste buds. A dour Somali met us at the door and led us to a dining room six steps down from the front landing. We found a half-dozen men eating at the picnic tables and benches, with room for a dozen more. The wooden floor was strewn with freshly cut grass, just as it would have been if this were a home or restaurant in Addis.

We washed our hands and took our seats, and at once a buxom woman arrived, bowing, wishing us good health, and placing water and two small flasks of golden yellow *tej* before us. The cornea of her left eye was milky white. Mesfin said her name was Tayitu. Behind her, a younger woman brought a tray of *injera*, on which were generous servings of lamb, lentils, and chicken.

"You see?" Mesfin said, looking at his watch. "I can eat here quicker than I can pump gas in my car. It's cheaper, too." I ate as if I had lived through a famine. The waitress in New York who first told me about the Queen of Sheba's had been right. This was the real thing.

Later, through a side window that looked out onto a sloping yard, I saw a white Corvette slide up. A shapely leg in heels emerged, the skin a café au lait color, with a shade of nail polish that B. C. Gandhi called "fuck-me red." A baby goat appeared from nowhere and danced around those elegant feet.

Soon a lovely Ethiopian lady came cautiously down the stairs, careful not to snag her heels. She said over her shoulder to the Somali, "Why is that silly boy letting the baby goat out at this hour? One of these days I'll run over it." Her golden-brown hair had red streaks, and it was cut in a perky, asymmetrical style that revealed her neck. She wore a maroon pin-striped blazer over a white blouse and skirt.

The Queen, for there was little doubt that this was she, bowed in our direction while continuing on to an office next to the kitchen. She stopped abruptly. She turned as if she had seen a vision and she stared. I was in my suit, my tie loosened—did I look that out of place? Within the confines of Our Lady of Perpetual Succour, all the tribes of Abraham were represented and I felt no more foreign than my patients or the staff. Now, as I attracted her attention, and that of the others there, I felt like a *ferengi* again.

"Praise God, praise His Son," the Queen said, her hands on her cheeks. She shifted her tinted glasses to her forehead, revealing eyes that were wide open in astonishment. I looked behind me; could she be talking to someone else? Her expression, at first quizzical, now turned joyous, showing brilliant white and perfect teeth. "Child, do you not know me?" she said, coming close, her rose-scented attar preceding her.

I came to my feet, still puzzled.

"I pray for you every day," she said in Amharic. "Don't tell me that I have changed that much?"

I towered over her. I was tongue-tied. She had been a mother and I a boy when I first met her.

"Tsige?" I said at last.

She lunged toward me, kissed my cheeks, held me at arm's length to better examine me, then pulled me to her to bump cheeks again and again. "My God, Blessed Mary and all the saints, how are you? Is it you? *Endemenneh? Dehna ne woy?* How are you? Can this be you? Praise God that you are here . . ."

After six years in America, it was only at that moment, standing in that yellow house, in her arms, cut grass under my feet, that I felt at ease in this land, felt my guard come down and the muscles in my belly and neck relax. Here was someone from my past, from my very street, someone whom I liked and with whom I had always felt a bond. I kissed her cheeks as vigorously as she kissed mine: Who would stop first? Not I.

Tayitu peered in from the kitchen. Two other women looked over the upstairs rail. Our fellow diners stopped to watch. They were displaced people, just like us, and they understood all too well these kinds of reunions, these moments when a piece of your old house comes floating by in the river.

"What are you doing here?" Tsige said. "You mean you didn't come to see me?"

"I came to eat. I had no idea! I've been living in New York for six years. I'm here just for the day. I'm a doctor now. A surgeon."

"A surgeon!" She gasped, falling back, clasping her hands to her heart. Then she kissed the back of my wrists, first one, then the other. "A surgeon. You brave, brave child." She turned to our audience and in the tones of a cantor she continued, still in Amharic, "Listen, all you unbelievers, when he was a little boy, and when my baby was dying, who took me to the right place in the hospital? It was he. Who called the doctor, who was his father, to see my child? He did. Then who was it who stayed with me as my baby fought for life? No one but him. He was the only one by my side when my little baby died. No one else was there for me, if only you knew . . ." The tears streamed down her face, and in an instant the mood in the room went from the joy of reunion to profound sadness, as if those two emotions were invariably linked. I heard sympathetic clucks and *tsks* from the men, and Tayitu blew her nose and dabbed at her good eye, while the other two women wept freely. Tsige was unable to speak, head bowed—she was overcome for a moment. At last she straightened her shoulders, raised her head, the lips parted to smile bravely, and she declared, "I never ever forgot his kindness. Even today, when I go to sleep, I pray for my baby's soul, then I pray for this boy. I lived across the street. I watched him grow up, become a man, go to medical school. Now he is a surgeon. Tayitu, give everyone their money back, for today is a feast day. Our brother has come home. Tell me, ye of little faith, does any one of you need some other proof that there is a God?" Her eyes glittered like diamonds; her hands, palms up, reached for the ceiling.

For the next few minutes I solemnly shook the hand of every person in the house.

. . .

LATER I SAT WITH TSIGE on a sofa in a living room upstairs. She had kicked off her heels and tucked her feet up under her. Still holding my hand, she touched my cheek often to exclaim how happy she was to see me.

I had plans to return to New York that afternoon, but Tsige insisted on sending Mesfin away. "You can take a later flight," she said.

"Are you sure I can find a taxi here?" I said, pretending to be serious.

After a beat, she threw her head back and laughed. "See, you have changed! You used to be so shy."

Through the window I saw six or seven baby goats in a large wire enclosure. Behind that was a chicken coop. A dreamy-looking boy with a long narrow head sat stroking one of the goats. "He's my cousin," Tsige said. "You can see the forceps marks on his forehead. He has some problems. But he loves to take care of the animals. You should come here when we celebrate Meskel on Meskerem Day. We slaughter the goats and cook outdoors. You will see not just taxis, but police cars. They come from the Roxbury and South End stations to eat."

Tsige said she left Addis a few months after me. A patron of the bar, a corporal in the army, had wanted to marry her. "He was nobody. But in the revolution, even the privates became powerful." When she declined his advances, she was falsely accused of imperialist activities and imprisoned. "I bought my way out after two weeks. In the time I was in Kerchele, they confiscated my house. He came to see me, pretending he had nothing to do with my arrest. If I married him, he said, everything would come back to us. The country was being run by dogs like him. I had money hidden away. I never looked back. I left.

"In Khartoum, I waited a month for asylum from the American Embassy. I worked as a servant for the Hankins, a British family. They were nice. I learned English by taking care of their children. That was the only good thing that came out of Khartoum. I don't mind the cold in Boston because every cold day reminds me how good it is to be out of Khartoum.

"I worked hard here, Marion. Quick-Mart—often I did two shifts. Then five nights I worked at a parking garage. I saved and saved. I became the first Ethiopian woman to drive a taxi in Boston. I learned the city. I found work for Ethiopians. Stock boy, parking attendant, taxi driver, or counter girl at the hotel gift shop. I lent money on interest to Ethiopians. Tayitu used to work for me in the bar, so when she came, I rented this house. She cooked. Then I bought the house. Now, my God, there is much to be done: grind *tef,* make *injera,* clean chicken, make *wot,* sweep the house. It takes three or four people. Ethiopians arrive at my door like newborn lambs, everything they have tied up in bedsheets, their X-rays still in their hands. I try to help them."

"You really are the Queen of Sheba."

There was an impish grin on her face. She switched to English, a language I had never heard her speak. "Marion, you know what I had to do to feed my baby in Addis. Then in Sudan, I was even lower than that—I was no better than a *bariya,*" she said, using the slang word for "slave." "In America they said you can be anything. I believed it. I worked hard. So when they say, 'Queen of Sheba,' I think to myself, Yes, from *bariya* to queen."

I told Tsige about seeing her on the day I left Addis so hastily, seeing her getting out of her Fiat 850. "Today, what do I see before I see your face? Your beautiful leg getting out of a car. The last glimpse of you in Addis was also your beautiful leg coming out of a car. I wanted to say good-bye to you then. But I couldn't."

She laughed, and self-consciously pulled her skirt down. "I knew you disappeared right after Genet," Tsige said. "No one knew if you were part of the hijacking."

"Really? People thought I was an Eritrean guerrilla?"

She shrugged. "*I* didn't think you had anything to do with it. But when I saw Genet, she never said anything one way or the other."

I was puzzled. "How could you have seen Genet? She left the same day I left. That's why I had to go—did you see her in Khartoum?"

"No, Marion. I saw her here."

"You saw Genet in *America?*"

"I saw her *here.* In this house . . . Oh my God. You didn't know?"

I felt the air leave my lungs. A sinkhole opened up under me. "Genet? Isn't she still fighting with the Eritreans?"

"No, no, no. That girl came here as a refugee, just like the rest of us. Someone brought her here. She had her baby in her arms. She acted as if she didn't recognize me at first. I had to remind her." Tsige's face turned hard. "You know, Marion, once we come here, we are all the same. Eritrean, Amhara, Oromo, big shot, *bariya,* whatever status you had in Addis it means nothing. In America you begin at zero. The ones who do the best here are those who were zero there. But Genet came here thinking she was special, not like the rest of us—"

"When was this?"

"Two, maybe three years ago. She said she'd lost touch with you. She didn't know where you went. She acted as if she didn't know you had escaped from Addis."

"What? She was lying," I said. "It was the Eritreans who helped me escape. She was their star . . . their big heroine. She must have known."

"Maybe she didn't trust me, Marion. I never knew her the way I knew you, never exchanged two words with her. People change, you know. When you leave your country, you are like a plant taken out of soil. Some people turn hard, they can't flower again. I remember she told me she got sick in the field. She got sick of the fighting, too, I think. She had the baby. Some women she knew in New York had a job for her and offered to help take care of the baby boy. So I didn't really have to do anything for her."

"My God," I said, sinking back into the sofa. I was glad I didn't know of this before, glad I didn't know she was in New York. "Is she still there?"

"No." Tsige hesitated, as if she wasn't sure whether to tell me the rest. "There were lots of rumors. What I heard is . . . she met a man and they got married. Something happened. She almost killed him. I don't know exactly why or how. All I know is that she's in prison. Her baby was given up for adoption . . ." Tsige saw the shock on my face. "I'm sorry. I thought you knew all this . . . I could find out if she is still in jail."

"No!" I shook my head. "You don't understand. I don't want to ever see her again," I said. I don't want to see her other than to spit in her face, I thought.

"But she was your own sister."

"No! Don't say that," I said sharply.

We sat there in silence. If Tsige found my reaction unexpected, I couldn't blame her. I had to wait a few minutes for the turmoil in me to subside.

"Tsige," I said, at last, reaching for her hand. "I'm sorry. I must explain. You see, Genet was not my sister. She was the love of my life."

Tsige was shocked. "You were in love with your own sister?"

"She's *not* my sister!"

"I am sorry. Of course."

"What does it matter, Tsige? If she was my sister or not my sister, either way I was in love with her. I couldn't change what I felt for her. We were going to marry after we finished medical school . . ."

"What happened?"

"My own brother betrayed me. She betrayed me." This was so hard to say. "They were pillows for each other," I said, using an Amharic expression.

I realized I'd just told Tsige what I'd never told anyone else, not even Hema. I'd come close to telling Thomas Stone in the restaurant, but I hadn't. There was such relief now in the telling. I left nothing out—my being falsely accused, Genet's genital mutilation, Rosina's death, Hema's suspicion that I was responsible. In six years at Our Lady of Perpetual Succour, with all the close friends I had made—Deepak, B.C., various medical students—not one of them had I told this tale.

Tsige's hand was over her mouth, her eyes showing her astonishment and empathy. After a while, she put her hand down and shook her head sadly. "Your brother wanted to sleep with me," Tsige said. She grinned when she saw my jaw drop. "Oh, yes. You both were young then, fourteen or fifteen. Not too young, though. Shiva was so direct. 'How much to sleep with you?' "

She laughed at the audacity of this, gazing out of the window, her mind conjuring up that faraway time.

"Did he?" I said at last, my throat so dry that the words could have set fire to the *tej* in my stomach. She had no idea how important her answer was to me.

"Did he what?"

"Sleep with you?"

"Oh, you sweet thing. No!" She pinched my cheek. "You should see your expression. No, no." I let out the breath I had been holding. "Don't you know that if it had been you, it would have been different? If you'd ever asked . . . I owe you, Marion. I still owe you."

I was sure I was blushing. As quickly as Genet had appeared in my head, she had disappeared. "You don't owe me anything, Tsige. And I'm sorry, I never should've asked you that—it's personal, your business."

"Marion, you must have lots of girlfriends. A surgeon in New York! How many nurses share your pillow, eh? Where are you going? Why are you standing? What's the matter?"

"Tsige, it is late, I'd better—"

She pulled me firmly down, so that I landed almost on top of her. She held me. The scent of her body and of her perfume had shot up my nostrils. My eyes were on her throat, her chin, her bosom. I had thought of her many a night in the house-staff quarters at Our Lady of Perpetual Succour, never imagining that I might really touch her. I was a board-certified general surgeon, but now I felt like a pimply adolescent.

"You are turning so red! Are you all right? Oh, bless me, Mary . . . blessed Gabriel and the saints . . . you are still a virgin, aren't you?"

I nodded sheepishly. "Why are you crying?" I asked.

She would only shake her head, studying my face while swiping at her eyes. At last, holding my cheeks in her hands, she said, "I am crying because it's so beautiful."

"It isn't beautiful, Tsige. It's stupid."

"No, it's not," she said.

"I saved myself for Genet. Yes, I know—ridiculous. But then when she and Shiva . . . I threw myself into my studies. The worst part is I still loved her. Shiva didn't. I loved her. I felt responsible when she almost died. Can you believe that? Shiva slept with her, and *I* felt responsible? Then, when she and her friends stole that plane, she betrayed me again. She never worried what might happen to me or Hema or Shiva. But at least at that moment, on the day I left Ethiopia, I was free of her. When I came here, I tried to forget her. I hoped she was dead in that stupid war—her damn war. Now I find she's here. Maybe I should leave the country, Tsige. Go to Brazil. Or India. I don't want to be on the same continent as that woman."

"Stop it, Marion. Don't talk foolishly. How much *tej* did you drink? This is a big country and you're a big man. Forget about her! Look where you are and look where she is. She's in *jail,* for God's sake!" She touched my hair, and then she pulled me to her bosom. "You are the kind of man that women dream about."

I was aroused. There was nothing about my life that I could hide from her, even if I wanted to. Not my shame, not my secrets, not my embarrassment.

She kissed me on my lips, a brief exploratory brush first, then a leisurely probing kiss. I could feel the adrenaline pouring out of me, the reserves of unused, stockpiled testosterone announcing their availability. So this is how it is going to happen, I thought. On the day I pass my surgical boards. How fitting. My hands reached for her.

She sighed and pulled back, pushing me upright, then straightening her hair. Her expression was serious, like that of a clinician making a pronouncement after the detailed physical exam.

"Wait, my Marion. You've saved yourself all these years. That is not a small thing. I want you to go home. After you have thought about it, if you want me, I will be here. You can come back here or we can go away, go on a trip together. Or I will come to New York and we will take a beautiful hotel room." She read the disappointment on my face, the rejection. "Don't be sad. I am doing this out of love for you. When you have something this precious, you must think carefully how you give it away. I'll understand if you don't give it to me. If you choose me, I will be honored, and I will honor you. Now, I'll get a taxi to take you. Go, my sweet man. Go with God. There is no one else like you."

This is my life, I thought, as my taxi slogged through heavy traffic and inched through the tunnel to Logan Airport. I have excised the cancer from my past, cut it out; I have crossed the high plains, descended into the desert, traversed oceans, and planted my feet in new soil; I have been the apprentice, paid my dues, and have just become master of my ship. But when I look down, why do I see the ancient, tarred, mud-stained slippers that I buried at the start of the journey still stuck to my feet?

CHAPTER 50

Slit the Thew

Now THAT I HAD the income of an attending surgeon, I bought a duplex at one end of a row of such units in Queens. The roofline above the dormer window on one side was peaked like an eyebrow, and it cast a proprietary gaze over an overgrown wedge of land, thick with maples. In summer, I put my jasmine pots on the little patio and I grew salad staples in a tiny garden. In winter, I brought the jasmine indoors while the empty wire cages outside stood as memorials to the succulent, blood-red tomatoes the earth had given up. I painted walls; I repaired roof shingles; I installed bookshelves. Uprooted from Africa, I was satisfying a nesting impulse. I'd found my version of happiness in America. Six years had gone by, and though I should have visited Ethiopia, somehow I could never quite break free.

One day, when coming out of an ice-cream shop, a tall elegantly dressed black woman, her leather coat dancing above her ankles, brushed past me. I held the door for her, and as she slid past, an intense disquiet came over me. She turned back to look at me, smiling. Another evening, while driving back through Manhattan from a trauma conference in New Jersey, a streetwalker caught my eye as she stepped out from under an awning near the Holland Tunnel. She was ghost lit by car headlamps and reflections off the puddles. She tit-flashed me in the rain. Or I imagined she did. I felt the disquiet again, like the hint of something afire, but one doesn't know where. I circled the block, but she was gone.

At home, I prepared for the next day's work. I could have gone into private practice when I finished my five-year residency, or else I could have gone to some other teaching institution. But I felt a great loyalty to Our Lady. And now, Brooke Army Medical Center in San Antonio and Walter Reed in Washington were sending us a few of their senior surgical residents. In peacetime, we provided the closest thing to a war zone, a place where they could hone their skills. I was Our Lady's Head of Trauma; we were blessed with new resources and more personnel. There was no reason for me to be unhappy. But that night, with a fire going in the grate, I felt restless, as if a paralysis would soon set in if I didn't take certain measures.

That weekend, I decided my life needed a dimension that did not involve work. I looked over the *Times* for events, readings, openings, plays, lectures, and other matters of interest. I forced myself to leave the house on Saturday and again on Sunday.

THE FOLLOWING FRIDAY, I came home after work and deposited my briefcase and the mail in my library. In the kitchen, I lit the candle, set the table, and warmed up the last portion of a chicken casserole that I had cooked the previous Sunday from a *Times* recipe.

There was a knock on the door.

I panicked.

Had I invited someone over for dinner and forgotten? Other than Deepak coming over once, no one had ever been here. Could it be that Tsige from Boston had decided to take matters into her own hands, since I had failed to call her? I'd picked up the receiver a dozen times, and then lost courage. Or could this be Thomas Stone knocking? I hadn't told him where I lived, but he could have found out easily from Deepak.

I looked through the peephole.

In that convex fish-eye image, I saw eyes, a nose, cheekbones, lips . . . My brain tried to juggle and rearrange the parts to come up with a face and a name.

It wasn't Stone or Deepak or Tsige.

There was no mistaking who it was.

She turned to leave, went down the two steps.

I could have watched her walk away.

I opened the door. She stood frozen, her body facing the street, her face turned back to the door. She was taller than I recalled, or perhaps it was that she was thinner. She looked to see that it was me, then she dropped her gaze to a spot near my left elbow. This allowed me to study her at will, to decide whether to slam the door on her.

Her hair was straightened, lank, without benefit of ribbons or bows or even a good combing. The cheekbones were intact, more prominent than ever, as if to better buttress those oval, slanting eyes which were her prettiest feature. Even without makeup, hers would always be a stunning face. Although it was summer, she wore a long wool coat tied tight around the waist, and she hugged herself as if she were cold. She stood there motionless, like a small animal caught invading the territory of a predator, paralyzed and unable to move.

I came down my steps. I reached my hand out and tilted her face up. Her eyeballs and lids rolled down just like the eyes of the dolls she used to play with. Her skin was cold to my touch. The vertical scars at the outer edges of her eyes were now seasoned lines, though I recalled the day Rosina's blade gave birth to them, and how they had been raw and choked with dark blood. I jerked her chin farther up. Still she wouldn't meet my gaze. I wanted her to see the scars on my body, one from her betrayal of me with Shiva and another from her becoming more Eritrean than any Eritrean, resulting in the hijacking that drove me out of *my* country. I wanted her to see my rage through my outer calm. I wanted her to feel the blood surge in my muscles, to see the way my fingers curled and coiled and itched for her windpipe. It was good she didn't look, because if she'd so much as blinked, I would have bit into her jugular, I would have consumed her, bones, teeth, and hair, leaving nothing of her on the street.

I took her by the elbow and led her inside. She came like a woman going to the gallows. In the foyer as I bolted the door, she stood rooted to the mat. I led her to my library—a dining room that I had transformed—and I pushed her down on the ottoman. She perched on its edge. I stared down at her; she didn't move. Then she coughed, a spasm that took fifteen seconds to pass. She brought a crumpled tissue to her lips. I looked at her for a long time. I was about to speak when the cough commenced again.

I went to the kitchen. I boiled water for tea, leaning my head against the refrigerator as I waited. Why was I doing this? One minute homicide, the next minute tea?

She had not changed her position. When she took the cup from me, I saw her unvarnished, chipped fingernails and the wrinkled washerwoman's skin. She pulled one sleeve down, passed the cup over, and repeated the process with the other, so as to hide her hands. Tears streamed down her face, her lips pulled back into a grimace.

I had hoped that my heart would be hardened to such displays.

"Sorry. I work in a kitchen," she whispered.

"After all you have done to me, you're sorry about the state of your hands?"

She blinked, said nothing.

"How did you find me?"

"Tsige sent me."

"Why?"

"I called her when I got out of jail. I needed . . . help."

"Didn't she tell you that I didn't want to see you?"

"Yes. But she insisted I see you before she would help me." She glanced directly at me for the very first time. "And I wanted to see you."

"Why?"

"To tell you I'm sorry." She averted her gaze after a few seconds.

"Is that something you learn in prison? Avoiding eye contact?"

She laughed, and in that moment I wondered if, with all she had seen and done, she was beyond being touched by anger. She said, "I was stabbed once for looking." She pointed down with her chin to her left side. "They took out my spleen."

"Where were you in prison?"

"Albany."

"And now?"

"I'm paroled. I have to see my probation officer every week."

She put her cup down.

"What else did Tsige say?"

"That you're a surgeon." She looked around the library, the shelves full of books. "That you're doing well."

"I'm only here because I was forced to run. Forced to leave in the night like a thief. You know who did that to me? To Hema? It was someone who was to our family . . . like a daughter."

She rocked back and forth. "Go on," she said, straightening her back. "I deserve it."

"Still playing the martyr? I heard you hid a gun in your hair when you got on that plane. An Afro! You were the Angela Davis of the Eritrean cause, right?"

She shook her head. After a long while she said, "I don't know what I was. I don't know who I was. The person I was felt she had to do something *great*." She spat out the last word. "Something spectacular. For Zemui. For me. They promised me that you and our family would not be harmed. As soon as the hijack was over, I realized how stupid it was. Nothing about it was great. I was a great fool, that's all."

She drank her tea. She stood up. "Forgive me, if you can. You deserved better."

"Shut up and sit down," I said. She obeyed. "You think that does it? You say sorry and then leave?"

She shook her head.

"You had a baby?" I said. "A field baby."

"The contraceptives they gave us didn't work."

"Why did you go to jail?"

"Must I tell you everything?"

She began coughing again. When the spasm was over, she shivered, although the room was warm and I was sweating.

"What happened to your baby?"

Her face crumpled. Her lips stretched out. Her shoulders shook. "They took my baby away from me. Gave him away for adoption. I curse the man who put me in that position. Curse that man." She looked up. "I was a good mother, Marion—"

"A good mother!" I laughed. "If you were a good mother you might be carrying *my* child."

She smiled through her tears as if I were being funny—as if she'd just remembered my fantasy of our getting married and populating Missing with our children. Then she began to shake, and at first I thought she was crying or laughing, but I heard her teeth chatter. I had rehearsed my lines in my head as I walked out of Asmara, walked all the way to the Sudan; I'd rehearsed them so many times since. I imagined every excuse she might offer if I ever met her. I had my barbs ready. But this quaking, silent adversary was not what I'd envisioned. I reached over and felt her pulse. One hundred forty beats per minute. Her skin, cool just a while ago, was burning to the touch.

"I . . . must . . . go," she said, rising but swaying.

"No, you will stay."

She was clearly unwell. I gave her three aspirin. I led her into the master bath and ran the shower. When it was steaming, I helped her undress. If earlier I had seen her as an animal in the predator's lair, now I felt like a father disrobing his child. Once she was in the shower, I tossed her underwear and shirt into the washer and ran the load. I helped her out of the shower. She was on glass legs. I dried her off and sat her on the edge of the bed. I put a pair of my winter flannels on her and tucked her in. I made her eat a few spoons of casserole and drink more tea. I put Vicks on her throat and on her chest and the soles of her feet, just as

Hema would do with us. She was asleep before I slid the woolen socks over her toes.

What was I feeling? This was a Pyrrhic victory. A *pyrexic* victory—the thermometer I slid under her armpit read one hundred three degrees. While she slept, I moved her wet clothes to the dryer and stuck her jeans in the washer. I put away the casserole. Then I sat in the library by myself, trying to read. Perhaps I dozed. Hours later, I heard the sound of a toilet being flushed. She was on the bed, covers thrown to the side, pajamas and socks off, wrapped in a towel and wiping her brow with a washcloth. Her fever had broken. She moved over to make room for me.

"Do you want me to leave now?" she said.

In that question, I felt that she was taking control because there was only one possible answer: "You're sleeping here."

"I'm burning up," she said.

I changed into my boxers and T-shirt in the bathroom, took a blanket from the wardrobe, and headed for the library.

"Stay with me?" she said. "Please?"

I had no reply planned for that.

I climbed into my bed. When I reached for the light, she said, "Please leave it on."

No sooner had I lain down than she pressed against me, smelling of my deodorant, my shampoo, and Vicks. She raised my arm and huddled in the crook of my shoulder, her damp body against me. Her fingers touched my face, very gingerly, as if she worried that I might bite. I remembered that night so many years ago when I had found her naked in the pantry.

"What's that sound?" she said, startled.

"It's the dryer alarm. I washed your clothes."

I heard her sniffle. Then sob. "You deserved better," she said, looking up.

"Yes, I did."

I stared at her eyes, remembering the little fleck in the right iris, and the puff of gray around it, where a spark had penetrated. Yes, it was still there, darker now, looking like a blemish she was born with. I traced her lips. Her nose. She shut her lids at my touch. Tears were sliding underneath them. She smiled a smile from our days of innocence. I took my hand away. She opened her lids, her eyes glistening. Hesitantly she kissed my lips.

No, I hadn't forgotten. At that moment, my anger wasn't so much with her as it was with the passage of time. Time had robbed me of such wonderful illusions, taken them away far too soon. But right then I wanted the illusion that she was mine.

She kissed me again, and I tasted the salt of her tears. Was she feeling sorry for me? I couldn't take that, ever. Suddenly I was on top of her, tearing away the sheet, tearing away her towel, clumsy but determined. She was startled, the muscles of her neck taut like cables. I grabbed her head and kissed her.

"Wait," she whispered, "shouldn't you . . . ?"

But I was already inside her.

She winced.

"Shouldn't I what, Genet?" I said as I bucked, my pelvis possessing some intrinsic knowledge of the movements needed. "This is my first time . . . ," I managed to say. "I wouldn't know what I should or shouldn't do."

Her pupils dilated. Was she pleased to learn this about me?

Now she knew.

Now she knew that there were people in this world who kept their promises. Ghosh, whose deathbed she never had the time to visit, was one such person. I wanted the knowledge to shame her, to terrify her. When it was over, I stayed on top of her.

"My first time, Genet . . . ," I said, softly. "Don't think that's because I was waiting for you. It's because you fucked my life up. You could have counted on me. Money in the bank, as they say here. And what did you do? You turned it all into shit. I wanted to make life beautiful for you. I don't understand it really, Genet. You had Hema and Ghosh. You had Missing. You had me who loved you more than you will ever love yourself."

She wept under me. After a long time, she gently caressed my head, tried to kiss me. She said, "I need to go to the bathroom."

I ignored her. I was aroused again. I began to move inside her once more.

"Please, Marion," she said.

Without removing myself from within her, I rolled onto my back, holding her, flipping her, and setting her on top of me, her breasts hovering over me.

"You need to pee? Go ahead," I said, my breath coming quick. "You've done that before, too."

I grabbed her shoulders and pulled her to me hard. I smelled her fever, and the scent of blood and sex and urine. I came again.

Then I let go. I let her slide off.

I woke late on Saturday morning to find her back in the crook of my arm, staring at me. I took her again—I couldn't imagine how I had denied myself this pleasure for so long.

When I awoke it was 2:00 p.m. and I could hear her in the kitchen. I went to the bathroom. It was when I returned to the bed that I saw the blood on the sheets. I stripped the bed and took the sheets to the washing machine.

She brought two cups of coffee, a serving of the casserole and two spoons to me. She was getting feverish again, the dressing gown not warm enough, her teeth chattering, and with spasms of a dry cough. I took the coffee from her. Her dressing gown came apart. She watched me remake the bed.

"Sorry," she said. "I am bleeding because the scars . . . I always bleed with . . . intercourse. Rosina's gift to me. So that I will always think of her when—"

"Is it painful?"

"At first. And if it's been a long time."

"What about this fever, how long have you been this way? Have you had an X-ray?"

"I'll be fine," she said. "It's a bad cold. Hope I don't give it to you. I took some Advil I found in your cabinet."

"Genet, you should—"

"Really, I'll be fine, Doctor."

"Tell me why you went to prison."

Her smile disappeared. She shook her head. "Please, Marion. Don't."

I knew then it was a story that would do me no good. I knew I had to hear it. Later, when the two of us were seated in my library, I insisted.

He was an intellectual, a firebrand, an Eritrean who like her had left the cause. He shall remain nameless—it's painful enough already. Suffice it to say he won the heart of her baby. (The baby's father had died in the struggle.) And then he won her heart—all this in New York, after her arrival. She felt her life was just beginning. They married. In a year she was pregnant with his child. She began to suspect that he was cheating on her. She found the whereabouts of the woman, the flat where they conducted their tryst. She broke in and hid in the woman's clothes closet and waited there for half a day till the couple arrived in the late afternoon. When her husband and his white lover were on her bed, seeking carnal knowledge of each other in a noisy, effortful way, Genet debated whether to announce her presence.

"Marion," she said, "as I stood in that closet, with this woman's belts in baskets like snakes at my feet, it all came back to me. Everything I had been through from the time of Zemui's death till then.

"I somehow came to America, and what did I do? For the first time in my life, for the one person who deserved it the least, I gave my love completely. I loved him—what is it you said earlier?—more than I loved myself. I gave it all up for this useless man. Standing in the closet, I knew that if I tried to get vengeance, I had to be willing to lose my life. There has only been one man in my life worthy of such a sacrifice, Marion, and it was you. I was too stupid to know that when I was young. I was too stupid.

"He wasn't worth it, but now I couldn't stop myself. You see, in loving him, it had happened again, Marion—I wanted to be great. I thought he was destined for greatness as an academic, as an intellectual, and my greatness would be in being with him.

"For the first time I understood who was the proletariat. The proletariat was me, the proletariat had always been me, and now I needed to act for the proletariat. I had my straight razor in my hand.

"I began to sing in my softest voice. They could not see me though I could see them.

"I opened the door of the closet with one intention for him: to slit his thew, slit it like a stalk of henna. You can only do that when you have loved someone so completely that you have held nothing back and there is nothing left of you—it has all been used. Do you understand?" I understood all too well. "Otherwise, I'd have said to her, *Take him and keep him. Good riddance.* Instead, I jumped on them.

"I cut them, but not as badly as I had in mind. They escaped. I waited for the police. I felt as if I had taken off handcuffs that had been on my wrists the whole time. I had been looking for greatness, and I found it then. I was free at the very moment when my freedom would end."

She saw my expression as I followed the story, and she smiled.

"Genet died in prison, Marion. Genet is no more. When they take your living child away, you die, and the child growing inside you dies, too. All the things that matter are gone, and so I am dead."

There was a tiny part of me that wanted to say, *You have me, Genet*. But for once, I stopped to consider myself, to save myself.

I felt compassion for her of a sort that I hadn't felt before: it was a feeling better than love, because it released me, it set me free of her. *Marion*, I said to myself, *she found her greatness, at last, found it in her suffering. Once you have greatness, who needs anything else?*

CHAPTER 51

The Devil's Choice

In retrospect, my illness began that Sunday morning in the crystalline moment of waking to a silent house in which I knew I was alone and she was gone. Forty-three days later, the first shudder of nausea arrived, an ocean surge as if a distant Vesuvius had collapsed into the sea. Next an ancient fog, an Entoto mist full of shifting shapes and animal sounds descended on me, and by the forty-ninth day I had lost consciousness.

How remarkable that a life should turn on such a small thing as a decision to open a door or not. I ushered Genet in on a Friday. She let herself out two days later without a good-bye, and nothing would be the same again. She placed a pinwheel cross at the center of the dining table, a gift for me, I presumed. That St. Bridget's medallion she wore on a necklace had been her father's, and it had belonged to a Canadian soldier named Darwin before that.

The tale of her ex-husband lingered like a nasty flu. I'd insisted on hearing the story. I discovered that Genet was capable of selfless love—just not with me. Still, in my home I'd found a momentary equilibrium with her, or the illusion of it, as if we were again like children playing house, playing doctor.

I hurried home each night after work, hoping to find her waiting on my stoop. My heart would sink when I glimpsed the yellow sticky I had left for her inside the screen door, telling her the key was with my good neighbor, Holmes, and to feel at home. Once inside, I felt compelled to retrieve my note, checking to be sure I had, in fact, written on it. I confess, I even left a stub of a pencil by the door in case she felt inclined to compose a reply.

By Friday, a week after I first dragged her into my home, the sight of that yellow square of paper screamed, *FOOL!* The stubby pencil said, *FOOL OF THE HIGHEST ORDER.* I tore up the paper and flung the pencil stub into the street.

I wasn't angry with Genet. She was consistent, if nothing else. I was angry with myself because I still loved her, or at least I loved that dream of our togetherness. My feelings were unreasonable, irrational, and I couldn't change them. That hurt.

Sitting in my library that night, having done more damage to a bottle of Pinch in four hours than I had in the year since I bought it, I replayed our last exchange. She'd been curled up in the chair I now sat in, wearing my dressing gown, the gown that I now wore. I came to her with tea—that signature move of fools, one of the stigmata by which you shall know us.

"Marion," she said, for she had been gazing at my library, my eclectic little collection. "Your father's apartment in Boston, the way you described it . . . it sounds so much like this."

"Don't be ridiculous," I said. "I built these bookcases myself. Half the books here have nothing to do with surgery. Surgery isn't my life."

She didn't argue. We sat quietly. At one point I saw her gaze flit to the rug on the floor between us—there was an intruder sitting naked on those synthetic fibers, a dark silent man with razor cuts to his body. His presence put a damper on our conversation.

When I announced I was going to go to bed, she said she'd be right along. She smiled. I didn't believe her. I thought I'd never see her again. But I was wrong. She joined me under the covers. We made love. It was tender and slow. It was the very moment when I thought, At last, she is going to stay, but in fact it was her good-bye.

TWO WEEKS AFTER SHE LEFT, I felt at odds with my house. I found my library oppressive. In the kitchen, I took out my dinner, which was a foil packet labeled FRIDAY in my handwriting; it was the last of what I had cooked, frozen, and packed in aliquots many weekends ago. Now I saw this categorizing of my freezer food as a sign of the true chaos inside my head.

Thank God for my good neighbor, Sonny Holmes. He heard me raging, he heard me bang my head against the fridge. Sonny Holmes had an inherent curiosity, an honest, all-American nosiness that came with crossing one's seventieth year and that did not try to conceal itself. He'd been aware of the coming of my guest—such a rare event—and he'd heard the headboard music and then the long silence.

"You need to hire a security firm," he said, coming to a quick diagnosis before I had even finished my story. Sonny believed in the enneagram, that Jesuit-invented classification of people into personality types. He was a One, willful and confident and certain. He had me pegged as a Three or a Four, or was it a Two? Whatever it was, it was a number that did not argue with Ones.

"I need a what?" I said.

"A private detective."

"Sonny, for what? I don't want to see her again."

"Perhaps so. But you need closure. What if she's in jail or in a hospital? What if she's trying desperately to get back to you, but can't?"

A noble motive, that was all a Two needed to continue an obsession. I latched on to that.

East Coast Investigations of Flushing turned out to be an earnest, blond youth by the name of Appleby, son of Holmes's late sister-in-law. Appleby quickly established that Genet had not returned to her halfway house. She hadn't gone to Nathan's restaurant, where she washed dishes. She had not checked in with her probation officer and she had not called Tsige. He learned these facts in no time. He even knew that Genet had been diagnosed with tuberculosis while in prison. She began medications, but then failed to report for her DOT—Directly Observed Therapy—after she was released. The cough, the fever, in all likelihood were her tuberculosis coming back. The disconcerting news was that if she ever materialized, I'd be third in line after the state health department and her probation officer. She would be headed back to jail. Appleby's source in jail could get his hand on her complete medical records if we wished, and Appleby said he'd taken the liberty of telling the man to proceed. I was concerned about violating her confidentiality. "Knowledge is power in these kinds of situations," Appleby added, and with that he won me over; any man who would use a quote that Ghosh loved was a man to trust. "You are paying to know," he added, "and I think we're obliged to know more."

"So what now?" I asked Appleby. I wasn't asking him about exposure to tuberculosis. I could handle that.

Appleby avoided my eyes. His cheeks and the tip of his nose were covered with twitchy blood vessels, ready to flush at the least provocation. His condition was *acne rosacea,* not to be confused with the pedestrian *acne vulgaris,* the bane of many teenagers. Appleby's nose would one day be burgundy and bulbous, the cheeks a meaty red. Already shy, his problems would get worse because strangers would assume incorrectly that his appearance was a result of drink. Here I knew about his future while paying him to tell me mine.

"Well, Dr. Stone," Appleby said, clearing his throat, his nose starting to redden, a sure indication that I would not like what he had to say, "Respectfully, I would say to check your silverware. Inventory your belongings. Make sure nothing is missing."

I looked at him for a long while. "But, Mr. Appleby, the only thing that matters to me is precisely the one thing that *is* missing."

"Yes, of course," he said.

The compassion in his voice told me he had known my kind of pain. There are legions of us.

AS FAR AS THE EVENTS of the next few weeks, I recall one night waking to the shrill ring of the telephone. Receiver in hand, I was lost, uncertain whether I was at Our Lady or back at Missing. I was the backup trauma consultant. But I couldn't decipher what the resident at the other end wanted. This isn't uncommon for the first ten seconds of a middle-of-the-night conversation. The caller understands. But, as we kept talking, the fog in my brain refused to lift. I hung up. I pulled the phone from its moorings. The next morning, my mind felt clear, but my body wouldn't rise off the bed. I was weak. The thought of food turned my stomach. I rolled over and went back to sleep.

Perhaps that same day, perhaps a few days later, a man was on the edge of my bed. He took my pulse, called my name. It was my former Chief Resident and now my colleague at Our Lady, Deepak Jesudass. I desperately held his hand and asked him not to leave—I must have recognized the danger of my situation.

"I'm not leaving," he said. "Just pulling back the curtain."

My memory is that I told him everything that had transpired. He examined me as I spoke. He pulled down my eyelids, interrupting me only to ask that I look down at my feet, or say "Ah!" At one point he inquired if I had a stethoscope in the house. I said, "Are you kidding? I'm a surgeon," and we laughed together, a strange sound that had been missing from my home. I said "Ouch" when he probed just under my ribs on the right. I found this funny. I heard him murmuring on the telephone. All the while, I did not let go of his hand.

Three men whose faces I knew arrived with a stretcher. They wrapped me in a flannel cocoon, carried me out to the curb, and lifted me up into their ambulance. I remember wanting to say something about the beauty of their motion, the inherent grace, and how incredible it was, this baby-kangaroo-in-pouch feeling. I apologized for not having appreciated their skill all these years.

Deepak rode with me. At Our Lady, he walked alongside my gurney, past the shocked faces of the staff we encountered in the halls and elevator. He wheeled me into the Intensive Care Unit of Our Lady of Perpetual Succour. My eyes glowed yellow under the harsh fluorescent lights, but I didn't know it. My skin, too. I bled wildly from every needle stick. Too late, the nurses tried to hide the ominous tea-colored urine in my catheter bag from me, but I saw. For the first time, I was very, very scared.

The increasing swelling in my brain made me desperately sleepy. I held on to consciousness long enough to ask Deepak to come near. "Whatever happens," I whispered, "don't take me from Our Lady. If I must die and can't die at Missing, I want to die here."

At some point I was aware that Thomas Stone came to my bedside and was studying me, but not with the concern of a clinician. It was the petrified look I knew so well, the look of a parent whose child had suffered some misfortune. It was at about this time that I lost consciousness.

As I learned later, the cable to Hema read: COME AT ONCE STOP MARION CRITICALLY ILL STOP THOMAS STONE STOP P.S. DO NOT DELAY STOP—and she did not. Hema called in her favor with the Comrade President-for-Life's wife, who understood all too well Hema's need to be at her son's sickbed. The American Embassy readily provided visas, and by day's end, Hema and Shiva were on their way to Frankfurt via Cairo. Then, still on Lufthansa, they crossed the Atlantic. Hema pulled out the telegram more than once, studying the letters, looking for a hopeful anagram. Over Greenland, she said to Shiva, "Perhaps this means Thomas Stone is near death, not Marion."

Shiva said with absolute certainty, "No, Ma. It's Marion. I can feel it."

At ten in the night New York time, they floated into the Intensive

Care Unit, a graying woman in a maroon sari, the face striking despite the raccoon rings around her eyes. With her was a tall youthful man who was so obviously her son and my identical twin.

They slowed outside my glass cubicle, weary Old World travelers peering into the glow of a New World hospital room. There I was, the son who went to the States for higher studies, who became a practitioner of the artful, lavish, disposable-everything, lucrative, and incredibly effective American brand of medicine, with no prices on the menu, so different in style and substance from what they did at Missing; only now it must have appeared to them as if the American medicine had turned on me, like the tiger turning on its trainer, so that I lay moored to a blue-gray ventilator, chained to monitors on the consoles behind my bed, comatose and invaded by plastic tubing, by catheters and wires. There was even a stiff wire like a nail poking up from my skull.

They saw Thomas Stone seated on the side of my room closest to the window, his head resting awkwardly against the bed's safety rail, his eyes closed as if in sleep. In the seventy-two hours since he sent the telegram, my condition had worsened. Thomas Stone opened his eyes, suddenly aware of them. He stood up, bedraggled, stiff, and somewhat shrunken in his borrowed scrubs, relieved but apprehensive. Worry lines ran into his eyes, and his face was drawn and pale under his shock of white hair.

The two old colleagues and combatants had last seen each other in a delivery room, moments after my birth and our mother's death. That was also when Stone had last seen Shiva: in Operating Theater 3, held tight in Hema's arms.

The bedside table and the ventilator blocked Hema's approach to the near side of the bed. She circled to where Stone stood, her eyes on me.

"He is 'critically ill' from what, Thomas?" Hema said, referring to the two words in the telegram that had most frustrated her. Her tone was professional, as if she were asking a colleague about a patient; it allowed her the pretense of being calm when inside she was quaking.

"It's hepatic coma," Thomas said, responding in the same manner, grateful that she'd elected to converse in the language of disease, a fallback which allowed even their son to be reduced to a diagnosis. "He has a fulminant hepatitis. The ammonia level is very high and the liver hardly functioning."

"What from?"

"Viral hepatitis. Hepatitis B."

Stone let down the bed rail and the two of them stood over me.

Hema's hand reached behind her for the tail end of her sari, the part that went over her shoulder. She brought it to her mouth.

"He looks anemic, not just icteric," she managed to say at last, clinging to the idiom of medicine to describe my pallor and jaundice. "What's his hemoglobin?"

"Nine, after four units of blood. He's bleeding from his gut. His platelets are down and he isn't making clotting factors. The bilirubin is twelve, and his creatinine just today is four, rising from three yesterday . . ."

"What's this, please?" Shiva said, pointing at my skull. He stood across from Thomas Stone, the bed between them.

"An intracranial pressure monitor. Goes into the ventricle. He has cerebral edema. They're giving him mannitol and adjusting the ventilator settings to keep the pressure down."

Shiva looked skeptical. "It goes through his skull, through brain into the ventricle just to measure? It does not treat?"

Thomas Stone nodded.

"How did this begin?" Hema asked.

As Thomas Stone recounted the sequence of events, Shiva freed the bedside table and found slack between the bed and ventilator. He let down the bed rail on his side. Moving with the slow efficiency of a contortionist, he slid under the tubes and wires. Deepak entered in time to see Shiva lying on his side next to me, his head touching mine. His being there looked both precarious and entirely natural. All Deepak could do was stare, noting, however, that my intracranial pressure tracing, which had done nothing but go up for three days, went down.

No sooner had Deepak introduced himself than Vinu Mehta, the gastroenterologist, filled the doorway, panting from taking the stairs. Vinu had been an internal medicine resident at Our Lady when I was a surgery resident. After specializing in gastroenterology, he'd joined a lucrative practice in Westchester but wasn't happy and had returned to the salaried staff of Our Lady.

"Vinu Mehta, Dr. Madam," he said, putting his palms together in a *namaste* before grasping Hema's hand with both of his. "And this must be Shiva," he said, unfazed at seeing Shiva in my bed. "I know this only because I am certain the other gentleman is Marion." He turned back to Hema. "What a shock this must be, madam. For everyone here, too. Our whole world is upside down! Marion is one of us." This sudden switch to the vernacular of feelings made Hema's lips tremble.

One look at Vinu and you knew the stories about him buying groceries for patients he discharged were probably true. I'd seen him extend a patient's stay to insulate her from some madness at home. He was the best friend to everyone on the staff and regularly baked cakes and cookies for me. I always sent him a card on Mother's Day, which pleased him no end.

"I was called the minute that Marion was brought here, Dr. Madam," Vinu went on. "Hepatology, the liver, that is my field. Hepatitis B swims around here. Lots of carriers, intravenous drug addicts and people who acquire it from their mothers at birth—very common in immigrants from the Far East. Madam, we see no end of silent cirrhosis and even liver cancer from this virus. But *acute* fulminant hepatitis B? In my career I have seen only two other patients quite this severe."

"Vinu, tell me the truth," Hema said, taking on a no-nonsense, Mother India tone with this young doctor who was all too ready to play the role of nephew. "Is my son a drinker?"

I suppose it was a fair question. I hadn't seen her in more than seven years. She knew it was in my genes. What did she really know of who or what I had become?

"Madam, categorically no!" Vinu responded. "No, no. A gem of a son you have."

Hema's stern expression softened.

"Although, madam," Vinu continued, "in the past few weeks, madam—don't take this wrongly—by the report of his neighbor, Marion had been troubled and drinking."

Deepak had found a new prescription in my house for isoniazid, a drug used to prevent tuberculosis. Isoniazid was also famous for causing severe liver inflammation. It was routine to check liver enzymes two weeks after starting treatment so the drug could be discontinued if there was any sign of liver damage.

"My hypothesis, madam, is that Marion-*bhaiya* started isoniazid on his own. The prescription is a month old. He probably didn't get his blood drawn to check liver functions the way he was supposed to. He is a surgeon after all, poor fellow. What does he know about these fine matters? If he'd only consulted me! I would have been honored to take care of him. After all, Marion-*bhaiya* took care of my hernia so lovingly.

"In any case, madam, I personally went to Manhattan, to Mount Sinai, and I chauffeured over the world's best liver man, the man who trained me in this specialty. I said, 'Professor, this is a not a case of hepatitis, but a case of my own brother.' He is in agreement that the alcohol and the isoniazid might be contributory, but there is no doubt that what we are dealing with here first and foremost is hepatitis B."

"What is the prognosis?" Hema said. "Will someone tell me that?" It was the most basic thing a mother wanted to know. "Will he get better?"

Vinu looked to Deepak and Thomas Stone, but neither man was willing to speak. The disease was, after all, Vinu's area of expertise.

"Just tell me. Will he live?" Hema spat out.

"It is undoubtedly very grave," Vinu said, and the fact that he was fighting back tears told her everything.

"Come on!" Hema said, annoyed by this and turning to Thomas Stone, and then to Deepak. "It's *hepatitis*. I understand hepatitis. We see the damage it does in Africa. But . . . here, America! In this wealthy place, this *rich* hospital"—she swept her hands at all the machinery—"surely here in America you can do more for *hepatitis* than to wring your hands and say *it is very grave*."

They must have winced when she said "rich." Compared with the state-of-the-art ICUs in the money hospitals, such as Thomas Stone's institution in Boston, ours was bare-bones.

"We tried everything, madam," Deepak said now in a more subdued tone. "Plasma exchange. Whatever anyone in the world can do for this disease, we are doing that here."

Hema looked skeptical.

"And praying, madam," Vinu added. "The sisters have a prayer chain going around the clock for two days now. Honestly, we need that kind of a miracle."

Shiva had quietly followed every word from where he lay.

Hema stood looking down at my unconscious form, stroking my hand and shaking her head.

Vinu convinced the two of them to retire to a room readied for them in the house-staff building; he'd even arranged for a light dinner of chapatti and dal. Hema was too tired to argue.

THE NEXT MORNING, Hema appeared in an orange sari, looking rested, yet as if she had aged a few years in the course of the night.

Thomas Stone was exactly where she had left him. He looked past her in the doorway, as if expecting Shiva, but Shiva wasn't there.

She stood by my bed again, anxious to see me in daylight. The previous night she'd found it all too unreal, as if it were not me on the bed but some extension of all the noisy machinery which had taken the form of flesh. But now she could see me, see the rise and fall of my chest, the puffiness of my eyes, my lips contorted by the breathing tube. It was real. She couldn't help herself, and began to weep silently, forgetting Thomas Stone was there, or not caring one way or the other. She was only conscious of him when he tentatively offered a handkerchief. She snatched it from him, as if he'd been slow to offer it.

"It feels as if this is happening because of me," Hema said. She blew her nose. "I know that sounds selfish, but to lose Ghosh, then to see Marion like this . . . You don't understand, it feels as if I have failed them all, that I let this befall Marion."

Had she turned, she might have seen Thomas Stone stir, seen him rub his knuckles against his temples, as if trying to erase himself. He spoke, his voice hoarse. "You . . . you and Ghosh never failed them. *I* did. I failed all of you."

There it was, Hema must have thought; it was both the sorry and the thank-you that was so long overdue, and the funny thing was that at this moment, she didn't care. It no longer mattered. She didn't even look his way.

SHIVA ENTERED, and if he saw Thomas Stone, he didn't acknowledge his presence. He had eyes only for me, his brother.

"Where were you?" Hema said. "Did you sleep at all?"

"In the library upstairs. I took a nap there." Shiva surveyed me, then he studied the settings on the ventilator, and then the labels on the fluid-containing bags hanging over my bed.

"There is one thing I didn't ask Vinu," Hema said to Stone. "How did Marion get hepatitis B?"

Thomas shook his head as if to say he did not know. But since she wasn't looking his way, he had to speak. "It . . . was probably during surgery. Nicking himself. It's an occupational hazard for surgeons."

"It can also be acquired by sexual intercourse," Shiva said, addressing Thomas Stone. Thomas Stone stammered assent. Hema glared at Shiva, one hand on her hip. She didn't get a chance to speak, because Shiva had more to say: "Genet was at Marion's house, Ma. She showed up there six weeks ago. She was sick. She stayed for two nights and then disappeared."

"Genet . . . ?" Hema said.

"There are two people in the waiting room you need to meet. One is an Ethiopian lady, Tsige. She used to live opposite Missing. Ghosh took care of her infant years ago. Marion met her again in Boston. The other is Mr. Holmes—he is Marion's neighbor. They want to speak to you."

BY MIDMORNING, Hema knew the whole story. Genet had been ill with TB. But Appleby had his hands on the prison health records and they showed what we had not known before: Genet was also a silent carrier of hepatitis B. She contracted it (or so the prison doctor postulated) from an improperly sterilized needle or a transfusion or a tattoo when she was in the field in Eritrea; she could also have acquired it sexually. Genet had bled readily when we slept together, and I had been generously exposed to her blood and thereby to the virus. The incubation period of hepatitis B fit Shiva's hypothesis: it was six weeks from her visit to my falling ill.

Hema paced the waiting room, cursing Genet and bemoaning my stupidity in letting Genet get close to me again after everything she had put us through. Had Genet appeared just then, I would have feared for her life.

WHEN DEEPAK AND VINU made rounds together that afternoon they shared the latest lab results: my kidneys were failing; my liver, normally the source of clotting factors, wasn't producing any. If there were any viable liver cells left, they were showing no signs of recovering. There was not a bit of good news they could convey. They withdrew, Shiva following them. Thomas Stone and Hema stayed, silent around my immobile form. Now it was a watching game, a vigil to the end. There was no hope. The two of them as physicians knew it all too well, but if anything, experience made it even less palatable.

AT NOON, an ICU nurse paged both Deepak and Vinu to a Stone family conference. They came to find Hema and Shiva seated across from Thomas Stone in the small meeting room.

Hema, weary, head in her hands and elbows on the table, gazed up at the two young doctors in white coats, her son's peers. "You wanted to see us?" she said impatiently to Vinu and Deepak.

Deepak looked puzzled. "I didn't call this meeting." He turned to Vinu, who shook his head.

"I did," Shiva said. He had a stack of photocopied papers in front of him. A yellow legal pad was covered with notations in his careful script. Hema noticed an authority to his voice, a sense of action and energy and initiative that no one else seemed capable of displaying in the face of my terrible prognosis. "I called the meeting because I want to talk about a liver transplant."

Deepak, who found it difficult to sit face-to-face with Shiva and not feel he was speaking to me, said, "We considered a transplant early on, Shiva. In fact, Dr. Stone and I talked about transferring Marion to Mecc—I mean to Boston General, Dr. Stone's hospital. Dr. Stone's team does more transplants than anyone on the East Coast. But we decided against it for two reasons. First of all, transplants are notoriously unsuccessful when the liver is being destroyed by fulminant hepatitis B. Even if we found a cadaver liver of the right blood group and size and we did the transplant successfully, we would have to use massive doses of steroids and other drugs that suppress the immune system to prevent rejection of the new liver. That would give the hepatitis B virus a field day and the new liver would be destroyed and we would be back to exactly where we are now."

"Yes, I know," Shiva said. "But what if the transplant is a perfect match? Not just the same blood group, but all six HLA antigens and other antigens you don't even measure—what if they *all* matched? Then no immune-suppressing drugs would be needed? Right? None. No steroids, no cyclosporine, nothing. Would you agree?"

"Theoretically, yes, but . . . ," Deepak said.

"A perfect match is what you would have if you took the liver from me," Shiva said. "His body would see it as self, not as foreign in any way."

The air had been sucked out of the room. No one spoke for a few seconds. Seeing Hema's expression, Shiva quickly explained, "I mean take a *part* of my liver, Ma. Leaving enough for me and taking out a lobe to give to Marion."

"Shiva . . ." It was on Hema's lips to apologize for Shiva—this clearly was not his field, or hers for that matter. But then she changed her mind. She knew something about his tenacity when it came to medical situations that others thought impossible. "But, Shiva, has that ever been done—transplanting part of a liver?"

Shiva slid one of the articles over to her. "This is from last year. A review by Deepak Jesudass and Thomas Stone on the prospects for *live donor* liver transplant. It hasn't been done in humans, Ma, but before you say anything, read page three where I have underlined. They say, 'Technically, the success in almost one hundred dogs, the ability to sustain life in the recipient and not jeopardize life in the donor, suggests that we are ready to perform this operation on humans. The risks to a healthy donor present a significant ethical obstacle, but we believe the critical shortage of cadaver organs obliges us to move forward. The time has come. Live donor transplant will overcome both the problem of organ shortage and the problem of cadaver livers that are damaged because it has taken too long to get consent and too long to remove the organ and get it to where it needs to be. Live donor liver transplant is the inevitable and necessary next step.' "

Shiva wasn't reading, but reciting word for word from memory. It didn't surprise Hema, but it astonished the other physicians at the table. Hema felt proud of Shiva. She was reminded how often she took Shiva's eidetic gift for granted. She knew he could draw the page he was reciting from, reproduce it on a blank piece of paper, beginning and ending each line just as it was on the original, down to the punctuation, the page number, and the staple marks and photocopy smudges.

Shiva, sensing that he had quieted Hema for the moment, addressed Thomas Stone and Deepak, the two surgeons: "May I remind you that the first successful kidney transplant by Joseph Murray involved a dying twin who received a healthy kidney from his identical twin brother?"

Deepak spoke, because it appeared that Thomas Stone was in a state of shock, "Shiva, we also state in the paper," Deepak said, "that there are ethical and legal implications—"

Shiva interrupted. "Yes, I know. But you also say 'in all likelihood the first donors will be a parent or sibling, because such a donor has a pure motive and takes on the risk willingly.' "

Deepak and Thomas Stone looked like defendants whose alibi had just been shot down by a surprise witness. The prosecutor was moving in for the kill.

But the attack came from another quarter. Hema said, "Thomas, tell me the truth: in the last four days, given that *this* is your area of interest"—she tapped the paper, her fingers bunched together—"seeing Shiva lie next to his twin, did the thought of this live donor operation not cross your mind?"

If she expected him to squirm and swallow hard, she was in for a surprise: Stone looked steadily at Hema, and after a beat, he nodded almost imperceptibly. "I thought of the Murray twins, yes. I thought of it. But then thinking of all the hazards . . . I dismissed it. This is much, much harder than removing a kidney. It's never been done."

"*I* never thought of it!" Vinu Mehta said quietly. "Madam, I *should* have thought of it. Shiva, I thank you. In anyone else with acute hepatitis B, a liver transplant would simply feed the virus. But with a perfect match . . . Of course, Shiva, the issue is really the risk to you."

My brother was ready, and he spoke without glancing at his notes, addressing his comments largely to Thomas Stone even though Vinu had asked the question. "Your estimate, Dr. Stone, based on cutting out one or more lobes from patients with liver trauma, is that the risk of death should be less than five percent for me, the donor. The risk of serious complications, such as bile leaks and hemorrhage, you said should be no more than twenty percent in an otherwise healthy donor." Shiva pushed a single sheet to Deepak and Thomas Stone. "I had my blood drawn last night. All my liver functions came back normal. As you can see, I am not a carrier of hepatitis B or anything like that. I don't drink or take drugs that might damage the liver. I never have." Shiva waited for Thomas Stone.

"You know that paper of ours better than I do, son," Stone said. "Unfortunately, those were estimates, a pure guess." He put his hands on the table. "We don't know how it might really work in humans."

"And if we fail," Deepak added gently, since Thomas Stone was finished, "we lose you who walked in here healthy *and* we lose Marion. Not to mention that we won't have a leg to stand on or that our careers could be over. Even if we succeed, we will be heavily criticized."

If they thought Shiva was done, they didn't know my brother. Hema was seeing her son anew. "I understand your reluctance. I wouldn't think much of you as surgeons if you agreed at once. However, if you *can* do this operation and if it has a reasonable chance, even a ten percent chance of saving Marion's life, and a less than ten percent chance of ending my life, and if you choose *not* to do the operation, then in my opinion, you would have failed Marion, failed Hema and me, failed medical science, failed yourselves. You would have failed my brother not only as his physicians, but as his friend, and as his father. If you *did* the operation and succeeded, you would not only save my brother, but you would have advanced surgery by a decade. *The time is now.*" He looked his father and then Deepak in the eye. "You may never get a chance like this again. If your rivals at Pittsburgh were facing this situation, what would they do? Would they not be bold?"

The prosecution rested. It was time for the other side of the table to respond.

"Bold, yes," Stone said, breaking the long silence, and speaking in an undertone as if only for himself, "but they wouldn't be operating on their own sons. I'm sorry, Shiva, I can't imagine this." He pushed back from the table, put his hands on the arms of his chair as if he were thinking of leaving.

"Thomas Stone!" Hema's voice was sharp as a Bard-Parker blade and it nailed him in his seat. "Once before I asked you for something, Thomas," she said. "It had to do with these boys. You walked away then. But this time if you walk away, neither I nor Ghosh can help these boys." Stone turned pale. He sat back in the chair. Hema's voice broke. "Thomas, do you think I would want to subject Shiva to a risk he couldn't surmount? Do you think I want to lose my sons?"

When she had composed herself, and after blowing noisily on her kerchief, she said, "Thomas, please dismiss from your head the idea that they are your sons. This is a *surgical* problem and you are in the best position to help them, precisely because they were never *your* sons. They never held you back, they never slowed your research, your career." There was no rancor in her voice. "Dr. Stone, these are *my* sons. They are a gift given to me. The pain, the heartbreak, if there is to be heartbreak, are all mine—that comes with the gift. I am their mother. Please hear what I say. This has nothing to do with your sons. Make your decision by deciding what you must do for your patient."

After an eternity, Deepak dragged the yellow pad from Shiva's side of the table and turned to a fresh page. He uncapped his pen and said to Shiva, "Tell me, why are you willing to subject yourself to such a risk?"

Shiva, for once, did not have a ready reply. He closed his eyes and made a steeple of his fingers, as if to shut out their faces. It worried Hema to see him this way. When he opened his eyes, he seemed for the first time since his arrival to be sad. He said, "Marion always thought that I never looked back. He saw me as always acting only for myself. He was right. He would be surprised if I were to risk my life to donate part of my liver. It isn't rational. But . . . seeing that my brother might die, I have looked back. I have regrets.

"If I was dying, if there was a chance he could save me, Marion would have pushed you to operate. That was his way. I never understood it before because it's irrational. But I understand it now." He glanced at Hema, then shouldered on.

"I had no reason to think about all this till I got here. But at his bedside . . . I realized if something happens to him, it happens to me, too. If I love myself, I love him, for we are one. That makes it a risk worth taking for me—it wouldn't be for anyone else, unless they loved him. I am the only one who is a perfect match. I want to do this. I couldn't live with myself if I didn't do this, and I think you wouldn't be able to live with yourselves if you didn't try. This is my destiny. My privilege. And yours."

Hema, composed till then, pulled Shiva to her and kissed him on the forehead.

Deepak, pen poised, had yet to write a word. He put the pen down.

At that moment it sunk in that they were going to go ahead with what had never been done before.

Shiva said to Deepak, "You said there was a second reason you had initially dismissed the idea of a transplant. What was it?"

Deepak said, "Before he lost consciousness, Marion made me promise not to transfer him. This hospital was special to him. It was more than a place for us foreign medical graduates to train. It welcomed us when other places did not. This is our home."

Hema sighed and dropped her head into her hands. Just when they had come this far, another obstacle.

"We can do it here," Thomas Stone said softly. He had listened to Shiva without moving a muscle, and those blue and steady eyes were now shiny and bright. He pushed his chair back and stood up, his movements purposeful. "Surgery is surgery is surgery. We can do it here as well as anywhere if we have the tools and the people. Fortunately, the world's expert in splitting the liver is sitting right next to me," he said, putting a hand on Deepak's shoulder, "and the tools, many of which he designed, are also here and will need to be sterilized at once. We have a lot to get ready. Hema, at any time if you or Shiva have a change of heart, all you need to do is say so. Shiva, please don't eat or drink anything from this moment on."

As he walked past Shiva's chair, he clamped his hand on my brother's shoulder, squeezed hard, and then he was gone.

CHAPTER 52

A Pair of
Unpaired Organs

A HELICOPTER FROM BOSTON GENERAL landed on Our
Lady of Perpetual Succour's helipad during the night. It brought
special instruments and the key personnel from Boston General's well-oiled liver transplant program. The corridor outside Our
Lady's operating suites, normally a desolate stretch where one might
find an empty stretcher or a portable X-ray machine parked while the
tech took a cigarette break, was now like battalion headquarters at the
start of a military campaign. Two large blackboards had been set up, one
labeled DONOR and the other RECIPIENT, each listing what had to be
accomplished with a check box next to the task. Our Lady of Perpetual
Succour's team with Deepak as lead surgeon would handle the donor
(Shiva's) operation, and the Boston General crew with Thomas Stone as
lead surgeon would staff the recipient (my) surgery. The Our Lady team
wore blue scrubs, while the Boston General crew wore white, and just
to be certain, the former had a big *D* (for "donor") marked on their hats
and scrub shirts with a black marker, whereas the latter had an *R*. The
adrenaline flow kept these disparate teams in good spirits; one Bronx
wag even suggested to his Dorchester counterpart that they could
call the teams Crackers and Homeboys. Only Thomas Stone and
Deepak Jesudass would be common to both teams, each man assisting
the other.

A dry run at midnight with dummy patients in both operating rooms
had uncovered a few critical glitches: anesthesia from Boston General needed a better orientation to the setup at Our Lady, and there
was need to anoint a "ringmaster" whose job was to be timekeeper,
to keep abreast of the activities of both teams, and who was the only per-

son authorized to carry and, most important, record all messages from Team R to Team D and vice versa. Two new blackboards were brought in to be placed *inside* each theater, and tasks to be ticked off written on these. Our Lady of Perpetual Succour was put on diversion, with trauma being rerouted to other hospitals in neighboring boroughs. By 4:00 a.m. it was time for the real thing.

Thomas Stone threw up in the surgeons' locker room. The Our Lady crew saw this as a bad omen, but the Boston General crew assured their counterparts that a pale, diaphoretic Stone augured a good outcome (though in truth, they had never seen him quite so pale and weak, lying prostrate on the bench, a puke basin at his side).

With so many people from two hospitals involved, it would have been difficult to keep the operation a secret. There were two television crews parked outside Our Lady. Newspaper editors were past the deadline for the morning paper, but they were preparing to weigh in on the ethics of this historic transplant, and now they could wait to see how it went before committing themselves.

Making history or keeping it a secret was the last thing on the surgeons' minds. Deepak, sitting on a bench separated by a row of lockers from where Stone suffered, tried to block out the sickening sound of his colleague's retching by reviewing a liver atlas.

At 4:22 a.m. Shiva was given diazepam and then pentothal, and a tube was passed into his trachea. The donor operation had begun. Thomas Stone and Deepak expected it to take anywhere from four to six hours.

IF THE BEATING HEART is pure theater, a playful, moody, extroverted organ cavorting in the chest, then the liver, sitting under the diaphragm, is a figurative painting, stolid and silent. The liver produces bile, without which fats are not digested, and the liver stores excess glucose in the form of glycogen. In silence and without outward signs, it detoxifies drugs and chemicals, it manufactures proteins for clotting and for transport, and it clears the body of ammonia, a waste product of metabolism.

The liver's smooth and shiny outer surface is monotonous and unexciting, and apart from a median furrow dividing it into a large right lobe and a smaller left, it has no visible cleavage planes. It is a surprise to find surgeons speak about its eight anatomical "segments"—as if they are discrete, as if they are like sections of an orange. Try pulling these segments apart and you'll have raw surfaces oozing blood and bile and a very dead patient. Still, the idea of segments allows the surgeon to define areas of liver that have a full complement of blood and bile conduits and that are therefore semiautonomous units, subfactories within the factory.

Four families of vessels enter or leave the liver. First, the portal vein, which carries all the venous blood leaving the gut and hauls it to the liver, blood that after a meal is rich in fats and other nutrients for the factory to process. The hepatic artery brings oxygen-rich blood to the liver from the heart via the aorta. The hepatic veins have the task of taking all the spent blood that has filtered through the liver and returning it to the heart via the vena cava. The bile formed by each liver cell gathers in tiny bile tributaries that merge and grow and eventually form the common bile duct that then empties into the duodenum. Excess bile is stored in the gallbladder, which is nothing more than a balloonlike offshoot of the bile duct. In keeping with the liver's chaste and understated demeanor, the gallbladder is tucked out of sight, just under the overhang of the liver.

DEEPAK, STANDING ON THE RIGHT, made the incision. The first step was to remove Shiva's gallbladder. Then, turning his attention to the stalk of vessels entering the liver (the *porta hepatis*), he dissected out the right hepatic artery, then the right branch of the portal vein and the right biliary duct. To get the right lobe free, he also had to cut through liver tissue and disconnect the hepatic veins at the back where they joined the vena cava—the dark side of the liver, the place where the surgeon might "see God" if there was bleeding. In removing a lobe of the liver for cancer, it is possible to control bleeding by pinching off the stalk of blood vessels in the *porta hepatis*—the Pringle maneuver. But this wasn't an option for Deepak, because it would compromise the function of the lobe they were removing, choke it half to death before giving it to me. There are now ultrasonic and even radio-frequency "dissectors" that make cutting through the liver easier, less bloody. But Deepak, with Thomas Stone as his assistant, had to resort to clamp crushing and "finger fracturing" to break through the liver tissue while avoiding the major blood vessels or bile ducts. Deepak worried about his senior partner: Thomas Stone's mind seemed to wander, something Deepak had never encountered before. Little did Deepak know that Stone was struggling to keep away the image and the memory of his futile efforts to save Sister Mary Joseph Praise, and his dangerous attempts at crushing a baby's skull.

The donor operation went without a hitch. At 9:00 a.m., I was wheeled into the operating room, and at 9:30 a.m., just as Shiva's right lobe was coming free, the Boston General team, without Thomas Stone, made a long incision across my middle, below my rib cage but above my belly button. They began mobilizing my liver, cutting away its ligaments and trusses.

Thomas Stone took Shiva's freed right lobe to a side table, where, with hands that were steadier than his insides, he flushed the portal vein with University of Wisconsin solution. Deepak, meanwhile, ensured that there were no bile leaks in the raw edge of what remained of Shiva's liver, which was largely his left lobe. He looked all around for any overlooked bleeders, repeated the sponge and instrument count twice, and then he closed Shiva's belly. In a month, Shiva's liver would regenerate to its previous size.

Now, Thomas Stone and Deepak donned fresh gowns and gloves and came to me to complete the removal of my liver. Because my clotting functions were poor, there were lots of tiny bleeders, particularly behind my liver as they freed it from the diaphragm. I required many units of blood as well as platelets. They carefully identified and preserved my bile duct, the hepatic artery, and the portal vein. It was one in the afternoon when my four-and-a-half-pound companion, which I had sheltered under my rib cage all these years, left me. A gaping cavity under the dome of my right diaphragm, an unnatural void, remained.

Connecting Shiva's liver, or rather his right lobe, was a laborious process. Bleeding had to be meticulously controlled in order to see clearly and for Thomas Stone, with Deepak's assistance, to suture artery to artery, bile duct to bile duct, and vein to vein. The scissors and needle holders were specially designed for microsurgery. Both surgeons wore headlights and magnifying loupes as they manipulated sutures that were finer than a human hair. One advantage of Deepak's decision to give me Shiva's right lobe was that it fit more naturally under the dome of my diaphragm, and its hilum—the place where the vessels entered—was oriented more naturally toward the vena cava. It made the surgeons' jobs a little easier.

The remnants of the D team took Shiva to the recovery room and then waited in the locker room. Their mood unexpectedly became somber. It was now out of their hands, and that made the tension almost unbearable.

An anxious Hema, with Vinu at her side, watched the clock in the waiting room. At first, she was thankful for her chatty companion, but then even he could not distract her. She kept thinking of Ghosh and wondering if he would have chastised her for letting Shiva take such a risk. *A stone in hand* . . . or was it "bird"? *Grass is greener* . . . he would have a maxim for the situation.

Word came from the operating room via the Ringmaster—he called at each stage of the operation—and Hema now wished he wouldn't, because the shrill ring never failed to startle her and made her imagine the worst, only to be told "They have begun" or "The portal vessels have been isolated" when what she wanted to hear is that they were done with Shiva. At last, she did hear those words, and soon she saw Shiva, awake but groggy in the recovery room and wincing in pain. She was giddy with joy, stroking Shiva's hair, and she knew that wherever he was, whatever form his reincarnation had taken, Ghosh, too, was relieved.

Shiva's eyes, coming into focus, asked the question. "Yes," Hema said. "They're putting your liver lobe into Marion right now. Deepak said the part you donated looked magnificent."

She wasn't allowed to stay long. Instead of returning to the waiting room, she decided to slip away to the chapel. A solitary stained-glass window allowed in very little light. When the heavy door closed behind her, she had to seek the pew with her hand and ease into the velvet-covered bench. She covered her head respectfully with the tail of her sari. As her eyes adjusted, she got the fright of her life, seeing a figure on its knees near the altar. An apparition! she thought. Then she remembered the prayer chain for Marion, the round-the-clock vigil in this chapel. As her pulse recovered, Hema settled back and observed the veiled head, the scapular falling back, stiff and separate from the pleated tunic. Hema realized that in importuning every deity she could think of, she had somehow neglected to appeal to Sister Mary Joseph Praise. The oversight caused a fierce and silly panic, blood surging up her neck. *Oh, please don't let that be a reason to punish my son.* She wrung her hands, squirmed and chastised herself for forgetting. *Forgive me, Sister, but if you only know how stressful this has been, and if it is not too late, please watch over Marion, please see him through.*

She felt the response arrive as distinctly as if it were a voice or a touch: first, a lightness in her forehead, then a calmness in her chest that said she had been heard. *Thank you, thank you,* Hema said. *I promise to keep you updated.*

She returned to the waiting room. She was so exhausted that she could only wonder how Stone and Deepak managed to stay upright. From the waiting room window the earth looked as if it were mostly sky and concrete—no real earth to speak of, no manifestation of nature on the ground other than the sun setting in that direction. It was so odd, and yet this was the view her son had known for the last six years.

At 7:00 p.m., Thomas Stone was at her side. He nodded, then smiled, an expression so rare that she knew it had gone well. He said nothing, and she, too, was speechless, tears running down her cheeks. In studying Stone's face, grooved where his magnifying spectacles and lamp had sat, and grooved also from worry and work, she realized with a start how old he had become, how old they had both become, and how if they had nothing else in common, they had this: that they were both still standing after all these years, and that her sons (his, too, at some level, she had to admit) were both alive.

Thomas Stone sat down, or rather fell into the sofa, and he didn't protest when she forced juice and a sandwich on him from Vinu's ice chest of goodies. Stone washed the juice down with a bottle of water and started on a second before life seemed to stir within him. His gaunt face filled out. "Technically, everything has gone well," he said. "Marion's new liver, Shiva's old lobe, was already making bile before we had even finished the anastomosis." He smiled again, a shy twist of the corners of his mouth, pride in his voice. The bile, he said, was an excellent sign.

"We had a scare," he added. "There was a moment when Marion's blood pressure dropped precipitously. No explanation for it. We were ahead on fluid and blood, but still his heart raced to one hundred and eighty beats a minute. We poured fluid in, tried this and that . . . and just as suddenly, the pressure came back up." She was about to ask him precisely what time that was, but then she didn't bother, because she knew. She closed her eyes and thanked Sister for her intercession. When she opened them, Thomas Stone was staring at her as if he understood. She felt so close to him, so grateful. She couldn't go so far as to hug him, but she did reach for his hand.

"So, I must leave now," he said to Hema after a minute. "It will be touch-and-go for a while for Marion, given how sick he was when we started. But at least he has a working liver. His kidneys are still not functioning, and he needs dialysis, but I trust it is just hepatorenal syndrome and the new liver will fix that." He was holding things back from her. He didn't tell her how, when things had looked so dire in the operating room, he'd looked up at the ceiling and prayed not to a God or to spiders, but to Sister Mary Joseph Praise, asking to be redeemed for a lifetime of mistakes.

THERE WAS REJOICING in the hospital, first that one of its own who had been near death was still alive, and second that Our Lady had made history. The Mass of Gratitude in the chapel was packed, Hema and Vinu in the front pew and the crowd spilling out to the cloisters.

Outside Our Lady of Perpetual Succour, the news vans were lined up—international as well as national. Every previous liver transplant in the world had its origins in a corpse-to-be, in someone who was brain-dead. A *living* donor—and an identical twin who had given half his liver to his brother—that was big news. The media didn't quite get that this technical breakthrough would be most meaningful to babies born with congenital biliary atresia—lack of bile ducts. Adult organs from people dying of trauma were scarce enough; a child donor was exceedingly rare. Stone and Deepak opened the way for a parent to donate part of his or her liver to save their infant.

By the second day, the ferreting journalists had connected Shiva to his fame as the fistula surgeon—"fixing holes is what I do"—and by the third day, they'd labeled Thomas Stone the "estranged father." It was perhaps only a matter of time before they discovered the story of Sister Mary Joseph Praise, though it would probably necessitate a reporter traveling to Addis to unearth that tidbit.

I CAME AWAKE on the fifth day. My first memory is that of floating up from the ocean bottom, my eyes still waterlogged and with what felt like scuba gear stuffed in my mouth and throat—I couldn't speak. As I broke to the surface, I understood that I was still in the ICU at Our Lady, but I heard nothing of what anybody said. I saw Hema and Stone and I looked for Shiva. He's decided not to come from Addis, I remember thinking, and I was disappointed.

Twelve hours later, in the late evening of the fifth day (though it was perpetual twilight in the ICU), I surfaced for good, relieved to see that Hema was there, and that I hadn't imagined her presence.

She stayed by my side, holding my hand. I craved her touch, fearful I might sink back into the abyss where it was all dark and from which there was no promise of return. But I would drift off into light sleep for short periods. Night turned to day, bringing with it a new bustle and energy and more traffic through our room.

On the seventh day, I was awake long enough for Hema to make the fantastic statement that half of Shiva's liver was in me. Sick patients need to have everything explained at least twice, because you can presume they will not have heard half of what you said. Hema repeated herself at least ten times, and it was only when she showed me the *Times*, and the picture of me and of Shiva, that I believed.

"Shiva is recovering," Hema said. "He's fine. But you've developed pneumonia and there is fluid collecting around your right lung. That's why you are still on the ventilator. But it's getting better, so Deepak says you will be off the ventilator tomorrow. Your new liver is functioning well, and your kidneys have bounced back." This was not the reunion I had imagined with Hema, but the expression on her face, her joy, her relief, were priceless. She rarely left my side.

I saw Deepak and Stone for the first time later that same day. I struggled with my emotions. I know I was supposed to feel gratitude. Sometimes I think we surgeons wear masks to conceal our desires, to hide our willingness to violate the body of another. Only the guarantee of amnesia, the fact that the patient will remember nothing but the anesthetist's saying "Sweet dreams," allows us to be surgeons. They stood before me, these perpetrators of organized violence on my body. The fact that both men were shy and unassuming seemed almost deceitful given the ambition, the hubris, that had allowed them to risk Shiva's life for mine. It was the only time I was thankful for that evil tube going down my throat and between my vocal cords, because what I would have said to them would have sounded ungrateful: *It's a good thing Shiva made it, otherwise I'd be after your hides.*

When I awoke sometime later, I forgot about the tube and tried to speak, which made me feel I was choking, which made me panic. My struggles triggered the ventilator alarm, and now I was terrified that the nurse would decide I was "fighting the ventilator," which could bring an order for intravenous curare. That drug, derived from the poison darts of Amazon tribes, paralyzes all the muscles, leaving you still as death, so that the ventilator can do its work unimpeded. But God help you if you aren't given a strong sedative along with it, because then you are awake, alert, but unable to twitch or even blink. The thought of being in that paralyzed, locked-in state had always horrified me, even as I blithely ordered curare (*and* sedation) for hundreds of patients. Now that I was a patient, my curse was that I knew too much.

With Hema's help, her soothing voice, I did my best to calm down, to let the machine push air into me, and the nurse retreated. When I felt better I wrote, *How is Shiva?*

She didn't have to reply, because just then my other half came in, led by Thomas Stone.

My brother, whom I had not seen for seven years, looked haggard, not at all like the picture in the *Times*. I felt vertigo in seeing my reflection moving independently of me. Shiva wore a hospital gown, one palm resting carefully on his belly, the other hand pushing his intravenous pole ahead of him, and using it as a walking stick. My brother wasn't given to laughing and most jokes were wasted on him, but when he saw me, he grinned like the chimp who'd locked up the zookeeper.

You monkey, you, I wanted to say, and I reached hungrily for his hand, our fingers interlocking. *You should laugh more, it suits you: see how the furrows around your brow vanish and your ears ease back?* I felt fluid running down my temples, and his eyes were full, too. I squeezed his fingers, a Morse code to convey what was in my heart. He nodded—*You don't have to tell me anything* is what he was saying. He bent forward gingerly, and I wondered what he was up to, surely not a kiss . . . He clinked his skull against mine. It was such an unexpected, jarring, and surprising act, a throwback to being little boys, the softest of *testas,* that it made me laugh, which made that horrible tube scratch the inside of my throat, and so I had to stop.

I pointed to Shiva's belly. He pulled aside his gown and I could see some of the incision, though a gauze pad with a drain passing through it hid the remainder. I raised my eyebrows at him, asking if it hurt. And he said, *Only when I breathe,* and we both laughed and both had to cut that off because of the pain. Stone stood looking on at this silent dialogue, amazed, a strange expression on his face.

Little did I know that Shiva's recovery had been complicated by a bile infection requiring antibiotics. Or that he had developed a blood clot in the vein in his right arm through which he'd been getting fluids. He was on a blood thinner, and the clot was resolving.

I held his hand for a long time, content to look at him, to thank him with my fingers, but he kept shrugging off my thanks. I reached for my pen, and Hema pushed the pad in front of me and I wrote, *Greater love hath no man—*

He didn't let me finish. He held my pen. He said, *You would have done the same.* I had my doubts, but he nodded. *Yes, you would.*

That evening, Deepak drained fluid from around my right lung, and my breath expanded in that direction. Then he took the wretched tube out of my throat. My first words were "Thank you," and when that ugly blue machine left my room, I fell into a deep sleep.

The next morning was full of small miracles: being able to turn and gaze at the window and see sky, being able to say "Ouch" when the movement pulled on my incision. Hema wasn't around. The ICU was quiet. My nurse, Amelia, was unnaturally cheery. I assumed it was still early morning. "We have an X-ray to do downstairs," she said, unhooking me from the tethers, and readying my bed to roll.

In Radiology I was lifted into the doughnut for a CAT scan, but oddly, it was of my head and not my belly. Surely it was a mistake. But no, the order was from Deepak, and it read, "CAT scan of the head with and without contrast."

Back in my room and by noon, still no sign of Hema, or Stone, or Shiva. Amelia said they would be along presently.

The physical therapist helped me stand beside my bed for a few seconds. My legs felt like Jell-O sticks. I took a few steps with assistance, then sat in the chair, exhausted, woozy, as if I had run a marathon. I dozed there, ate what little I could. After lunch, I took a few more steps, and even peed upright. The nurses helped me back to bed. In retrospect, they seemed pleased to get out of my room.

IT WAS 2:00 P.M. when Thomas Stone appeared at my door. There were dark circles around his eyes. He sat self-consciously on the edge of the bed. He touched my hand. His lips parted.

"Wait," I said. "Don't say anything yet." I looked out of the window at the clouds, at distant smokestacks. The world was intact now, but I knew once he spoke it wouldn't be so.

"Okay," I said. "What happened to Shiva?"

"He had a massive bleed in his brain," he said, his voice hoarse. "It happened last night, about an hour after we left your room. Hema was with him. He suddenly clutched his head in pain . . . Then, in a matter of seconds, he was . . . unconscious."

"Is he gone?"

Thomas Stone shook his head. "He bled from an arteriovenous mal-formation, a cavernous tangle of blood vessels in the cortex. He has probably had it all along . . . He was on anticoagulants for the blood clot in his arm . . . In a week we would have stopped."

"Where is he?"

"Here. In the ICU. On a ventilator. Two neurosurgeons have seen him." He shook his head. "It isn't feasible to evacuate the bleed. They think it's too late. And that he's brain-dead."

I didn't register much of what he said after that. I remember he said that my CAT scan showed a similar but smaller spider knot of vessels, but mine wasn't bleeding, a miracle of sorts, I suppose, since I'd bled from everywhere till I got Shiva's liver.

A few minutes later, Hema, Deepak, and Vinu came into the room. I understood now that Stone had been delegated to break the news.

Poor Hema. I should have tried to comfort her, but I was too full of grief and guilt. I felt so very tired. They sat around my bed, Hema weeping, bent over, resting her head on my thigh. I wanted them to leave. I closed my eyes for a moment. I woke up when a nurse came in to silence one of the intravenous pumps. There was no one else in the room. I had her walk me to the bathroom and then I sat in the armchair. I wanted my strength back.

WHEN I AWOKE, Thomas Stone was by my chair. "He can't breathe on his own, and there are no pupillary or other reflexes," he said in response to my silent query. "He's brain-dead now."

I said I wanted to see him.

My father wheeled me down the hall where Shiva lay. Hema was with him, her eyes puffy and red, and when she turned to me, I felt ashamed to be alive, ashamed to be the cause of her sorrow.

Shiva looked asleep. It was his turn to sport the spike coming out of his skull—the intracranial pressure monitor. The endotracheal tube skewed his lips, angling his chin up unnaturally. The rise and fall of his chest from the ventilator offered a spot on which to rest my eyes, and my ifs were coming in that rhythm: If I hadn't come to America. If I hadn't seen Tsige. If I hadn't opened the door for Genet . . .

. . .

HEMA WHEELED ME BACK to my room, helped me back in bed.

I said to her, "It would have been better if you and Shiva had buried me. You'd be on your way to Missing now with your favorite son."

It was a stupid, churlish thing to say, a primitive and subconscious urge to wound her so as to assuage my pain and guilt. But if I expected her to strike back, she didn't. There is a point when grief exceeds the human capacity to emote, and as a result one is strangely composed—she had reached that point.

"Marion, I know you think I favored Shiva . . . And maybe I did. What can I say but that I'm sorry. A mother loves her children equally . . . but sometimes one child needs more help, more attention, to get by in the world. Shiva needed that.

"Marion, I have to apologize to you for more than that. I thought you were responsible for Genet being mutilated, circumcised, and all that followed. I held that against you. When we came here, Shiva told me everything. My son, I hope you can forgive me. I'm a stupid mother."

I was speechless at this news. What else had gone on when I was unconscious?

Outside a siren drew closer and closer, an ambulance coming to Our Lady.

"They want to discontinue the ventilator on Shiva," Hema said. "I can't bear for them to do that. As long as he is breathing, even if it is the ventilator breathing for him, he's alive for me."

The next morning, after the nurse seated me in the shower and helped me with my first bath, I put on a fresh gown and I asked to be wheeled to Shiva's room.

"Stop here," I said, well before his room, because I saw through the half-open door that Thomas Stone was seated by Shiva's bed, just as I was told he had sat by mine. His fingers rested on Shiva's wrist, feeling the pulse. His hand lingered there long after he had registered the heart rate. I wondered what he was thinking. I watched him for a full ten minutes before he stood up and came out, his eyes haunted and red. He didn't see me as he walked off in the other direction.

I rolled my chair after him. "Dr. Stone," I said. Every fiber of my being wanted to cry out, *Father!*

He came to me. "Dr. Stone," I said. "Surely an operation . . . is his only chance. Can't the neurosurgeons go in, tie off the tangled vessels, and evacuate the clot in his brain? So what if it's a long shot? It's his only shot."

He considered this for a while.

"Son, they say the tissue in there is—sorry to say this—the consistency of wet toilet paper. Blood mixed with brain. The pressure's so high, if they so much as touch him, they tell me it'll only make him bleed further."

I didn't want to accept that. "Can't *you* do it? You and Deepak? You've done burr holes. I've done burr holes. What's there to lose? Please? Let's give him that chance."

He waited so long that even I could hear the fallacy of what I was suggesting. My father put his hand on my shoulder. He spoke to me gently, as to a junior colleague, not to his son. "Marion, remember the Eleventh Commandment," he said. "Thou shall not operate on the day of a patient's death."

When I was back in my room, Thomas Stone brought up Shiva's CAT scan. I was shocked to see the huge white splotch—which is how blood looks on a CAT scan—involving both hemispheres and spilling into the ventricles. It compressed the brain within the rigid confines of the skull. I knew then that it was hopeless.

BECAUSE OF THE ANEURYSM or tangled vessel malformation in his brain, Shiva was not a potential donor for heart or kidneys, for fear there might be similar changes in those organs.

Hema didn't want to be there when the ventilator was discontinued. I said I'd be with him. I asked to be alone with Shiva when he passed.

Hema said her good-bye first.

I was outside the room when Vinu escorted her out. It was a heartbreaking sight to see my mother, the tail end of her sari draped over her head, her shoulders slumped, leave her still-breathing child. It must have felt to her as if she were abandoning him. Every eye in the unit was on her, and not one was dry, as her shimmering, sari-clad form floated down the hall on her way to the Quiet Room.

With Deepak's assistance I climbed onto Shiva's bed. It was eight in the evening. I settled myself next to him. Everything but his breathing tube and an intravenous line had been removed. Deepak peeled away the tape that held the tracheal tube to Shiva's cheeks. Then, with a nod from me, he injected morphine through Shiva's intravenous tubing. If any part of Shiva's brain was alive, we didn't want it to sense pain, or fear, or suffocation. Deepak turned off the ventilator, silenced its immediate shrill protest, slid the endotracheal tube from Shiva's mouth, and then he left the room.

I LAY THERE, my head against Shiva's, a finger resting on his carotid pulse. His body was warm. He never took a breath after the tube came out. His facial expression never changed. His pulse stayed regular for almost a minute, then it paused, as if it had just realized its lifelong partner—the lungs—had quit. His heart sped up, became faint, and then, with a final throb under my fingers, it was gone. I thought of Ghosh. Of all the pulse types, this was both the rarest and the most common, a Janus quality that every pulse possesses: the potential to be absent.

I closed my eyes and clung to Shiva. I cradled him, his skull buttressed against mine and now wet with my tears. I felt physically vulnerable in a way I'd never felt when we were a continent apart, as if with his death my own biology was now altered. The heat was rapidly leaving his body.

I rocked Shiva, wedging my head against his, remembering how for so long I was unable to sleep except like this. I felt despair. I didn't want to leave this bed. Chang and Eng had died within hours of each other, because when the healthy one was offered the opportunity to be freed from the dead one, he declined. I understood so well. Let Deepak give me a lethal dose of morphine and let my life end this way, let my respiration cease, my pulse fade and then disappear. Let my brother and me leave the world in the same embrace with which we began in the womb.

I PICTURED SHIVA getting the telegram, his coming to me, then putting himself at risk to save me. Would I have done the same for him? Perhaps when he saw me, he'd felt the way I did now: that it didn't matter what might have transpired between us, but life would not be worth living and would end soon if something happened to the other.

His body continued to lose heat in my arms as if I were drawing it away, siphoning it over. I remembered the two of us running up the hill in a relay, carrying a lifeless and cold child to Casualty, the parents trailing behind us. He was now that lifeless child.

The minutes passed.

Ultimately it was the rude coldness of Shiva's skin, the terrible separation it delineated of the living and the dead, the disarticulation of our bound flesh, that forced me to a new understanding, a new way of seeing us in the face of such rapid attrition, and this is what I came to:

Shiva and I were one being—ShivaMarion.

Even when an ocean separated us, even when we thought we were two, we were ShivaMarion.

He was the rake and I the erstwhile virgin, he the genius who acquired knowledge effortlessly while I toiled into the night for the same mastery; he the famous fistula surgeon and I just another trauma surgeon. Had we switched roles, it wouldn't have mattered one bit to the universe.

Fate and Genet had conspired to kill my liver, but Shiva had a role in Genet's fate, and hence my fate. Every action of ours turned out to be dependent on the other. But now by a brilliant and daring rearrangement of organs, ShivaMarion had readjusted. Four legs, four arms, four kidneys, and so on, but instead of two livers, we had downsized to one. Then karma and bad luck took us even further, forced further concessions: we lost ground on his side, a few organs died. Okay—just about everything on his side died, but we retained half his liver, and it was thriving. What we had to do now was economize further, go halves again, tough measures for tough times: two legs sufficed, so also with eyes, kidneys. We'd go with half a liver, one heart, one pancreas, two arms . . . but we were still ShivaMarion.

Shiva lives in me.

Call it a far-fetched scheme that I conjured up to allow me to go on . . . Well then, it allowed me to go on. It gave me comfort. It dried my tears, helped me untwine my arms and legs from the body that we were discarding. In the eerie quiet of that room, so primed for machines but with the machines all silent, the blinds closed, and with an icy corpse next to me, I felt Shiva was instructing me. He had rowed over from the sinking ship and he was telling me to think this way, and it was just Shiva's kind of logic. *One being at birth, rudely separated, we are one again.*

THEY WERE ASSEMBLED outside, a ghoulish receiving line was what I thought at first. But they couldn't know what had just transpired, and so I didn't blame them. Their hearts were in the right place. Thomas Stone, Deepak, Vinu, and so many of my nurses and nursing assistants— my friends, my Our Lady family before they became my caregivers. I shook each hand, and thanked them for the two of us. I believe they will tell you my manner was composed, far different from what they expected. I left Thomas Stone for last. After I shook his hand, I followed an irrational instinct—Shiva's, I believe, certainly not mine—which told me to hug him, not to get but to give. To let him know that as a father it turns out he'd done what he was meant to do; he lived on in us and we lived because of his skills. The way he clung to me, held me as if he were drowning, told me I'd made the right choice, or Shiva had, awkward as it was.

I walked slowly down the hall to our Quiet Room, a euphemism for the place we chose to give bad news, a place with chairs, a table, a sofa, a big picture window, a cross on the wall, but no TV, no magazines, only a solid and soundproof door. How many times had I made this walk as a trauma surgeon? So often I had lingered outside the door, conscious of the devastation my news would be bringing. Had I honored the feelings and the dignity of those who waited in that room, the parents, siblings, spouses, and children, even if what I had to say dashed all their prayers? I could remember every such encounter; I could recall each face as it turned in hope and apprehension when the door opened.

I FOUND HEMA, hands crossed in front of her, gazing out of the window at the lights of the Battleship housing project that abutted our house-staff quarters, and the distant outline of the bridge beyond. Her back was to me. She saw my reflection in the glass before she saw me, but unlike every single person I had ever come to see in this room, she did not spin around. Instead, she stood like a statue, staring at my reflection in the window. I stopped where I was, holding the door open. I saw in that glass her eyes widen, the eyebrows rise. She held my gaze for the longest time. Her face showed surprise . . . as if who she saw wasn't the person she had expected to see.

"Here we are, Ma," I said.

She cocked her head at my voice. She brought one hand up to her chin, her fingers aligned and locked together and resting contemplatively along her cheek, her movements exaggerated. She studied my face, my reflection, just like a village girl who is surprised in the act of drawing water at the well, and who must now read the intentions of the tall, smiling avatar whom she sees standing behind her.

Then, in slow motion, as if this were a dance, and both of us dancers, she turned and faced me.

I moved to her. "Here we are," I said again, my arms extending toward her. "We can go home now, Ma."

It must have seemed to her a very strange thing, even the wrong thing, to say. To live purely in the here and now, to look forward but never to the past—that was vintage Shiva. "Here we are," I said.

She came into my arms.

We held her tight.

CHAPTER 53

She Is Coming

O N A BEAUTIFUL MORNING, just three weeks after Shiva's transference, Hema and I took leave of Our Lady of Perpetual Succour. Thomas Stone insisted on being our escort. We stepped outside into air so crisp I felt a cough or a sneeze would shatter it like glass. The brick façade of Our Lady of Perpetual Succour glistened with dew as we said our good-byes. The hospital's recent turn in the limelight had brought in special city funds and sparked emergency repairs; as a result, the monsignor in the fountain was no longer tilting, his swizzle stick was gone, as was his crusting of bird droppings. Polished and sanguine, he looked emasculated and alien to the place where I had spent the last seven years of my life.

Our yellow cab sped across the Whitestone Bridge to Kennedy Airport. The sun had barely come up, and yet the freeway was thick with cars, the solitary drivers insulated from one another in wafer-thin metal, which at these speeds offered only the illusion of protection. We merged like wingmen rejoining the formation. Hema looked out meditatively just as I had when I arrived seven years before. I wondered if she could hear the hum of the überconsciousness, the superorganism who kept this from descending into chaos.

The year 1986 was a disaster for our family. Hema believed that it had something to do with the number, because it had birth in the 1 and destiny in the 8. Nineteen eighty-six had started off terribly with the *Challenger* spacecraft exploding on January 28 (which was month 1, and there was the number 8 again). Then the Chernobyl tragedy was exactly eighty-eight days after the *Challenger* disaster. On that scale, the death of one twin—on the eighteenth of the month—hardly registered.

There was yet another death eight days later that had bearing on us: my neighbor Holmes came with Appleby of the detective agency to let me know that Genet had passed away in a prison hospital in Galveston just as I was regaining my strength. Genet's son had been adopted by a family in Texas, and she had gone in search of him. She'd been living hand-to-mouth in a cardboard lean-to a few blocks from the seawall when she was picked up. She was a mere skeleton and survived just two days in the prison infirmary. She had supposedly died of adrenal failure caused by tuberculosis. I knew better. She had died chasing greatness and never saw it each time it was in her hand, so she kept seeking it elsewhere, but never understood the work required to get it or to keep it. I'm ashamed to say I felt relief when the word came; only her death could ensure that we didn't keep tearing each other apart for what remained of our lives.

IN THE INTERNATIONAL DEPARTURE HALL, I heard snatches of Bengali, Arabic, and Tagalog. A man bound for Lagos protested in screeching pidgin about the unfairness of British Airways, because there was no way he was four pounds over. In this setting, Thomas Stone, without his white coat or scrubs, looked like the newly arrived foreigner.

"Will you be back, Marion?" he asked when it was time for saying good-bye.

All I knew was that I wanted to be with Hema when she interred Shiva's ashes between Ghosh and Sister Mary Joseph Praise. The grotto by Missing's back wall and in earshot of the little creek was rapidly becoming the family burial plot. I was going back also to see Matron, Almaz, and Gebrew. I knew that my presence would help console them. Beyond that, I hadn't given great thought to my future.

"Of course I'll be back," I said. "I still have my house, the car, my job . . ."

"Be careful what you eat, drink . . . ," he said. It was his way of telling me to protect his handiwork.

I felt better than well. Other transplant patients had to fight to keep their bodies from rejecting the lifesaving organ. The cortisone they took led to cataracts, diabetes, hip fractures, and other side effects. I was blessed not to have to swallow a single pill. I felt no pain if you didn't count the twinges under my ribs, which I considered promising and not painful; they were the sign of Shiva's half liver growing to fully occupy its new home.

"How about you?" I had yet to find a comfortable way to address my father; it was "Dr. Stone" in the hospital and nothing at times like this. "Will you have a job to go back to?" I teased. He hadn't seen Boston since I fell ill.

His slow smile only exaggerated the sadness in his face. He took Shiva's death personally, as if fate had never forgotten that he'd once attempted to destroy Shiva, and so when he had operated to save Shiva, his original intent had betrayed him.

My father made no attempt to shake my hand. Our one hug after Shiva's passing was good for a lifetime. We parted with a nod.

Hema, however, took Thomas Stone's hand in both of hers. I had missed their reunion at my bedside. Now, I watched like a nosy child.

"Thomas, stop this at once!" Hema said, chiding him for his melancholic expression. "You did everything you could, do you hear me? You did your best for your sons. No one else in the world could have done what you did. Thomas, if Ghosh were here, he'd say the same thing. He'd have been so proud of you and he'd say, 'Go on with your work because it is so important.'" She released his hand, after patting it one last time, then she turned and walked away.

Later, as our plane banked over Queens and headed for open water, I thought about Hema's parting words to Stone. Buried in there had been her apology for having fashioned him into a monster in her mind for all these years. In patting his hand and walking away, she was releasing herself.

Alitalia took us to Rome. Mechanical problems on the connecting flight had the agent projecting a fourteen-hour layover. It gave me an idea. In no time Hema and I were once again in a taxi on a freeway, but this time we were heading to downtown Rome. We were like children playing hooky from school.

Hema had needed little convincing. We went to a first-class hotel, the Hassler, Rome's best, I was once told. It was a grand building that overlooked the Spanish Steps. From the rooftop at dusk the sky's red hue outlined the dome of St. Peter's in the distance.

Each morning we set out for the briefest sightseeing. We returned to our hotel for lunch and a long afternoon nap. The evenings we wandered down the streets and alleyways beneath the Spanish Steps. Eventually we'd pick an outdoor café for dinner. "It's so familiar, isn't it?" Hema said. "These menus, typed out and mimeographed, minestrone and *pasta fagioli*, the waiters with white shirts, black pants, white aprons . . ." I knew what she meant. The Italians had brought it all to Ethiopia, right down to the umbrellas that hung over the little Formica-topped round tables. Hema's face at dinner was as tranquil as I'd seen it since I became conscious of her at my bedside at Our Lady. "I wish Ghosh could have been with us. How he would have enjoyed this," she said, smiling.

ON THE FOURTH MORNING, we let the concierge talk us into a private tour with a guide from our hotel. What did we want to see? Surprise us, we said. Take us off the cow path. Places where there isn't too much walking or waiting in line.

He began with the Santa Maria della Vittoria, a ten-minute ride from our hotel. It was a homely church, sitting right on the street, cars passing by, the elaborate façade looking as if it had been slapped on to the front of an unadorned stone box. Our guide said it was built about 1624, first dedicated to St. Paul, and later to the Virgin Mary. The interior was small—tiny when compared with St. Peter's—with a short nave under a low vault. Off to the side, Corinthian pillars flattened into the wall demarcated three "chapels" which were nothing more than recesses, each with a rail for private prayer and a place to light candles. As we came to the end of the nave, our guide turned to the left and pointed. "This is the Cornaro Chapel. It is what I wanted you to see," he said.

It took a few seconds for my eyes to relay the sight to my brain, and longer still for my brain to believe. The blue marble sculpture floating before me was Bernini's *Ecstasy of St. Teresa*. I wanted to silence our guide and say, *Stop, I know this sculpture.* But in truth what I knew was only a print that found its way onto a calendar which my mother had then thumbtacked to the wall of the autoclave room. It had been up for perhaps thirty years before Ghosh had taken that aging piece of paper and framed it for me, to protect it from further deterioration. The print meant the world to me, yet it had never seemed at ease on my walls in America, where it looked like the cheapest kind of tourist gewgaw. I'd packed it with me on this journey, planning to restore it to the one place where I knew it was at home, the autoclave room.

I looked over to Hema. Her face was aglow. She understood. What providence had brought us to this spot? Surely this was Ghosh announcing his presence, because Ghosh was the sort of man who could be counted on to know that Bernini's *Ecstasy of St. Teresa* was minutes from our hotel, even if he'd never been to Rome before. Ghosh had brought us here, led us to this spot, not to see St. Teresa in marble, but to see Sister

Mary Joseph Praise in the flesh, for that is what the figure was to me. *I have come, Mother.*

WE LIT CANDLES. Hema fell to her knees, the flame throwing a flickering light on her face. Her lips moved. She believed in every kind of deity, and in reincarnation and resurrection—she knew no contradictions in these areas. How I admired her faith, her lack of self-consciousness—a Hindu lighting candles to a Carmelite nun in a Catholic church.

I knelt, too. I addressed God and Sister Mary Joseph Praise and Shiva and Ghosh—all the beings I carried with me in the flesh and in spirit. *Thank you for letting me be alive, letting me see this marble dream.* I felt a great peace, a sense that coming to this spot had completed the circuit, and now a blocked current would flow and I could rest. If "ecstasy" meant the sudden intrusion of the sacred into the ordinary, then it had just happened to me.

My mother had spoken.

What I didn't know then was that she had more to say.

CHAPTER 54

Homefires

I T WAS DUSK when we landed. I had been away from Addis for seven years. The white buildings of Missing looked rounded at the edges, worn down, as if they'd been excavated in an archaeological dig but not restored.

When the taxi reached Shiva's toolshed I had the driver let me out. I told Hema to go on because I wanted to walk the rest of the way.

I stood listening once the car pulled away; the dry rustle of the leaves was like a child's hand sifting through a box of coins. The sound had lost all its menace for me. I found that dented and bent curb, which had stopped a motorcycle but not its rider. I looked down into the trees and the shadows where he fell. The spot no longer generated any dread for me. All my ghosts had vanished; the retribution that they sought had been exacted. I had nothing more to give, and nothing to fear. I looked out over trees to the city. The sky was a mad painter's canvas, as if halfway through the artist had decided against azure and had instead splashed ochre and crimson and black on the palette. The city was alight, glowing, but here and there it was obscured by great puffs of mist which smudged my view, like the smoke of many small battles.

I walked up the hill to the house, a thousand memories now of Shiva and me doing our three-legged race to be in time for dinner, or the two of us and Genet walking back with our school books, of Zemui coming up with his motorcycle and then coasting the last hundred yards. Up ahead I could see the figures huddled around our taxi and around Hema. Then Matron, Gebrew, and Almaz separated from the vehicle, silhouetted against the last embers of the sky, and they waited for me.

I'D BEEN BACK just three days when Matron summoned me to Casualty. A young girl with a bull-gore wound to the abdomen was exsanguinating before our eyes. The child would have died if we'd tried to send her elsewhere. I took her to Operating Theater 3 at once, and found the bleeder. What followed next—cutting out damaged bowel, washing out the peritoneal cavity, fashioning a colostomy, was routine, but its effect on me was anything but. I felt I was on consecrated soil, standing on the same spot where Thomas Stone, Ghosh, and Shiva had stood, each with scalpel in hand. At the end of the surgery, when I turned to leave, weaving around the bucket and wires on the floor, I looked up and saw Shiva in the new glass that separated Theater 3 from its spanking-new mate, Theater 4. The sight took my breath away. I remembered Shiva's first words when the killing of Koochooloo's puppies prompted him to break years of silence: *Will you forget if someone kills me or Marion?*

No, Shiva, we'll never forget you, I said to my reflection. In saying that I think I decided my future.

AMONG SHIVA'S BELONGINGS in his room, I found a key on a keyholder shaped like the Congo. In Shiva's toolshed was a strange-looking motorcycle, with bright red, stubby fenders, a teardrop-shaped red fuel tank, handlebars that would have been called ape hangers in America, and lovely chrome wheels. Hema said that Shiva had bought the bike secondhand a few years back and that he kept tinkering with it. She said he had only ridden it late at night when there was no traffic. The udder-like engine looked very familiar, and its low rumble when I kick-started it gave away its true identity.

I operated three days a week, and when my return ticket to New York was about to expire, I did nothing.

Shiva's liver functioned beautifully in me year after year. The shots of hepatitis B immunoglobulin helped. The virus became so dormant that my blood tests showed I wasn't a carrier, and that I couldn't infect anyone. Matron insisted it was a miracle, and I had to agree.

In 1991, five years after my return, I stood by the gates of Missing just as I had when I was a child, and I watched the forces of the Tigre People's Liberation Front and other freedom fighters make their way into the city. They were dressed in the same functional shirts, shorts, and sandals of the guerrillas I had seen in Eritrea, bandoliers crisscrossing their chests, rifles in their hands. They didn't march in formation, yet their faces showed the discipline and confidence of men who believed in their cause. There was no looting, no mayhem. The only looting was by the Comrade President-for-Life, who emptied the Treasury and flew with his loot to Zimbabwe, where his fellow looter, Mugabe, gave him refuge. Mengistu was a despised figure, a blight on the nation, a man about whom to this day no one can find a good word to say. Almaz said that the souls of all those he murdered were assembled in a stadium, waiting to give him a reception on his way to hell.

EVERY EVENING I checked on Matron before I went to bed. She was so tremulous and bent over with age, but her joy in life was unchanged. We would have a cup of cocoa together. Her only LP—Bach—played in the background on the small gramophone I had bought for her. She never tired of the "Gloria," which I will always associate with her. As I'd sit with her, she would look over and smile as if she always knew I'd come back to the land I had once disowned. It had been Matron's wish that God might call her either during her prayers or her sleep, and He obliged. It was 1991, a few months after the President-for-Life fled; I found her in her chair, the record still spinning on her gramophone. Just the previous morning she had been supervising the planting of a new cultivar, the *Rosa rubiginosa Shiva,* which she had officialy registered with the Royal Society. To me it looked as if the whole city, rich and poor, turned out for her funeral. Almaz said that the streets to heaven were lined by the souls of those who were grateful to Matron, and that her throne was next to Mary's.

Almaz and Gebrew were retired and ensconced in new, comfortable quarters built for them at Missing, free to spend their time in any way they chose. I suppose it should not have surprised me that they would spend it in fasting and prayer.

The Shiva Stone Institute for Fistula Surgery with Hema as its titular head grew, as did its funding. Hema worked every day, and zealous young gynecologists from within the country, but also from other African nations, came to train and take up the cause. The Staff Probationer, whose room I had visited so many years ago, had become a skilled assistant under Shiva's tutelage, and now, with Hema's encouragement, she was a confident surgeon on her own, well suited to the painstaking task of training the young doctors who came to learn how to treat this one condition. I insisted on learning her real name, and reluctantly she told me it was Naeema. But it was not a name she ever used; she had become the Staff Probationer even to herself.

In going through Matron's papers, I discovered that the anonymous donor who had modestly funded Shiva's work for so many years was none other than Thomas Stone. Now he worked to direct other donors and foundations to support Missing.

I HAD TO WAIT till 2004 for Sister Mary Joseph Praise's message to reach me. It happened just after New Year's on the Western calendar, a time when the mimosa trees that surrounded the outpatient building had sprung their violet and yellow blooms and Missing was enveloped in the scent of vanilla.

I'd gone into the autoclave room between patients. The framed print of Bernini's *Ecstasy of St. Teresa* looked slightly askew. In straightening it, I found the hook was loose. When I took the frame down to tighten the hook, I noticed the thick paper backing had come unglued at one edge. The room stayed humid because of the autoclave, and it appeared to have weakened the glue. On trying to get the backing to stick again, I spied a gossamer-thin letter paper folded and ensconced behind that backing, the lines of blue writing showing through.

I fished it out.

I slumped back into my chair. My hands never tremble, but for some reason that delicate slip of paper shook.

The letter looked discolored by age, almost transparent, in danger of crumbling into dust. Like Ghosh, I had a moment to decide whether to read a private letter that was meant for another. I was certain that this was the letter my mother had penned just before I was born. Then it was in Ghosh's possession. When I was twenty-five years old, the letter came to me. I had carried it to America, then I had brought it back. For twenty-five years I was unaware that I had it. Until today. "When are you coming, Mama?" I used to ask when I was a small boy, gazing up at the picture. She had come at last.

CHAPTER 55

The Afterbird

September 19
Dear Thomas,

Last night, God told me I must confess to you what I have never confessed, even to God. Years ago, in Aden, I turned from God as He turned from me. Something happened to me there that should not happen to any woman. I could not forgive the man who harmed me. I could not forgive God. Death would have been better than what I endured. But I came here, to Missing. I came in the dress of a nun to hide my bitterness and shame from the world.

In Jeremiah 17 it is written, "The heart is deceitful above all things and beyond cure, and who can understand it?" I came to Ethiopia in deceit.

But our work changed me. I would have been your assistant till my last breath. Now, things have changed again.

A few months ago, you were like a man possessed, and I tried to comfort you. Now I am with child. Do not blame yourself.

It was difficult to hide my body from Matron and the others. Many times I thought of telling you. I could never find a way. But now I am frightened. My time is short. Last night the movements became strong. It made me think, What if Thomas wishes me to stay? I should not leave in the way I came to Missing and to you, hiding and in deceit. That is why I write.

I must flee Missing to spare it my shame just as I once fled to it to hide my shame. If you come to me when you get this letter, I will know that you wish me to be with you. But whatever you do, my love will always be the same.

Mary

It took such concentration to finish my last surgical case—a routine vagotomy and gastrojejunostomy for a duodenal ulcer—and not let my mind wander. At last, with that letter in hand, I walked back to my quarters, feeling as if I had never come up this path before.

She loved him. She loved him so much she ran to him from Aden. The bloodstains with which she came to Missing told me what she could not. She made her way to the doctor—the man—she had met on that ship out of India. And then, years later, she loved him so much she was ready to leave him. At the eleventh hour she decided to write and tell him. Then she waited for him to come, or not.

But Thomas Stone did come. Surely she would have registered his arrival. As he picked her up, carried her, ran with her, every tear that fell from his eyes onto her face she would have interpreted as affirmations of his love. He came not because of the letter: he never got it. He came because some part of him knew what he had done, and what he had to do: some part of him knew what he felt.

I pictured Ghosh visiting Thomas Stone's quarters after my mother's death, searching for him. He would have seen on Stone's desk the new textbook and bookmark, and on top of them, conspicuously perhaps, this letter. Thomas Stone never saw the book or the letter because he spent the previous night sleeping in the lounge chair in his Missing office, as he often did, and then after my mother's death he never returned to his quarters. Why hadn't Ghosh simply mailed the letter directly to Thomas Stone? Thomas never wrote or communicated; Ghosh had no address at first. But as the years went by, Ghosh could probably have found Stone's whereabouts. After all, Eli Harris had always known them. But perhaps by then Ghosh was hurt by Stone's silence and his willingness to forget his old friend and leave him caring for his children as he ran from his past. As more years went by, Ghosh might have pondered the effect of the letter on Stone—perhaps it would in fact be a disservice to send it to him. It might have precipitated another meltdown, or, as Hema had always feared, Stone might have returned to claim the children. And perhaps Stone wouldn't understand—or believe—anything the letter said.

Then, as death approached, it must have worked on Ghosh's conscience to be the keeper of this letter. What if the contents could save Stone, put his heart at ease? What if it made Stone do, even belatedly, the right thing by his sons? By this time all Ghosh's resentment for Stone, if he ever had any, had vanished.

So ultimately Ghosh gave the textbook and bookmark to Shiva, and the letter to me, but hidden from me. I marveled at the foresight of a dying man who would entomb a letter within a framed picture. He would leave it to fate—how like Ghosh this was! When would I find Thomas Stone? When would I find the letter? If and when I found it, would I give the letter to its intended recipient? Ghosh trusted me to do whatever it is I would choose to do. That, too, is love. He'd been dead more than a quarter century and he was still teaching me about the trust that comes only from true love.

"Shiva," I said, looking up at the sky where the stars were warming up for their nightly show while I recalled the night I fled Missing in haste, and how Shiva had thrust at me my father's book—*A Short Practice*, that bookmark inside. The few words on the bookmark penned by my mother were the only way any of us knew a letter even existed. Years ago, over the telephone, I had asked him, "Shiva, what made you give me the book?" He didn't know. "I wanted you to have it" was all he could say. The world turns on our every action, and our every omission, whether we know it or not.

WHEN I REACHED MY QUARTERS, I sat down and spread the letter on my lap, and with shaky hands I dialed Thomas Stone's number. My father was well past eighty now, an emeritus professor. Deepak said the old man's eyes were fading, but his touch was so good he could have operated in the dark. Still, he rarely operated anymore, though he would often assist. Thomas Stone was once known for *The Expedient Operator: A Short Practice of Tropical Surgery.* Now he was famous for pioneering a breakthrough transplant procedure. I was proof that the operation worked, but Shiva's death was proof of the attendant risks. Surgeons around the world had learned to do the operation, and many infants born without a working bile-drainage system had been saved by a parent's gift of a part of his or her liver.

IN MY EARPIECE I heard the hush of the void that hangs over the earth, and then out of that ether, the sound of the phone ringing far away, its high-pitched summons so brisk and efficient, so different from the lackadaisical analog clicks and the coarse ring when I dialed an Addis Ababa number. I pictured the phone trill and echo in the apartment that I had visited once, and which I had left open like a sardine can so that Thomas Stone would know that his son had arrived in his world.

I thought of my mother writing this letter, her whole life compressed on one side of this parchment. She had probably delivered it (and the book with bookmark) in the late afternoon when the pains hit her. She had worsened in the night, slowly slipping into shock, and then the next day she died. But not before Thomas Stone came to her. It was the sign she had waited for. He did the right thing, and yet for the last half century, he was unaware that he had done so.

Thomas Stone answered after the first ring. It made me wonder if he were wide awake even though it was the middle of the night in Boston.

"Yes?" My father's voice was crisp and alert, as if he expected this intrusion, as if he were ready for the story of trauma or massive brain bleed that made an organ available, or ready to hear of a child, one in ten thousand, born with biliary atresia who would die without a liver transplant. The voice I heard was that of someone who would bring all the skill and experience he carried in his nine fingers to the rescue of a fellow human being, and who would pass on that legacy to another generation of interns and residents—it was what he was born to do; he knew nothing else. "Stone here," he said, his voice sounding so very close, as if he were there with me, as if nothing at all separated our two worlds.

Acknowledgments

THIS IS A WORK OF FICTION, and all the characters are imagined, as is Missing Hospital. Some historical figures, such as Emperor Haile Selassie and the dictator Mengistu, are real; an attempted coup did occur in Ethiopia, but five years earlier than the one I describe. The Colonel and his brother are loosely based on the real coup leaders. The details of their capture and the words at the Colonel's trial and before he was hanged are from published reports, particularly Richard Greenfield's *Ethiopia: A New Political History;* John H. Spencer's *Ethiopia at Bay: A Personal Account of the Haile Selassie Years;* the published work of Richard Pankhurst for historical backdrop; and Edmond J. Keller's *Revolutionary Ethiopia: From Empire to People's Republic.* A remarkable physician by the name of John Melly died after being shot by a looter, but his dialogue with Matron is imagined. The Ibis and other bars are inventions. The LT&C school is imagined; any resemblance to my wonderful school (where Mr. Robbs and Mr. Thames encouraged my writing) is not intentional.

The following sources, books, and people were invaluable: The birth scene and the phrases "white asphyxia" and "in the obscurity of our mother's womb" are inspired by the wonderful memoir of the late great Egyptian obstetrician and fistula surgeon Naguib Mahfouz, *The Life of an Egyptian Doctor,* as is the idea of the copper vessel. Nergesh Tejani's essays describing her experiences in Africa with version clinics and with fistula, as well as our correspondence, were extremely helpful. I consulted the published work of Dr. Reginald Hamlin and Dr. Catherine Hamlin, pioneers of fistula surgery. As a medical student, I would see them and was very aware of their work. Recently, I had the opportunity to visit the "Hospital by the River," which is also the title of Catherine Hamlin's lovely memoir. The fistula surgeons in my book are not in any way based on the Hamlins. The late Sir Ian Hill was in fact the dean of the medical school, and if I use his name, and that of Braithwaite, in the book, it is as a tribute to two people who took a chance on me. The attempted hijackings of the Ethiopian Airlines jets during the 1960s and 1970s are historical facts; one would-be hijacker was my senior in medical school; she and her fellow hijackers perished in the attempt. The present prime minister of Ethiopia, Meles Zenawi, was one year my junior in medical school; he became a guerilla fighter, ultimately leading the forces that toppled Mengitsu. The heroism of the security crew and the incredible skill of the pilots are very real. Ethiopian Airlines remains, in my opinion, the safest and best international airline I have flown, with the most hospitable and dedicated flight attendants. Louse-borne relapsing fever was studied by the late Peter Perine and the late Charles Leithead, and I had the pleasure of seeing patients with both men when I was a student.

For information about Teresa of Avila, and the description of Bernini's statue, I drew on *Teresa of Avila: The Progress of a Soul* by Cathleen Medwick. Even after seeing the original in Rome, I found Medwick's descriptions so insightful. Any of St. Teresa's words that I quote, as well as the ideas about faith and grace, and the idea of Sister Mary Joseph Praise reciting the *Miserere* at her death and the idea of the inexpicably sweet scent, are based on Medwick's account of the life of Teresa. The words "celestial billing and cooing" are from H. M. Stutfield quoted in Medwick's book.

The line "I owe you the sight of morning" is by W. S. Merwin from the poem "To the Surgeon Kevin Lin," originally published in *The New Yorker*. A limited-edition print of this poem prepared by Carolee Campbell of Ninja Press and signed by William Merwin hangs in my office. I owe a great debt to physician, writer, and friend Ethan Canin for first inviting me to the Sun Valley Writers Festival and thereby introducing me to Reva Tooley and the remarkable people who gather there.

The line "her nose was sharp as a pen" is from *Henry V, Part II* and relates to my belief that it represents Shakespeare's astute clinical observation, which I described in "The Typhoid State Revisited," in *The American Journal of Medicine* (79:370; 1985).

My own impressions of Aden and my memories of sitting in khat sessions were aided by the most vivid descriptions in Eric Hansen's wonderful book *Motoring with Mohammed: Journeys to Yemen and the Red Sea* and also *Eating the Flowers of Paradise: One Man's Journey Through Ethiopia and Yemen* by Kevin Rushby. The image of the woman with the charcoal brazier on her head and also the wheelbarrows transporting people come from Hansen's book.

The Italian occupation, the description of Aweyde, and many aspects of the Italian-Ethopian conflict, including the desire to win by any means—*Qualsiasi mezzo*—were informed by Paul Theroux's wonderful *Dark Star Safari: Overland from Cairo to Capetown* and many other sources.

"Squared her shoulders to the unloveliness" is a paraphrase of James Merrill's line in the poem "Charles on Fire": "No one but squared / The shoulders of his unloveliness."

Bliss Carnochan showed me an early edition of his *Golden Legends: Images of Abyssinia, Samuel Johnson to Bob Marley* and helped me see how Western ideas about Ethiopia were shaped.

I and countless Commonwealth medical students admired *Bailey and Love's Short Practice of Surgery;* Stone's imagined textbook is based on *Bailey and Love,* and the wombat and the appendix story is from there. As a student I was impressed with the photograph of Bailey and his nine fingers. Other than that, the character of Stone has no connection with Hamilton Bailey, who practiced only in England before retiring.

"A careful decision was needed so as not to blunder again. It was often the *second* mistake that came in the haste to correct the first mistake that did the patient in" and "A rich man's faults are covered with money, but a surgeon's faults are covered with earth" are both from *Aphorisms and Quotations for the Surgeon* by Moshe Schein. For these and many other surgical notions, I owe Moshe, maverick surgeon, brilliant teacher, author of several wonderful surgical textbooks, essayist, and friend. He not only read early drafts but also introduced me to the community of surgeons on SURGINET. I delighted in, learned from, and borrowed ideas from their musings, particularly the vasectomy details, which made for a series of memorable exchanges. Karen Kwong shared with me her experiences (and those of her husband, Marty) as a trauma surgeon, and she was a careful reader of the manuscript both early and at the end. Her long, thoughtful e-mails were precious, and I cannot express to her sufficiently my gratitude and admiration. Thanks also to Ed Salztein, Jack Peacock, Stuart Levitz, and Franz Theard. I met Thomas Starzl when I was a Chief Resident in Tennessee and have since renewed the acquaintance. He is truly a surgeon's surgeon, and his pioneering work establishing the field of liver transplantation is no fiction; I refer to him in the book in tribute. Thomas Stone is his fictional contemporary. Francisco Cigarroa, president of the University of Texas Health Science Center, San Antonio, was kind enough to let me watch as he performed a liver transplant on a child. The remarkable group in San Antonio, led by Glenn Halff, who make liver transplant appear almost routine, are part of Starzl's legacy—until very recently, it was fair to say that every liver transplant surgeon in the world was trained by Starzl or by someone who trained with Starzl.

"Birth, and copulation, and death / That's all the facts when you come to brass tacks: I've been born, and once is enough" is a partial quote form T. S. Eliot's *Sweeney Agonistes.*

"Indeed to think of life as tragic is a posture of delusion, for life is uniformly worse than tragic" is a line from Heinrich Zimmer's *The King and the Corpse,* edited by Joseph Campbell, as is "Not only our actions but also our omissions become our destiny."

"They saw in the plague a sure and God-sent means of winning eternal life" is from Camus' *The Plague.*

I am greatly indebted to the late Ryszard Kapuściński's take on a city and a country which I thought I knew well. Details of the Emperor's court, the palace, the funding of the health departments, the Amhara character, the motorcycle escort, the Minister of the Pen, and the palace intrigues were things most residents knew about and had in some cases seen firsthand, but Kapuściński's particular talent was, as an outsider, making those things more visible to us, which he did in his extraordinary book *The Emperor.*

"The crookedness of the serpent is still straight enough to slide through the snake hole" is paraphrased from one of the Bhakti poems in *Speaking of Siva,* edited by the late, great A. K. Ramanujam.

For information about the Carmelites I thank Fred de Sam Lazaro and Eliam Rao and the incomparable Sister Maude. There is no convent of Carmelites to my knowledge in Egmore.

The details of the the Rock of East Africa, AFRS Asmara, are from http://www.kagnewstation.com/.

For the scenes of the escape from Asmara, I thank Naynesh Kamani, who was my senior in medical school and who made that heroic walk; he read the manuscript and had many corrections and suggestions. I was greatly influenced by Thomas Kennealy's wonderful novel *To Asmara,* with its observations about the Eritrean guerrilla camps which Kennealy appeared to have visited; he remains a champion of the Eritrean people. I should state that my affection is equal for both Ethiopia and Eritrea, and I have dear friends in both places.

"As if I had given him the greatest gift a man could ever give another" is a paraphrase of a line in Raymond Carver's "What the Doctor Said," from *New Path to the Waterfall*.

For the scenes at the tuberculosis sanatorium, I am indebted to Jean Mason's "The Discourse of Disease: Patient Writing at the 'University of Tuberculosis,'" which I was fortunate to hear at the Psychoanalysis and Narrative Medicine Conference, University of Florida, Gainesville, in 2002.

"May no English nobleman venture out of this world without a Scottish Physician, as I am sure there are none who venture in" was said to be a toast used by William Hunter, M.D., the elder of the Hunter brothers. I have paraphrased this as a toast that B. C. Gandhi uses.

"Call no man happy until he dies" is what the Athenian Solon tells Croesus, the wealthy king of Lydia, according to Herodotus. These are words that Sir William Osler quoted on hearing the news of his beloved son Revere's death at Flanders. The imagined nursing textbook that describes Sound Nursing Sense is a recasting of one of Osler's aphorisms.

For the information on psychosomatic ailments among Ethiopians, I am grateful to my friend Rick Hodes, M.D., internist, writer, and mensch. His life in Ethiopia is a story of its own. Thanks to Thomas "Appu" Oommen for his incredible recollections of his time in Addis as a schoolboy and later as a journalist, and of the period of the coup. An e-mail Appu shared with me from Yohannes Kifle gave me great insight into Kerchele. My parents, George and Mariam Verghese, shared their memories, and my mother made extensive notes just for my use. To them I have dedicated this book.

In the course of writing this novel over several years, I consulted many other works, most of which I hope are listed in the bibliography, and any failure to acknowledge a person or source is something I would like to correct. The scene of Genet's damp gift to Marion was inspired by a similar scene from a novel or short story whose authorship I cannot recall; similarly, the metaphor of Aden as a city at once dead yet alive like maggots on a corpse (or words to that effect) is one that I would love to attribute to a source.

I am grateful to the extraordinary Advisory Board in San Antonio that allowed us to build a Center for Medical Humanities, but even more grateful for the personal friendships I formed with its members. Steve Wartman, my tennis partner and friend, recruited me to San Antonio when he was dean. Edith McAllister was my teacher, my coach, my inspiration, and the person who understood better than anyone the need I had for protected time, even if it meant my leaving; in my next life my ambition is to come back as her. For Marvin and Ellie Forland and for Judy McCarter, words cannot do justice to the support and love they gave me; to hold a distinguished professorship named after Marvin, and a distinguished chair named after Joaquin Cigarroa Jr. (both consummate internists), was the greatest honor. Judy remains my counselor and conscience; with every passing year I grow in admiration of her wisdom. Thanks to UTHSCA, to the extended Cigarroa family, Bill Henrich, Robert Clark, Jan Patterson, Ray Faber, Tom Mayes, Somayaji Ramamurthy, Deborah Kaercher, the late David Sherman, and so many others who made it a special place to work; so also to Texas Tech, El Paso, where this work first began. Dr. Erika Brady of Western Kentucky University's folk studies department was an expert in matters ranging from Alpha Omega Alpha to Religio Medici to details about prayers and dress; I could always rely on her research. Michele Stanush also helped me with research, and I am most grateful.

My Wednesday-morning brothers (Randy Townsend, Baker Duncan, Olivier Nadal, Drew Cauthorn, Guy Bodine, and especially Jack Willome) and their wives (and especially you, Dee!) gave me love and faith and held me accountable. "No greater love . . ."

Tom Rozanski, neighbor, colleague, and urologist, gave me advice on the vasectomy scene as well as other surgical issues, for which I am most grateful. Rajender Reddy and Gabe Garcia helped me think through issues related to hepatitis B.

Anand and Madhu Karnad, my dearest and oldest friends, read and heard many sections of this and all my previous books over the years; they gave and continue to give me love and sustenance, and I know I have a home wherever they are.

I am grateful to John Irving for his friendship all these years. I have learned so much from him both in our correspondence and in his published work.

Ralph Horwitz, M.D., chairman of medicine at Stanford, created a home for me; I am so grateful for his vision and his and Sally's friendship. I thank my brother, George, and his wife, Ann, and the Kailaths, as well as Helen Bing, for introducing me to Stanford's charms years before I dreamed of coming here.

My lovely wife, Sylvia, spent hours entering the changes that I would write on the manuscript and did this several times over the years. She more than anyone, but also Tristan, Jacob, and Steven, put up with my absences from society and sustained me through the ups and downs in the writing of this book. *Gracias mi amor; con los años que me quedan . . .*

Mary Evans, my agent, sold my first story to *The New Yorker* before we met in person, and she has kept the faith with me since those days in Iowa in 1991. Her discerning eye and wise counsel have made a writer of me, and her friendship has made me a better person. Robin Desser had a hand in my first book, and it was a privilege to get to work with her on this one. Robin saw this book through its many iterations and spent innumerable hours with it and with me, and I am so indebted to her. I have often thought that the grace, passion, humility, and extraordinary skill she brings to her craft are attributes she shares with the physicians I most admire. My thanks also to Sarah Rothbard, Robin's wonderful assistant. I am most grateful to Sonny Mehta for his enthusiasm for this story and his steadfast support of my writing.

Medicine is a demanding mistress, yet she is faithful, generous, and true. She gives me the privilege of seeing patients and of teaching students at the bedside, and thereby she gives meaning to everything I do. Like Ghosh, every year, at commencement, I renew my vows with her: *I swear by Apollo and Asclepius and Hygieia and Panaceia to be true to her, for she is the source of all . . . I shall not cut for stone.*

Abraham Verghese,
Stanford, California, June 2008

Bibliography

Anderson, R., and R. Romfh. *Technique in the Use of Surgical Tools.* New York: Appleton-Century-Crofts, 1980.

Ayele, N. *Wit and Wisdom of Ethiopia.* Hollywood, Calif.: Tsehai Publishers and Distributors, 1998.

Bailey, H. *Pye's Surgical Handicraft.* 17th ed. Bristol, England: John Wright & Sons, 1956.

Bierman, J., and C. Smith. *Fire in the Night: Wingate of Burma, Ethiopia, and Zion.* New York: Random House, 1999.

Coleman, D. *The Scent of Eucalyptus: A Missionary Childhood in Ethiopia.* Fredericton, New Brunswick, Canada: Goose Lane Editions, 2003.

Cook, H. *Fifty Years a Country Doctor.* Lincoln: University of Nebraska Press, 1998.

Cope, Z. *The Diagnosis of the Acute Abdomen in Rhyme.* London: H. K. Lewis & Co., Ltd., 1962.

Dreger, A. D. *One of Us: Conjoined Twins and the Future of Normal.* Cambridge, Mass.: Harvard University Press, 2004.

Gould, G. M., and W. E. Pyle. *Anomalies and Curiosities of Medicine.* New York: W. B. Saunders, 1896.

Habte-Mariam, M., and C. Price. *The Rich Man and the Singer: Folktales from Ethiopia.* New York: E. P. Dutton, 1971.

Hertzler, A. E. *The Horse and Buggy Doctor.* Lincoln: University of Nebraska Press, 1938.

Humphries, S. V. *The Life of Hamilton Bailey.* Beckenham, England: Ravenswood Publications, 1973.

Keller, E. J. *Revolutionary Ethiopia: From Empire to People's Republic.* Bloomington: Indiana University Press, 1991.

Lambie, T. A. *Boot and Saddle in Africa.* New York: Fleming H. Redell Co., 1943.

————. *A Doctor Without a Country.* New York: Fleming H. Redell Co., 1939.

Marcus H. G. *The Politics of Empire: Ethiopia, Great Britain and the United States, 1941–1974.* Lawrenceville, N.J.: Red Sea Press, 1983.

Marston A. *Hamilton Bailey: A Surgeon's Life.* London: Greenwich Medical Media Ltd., 1999.

Melly, A. J. M. *John Melly of Ethiopia.* Ed. K. Nelson and A. Sullivan. London: Faber & Faber, 1937.

Speert, H. *Iconographia Gyniatrica: A Pictorial History of Gynecology and Obstetrics.* Philadelphia: F. A. Davis Co., 1973.

Smith, I. *Wish I Might.* New York: Harper & Brothers, 1955.

Waugh E. *Waugh in Abyssinia.* Harlow, Essex, England: Longman, 1936.

ABRAHAM VERGHESE is Professor and Senior Associate Chair for the Theory and Practice of Medicine at the Stanford University School of Medicine. He has served on the faculty at East Tennessee State University, the University of Iowa, Texas Tech University, and the University of Texas Health Science Center, San Antonio, where he was the founding director of the Center for Medical Humanities & Ethics and where he holds an adjunct professorship. A graduate of the Iowa Writers' Workshop, he is the author of *My Own Country,* a 1994 NBCC Finalist and one of five books chosen as Best Book of the Year by *Time,* and *The Tennis Partner,* a *New York Times* Notable Book. His essays and short stories have appeared in *The New Yorker, The New York Times, Sports Illustrated, The Atlantic Monthly, Esquire, Story, Granta, The New York Times Magazine, The Wall Street Journal,* and elsewhere. He lives in Palo Alto, California.

A NOTE ON THE TYPE

THIS BOOK was set in a modern adaptation of a type designed by the first William Caslon (1692–1766). The Caslon face has enjoyed much popularity in modern times. Its characteristics are remarkable regularity and symmetry, and beauty in the shape and proportion of the letters; its general effect is clear and open but not weak or delicate. For uniformity, clearness, and readability it has perhaps never been surpassed.

Composed by Creative Graphics,
Allentown, Pennsylvania
Printed and bound by Berryville Graphics,
Berryville, Virginia
Designed by Virginia Tan